Glittering par...
passion...

Regency

HIGH-SOCIETY AFFAIRS

They're the talk of the Ton!

The Outrageous Débutante
by Anne O'Brien

&

A Damnable Rogue
by Anne Herries

The Regency

HIGH-SOCIETY AFFAIRS

Regency

HIGH-SOCIETY AFFAIRS

Anne O'Brien &
Anne Herries

M&B™ and M&B™ with the Rose Device
are trademarks of the publisher.
Harlequin Mills & Boon Limited, Eton House,
18-24 Paradise Road, Richmond, Surrey TW9 1SR

First published in Great Britain in 2005 and 2003

REGENCY HIGH-SOCIETY AFFAIRS
© Harlequin Books S.A. 2009

The publisher acknowledges the copyright holders of the
individual works as follows:

The Outrageous Débutante © Anne O'Brien 2005
A Damnable Rogue © Anne Herries 2003

ISBN: 978 0 263 86869 2

052-1209

Printed and bound in Spain
by Litografia Rosés S.A., Barcelona

The Outrageous Débutante

by

Anne O'Brien

Anne O'Brien was born and has lived for most of her life in Yorkshire. There she taught history before deciding to fulfil a lifetime ambition to write romantic historical fiction. She won a number of short story competitions until published for the first time by Mills & Boon. As well as writing, she finds time to enjoy gardening, cooking and watercolour painting. She now lives with her husband in an eighteenth-century cottage in the depths of the Welsh Marches. You can find out about Anne's books and more at her website: www.anneobrien.co.uk

The Outrageous Débutante is the second book in
Anne O'Brien's exciting trilogy,
THE FARINGDON SCANDALS – look for
The Enigmatic Rake next month!

Prologue

The sun beat down from a sky so pale with heat as to be almost colourless. From the deep ochre sand and rock of the Syrian desert, ruins of a Roman town stood proud, as if grown from the earth. Arches lifted their broken heads to the heavens, columns rose with splintered capitals and walls crumbled into dust. They might have stood there since the beginning of time, and would continue to stand until the hot winds and cold nights reduced them once more to nothing but grains of sand. Nothing moved in the landscape except for a pair of lazily circling eagles and the lizards that basked on the hot stones. Nothing moved until two figures emerged from the distant heat haze, to fly across the firm sand towards the ancient town. A pair of fine Arabian horses, their riders crouched low as they encouraged them to pit their strength and speed against each other. Far behind followed a small group of riders, at a more sedate pace, leading well-laden pack horses.

The two riders drew rein before the remains of a magnificent triumphal arch. The animals danced at the curbing of their energies and tossed their heads. They were beautiful, both satin-skinned greys with the short curved necks and small heads of true Arab breeding. The riders controlled them with ease as the horses resisted the firm hands on the reins and fought to run.

As they finally settled and consented to stand, sides heaving, the riders dismounted. They walked towards the crumbling stonework and, securing the reins to fallen masonry, sank down in the shade. Then they proceeded to unwind the scarves that had been draped around head and face against the sun and sand and to loosen the all-encompassing robes that protected their clothes— to reveal that the riders were female.

'That was wonderful! So much light and space. I love the elemental heat of it—even when my nose is pink and I have sand in my mouth!' The younger woman wiped the back of her hand over her dry lips as she watched the slowly approaching caravan, then turned her brilliant blue eyes on her older companion. 'You have no idea how much I shall miss this place, Mama.'

Lady Drusilla Wooton-Devereux smiled her understanding, in complete accord with her daughter. 'I, too, regret leaving it, Thea. And Sir Hector would not be averse to remaining at the Court of Constantinople for a few more years. But his position does not allow him free choice in the matter. We must make the most of the remaining days here.'

Theodora Wooton-Devereux pulled the long veil completely from around her head, to reveal the interesting fact that her hair was of a rich gold, a burnished cap in the sunlight and cut as short as any boy's. She ran her fingers through the short strands where the wisps stuck to her heated forehead and cheeks. Unconventional it might be—shockingly so, some might say—but it drew attention to the face of a Beauty. Glorious deep blue eyes, the dark, elegantly arched brows, the fine cheekbones and straight, almost masterful nose. Miss Wooton-Devereux's delicious mouth with its full bottom lip curved in unalloyed pleasure. She was without doubt a striking young woman.

'What will it be like in Russia when Papa is sent to St Petersburg?' she asked. 'Cold, I expect.'

'Not so much now in the summer months. But in winter, yes. A land of ice and snow, temperatures so low you could not believe it. Even the rivers freeze over.' Lady Drusilla smiled at the memories, surrounded as she was by extreme heat and dust. 'Your father and I spent a few months there—he was in a lowly position in the diplomatic ranks in those days, of course—before you were born, Thea.'

'How exciting it must have been—you as a young bride. I shall like to see it. And the court of Tsar Alexander, of course. Do you suppose he is as handsome as they say? We shall need furs and woollen cloth, not these wonderful light garments.' Thea leapt to her feet, unwilling to sit longer when energy surged through her veins, and strode around so the robes billowed about her, robes such as a Bedouin in the desert would wear, revealing that beneath them she wore wide breeches as the Turks might, tucked into the tops of long leather boots. 'I think that wherever we go, this will always be my favourite place. Riding for ever with the distance never seeming to come any closer. Sleeping outside under the stars, which shine with such brilliance.' She spread her arms and danced a few short steps of joy. 'But I expect Russia will hold as many delights. How long do you suppose before Papa is transferred?'

'A few months, perhaps as long as six. We should be fixed in London for the time and so will take a house for the Season.' Lady Drusilla watched her daughter, unwilling to curb Thea's delights. But she knew she must. It was more than time for her to remember her duties as a mother to this enchanting daughter.

'Thea—I do not think that you should come with us to Russia.' The words came out as a bald statement.

The dance across the sand stopped. The dancer turned, her face registering a sharp mixture of shock and surprise. A sudden fear.

'Not come with you? But why not? I have always travelled with you. Saint Petersburg cannot contain more dangers than Constantinople, surely. And if *you* are to accompany Papa, there is no reason for me not to do so.'

'It is not a matter of safety. That has never been an issue, as you are well aware.' Lady Drusilla turned her eyes away, unwilling to see the hurt that she must surely inflict. She knew her daughter's temperament too well. Had she not herself fostered the strong streak of independence, the love of travel and adventure? But there were now steps that must be taken. 'It is time that you married, Thea.' She kept her voice light and gentle. 'You are now one and twenty, high time that you were wed. I had been married all of two years when I was your age.'

'There is plenty of time for that.' Thea came to sit beside her mother, intent on persuasion. In her short life she had rarely found it difficult to get her own way. But Lady Drusilla, fully aware of her daughter's tactics, shook her head and resisted the clasp of the urgent hand on her arm.

'No. We have been too selfish with you, my love. Enjoyed your company far too much. I shall miss you dreadfully.' She closed her hand over Thea's, to still the restless fingers. 'But it is time that you had a husband and your own home. Children, of course. We must not leave it longer. It would be most unwise.'

'Mama—do I really need a husband? I would far rather come with you to Russia. Perhaps in a few years when—'

'No! You are older than a traditional débutante for her coming out as it is, Thea, and that is my fault. You should have a Season in London—you deserve one. You are a beautiful young woman and should not be denied a formal introduction to London society. Besides, I want a rich and titled husband for you, so that you might be comfortable.'

'But I am an heiress. I don't need more wealth.'

'Perhaps not. But you certainly need a husband. I do not wish to think of you growing old as an eccentric and lonely spinster, roaming the deserts with no company but your servants, the object of gossip and speculation from everyone you meet. That is not what any mother would want for her daughter.'

'I would not be lonely. I should take a lover!' The lady lifted her chin, deliberately intending to shock her mother, horrified at this sudden arrangement of her future life without any consideration for her own wishes.

'You will do no such thing, Theodora. Your upbringing might have been somewhat out of the way in comparison with that of most young girls, but I will have no truck with the scandalous, the improper!'

'I see.' Thea lowered her chin, her mind working rapidly. 'Does Sir Hector agree with this plan?'

'Yes. Of course. We have talked of it.'

Of course they would have. And Sir Hector would undoubtedly be swayed by Lady Drusilla's forceful arguments. All the joy, all the brightness, seemed to have gone out of the day. 'Very well.' What other could she say? 'I suppose I shall have to be more conventional in London.'

'Assuredly. I think I have allowed you far too much licence in the past.' Lady Drusilla frowned a little at her daughter as she considered her sudden compliance.

'No. Never too much. It has been wonderful, Mama. Can I gallop my horse in London?'

'Certainly not. Nor wear the garments you enjoy at present, as you are very well aware.'

'Or ride astride?'

'Theodora! You must behave with decorum and dignity. Your purpose in London will be to attract a husband, not frighten him away with an exhibition of unseemly manners. I would not wish you to become an object of gossip or shunned because the *ton* considers you ill bred.'

'Oh, dear! It all seems very dull.'

'By no means. I wager that you will find it most entertaining.'

'Well, I shall certainly do my best to make it so, as you know, Mama. I have never yet been bored. I suppose that London can offer as much to attract and occupy me as Constantinople or St Petersburg.'

'Thea!' Lady Drusilla warned as she recognised the glint in her daughter's eye.

'Don't fret, Mama. Of course I shall behave.' After a little thought, Thea's good humour had quickly reasserted itself and she laughed. 'Perfectly, in fact. I shall set my cap at a fabulously rich Earl and ensnare him, just to please you.' Her eyes twinkled at the prospect, but she managed to keep an expression of innocent compliance in place. Perhaps London might not be so dull after all.

Chapter One

In the county of Herefordshire, far removed from the exotic delights and windblown sands of Arabia, Lord Nicholas Faringdon opened a letter with utmost reluctance, a letter that was destined to disrupt the unchanging predictability of his life.

His lordship had spent the morning, unaware of the devious workings of fate, in the company of George Dinmore, agent to the estate of Burford. A fine sense of optimism warmed his blood, as satisfying as the first real heat of early summer that brushed his skin. It was too early to tell if the harvest would be good but the crops were coming on well, the arable fields sheened with bright green. Now it was up to sun and rain and the will of God. There had been too many cold and wet summers of late. But the cattle and sheep were thriving, as were the horses on his own estate at Aymestry Manor. It could not be said that Lord Nicholas neglected his duty to his family in his role as trustee for Tom, his young nephew, who held the title and inheritance as Marquis of Burford.

The little town of Kingshall, its wood-and-plaster dwellings clustered around a central market square, hummed with life. Outside the Red Lion, Lord Nicholas had paused to listen to the landlord, who could be relied upon for knowledge of any local happenings. Nicholas made it his business to enquire and keep

abreast of developments or hints of unrest. The local cottage in-
dustries were thriving well enough. There was no serious competition here from machines. He knew that if he rode down Back
Lane, he would see the women who made the beautifully sewn
gloves from the palest, finest of leathers, sitting working on their
doorsteps in the sun. But another bad summer, another autumn
beset by storms and heavy rain, would push up the price of grain.
Lack of food, as Nicholas well knew, led to mutterings in the Red
Lion over a draught of ale. The lord would be the easiest target for
such discontent when tempers ran high. Lord Nicholas Faringdon
had no intention of allowing his nephew's inheritance to be destroyed or compromised in any way, even if his nephew was living in New York with Nell, his mother, and nearly four years old.

As soon as the pasture had opened up on the edge of the town
he had urged the young chestnut mare out of her somnolence into
an easy gallop. She had willingly extended her stride until they'd
flown across the grassland in perfect unity, disturbing a small
flock of Ryeland sheep. He rode well, could never remember not
being at home on horseback. The speed, the breeze which had
ruffled and tugged at his dark hair, the sun which had glittered
on the still waters of the mere, had all served to lift his spirits,
banishing the niggling worries that had plagued him of late.

He did not know why he had been so beset. There was no obvious cloud of concern on his horizon, nothing which could not
be managed between himself, Dinmore and Hoskins, the family
lawyer in London. Nicholas had frowned as he breasted a rise
and the lovely, familiar view of Burford Hall had opened up before him, its mellow stone glowing in the sharp midday light. For
some reason life was a little flat. Even a little lonely. The house
was empty apart from himself and the servants and would be so
as far into the future as he could see. His brother Hal and Nell,
now his wife, were firmly settled in New York where the firm of
Faringdon and Bridges occupied Hal's business acumen. His eldest brother Thomas had been dead now more than three years.
So the Hall was empty. As was his own attractive manor at
Aymestry.

Perhaps a visit to town was the remedy for this vague sense of *ennui*. It was a year or more since he had last taken up residence for any length of time at Faringdon House in Grosvenor Square. The Season would be at its height with all the Polite World in town. It would not do for him to rusticate completely, to become nothing but a county squire, buried in soil and hunting with pretensions to neither fashion nor style. Nicholas smiled at his own harsh judgement. There was little chance of that. He could rise to the occasion as well as any and play the sophisticated man of fashion.

Lord Nicholas's arrival on the sweep of gravel before the steps of Burford Hall had coincided with that of the post boy from Leominster, so that now he stood in the library, wine glass in hand, having leafed through the letters before casting them on to the desk. But not all. One of them, the fatal one, had caught his attention—he had recognised the handwriting immediately. It caused him to groan quietly. He might have wished for a change of pace and scenery, but that did not include the interference of Aunt Beatrice. He could guess at the content before he even unfolded the thin sheets of paper with Lady Beatrice's distinctive scrawl. Carrying it to the window seat, he sat and prepared to read.

> *My dear Nicholas,*
> *Although the Season has been under way for some weeks, it has come to my notice when visiting Judith in Grosvenor Square that Faringdon House has remained closed up with the knocker off the door and we have not had the pleasure of your company. I took the liberty of calling to ask Elton if he had any knowledge of your sudden arrival—which he had not. I am sure that it is not good for you to bury yourself in the country. You need to come to town, my boy.*
>
> *I know that it will be no surprise to you if I suggest that matrimony should play a significant part in your planning. You are young, well set up with your own income and property, both of which are substantial, and I do not hesitate to*

*say that you are not unattractive to the opposite sex. It is time
that you took a wife—indeed, I consider it to be your duty.
Now that Henry and Eleanor are settled in New York—although why that should be I cannot imagine—it behoves you
to consider setting up your own nursery. I am sure that you
take my meaning. I believe that life can be considered cheap
Across the Sea.*

*How can you expect to meet anyone suitable if you are bur-
ied at Burford Hall? Not that it is not a delightful place—I
remember exceptional house parties there in your dear
mother's day—but not in April when you should be in London for the Season.*

I cannot insist that you come to town, of course—

Really! Nicholas's lips curled in appreciation of his aunt's
forthright style, against which few members of the family were
ever prepared to take a stand.

*and I am sure that you can find any number of excuses why your
time at Burford is invaluable, but it would please me if you
would present yourself in Berkeley Square for my own ball in
three weeks. I will take the opportunity to introduce you to this
year's crop of débutantes. Some very pretty well-bred girls,
who would be valuable additions to the Faringdon family.*

There is no need to reply to this letter. Merely arrive!

Your loving aunt

Beatrice

He cast the letter on to the desk to pour a glass of claret from
the decanter, which the footman had brought in whilst he read.
Merely arrive!

Well, he had thought of going, had he not? But not if he was
to be an object of Beatrice's interest. Like a rare insect under a
magnifying lens.

Marriage. Of course she would interest herself. Her advice in
the letter was nothing new. But Beatrice—damn her!—had

pricked at his sense of duty and he could not but acknowledge the weight of her argument. Even so, the prospect of dancing attendance on any number of young girls at Almack's and other fashionable squeezes filled him with something akin to horror. Eyed, assessed, gossiped over by their avaricious mamas, his income, rank and future prospects a matter for public speculation. The daughters hanging on his every word, hoping for a declaration of undying love or at least the invitation to accept his hand in marriage and take up residence at Aymestry Manor. Or, even more enticingly, at Burford Hall in the absence of the Marquis. Thomas, with considerable aplomb and good humour, would have laughed it off and enjoyed the flirtation and the female fluttering for his attention. Hal would have simply made himself scarce. He, Nicholas, in the circumstances, could do neither. The bonds around him, the silken ties of family responsibility and duty, tightened around him even more. Unbreakable, even though constructed from love and care.

Nicholas poured another glass of claret and frowned into it. Hal had the right of it when he took himself off to New York. But, of course, he had Nell with him now, the love of his life.

He supposed he could simply stay buried here, as Aunt Beatrice had so tactfully phrased it. Offer for the hand of Amelia Hawkes, daughter of the hard-riding, hard-drinking baronet whose land marched with the Faringdon estate in the west. She would like nothing better than to be Lady Nicholas Faringdon, and many would see it as a good match. An excellent rider to hounds, well connected locally, Amelia would take over the running of Aymestry Manor with the same style as she had run her father's establishment since her mother's death. She had probably been waiting for an offer from him for the past half-dozen years, he decided, with more than a touch of guilt. Not that he had ever encouraged her to believe that marriage was in his mind—but neither had he discouraged her. With some discomfort he saw the situation from Miss Hawkes's perspective. They met frequently in the hunting season. He stood up with her at local assemblies in Ludlow and at private parties. Her father, Sir

William, certainly would have no objection to such a match. Why not offer for the girl and tell Beatrice that she need dabble no longer—it would be comfortable, easy, familiar?

No, he could not do it. He put down the neglected wineglass with a sharp snap. Poor Amelia. He had not been fair with her. The plain truth was that he no longer wanted comfortable, easy and familiar. She was an attractive girl and would no doubt make some man an excellent wife. He liked her well enough. But love? Amelia never caused his blood to run hot or his eyes to spark with the possessive emotion that he had seen in Hal's when he turned his gaze on Nell. Nor was the lady blessed with a well-informed mind. They could exchange views on horses and hunting, the desirability of pheasant at the end of the season when *stringy* could be something of a compliment. But if he ever took the conversation into any other channels—the new ideas on farming—or, God preserve him, the political situation—her eyes glazed over and she had no opinion or knowledge to volunteer. And, he realised as the image of Miss Amelia formed in his mind, she had absolutely no interest in clothes and her appearance, spending most of her days in a riding habit. Nicholas, he discovered with some surprise, since it had never crossed his mind before, was sufficiently fastidious that his future wife must look and play her part with style, whether it be in a fashionable drawing room or on the hunting field.

No. Miss Amelia Hawkes would never be mistress of Aymestry Manor. He supposed it would have to be Aunt Beatrice and the débutantes. He hoped to God that since it was undoubtedly his duty to marry and his heart was clearly not engaged elsewhere, he could meet someone suitable, someone intelligent, stylish and conventional, within a few weeks of his arrival and get it over with. As long as he did not repeat the experience he'd had with Georgiana Fitzgerald. He'd thought he had been in love. The lovely Georgiana Fitzgerald had flirted and smiled, had led him to believe that she would look for more than a light friendship—indeed, a deeper, lasting relationship. For his part he had been entranced by a lively and confiding manner and lovely face. And then, when he had been on the point of declaring himself, she had thrown him over to become the object of interest to an extremely wealthy Viscount on the trawl for a wife. She had wanted a title and fortune, not the heart and devotion of a younger son with a mere easy competence. Nicholas, distinctly disillusioned, had been left to consider the folly of allowing his heart to become engaged when considering matrimony. But that did not make Miss Amelia Hawkes any more acceptable!

On which negative note, Lord Nicholas tossed off the remainder of the claret and left the haven of his library to give instructions for his visit to town. With perhaps, in spite of everything, a lightening of his heart.

Chapter Two

~~~~~~~~

Judith, Countess of Painscastle, sat alone in the supremely elegant withdrawing room of the Painscastle town house in Grosvenor Square. Thoroughly bored. she leafed through a recent edition of *La Belle Assemblée*, but the delicious fashions for once left her unmoved. She closed the pages and frowned down at the fair and innocent beauty who graced the front cover. There was absolutely no reason for her lack of spirits! There were so many possible demands on her time, and all of them designed to please and entertain. A soirée at the home of Lady Beech that very night. Lady Aston's drum later in the week. A luncheon party. An essential visit to the dressmaker. What more could she require in life? She was truly, deliriously happy. But her husband Simon had found a need to visit Newmarket. He would return before the end of the week. But she missed him more than she would ever admit.

Now a married lady of almost seven years, Judith had changed little from the flighty, gossip-loving débutante who had stolen Painscastle's heart. Her hair was as wildly red and vibrant as ever, her green eyes as sparkling and full of life. Only the previous year she had fulfilled her duty and presented her lord with a son and heir. She was inordinately proud and loved the boy beyond measure. But she could not devote all day and every day to her child. She needed something, or someone, to entertain her.

She sighed again, flicked through the pages again, tutted over an illustration of an unattractive and certainly unflattering walking dress with heavy embroidered trim around the hem and cuffs when, on a polite knock, the door opened. Matthews, her butler, entered and presented a silver tray with a bow.

'Forgive me, my lady. A morning visitor.'

She cast aside the magazine at once and sprang to her feet. A diversion!

'A visitor!'

'A young lady. She says that she is unknown to you, but was advised to call by Lady Beatrice Faringdon.'

'Mama told her to come? Did she, now? She did not tell me.' Judith picked up the visiting card from the tray. 'I do not recognise this name. But if Mama sent her… Pray show the lady in, Matthews.'

'Yes, my lady.' There was a stern expression on his face as he retreated from the room to usher forward the lady in question.

'Miss Wooton-Devereux, my lady.'

'Thank you, Matthews. Would you be so kind as to bring ratafia?'

'Of course, my lady.' With a distinct frown, the butler retired.

The lady curtsied. Judith did likewise.

'Forgive me, my lady.' The lady spoke with confident assurance in a low, rather husky voice. 'I know that it is not usual to pay a morning call on someone to whom one has not been formally introduced, but my mama and Lady Beatrice have exchanged some correspondence of late. Lady Beatrice suggested that it would be of advantage to me to make your acquaintance as we are to be here in London for a little time. Being of a similar age, you understand.' She saw the lack of comprehension in Judith's face. 'I gather that your mama has not told you of this.'

'No. Nothing.'

'Forgive me. Perhaps I should not have presumed.'

'No, no—I am delighted that you did.' Judith thought that the lady did not look particularly sorry. 'Come and sit.' She waved an expansive hand towards a chair. 'I was only a moment ago thinking that I was in need of a distraction.' And this, she thought, after an equally brief moment of being in the lady's company, might be exactly the diversion she needed.

As the lady settled herself on the cream-and-gold striped chair, shaking out her skirts and removing her gloves, Judith took stock of her visitor.

'I am Theodora Wooton-Devereux. We—my parents and I— have just arrived in town. My mother is set to launch me into society, you should understand.' The lady's opinion of this intent was signalled by the faintest of curls to her beautiful lips.

'Indeed.'

The lady who sat before Judith in her withdrawing room, and somehow seemed to fill it with her personality was, well, striking, Judith supposed. Perhaps not classically beautiful exactly. Stunning might be a better word. She would certainly draw all eyes when she entered a room. She did not wear a bonnet. Her fair hair shone and—oh, my—it was cut quite short into the neck with curls that lay softly, without artifice, against her cheeks and forehead. When it was all the rage to wear ringlets falling to the shoulder from a high crown, Judith could not but stare. It was quite outrageous. But quite—charming, if one had the courage to wear it so. Judith knew that she would never dare. As Miss Wooton-Devereux turned her head, there was a touch of burnished copper amongst the gold where the sun caressed it. And those dark lashes and brows—an interesting combination with the deep blue of her eyes. Were her lashes actually dyed? And was there just a hint, the faintest brush of cosmetics on that flawless skin? Judith feared so—and was entranced. Her gown was both expensive and tasteful, but definitely not that of a débutante, shimmering as it did in pure silk of deepest amethyst, trimmed with knots of ribbon and a profusion of tiny silk flowers, in the same hue, around the hem and low-cut neckline.

Definitely *not* a débutante! Judith decided.

Nor did she wear the single strand of pearls so appropriate to a young girl on the brink of her presentation to society. Instead, a golden necklace of tiny entwined flowers and leaves lay against

her throat, coloured stones winking in their depths, and matching earrings dripped exotically from her delicate ears. A stole was
draped in artistic folds over her arms, of distinctly eastern pattern with just the hint of sparkle in the weave and the long
fringes. Her hands, now revealed as she placed her gloves and
reticule on the occasional table beside her, were long-fingered,
slender, with a number of intricately worked rings that gleamed
gold and silver in the sunlight.

The vision immediately stirred Judith's jaded appetite. It was
as if some exotic butterfly had taken it into its head to land in
her withdrawing room and bring it to life.

'You said that your name was Theodora?' Judith enquired
when she had completed her survey as tactfully as she might.

'Yes. My mama, Lady Drusilla, called me for the Empress of
the Roman Empire, the wife of the Emperor Justinian. She admired her, I believe. But do call me Thea.'

'Thea. Yes, of course. An unusual name.'

'Unfortunately. We do not choose our own and my mama has
eclectic tastes.' A glinting smile touched Thea's face. 'I have to
be grateful that she did not name me Cleopatra. Or Dido.'

'No, indeed! That would be most unfortunate!' The Countess
of Painscastle had no idea who Dido might be but decided that
it did not matter. 'Ah—you must call me Judith. You say that you
are to have a London Season?'

'Yes.'

'Forgive me, but…'

'I know what you are thinking.' Thea smiled with cheerful
composure. 'You think that I am too old to be a débutante. My
mama warned me that it must be so.'

'Well… That is to say… You are very forthright!'

'I was brought up to be so. And your comment is certainly
accurate. It is not my choice to have a Season at all. I wish to go
to Russia instead. But my mother insists. She wants an Earl for
me, you see.'

'Really.' Judith blinked. 'Well—that is to say…I expect she
might…'

'Yes. So my father has taken a house in Upper Brook Street and we are set to entertain. Your mama is acquainted with mine—and so suggested that you might give me some advice—how to go on here. I know the protocol in Paris and Constantinople. Even Vienna. But I have never lived in London before.'

'I see.' Judith didn't, but she was sure that this fascinating creature would soon explain.

'And so I thought I should come and see if you are willing—or if you would rather not. I hope that you would tell me what you truly feel. Parents can be so thoughtless and inconsiderate when they compromise their offspring—particularly when that offspring has no inclination for it at all!'

'Very true.' Judith found herself returning the smile in astonishment—and total agreement.

'Perhaps I should have not come here before we were introduced. Perhaps it is not *comme il faut?*'

Judith found herself sitting on the very edge of her seat. 'Perhaps not—well, no, it is definitely not the done thing, but I am delighted that you did. I was suffering from such a megrim before you arrived.'

'I have never suffered from a megrim in my life, but it pleases me that I can restore your spirits.' Miss Wooton-Devereux laughed gently, showing perfect teeth, her eyes gleaming with amusement. What an odd creature she was, to be sure.

'Tell me—' Judith had to satisfy her curiosity and decided that she felt no compunction in asking '—why have you not been presented before?'

Thea was perfectly willing to explain. 'My father, Sir Hector, is in the diplomatic service. He has been Ambassador to the Court of Constantinople of late. And we have travelled extensively so I have never had the opportunity to stay long in London or enjoy a Season. But now he is between posts. He expects to be sent to St Petersburg later in the year, but for the present we are to remain in London.'

The simple explanation was interrupted by Matthews, who brought in a tray bearing a decanter of ratafia, two glasses and a plate of little biscuits. He arranged them on the table beside Judith's chair and left, but not before directing another disapproving glance in the direction of their guest.

'I can not think what is wrong with Matthews.' Judith watched him as he left the room, shoulders rigid.

Thea laughed again, an infectious low chuckle that instantly encouraged Judith to smile in response. 'I believe that I have the answer. *I* am the cause of your butler's disapproval.'

'Why? What can you have done?'

'I came unchaperoned. Without my maid. He appears to disapprove.'

'Yes. I imagine that he would.'

'But it is only a step,' Thea explained. 'Hardly a stroll. Why should I need a maid with me? I am hardly likely to be set on by footpads in Mayfair in broad daylight, I presume.'

'No. Of course not. But it is most unconventional. It is not considered…seemly for an unmarried lady to venture on the streets unaccompanied.'

'I do not see—' She broke off as Judith handed her a glass of ratafia. She sipped it reluctantly, but with a practised pretence at enjoyment.

'It would not be good for you to be seen as *fast*,' Judith explained after taking a sip from her own glass, 'if you are to be accepted by the *haut ton*. You are not in Constantinople now— or Vienna.'

'I suppose not. I think your mama had the right of it. I need advice. Are you indeed willing to give me your support, Judith?'

'I think it would be the most delightful thing.' Judith put down her glass and all but clapped her hands with pleasure. 'It is just that you must be careful not to offend. You will wish to acquire tickets for Almack's, I suppose. And the patronesses are so strict, unpleasant even. The slightest whiff of scandal and they could refuse—and that would be fatal for anyone wishing to cut a dash in London.'

'Oh, there is no problem there.' Thea wafted away the problem with an elegant sweep of her hand. 'My mother is thick as thieves with Princess Esterhazy. They have known each other for ever—in diplomatic circles, you understand.'

'Oh dear. I did not mean to imply…' Instant colour rose in Judith's cheeks to clash with her hair.

'No matter. I know that she is not liked. But she can be very informative when she is not lecturing or finding fault. Perhaps you would be so kind as to drive or ride with me in the Park and point out some of the people I should know. And *not* know, of course, for I have not the least idea. Unless they are *very* entertaining. Have you noticed that those who are most scandalous and shunned by polite society are the most pleasurable to know?'

'I suppose so. I had not thought.' Judith's eyes grew round with astonishment.

'One has only to look at Lord Byron. Most unacceptable, but totally fascinating.'

'Well—yes. I agree. I suppose… Are you acquainted with my Lord Byron?'

'I know of him—all the scandals and the notoriety that he enjoys. And read his works of course. I thoroughly enjoyed *The Corsair*, but I think my mother would not welcome his lordship as a visitor to her withdrawing room. However free thinking she might claim to be, she disapproves of unbridled volatility above all things.'

Judith could think of no reply to this revelation.

'So will you help, Judith?' Thea returned to her original plea. 'I think we should deal well together.'

'I should be delighted.' Judith found her voice at last. And felt as if she had just been swept along by a positive whirlwind!

'On first acquaintance, I think that London could offer me a deal of pleasure.' Thea took another sip of ratafia with remarkably smooth features and looked hopeful.

'Oh, yes.' Judith gave a sigh of satisfaction and silently thanked her mama. Theodora Wooton-Devereux could just be a gift from heaven. But what polite society would make of Miss Wooton-Devereux, Judith could not imagine. It would be just too fascinating to discover. She decided to take the matter in hand immediately.

'If I might say, Thea—that is a very pretty stole. Quite eye-catching.'

'Yes. I like it.' Thea rearranged the folds of the scarf. 'I bought it in Palmyra. It is considered to be very typical of the delicate work produced in that city.' She caught a look in Judith's eye. 'Is there perhaps a problem with it? You must tell me, for I have not the slightest inclination.'

'Well—yes, it is certainly very attractive—but perhaps not for morning wear, you understand, as it is rather…decorative! For an afternoon visit it would be unexceptional. Or an evening at home. I hope that you do not mind me mentioning it?'

'Why, no.' Thea held up the luxurious fringing for inspection. 'Really? I would not have known. And I would dislike above all things to be considered lacking in taste. There! I said that we might deal well together, dear Judith.'

'I do hope so.' The Countess nodded with satisfaction.

'Now, enough of me. Tell me about yourself and your family.' Thea folded her hands in her lap and set herself to be sociable. 'Is your husband at home?'

'No, he is not. Simon has gone to Newmarket! I am quite vexed about it.'

'Ah! I understand that you have a young son.'

'Oh, yes. Giles. Now he is quite adorable. Come and see.'

Thea sighed a little, but was determined to fulfil her social duties. After all, she owed Judith much for her unaffected welcome of an unknown lady to her home, and suspected that she would owe her more before her sojourn in London came to an end. With a not quite enthusiastic smile, but a sharp relief at being able to abandon the much disliked ratafia, she followed Judith up the sweep of the staircase to the nursery to meet the heir to the Painscastle inheritance, prepared to admire and be charmed as was required.

Why her mother thought she needed a husband and children of her own, she could not imagine!

Thea returned to the smart rented property in Upper Brook Street, worthy of one of his Majesty's Ambassadors, to find a chaotic scene of boxes and packages littering the generous entrance hall. Their luggage, it appeared, had finally caught up with them. Servants, hired with the house, were in evidence and in the centre of it all, directing operations with imperious manner and a list in her hand, was Lady Drusilla. As wife to the Ambassador, she had successfully moved homes—and countries—many times. Sir Hector was, sensibly, nowhere to be seen. There was no hope, Thea realised, of her making an entrance undetected, so she did not try.

'Theodora! Where have you been? And without your maid—do not even try to deny it! Agnes informed me of your *sneaking* off within minutes of your leaving the house! As you must know she would!'

Thea bridled at the onslaught, even if it was expected. It was simply one more nail in the coffin of her much-prized freedom. 'If you had wished me to follow every social convention, you should have brought me up differently, Mama.' Her eyes snapped with irritation. She would have a few well-chosen words with Agnes Drew, her childhood nurse and now her maid—or perhaps more of a companion and confidante—whose loyalty seemed to be as much to Lady Drusilla as to herself.

'True. I myself have no time for many of them. That one. And that.' The lady pointed at two boxes and crossed them off her list as they were carried away. 'But here in London—it is important to have a care.'

'I have been out of the house barely two hours—and done nothing to draw attention to myself.' Thea narrowed her eyes at her mother's back. 'How should you think otherwise! Your opinion of me is not flattering, Mama.'

'Nonsense! My opinion of you is of the highest as you are very well aware. But by the end of the Season I hope to have acquired a rich and titled husband for you.' She announced her intentions with supreme disregard for the interested audience of maids and footmen around her.

'I know. An Earl. Any one of them will do, however old and ill favoured. As long as he is titled and rich! And available!'

'Now, Theodora! I have it on the best authority—from your father, no less—that the Earl of Moreton is in town. He is neither old nor ill favoured and has, I am given to understand, considerable address. Since he also has the advantage of being unmarried, he sounds to be just the thing. I have every hope.' For the first time, Lady Drusilla gave her daughter her full attention and noted the heightened colour in her cheeks, hardly engendered by a gentle stroll along Upper Brook Street, plus the sparkle in her eyes, which denoted a flash of temper. 'What have you been doing to put yourself so out of countenance?'

'Nothing. I am *not* out of countenance.' Except that she was after listening for an hour—was it only an hour?—to Judith singing the praises of a husband who seemed pleasant enough, but dull in the extreme. An equally tedious lifestyle of trivial pursuits and pastimes in London, of visits and conversations with the same set of acquaintance day after day, week after week. Winter spent incarcerated in the depths of the country, trapped by bad weather and worse roads. Was that the life for which she was destined? She shuddered at the prospect. There was no point telling her mama, who had quite made up her mind, of her fears, her depressing thoughts. But she did not have to like it. Or the unknown Earl of Moreton!

'So, where have you been?'

'To pay a morning call on Lady Painscastle.'

'I see. I am quite sure that you should not have done that without an invitation, Thea.' Lady Drusilla frowned her disapproval, but kept her tone light.

'Oh, she did not mind. I liked her. And she did not turn me from the door—although her butler would have dearly liked to.' A faint smile illuminated Thea's face at the memory.

'It is all your own fault if you allow servants the opportunity to patronise you, my dear.' Thea had to admire her mother's worldly wisdom expressed so casually. 'Take your maid in future! And wear a hat. I expect it is not at all the thing to go about with your head uncovered. At least you had the sense to wear gloves.'

'Yes, Mama.'

'So?' Lady Drusilla raised her brows. 'What has ruffled your feathers?'

Thea sighed a little. 'Do I really need a husband?'

'Yes. We have had this conversation before. You know my reasons—and your father's, of course.'

'But I have enjoyed independence for all my twenty-one years. Travel. Culture. Pleasing myself. Why can I not continue to do so?'

'You cannot travel for the rest of your life, Theodora. It is not suitable.'

'But you have.' Thea sat herself down on one of the unopened wooden packing cases, swinging her reticule carelessly by its silken strings.

'I had the felicity to meet and marry your father. Such opportunities as wife to a royal Ambassador are not given to everyone. You need a husband who will admire you for your qualities and allow you freedom to express yourself. As Sir Hector allowed me. I hope you will not *break* anything in that case on which you are sitting!'

Thea hid a smile. Secretly she doubted that Sir Hector had had any choice in his wife's chosen lifestyle. 'Does such a husband exist for me, do you suppose?'

'Of course.'

Thea pursed her pretty lips, looking sceptical, but made no reply.

'It is merely a matter of learning a few rules, knowing how to go on. And if you could pretend to be demure and biddable for a few weeks—'

'Ha!'

'And converse in a genteel and respectful manner, without interruption—'

'About fashion and embroidery, the latest dance and the latest *on dit*.'

'Exactly.'

'Oh, Mama. What have you committed me to!'

'It is not purgatory, my love.'

'And growing my hair into curls and ringlets again, if the glances I received today are anything to say to the matter.'

'I told you that you should not have been so extravagant! But you would do it!' Lady Drusilla stepped round a pair of leather travelling cases and leaned to kiss her daughter lightly on the cheek. She understood and sympathised with her concerns very well. 'You are a lovely young woman of whom I am very proud. Whether you grow your hair again, my love, is purely a matter of your own personal choice.'

'I have no intention of doing so.' Thea returned the salute and rose to her feet. 'By the by, I arranged for us to pay an afternoon call on Lady Beatrice Faringdon tomorrow if that suits.'

'Certainly. An excellent idea. My acquaintance with Lady Beatrice is from the very distant past, when we were still girls, but she is, I think, knowledgeable and accommodating. And, most important, has entrée to the best families in London. So begins our first step in the campaign.' Lady Drusilla crossed off two more items on her list. 'Did you learn anything other of import?'

'No. Except that this stole is pretty enough, but far more suitable for evening wear than for a morning visit.' The lady raised her brows, her mouth curling into a mischievous smile, as she lifted the delicate scarf from her shoulders.

'Oh.' Lady Drusilla inspected the garment with sudden interest. 'Perhaps we shall need a new wardrobe. It would not do to be regarded as *provincial*. Or oriental in our case! What is suitable in Constantinople is quite plainly not suitable here.'

The two ladies exchanged smiles, their differences reconciled.

'Let us go and discuss the matter with your father. Who, you will notice, has absented himself from all this.' She waved her hand in an expansive gesture at the chaos around her feet, then handed her list with great willingness to one of the footmen. 'And then, dear Thea, when we have some funds at our disposal, perhaps a stroll down Bond Street would be in order.'

* * *

On the following afternoon Lady Drusilla Wooton-Devereux and her daughter, with Agnes Drew discreetly, if a trifle smugly, in attendance, applied the knocker to Lady Beatrice Faringdon's imposing establishment in Berkeley Square. Expected, they were admitted and ushered into the lady's withdrawing room.

'Drusilla. My dear.' Lady Beatrice surged to her feet with a rustle of the puce damask that shrouded her opulent figure and clashed uncomfortably with her fading red hair. 'And this must be your daughter. Theodora.' She held out a hand in greeting, then halted, the hand falling to her side, and raised her lorgnette to deadly effect. She did not need to apply the lens as her eyesight was perfect. But the gesture was guaranteed to make an impression. She levelled the glass at her friend's daughter, surveyed her with a critical thoroughness from head to foot, and drew in a breath.

'Well. Caro Lamb, as I live and breathe!'

Which unwise comment was guaranteed to bring about a distinct pause in the proceedings. Lady Caroline Ponsonby, as she was before her marriage to William Lamb, Viscount Melbourne, was a spoiled capricious beauty whose appearance, behaviour and wild, tempestuous affair with Lord Byron some years previously had scandalised a notoriously decadent society.

Theodora took it upon herself to reply, with the politest of smiles, before her mother could intervene. But there was a noticeable edge to her voice and a glint in her eye, which might be interpreted as a challenge to their hostess. 'I hope that my upbringing has been more respectable than that of Lady Melbourne. It is certainly not my intention to distress my relatives by my outrageous behaviour or to take the town by storm in quite the same manner as that unfortunate lady. I would consider it exceptionally bad *ton* either to fly into a fit of rage in public, or to attempt to slash my wrists with broken glass.'

Lady Beatrice actually coloured at the implied set-down.

'Forgive me, my dear girl! Drusilla! It was not my intention to be so ill mannered. It is just… The hair, you understand. So fair…and so short. And so slender a figure. A mere fleeting impression, I do assure you.' She thought for a moment and raised her glass again. 'You have not been *ill*, have you?'

'Of course she has not.' Lady Drusilla stepped into the breach with calming words, a gracious smile for Lady Beatrice and a narrowed glance toward her daughter. 'We have travelled extensively in recent months in Arabia to see some of the archaeological sites. Theodora found it expedient to cut her hair. The sand is a great trial, you understand, and not kind to long hair. Theodora is always excessively healthy!'

'Of course. Forgive me, dear Drusilla...' Lady Beatrice almost gushed.

'And is nothing like poor Caro Lamb.'

'Indeed no. My wits must have abandoned me.' Lady Beatrice managed to recover her air of self-assurance and smiled with a trifle more warmth at the young lady who still regarded her with the coolest of expressions. 'And so charmingly dressed. I remember seeing Lady Melbourne in the most inappropriate gowns—if you could call them that—with not a stitch on beneath them, I warrant. Little wonder that she always looked as if a brisk breeze would demolish her. Some of the young girls today...' Lady Beatrice shook her head and brought her thoughts in line. 'But that is of no account. I am so delighted to see you again. Come and sit. And you, Theodora. How long is it since we last met, Drusilla?'

'Far too long to contemplate!'

The difficulties over, the three ladies sat, the two older ones intent on catching up over a dish of tea. Their paths had not crossed since school girls at Miss Felton's Academy for Young Ladies in Bath. Drusilla Hatton, as a daughter of wealthy parents, had even then nursed ambitions to travel and experience for herself what life could offer. Beatrice had been destined for a Season in London and as advantageous a marriage as she could achieve. The two girls had parted with many tears and protestations of undying loyalty. They would keep in touch. But they had not. And so of necessity the ladies had grown apart.

As the two ladies set to reminisce, Thea let her thoughts wonder, listening with only half an ear to the less than exciting do-ings of her parent at the Academy in Bath. What could they find to talk about that was of interest after all these years? It all sounded desperately dull and hedged about with restriction and parental expectations. She hid a yawn with considerable expertise. It reminded her of the worst of formal diplomatic receptions where nothing happened to relieve the tedium and no one had anything of moment to say after the introductions had been made. Thea fervently wished that she had found another occupation for the afternoon—until a stray comment from Lady Beatrice caught her attention.

'You had a sister, I remember. A year or so older, at school with us. Mary, I think.'

Thea's eyes snapped to her mother's face.

'Yes. You have a good memory.'

I did not know that my mother had a sister! Why did I not know? Lady Drusilla's reply was smooth enough, and yet Thea sensed the slightest of hesitations, a hint of reserve in her voice. She turned her attention fully.

'Does she live in London?' Lady Beatrice went on to enquire.

'No. Mary lived her whole life in the country. And is now dead. Some years ago.'

'I am sorry. Did she perhaps have family?'

'Yes. Two…two children. But we had not kept in touch. There was… an estrangement. Her marriage was not an easy one. I was not made welcome in her house.'

'You need not tell me about difficult marriages…'

The conversation moved on, leaving Thea to wonder about this branch of the family of which she was completely unaware.

The visit drew to a natural close when the ladies ran out of events and people to recall, criticise and chuckle over.

'As you know, we do not expect to remain long in London.' Lady Drusilla drew on her gloves in preparation to making her departure. 'But it is my wish to see my daughter married. You were kind enough to offer to ease our entrée into London society. I cannot express my gratitude sufficiently, Beatrice.'

'It will be my pleasure. At the end of the week I have an invitation to Lady Aston's drum. All the world and his wife will be there, I expect. It has been my intention to get up a small party—just family and close friends, you understand. I am expecting my nephew Nicholas to arrive here from the country any day—that is, if his recent correspondence rings true. But he is a difficult boy to pin down, with a mind of his own, and getting him to put in an appearance in town is more aggravating than you could possibly believe...' Lady Beatrice shook her head and huffed in indulgent irritation at the vagaries of her wiful relative. 'But that aside—you, my dear Drusilla, must come as my guest. It will be the perfect opportunity for you. And for Theodora to make some acquaintances.'

'We shall be delighted.' Lady Drusilla rose to her feet. 'It is my intention to entertain from Upper Brook Street, but we are not yet fully settled, as you might imagine.'

'Perhaps I might suggest—' Lady Beatrice cast another assessing glance towards Thea, who stood demurely beside her mother as if the visit had provided her with nothing but delight '—the matter of suitable dresses for dear Theodora. Not that she does not look charming. But...'

They both eyed the lady in question as if she were a strange object from antiquity.

'I thought she looked particularly fetching this afternoon.' Lady Drusilla stood back to take in the overall impression created by a high-waisted walking dress with long tight sleeves and a ruched hem in an eye-catching emerald and cream stripe.

'Yes. There is no question of that...' Beatrice was quick to soothe. 'But not quite in the way of a débutante.'

Lady Drusilla gave a little sigh. 'I have to admit that my daughter is not perhaps quite in the way of the usual débutante! I fear that it is my fault.'

'How old are you, my dear?' Lady Beatrice asked.

'I am twenty-one, Lady Beatrice.' Then, after a moment's hesitation, Thea could not prevent herself from adding, 'I fear that I have no control over that unfortunate situation.'

'Mmm.' The lorgnette came into play again. Lady Beatrice came to a rapid and sensible decision. 'Well. We will not allow it to be a problem. Perhaps we should say that Theodora made her curtsy to the Polite World in Constantinople. I am sure there were any number of official functions there which she attended.'

'Indeed she did. She helped me entertain on numerous occasions. She is perfectly versed in how to go on in such circles, so I have no fears on that account.'

Thea set her teeth against being talked over and around in such a fashion but, more amused than discomfited, allowed the ladies to continue their plans.

'She will need some suitable dresses. With a less—shall we say, *exotic* flavour. I am not sure what it is, but… Such a vibrant shade with such intricate decoration is not quite *suitable* for a young girl…'

'Very well. I bow to your judgement. Perhaps tomorrow morning we should visit the modistes in Bond Street. If you could recommend…?'

'I shall do more than recommend, dear Drusilla. I shall be delighted to accompany you…'

And so it was all settled. Theodora would make her curtsey at Lady Aston's drum, tastefully dressed, as far a possible, *à la jeune fille*.

The ladies parted in complete accord and satisfaction.

'Why did I not know of your sister? That I have cousins?' The two Wooton-Devereux ladies strolled home along Park Lane, parasols angled to shield their skin from the rays of the sun.

'The subject never came up.' Thea detected the slightest of shrugs as her mother replied. Nor was she fooled by the bland expression on her face.

'Mama!'

'We—Mary and I—were estranged,' Lady Drusilla explained further. 'I found it…painful. As I told Beatrice, we had had no contact for many years.'

'But you knew that she had died.'

'Yes. It was reported in the *Morning Post*. When we were in Paris.'

'I just thought you would have mentioned it—the fact that there were members of the family whom I had never met.'

'I suppose that I did not see any reason to do so. I had no intention of picking up the connection with that side of the family. There was nothing more sinister than that, I do assure you, Thea. Such estrangements happen in families. You have only to look at your father's cousin. He has not spoken to his own son for the best part of a decade.'

'I see.'

'Mary and I simply did not get on.'

Thea let the matter drop, but did not forget it. And it struck her some time later that during the whole of Lady Drusilla's explanation her eyes, usually so direct and forthright, had never once met those of her daughter.

Chapter Three

Lady Beatrice finally gave up on appearances, closed Miss Austen's *Emma*, which she had been assured was most refined and enjoyable, but over which she had been yawning, and allowed her eyes to close. After an exhausting morning spent choosing a new pair of evening gloves to wear at Lady Aston's drum, Lady Beatrice desired nothing more than to settle on to a comfortable sofa in a quiet parlour with the shades drawn and rest her eyes. She certainly had no intention of being at home to visitors. Instead, within minutes, she found herself playing hostess to Judith, who arrived in a flurry of energy to discuss with her mama their new friends. And then, following quickly on her heels, Lord Nicholas Faringdon.

'Nicholas. I had quite given up hope of seeing you this week. When did you arrive?' Lady Beatrice stretched out her hands in sincere pleasure, but did not bother to struggle to her feet. 'Ring the bell, Judith, for tea.'

'Would I dare ignore your summons, Aunt? I came yesterday evening.' Nicholas strode across the room to where his aunt was seated, raised her hands and kissed her fingers with rare grace. 'You look in excellent health, as ever.'

'Never mind my health! Let me look at you.' But she smiled almost girlishly at her nephew's elegant gesture as she surveyed him from head to foot. It was a relief to see him in town rig. For although he was no dandy and might have rusticated at Burford for over a year, there was nothing of the unfashionable country squire in the gentleman who graced her withdrawing room. The close-fitting coat of dark blue superfine, with all the hallmark of Weston's exquisite tailoring, was unexceptional. As were the pale biscuit pantaloons, polished Hessians and the sober but tasteful waistcoat. His neckcloth had been arranged with meticulous attention to detail. Altogether, a Man of Fashion.

'Very fine!' was the only comment she made. 'My letter was not in any way a summons. Merely a request. And, yes, you have been ignoring my advice for any number of years. Ever since you attained your majority, I shouldn't wonder.'

'I was not aware that I was so disobliging.' Nicholas turned to drop a light kiss on his cousin's cheek. 'Judith—and how is the heir to the Painscastle acres?'

'Giles is in excellent form. You must come to visit us, of course.' She patted the seat next to her. 'It is good to have you here Nick. We had thought you were becoming buried alive at Burford. Don't tell me that you have a young lady there who lures you into rural seclusion.'

'I shall tell you no such thing.' He showed his teeth in a quick smile, refusing to be baited.

'So you don't have a lady who is the object of your gallantry to while away the winter evenings?' She laughed, slanted him an arch look, glinting with mischief. 'I cannot believe that the ladies of Herefordshire are so blind to your charms. No cosy armful tucked away in the depths of Aymestry?'

'Judith! Such levity! It does not become you.' Beatrice frowned, rescued Nicholas and steered the conversation into the area of her own choosing. An area no less full of subtle—or not so subtle—suggestion.

'Now, tell us—how is Henry? And Eleanor. We have not heard for some months.'

'Hal is very well.' Nicholas leaned back and prepared to do his bit for family news and deflect any personal comments from either his aunt or his cousin. 'And he is now in possession of a thriving business, it seems. They have moved into the house. Eleanor said she was delighted to have her own front door at last. Her letter was full of furnishings and decorations as I recall. Hal's pockets will have to be bottomless if she is to have her way.'

'Eleanor is in an *interesting condition*, I believe.'

'Yes. She is. They are very happy.'

'As they deserve to be.' Beatrice nodded. 'What a blessing it was that they escaped the toils of that truly appalling man Edward Baxendale.'

Baxendale!

The name would have twisted Lord Nicholas's lips into a snarl if he had not been sitting in the civilised surroundings of Lady Beatrice's withdrawing room. Even now, after two years or more, it had the power to heat his blood and fill him with immoderate fury.

Sir Edward Baxendale had claimed that the marriage of Eleanor to Nicholas's eldest brother Thomas was illegal, and thus her baby son not, as all believed, the Marquis of Burford, but stained with the stigma of illegitimacy. He'd presented his own wife Octavia, with diabolical cunning, as Thomas's true wife, the true Marchioness of Burford. Since Thomas had died in a tragic accident, the shocking tale had cast the family into instant scandal, only salvaged by the efforts of Nicholas and his brother Hal proving that Eleanor's marriage to Thomas had indeed been valid and Baxendale nothing but a malevolent trickster. Hal had then declared his love for Eleanor and, with typical highhandedness, taken her and the baby off to New York. But all could so easily have been a disaster if Baxendale had triumphed. So much pain deliberately inflicted by the greed of one man. No wonder Nicholas detested Sir Edward with every sinew in his body, every drop of blood.

By sheer effort of will, Nicholas forced his muscles to relax, his hands to unclench, as Lady Beatrice continued with her social catechism, unaware of the impact of her chance comment.

'And Tom. He will be more than three years old now.'

'Four more like. Time passes. Eleanor said that Hal was teaching him to ride.'

'Do you think they will ever return?' Judith asked a little wistfully.

'No. I do not. I think Hal's life is there in America.'

'And the estate?' Disapproval was clear in Beatrice's tight-lipped mouth. She simply could not accept that the young Marquis of Burford should be allowed to live in America, far from his family, his land and his responsibilities. It was beyond anything. 'What will happen to it? It is all very well—'

'I don't know,' Nicholas broke in before she could get into full flow. This was not a new situation over which they disagreed. 'That is for the future. For the present it is carefully administered. I shall not permit anything other. What Hal will choose to do is entirely his own concern. And nothing to do with me—or, with respect, with you, Aunt Beatrice!'

Which statement, Lady Beatrice decided with something akin to shock, was certainly guaranteed to put her in her place!

'No. And of course you will act in the best interests of the family. I would expect no less and I intended no criticism of your trusteeship.' Beatrice controlled her concerns, leaned over to pat his arm. 'There is no point in discussing it further. Forgive me, Nicholas.' With respect, indeed! Now here was a novelty! 'Now, since you are here at last, perhaps you can escort us to Almack's one evening.' She hesitated only momentarily before launching in. 'There are some very pretty débutantes this Season.'

'I am sure there are.'

'One or two are quite exceptional. Sir John Carver's daughter, for instance.'

Nicholas raised his hand, turning a stern gaze on his aunt. His eyes, often so friendly and full of laughter, had the quality of ice. As had his voice. He may as well, he decided, nip this in the bud immediately. 'Aunt Beatrice, I wish that you would not. I am perfectly capable of selecting a wife for myself without any help from you, *when* I decide that I wish to marry. I agree with you that I should consider it, but it will be in the time of my choosing, as will be the identity of the lady who I eventually ask to become my bride. Do we have an understanding?'

There it was, laid out for her. Beatrice stiffened at the snub, taken aback for the second time since Nicholas had entered the room. She had forgotten that her nephew was no longer a young and impressionable boy. It was so easy to forget when he was the youngest in the family. But the years had moved on and he had put her firmly in her place twice within as many minutes with a perfect exhibition of suave, cool—and implacable—good manners. Beatrice took in the stern mouth, the austere features, and wisely retreated.

'Of course. I would not dream of interfering in your affairs, my boy—'

'Yes, you would. But I ask that you do not. I would not wish to feel obliged to refuse your kind invitations. And I will if necessary.' He was clearly not prepared to compromise over this. 'I am sure that you take my meaning?'

Oh, yes. She took his meaning very well—and realised that she must reassess Lord Nicholas Faringdon. She raised her hands and let them fall in her lap. 'Of course. I will do nothing that you do not wish for, Nicholas.'

'I should be grateful, Aunt.' He deliberately changed the subject. 'So, how is Sher? I have not seen or heard from him for well over a year.'

Lord Joshua Sherbourne Faringdon. Undoubtedly the black sheep of the otherwise impeccable Faringdon family. And the bane of Lady Beatrice's life.

'My son Joshua is still in Paris.'

'Is he well?'

'I presume.' The response from the less than doting mama was tight-lipped. 'All we hear is scandal and gossip.'

'He has a new mistress,' Judith added with an irrepressible twinkle. 'An actress, we understand.'

'I think that is not a subject for my withdrawing room, Judith. Joshua will go to the devil in his own way. There is no need for us to show interest in it. Now…did you know that Simon has been to Newmarket? One of his horses is expected to do particularly well on the Turf this year…'

The conversation passed into calmer waters, Nicholas turning to Judith for news of Simon and the promising stallion.

Beatrice watched the pair as they sat at ease, reliving old times, discussing friends in common. It was time Nicholas married. He needed a family. Not merely the responsibility of the estate—God knew he had enough of that!—but responsibility for a wife and children. He had been too long pleasing himself. He needed someone to ruffle his equilibrium, to shake his self-confidence. It appeared that he could be as difficult and opinionated as all male Faringdons. Look at Henry. A law unto himself, taking himself and Eleanor and the child off to New York without a word to anyone! And as for her own dearest husband, now long deceased, and her son…whom she did not even wish to contemplate. They were all the same—excessively handsome with all the charm and address in the world, but all with that fatal streak of arrogance and self-worth. And Nicholas, to make matters more difficult, had that cool reserve which was difficult to shake. When *that* had developed she did not know, but the aura of cold detachment and control coated him with a hard brilliance.

At least Judith was easy to deal with—she was like an open book! Beatrice watched with affection her daughter's expressive face as she laughed at some comment from Nicholas. That was from *her* side of the family, of course, just as much as the red hair and green eyes. Nicholas was a Faringdon from his dark hair and equally dark brows to his toes of his polished boots. And he needed someone who would challenge his intellect and keep him on those toes—give him something to think about other than farming and cattle and such.

She watched, tapping her lorgnette against her lips as she studied him, the lad whom she had known from birth and had watched grow into this spectacularly handsome young man. Even tempered, easy to converse with, but underneath…Well, they said still waters… She was quite sure that he could acquire a bride with an arch of those expressive brows or a crook of his finger. But not *any* débutante would do. He needed someone to stir him out of his complacence. He was too much in the habit of going his own way with no one to question his decisions or his opinion.

Lady Beatrice blinked as the thought slid so simply, so effortlessly into her mind, the image as clear as an etching on crystal. Now *there* was an interesting prospect. Beauty. Money. Excellent breeding. But also strong-willed, independent, outspoken and… Well! What could be better?

'Nicholas…' She interrupted the exchange of news between her nephew and her daughter. 'Will you be very busy during your stay in town?'

'Nothing out of the way. I have an appointment to see Hoskins. My tailor will no doubt see me. Friends, of course. I have no definite plans. Why?'

'No reason.' Her smile was pure innocence. 'Perhaps you would care to attend a number of social engagements with us? An extra gentleman is always valuable in a party. And you dance so well.'

'Why not? Since you are concerned to flatter me…' His tone and demeanour had reclaimed their habitual warmth, the chill forgotten. He saw nothing suspicious in Beatrice's bland smile and innocuous request, believing that he had made his opinions on the matter of marriage quite clear. Why should he harbour suspicions? And it would be good to circulate in society again.

'Tomorrow we are engaged to attend Lady Aston's drum. A large affair, totally lacking in exclusivity as such things usually are, but entertaining enough. I have got up a small party. Perhaps you would care to join us? We have some new acquaintance in town. One of them is to be our Royal Ambassador to the Russian Court. I am sure you will find him interesting company.'

'I am sure that I shall.'

Beatrice glanced over at Judith, smiled, her eyes guileless. And Judith, in spite of no words being spoken between them, was in no doubt as to exactly what her mama's plan might be.

'Do come.' Judith turned her persuasive gaze on her cousin. 'It should be a most entertaining evening.'

Unaware of the machinations of his female relatives, ignorant of the trap about to close over his head, Lord Nicholas bowed his agreement.

In Grosvenor Square on the following morning, very early, it was brought home to Nicholas how long it had been since his last visit to town. His body and mind were not in tune with town hours where it was customary to sleep and rise late. A combination of rural habits and the early sun through his bedroom window over and above the array of noises of a large city awakening to a new day—all assaulted his senses to ensure that he was wide awake. So he rose, dressed and headed for the stables behind Faringdon House. He might as well make the most of the opportunity to ride in Hyde Park so early as it would be mostly deserted; since he had no particular desire to converse with those who wished to parade and make a fashionable statement, it was the ideal time. There was a young horse that would benefit from a confidence-boosting outing without the habitual bustle and racket of London streets.

It was a perfect morning. He breathed deeply, encouraging the mare into a brisk walk through the light traffic. Through the ornamental gates and there, with an easing of the reins, he allowed the horse to break into a sedate canter along the grassy edge to the walk. And smiled his satisfaction. She was just as fluid and easy in her action as he had hoped.

In Upper Brook Street, Theodora woke from a restless sleep, certain that she would positively burst if she did not escape from the house and take some exercise, unwatched by either her mama or the ever-vigilant Agnes Drew. London was noisy, exciting, fascinating, all that she had hoped. But the restrictions irked. She was never alone. If she set foot outside the front door, Agnes had been instructed to be in attendance, even if all she did was step out to Hookham's Circulating Library, no further than Bond Street. She found it difficult to accept this necessity. She was hardly likely to be accosted by armed tribesmen or bands of fearsome robbers as might have been expected anywhere on their perambulations through Arabia. She closed her mind against that thought with a little shake of her head. She would not think about it…not now.

Therefore, driven by a need for open space and not a little adventure, Thea rose early before even the servants were afoot. No one would know if she rode in Hyde Park. She would be home long before one of the maids brought her morning cup of hot chocolate, long before anyone else—Agnes!—had the opportunity to miss her. And there would be no one in the park at this hour who would even take note of her, much less recognise her in the future. Perfect!

Thea stood before the doors of her closet. Then her face lit with mischief on a sudden thought. Of course. Why not? No one would ever know. She closed the door on her riding habit and, in a moment of delicious rebellion, turned from the closet and unearthed her travelling clothes from the chest in her dressing room. Without another moment to consider the impropriety of what she was about to do, she donned a long-sleeved shirt, a striped loose-weave waistcoat, loose breeches and boots, covering all with the light cloak she had worn in the desert, finally wrapping the long scarf round her hair. There. Her disguise was complete. She postured before the mirror. She would defy anyone to recognise her in future, at some social event, even if they did catch a glimpse of her that morning. Had she not been so very good and accommodating of her parents' plans for so long? Days at least! She deserved a treat, a moment of freedom.

Even the stables were deserted. She saddled her own mount, The Zephyr, one of the grey Arabs that they had shipped to London who was also in need of a good run, tossing her head and snatching at the bit with anticipation. It took no time at all to negotiate the empty streets, and if the shrouded figure earned some surprised glances and muttered comments, Thea was either unaware or simply did not care. The magnificent gateway opposite Apsley House beckoned. Once through Thea took a deep breath. She had been right to come. This was just what she needed. She eased into a canter, and then, the breeze tugging at her robes, she pushed the horse on into a gallop. The Arab responded with alacrity, leaping forward against the bit, its neat hooves skimming the ground as it fought for its head. Thea leaned into the movement with a little crow of pleasure, revelling in the speed and excitement. Exhilaration sang in her blood, rich as red wine, just as intoxicating. She gave herself over to the splendour of the moment, oblivious to everything around her but the pound of the hooves, the whip of the soft air on her face, the satin-smooth ripple of the horse's muscles beneath her.

Nicholas's mind was filled with nothing very much, apart from the excellent confirmation of his young mare as she answered the demands of heel and thigh. Nothing to disturb the placid tenor of the morning until he heard the sharp beat of hooves on grass, at speed coming from his left. He turned his head, his attention immediately caught. At considerable speed, he realised. He reined in the mare to look, squinting against the early rays of the sun, and saw a figure approaching at an angle, surely at full gallop, the rider crouched low in the saddle as the animal extended until it flew across the ground. Surely it was out of control. No one galloped in Hyde Park as though it was the hunting field. Or more like the Turf at Newmarket, given the speed of the animal. No one would choose to ride hell for leather here.

For the briefest moment Nicholas allowed himself to admire the fluid lines of the grey, the excellent conformation, the sheer beauty of the sight, but for a moment only. On a rapid decision, he kicked his mare on to intercept as the prospect of danger touched his spine with a shiver of unease. If the rider fell at that speed, there could be serious consequences. The animal could stumble, shy—and it seemed that the rider had no chance of drawing it to a standstill. Nor would intercepting be an easy matter on an untried young horse. But he must try.

Since the galloping animal kept up its headlong flight, Nicholas was forced to extend to head it off. His mare responded readily. The grey became aware of his approach, her ears twitching, even if her rider did not appear to react. She veered as he drew abreast but did not check her stride. If anything, she increased her momentum.

For what seemed like minutes—but was more likely seconds only—the two horses galloped side by side, the enforced rivalry adding an edge to the grey's speed, until Nicholas moved close enough that he could lean across the gap between them and grasp the bridle just above the bit, trusting his own animal to remain on course. She did, allowing him to tighten his muscles in arm, shoulder and thigh, grimacing at the strain as he drew both horses to a more seemly speed and finally to a trembling halt, their sides heaving with effort, nostrils wide, eyes rolling. At the same time he grasped the wrist of the rider in a firm hold, in case the grey jinked in sudden panic.

'You are quite safe. You are in no danger now.'

Nicholas's breathing was a little unsteady as he continued to control the reins of both horses. He looked down at the rider— a young boy, he thought, at closer inspection—to see if his reassurances were necessary, only to be struck by a pair of furious blue eyes turned on him, blazing with…what? Anger? Shock? But also more than a hint of fear.

'You are quite safe,' he repeated. Of course, the rider would be unnerved after such an uncontrolled bolt across the Park.

Before he could say or do more, the boy raised a riding crop and brought it down in a deliberate and painful blow across Nicholas's hand where he still had hold of the rider's wrist. Nicholas flinched, hissed, took a sharp intake of breath, perhaps more in amazement than pain, as a red welt appeared across the width of his fingers.

'What the devil…!'

'How dare you! Take your hands off me!' The rider pushed back the scarf—and Nicholas looked down into the face of a woman.

'How dare you interfere!' Her blue eyes were dark, almost black with emotion.

'I thought, madam, that your horse was out of control.' It was difficult to know what other to say. The last thing Nicholas had expected was to be under attack for his gallant, and supremely successful, attempt to rescue a damsel in distress. The absurdity of the situation might have amused him. It might if the blow on his hand was not so searingly painful!

'No, I was not out of control.' There was now the hint of a tremble in the angry voice. 'You had no right.' He watched as a range of emotions flitted across her face. Uppermost it seemed to him was a determination to regain control of a fear that threatened to overwhelm her.

He discovered that he was still grasping her wrist.

'I said, let go!'

Their eyes met and held for a long moment which seemed to stretch on and on. They remained frozen in the little tableau as the air positively sizzled between them, around them, as when lightning strikes in a summer storm—rapid, without warning, and possibly devastating. Nicholas was the first to break the contact.

'Forgive me.' He released her, cold now, all humour banished under the lash of her words and the shock of his reaction to her. 'I thought you were in distress.'

'No, I was not.'

'My mistake.' Reserve infiltrated his voice, but he still watched her carefully. There was some problem here of which he was unaware. 'Next time I will allow you to fall and break your neck.'

'Do so. There will not be a next time. I do not need your help. How dare you put your hands on a lady in this manner!'

Any latent sympathy Nicholas might have felt promptly vanished. 'You must excuse my concern, madam.' He looked her over from head to foot, taking in the whole of her appearance. 'I did not realise. I would not expect to see a *lady* galloping in Hyde Park. Please accept my apologies.' The emphasis in his words was unmistakable and made Thea flush, angrier than ever.

'Let go of my reins.'

He did with alacrity and reined his own animal away from her. In that one moment he thought, although perhaps he was mistaken, that there was a hint of tears in those eyes, which still snapped with temper.

The lady, if such she was, gathered up her own reins, kicked the still lively grey into action and set off in a canter towards the distant gate without a backward look.

Leaving Nicholas to sit and stare after her.

Thea arrived home, delivered The Zephyr into the hands of a sleepy groom who gazed at her in wordless astonishment, fled to her room and locked the door. There she stripped off her incriminating garments, folded them back into the chest and tied a ruffled, feminine muslin wrapper around her. Then, as the furious energy drained away, she sank on to the bed and covered her face with her hands.

What had she done? Not the gallop in the park. She could never regret that. How the grey had flown, fast as a desert hawk towards its prey. But she had struck him. The man who had come to her rescue. However unnecessary it might have been, he had thought she had been in danger and had ridden to her rescue. And what had she done? She had marked him with her riding whip. And then she had been so rude. Unforgivably so. She could not remember her exact words, uttered in the heat and confusion of the moment, but knew that they had been ungracious. Vicious, even. What would he think of her? How could she have allowed herself to do that?

But she knew why. And whatever the extenuating circumstances, she blamed herself totally.

She relived the events in her mind as she curled on to the bed in that sunny room. She had been unaware of his approach, so lost in the unity of horse and rider, in the glorious speed. But then, in that moment when his horse had stretched beside hers, when he had leaned and grasped her reins, his strong hands forcing her to come to a halt, the past had rushed back with all its pain and fear. She had thought it was forgotten, or mostly so, pushed away, buried deep within her subconscious, only to emerge with infrequent intensity when nightmares troubled her sleep.

She had been very young, hardly more than a child. On one of their journeys they had been beset by robbers in spite of the size and strength of their entourage. Forced to halt, to dismount, to stand and watch as her mother's jewellery was stripped from her, as her father was threatened at the point of a knife. The fear had been intense. They had been allowed to go free at the end, but the terror of that moment when they were held captive and in fear for their lives had not quite gone away.

Thea shook her head, scrubbed her hands over her face as if to dislodge the thoughts. She should not be so fearful now—but she had been only a little girl, after all. And her arm had been broken when she had been pulled from her horse. She rubbed her forearm as if the pain, inflicted so long ago, still lingered, as the image still lingered in her mind.

So when he had forced her to halt, had grasped her wrist in such a strong hold, the memory of the robbers, of being constrained and hurt and frightened, had rushed back and she had struck out blindly. At an innocent victim.

And he had reacted with disgust at her bad manners, her lack of gratitude. Her face flushed again with humiliation as she remembered the look of astonishment on his face. And what a face. Strikingly handsome. Heart-stoppingly so. But how he had looked down that high-bred nose at her, with such chilling hauteur. Eyes as glacial as chips of ice. Lips thinned in distaste—and probably pain, she was forced to admit. And she remembered his voice. Warm, reassuring at first when he had thought to comfort her, then cold and flat when she had actually accused him of trying to harm her.

She groaned aloud and twisted to bury her face into the coverlet. If she tried to put the blame squarely on her unknown rescuer for daring to interfere, her innate fairness quickly stopped her. Her behaviour towards him had been despicable. He had suffered for his quixotic actions because she had used enough force to mark his skin and inflict pain.

And then there was that strangest of moments. A little shiver ran over her skin as she felt again the force of it. She had no experience of such things. But as her eyes had met his, she could not look away, her breath had foundered in her lungs. She could still feel the hard imprint of his fingers around her wrist. What was it that had united them in that one moment of uncontrolled emotions, had robbed her of words, of actions? All she had seen was the beauty of his face, the run of emotions across it. And in that one fleeting moment she had wondered what it would be like if those firm lips had moved a little closer and actually touched hers.

Thea stood up, astounded at the direction of her thoughts.

All she could hope for was that she would never have to meet him again! In her usual forthright manner, Thea knew that she could not worry over what she could not undo. She must compose herself or her mother would ask far too many questions.

But she could not forget him, and her heart was sore.

Lord Nicholas Faringdon rode back to Grosvenor Square deep in thought, allowing the mare to choose her own pace. All he could think about was that lovely face when she had removed the enveloping scarf, and her hair—short and shining like a golden halo round her head. But she was no angel. He smiled a trifle grimly at the thought. Those furious eyes. Imperious as she lashed at him with whip and words. And there had been fear there. And at the end—distress? Had she actually flinched from him, cowered even for that one moment when he grasped her wrist? And whereas he might have expected her to be flushed from her exertions, her face had been white, all the blood drained from her cheeks as she had looked up into his face, until she had recovered and wielded her riding whip with considerable force and accuracy.

He was not sure, but her violent response seemed to be as much from fear as from anger. But why? Apart from bringing her horse to a halt, he had done nothing to threaten her. Could she really have believed that he was attempting to molest her, to force himself on her in so public a place? Or anywhere for that matter!

Take your hands off me!

Her tone and words were clearly imprinted on his mind. She had been terrified. Furthermore her whole appearance was—unusual, to say the least. Remarkable clothes, enveloped in some sort of eastern robe. And alone. No sign of a maid—not surprising in the circumstances—but neither was there an accompanying groom, not even in the distance. And—of course! Something else that now struck him: she had been riding astride. And if he had not been mistaken, there had been no sign of cumbersome skirts and petticoats. She had been wearing breeches and boots! Well, now!

Perhaps, then, she was merely some less-than-respectable woman to indulge in behaviour so particular—yet he did not think so. The impression was that she was undoubtedly a lady. Certainly not in the style of the notorious Letty Lade, who might have been an excellent horsewoman but who also had claims to being a highwayman's mistress before her advantageous marriage. No—there was a distinct air of class and style attached to this mysterious horsewoman who had just crossed his path. Moreover, the grey Arab had taken his eye. Now there was an example of superior horseflesh and breeding. And whoever she might be, he had to admit that the lady could ride!

Nicholas turned out of the park and allowed himself to think of that instant of—of connection, he supposed. He had not imagined it. It had held them both in thrall as the world continued round them. Shrugging his shoulders against a slight chill of discomfort, he pushed the memory away of the sudden heat that had spread through his blood as he had tightened his fingers around her wrist and felt the beat of her heart through her pulse. It had taken him aback. But it did not matter since they were unlikely ever to meet again. And what did he want with a woman who galloped her horse across Hyde Park, clad in unseemly garments, and responded to kindness with rude and insulting words? Yet a tinge of admiration crept under his skin, recognition of her courage and spirit, until he deliberately, ruthlessly thrust it away.

Lifting his hand from the reins, he stretched it, then made a fist with a grimace. The welt was red, a little swollen where the blow had broken the skin. He swore at the sting of pain.

Of one thing he was quite certain, he decided, as he turned into the entrance of Grosvenor Square. He had never met the woman before. And he would not be sorry if he never saw her again.

'It is a very pretty dress,' Thea acknowledged with what could be interpreted as a most accommodating smile, if one did not know the lady. 'And I am sure that the colour is most suitable and flattering to any young girl. But I will not wear pale pink.'

'But it is *Maiden's Blush*, miss.'

The four ladies all surveyed the gown being displayed in the arms of the assistant at Madame Therese's in New Bond Street with varying degrees of appreciation. The assistant frowned, impervious to the débutante's smile. As Madame Therese's senior assistant, she was used to dealing with their noble customers with superior and knowledgeable condescension. Dealing with this exacting, although exceedingly polite young lady, she felt her temper was beginning to fray.

'*Maiden's Blush* it may be, but it is still pale pink. It is entirely inappropriate for my colouring, either my hair or my skin. I will not wear it.' Thea's opinion was expressed in the gentlest of tones, almost apologetic in its denial, but her refusal could not be in doubt. The assistant's frown had no effect.

'Perhaps this would be better suited to you, miss.' The harassed lady laid the offending gown with its delightfully ruffled skirt and pearl-buttoned sleeves—the epitome of the art of dressmaking and one of their finest designs—across a chair and lifted another with tender care. 'This is *Evening's Kiss*. A most fashionable colour this year. A most exclusive garment, as you can see.'

'That is pale blue.'

'Indeed, it is very attractive, Thea. Such precise but delicate embroidery, don't you think? Will you not try it?' Lady Drusilla saw the set of her daughter's lovely mouth, despite the smile, and her heart sank. Not stubborn exactly, just…well, *decided*. Dressing Thea was never easy.

'I do not wish to wear pale anything, Mama. How can you ask it of me? You know that I look far better in something with a little—intensity, with depth.'

'But it is most becoming for a débutante.' The assistant appeared close to tears. This was the sixth gown that had been rejected out of hand and one of them had been *Damsel's Dreams*. How could any young lady reject such a confection of white organdie sprinkled with knots of forget-me-nots?

'No.'

'Jonquil?' suggested Judith. 'It is such a soothing colour, I always think, and unexceptional for morning wear.' The Countess of Painscastle had joined them at Madame Therese's with apologies for her late arrival. Simon had returned home earlier than she had expected, she explained, with a becoming flush to her cheeks. She had been detained.

Thea turned unbelieving eyes on Judith. 'Pale yellow? It will rob my hair of any colour at all! I shall look even more sallow. How I wish that I had been born a brunette with dark eyes! Or a redhead like you.' She turned her gaze back to the blue creation, determined that she would not grace Almack's, or any other occasion, in such an insipid dress, however fine the embroidered hem.

Lady Beatrice sighed and shuffled on her chair. This was going to be just as difficult as she had expected. Theodora had a most unfortunate strength of will. And her mama had apparently encouraged her to exert it with flair and confidence at every possible opportunity. The *Evening's Kiss* had been so pretty...

They were interrupted from any further discussion over the maligned gown by a slight, dark lady coming into the room. Her face was thin, her features narrow and prematurely lined, but her eyes were quick and assessing of the situation.

'Madame Therese.' Lady Beatrice hailed her in the light of a saviour. 'Yours is just the advice we need. Here we have Miss Wooton-Devereux who is to go about in society. She is reluctant to wear the dresses we have seen that are suitable for a young girl who is to make her début. Perhaps *you* can persuade her where *we* have failed.'

Madame Therese smiled a greeting. 'I will try. Let us consider what we might achieve for the lady.' Her accented voice was genuine. A French *emigrée* who had fled from her home in Paris, she had been forced to sell her skills. She had a decided air of fashion and an excellent eye for what would suit, so she was soon in demand when she opened her select little establishment in the heart of Mayfair. Rumour said that she had been a countess in her past life. It added a cachet so she did not disabuse her customers.

'Come, *mademoiselle*.' She took Thea's hand to draw her to her feet. 'If you would stand. And turn a little. You have an excellent figure, if I might venture. And such a slender neck. It will show to good advantage in the low necklines that are so fashionable this year. And with your hair so short—*c'est magnifique*. You are tall enough to carry the slender skirts with style. I think we shall manage very well. Tell me what *you* would choose to wear.'

The result was a comfortable and detailed conversation between Madame Therese and Miss Wooton-Devereux, which resulted in the hovering assistant being dispatched to collect a number of garments from the workroom at the back.

'You are not the traditional débutante, not the shy *ingenue*. I agree.' Madame Therese spoke her thoughts. 'I think we should—ah, experiment a little. I believe that we should try for a little restrained sophistication. For youth, of course, but with a layer of confidence. We will keep it simple but add a little gloss—how you say—town bronze.' She nodded, pleased with the direction of her thoughts. 'What a challenge it will be to promote a new style for a young lady who is not merely a child. I think that we might take the town by storm. I vow that you will wear any of my creations with panache, *mademoiselle*.'

'I do not think that we wish to draw too much attention…' Lady Drusilla was quietly horrified. It would take little to encourage Thea. Taking anything by storm was not a careful mama's intention. A quiet, demure introduction would be much more the thing and far more likely to attract the titled gentleman she had in mind.

'No, no, Mama.' Thea's eyes sparkled with enthusiasm for the first time since they had set foot inside the establishment. 'Madame Therese understands perfectly.'

'I do indeed.' The dark eyes reflected the sparkle. 'There is no need for concern, my lady,' she was quick to reassure Lady Drusilla. 'We shall consider nothing outrageous or unseemly. All will be tasteful and elegant. Now. Might I suggest…'

The next hour passed rapidly. An array of dresses appeared as if by magic for *mademoiselle* to try. Dresses for morning wear, for afternoon visits, for walking or driving in Hyde Park. Silk spencers for when the day was inclement. Gowns for an informal soirée at home, or an evening at Almack's. Even for a formal ball with a matching cloak and satin slippers. The prevailing style suited Thea to perfection, Judith had to admit with only a hint of jealousy, as she watched her new friend execute a sedate twirl in a high-waisted, low-necked column of shimmering gold with a transparent gauze overskirt. She was as tall and stately, as coolly elegant, as a *regale* lily until you saw the flash of fire, of sheer enjoyment in those dark blue eyes.

The gowns were, as Madame Therese had promised, simply constructed, with little decoration except for some silk lace to trim, a row of scallops or a neat ruche of ruffles. Perhaps a little satin ribbon or tiny pearl buttons, but nothing *outré*. But what an air. What style. And in such colours. Celestial blue, as deep as a robin's egg. A rich, clear pink, nothing like *Maiden's Blush*, but one which glowed like a newly unfurled rose in morning sunshine.

Thea was even talked into the palest of *eau de nil* silk, *Breath of the Sea*, she was assured—deliciously enhanced by an overskirt of spangled lace. It glittered as the light caught the spangles, gleamed as if under water where the light refracted into a million facets, turning her into a veritable mermaid. Who could resist such gowns?

Finally Madame Therese stood back, hands folded in complete satisfaction.

'*Enchanté!* It has been a pleasure to dress you, *mademoiselle*.'

If she knew the fashion world, as she undoubtedly did, she would wager the cost of the deep blue gown, which, at this moment, was turning Thea into the breathtaking image of a stately but delicate delphinium, that there would be any number of mamas wearing a path to her door to demand that she dress their daughters in such understated but sophisticated glory. But not all would carry off such simplicity as superbly as Mademoiselle Wooton-Devereux.

And as Sir Hector was generous to a fault where his daughter was concerned, Thea had no compunction in giving in to overwhelming temptation and purchasing a number of gowns for immediate delivery to Upper Brook Street.

There was relief on all sides. Not least Lady Beatrice, who responded to the final decisions as if she herself had achieved the unachievable. Miss Wooton-Devereux was now presentable. She raised the lorgnette, admiring a delectable cream and gold creation, most discreet, with a ruched satin border and a neckline enhanced by tiny satin pleats. And if it was made known— the quietest of whispers, in confidence, would do the trick—that the lady was set to inherit a considerable fortune from her beloved papa, Lady Drusilla might just achieve her heart's desire. Theodora might prove to be quite irresistible.

'I think that you are now ready to be presented, Theodora.' Lady Beatrice inclined her head in approval, the ostrich plumes in her bonnet nodding.

'So do I.' Thea surveyed herself in the long mirror. Her lips curved. Her mother had been right. London had much to recommend it.

Lady Aston's drum was everything that Lady Beatrice Faringdon anticipated it to be and more.

Dazzling. Crowded. Humming with gossip, intrigue and comment. Attended by every member of the *haut ton* who happened to be in London. Lady Aston would be able to crow with delight to the discomfiture of other hostesses who had enjoyed far less success since the beginning of the Season. It provided an excellent opportunity to bring Miss Theodora Wooton-Devereux to the combined and critical attention of the Polite World and launch her into society.

'Are you nervous?' Judith asked. 'You don't appear to be so.

How lowering!' Thea and Judith waited in a little anteroom as a flock of servants descended to relieve the party of their evening wraps. 'I remember some of my first balls and soirées. I was horribly nervous, almost so much that I did not enjoy them. Once I spilt a whole glass of lemonade, all down the front of a new gown. It was very expensive with Brussels lace over the bodice and—' She caught the amused glint in Thea's eyes. Short though their acquaintance might be, Judith's obsession with pretty clothes was an open secret. 'Well! Anyway, Mama was furious and threatened not to let me out of the schoolroom again until I could behave with more elegance.' She smiled at the memory. 'I suppose I was too naïve for words, but I was only seventeen.'

Thea nodded in sympathy as she arranged her stole and unfurled her fan. 'No. I am not nervous. But then I have an advantage over your position. I have attended any number of such events as this. I presume that I am suitably got up for this momentous occasion?' She arched her brows in gentle mockery, held out her arms for Judith's inspection. 'My mama considered me to be in relatively good looks and Sir Hector huffed at the bills, but did not object.'

Judith could not help but laugh. 'I think that Lady Drusilla had the right of it. You look quite the thing!'

Thea was in her guise of mermaid in the deliciously spangled *eau de nil* body with the delicate lace overskirt. She had competed her *toilette* with long silk gloves, a pretty beaded reticule and the ivory-and-feather fan. The spangled scarf from Madame Therese matched the overskirt. A pearl necklet and pearl drops in her ears completed the ensemble with the exact touch of sophistication. Judith was left to contemplate that in relatively good looks did not quite do justice to this apparition, but she had already come to the conclusion that the relationship between Thea and her mother was not of the common order.

'Good. Now I can enjoy myself.' Then the two young women turned to follow Lady Beatrice into the ballroom where their hostess was in the process of receiving a steady stream of guests, the majority of whom she had no idea she had invited.

The Faringdon party found itself absorbed happily into the throng and it was soon abundantly clear that Theodora was in her element in such surroundings. It was also abundantly clear that she would not lack for partners. She was introduced to so many gentlemen, all eager to salute the fingers of the willowy golden-haired beauty who would one day inherit a fortune, that she all but lost count. She chatted, sipped champagne and promised herself for any number of dances, with grace and aplomb and all the assurance of having acted as her mama's deputy in formal and diplomatic circles.

Lady Beatrice subjected her to more than one sharp glance, but soon was forced to accept that there was no cause here for anxiety that the girl might not know how to conduct herself. Her upbringing might be unusual, she might be of a forthright disposition, but her social skills were excellent and she would do nothing to bring a blush of mortification to her hostess's face. True, there might have been some concern over whether she should grace the ballroom in the waltz or not. But Lady Drusilla approved. If Theodora could waltz in Paris, she could waltz in London. So waltz she should, and most competently, thus Beatrice shrugged off all responsibility. After which decision, there was nothing to spoil the night.

For her part, Thea took her place in one country dance after another, never flagging. Sufficiently experienced, she did not lack for conversation, but could mind her feet and her tongue at the same time as she twirled and stepped with precision and elegance. Nor was she averse to a little light-hearted flirtation. She could use her fan most adeptly to draw attention to her glorious eyes, whose sparkle rivalled the crystal drops above her pretty head. Laughter and a bright spirit flowed from her. Who would not desire to dance with such an enchanting young lady? No fear that she would ever be a wallflower, destined to sit and watch as others trod the stately or lively measures. And if no unwed earl was present so far to ask for Miss Wooton-Devereux's hand in the next waltz, not even the Earl of Moreton, still Lady Drusilla could not be disappointed with the proceedings.

As for those who observed and assessed and might have stared in cold and stuffy disapproval, they came to the conclusion that Miss Wooton-Devereux was indeed something out of the way, but not unbecomingly so. And her mama. Well, perhaps Lady Drusilla was a little eccentric with the draped turban on her greying curls, all hung about with jewels and feathers, rather in the manner of an eastern potentate. And the quantity of gold chains on her bosom. Rather strange but…interesting. And Sir Hector—of course—so distinguished and responsible. If the Princess Esterhazy herself greeted Lady Drusilla with warm condescension and a light kiss on the cheek, then there was no matter for concern. And if the girl had been brought up in the courts of Europe, then that would account for any oddity in her manner. But her breeding and her appearance, it was decided, were beyond question. Of course, the prospect of money would win over even those who might still look askance at a girl who was one and twenty before making her formal curtsy.

At some point towards the hour when a light supper would be served, Thea returned from a sprightly reel with Simon, Earl of Painscastle, an enthusiastic if inexact exponent of the art of dancing, somewhat heavy on his own feet and those of his partner, to find Lady Beatrice, Sir Hector and Lady Drusilla in deep conversation with a newcomer to their party. He stood with his back to her. And laughed at something that had been said as they approached.

'Ah!' Simon pressed Thea's hand as it rested on his sleeve. 'Now here is a man I am pleased to see. And so will you be, I wager. Come—I will introduce you.'

He struck the gentleman on the shoulder, a light punch to draw his attention.

'Better late than never, Nick. We had quite given up on you. Your dancing skills are needed here by the ladies—and I can retire for a hand or two of whist.'

The gentleman turned, his face still alight from the previous laughter.

'Simon. Good to see you. Judith says that you are well.'

'Of course. Burford Hall keeping you busy?'

'A little. I have been told that I must visit you and admire your son.'

'Without doubt. Judith invites everyone to admire him!' But there was no mistaking the pride in his voice. 'You should try it yourself, my boy!'

'Not you as well!' Nicholas smiled, a quick and devastating grin. 'I am assaulted from all sides.'

'I'm sorry.' Simon risked a glance towards Lady Beatrice. 'I can imagine.'

'Never mind that. I hear you have a stallion for sale!'

'For sale? Not at all. Unless you can tempt me with gold!'

'I might, if he is superior to my own animals. Which I doubt!'

At which descent into purely masculine topics of conversation, which threatened to occupy them for the rest of the evening, Lady Beatrice grasped her son-in-law's arm with one hand and tapped her nephew's with her fan to remind them of their surroundings.

'Don't start talking horseflesh, for the Lord's sake.' But her tone was indulgent enough. 'Nicholas. I must introduce you…'

During the whole of this interchange, Thea had been standing a little to the side, out of direct line of sight. Out of neither cowardice nor shyness, but standing rooted to the spot, her heart beating rapidly, her mouth dry, for here was the gentleman of the Park. And, she realised in that one moment, the length of a heartbeat, that any memory she had of him bore no comparison with the reality that now stood before her. He took her breath away. Splendidly handsome, as she had realized, but now she had the opportunity to study him in the dark severity and elegance of formal evening clothes, at the same time horribly aware that he could reveal her unmaidenly behaviour to all. She had hoped never to see him again, but there was no escaping this introduction.

'Theodora, my dear.' Lady Beatrice drew her forward. 'This is my nephew, Lord Nicholas Faringdon. Nicholas, allow me to introduce Miss Theodora Wooton-Devereux, Sir Hector and Lady Drusilla's daughter. This is her first Season in London.'

Nicholas turned to the lady presented to him—and found himself looking into the eyes—those deep blue eyes fringed with the darkest of lashes—that had last flashed with anger and fear as his hand closed around her wrist. But here any similarity ended. Here was wealth, understated taste, elegance. Yet he felt the strange affinity again, rippling over his skin as if brushed by a chill draught of air.

Good manners prevailed, of course. Theodora curtsied in her best court manner, eyes demurely downcast, a smile pinned to her lips, her pretty hand extended to the gentleman. Just as she ought. Nicholas took the offered hand in his own and bowed, a formal inclination of the head, just touching his lips to her fingers. The epitome of the well-bred gentleman of fashion. They straightened, disengaged, the tension between them invisible to all, but palpable none the less.

Thea waited, swallowing against her panic. Was this the moment when he would acknowledge that he had met her before? Would he announce to one and all that she had been galloping in Hyde Park—and wearing boots and breeches? She could not prevent her eyes dropping to his right hand where the whip mark was clearly visible, still a vivid red scar. When he did not and the moment passed, relief surged through her blood, but she did not enjoy the sensation. Her previous behaviour had effectively thrown her into his hands, at his mercy. Resentment quickly overpowered the relief.

Meanwhile Nicholas fought against an equally strong torrent of anger. So this was his aunt's plan, in spite of his warning. It had all the hallmark of Beatrice Faringdon about it: devious, persistent, interfering. Introduce him to a débutante, wait for the knot to be tied and, in the event of any harm befalling Hal and the young boy in America, the Faringdon succession would be secured to her satisfaction. Furthermore, a débutante whose behaviour had been indecorous in the extreme. Well, he would not. He would not give Lady Beatrice the satisfaction of falling in with her plans. He might keep his face politely bland, his eyes flat, but inside he fumed.

Never had a meeting between lady and gentleman in a ball-room been so fraught with overtones and supposition.

'Why don't you invite Thea to dance, my dear Nicholas?' Beatrice remained oblivious to the passions seething around her.

'Of course, Aunt. It would be my pleasure.' His lips curved into a semblance of a smile, but there was no warmth in it. He fixed his gaze on Theodora. 'Although I presume that you do not waltz, madam,' he remarked as the musicians struck up.

'I do indeed, my lord.' Equally cool.

'Ah.' His raised brows were not quite a criticism.

'I have waltzed in Paris and Vienna, my lord. My mama sees no objection and I have every reason to believe that I have the blessing of the Princess Esterhazy. So I will willingly accept your invitation.'

'Then I shall be honoured.' Nicholas bowed in acknowledgement, led Thea on to the dance floor without further comment, where he turned her with one arm around her waist and began to circle to the music. She fit perfectly against him and moved smoothly, gracefully, through the simple demands of the dance. And as in Hyde Park he was stunned by his physical reaction to her. It was a body blow, like a fist to his gut, a tingle along his veins, an outrageous desire to lift her face and cover that enchanting mouth with his own. To kiss her slender fingers in a formal salute was simply not enough. No matter that the whole world might be watching—in that moment he did not care.

And then: *I do not want this!* His expression as he glanced down at her was almost fierce. Together with the overwhelming wave of lust came the knowledge that this girl was dangerous and his reaction to her was too extreme for comfort. He set himself to resist. He knew that her conduct could be far outside the acceptable and he could not afford to tolerate that. There had been enough scandal in the Faringdon family of late to last a lifetime. He must resist at all costs!

And Theodora? She was aware of none of these thoughts. Aware of nothing but the weight and strength of his arms around her, the clasp of his hand on hers, cool skin against cool skin, the slightest pressure of his body as it brushed hers in the demands of the dance. The memory of the touch of his lips on her hand still burned as a brand. She had waltzed with other partners with mild pleasure. But never anything like this. Lord Nicholas Faringdon quite simply caused her heart to beat against the confines of her bodice like a wild bird in a cage, until she was sure that he would feel the force of it against his chest when he held her close. Just as he had destroyed her composure when his hand had closed around her wrist with such mastery in Hyde Park.

This was no good! Thea knew that she could not remain silent.

'I have to thank you, my lord.' Thea raised her eyes to his as they settled into the rhythm of the music. Her colour was a trifle heightened, he noted as dispassionately as he was able, tinting her cheeks a delicious rose, but she was not shy. All he could think about was the sensation of holding her in his arms. He did not want this attraction.

'Why?'

She was taken aback by this somewhat curt response. And were not his eyes unsettlingly, chillingly grey rather than blue? Perhaps she had simply mistaken it and struggled to find the right words. 'I am not unaware of the debt I owe you. It would have been most uncomfortable for me if you had revealed the…the circumstances of our previous meeting. You deserve my gratitude, my lord.'

'It is not necessary.'

'And…and I should apologise for my…behaviour towards you,' she persisted. 'It was most regrettable.'

'There is no need.'

'But I hurt you!' Her eyes snapped up to his in some confusion. She could not read his expression behind the bland mask. No, she realised, it was not bland but icy with controlled temper. 'I see the evidence of it on your hand—you cannot deny it.'

'Very well, then. Yes. You did. Unnecessarily, as it happened. I had no intention of either harming or molesting you, Miss Wooton-Devereux.'

'I realise that… I should explain.' She was getting nowhere here. 'There were circumstances…' What should she say? She did not wish to bare her soul over the matter of her past experiences, her innermost fears, and certainly not in the centre of a ballroom with a partner who had an amazing effect on her senses and who was less than accommodating to her attempts to make remission. She had apologised and he was totally insensitive to the fact. What could she say? How could she explain? In the event she did not have to.

'I need no explanation, madam.' If his eyes froze her, his voice would reduce her to an icicle if she allowed it. 'You reacted as you saw fit.' Why did those words have all the air of a snub rather than a soothing offer of forgiveness? She could not be mistaken. There was a cold condemnation in that smooth voice and she did not know what she had done to deserve quite so harsh a judgement. 'I do not need to know,' Lord Nicholas continued in preparation for launching the final deadly arrow. 'But at least you are more conventionally dressed tonight than when we last had the misfortune to meet.'

Any number of sharp replies coming into her mind, Theodora opened her mouth to utter them. Then closed her lips. *Since when are you free to comment on what I might or might not wear, my lord?* She could not say that aloud, of course—or not here! This was not the time or place to create a scene. The fact that she had indeed been in the wrong ruffled her temper further but she kept a firm hold on it. She smiled, a miracle of control, and chose her words with deadly precision. 'Yes, I believe that I am, my lord. Everyone who has danced with me has complimented me on my stylish dress *à la mode* and the appropriateness of this particular creation. Madame Therese is a true *artiste*, is she not?'

He could not deny the delicate gloss of sarcasm over her words and had the grace to wince a little. But only inwardly.

'I am delighted that you approve my appearance, my lord. It gives me so much confidence. Without your approval I should be desolate indeed.' Thea did not let up. But *why* was he so cold? Perhaps she must accept that, in all truth, being struck by a riding whip would make him so. She had read the contempt in his eyes as their first meeting drew to its unfortunate ending—an infinite quality of disdain—and there was no difference now. But she denied his right to taunt her!

'I think that you do not lack for confidence, madam.'

A flash of anger darkened her eyes at this lethal sniping. She bit down on any further sharp response. She could not understand the reason for it, but gathered all her social skills about her.

'Perhaps we should talk of something less controversial, my lord? A ballroom is no place for such a frank exchange of views.' The smile was still in place. She would keep it there if it killed her!

'Of course, Miss Wooton-Devereux.' Nicholas, too, bared his teeth in what could have passed for pleasure if anyone was observing the handsome couple. 'What do you suggest that we might have in common to discuss?'

Before she could think of anything polite to reply to this challenge, the waltz had drawn to an end and he escorted her with frigid good manners back to where her parents and the Faringdons were ensconced. He bowed to her, and with equal chill to Lady Beatrice. Thea's hand was soon claimed. She saw Lord Nicholas treading the measure of a country dance further down the set with Judith.

Nicholas made no attempt to approach Thea for the rest of the evening. Theodora made sure that her eyes did not follow him as he danced with other ladies of his acquaintance.

'Nicholas is quite my favourite cousin,' Judith observed in a deceptively neutral voice in an interval between dances.

'Is he?' Thea studied her dance list intently.

'And he is so handsome. Do you not agree?'

'Certainly. I doubt any woman here tonight would disagree.'

Judith gave up, not a little surprised at the lack of interest between them. Nicholas had not set foot near Thea since that one first waltz. But there would be time and enough for them to get to know each other. She would see to it that they did.

Nicholas returned to Faringdon House in a thoroughly bad mood. He was furious with Beatrice. Even after he had warned her off, his aunt had produced a beautiful débutante—he could not deny her lovely face and figure—whom she considered suitable. *Suitable?* She had no idea! He was also furious with himself for taking out his ill temper on the girl. He might have kept the semblance of good manners, but his comments had been unwarrantable. And he was equally furious with Theodora Wooton-Devereux, whose presence in his arms had left a lasting and most uncomfortable impression on him. He resigned himself to an uneasy night.

Theodora returned to Upper Brook Street equally angry and confused, despite the success of her first public occasion in London. How dare he treat her so! She did not deserve his damning opinions of her or his icy set-downs. And why should he react quite so violently against her? Was he so dull and hidebound that he should condemn her for one social solecism? Well—she did not care! But she determined as she removed the pearl drops from her ears that she would get the better of Lord Nicholas Faringdon!

Chapter Four

❦

Since both Lord Nicholas Faringdon and Miss Theodora WootonDevereux moved in the first circles in London society, it was to be expected that their paths would cross with frequency. And they did. If they had not done so by accident, they would certainly have done so by design. For both Lady Beatrice and the Countess of Painscastle considered Theodora to be a most suitable and enlivening match for their uncooperative relative, and Nicholas an equally desirable husband for so delectable a débutante. The opinion of neither lady nor gentleman was sought.

So they came quite naturally within each other's orbit at the social events of the Season, whether it be alfresco breakfasts, riverboat parties on the Thames or the more conventional soirées and balls. Unfortunately for those most interested in the match, who watched the pair with keen eyes, it appeared that there would be little chance of his lordship fixing his interest with the lady. For there was a decided edge to their meetings from the very beginning.

'Lord Nicholas.' Theodora curtsied and smiled politely upon meeting his lordship as she descended the steps from the Painscastle Town House in Grosvenor Square, closely followed by Judith, two days after Lady Aston's drum. 'I had thought you might have returned to the country.'

'My estate will survive a day or two without my presence.' He bowed his head unsmilingly.

'I expect it will.' She unfurled her parasol with graceful expertise and only mild interest. 'I understand that the land belongs to your nephew?'

'Yes. He is the Marquis of Burford.'

'Tom is hardly more than a baby and lives in New York.' Judith added the explanation, struck by the unexpectedly stark confrontation.

'And you administer it, my lord.'

'I do.'

'I see. A worthwhile occupation, I expect.'

Lord Nicholas inclined his head. Now, why did he get the impression that she disapproved, that she had judged him as some variety of noxious parasite to live off the wealth and achievement of others? It ruffled him more than he cared to admit. But he strove with perfect success to preserve a courteous and faintly amused expression.

'Does it not meet with your liking, madam?'

'I am sure that it is no concern of mine, my lord, how you choose to live your life.'

'Very true. It is not.'

Accepting the put-down with raised brows, Miss Wooton-Devereux persisted. Of course he was ruffled. She would teach him to look at her with such arrogant superiority! 'I would have thought a man would want to develop his own land, my lord. Not that of another, however close the relationship with the owner.'

His voice became positively glacial, his eyes a distinct quality of arctic grey. 'It is a responsibility to my family, and so it is my duty. I am trustee for the estate's well-being.' So, she would have the temerity to hold his lifestyle up for criticism, would she? And why was he actually explaining his views to the woman…?

'Of course.' Theodora simply angled her head and smiled.

Nicholas felt the muscles in his jaw clench. Was she deliberately baiting him? Surely she was!

Judith leapt into the breach. 'You should know, Theodora, that Nicholas has his own estate at Aymestry Manor.'

'Ah.'

'He breeds horses.'

'How interesting.'

And although Theodora would have dearly loved to have entered into a discussion of the rival merits of English thoroughbreds against Arab bloodlines, she restrained herself. She would not admit to any similarity of interest with his lordship.

Damn her! Nicholas watched as the two ladies made their way out of the Square. Why should it matter what Miss Wooton-Devereux thought of him?

But it did.

And became increasingly important as the days passed. Although he would have been the first to deny it, Nicholas could not help but be aware of the lady. Not that he approved of her to any degree! Her behaviour was always within the bounds of acceptance—yet not the demure and decorous demeanour to be expected of a débutante. Her appearance was noticeably unconventional with her short hair and striking gowns. She flirted outrageously, showing particular skill in the use of her fan and those miraculously long and thick eyelashes. Not that he had noticed them, of course! She was outspoken to a fault on all manner of subjects, from the politics of the day to the unfortunately corpulent and badly dressed figure presented by the Prince Regent.

When she danced with the highly eligible and extremely rich Earl of Moreton, her mother's chosen favourite in her plan to find a wealthy, titled husband for her daughter, Nicholas could do nothing but turn his back and invite another lady to partner him. He would not give her the pleasure of seeing him watch her circle the ballroom, however graceful and elegant she might be. He would not. And when his aunt once more invited him to take dear Thea into supper, or partner her in a country dance, he would bow and comply with firm composure as if it were a matter of no possible consequence to take that long-fingered hand in his—or else he would discover an instant excuse for his attendance elsewhere. But he would not single the lady out. He would not give the lady or Lady Beatrice the opportunity to gloat!

But if that were so, why was he still in town? Nicholas refused to consider the implication of such perverse behaviour.

Meanwhile, Thea refused to notice or to be disappointed when his lordship led another pretty débutante into a country dance set. Or failed to put in an appearance at Almack's when she had chosen to wear a particularly flattering gown of emerald silk overlaid with silver-grey lace. Instead, she took every opportunity to be deliberately provocative—a task that she found surprisingly easy. Quite as effortless as Lord Nicholas in taking her to task for her somewhat slighting remark on the overbearing tactics of the Duke of Wellington in the government of the day.

'Is that your own opinion, madam? Or that of Sir Hector?' Unable to ignore her in so small a gathering, Nicholas handed her a glass of champagne at Lady Beatrice's small soirée, his expression one of distinct disapproval.

'My own, of course.' Thea sipped the golden bubbles with a little smile.

'I did not realise that your interests stretched to politics, Miss Wooton-Devereux.'

'And should they not?'

'It is not always to be expected in a débutante.'

'It is important to be well informed, I believe.'

Lord Nicholas merely observed her without reply, one brow lifted a fraction of an inch.

Well! She could not allow so negative and *patronising* a response go unanswered!

'Can it be that you are criticising my upbringing and education, my lord?' Thea's brows rose in delicate arcs. She watched him over the rim of her glass.

'I would not be so bold, ma'am.'

'My upbringing has been impeccable,' the lady informed him, 'according to the advanced ideas of the philosopher Rousseau.

And as advocated by Maria Edgeworth, no less, in her *Practical Education*.'

'I can well believe it.'

'It is essential,' continued the lady, 'that every child and thus every adult be treated as an individual to develop his or her innate talents and abilities.'

'Most estimable, to be sure.'

'Thus I would consider it necessary that every intelligent woman be aware of the policies of our government and the political figures who influence them. Which makes me free to be critical if I find the Duke's approach not to my taste.'

'As I would agree.' Nicholas smiled with all the friendliness of a kestrel eyeing a tasty mouse. 'But even Rousseau considered the opinions of the female sex to be far inferior to those of the male.' He raised his glass in a little toast and drank from it. 'I am certain that, educated as you are, you see the force of my argument.'

'No! I do not, my lord!' Thea felt a warmth of colour touch her cheek at his underhand tactics.

'Now, why did I think that would be your answer?'

Which left Theodora without a parting shot.

And gave Lord Nicholas a degree of satisfaction.

But within the third week of their distinctly uneasy acquaintance, there was a particular development in the nature of their relationship, a strange little event that gave both lady and gentleman much to consider. As Nicholas drove his curricle through the city, having visited his bank, he spied a familiar female figure. There, standing on the pavement, on the corner of Chancery Lane and Fleet Street, was a lady whom he could not possibly mistake. She held her reticule, gloves and parasol in one hand, and a guide book, compiled for those travellers who might wish to enjoy the sights of London, open in the other. She was clearly oblivious to the small crowd of urchins and undesirables who had gathered, attracted by her obvious wealth and her unaccompanied state.

He drew in his horses beside her, a heavy frown apparent.

She looked up, a delightful picture in a gauze and satin straw bonnet, but her words did not hold the same charm.

'Do not say anything, my lord!'

So he obligingly did not, but made no attempt to hide his disapproval of her unchaperoned situation in the City as he held his matched chestnuts under firm control. What was she thinking! The fact that her presence here had caused him a ripple of concern for her safety was rapidly discarded.

'I am lost,' Thea snapped. Of all people, why did it have to be Lord Nicholas Faringdon to drive past, to look down his arrogant—if beautiful—nose at her as if she were a beetle in his path? 'I should not be here—and certainly not unchaperoned. I should have a maid with me. I should not be drawing attention to myself. Anything else, my lord?'

She had read him to perfection. He suppressed any sign of wry amusement, so his reply was cold and curt.

'I cannot think of anything at the moment. You appear to have covered every aspect of this unfortunate situation.'

He dismounted, handing the reins to the groom, his expression not pleasant at the inconvenience. 'I think I should return you to your family, ma'am.'

'Why should you? I would much rather go to St Paul's.'

Without a word he held out his hand and, when she complied—she could hardly do other in this busy street—helped her up into the curricle.

'And why *are* you without your maid?' Nicholas took his seat and the reins again, and the chestnuts stepped out with well-bred conformation.

'Agnes is not well. A cold. It would be more than cruel of me to drag her on a sightseeing expedition.' Theodora set her teeth, determined to remain composed. How like him to question her behaviour!

'Would not my cousin accompany you if you were intent on exploring?'

'Judith had other engagements.' Her tone became noticeably more clipped.

'You are too cavalier, ma'am. Do you have no regard for convention? What will people think? You cannot afford to set up the backs of those who are too quick to damn a lady's reputation. The town tabbies are quick to gossip.'

'Really?' With his concentration on the traffic, he did not see the angry glint in that lady's eyes. 'I know you disapprove of me, my lord.' She had given up any pretence at mild conversation. 'How can I spend my life worrying about what people think?'

'That may be all very well in the deserts of Syria or wherever you spent your formative years, with females such as Hester Stanhope setting herself up as the Queen of the Desert or some such nonsensical thing, but I fear it will not do here.'

'This is not Syria!'

'I am aware. But walking alone through the city? It is not appropriate, Miss Wooton-Devereux. As you well know.'

And she did—more than aware of the stark comments of Lady Drusilla if it ever came to her ears, which stirred her wrath even further. Without considering her words, she directed that wrath at Lord Nicholas. 'How dull life would be if I worried constantly about the possibility of getting lost.' She was soon in her stride, his reprimand a light to dry tinder. 'How restricting and tedious if I did nothing in the chance that I became the object of social condemnation. If I stayed at home because I feared to suffer an injury, or was captured by a band of robbers who…' Her words dried up. A stricken look on her face, Thea closed her mouth firmly and looked away so that he might not see her heightened colour.

Ah! So that was it!

Nicholas waited in silence, steering the chestnuts around a large wagon that had come to a halt in the street. He would give her time to regain her composure. He had heard the note of distress, hastily suppressed.

It worked. As the chestnuts settled again into an easy trot, Thea did not return to the dangerous topic, choosing something mildly innocuous, but continued placidly enough. 'It was such a lovely morning, it was impossible not to take advantage of it…'

So she will not talk of it. But it distressed her considerably. Nicholas immediately pulled his horses to a standstill against the curb, to her surprise.

'Thea…' He touched her hand, which held tightly to her parasol, her fingers white against the ivory of the handle. 'Is that what happened to you?' If it drew their attention to hear her given name on his lips, neither of them gave any sign.

'I should not have spoken.'

'Why not? Is that why you reacted as you did in the Park, the day you struck out at me? Had you been accosted by robbers?'

'I do not wish to speak of it.' She shook her head, would not look at him.

'Will you not tell me what happened?'

'I cannot. I won't talk about it.' There was real distress now, in her voice and in her face.

'Very well. I cannot force you. And would not wish to give you more cause for pain.' His voice was low, soothing. 'But if you ever wish to, I will listen.'

Ignoring their very public surroundings, Lord Nicholas took possession of her hand, to lift it to his lips.

'I am grateful.' Her hand was as cold as ice and just as rigid as it lay in his. A strained silence developed that Thea would not—or could not—break. She had not expected such compassion from him. Just as he had not expected such an admission from her.

Eventually she risked a glance at him, seeing nothing but warmth and sympathy replacing the harsh condemnation in his eyes. It drew from her an instant need to apologise. 'I am nothing like Lady Stanhope!'

'No.' He could not stop the smile.

'I would never do anything so outrageous as to wear male clothing and take a lover in the desert! Well, not often—the clothing, that is!'

'Of course not.'

'I am sorry if I was impolite.'

'I must admit that you were under extreme provocation.'

'Are you laughing at me?' She sighed as she saw the telltale curve of his lips. 'Yes, I was provoked—but I am grateful for the rescue. I knew that I was in the wrong.'

'Such an admission makes me think that you are more distressed than I had believed!' It roused a chuckle from her, which pleased him. 'It gave me pleasure to be of service to you on so beautiful a day.'

There was a tone in his voice that Thea could not quite interpret, forcing her to look up. And then she could not look away. Equally held in the moment, Lord Nicholas raised her hand again to press his lips to her fingers, a distinct pressure, far more than a formal salute. And lingered a little until a polite cough from his groom caught his attention.

'Some interested parties around, m'lord.'

Which brought him back to the fact that they were indeed in a very public street, which was no place to be drowning in the depths of a pair of sparkling sapphire eyes. Or enjoying the touch of silken skin. He laughed softly, perhaps to dispel his astonishment in being driven to such indecorous behaviour. But he did not let go of her hand.

'Will you take me home then, my lord?' Thea was as much held by the moment as he.

'Why, no.' He released her to pick up the reins again. 'I think that we go on to St Paul's. What do you say, Theodora?'

He was rewarded with the faintest hint of a smile, as if the lady had come to a momentous decision. As perhaps she had. 'I should like that above all things. How kind you are.'

It warmed his heart.

Which little episode led to a subtle change in their response towards each other. Theodora was nothing at all like the lady whom Lord Nicholas might consider setting up as his latest flirt. He was uneasy about his reactions to her, whereas Theodora still smarted under his stern gaze and disapproving demeanour.

But each was drawn to the other as a moth to a fatal flame.

It became an accustomed sight, giving Lady Beatrice a blaze

of triumph, to see the beautiful Miss Wooton-Devereux partnering the splendid Lord Nicholas Faringdon in the waltz. He was seen to invite the lady to drive with him in Hyde Park at five o'clock, the hour of the fashionable promenade. He even volunteered his services to squire the ladies to Almack's, giving the Earl of Painscastle reason to comment that he must be a lost cause indeed. But Lord Nicholas shook his head, admitting to himself that he was in a serious state of indecision. Yes, the lady was beautiful, interesting, intelligent—but equally outspoken, argumentative and opinionated. Not to mention given to unreliable quirks of behaviour that might make her the talk of the drawing rooms. But there again, when she walked into the room, the very quality of the air that he breathed seemed to change. He found himself entirely captivated…

Theodora was equally preoccupied, her eyes quickly scanning any room to note if he were present. And if she saw his tall figure, his dark hair, her evening took on a glow of its own. If he did not put in an appearance, the event, no matter how entertaining, was distinctly flat. She took to noticing his strong but fine-fingered hands as they controlled the reins of his high-spirited horses. The firm strength of his arm when he held her close against him in the waltz. The elegant grace when he presented her with a posy of flowers or held her reticule as she unfurled her parasol. The power of his body when he took her hand to help her take her place in the high-perch phaeton that he sometimes drove with such masterly skill. The sheer magnetism of his presence when their eyes met and neither could look away. A sad case, she decided, as delicious shivers fluttered over her skin. They were drawn to each other whether she wished it or not. She found him kind, generous, with a depth of compassion—despite his somewhat over-bearing personality and his liking to get his own way!

And if it was becoming clear to Theodora, it was becoming equally evident to Lady Drusilla that Lord Nicholas was winning a place in her daughter's usually sensible heart. When Drusilla frowned her disapproval at Thea's standing up with his lordship for the second time in an evening, it had absolutely no effect on her wayward offspring. And when Drusilla smiled her agreement to Thea's accepting an innocent invitation to drive in Hyde Park with Judith, there was little she could do when she discovered that Lord Nicholas was also to be included in the invitation. Furthermore, it was patently clear that the undoubted charms of the wealthy Earl of Moreton were no competition at all against the dark good looks and dashing grace of Lord Nicholas Faringdon.

Had Lady Drusilla but known it, the matter had progressed much further than even she had believed. Lord Nicholas had organised an evening of entertainment and pleasure at Vauxhall Gardens in the form of a masked supper for family and close friends. There would be music and dancing, of course, with an orchestra to play works by Handel in the concert hall during supper. A simple enough meal with champagne and punch and the specialities of the Gardens—cold chicken and wafer-thin slices of ham, all partaken in a private supper box, hired for the occasion. A most tasteful and unexceptional occasion.

Thea was both amused and entranced, never before having visited Vauxhall with its exotic attractions. She declared the enticing groves, the maze of secluded alleys and the secret arbours and grottoes to have great charm.

'The darkness lends enchantment, I fear.' Lord Nicholas smiled at her obvious enjoyment. And her delectable appearance. Her gown was covered by a shimmering domino of silver silk tissue, a matching silver mask covering her face, but with no pretence at disguise. Nor for Lord Nicholas, his evening rig cloaked in severe and elegant black.

'You are too cynical, sir. And superior. I like it very well. It reminds me of one of Mrs Radcliffe's Gothic novels. All the caves and waterfalls. I have never seen so many temples and pavilions and rotundas, all in one place, in my life. Even you must admit to the lamps in the trees being very pretty, my lord.'

'I will admit nothing.'

'I suppose that you prefer the rustic and natural delights of your manor at Aymestry.' Thea angled a glance in arched enquiry, having heard something of the delights of Lord Nicholas's home.

'Perhaps I do.'

'I would wish to see it.' Her gaze within its silver frame remained steady on his.

'And I would wish to show it to you.' A little silence lengthened between them, until Nicholas took himself in hand. 'But that aside, the lights here hide a multitude of sins.'

'Perhaps. But I will not allow you to spoil the evening by drawing attention to it!'

He hesitated again, the length of a breath. 'I would not wish to do so. That would never be my intent.'

'I know it.' And although she spread her fan with a flirtatious turn of her wrist, he could not mistake the solemn appraisal in her eyes, before she turned to answer a query from Lady Beatrice, formidable if incongruous in her deep purple domino.

After supper the younger members of the party dispersed to stroll down the lamp-lit walks, assuring Lady Beatrice and a reluctant Lady Drusilla that they would most certainly remain within sight and sound of Agnes Drew, their designated chaperon for the occasion. But it was clearly destined for Lord Nicholas to draw Miss Wooton-Devereux's hand through his arm, just as it was astonishingly easy for them to lose their companions in the deeply shadowed pathways.

'Which do you prefer, lady. Dark Walk or Druids Walk?' he enquired as they came to a parting of the ways.

'Definitely Druids. Do you think we might see some after all these hundreds of years? Lurking in the groves of Vauxhall with their oak leaves and mistletoe.'

'I doubt it—but let us try.' He guided her along the appropriate path.

'But we may hear nightingales, I expect.' She slanted a look.

'I have arranged it specially for you, lady.'

He sensed her smile in the darkness. They strolled in silence for some little way.

'It appears that we have lost our companions,' Theodora commented.

'So it would seem.' Nicholas came to a halt and turned to face her. 'Your mama would not approve.'

'No. She would not.' It did not seem to trouble Theodora unduly.

The night enclosed them in deep silence, the scents of earth and flowers, soft but intense. Every sense was heightened. Nicholas could catch the perfume that Theodora wore, was supremely aware of the light touch of her fingers on his arm. When he raised a hand to loosen the strings of her mask she made no resistance.

'Well, Miss Wooton-Devereux. I should never have known it to be you.' He removed his own mask.

'Your disguise was perfect, my lord.'

He bent his head and kissed her. A brush of lips against lips, soft as a sigh. Then he raised his head to look at her. 'I should not have done that.' A sardonic smile touched his austere features.

'Did you not wish to do so, my lord?'

'Why… Yes. I did. Very much.' It was an admission to himself as much as to the lady.

'And I should not have allowed it.' Obviously a night for admissions.

He kissed her again, savouring the warm softness of her lips as he increased the pressure. She was quite irresistible.

And Theodora was breathless. 'I am very glad that you did. How forward I am tonight! There is no hope for me. My reputation will be quite ruined.'

'Do you often allow gentlemen to kiss you?' Nicholas found himself asking. Part humour, part unease at her flippancy. Her answer suddenly mattered very much.

Serious, deadly serious, Theodora raise a hand to touch his lips 'Oh, no. Not at all. Do you often kiss ladies in Vauxhall Gardens, my lord?'

Well, he had deserved that, had he not?

'Certainly not! So, since neither of us is in the general way of kissing other people…I will kiss you again, Theodora, if it pleases you.'

'Yes, Nicholas, it does.'

So he did. His hands tightened over the silk at her shoulders, to draw her closer so that his arms could enfold, his lips take possession. Still persuasive against her soft mouth, still gentle, a promise rather than a demand. But he felt her shiver against him. And Theodora could think of nothing but the incredible sensation of being kissed until sparkling bubbles raced through her blood, as fine as any of the champagne she had drunk that night. Was aware of nothing but the heat that spread its fingers from the region of her heart to every extremity. Her experience of life had never prepared her for anything such as this. If she were breathless before, now she was positively light-headed.

Much as Lord Nicholas was stunned by his reaction to this delightful creature who melted into his embrace and returned his kisses with such sweetness. He wanted her. Wanted to touch her. Wanted her for his own. He thought it would be the easiest thing in the world to fall in love with her.

Which exactly mirrored Theodora's thoughts.

Her mother would indeed have been horrified.

Chapter Five

'We need to talk, Hector.'

Because his wife, always an exemplary diplomat's wife, rarely interrupted him when he had urgent business to complete, Sir Hector put down his pen and held out his hand in welcome to Lady Drusilla. She had come to a halt just inside the door of the library in Upper Brook Street.

'What is it, my love? I thought you were already gone—I forget where, but somewhere with Thea.'

'No. I have sent Thea off with Lady Beatrice and Judith. I need to talk with you and it would be better if Thea were not here.'

'Very well.' Sir Hector now saw the strain on his wife's face, so immediately rose to his feet and approached to draw her into the room. 'What has happened to put such a heavy line between your brows.' He rubbed at it with his thumb in a quaint gesture of deep affection. 'Is it Thea? What has she done now?'

'No, it is not Thea—well, yes, it is, in a way.' Drusilla caught her bottom lip with her teeth and sighed as if at the culmination of much painful thought. 'We have to tell her, Hector.'

'Hmm!' Hector drew his wife to sit beside him on the sofa before the empty fire grate. 'But why?' It was clear that he knew beyond question the cause of her distress and the meaning behind her enigmatic statement. 'We have kept it close for so long—all of twenty-one years. As you wished. Why stir up the mud in that particular pond now?'

'I know I wanted it,' Drusilla admitted. She looked down at their clasped hands and held tight. 'Because she is *our* daughter. She is ours—yours and mine—in upbringing, in character, in education—and in love. What does blood matter? I love her so much, Hector.' Tears began to track their path down her cheeks and she was unable to stifle a sob.

Hector sought in his pockets and began to apply his handkerchief with great tenderness. 'I know that you love her, Drusilla. As do I. No one could have been a better mother than you—and no daughter could be such a credit to our love and care. So, as I said—why has it become so imperative to break silence now?' His voice was all gentleness, but she was not soothed.

'Because it is becoming too dangerous *not* to tell her.'

'I don't see…'

'I think…I believe that Thea is falling in love with him. And he with her.'

Sir Hector frowned a little at what was obviously news to him. 'I thought your preference was fixed on the Earl of Moreton.'

'It is what I might prefer—all that wealth and consequence rather than a younger son—but Thea thinks only of Lord Nicholas Faringdon. I fear that the Earl does not compare favourably. And, in truth, I cannot blame her. Lord Nicholas has such address, such style. And is so very handsome. What young woman would not lose her heart to him—particularly when he has clearly set himself out to attract.'

'Drusilla! Are you as captivated as our daughter?'

'If I were twenty years younger, you would have serious competition, sir!' She managed a wan smile through her tears. 'You must acknowledge—he has considerable charm.'

'Mmm.' Sir Hector smiled in reply, quite sure of Drusilla's heart. 'And you think that it is more than a superficial attraction? Surely not, my dear. She has known him less than a month, after all.'

'What does that signify? *I* fell in love with *you* in less than twenty-four hours after I met you at the Pakenhams' ball. But that is of no consequence. I think that Thea is fast losing her heart. Whether she acknowledges it fully to herself, I am not sure. But she is very like me.' Drusilla took the damp square of linen from her husband and wiped away more tears. 'When she gives her heart, it will be without reserve. And I am very much afraid that her heart could be broken as a result.' She looked up at her husband. 'I don't want that for her. I would do anything to spare her pain. I had hoped to deflect this friendship—to stop it developing beyond a mere acquaintance—but I failed. There is a…a feeling between them—it is so strong that you can sometimes feel it when they are in the same room together. I see it in his eyes when he looks at her—and in hers, too.'

Sir Hector looked skeptical, but did not demur. Then, 'It may not come to anything, of course,' he considered after a moment's thought.

'Oh, Hector. He sends her posies of flowers. He takes her driving in the Park. He brought her a copy of Dr Clark's *Russia,* which apparently she expressed a desire to read, and yesterday he took her to the British Museum because she declared an interest in seeing the Parthenon Marbles. Does that not sound like a man in love to you?'

'He must be, by God!'

'*You* took *me* to an exhibition of minerals and fossils when you were trying to fix your interest with me!' she recalled with some asperity. 'And you loved me!'

'So I did. And have loved you ever since!' He kissed her damp cheeks. 'But look, Drusilla—would it really matter if we did not tell her? Would the truth ever have to come out? It was never a secret as such, but it has been of interest to no one but ourselves for more than twenty years. If no one has bothered to make the issue, why in Heaven's name should they do so now?'

'Because, until now, nothing has brought it to mind. But if there was an understanding to grow between Thea and Lord Nicholas, it might bring old memories to life. What if someone who knows the truth—and there must be members of the family who do—what if they make the connection and speak out?'

Drusilla's lips thinned into a bitter line. 'It would not have mattered at all, of course, if it had not been for that terrible scandal here in London when we were in Constantinople. Hector—you must see what could now occur if tongues start to wag.'

'It is always possible,' he agreed, but still not convinced. 'Did you not think of that possibility when you engaged the help of Beatrice Faringdon?'

'No. I did not. Perhaps I should—but when Beatrice offered her kind auspices to introduce Thea into society, I did not expect Thea to fall in love with her nephew!'

'Well, Faringdon is a man of sense from my reading of him. And if he loves Theodora I do not see the problem. She would be merely an innocent party in all this.'

'Are you prepared to take that chance?'

'I just don't see that he could blame her for anything other than a blood connection. And one of which she knew nothing.'

'But if the hatred were strong enough, and sufficiently long-lasting, Nicholas could equally condemn Thea. Can you imagine if he were driven to turn from her in disgust? It would break her heart! We dare not risk it, Hector.'

'We could, of course, just forbid her to develop the connection further.' The experienced diplomat, ever willing to consider all angles in an area of difficult negotiation, raised his brows in some speculation.

'Ha!' Drusilla was not impressed. Her husband sometimes thought that his reputation was as dust beneath her feet. 'Sometimes, Hector, I do believe that you have no knowledge or understanding of your daughter. To forbid would be fatal in these circumstances. And to reason with her… She is always open to reason, as I know—but when does reason carry weight if love is in the balance?'

He took her in his arms as tears threatened once more. 'There now, Drusilla. Don't cry again.' He held her close, his heart troubled as his mind mulled over the possible repercussions for Theodora. 'Then I suppose that we must tell her.'

'Yes.' She nodded against his chest. 'It will allow her to end this understanding between them before further damage is done. Before her heart is engaged irrevocably.'

Drusilla stood with a final brisk application of Sir Hector's handkerchief and walked to the door, her habitual composure once more in place. There she halted and turned on a final thought.

'Because there is one fact in this whole sorry mess of which we are certain,' he informed her husband. 'After Sir Edward Baxendale's devious and despicable behaviour, Lord Nicholas Faringdon will have nothing good to say about anyone with the name of Baxendale.'

Had her parents but known it, Thea's heart was already lost. Lord Nicholas Faringdon had fixed his interest with her with considerable success. From that very first moment when their eyes had locked as he forced her mount to a standstill, Thea had been aware of Nicholas Faringdon with disturbing intensity. His proximity, the mere anticipation of seeing him at some point during the day, of perhaps feeling the brush of his lips against her fingers, all spread a warm tingle of longing through her bloodstream. And what if he were tempted to repeat that more intimate touch of mouth against mouth. Her breath shortened. How scandalous! How delicious! The longing tightened as a band around her heart.

When, later that morning on her return to the house, Thea was requested by a footman to attend her parents in the library, she found nothing out of the way. They had always been a family who had talked together. But the serious and solemn expressions on their faces, their unified stance before the window, brought her up short. They had not been admiring the view.

'What is it? Have you had bad news?' Thea stepped forward, casting aside reticule and parasol, untying the satin ribbons of her bonnet.

'No. Dear Thea.' Her mother immediately came to take her hands and draw her towards the sofa. 'Come and sit down. We have something that we…that we have decided we must tell you.'

Thea was not in any way put at ease by these words, but she sat and looked from one to the other, aware that Sir Hector and Lady Drusilla also exchanged glances with considerable unease.

'Please don't keep me in suspense.' She tried a little laugh, but it dried in her throat. 'I cannot imagine what should make you so stern.'

Her father took his seat behind his desk, fixed her with a direct stare and began. 'Theodora, your mother and I have decided that we should put you in possession of a number of important facts.'

'Hector—for Heaven's sake!—you are not addressing a meeting of the crowned heads of Europe.' Drusilla took her daughter's hands. 'Listen, Thea, first I need to say that we love you dearly. And nothing can or will ever change that.'

'I know that—but what can it be that—?'

Lady Drusilla took a breath, determined to step into the raging torrent. 'You have to understand—' there was no easy way to put it '—you are not our daughter, dearest Thea. We are not your parents.'

Thea blinked. Looked from one to the other. Could find no words. 'Not my parents? I do not understand. How should you not be?'

'Your mother is—your *true* mother was my elder sister Mary.'

'Oh.' Thea simply could not *think*. 'Forgive me. I find it difficult…' Her hands tightened on those of the woman whom she had always known as her mother as if in a death grip. 'Please… will you tell me?'

'Of course.' Lady Drusilla leaned forward to place a light kiss on Thea's forehead. There was the suspicion of tears in her eyes, in spite of all her intentions to remain calm and composed as she explained. 'Two weeks after you were born, your father died. Mostly from a dissolute life and too much alcohol—I hesitate to say, but it is true. Your mother—my sister—fell into a decline and took to her bed with smelling salts and laudanum. We—Sir Hector and I—were informed. In those days I still had some contact with my sister, although we had found her husband beyond bearing. When we arrived at the Great House—her home—she was in a state of collapse, incoherent and hardly aware of her surroundings. And we found you, in your crib, not to put too fine a point on it, neglected and unwanted. You were hungry, I recall, not over-clean, and you were crying. A poor little scrap. At that moment my heart went out to you. I could not leave you like that and Mary certainly could not deal with you. There were serious money problems, we were to discover. The other two children were in the care of a governess of sorts, but there was no nurse to take charge of you. It was decided that we should take you and bring you up as our own. Mary was in full agreement, as much as she could agree to anything considering her tears and vapours. Sir Hector and I had no children.' She met his eyes again for support and smiled a little as he nodded. 'And so we took you. You were just a month old. We gave you a name of our own choosing. And from that day we brought you up as if you were our daughter.'

'I cannot think what to say. I had no idea.' Thea struggled to come to terms with the shattering revelation, her mind repeating over and over her mother's words.

For a little while they sat in silence to give Thea time to take it all in.

Finally she turned to Drusilla. 'And you said that your sister— my mother—agreed to this?'

'Yes, she did. I would not willingly choose to speak ill of the dead, and not of my own sister, but she did not want you.'

'Did she never ask after me, not in all the years when I was growing up?'

'No.' Drusilla lifted an unsteady hand to stroke her daughter's bright hair in sympathy. 'I could lie to you and tell you that she did. But I will not. I can make excuses for her, of course—she was unwell and even as a girl had never had the strongest of minds. And now she was alone with two young children, a new baby and a dead husband. I do not think that she wanted the responsibility of your upbringing. And perhaps you reminded her of her husband's death. Not that *he* was any loss to her. But, no, she never did. She told us that she never wanted to see you—or us—again. I think that she was perhaps more than a little deranged.'

'I see.'

'We occasionally sent money—so that she should not be completely without funds. But she never replied to my letters. They were returned unopened, although the money was always accepted. Perhaps she was ashamed. I never saw my sister again after the day I left her house with you in my arms—and she never saw you.'

'But her loss was our gain, Thea,' Sir Hector added. 'We could not have had a more loving daughter if you were our own child. We are and always have been very proud of you and it delights me that you will be my heir. You must never think otherwise.'

Thea managed a smile as this simple declaration began to thaw just a little the crystals of ice in her blood.

'But she—your sister—' she turned to Lady Drusilla again '—she is now dead, as you told Lady Beatrice.'

'Yes.'

'And I have a brother and a sister?'

'Yes. Edward and Sarah.'

'Do they know about me?'

Again that look passed between Sir Hector and Lady Drusilla.

'We do not know. Your birth must have been recorded within the family and that record was never altered to our knowledge. You were certainly baptised. As head of the family Edward is probably aware. And perhaps he was old enough at the time to understand the sudden absence of his baby sister. Other than that, I think that Mary would not have seen fit to discuss the matter with her other children. Why should she? It would not reflect well on her, after all.'

'So I was not always Theodora.' A genuine smile touched her mouth.

'No. That was a name of our choosing. Your baptismal name was Sophia Mary Baxendale.'

'I like Theodora better!' Thea sat and thought. And then spoke in her usual clear manner, although her mother saw the depth of sadness in her eyes and there was the slightest hitch in her voice before she steadied. 'It is very strange. But I find that I can feel little emotion towards either a father who did not know me or an unknown mother who effectively disowned me. Neither love nor contempt. Regret, perhaps.' She looked up at the two people who had taken her as their own, loved her and cared for her, showered her with every family blessing. How hard it must have been for them to tell her. How painful it must be to wait—as they were waiting now in silent anguish—to know what her reaction would be towards them.

Thea's heart swelled with sudden love for them. 'You are the mother and father whom I have always known and whom I love,' she explained. 'What you have told me—it makes no difference to my love for you. But…' a frown touched her brow '…why tell me now? I do not understand why you should have found a need to tell me, if you have kept the secret for so many years.'

Her parents once more looked at each other, as if to draw strength.

'It could have a bearing on your future,' Sir Hector began. 'On your happiness. We thought that you should know. It is not an edifying tale. I think your mother will tell it better than I.'

So she did, and throughout the telling of it, with all its implications, Thea's blood ran cold. 'A little over three years ago, Edward Baxendale, your brother, attempted to discredit the good name and the validity of the marriage of the Marchioness of Burford and her recently dead husband, the Marquis.'

'Nicholas's eldest brother?'

'Yes. We do not know the full facts. We were not in England and, although rumour and scandal were rife, the Faringdon family kept the matter close to protect the Marchioness and her young son. But we understand that there were accusations of a bigamous marriage and a vital claim on the Faringdon estates was made. Edward's wife, Octavia, too was involved in the charade. We believe that the motive was money—which would not be beyond belief. More than that we cannot say.'

'So how does this…?' But light began to dawn in Thea's mind. It was searingly bright and struck her with a wrenching dread.

'Whatever the content of the deceit, the result was the breaking of a scandal in London. The private affairs of the Faringdon family were held up to public scrutiny, stripped bare for all to pick over and speculate. They were the latest *on dit* during that Season, discussed as a matter for open conjecture in every drawing room and every club—until Lord Henry and Lord Nicholas apparently unmasked Edward for the villain that he undoubtedly was. Your brother could have done irreparable harm to the family. He must certainly have caused the young Marchioness great distress.'

'That would be Eleanor, who went to New York with Lord Henry.' Thea nodded as she put her knowledge of the family into place.

'Yes. What I need to ask you, Thea, is this—what are your feelings towards Lord Nicholas?'

'I…' Thea flushed as she considered her reply. 'I…' She lifted her hands in a hopeless little gesture.

Her father came to the rescue.

'Your mother thought that perhaps you were not…uninterested where Nicholas Faringdon is concerned. One thing we do know, dear girl, is that the outcome of the scandal must have left a residue of deep hatred between Faringdons and Baxendales.'

'If Nicholas learns from some interested source that you are the sister of Sir Edward Baxendale,' Drusilla continued, watching her daughter's reaction anxiously, 'we fear his reaction towards you.'

'I see.' Amazingly, Thea discovered that she could keep her voice cool and controlled when her inclination was to cry out in the sudden intolerable pain from the wound inflicted by the knowledge of her past. 'That he would condemn me by association, I suppose.'

'Yes. Because you, too, are a Baxendale. As much as Edward is.'

'I understand. The lees in that particular cup must be bitter indeed. But…' She sought for a way through the terrible morass of grief that appeared to be building within her chest, hampering her breathing. 'Why should anyone speak out after all this time? Why would it be of interest to anyone now after all these years? Would anyone even remember that I am a Baxendale by birth?'

'They may not, of course.' Sir Hector would have given the world to be able to offer a vestige of hope, to wipe away the distress that his daughter covered so admirably. He could not do it. 'But it is a risk, a serious risk, now that you are well known in London circles. And if gossip begins to unite your name with that of Lord Nicholas, however loosely… We did not think it wise for you to base a relationship with Nicholas on a lie.'

'Oh, Thea.' Drusilla swallowed against the imminent threat of tears. 'We did not want him to break your heart if you fell in love with him, you see.'

'I do see.' And perhaps, as of this moment, her heart was broken anyway.

'You do understand why we had to tell you, don't you?'

'Of course. Such information could destroy any relationship between us.'

'I fear it.'

'So, what do you advise?' Thea straightened her shoulders, took a deep breath, and tried to still her fingers, which plucked at a satin ribbon on her morning gown.

'I think you know. You have always been open to sense—to reason.' Overflowing with admiration for her spirit, Drusilla worked hard to put on as brave a face as her daughter. She could do no less. 'We think it would be best if you kept your distance from Lord Nicholas. You should do everything possible to discourage any connection between you. It should not be difficult.'

Difficult? It would be well nigh impossible! Perhaps the hardest thing she had ever been asked to do in her life.

'And if I don't?' But in her heart she already knew the answer.

'Maybe nothing. Perhaps you would fall in love. If he offered for you, then you would marry. But if he discovered the truth of your birth, that you are in truth Edward Baxendale's sister, would Lord Nicholas continue to look on you with love—or would he turn his back with condemnation and contempt?'

'I could not bear that.' A tear stole unnoticed down Thea's cheek to soak into the little satin ruff of her gown.

'No. It would be beyond anything. You must end it, Thea. I knew you would be sensible if we explained the situation to you.'

'Sensible? No—it is not that.' Thea wiped away another tear with an impatient hand. 'It is simply that I find I have no choice.'

Leaving the library almost in flight, Thea took herself, with the long-suffering and loudly-complaining Agnes Drew, for a brisk walk in Hyde Park. The sun had vanished behind a thickening layer of high cloud and a sharp little breeze had sprung up to shiver the new leaves. The grey light and the hint of rain exactly suited her mood, so she strode out, taking no thought to the possible threat to her new French straw bonnet with ribbon and flower trim. What did a bonnet matter, however fetching, when placed in the balance against the disturbing developments of the past hour?

She needed the space in which to think, without the tortured presence of Sir Hector and Lady Drusilla both watching her with loving but anxious eyes. How she would have loved to gallop across the grass, she thought, as she saw others on horseback along the rides, although at a more seemly canter. To gallop without restraint, to allow the speed and exhilaration to cleanse her mind of the weight of knowledge that had been laid upon her. And the wave of despair that threatened to engulf her as she recalled that first fateful meeting with Lord Nicholas when their eyes had met and held, his hand clasped so firmly around her wrist. How she wished that she could experience his touch, his closeness, again. And yet, if her mother's fears held weight, it appeared that any future together, any blossoming of love between them, could never be.

Her parentage, Thea quickly discovered, interested her very little—apart from a mild curiosity. This shocked her. Surely it should have some meaning for her to know more of her blood relatives—that her father had been a dissolute gambler who had drunk himself into an early grave, her mother apparently a weak, pathetic creature who had withdrawn into a laudanum-created haze rather than face up to the responsibilities of her family. Thea frowned at the image painted by Lady Drusilla's words. There appeared to be absolutely no connection between these two shadowy people and herself.

She found herself heartily thanking God for Sir Hector and Lady Drusilla, who had moulded her by example and loving care into much sterner stuff. She should be grateful indeed that her mother—Mary Baxendale—had seen fit to give her away! So, after worrying at the matter for a bare five minutes, she simply discarded it as something of no real importance and no bearing on her life. Sir Hector and Lady Drusilla were her parents. The Baxendale family was nothing to her. There was nothing other to consider.

But the repercussions… Ah, now there was an intricate weave of possible consequences that would threaten her happiness, would effectively shatter the new sensations which she had just begun to experience. Even now, these consequences kept her mind occupied until she felt the beginnings of a headache build behind her eyes. Theodora never suffered from the headache! But she did now, exacerbated when she could find no simple solution. Only one path presented itself to her and she cringed from it. But the fear that she had no choice weighed on her soul.

The true state of her heart with regard to Lord Nicholas Faringdon she hastily pushed aside. She could not think of that now. But what exactly had Sir Edward Baxendale—her brother!—done? Had it been so *very* bad that Nicholas could harbour an undying hatred for anyone of the name of Baxendale? Would he indeed consign her to the fiery pit of hell in company with Sir Edward simply because of their shared parentage? Even though she had not even been aware of it until an hour ago? Was it possible that her parents had got it wrong—had read too much into the gossip that they must have heard at least second-, if not third-, hand? It was not difficult for gossip to embroider and exaggerate the true state of affairs. Perhaps it was all a terrible mistake, over which she might laugh in glorious relief when she knew the truth of it. But if what Lady Drusilla had intimated was indeed true, how the family must have suffered, particularly Eleanor on behalf of her child who would have been disinherited. Yet it all sounded highly far-fetched.

The morass of conflicting thoughts and fears in her head brought Thea to an abrupt halt in the centre of the path, causing Mistress Drew to hastily side-step with more muttered comments on inconsiderate young ladies who had no concern for those with ageing bones and with no wish to take long and energetic walks when a downpour was imminent. In quick sympathy and apology, Thea closed her hand on her maid's arm, but quickly turned her face away to disguise the emotions that she could not hide.

She stared across the vibrant spring grass towards the distant stand of trees, knowing that if she closed her eyes she would be faced with a stark image of Nicholas. She would read his reaction to her if the facts of the Faringdon scandal were true—the icy hauteur in his eyes, the thinned lips, the disdainful inclination of his head when pride and self-control took command, as in their first introduction in Lady Aston's ballroom when other influences were allowed to stand between them. How far they had progressed since that cold meeting. Now Lord Nicholas's face lit with a subtle glow when his eyes made contact with hers, when he turned and saw her across a room, his smile…

No! She could not think about the contempt that would surely colour Nicholas's vision of her if Sir Edward were the evil villain of her parents' fears. Thea tightened her hold on her parasol, ignored the shiver brought on by the sudden chill, and stepped out again. Agnes sighed and followed.

So, rather than being emotional, she would be practical. She was good at that. Considering the practical, then, how should she discover the truth?

The obvious source was Nicholas, but that was not a path which she could take. She shuddered at the prospect. So, the next alternative? Judith, of course. Judith, who would know the full truth of Faringdon family affairs and was never reluctant to indulge in a little gossip.

How could she go about it? Simply ask, of course. Thea nodded to herself. It should be perfectly straightforward. She had heard a whisper of an old rumour. What could it have been about? This would give Judith the perfect opening to reminisce and inform her in more, and doubtless accurate, detail, without any fear that her own unfortunate connection with the Faringdon family history would be detected.

Because, whatever the outcome of her uncharacteristic subterfuge, however unpleasant and unpalatable the outcome, she must discover the truth. She was not prepared to live with less. But, oh, how she prayed that it would all be false. Her mother had feared that she might lose her heart to Nicholas, that it might be broken. Thea, with typical self-analysis and painful honesty, feared that *that* particular part of her anatomy was already in serious danger of being lost to her. Whether he was aware or not, Nicholas held the key to her happiness. To lose him now was a sharp sword of pure distress of which she had no previous experience.

So, she must ask Judith in the most innocent manner to divulge the family secrets. On which decision, Thea turned around and retraced her path home at an equally brisk pace. Surely it was all a terrible mistake. And Judith would be able to put her mind at ease.

Miss Theodora Wooton-Devereux discovered that, perhaps as a diplomat's daughter, she had a talent for devious and cunning manipulation. And an equally well-developed one for hiding her true thoughts and feelings.

'Judith. I heard such a strange thing yesterday.' The two ladies were taking the air in Lady Painscastle's smart new barouche. Thea's mind was far from the delightful picture they made, or the admiring glances that might be turned their way. The deep blue afternoon gown with the darker velvet spencer and matching flowers on her rakish little hat did nothing to raise her spirits. This was the best opportunity that she would be given and so took it with hardly a qualm. 'I know it is none of my affair—but I would not wish to do or say anything inadvertently that would disturb Lord Nicholas.'

'What on earth could you have heard?' Judith raised her kid-gloved hand in recognition of the occupants of a passing landaulet, but turned humorous and enquiring eyes toward her companion. 'I may of course have been mistaken, but I had thought that you *did* wish to disturb Nicholas!'

Thea flushed with discomfort. How cheap it made her feel, to be using the situation to lure her unsuspecting friend into innocent gossip! But there was no help for it.

Judith misinterpreted the rose tint. 'There! I knew I was not wrong, as I told dear Simon only this morning!'

Thea managed an ingenuous smile, a slight flutter of lashes. 'I am sure that I do not know what you mean! But as I was saying—yesterday I overheard, when I was taking tea with Mama in Gunter's, a mention of a…of a *Faringdon scandal*. And the name—Baxendale, I think? Could that have been so? I trust that it was nothing of a serious nature!'

'So *that* unfortunate affair has resurfaced. We had hoped that it would die a permanent death.' The bright interest in Judith's face disappeared behind a thin cloud of anxiety. 'I wish it had not—it can bring nothing but distress to all involved.'

Thea felt her throat tighten as she swallowed against a moment of pure panic. 'Was it very bad?'

'A disaster. Poor Eleanor—you cannot imagine!'

Worse and worse! 'The Marchioness?'

'Yes. It could have ruined her life and that of Tom, her son. If it had not been for Hal and Nicholas, I fear that it would have succeeded.'

'Oh! Was the outcome—was the final outcome satisfactory?' Thea felt her heart grow cold within her, a leaden weight that seemed to fill her chest. It could not be!

'Forgive me, Thea.' Judith's face was now emotionless, her expression closed. 'The secret, the terrible scandal—is not mine to tell and I would not wish to dredge it up again. Suffice to say Edward Baxendale was a rogue, a villain who would have destroyed the honour and integrity of our family. I will not say more.' Which was so unlike Judith as to speak volumes in itself.

'Oh. I had no idea…' Thea sought for something to say. 'It must have been when Sir Hector was still resident in Constantinople.'

'Yes. More than two years now. We shall never forgive him— Edward Baxendale. The name is not mentioned. His wife was also part of the tissue of lies. Even his sister Sarah was involved. You have no idea—it was a terrible thing.'

'I see.' But, of course, Thea did not. Only that it must have been terrible indeed if the effect was to close Judith up like an oyster over its pearl. Both Edward Baxendale and his sister. There was no hope for her.

'I know that you will understand.' Judith folded one hand in neat precision over the other as if that finished the matter. As it did. 'Baxendale is a black name in our family.'

Despair crawled along Thea's veins from head to toe And with it not a little anger at the twists and turns of unfeeling Fate—that the sins of a brother should be visited on a sister, even when that sister had not even known of his existence until two days ago.

'Of course. I understand.' Thea continued with the charade, her composure quite remarkable in the circumstances. 'I am sorry that I should cause you to remember something that obviously resurrects so much pain.'

The rest of the afternoon passed in something of a haze for the lady. She managed to chatter and gossip, wave and exchange greetings as if she had no care in the world. But when she arrived back in Upper Brook Street her emotions felt as if they had been completely wrung out. She neatly avoided Lady Drusilla to shut herself in her bedchamber, to look out over toward the Park where she had first met Nicholas. But she did not see the view from the window. Finally she turned from it, straightened her spine and rubbed her hands over her face where the muscles felt strained and stiff with the pretence of smiling and being happy. Now she felt that she would never be truly happy again.

But she knew what she had to do. Thea looked at herself in the mirror of her dressing table. She must set herself to destroy any vestige of the relationship that might have begun to blossom between herself and Lord Nicholas. It should not be too difficult, should it, to give him a disgust of her if she really tried? To make him wonder what he had ever seen in her to attract. To turn his attention to other fortunate débutantes who would not fear the outcome of falling in love with him.

And for herself? There might even be hope for her mama's Earl yet. Thea found that she could not smile at the prospect.

She wiped tears from her cheeks surreptitiously. She never cried. Just as she never had the headache. There was absolutely no purpose in either. She must be *sensible*—that was the word— hiding her shattered hopes and damaged heart from everyone. No one must guess. Not Lord Nicholas. Not ever Nicholas. And certainly not her mother, who would blame herself for the rest of her life if she were allowed to sense her daughter's despair.

And whilst his love found herself reduced to the blackness of utter misery, Lord Nicholas Faringdon was equally prey to extreme emotions. Against all the odds, against all his inclination to thwart the plotting of Lady Beatrice, against every vestige of will-power, he had fallen in love. Although his acquaintance with Theodora could be measured in weeks—days, even—there was no room for doubt in his mind. He wanted nothing more than to ask for the lady's hand in marriage and carry her back to Aymestry. Could think of nothing better than to make a life with her, create children with her. She fired his blood. She intrigued him. She entranced him. If he had his way, Miss Theodora Wooton-Devereux would become Lady Nicholas Faringdon in the shortest possible time. And a smile of satisfaction touched his mouth—there was nothing in the manner of that lady towards him that might indicate that she would not welcome his addresses.

Chapter Six

So Theodora set out to destroy any warmer feelings that Lord Nicholas Faringdon might enjoy towards her, to build a barrier that he would not care to scale. She considered it all very carefully through a sleepless night. As dawn light touched the trees in the Park with gold, she had decided that she could not bear that he hold her in total contempt. The thought of that almost drove her to abandon her planning and simply allow fate to take its course, to allow love to develop between them and risk the chance of cruel revelations of her past. But she dare not. Therefore, she would allow herself to be just sufficiently undisciplined, just sufficiently outrageous, perhaps even a little *fast,* so as to drive a wedge between them. Just enough to persuade Lord Nicholas that he did not wish to squire so volatile a lady to supper. He would not choose to be seen in company with so outré a débutante in Hyde Park. He would not feel obliged to solicit her hand to partner him in the waltz on even *one* occasion in an evening if he considered her upbringing and behaviour not quite *the thing*. And he certainly would not desire to take her pretty lips in a kiss, the memory of which still had the effect of bringing a heated flush to her face when she was foolish enough to remember. Or even to brush his smiling mouth across the tips of her fingers. And if she could achieve all that, the distance between them would be vast and there would be no danger of either of them falling in love with each other. And no reason for anyone to remember the old scandal and the secrets behind Thea's own lineage. Thea would never have to experience the horror of the man whom she…whom she…*liked* a little…turning from her in contempt and harsh judgement. A little chilly distance was all she needed to achieve.

Therefore Thea applied herself to it with all the attention to detail of a battle campaign. She would rejoice when he bowed over the hand of other damsels, or held them within the circle of her arm in a waltz. And she would weep bitterly when she saw the depths of hurt in his eyes before pride came to his rescue and swiftly masked it. Anything was better than allowing a declared love to be blighted by the revelation that she was really Sophia Mary Baxendale.

She set herself two weeks in which to change the course of her life. And discovered that even within one week her irreverent and cavalier behaviour had achieved a splendid success.

Astonished at her skill, Thea slipped into the role of outrageous débutante with ease. Flirting irresponsibly with the Earl of Moreton, she repressed the sharp twinge of guilt when that gentleman responded with some surprise, but apparent delight. She made great play with her lashes and her fan, practising a coquettish turn of her shoulder, a particular angle of her head that might encourage intimacy, an unspoken encouragement to the Earl—*Frederick*—to invite her to dance. She made sure to accept his invitations on sufficient occasions that would rouse comment from those who watched the developing relationship. And a heavy sigh from Lady Drusilla, who knew just what her daughter was about. If her new gown was cut slightly too low across the bosom for modesty, Thea smiled brightly and dared anyone to comment. When Nicholas approached and requested a dance, it was amazing how frequently Thea discovered that her dance card was already full. Even for the country dances. She would have loved to partner him, but…she explained with an arch look. She was never in need of a gentleman to escort her in to supper.

Well—so much for the evenings!

With her mother's wincing and critical collaboration, Thea purchased a satin straw bonnet. It resembled to a remarkable degree a coal scuttle with a large crown and a deep, enclosing and unflattering brim lined with pleated satin. The ribbons and flowers were in varying shades of purple, the daisies sporting large yellow centres.

'I have rarely seen anything quite so ugly—or so common!' Lady Drusilla frowned at the monstrosity. 'Are you sure about this, Thea?'

'I know it is—but think of its effect.' Thea closed her eyes as she did indeed think of it. But she could not retreat now. 'Think how disagreeable it will be when it comes into lurid proximity with my hair.'

'I am! Indeed, I am thinking about that very thing!' Thea's mama shuddered visibly. 'It is unbelievably dreadful. Never would I have thought a daughter of mine, with a nice degree of taste…'

Agnes was even more outspoken. 'Are you trying to set yourself up as a joke, Miss Thea?'

No! There was nothing amusing at all about this. Thea set her lips in a determined line as she tied the offending ribbons. Nicholas could not possibly admire either her appearance or her taste in fashion when he caught sight of her in this impossible creation!

So, when she wore it to a shopping outing with Judith and Lady Beatrice, it drew all eyes. And not a few unkind comments with hastily suppressed giggles. Lady Beatrice found a need to use her lorgnette once more and failed to hide her displeasure. And Nicholas, whom they just happened to meet in New Bond Street? Although not so well versed in ladies' fashions, Thea could not mistake the faint hint of shock in his eyes.

But two wearings for the detested bonnet were quite enough. She could not bring herself to don it again and, when her mama positively forbade it, consigned it to the rear of her closet.

So far, so good.

With what she considered a brilliant ruse, Thea next arranged the loan of a high-perch phaeton from an acquaintance of Sir Hector. A remarkable vehicle with its height and huge wheels, not frequently seen as a vehicle for a lady, in itself it would have drawn all eyes. But Thea chose to drive it in the Park, at the optimum time of day, without either her maid or an attendant groom. And, far worse, insisted on wrapping herself in her desert robes with the scarf around her hair. The strangest sight! With enough comment to satisfy her, some raised brows—even better. Thea set her teeth and bowed to a startled pair of ladies in a passing landau as she applied her long-handled whip with considerable expertise. Definitely fast! She would have worn the boots and breeches if she had the nerve. But even Thea did not dare.

Now for a more personal encounter with Lord Nicholas. It tore her heart in two!

On the day of the Sefton ball, Thea accepted the delivery of a tasteful posy of flowers in a filigree holder. It was delightfully delicate, white and cream blooms bound with silver ribbons. From Nicholas. She had not yet managed to drive him away and the little confection would be perfect with her dress. Regretfully, she stroked the dewy petals, then laid them aside. She must not carry them. It might proclaim the message of her heart, but she must be prepared to take a stronger stand. She had never been closer to weakening as at that moment, but no. She sent Agnes to purchase a less-than-tasteful cluster of yellow roses, far too large for a lady to carry to a ball. She positively flinched when she saw them with her glowing, delphinium blue gown, but carry them she would. And it would not be difficult to hint that they had been given to her by another admirer. Which should effectively destroy any desire on Nicholas's part to single her out!

And as Nicholas, on seeing the golden bouquet, bowed and withdrew to lead a sprightly dark-haired damsel into a waltz, his face coldly stern, Thea knew the glorious heights of success. And the abyss of black despair.

Thea's talent for deception continued to grow. Taking Agnes into her confidence, she arranged a cruel little scene, knowing that Nicholas would be present to witness it, and would not enjoy the experience of seeing the superior Miss Theodora Wooton-Devereux at her most callous. Emerging from Gunter's with Judith and Nicholas, it had begun to rain. Thea immediately dispatched Agnes to find a cab to take them home in some degree of comfort. When Nicholas would have objected and stepped out himself, Thea demurred.

'But it is now raining heavily.' She could not ignore the sharp criticism in his tone or the hardness in his gaze. 'Mistress Drew will be wet. That should not be.'

Thea shrugged, a nasty, selfish little gesture that she had practised before her mirror. 'But she is my maid. She will find a cab. It would not do for you to get wet, my lord.' She tried not to be wounded by the narrowed glances of both Judith and Nicholas.

The outcome was painful but satisfactory. Nicholas, with a firm gesture of his hand to Agnes to remain where she was, stepped out into the rain to summon a cab. Then handed Thea and Agnes up into the vehicle—but both he and Judith, somewhat stiffly, declined an invitation to accompany the ladies. So they did not see Thea enfold Agnes into a quick hug with a kiss for her cheek. Or the tears that she was forced to brush away from her lashes with an impatient hand when her nurse, who had always been there to comfort her since she was a child, returned the kiss.

'I trust that you are satisfied, Miss Theodora.' Agnes looked skeptical, but patted her charge's hand.

'I must be, dear Agnes. I think he now has a disgust of me, do you not?'

'I would certainly expect so!'

Perhaps just one more little event was needed to hammer the final nail into the coffin of their relationship. Ordering Agnes to remain at home, Thea donned an eye-catching gown of rich rose pink, tilted her silk and lace parasol at an elegant angle and proceeded to walk—to *saunter*, in effect—down St James's Street. She could feel the eyes of the dandy crowd from the Bow Window set at White's follow her every movement. They raised quizzing-glasses. Leers and smirks. The only blessing was that she was unable to hear any of the comments the gentlemen might make. But with a smile pinned to her lovely face, she completed her promenade—and prayed that she would never have to accomplish anything quite so obnoxious again. But, as she had intended, the gossips would undoubtedly tattle.

'What are you about, Thea?' Judith accosted her at a little soirée that they both attended that night. Her expression, for Judith, was austere, and there was a noticeable reserve in her demeanour. 'Are you deliberately wishing to make yourself the talk of the town? You are certainly succeeding. Why would you do something so particular? I must say, I had not thought it of you. If you do not take care, people will not wish to acknowledge you. And then where will you be?'

From which troubled comment, Thea presumed that her plan had achieved its ends.

She knew for sure when approached by Nicholas at Almack's on the following evening.

With a formal bow, Lord Nicholas Faringdon requested the honour of a dance.

With a bright smile, Miss Theodora Wooton-Devereux made her excuses.

'You appear to have developed a sudden aversion to my company, madam.'

'An aversion?' She laughed with a distinct toss of her head. She found that she could not read his thoughts behind the cool demeanour. 'Nothing so melodramatic, my lord.'

'I had hoped that we had an understanding.' Again that dangerous calm.

'An understanding? I am not sure of your meaning.' *Oh, Nicholas, forgive me!* 'We have certainly flirted. And most successfully. But an understanding? Why, no, my lord!'

'No. Forgive me for imposing on your time. I was clearly mistaken. I will relieve you of my presence.'

'If you wish it, of course.' And again that brittle little laugh.

For a long moment he looked at her, from her golden hair to the toes of her satin dancing slippers. 'I believe that I do, madam. I fear that I misread you in many ways. But you will not be without a host of suitors to your hand.'

'Why, no.' Thea was forced to take a breath against the lance of pain that struck at her heart, but her words were flippantly light-hearted. 'As you know, I am very rich. Of course I am most sought after. I would expect it. All I need is a title. My mama is very keen to see me settled and I agree with her.'

'I wish you well in your search.'

He bowed with glacial elegance and economy of movement and turned on his heel. He did not look again in her direction for the whole of the evening.

In their carriage on Thea's return to Upper Brook Street after one of the most miserable evenings of her life, tears fell. She could not stop them. Her mother put her arms around her in the darkness, struggling against the wave of guilt that swept through her at her daughter's distress. If she had not divulged her fears, the secrets of the past, this would never have happened. But what use now with regrets?

'It is very hard.'

'Yes.'

'It is for the best, Thea. You will meet someone whom you can love. Where there is no past to stand barrier. You will be happy again and your heart will mend.'

'If you say so, Mama. I cannot see it.' Theodora tried for a smile when she saw her mother's worried expression as they passed a lighted flambeau on Park Lane. 'At least if he has taken me in dislike, he will go home to Burford Hall and I can stop being quite so outrageous. It is far too exhausting.'

She rested her head against her mother's shoulder and prayed that he would go, whilst Lady Drusilla's heart was sore indeed that her advice had caused her daughter so much pain. She prayed that her daughter's strength of will would prevail, but how her heart went out to her child in her sufferings as her tears fell undetected on to Theodora's bright hair.

'I thought you liked Nicholas.'

'Nicholas?'

'Yes. My cousin.' With a sharpness quite alien to Judith, she pinned her companion with an accusing stare. 'With whom you have danced and dined and walked and driven…'

'I do not dislike him.'

'You know what I mean. He no longer seeks you out. You turn away from him. You refuse to dance. Have you quarrelled?'

'No.'

'And all that strange behaviour. I thought I would die when I saw you in that purple-flowered monstrosity! And as for St James's Street! Don't tell me there is nothing wrong!' Which was very percipient, Thea decided, for Judith. And also too close to the truth for comfort.

'I cannot say. Forgive me, Judith. I cannot say. I only hope that I have not hurt him.'

'I expect you have—although you would not know it. Nicholas always was good at hiding his feelings. But it seemed to me that you deliberately set out to do so.'

Thea found that she could not look at her friend. 'I…I hope that it will not matter to him—that he will soon forget…'

'I would never have believed that you could be so cruel and hard, Thea.'

'Forgive me.' Thea fled from the room.

She wept bitter tears.

Not only had she destroyed the promise of any love between herself and Nicholas, she had also damaged her friendship with Judith.

Was it worth it? Would it not have been better to let events take their course? How many times had she asked herself that question?

Judith had the right of it. She had indeed been cruel and hard. But into her mind crept another image. Of her standing before Nicholas. And in his eyes a fervent hatred that she was the sister of Edward Baxendale, the man who had deliberately set out to destroy the integrity of the Faringdon family for his own ends.

Oh, yes. It was worth it. She could not bear that. Nor could she bring such lasting pain to Nicholas. A little present discomfort, even heartache, would soon fade and would be forgotten as his life continued without her.

But her tears, privately shed, were bitter indeed.

And Lord Nicholas?

Nicholas found himself in an unusual and unpalatable state of mental upheaval. How could he have been so mistaken in his reading of the character of the lady? In the past week, such a short time, he had discovered her to be any number of things that he actively disliked. It was, he decided, like a nightmare from which he could not wake. He had seen her to be thoughtlessly unkind, lacking in all aspects of both good manners and breeding, and with a wilful rejection of acceptable standards of behaviour and taste. She was both spoiled and selfish. And an accomplished and heartless flirt. Surely he could not have read her so wrongly? A lovely face, he realised, had little to recommend it when overshadowed by the faults of character that he had the misfortune to encounter in the past seven days.

And he had come perilously close to allowing his heart to slip from his control and into those undoubtedly pretty but careless hands.

The thought angered him as he leafed through the pile of invitations that had arrived at Faringdon House, leaving him with a ridiculous sense of betrayal. He cast the gilt edged cards on to a side-table and shrugged. Better to discover now before he was entirely caught up in her sticky spinnings. It was not a web to his liking. He simply had to accept that she was nothing but a rather common flirt who had been allowed far too lax an education and now had her sights set on as elevated a title and as well-lined a pocket as she should achieve. He would have no further part in the scheming of this particular spider. He would not be made a fool of by a delicious smile or a pair of entrancingly blue eyes.

As for her attention-seeking perambulation around the Park in unacceptably exotic costume, and her scandalous flouting of convention by daring to walk down St James's Street, leaving herself open to being ogled by any man on the strut—she must have known that such behaviour would ruin her reputation. No. He wanted no more breath of scandal in his life. She was welcome to the Earl of Moreton, if that was what she wanted. And the Earl was welcome to her!

It struck him as he descended the stairs on his way to Brooks's that he had had quite enough of London. There was nothing to keep him here but pride—which would ensure that he remain for a little longer. He would not be seen to run from a connection that he had deliberately sought. But pride and self-control would keep him well out of Miss Theodora Wooton-Devereux's manipulative orbit. There was no need for him to consider her ever again.

So Nicholas stayed on for a few days. Keeping his mind closed to his motives, he made sure that he was seen squiring other eligible débutantes in his curricle in Hyde Park, at private parties and at Almack's. He even went so far as to organise another small party for an evening among the pleasures at Vauxhall Gardens, but deliberately did not invite Miss Theodora Wooton-Devereux, who would find out about it eventually from Judith, of course. And be hurt.

He found no interest in kissing anyone in the shadowed groves of Druids Walk!

After which superb show of indifference, Nicholas would go home to Aymestry Manor, and Burford Hall. But all he could see was a tall, slender, fair-haired lady who had enticed and then rejected him, leaving an ache in the region of his heart. Love? Of course not. Simply a mild interest, which would pass and the ache with it!

It had before.

It would again.

* * *

Theodora saw the results of her campaigning all too clearly. Nicholas was rigidly, freezingly polite when they met. He bowed in stern acknowledgement, but took care not to touch her. Not even her hand. He certainly did not seek her out. In fact, he remained as little time in her company as was politely possible. He did not smile at her or allow his eyes to meet with hers. They might have been mere distant acquaintances who did not like each other overmuch. Occasionally she surprised a quizzical look on his face as if he could not quite understand her. And he never flirted with her!

So why was she so unhappy? She had achieved exactly what she had set out to achieve. And in so short a time as to be almost miraculous. Perhaps she had missed her calling and should go on the stage!

At night she turned her face into her pillow, as if to block out the image of his face that haunted her waking and sleeping hours, and longed to feel the strength of his arms around her again.

'You are sadly out of countenance, my love.' Lady Drusilla eyed her daughter over the breakfast table and decided that the time had come not to mince words.

'It was late when I arrived home last night,' Thea explained in a somewhat colourless manner. 'The musical evening at the Southcotts', if you recall. I think you made an excellent choice not to attend, Mama. I have rarely spent a more tedious evening.'

'It is not lack of sleep that makes you so pale. I have known you to dance until dawn without ill effects. So, listening to music…' She paused. 'He has gone, Theodora. It is over. You know it was the best decision to make and you must accept it.' Her tone was bracing, but not without compassion.

It was three weeks since Lord Nicholas Faringdon had made his perfunctory excuses to his family, closed up Faringdon House and returned to Burford Hall. He had obviously made no attempt to see Theodora.

'I know.' Thea managed a smile as she reduced the warm roll to crumbs on her plate. 'You will note that I am making every attempt to fulfil your wishes for me. Frederick is becoming quite hopeful.'

'Unless he is driven away by your fading looks! I think you need a change of air, my dear. To leave London.'

'Will you let me accompany you to St Petersburg?' Thea looked up hopefully from the crumby disaster. *At least in Russia I would be as far from Nicholas as it would be possible to be!*

'No!'

'But why should I leave London now? In the middle of the Season?'

'Only for a short time. A few days. Until you have regained your looks. And I anticipate that the Earl will miss you—and be even keener to fix his interest with you on your return.'

'Or take up with another débutante in my absence. A sad case of out of sight, out of mind.' Not that she cared! 'Miss Walworth is very pretty, do you not think?'

'You need some colour in your cheeks.' Lady Drusilla recognised the diversionary tactics and refused to co-operate. 'And I think that you have lost weight. Furthermore, there are distinct shadows under your eyes this morning. It really will not do, Thea.'

Thea sighed and gave in, even as she took herself to task for lack of spirit. 'So, where are you sending me?' Perhaps a change of scene would restore her energies. She was simply not used to feeling so *down*.

Since Lord Nicholas's departure, Thea's errant behaviour had been transformed almost overnight, the unfortunate hitches forgotten, her social solecisms glossed over. Judith had apparently forgiven her, although she still expressed disquiet over her treatment of poor Nicholas. Lady Beatrice frowned and was inclined to refer to *that incident in St James's Street,* but was prepared to accept that perhaps Theodora had not realised the enormity of her transgression. Frederick was attentive. Smitten, Judith suggested with a suppressed chuckle. So all was comfortable again.

The only problem was with Thea's heart, which refused to return to its previously unawakened state and its normal steady rhythm.

'I have had an idea,' Lady Drusilla announced. 'I have an ancient cousin, Jennifer Hatton. She is mostly housebound and very deaf, but she is my only close relative. I have no wish to visit her in her rural solitude, but should enquire after her before we leave for St Petersburg. *You* could go, instead. With Agnes, of course. It would be the perfect solution. You will enjoy the freedom from London restrictions and a visit into the country will do you good.'

'Very well.' Thea abandoned her attempt at breakfast. She felt no great enthusiasm, but perhaps it would be better than allowing her eyes to search every soirée, every ballroom, every street, for a glimpse of Nicholas, when she knew for certain that he was no longer in town. And certainly better than suffering a severe attack of the nerves when she saw a dark-haired, broad shouldered gentleman. It was hopeless! She *never* suffered from nerves!

'There is one problem.'

She tuned her mind back into her mother's words.

'Cousin Jennifer lives in Tenbury Wells. In Herefordshire.'

'Oh!' *Burford Hall is in Herefordshire!*

Lady Drusilla caught the interested gleam in Thea's eyes. 'I expect you to be sensible, Theodora,' she declaimed in firm accents. 'On no account are you to make contact with Lord Nicholas. Not after all your hard work to distance yourself from him—it would be foolish in the extreme to put yourself in his way. It is an advantage that you will not be called upon to socialise while you are there in Tenbury Wells. My cousin is too elderly to visit or to keep open house.' She surveyed her daughter and wondered if her suggestion had been quite wise. There was a distinct return of colour to Thea's pale cheeks. 'You will do nothing to draw attention to yourself. You will go nowhere near Burford Hall. Fresh air, new surroundings, and back here at the end of the week. Do I make myself clear?'

'Yes, Mama. Very clear.' Thea smiled in perfect serenity. 'I will do just as you say.'

'You do not visit Burford Hall!'

'Of course not, Mama.' Of course she would go nowhere near Burford Hall.

But Aymestry Manor, Nicholas's own property, which her mama appeared to have overlooked, was not so very far from Tenbury Wells. Would she be able to resist going to see Nicholas's own home? If she were sensible, she would remain as distant as possible from it. How foolish it would be to even risk a chance meeting. But the temptation to see his home for herself was well-nigh irresistible…

Her spirits lifted as she left the breakfast parlour, informing her mama that she would go and supervise the packing for a visit into the country. She could not quite quell the little surge of— what? Hope? Anticipation? How foolish she was, but energy once more sang in her blood.

Lady Drusilla frowned at her daughter. 'Are you humming, Theodora?' she asked, her suspicions aroused, as the lady walked to the door with a lively flounce to her skirts?

'Humming? Certainly not, Mama. I never hum!'

And with that Lady Drusilla had to be content.

Chapter Seven

Thea discovered her mother's brief description of Cousin Jennifer to be exact to a point. Of advanced age, she lived retired from society, profoundly deaf and intolerant of those around her except for the equally elderly servants who ministered to her needs. Her days were spent in reading, tending her beloved garden and drinking a quantity of vintage port. She made Thea welcome in a casual manner, but, although friendly enough, made no alteration in her own itinerary beyond giving instructions for Thea's comfort in the house as long as she cared to remain there. She had clearly expected no visit from Lady Drusilla. Thea decided that it had all been a ruse on her mother's part to remove her from town for a little while, but accepted the cunning but obvious subterfuge with equanimity. She had enjoyed the journey in the company of Mistress Drew and her groom of long standing, Edward Dacre. Sir Hector had also insisted that a servant accompany her to handle her luggage, arrange her accommodation at hotels and inns *en route*. So they had made quite an entourage and Thea had found nothing demanded of her but to relax and enjoy the experience. Sir Hector had provided a light travelling coach for her comfort so she travelled in style and also had her grey Arab mare, The Zephyr, with her.

At Tenbury House, on the outskirts of the little town, Thea set-

tled in. Nothing was required of her by her hostess, which gave
Thea the opportunity to enjoy as much fresh air and freedom as
her mother had recommended. She explored the little town, a
minor spa graced with a parade of shops, an ancient church and
a swiftly flowing river with swans and ducks. But, attractive as
it was, its pleasures were soon exhausted.

So, now what should she do with her time? Thea discovered
a little pamphlet describing the local sights worthy of admiration. She riffled through the pages with eyes that did not quite
focus on the words and illustrations on the page. Because in the
back of Thea's mind lurked the prospect of Aymestry Manor. It
glowed like a jewel on black velvet. It lured her, enticed her,
wearing down her good intentions. It was so close, after all.
Surely a brief visit, just to *look*—from a distance, of course—
would be acceptable? Conscience and common sense warned her
of the dangers of such an escapade. Her own inclination was reluctant to listen. Her common sense took on the tone and accents
of Lady Drusilla at her most imposing.

You must not go there, Theodora!

But why not?

*What good would it do to meet Nicholas again? You know all
the arguments, all the dangers, only too well.*

He would not be there!

It would be wrong to see him. You care for him too much.

I have no intention of seeing him!

So what is the point of going?

Because…because I want to see the house that is his very own,
which he cares for, which is close to his heart.

And what good would that do, pray?

I don't know. I simply want to see something that matters to
him. There is no danger in that, is there?

So you are merely inquisitive? Really, Theodora!

Yes! And what is wrong with that?

Her common sense (and Lady Drusilla) gave up and lost the
argument.

* * *

As a result, on a bright morning, the lady took Agnes Drew, Edward Dacre and their servant on a mounted expedition to Aymestry, a journey that could easily be managed in a day. A pleasant journey where they were free to admire the gentle rounded hills, wooded valleys, the flash of the deep and secret River Teme as it emerged from the undergrowth. Wild flowers cloaked verges with buttercups and ox-eye daisies. The apple trees were laden with blossom, promise of a good harvest.

Asking directions, they turned on to a little track that wound between high grass and old hedgerows. And there it was, in an open valley, surrounded by pasture and stands of oak and beech. Thea reined in The Zephyr on a rounded knoll to get a better view. Nicholas had spoken of Aymestry Manor often, not in any great detail, but with deep affection. Now she understood why, knowing that it had been willed to him from the family estate, originally part of a dowry from his mother's family.

The first impression to strike her was that it was not classically beautiful. No clean lines or porticoes, no symmetrical windows, no pillars or imposing steps. It was a hotchpotch of old construction over the centuries, with the addition of more recent wings and storeys. A mellow stone wing from the seventeenth century butted against wood and plaster half-timbered walls and gables. A carved entrance porch led to an arched doorway that smacked of medieval origins. One recent addition with a little tower rose above a double-hipped roof-line. Beside it, around a paved central courtyard, were half-timbered barns, a red-brick dove cote, a pair of oast houses with their tilted stone roofs and a range of stone and plaster stabling. It was not classical, but it was charming, offering an immediate warmth and welcome.

It was, she thought, on a sudden impulse, a *home*. But she knew that Nicholas, by necessity, spent little time there.

Around the house she could see evidence of gardens, both informal and formal, a ha-ha protecting them from the predations of animals that grazed in the open pastures beyond. Thea sighed and tried to ignore the little tug at her heart as the sun encouraged the roses along one gable-end to unfurl their petals and the doves flew in a flurry of white wings, to settle once more on their perches.

Yes. It looked like home. And had been over the centuries. A settled place, something of which she had no experience in her short life.

Agnes, seated beside her on a stolid gelding, interrupted her reverie. 'I think we should go back, Miss Thea.'

'No. I want to go closer.'

'It is not wise. His lordship might be here. And then where shall we be?'

'No.' Thea was certain. 'He visits only rarely, when business permits.'

Before Agnes could object further, she kicked the little mare into a descent from their vantage spot. All she wanted was to see what lay so close to Nicholas's heart. To know a little more about him, even if it would increase the pain, even if they were destined to live apart. She nodded in quick decision. It was worth the risk.

At close quarters the house was just as entrancing. Gardens carefully tended without being fussy, perhaps lacking the hand of a woman, Thea found herself thinking before she stopped herself. Voices from the further side of the house drew her to approach a small paddock where two mares with their new foals grazed, watched by a pair of grooms who leaned on the fence. But no sign of Nicholas.

Well, she was here. She would see what enthralled him about this place. She walked The Zephyr up to the paddock, leaving Agnes and their escort some way behind, and brought her to a halt.

An elderly man with grizzled hair and weatherbeaten face, with some authority on his shoulders, emerged from one of the barns at her approach. Touched his hand to his hat as he took in the quality of the visitors, and, more importantly, their horseflesh. Thea dismounted.

'Good day, miss.' He came over to hold her reins, a little bent with age. 'Can I be of help?' His voice held the soft Marches' burr.

'No. I was passing…visiting in the area…a cousin lives near

Tenbury. I am a little acquainted with Lord Nicholas Faringdon. Is he perhaps here?'

'No. Expect he's over at Burford. I'm Furness, his lordship's head groom 'ere at Aymestry.'

A curious mix of relief and disappointment flooded through her. Deciding that relief was the more apt of the two, she smiled at the groom. 'It is lovely here, Master Furness.'

'It is that.'

'Lord Nicholas has spoken often of his horses.'

'Prime beasts, miss.' He turned back to admire his charges, pride clear on his lined face. 'We hope to do well on the turf. Good lines in this breeding, y'see. These little 'uns are both thoroughbred. Much in demand in the hunting field too.'

'I can see.' She smiled at his enthusiasm and stretched out her fingers to scratch the forehead of an inquisitive mare.

'His lordship—he doesn't get enough time to concentrate on 'em. Not as much as he'd like. Too much business over at the big house and estate.'

'It takes a lot of his time?' The mare pushed at her hand, perhaps hoping for an apple. She laughed and shook her head.

'Too much, I'd say. His're the only shoulders to bear it, y'see—the Marquis being only a little lad and in foreign parts an' all.' Furness searched his pockets to find a wizened fruit, which the mare promptly crunched.

'Yes. I see. He is a conscientious landlord?' Thea discovered that she had no pride when it came to questioning the groom about his master. She flushed a little at the realisation. Thank God her mama was not within hearing distance!

'Aye. No hard feelings round here. Or none to speak of.'

'No. I suppose not. Is there much unrest?'

'Some. We hear rumour of it on Lord Westbourne's estates, which run between here and Tenbury. And in Leominster, o' course. But not at Aymestry. Or Burford. Even when we've had hard times—harvest bad and famine at hand—he cares for his own, does Lord Nicholas. Puts money from his own pocket back into the land. Keeps rents down, d'you see. Not like some I could name round 'ere. Lord Westbourne, for one. Them as thinks of nothing but their own comfort and pleasures.' Furness spat on the ground. 'Beggin' your pardon, miss.'

'You are fortunate indeed, Master Furness.'

He nodded. 'Not all agree. The markets are bad, but we do well enough. The cattle and sheep are sturdy breeds. Ryelands over there—see.' He pointed with gnarled fingers. 'And Herefords in the far pasture. New blood brought in to improve the stock. Lord Nicholas keeps up with the trends—always reading some pamphlet or other. Different from in my dad's day—when he was groom 'ere.' The old groom, it seemed, needed no encouragement from Thea to express his admiration. 'His lordship now—he's done it since he was nobbut a young lad, as well, his brother dying so young and Lord Henry being in New York.'

'Yes. Of course.' Thea found words difficult. Her heart swelled within her breast and emotion tightened its hold on her throat, surprising her with its intensity. To hear such praise from Master Furness. And she had to admit to the sly finger of guilt that touched her spine. She had been more than ready to condemn Nicholas as a frivolous, self-serving landlord with no thought for his tenants. And living on his nephew's inheritance too! How far, it seemed, she had been from the truth.

'I must go,' she decided eventually, giving the mare a final caress on her soft nose. 'I have enjoyed our meeting, Master Furness.'

'A nice horse you have there, miss.' He cast his eye over the grey, then leaned down to run his hands down her forelegs. 'His lordship could make good use of some swift Arab blood in the breeding. I reckon she runs well.'

'Yes. Like the wind. Sometimes she is difficult to stop.' Memories were suddenly stark in her mind. She had stayed long enough. It would not do to tempt fate further.

'I must go,' she repeated.

'Who shall I say that called, miss?'

'No matter. Goodbye, Master Furness.' She turned to go, suddenly aware of a hiss of expression from Agnes Drew.

And there he was.

* * *

On his return from London, Nicholas had found himself seamlessly absorbed into estate matters. It was not difficult. Lambing and calving continued apace at Burford and he was readily involved. Riding the family acres, a small glow of satisfaction touched him that he had thwarted Beatrice's less than subtle plans. He fervently hoped that she was feeling put out that he had escaped her clutches. Without doubt, he had enjoyed the pace and glamour of the London scene, but he was not sorry to be back. The stern lines of his face relaxed into a smile as he watched a pair of swans with their fluffy if unmanageable brood take to the water on the mere.

But the smile faded.

Theodora.

He would not think of her! She meant nothing to him. He looked down, a line developing between his brows as he rubbed at the skin on his hand where the mark of her whip had just faded to the slightest discoloration. A woman who was volatile and unreliable, spoilt, privileged and indulged from childhood. A lucky escape indeed to see her in her true colours when he might have been in danger of allowing himself to enjoy her company too much.

So why did the thought of her, the memory of her laughter, the sparkle in her magnificent eyes, still heat his blood? And trouble his sleep? Unwise enough to recall the softness of her mouth against his in those few stolen kisses in Vauxhall Gardens, the muscles in his loins tightened uncomfortably. Desire ran hot through his veins. He bared his teeth and kicked his horse into a canter. But the speed of the animal did nothing to distance him from the apparent hold Miss Wooton-Devereux continued to exert over his very masculine reaction to her. Against all logic, all good sense, he continued to be driven by the thought of taking Theodora to his bed, of claiming her lips in a furious possession that did not include gentleness. Igniting all that fire and energy in his arms. If only she hadn't been so irresponsible and wayward. Frustration made him groan and set his teeth. It could, he decided, be the death of him!

When matters at Burford allowed, Nicholas decided on impulse to spend some time at Aymestry Manor. It was a fine day and an easy ride through undemanding country. He did not need an excuse, but if he did, some of his mares would be ready to drop their foals. Furness would deal with it, of course—he had worked with horses all his life, and his father before him—but Nicholas wanted to see the fruition of his long-term planning for himself. He dropped down through the woods behind the little Manor, remembering boyhood adventures there with his brothers, and so was perhaps, a trifle melancholy, only to see a little group of visitors with their horses standing beside one of the paddocks. This was nothing out of the way. Most likely lost travellers stopped to ask direction. A lady was in conversation with his groom, another female companion and an escort in attendance. His first thought was that the lady held the reins of a prime piece of horseflesh. He cast an experienced eye over the short arched neck and glossy, deep-chested body, the powerful, glossy flanks. A pretty animal—and perhaps not unfamiliar? Then the lady turned, gathering up the reins and taking hold of the saddle to mount. At the same moment, as if on cue, the sun emerged from behind a little cloud to illuminate the scene.

Nicholas reined in his horse sharply, with a less-than-smooth gesture, causing his mount to toss its head in immediate resistance to the unusual treatment. Then he simply sat and stared through narrowed eyes.

Golden hair, curling neatly into her neck, a rakish little hat trimmed with a soft feather that curled to brush her cheek. A deep blue riding habit in some soft material that draped and clung to her tall, elegant figure. A heart-lifting smile as she turned her head to reply to some comment from Furness.

Oh, God! No!

Nicholas closed his eyes against the vivid scene. It was bad enough seeing her in his dreams, imagining her dancing in London in some other man's arms. Probably the damned Earl of Moreton! But not here! Not now!

But when he opened them, the vision was still there. The sun felt too hot on his skin, the light around him too bright to bear. Everything was in sharp focus as he heard her soft, infectious laugh, as his heart beat heavily against his ribs. Then, with a touch of his heel, he urged his horse forward.

Thea had no presentiment of his approach until the sharp hiss of warning from Agnes Drew caused her to turn her head. A figure mounted on a magnificent dark bay thoroughbred rode toward her, came to a halt, the sun behind him gilding his outline, casting his face into shadow. But she knew immediately—and froze, hands tight on her reins. He dismounted.

They simply stood and looked at each other. As if they were alone in the universe.

It was almost a month since they had set eyes on each other. Thea felt that it could have been yesterday as her gaze searched his familiar features.

Tension held them silent in its grip. Eyes locked as emotion arced between them. Attraction or latent hostility? A nameless desire? Neither could or would have named it, but it held them captive, unaware of either their surroundings or the more-than-interested audience. Until it was suddenly brought to Nicholas's mind, the recollection of the almost physical charge between his brother Henry and Eleanor, the love of his life, when they were in the same room together. No. There was nothing similar here. It could not be! And Thea found herself dissecting her motives in proposing this visit. Had she wanted this meeting all along? In honesty, she did not know. But her heart seemed to be lodged somewhere in the region of her throat. She could find no words to say.

Furness coughed respectfully. 'There now, miss. Here's his lordship. Timely come, I reckon. Just as you was about to leave, an' all.'

It broke the spell. The focus softened and the actors in the little scene fell back into accustomed responses. Lord Nicholas stepped forward, handing his horse over to Furness. Bowed formally in acknowledgement of Thea's presence. Inclined his head to Mistress Drew. Thea curtsied. Neither smiled.

'Miss Wooton-Devereux. Mistress Drew.' His bow was impeccable, worthy of a town withdrawing room, no indication of the churning surge of emotions through his body. They might have been the casual travellers he had first thought them to be. 'Welcome to Aymestry Manor. I would not have expected to see you here in this part of the country.' *Why are you here?*

Thea determined not to show her discomfiture. She could be just as cool as he. 'I am visiting an elderly relative, my lord—a cousin of my mama—in Tenbury Wells.' *I should not be here. What a terrible faux pas.* 'I remembered your description of your home here, and since it was so near… Master Furness has been telling me about your horses.'

'We are proud of them.' *It is too painful you being here. I wish you had not—and yet…*

'And rightly so. I have been admiring the foals…' *He is so cold, so stern. As if my sudden appearance at his door holds no significance for him. So what do I read in his eyes when he looks at me, when I am unable to look away or hide my own feelings?*

'Ah, yes. We have a new stallion. We are breeding for speed as well as endurance…' *She is so polite and composed. As if it is nothing to her that I have discovered her at my home. And that there is a passion which runs between us, almost visible as a shimmer in the air, which cannot be gainsaid, however much I would deny it.*

He was just as she remembered. Tall, imposing, his dark hair lifted by the light breeze. The straight nose and fine brows of all the Faringdons. Absurdly handsome in a distinctly masculine fashion, features dramatically sculpted with light and shadow. She had been used to seeing him elegant in town clothing. Now he wore the double-breasted riding coat, breeches and riding boots of the country gentleman, just as becoming, the dark green cloth of the coat emphasising his lithe, well-muscled build and broad shoulders. But his mouth was stern, his eyes cold, blue fire that held no warmth. Whatever flashed between them, shattering in their mutual awareness, was not a welcome—but of course she had destroyed the possibility of that, had not she?

'Perhaps you will stay for some refreshment, Miss Wooton-Devereux? Before your return to Tenbury.' *It would be better if you did not!*

'Why no. Thank you, my lord, but we must go back. My cousin…' *Once he would have called me Thea.*

'I am sure Mistress Drew and your groom would appreciate the opportunity to rest and refresh themselves.' The arch to his brows became more pronounced.

'Very well, my lord.' She accepted the inevitable with a gracious but chilling smile. 'It will be my pleasure.' She had noted the hint—the merest hint of arrogant criticism. How dare he make her aware of her responsibilities!

Lord Nicholas nodded as if he had no doubts of her acquiescence. 'I will go on up to the house. Furness here will take your animals and direct you. Mrs Grant, my housekeeper, will see to your comfort.' He turned on his heel and strode off towards the main wing of the house, leaving the ladies to follow at their leisure and Dacre to remain to discuss the finer points of horseflesh and enjoy a tankard of ale with Furness.

'I told you we should not have come!' Agnes's voice took on the tone of Thea's childhood nursemaid. 'Why would you not take my advice?'

'I know, I know! But we did and we have met him. Don't tell my mother!'

'Hmm!' Agnes huffed, but beyond glaring at her wilful mistress, she knew there was no ground to be made in saying more. At least she could rely on Lord Nicholas to behave as a gentleman should. His manners, in the circumstances, had been impeccable. She could not but admire him.

They were welcomed into the Manor by an elderly lady, clearly a family retainer, clad in black silk with the keys of the household secured by a silver chatelaine to her waist. She curtsied with placid composure, smiled in welcome and showed them into a sunny parlour where she invited them to sit at their ease. 'We do not see many visitors these days at Aymestry. Master Nicholas does not stay here often,' she explained, with the familiarity of long service to the family. 'It is good to have people about the place. Sometimes it is too quiet. His lordship said to bring you whatever you required. I shall bring tea, perhaps?'

'If you would be so kind, Mrs Grant. It is a beautiful old house.' Thea cast her eyes in admiration round the cosily panelled room, in the Tudor wing of the house, with its polished furniture and rich deep-red drapes.

'Indeed it is. I wish… But there. Master Nicholas will do just as he wishes! I shall bring the tea tray.' Leaving Thea to contemplate the knowledge that *Master Nicholas* probably always did *exactly* as he wished. Only to be interrupted by the return of the gentleman himself with Mrs Grant and the tea tray hard on his heels.

Without a hostess, Thea was called upon to preside over the little ceremony of brewing the tea which she did with consummate skill, calling on all her social skills to remain serenely at ease. As she poured the fragrant brew into delicate china cups, Lord Nicholas and Miss Wooton-Devereux indulged in polite and meaningless conversation about the scenery, the condition of the roads, the prospect of the harvest, the horses. Both lady and gentleman found themselves most adept at exchanging a number of opinions, in which neither had any particular interest at that moment, and in the coolest manner possible. And between them Agnes for the most part sat and listened. When called upon to give an opinion, she did so in brusque but not unfriendly manner, intent on watching the skilled thrust and parry that disguised far deeper emotions, emotions which had the edge of a honed duelling blade.

It was a relief for everyone when conversation was interrupted by a distant rumble of thunder.

'We should be going, Miss Thea,' Agnes interrupted with a glance at the thunder clouds now clear through the window. 'It may be nothing, just a summer shower, but we should not wish to be drenched.'

'Too late, I fear.' Nicholas stood as a flash of lightning pierced the shadows. They had failed to see the growing gloom in the room. 'I will ask Mrs Grant to prepare rooms. You will stay here for the night.'

Again the presumption that they would do as he said! Well, she would not. 'No, my lord. There is no need. I am sure it will soon blow over—and we will be home before dusk.'

'That would be a foolish decision. You will be quite safe here, Miss Wooton-Devereux.' Nicholas's lips curled in what might have been reassurance—or more likely a touch of derision. Thea was in no doubt. 'Mistress Drew is chaperon enough for you, I believe. Your reputation will not suffer under my roof. Do I need to send a message so that your cousin will be at ease?'

'I doubt she will notice our absence. She is somewhat cut off from the world.' Thea resented the sharp cut at her previous immoderate behaviour but had little choice except to let it go, even if she had to clench her hands into fists within the folds of the dark velvet to achieve it. The rain began to beat against the window, heralding an imminent downpour. It prompted her decision even as she hated the necessity. 'It seems that we must accept your kind invitation, my lord. We are most grateful.'

'Very well.' His lordship gave no indication that he had heard anything in her reply but the gratitude she professed. He inclined his head. 'Perhaps you will dine with me later? Mrs Grant will arrange all. Now…if you will excuse me, I need to conduct some business before the rain gets any heavier.'

And that was it. All icy good manners. *Damn him!*

'I told you—' Agnes began as soon as the door had closed after him.

'I know! Don't fuss.' Thea allowed her ruffled sensibilities to show. Why did she feel that she had been outmanoeuvred? 'I freely admit I was in the wrong. Does that make you feel any better?'

'No. It does not! We should not be staying here.'

'I know that too, Agnes.' She allowed herself a wry smile as the absurdity and potential discomfort of the situation struck her. 'You can sleep across the threshold of my room if it makes you feel any better.'

'No, it won't. Not that I would need to. I don't know what it is between you two—but I don't think his lordship likes you very much.'

'Good. Neither do I like him. And that is exactly how it should be, if you recall.' Thea stood, carefully replaced the china teacup on the tray and shook out her skirts. What was the use of regret? She must deal with what she could not change. 'We will leave Aymestry tomorrow morning and we can forget we were ever here. All I have to do is survive an evening of dining with him.'

'Hmm!'

'I trust the food will be warmer than his manners!'

'And perhaps sweeter and more palatable than yours, Miss Thea!'

On which tart word of warning, and ignoring the lady's answering flounce, Mistress Drew stalked from the room to discover the whereabouts of Mrs Grant.

Thea was shown into a bedroom in one of the more recent additions to the house where the panelling had been replaced with papered walls in white and cream stripes. Small and intimate, full of light, she had the impression that it had once been the room of a Faringdon lady. There were no personal touches now, but a pair of delicate watercolour paintings of country scenes hung beside the fireplace, a small dressing table with a mirror graced the window embrasure and there was a lingering smell of herbs— of lavender and perhaps rosemary. The bed hangings and window drapes were old, but distinctly feminine, in pale blue embroidered silk, well cared for, and had once been very fine.

She took off the close-fitting coat of her riding habit, shook out the lace ruffles on her cuffs and brushed her heavy skirts of any lingering dust from her ride. It was the best she could do. Hot water had been provided for her, so she washed her face and combed her hair with the ivory comb thoughtfully placed for her use on the dressing table.

Then she sat and looked out of the window at the new green leaves giving shape to the herbaceous border where it bloomed against the warm stone of the kitchen garden wall.

Now what? It was all very simple, she decided. As she had told Agnes, they would dine, she would try for sweetness and a

soft response to every topic of conversation—if it killed her!—
and she would leave tomorrow. There need be no complications
here. But Lord Nicholas's proximity brought a shiver of anticipation along her skin, as if a gentle breeze had got up with the
onset of evening to caress her arms and throat. A heightened colour touched her cheeks with rose. Recognising it, accepting it,
Thea warned herself to have a care, and believed that she could
rely on Nicholas to treat her with such icy indifference and formality that she would feel no inclination to behave in a less-than-
maidenly manner. She knew exactly how to conduct herself with
sufficient social skills to grace any occasion.

As the light began to fade, a footman came to lead her to the
dining room, again one of the old panelled rooms. Everything
had been made ready, with a fire lit against the chill of the early
summer evening and the dining table formally set, but with only
two places. Agnes was probably tucked up in a cosy gossip with
Mrs Grant, Thea decided with some envy.

Nicholas bowed Thea into the room and held her chair as she
sat, before taking his own place at the opposite end. So they were
to dine formally. She considered this decision on Nicholas's part.
Perhaps it was for the best.

A simple meal was served to them by two self-effacing footmen. The polished surface of the table stretched between them,
weighty with silver and crystal, discouraging conversation on a
personal level. The wide expanse exactly mirrored the distance
between the two who shared the meal.

It was the strangest meal, Thea decided, that she had ever
eaten in her life. The tension in the air robbed her of any real appetite but she did her best to do justice to Mrs Grant's kind preparations. The conversation that flowed so easily—cool, practised,
trivial, uncontroversial conversation—hid the charged undercurrent that wound the tension to snapping point, as taut as a watch
spring. His face was calm, expression enigmatic. She presumed
that hers was the same. Their manners could not be faulted.

But all the time that same undercurrent curled, as strong as the lethal drag below the surface of a placid millpond, spelling disaster to the unwary. Whenever their eyes met across the expanse of china and glassware, it held them, until one of them deliberately broke the contact by sheer effort of will. It was almost a courtship, held suspended in icy restraint. Thea found that her breathing was shallow and, despite an excellent wine, her mouth was dry. The words that they addressed to each other did not express what was in their hearts. And both knew it. It was almost as if the air around them held its breath for the outcome.

Eventually the footmen withdrew, leaving fruit, sweetmeats, a decanter of port. Candles were lit against the shadows, the drapes closed, enclosing Nicholas and Theodora in a small personal world of heightened emotion. The flickering lights glowed on the soft velvet of her gown and on the bright curls of her hair. It sparked fire from the diamond pin in his cravat. Her beauty struck him once again, rare as the jewel at his throat, as she looked up from the apple that she had begun to pare. An urge to push the situation on—to some sort of conclusion—gripped him. Indeed, he realised that he had no choice.

'Do you wish to withdraw to one of the parlours, madam? Or retire?' His voice was low, as if deliberately controlled. It made her shiver. Here was the ideal chance to escape his dominating presence and she knew that she should take it. Then tomorrow she could leave—and the visit would be over with no lasting repercussions for either. She had made a mistake in coming here, but it would soon be rectified.

She should say yes, should return to the restful solitude of her bedchamber, where she could breathe again.

'No. I would stay here,' she heard herself say. Her pulse began to beat, an insistent throb in the tender hollow at the base of her throat.

'Of course.' He appeared to accept her decision with equanimity and poured a glass of port for both of them.

She accepted it. Raised it to her lips, took a little sip. 'It is a beautiful house. You are very fortunate, my lord.'

He watched her, caught up by the trace of wistfulness here.

All he could think was that here was no vestige of the flighty débutante who had played fast and loose with his emotions and then deliberately driven him away, as carelessly as she might discard a dress that no longer became her. She sat at the end of the table, the candlelight in her eyes and gilding her skin, composed, beautiful and most desirable. Neither flighty nor frivolous.

'I like it,' he replied. 'But it seems that I am not destined to spend much time here.'

'So Master Furness told me. You have loyal people around you.'

'I suppose. I inherited most of them. Perhaps I am fortunate.' He hesitated. Then, for the first time, he introduced a personal note into the dialogue between them. 'Where do you call home?'

'I have never had a settled home,' she replied willingly enough, but looked down at the rings of apple peel. 'We have a small estate in Yorkshire, but we have tenants who occupy it because of our long absences. All I recall from when I was a young girl is living in embassies and rented town houses. Always very comfortable, some of them luxurious even. The one in Paris was so splendid as to be positively intimidating.' She laughed a little at the memory of the overpowering grandeur. 'But it was not home, you understand…' Again that breath of regret, of which she was perhaps unaware.

Silence stretched between them, broken only by a faint crackle from the fire and the soft ticking of a long case clock.

Then, 'Why did you come here today, Thea?'

She looked at him down the length of the table, astonished that he should ask so direct a question, thinking quickly. The truth could be dangerous. It could indicate the state of her heart. It could destroy all her careful and painful strategy. And she would have no one to blame but herself if she showed her vulnerability to him. Yet she found that she had no compulsion to lie.

'Because I wanted to see your home.'

Nicholas sat for a long moment, fingers holding the stem of his glass, considering her reply.

'Why did you deliberately reject me in London, Thea?' Thea was not the only one driven by honesty, it seemed.

'I did not!' A wash of shame brought guilty colour to her face and made her dissemble, which made the guilt even stronger.

'You did. I would suggest that it was a carefully constructed little charade to drive me away.' His voice remained low, soft, but there was an implacable quality about it. 'I did not see it at the time. But I do now. The girl I saw in London who went out of her way to ruffle so many feathers—and with remarkable success—was so out of character, I think, as to be ludicrous. I should have seen it, but did not. Perhaps because it touched me so personally.' He watched her every move, every expression that flitted over her lovely features, his eyes demanding that she tell him the truth. 'Why did you do it, Thea? You cannot deny what is between us, however uncomfortable it might be. However much we might wish that we could.'

She raised the tips of her fingers to her lips as if to stop incriminating words. For once she did not know what to say.

He rose to his feet with fluid grace and came towards her. Held out his hand. For a moment she looked at it and then up into his face. Finding that she had no will of her own against such silent insistence, she closed her fingers over his. Stood and moved away from her chair, where they faced each other in the centre of the room, both her hands clasped in his.

'Tell me the truth, Thea. You are attracted to me as much as I am attracted to you. Don't tell me that you do not feel it.'

'Yes.' It was hardly more than a whisper, but she did not hesitate. 'I feel it every time that you look at me.'

'So what was all that about, when you resisted every attempt of mine to spend time with you? When you tried to give me a disgust of you?'

'I cannot say.' She swallowed against the dryness in her throat, but kept her eyes on his. It was suddenly imperative that he did not doubt her. 'But however it might have seemed, my lord, I did not deliberately intend to hurt you.' She sighed a little. 'I would never do that.'

'Very well.' He could press her for more, knew that he needed to do so. But intuition told him that it was not the time. He would leave it for now.

Time stretched out as they looked at each other—a minute, an hour…it could have been a lifetime. Then he drew her slowly forward into his arms. Giving her the chance to refuse if that was her inclination. His intention was clear.

'Tell me no, if you do not wish for this, Thea.'

'I cannot, my lord.'

'Call me by my name.'

'Nicholas.' A sigh, as soft as a caress, skin against skin. This was fatal! But she could not resist. She wanted more than anything to feel the strength of his arms around her, the demand of his mouth on hers. So she stood as Nicholas ran his hands in one long caress from wrist to shoulder and then on to frame her face. With gentle fingers, a little callused, he traced along the line of her eyebrows, across her delicate cheek-bones. Then to follow the same path, equally gently, with his lips. She held her breath at the featherlight touch, closed her eyes at the sensation of his fingers and mouth, his own breath a whisper against her hair.

'Open your eyes, Thea.'

As she did so, obedient to his every demand, he lowered his head, holding her in submission. Not that he needed to do so. She could not have moved, drawn into the enchantment of the occasion. Aware only of his lips, firm and cool. Seeking and exploring, without haste. Yet it was not the chaste kiss that they had shared in London—far from it, as he changed the angle for his own pleasure, increased the pressure, until her lips parted beneath his. He allowed his tongue to caress the soft skin, outlining her lips. Still gentle, as if he, too, were holding his breath against the promise of passion.

She was soft and responsive and willing. He knew that he should be filled with exhilaration at holding her in his arms at last. And yet… It was not a straightforward matter at all. He determined to close his mind against the sharp edge of doubt, almost in the way of a premonition, which refused to let him rest, and concentrated on enjoying the awakening of her responses to him. On keeping his own demands light and uncomplicated, mindful of her inexperience. But it became increasingly difficult when she sighed against his mouth, when her fingers dug into the hard flesh of his shoulders as if to anchor her in the present, when she took a little step, moulding her body against his, hip and thigh and breast.

She was everything he could ever want in a woman. And he was afraid—of her and of the emotions that she aroused in him.

With a low growl in his throat, Nicholas was the one to end the kiss, lifting his head as he put her away from him. Dropping his hands from around her slender body, he stepped back, his breathing as heightened as hers. When Thea lifted her hands to stop him, he took another careful step in retreat, his face austere as if he had just made an almost impossible decision.

'Why?'

He knew her meaning. 'I must not.'

'I am not resisting you, Nicholas.'

'I know. And that is part of the issue! If we are into honesty, which we appear to be…' a touch of humour deepened the colour of his eyes '…it is my inclination at this moment to take you to my room—to my bed. I doubt that you are aware of how much I want you. Your innocence would be no shield against the passion that fires my blood when your lips open beneath mine.'

Her breathing caught at his outspoken intent. But she was not shocked. 'And if I agreed?'

'No.' Another step away. 'You must not. And I will not.'

'I see. I have no experience of this. So you will not.' A little smile curved her mouth, but her face was sad. 'Because, in spite of your…your desire, you do not like me enough?'

'Because it would be unworthy of me to take advantage of that innocence.'

'And if I am willing?' She tilted her chin, a hint of challenge in the gesture. The sapphire glint in her eyes bridged the gulf between them. Unmaidenly indeed!

'No. You do not understand. How could I risk your reputation? As a gentleman my honour is at stake. And of course there must be no breath of scandal around your name that is of my making.' He suddenly turned on his heel, presenting his back to her, so that he could not see the invitation in her face. 'I wish you had not come here today, Thea. It compromises my control where you are concerned.'

'And you would not risk scandal.' A statement rather than a question. Perhaps she knew why. Of course she knew why!

'Never. For scandal can wound beyond bearing. Can destroy.'

'For you or for myself?'

'Thea…' He sighed 'You do not know what you ask of me.'

'I do. And now I am the one to be rejected.' She stepped forward across the space that he had deliberately created. 'Is this a punishment? Because I hurt you?'

At first he did not respond, nor did he turn towards her. Instead he picked up the neglected glass of port and drank it in one swallow, then twisted to face her again and answered, a hint of weariness in his voice, 'No. Such a suggestion would dishonour me.'

'Forgive me. I know that it was unworthy. It is just that…it hurts.'

She looked so desolate as she turned her face from him and, in so doing, destroyed all his honourable intentions to preserve the distance between them.

'Theodora…' He reached for her, encircling her once more into his arms. The gentle encouragement of his previous kisses deserted him. Possession. Demand. His need for her swept through him as his mouth ravaged hers, the glorious curve of her throat, the lovely slope of her shoulders to the lace edging of her garment. His arms banded round her as steel, preventing any escape. But in Thea, under the onslaught of new emotions and sensations, there was no desire to escape and he sensed it as she allowed him to take her mouth in a searing possession. Her innocence was a delight, but her willingness fanned the flames to a raging fire. For Thea, the searing kisses forced her to acknowledge finally and without question the ultimate loss of her heart to Lord Nicholas Faringdon.

At last he released her, but not before he pressed a final salute to her hair, to the tender skin at her temples, deliberately gentling the touch of his hands at her shoulders. 'It is better that you go to bed alone.' He smiled to reassure her, just the slightest curve to his mouth, then took her hand as if she were a child and led her from the room to the foot of the staircase. There he lit a candle for her, then bowed low and lifted her hand as if to kiss it in a formal leave-taking. Instead he turned it, cupping her hand in his and pressing his lips to her palm in the most intimate of caresses, then closed her fingers over it before he released her.

'Nicholas…'

He shook his head to stop her. 'Go up, Thea. There are limits to my control. I would not wish to regret my actions tomorrow in the cold grey light of dawn.'

Her lips parted, as if to argue, to beg even. Where were all her good intentions now? Destroyed to ashes, consumed in the fire of passion, ignited by his lips. She had all but thrown herself at him. And he had refused. And she knew why—and could hardly blame him. She could ask nothing from him that he was not prepared to give. She allowed her lashes to veil the sense of hurt and loss that assailed her as she realised that there was no possibility of a future for them together. So be it. With a deep breath she called on all her pride and dignity. Now she was cool and calm again.

'Of course. Forgive me, if I have made your situation difficult.'

'There is no need for forgiveness. Perhaps neither of us has shown wisdom this night.'

She trod the stairs, aware of his tall figure standing quietly. How foolish she had been to press him—and how forward. Her mother, however liberal Lady Drusilla might be, would be horrified if she had seen and heard her daughter this night. But the touch of his mouth, the power of his body, the timbre of his voice, every quality of Lord Nicholas Faringdon was imprinted on her soul. She must leave as soon as she could. It would be unfair of her to do any other.

Nicholas stood and watched her until she turned the bend in the stairs and vanished into the gloom of the corridor, only the faint glow from her candle marking her passage. He pushed his fingers through his hair. What an incredible complication this

was. And one that he did not fully understand. Theodora—a
complicated weave of contradictions. He liked her—more than
liked her. Oh, God, he wanted her! Imagined stripping the soft
velvet from her body, lifting her in his arms to lay her on the cool
sheets of his bed and to cover her body with his own. To possess
those elegant, slender limbs with hot caresses and wild kisses,
giving her no choice but to shiver beneath him with a passion of
her own. She had no knowledge of such things, as she had said.
It would delight him to give her that knowledge, to take that innocence for himself until she cried out with uncontrollable longing. And he would bury himself in her, possess her utterly. The
thought, the taste of her lips, her skin, heated his blood beyond
bearing. He returned to the dining room to pour another glass of
port and pace a track between window and fireplace.

Perhaps he had seen the true Theodora tonight. A little vulnerable. Haunted, surprisingly, by a longing for a home of her
own. And perhaps he had seen himself. His own desires, rather
than those demanded by his family. He wanted her. Her kisses
had roused him beyond sense; her honesty, her openness, her intelligence, had touched a chord within him. But there was something between them, something to cloud the brilliance of her
eyes, to draw a faint line between her brows. Something which,
in London, had driven her to put a distance between them. He
did not know what—and she had refused to explain her deliberate wilfulness. Perhaps it would be wiser to keep his distance
after all. He had without doubt made the best decision possible.

At this moment, wisdom was far from his thoughts.

Chapter Eight

~⚜~

On the following morning over breakfast in a sunny parlour, Thea, with the brightest of smiles, assured Agnes that she had slept perfectly well, not stirring until a maid brought her a cup of hot chocolate. Agnes, on seeing the rather strained expression on Thea's face and even the hint of a shadow beneath her lovely eyes, could have argued the point, but realised that there was nothing to be gained and so remained silent on the subject. Nor did she ask about Lord Nicholas, who had already broken his fast and was, they were given to understand by Mrs Grant, somewhere about the stables and had been since dawn.

'I see that you survived the ordeal,' Agnes ventured, watching carefully to see Thea's response.

'Yes, indeed.' Thea smiled brightly. 'You would have been proud of me. We did not discover one topic to disagree over throughout the whole of the meal.'

'Remarkable. A miracle, some would say.'

Thea might have replied with some acerbity, but a footman entered the room to inform them that their horses were ready and awaited their convenience, which silenced her as she finished the meal, understanding Nicholas's decision to make the parting as public and as impersonal as possible.

* * *

So their final meeting, as he had planned, was in the court-yard beside the stables. He smiled at their approach, inclined his head in greeting, wished the ladies a good morning. But his eyes were flat, not reflecting his smile. And he did not touch her, al-lowing Dacre to hand her up into the saddle of The Zephyr as he himself aided Agnes. But the memory of that shared moment of passion when he had kissed and held her, as if he wanted noth-ing more in life than to keep her with him, lingered around them, an almost visible swirl of emotion, like smoke on an autumn day.

'You should make good time.' He spoke to Edward Dacre as the groom and the servant mounted. 'Take care of them. Any problems on the road, don't stop. You should be safe enough on the Aymestry and Burford estates.' He thought that he should pro-vide the little group with an escort, but understood that the lady would be more than likely to refuse. There were ways around that which he was prepared to take.

He approached the shoulder of the little mare for a final leave-taking.

'Goodbye, Miss Wooton-Devereux.' Not farewell or adieu. Or Godspeed. Thea noted and understood the deliberate choice of words and followed suit.

'Goodbye, my lord. We are grateful for your hospitality.' Her voice as light and uninvolved as his. And her eyes just as care-fully guarded.

But now, as if it were beyond him to resist, he took her hand from where it lay loosely on her reins and raised it to his lips, first turning it, as he had the previous night, to press his mouth to her palm, then released her. She raised that hand for just a mo-ment, tempted to bend and touch the dark hair where it lay at his temple. But did not, of course, could not prolong the pain of this brief and dispassionate farewell for either of them. But she pressed her palm with its burning imprint against the bosom of her velvet jacket, against her heart.

He watched her go. If Furness thought his expression a little bleak, he decided that it had more to do with a colicky mare than the departure of the guests.

'Jed.' Lord Nicholas beckoned one of the stable boys, a likely lad, who was emerging from the stable. 'Follow them. Take someone with you—George Abbot, perhaps. And keep your eyes open on Lord Westbourne's acres.'

'Afraid of trouble, my lord?' Furness frowned, not liking the possibility.

'No. But I would not wish harm to come to them. I have heard that the Maidens have been active this fortnight.'

Stepping forward to hold Jed's mount steady, Furness grunted his disgust. 'Men dressed as women!'

'Disguised they may be, but they are a rough crowd with little respect for the law when their wages are low and their children starving.' Lord Nicholas turned back to the lad as he mounted. 'Stay with them until Tenbury is in sight, Jed. Anything that worries you, anything at all, one of you ride to get help.'

Some little time later Nicholas, sleeves rolled up, was inspecting a newly arrived foal, all long legged and satin smooth, as it lay and dozed in the sunshine beside its protective mother. He looked up and rose to his feet, a finger of disquiet touching his spine, as Jed galloped into the courtyard with a hasty clatter of hooves, the horse in a lather.

'What?' Nicholas strode over.

'The Maidens're out, m'lord.'

'Are they on the road?' Nicholas grabbed the bridle in an urgent hand, muscles suddenly tense at the news.

'Aye, my lord. Met Nol Price from the Westbourne estate by the packhorse bridge,' Jed gasped, not bothering to dismount. 'The word is out. Riots, m'lord. Labourers have gathered—most like the Maidens—decked out in skirts and shawls and such. Nol said a big group, out for trouble against my lord Westbourne. Burning ricks. And I saw black smoke in the distance.' He ran a hand over his face, which was red from his efforts. 'I didn't know…I thought I should come back here for help. George went on to warn them…or lead them to safety. But if the Maidens're out in force and it's mischief they're after…'

Nicholas did not linger. The relaxed country gentleman underwent an instant transformation. 'You did the right thing, Jed. Get a fresh horse and tell Mat to join us.' He was already grabbing saddle and bridle and opening the door of the bay stallion's stall. 'Come with me, Furness. We'll take the pistols—better safe than sorry. And move it!'

The scenery on that bright morning, which had so captivated Thea when she rode to Aymestry on the previous day, now meant nothing to her. She travelled in silence, lost in her own thoughts, blind to the beauty around her. Sensing her abstraction, Agnes, too, kept her own council and any comments she might make were directed at Dacre. She was aware of the new level of tension between her mistress and Lord Nicholas—who could not be? Yesterday, the atmosphere in the stable yard and when they had take tea had been strained, even uncomfortable. But now? Agnes would have given her best kid gloves to know what passed between them the previous evening when they had dined together. But whatever it was, it had brought neither of them happiness. She could have cut the atmosphere this morning with the silver scissors in her reticule.

Thea was oblivious to Agnes's speculations, to everything but the ache that was almost physical around her heart. It gnawed at her, intensified by the anguish of the knowledge that, however much she might love him, however much he might be drawn to her, fate had determined that she would never see him again. Or be allowed to love him as she wished.

Thea deliberately straightened her shoulders, shortened her reins as The Zephyr tossed her head. There was nothing she could do about it, she lectured herself. She must forget Lord Nicholas Faringdon and turn her thoughts to the future. But she could not. The memory of the possessive touch of his mouth on hers remained a tangible presence, his rejection of her an impenetrable mist of sorrow.

Dacre's voice jolted her out of her preoccupation.

'Look to the left, Miss Thea. Smoke over by those barns. Looks like a large fire.'

Thea blinked, realised that they had already left the Burford estate and were crossing the arable fields of a neighbouring landowner. And, yes, there was a large fire, dark smoke billowing, flames clear as they leapt into the sky from the dry timber and straw.

She pulled the grey mare to a halt. 'Does the road go near? I don't remember.'

'No, Miss Thea. It curves to the east. It should not be a problem.' But Dacre, although unwilling to voice it, kept Lord Faringdon's warning in mind.

The little party continued, more cautiously now and with closed ranks, keeping a watch on the road ahead. It dipped towards a small copse and they could see a crossroads where a wider track, obviously a drove road, came in from Ludlow to the west. The fire was now closer, with the dense smoke beginning to drift across their path in the still air, but did not necessarily give any cause for concern.

'Only some old hay ricks.' There was relief in Dacre's voice. 'No danger, I think.'

'But look at the crossroads.' Thea raised her hand to point to the meeting of the tracks.

A little crowd of people, perhaps a dozen or more, had gathered. Still too far away for any detail, they could hear raised voices and the movement of the bodies suggested some agitation. Thea squinted against the sun and then it struck her.

'Why, look. They are women.' She could see the heavy skirts and bright shawls habitually worn by countrywomen in the fields, their heads covered by scarves or white cotton bonnets. 'What can it be?'

'I mislike it.' Dacre pushed his horse parallel with Thea's and motioned the servant to take closer order behind him next to Agnes Drew. For indeed there was a tension about the little group, despite their distance.

'It may be that someone has been hurt in the fire,' Agnes suggested. 'A child perhaps.'

They continued to approach with some caution, too conscious of the harsh tone in the voices that now carried to them. Women they might be, but something had occurred to reduce them to stark anger.

'But they are not women.' Thea's sudden and surprised statement brought the travellers to a halt again, for, despite the swirl of skirts, the layers of scarves and shawls, the forms beneath were now clearly masculine, long limbed and broad shouldered, as were the harsh voices that shouted and demanded attention. Now it could be seen that their skirts, hitched up from the ground for ease of movement, covered breeches, rough stockings and heavy work boots. And they carried a range of sticks and scythes and even an old shotgun, all being wielded with evidence of high-running emotions.

The Maidens!

Dacre immediately, acting on pure instinct, stretched out his hand to snatch at Thea's bridle, whether she would approve or no. Emotions were indeed running high. One of the group had swung himself up on to a tree stump and was haranguing the rest, emphasising his points with fierce gestures. There could be danger here for the well-born travellers.

'We have no quarrel with them, nor they with us.' Thea glanced at her groom with raised brows and not a little anxiety. 'Why should they harm us?' She twitched her bridle free and applied her heels to the grey's flanks. Better to get past the danger as quickly as possible. Nothing could be gained by sitting here in the road, simply waiting for God knew what outcome. But as they walked their mounts forward, confidently enough in appearance, shouts broke out. They were able to hear, one overlapping another, as the men addressed their leader who had taken up a stance on the fallen oak, his skirts flapping round his legs in his agitation.

'We'll starve if he has his way…'

'The bastard cares nought for us, now that…'

'He's told us we'll be laid off come summer…'

'Wages be so low…'

A litany of rural complaint that had been given a sharp edge by some local crisis.

Thea refused to halt, determined to press forward. She might sympathise, but the responsibility was not hers to remedy. Rather her need and her duty was to ensure the safety of Agnes and her servants. She found herself praying that the volatile gathering would accept their ignorance of local affairs and allow them to pass with nothing more than harsh words and accusations. Besides, there was no help to be sought in the circumstances. They must brazen it out.

Then a shawl-draped head in the crowd turned at the beat of the hooves and saw them.

'What have we here? Fine feathers on even finer horseflesh.' He laughed derisively at the prospect of such wealthy prey.

The crowd turned, harsh, masculine faces ridiculously framed by scarves and shawls and bonnets. But there was nothing ridiculous in the scene. The faces turned towards them were twisted in anger and despair. There would be no sympathy here for their innocence.

'They're not from round 'ere.' One voice, perhaps of reason, drifted on the charged air. 'They've nothing to do with Lord Westbourne and his damnable machines…'

It was only one voice, easily swamped by the rest.

'They do well from our labour by the looks of 'em…'

'Look at those horses—we can sell 'em…'

A stone was thrown. Then another. And, as one, the crowd rushed towards them, intent on stealing anything of value from the hated landlord class.

For Thea, everything afterwards happened in a mad rush of uncontrolled and confused aggression. A well-aimed stone struck Agnes on the side of her head, causing her horse to shy, and she fell heavily on to the road. Thea cried out in alarm and tried to reach her. Dacre's bridle and that of their servant were both seized, preventing them from either going to the rescue or riding to secure help. Thea also found herself surrounded by a sea of bodies, ungentle hands grasping at her bridle, her saddlebags, her long skirts. She could do nothing but fight to prevent herself being pulled from the saddle as The Zephyr stamped and fidgeted, head tossing in increasing unease at the harsh treatment.

'She'll 'ave something of value 'ere… And this animal's worth a pretty penny…'

Suddenly the outcome, or any sense of the present outrage, was taken out of Thea's hands. She simply froze in a blind, unreasoning panic. Memories flooded back, vivid and intense, to rob her of all sense. She knew in her mind, clear as faceted crystal, that she should ride for help. She should go to the aid of Agnes, who lay on the ground amidst the stamping hooves and the swarm of attackers. As if from a distance, she watched herself in mounting horror. She could not move, could not force her body to follow the dictates of her brain. Her whip was snatched from her unresponsive hand. She was unable to breathe, her ribs constricted by sheer irrational terror. Pulled from the saddle, she landed on her knees on the stony ground. She did not even feel the sharp edges that cut into her flesh, only felt the hands that grasped her arms, and urged her to stand. She could see where Agnes was trying to sit up and knew that she should go to her—but could not. Dacre attempted to push his horse between the rabble and his stricken mistress, but to no avail. They were outnumbered and in the violent control of their attackers.

'Let's make an example of 'em…show his bloody lordship that we mean business… He'll 'ave to listen to us…'

Again it was only one voice. But it was enough. Shouts of enthusiasm and encouragement exploded round them.

Thus the outcome for the travellers was fraught with more than the danger of being robbed. And yet for Thea, dragged to her feet, dishevelled, skirts covered with dust, it had no meaning. Terror continued to hold her, cold and immobile in its grip.

The sound of a single shot brought the furious rabble to a halt, caught in a strange moment of silent stillness. Even the birds were shocked into silence.

Lord Nicholas Faringdon, accompanied by Furness and his two grooms, had come to a halt on the little rise above the crossroads, just long enough to assess the situation. It took no more than a moment to see the intent, if not the detail of it. And it was clear that one pistol shot fired over their heads would not disperse this enraged gathering. Nor could Nicholas risk firing again. It would be impossible to ensure the safety of Thea and her escort in the seething mass before him.

'What the hell in going on here?'

'They're Lord Westbourne's tenants, m'lord.' Furness pulled up beside him, pistol in hand.

'So I see.' It explained all.

Lord Nicholas could see Dacre still trying to escape the attentions of three skirt-clad individuals. He could not see Agnes at all. And Thea? There was a flash of blue velvet in the very heart of the group. And he glimpsed her plumed hat being whirled aloft by a shawl-swathed arm. His blood ran cold in spite of the heat of the day and the sweat which trickled between his shoulder blades after their hard ride.

'Ride on!' His voice was urgent but betrayed none of his fear. 'But don't risk firing.'

Without another thought, even though desperately outnumbered, they kicked their mounts into action, relying on fists, the power of their horses and any remaining vestige of authority that Lord Nicholas might have with the Maidens.

The rioters gave way at the initial charge, but were not to be overawed or intimidated by a mere four men and surged forward again. Using his riding whip and the force of his horse, Furness managed to thrust his way to Agnes's side where she still half-lay in the dirt. Nicholas aimed his horse towards Thea. A heavy blow on his shoulder from an accurately wielded length of wood caused him to wince and snarl though his teeth, but did not deter him. He turned his body to use his booted foot to push aside a man with a pitchfork. A sharp right jab deterred another from attempting to pull him from the saddle. He pressed on.

And recognised a face amidst the mêlée. Lewis Bates, Lord Westbourne's head groom. A man who had always impressed Lord Nicholas with his good sense and calm demeanour—or at least in his dealings with Westbourne's well-bred and highly strung hunters. Nicholas found himself praying that the same good sense and moderation might be prevailed upon in this crucially dangerous situation.

'Bates!' he shouted. 'Lewis Bates!' He pressed his horse against the tide of violent humanity, over to the man's side. 'What in God's name are you doing? What are you about?' Nicholas took hold of a fistful of woollen shawl and shook the man, dragging him closer. 'Two unarmed women? They're no danger or threat to your livelihoods. You do your cause more harm than good, man.'

'You don't know the half of it, m'lord.' Bates snarled his answer.

'Perhaps not. But this is no way to gain a sympathetic ear. Have sense, man. What will it bring you if they are injured? Only condemnation and a bad name. Who'll listen to you then?'

Bates squinted up with narrowed eyes, whiskers and a weatherbeaten complexion incongruous beneath the grubby cotton bonnet.

'Lord Westbourne, damn him to hell, is laying 'em off. They're out for blood, m'lord.'

'I can see that. And a liberal helping of ale has removed any sense they may have had. But they'll listen to you. For God's sake, Bates…'

The man looked at his lordship, considering his words. The outcome of the ugly incident hung in the balance.

'Your quarrel is with Westbourne, Lewis. Not with chance travellers who have been my guests.'

It tipped the balance.

'Aye. Reckon you're right. As a landlord, you're better'n most.' Bates raised the shotgun and fired into the air, then leapt back on to the oak stump, agile in spite of the hampering skirts. The loud explosion at close quarters once more brought the proceedings to a halt, just as The Zephyr, her composure finally deserting her, pulled free from her captor and bolted down the road, back in the direction of Aymestry.

'It's my lord Faringdon, lads.' Bates's voice rolled over the restive gathering. 'We have no quarrel with him.'

'They're all landlords. They're all rich on our backs.' A short, stocky man, younger that most, pushed back his shawl and glowered up at Bates. 'Why should we treat him any different? Or them?' He swung his arm to indicate their erstwhile captives.

'Not all are as bad as Westbourne, Sam.'

'Are you in league with them, then? Are the landlords paying you?' Sensing defeat, Sam's features registered thwarted anger. He spat his disgust into the dust at his feet. 'And who says you're our spokesman?'

'I do. As for being in league with the landlords—don't be a damned fool, Sam Dyer.'

'I don't like it!' Dyer would not let go, like a terrier with a rat.

'Neither do I. But you'll do as I say.'

Their eyes met, a challenge until the younger man backed down with a snarl and a muttered oath.

'As his lordship says,' Bates addressed the men who now waited uncertainly, 'better that we don't antagonise the whole countryside, lads.'

'Why not? What have we to lose? We've nothing left as it is.' A voice from behind Sam Dyer expressed the desperation of all present.

'We may need friends. Them as'll stand up and speak for us.'

'It'll not look good if you harm two women.' Lord Nicholas added the weight of his argument, his eyes fixed on Thea where she stood, completely unmoving and apparently unaware in the centre of the group.

'Keep out of this, my lord, and go while you still can,' Bates hissed in a low voice. 'Not your concern.'

'As JP it is my concern.' Nicholas would not turn and run from the confrontation. He allowed his eyes to travel the crowd before him, the expressions ranging from fury to drunken exhilaration to careworn despair. 'And you can be sure that I will see justice done. For the landlords. And also for you.' His firm gaze, which took in the throng, holding every pair of eyes that stared back, was both a challenge and a promise. Would they resist his authority? Or would they accept his word for honest dealings with the law? 'But it is not justice to rob and hinder innocent travellers.'

'Not now, my lord.' Bates's quiet voice came from behind him. 'Not now. I suggest you leave. We'll not hinder you. And you should forget what you've seen here this day.'

Nicholas saw the sense of it. They were outnumbered and the mutterings were still ugly with suppressed violence. Bates might have deflected their anger, but for how long? He nodded in recognition of his debt. 'I owe you, Lewis.'

'I'll remind you of it, my lord.'

The crowd withdrew into a little group. Still sullen. Still angry and silently threatening, but willing to accept the logic of Bates's argument as Lord Nicholas and the travellers made their preparations for departure. The grey, severely lame from an uncontrolled stumble on the boulder-strewn path, was rescued by Mat and led gently back. Dacre, suffering the after-effects of a number of hard blows to his back and shoulders, regained his composure with gruff thanks to his lordship, and went to help Mistress Drew. She was lifted to her feet with a damaged arm and painful temple where the stone had struck. It might have broken the skin, but not her spirit. Having been lifted on to her horse, she insisted that she was quite all right and could ride on without aid. Better to look to Mistress Thea. She glowered at the band of *women* who, she announced in loud accents, should know better than to attack helpless females. She would have gone to Thea's side, but Nicholas shook his head. Furness looped her reins with his and led her away before she could say more to antagonise the still-hostile labourers.

And Thea? When Lord Nicholas finally made his way to her side, she simply stood in the road in a paralysed state of shock. Eyes glassy and unfocused, skin pale and clammy, she appeared not to recognise her rescuer when he took her arm and gently led her toward his horse. He mounted.

'I'll take her. She is not fit to ride alone. If you will lift her…'

Dacre steadied his mistress in his arms and lifted her, allowing his lordship to take her and settle her in the saddle before him. She made no response other than a little sigh as she allowed her head to rest against his shoulder. But her whole body was tense and rigid, as if held in check against some unseen enemy. And although he spoke, soft words of comfort and reassurance, she made no response. In the end he simply held her, one arm firm about her waist, aware of nothing but the rapid beat of her heart against him, as a helpless bird would flutter for its freedom from a trap.

And on that journey back to Aymestry Manor, in a blinding revelation, Lord Nicholas Faringdon knew that all he had ever wanted in life, all he had dreamed of, lay at that moment in his arms, held tight and safe against the world, her hands clutched in the material of his riding coat. He could do nothing but take her back to Aymestry. He had persuaded himself that Theodora should have no place in his life. He had made that decision. But now, for better or worse, fate had determined that he have no choice in the matter.

At Aymestry Manor, Lord Nicholas sent servants scurrying with brisk and practical instructions that hid the depth of anger and fear which still rode him. Jed was ordered into the house at a run to warn Mrs Grant of the urgent needs of their guests. The little grey, limping and distressed from a severely strained fetlock, was dispatched to a vacant stall in the stables with orders to one of the stable lads to prepare and apply a hot poultice to reduce the swelling in the injured leg.

Mistress Drew was helped from her horse by Furness, who took it upon himself to escort her into the house. There she was immediately taken under the wing of Mrs Grant, ushered up to her bedchamber with promises of tea and a sympathetic ear. A housemaid was sent for hot water and bandages. A bottle of spirits. And Mrs Grant assured the lady that Furness could set a broken limb as well as any doctor, as she would soon see for herself. In a little while, the pain would be eased and then all Mistress Drew would have to do would be rest and allow the bone to knit. There was no need for her to concern herself over Miss Thea's well-being. They would take good care of her. Just the shock of the events. The young lady would soon feel more the thing and Mistress Drew could visit her as soon as she wished. What was the world coming to, that law-abiding citizens were not free to travel the king's highway without fear for their property and their lives from men who should know better…The Maidens, indeed! The sound of Mrs Grant's soothing voice disappeared into the echoes of the upper landing.

Meanwhile Lord Nicholas carried Thea into the entrance hall where he gently stood her on her feet and allowed his arms to fall from around her. She still appeared strangely disoriented and clung to his arm with rigid fingers. Her face was unduly pale with a slight sheen of sweat on her brow and upper lip. The pulse at the base of her throat fluttered light and fast. When she raised her head to take in her surroundings, her eyes still lacked focus and she appeared not to recognise where she was.

'I…I'm sorry. I don't…' She gazed at him as if unsure of his identity. 'I don't quite remember…'

Nicholas frowned. Shock at the attack, yes. But this was more than could be expected. What had happened to cause her such distress? He made a rapid decision. 'Elspeth.' He summoned one of the hovering maids. 'Fetch tea and a bottle of brandy. Hot water and towels. Bring them up to Miss Thea's room. She needs to rest.'

'No…' Thea's reply was strained, hesitant, quite unlike her usual firm voice and manner. 'I shall be quite well if I can just sit… Poor Agnes needs more care than I… I must see her…'

'You will rest.'

'But I…'

Ignoring her reluctance, and with a suppressed oath at his inability to deal effectively with this situation, Nicholas simply swept her up into his arms again, up the staircase and into the room that she had previously occupied. There he lowered her feet to the floor, noting that any resistance had disappeared. She frowned a little as if unsure what she should do next, so, with a typical masterful demonstration, he made the decision for her and began to unbutton the velvet jacket of her riding habit and ease it down her arms. She allowed him to do so, standing before him as lifeless as a doll. Eyeing the lace ruff at the high neckline, he contemplated dealing with the tiny pearl buttons. No. He would not. But he unpinned the diamond-and-sapphire brooch at her neck and laid it on the dressing table. Then, with gentle sensitivity, he took her by the hand and led her to the bed where he pushed her to sit. When she obeyed, he knelt before her to pull off her soft riding boots, all the while keeping up a steady stream of comment in a calm voice, notwithstanding her wordless acceptance of all his actions, however intimate they might be. The little grey would soon recover—it was a sprain only and she would be sound enough. Furness was a worker of miracles. Mistress Drew would no doubt find cause to complain, but Furness would have her put to rights. A man of great skill, with horses and humans. They could stay comfortably at Aymestry under Mrs Grant's care. He would dispatch a message to her cousin in Tenbury that very hour, that she would not worry, and perhaps send clothes and other necessities back for the ladies. The dangers were over. She was quite safe here.

Thea did not answer, but sat and watched him with utmost concentration.

As soon as Nicholas had removed her boots, he sat beside her and lifted her inert hands from her lap. He found them cold, shockingly so in the warmth of the room and despite the perspiration on her face, as if all the blood had retreated from the surface of her skin. He enfolded them to warm them between his own.

At that she looked up at him. Bloodless lips parted, eyes wide and anxious.

'I have to thank you.' Her voice caught. 'I think…I think that you saved our lives.'

'Nothing so momentous.' He tried to reassure with a smile and a gentle pressure on her fingers. 'But it was a timely intervention. You were unlucky to be there at the moment that the Maidens fired the ricks.' Despite the lack of comprehension in her gaze, he continued to explain, hoping that the sound of his voice and the calm that enveloped them in the sunny room would help to restore her composure. 'I had your little party followed—to be certain of your safe-passage to Tenbury. When one of my grooms saw the dangers he rode back. So I was able to be there before more damage could be done.'

'Yes…' Her eyes continued to search his face as if for enlightenment. 'I am sorry to be such a trouble to you. To return here when you did not wish me to do so…'

And Theodora promptly startled both of them when she pulled her hands free of him, covered her face with her hands and disintegrated into tearful sobs.

Nicholas had no choice. He did the only thing any man could do faced with such distress. He drew her into his arms and let her cry against his chest, holding her close, his cheek resting gently against the crown of her head. Saying nothing, but just holding her and allowing her to sob out all the fear. She seemed so fragile, so vulnerable. All he wanted to do was protect her, hold her, keep her unknown fears, whatever they might be, at bay. There was nothing that he could find to say to her in this situation as, without doubt, she was not receptive to any words of comfort. So he simply kept silence, submerging an urgent need to pour out his own love and his desire to protect her for ever. That was not what she would wish to hear.

Gradually her sobs quietened. Only then did he ease her away. With a hand beneath her chin, he made her lift her face and used his handkerchief to wipe away her tears, when Elspeth arrived with another of the Aymestry maids and a loaded tray.

Nicholas stood, admitting to some relief. Oh, he would have stayed and held her in his arms for ever if she had need of him. But she needed a woman's ministrations more and would not thank him for lingering. It would be too humiliating for her when she came to her senses, realising that he had seen her when her distress had overcome her pride and reduced her to such desolation in his arms.

'Elspeth.' He stepped away from the bed, putting a distance between them. 'I will leave Miss Thea in your care for now. She needs to eat and drink. Then let her sleep. But leave one of the maids with her.' He did not want her to awake alone and be afraid.

'Of course, my lord. The young lady will do very well.'

'Let me know if there is any problem—if the lady needs anything.'

'Of course, my lord.' Elspeth almost swept him from the room. Clearly in her eyes, this situation held no role for a man.

With a final glance towards Theodora, who had raised her hands again to hide the ravages of her tears from him, Lord Nicholas took his leave.

He took himself to his own rooms where he proceeded to strip off his soiled and damaged coat and shirt, to flinch as the movement put pressure on his arm and shoulder. There were already signs of livid bruising, as he could see, although the skin was not broken. As he shrugged carefully into his clean linen, he let his thoughts roam over the past few hours. A serious affair, perhaps more serious than he had first believed. It had been diffused of course, thanks to Lewis Bates, and he was not the target of the violent hatred, but it was not a situation he could ignore when he and his guests came under attack. There were troublemakers amongst that little gathering who might not be willing to listen to the dictates of reason and the law again in the future. Samuel Dyer was a name to remember, perhaps. And the deliberate disguise of women's clothing showed a depth of organisation that he would not previously have considered. Perhaps he should talk with Lord Westbourne to find out the background. But Westbourne was known as a harsh landlord, with little sympathy for those who might stand in the way of what he saw as progress. Nicholas grimaced as he worked his arm back into a coat. Whatever the cause of today's disturbance, he did not want such discontent to spread to the Faringdon estates.

But such matters, serious as they might be, did not retain his attention beyond the changing of his clothes.

For there was Theodora. The complications and contradictions of that beautiful girl swamped his thoughts. There was so much that he did not understand.

As he headed towards the stables to check on the progress of The Zephyr, he remembered Thea's first reaction to him when he had intercepted her horse in Hyde Park. Not as extreme as this, of course, but the same uncontrollable panic that robbed her of thought, the same inordinate amount of fear. When he had asked her before, she had refused to explain further than that one obscure statement. Shrugged it off as of no account. Obviously it was not.

Well, if Thea would not tell him, he must use other means to discover the truth. He would have an honest and direct conversation with Mistress Drew. Because he was forced to acknowledge the fear in his own heart at the thought that she might have been injured, a fear that had been sharp and lethal when he saw her at the mercy of that rabble of a drunken mob. His blood still ran cold as the scene replayed itself in his mind, when he had been helpless and outnumbered against their hostility. He could no longer deny the strength of his feelings for Theodora. It would be foolish to even try.

Thea woke from a restless sleep where dreams had chased her relentlessly. Of faceless riders who shouted orders at her. Forced her to rein in her horse and dismount. To stand under the beating desert sun. Riders wrapped in the loose robes of the desert meshed into men who wore skirts and shawls, men with hard, merciless hands and cruel smiles. It was a relief to escape into reality, into the still quietness of the familiar room. She lay for a little while, allowing her fears to subside, her breathing to quieten, enjoying the rays of sunshine through the window. She could not remember where she was at first, but it did not seem to matter. The bed was soft, the air warm and comfortable, the atmosphere still. She lay and drifted, making no attempt to draw her thoughts back to the present. Until she heard a little movement. Turning her head, she saw a maidservant sitting beside her, with sewing in her lap. The young girl smiled as she waited for Thea to speak.

'Hello.'

'There, mistress. You look so much better.'

'I don't remember very much.' Did not wish to remember!

'You fell in with some of the rioters from Lord Westbourne's estate. The Maidens, Mr Furness said.' The word had spread around the household with the rapidity of a heath fire. 'Lord Nicholas came to rescue you. You were a bit shocked, that's all. You fell from your horse. But now you are safe.'

'Oh.' She thought for a moment. 'Am I at Aymestry Manor?'

'Yes, miss. Don't you recognise the room?' The girl smiled with gentle encouragement.

Of course. She remembered everything, allowing the vivid pictures to slide back into her mind. And how frightened she had been, how useless when Agnes had been struck, incapable of doing anything of any value to help herself or her escort. The humiliation and shame ran deep. What on earth would Nicholas think of her? And had she really wept in his arms? She feared that it was so.

'I must get up.'

'No need.' The maid's voice soothed with its Marches' burr. 'You did not sleep for very long, miss. His lordship says you need rest. There is nothing to get up for. Lord Nicholas will take care of everything, you'll see.'

'I suppose he will.'

Which she accepted, and allowed herself to sink once more into sleep. Deep and dreamless and healing. For some strange reason that she could not comprehend with her tired mind, she felt totally reassured that Lord Nicholas would indeed take care of everything.

'Mistress Drew. Are you sufficiently restored to talk to me?'

Agnes Drew sat in Mistress Grant's little parlour, that lady having taken herself off to overlook preparations for the evening meal, giving his lordship the opportunity for a private conversation as he had requested. Agnes's wrist was bandaged and immobilised against her flat chest. The wound in her hairline had been bathed, but she had refused a bandage. The headache was unimportant, she would simply ignore it. A restorative glass of claret stood at her elbow, a book lay open on her lap. Perhaps there were lines of strain around eyes and mouth, and a faint frown between her brows, but, considering her ordeal, she was remarkably composed.

'Of course, my lord.' She would have struggled to her feet, but Lord Nicholas restrained her with a gentle hand to her undamaged wrist. 'It will take more than that rabble to see me off. I have to thank you. And for Miss Thea. If any harm had come to her…' For the first time there was fear in Agnes Drew's eyes.

'It is no matter, Mistress Drew.'

'It is. I know the dangers we were in today. I have been to see my mistress. She is resting well.'

'It is about Thea—your mistress—that I wish to speak.'

Agnes's brows rose a little in some surprise at his direct approach, his use of Thea's name, but she waited for him to speak.

He did, without preamble. 'Will you tell me what happened to her, Mistress Drew? Some time in the past. Something that causes her to react with such withdrawal, such extreme shock, when faced with certain situations.'

'I don't—'

'I have seen it twice. I know that I have not imagined it. Please do not denigrate my intelligence by denying the existence of any problem. Thea herself once hinted at it.'

Mistress Drew flushed at the gentle criticism. 'I think that Miss Thea would not wish me to say. It is not my story to tell. My loyalty is to her, my lord, not you.'

'But it causes her considerable distress. I would know what it is.'

Agnes pursed her lips, sharp eyes considering his lordship. Here was a man of strong will, as wilful as Theodora. And there was undoubtedly that *connection* between them. But should she tell?

'I will not tell her what you tell me, if you do not wish it.' Nicholas's lips twitched into a dry smile as he acknowledged Mistress Drew's silent and frank assessment of him. 'But I find that her well-being has become a concern for me.'

Such honesty! Perhaps he deserved to know. And there was no doubt that they owed him much.

'Very well. I will tell you what I know.' Agnes waited as his lordship pulled up a chair. 'I was not there when it happened. But I can tell you of the effects that I have seen for myself. As have you, my lord.' She took a sip of the claret as she marshalled her thoughts, then proceeded to tell him of Theodora's terrifying experience in the desert near Palmyra as a child. 'It was a frightening experience for a young girl and has left a lasting fear, a weakness if you will.' Agnes hesitated. 'Miss Thea is as brave as a lion, but not when surrounded by noisy yelling crowds who might be interpreted as a threat. In Constantinople she was caught up in a large family group who were celebrating a wedding. Her reaction was just the same, even when there was no threat at all to her, only noise and high spirits. She has no control over it, poor girl, but then recovers as if nothing was amiss. That is all I can say—but it explains her withdrawal from reality today.'

'Yes. It does.' It explained much. 'Thank you, Mistress Drew. I value your confidence.'

'I would rather you did not say that I told you.' Mistress Drew's face was stern even as she asked for Nicholas's silence. 'It embarrasses her—because she can not control it. She sees it as a *fault,* you understand—and would not have it known.'

'No.' He smiled at the lady, deliberately taking possession of her good hand and raising it to his lips. 'I will not tell her. Your secret is safe in my keeping.'

Agnes found herself blushing—as if she were a young girl, indeed!—at the unexpected and completely charming gesture, but her voice was firm, her gaze direct when she made her answer with deliberate honesty for her reading of the situation between her mistress and Lord Nicholas Faringdon. 'Take care of her, my lord.' Their eyes held, united in understanding and concern for Theodora. 'She is worthy of your love.'

'Of course.' He rose to his feet and bowed. 'It is my intention.'

He made his way down to the library, deep in thought. He had not thought himself to be so transparent, but perhaps where

Theodora was concerned, his emotions were clear to all. And now he knew. That was one of her secrets laid bare. Would she be willing to tell him herself? But there was, of course, a far deeper mystery. Would she ever be willing to tell him why she had worked so hard to end any relationship between them? Her explanation that it was too complicated to explain her aberrant behaviour was no answer at all.

And that, he knew with some disquiet, was no sound basis for any lasting relationship, no matter the undoubted attraction between them.

Yet after all that, did it matter? The connection between them, some basic inexplicable attraction, had not been severed in spite of all Theodora's amazing efforts to give him a disgust of her. His mind might say that it did, but his heart would deny it.

Thea awoke from a deep healing sleep and stretched luxuriously, at one with herself and the world. No dreams had troubled her, no memory of the horror of the Maidens' attack now assailed her. She pushed herself up on to her elbows, her spirits fully restored. It was late evening, as she could see by the quality of the light—she must have slept for hours. Shadows lurked in the corners of the room and encroached on to the edge of the bed, yet she felt alert and restored.

The little maid who still sat beside her smiled.

'Are you well, mistress?'

'Yes.' Thea returned the smile. 'I feel alive again.'

She got up, dismissed the maid with grateful thanks, and lifted the cover on a little tray that had been left for her, since it seemed that her appetite had been restored also. She drank a glass of wine, ate a little bread and cheese and fruit. Having no clothes other than the riding habit in which she had arrived the previous day, she donned her riding skirt—brushed clean of the dust of her adventures—and the long-sleeved blouse, pinning her sapphire and diamond brooch at the high neck.

She must see Agnes, of course.

One of the maids escorted her to Mistress Drew's room. Since she found that lady tucked comfortably into bed and sleeping, with no sign of fever or discomfort, her bound wrist resting easily on the coverlet, Thea withdrew. And then her courage wavered. She stood outside Agnes's room and thought as the somewhat hazy memories crowded in. She must now find Lord Nicholas. She must thank him for his timely rescue, apologise for her appalling weakness when she had lost all control over her senses and actions. Overcome the embarrassment which even now brought colour to her cheeks as she recalled how she had wept in his arms and, with so little will of her own, had allowed him to carry her to her room. Not that she remembered much of that. What must he think of her? She must explain somehow. It was not a task she relished.

So first she would see how her mare had fared.

It was an easy matter for her to find her way to the stables. They were now deserted of the grooms and Master Furness, dim and warm at the end of a sun-filled day. Silent except for the shifting of hooves on straw, the occasional snort and wicker of a restless horse. Stray beams of sun, the final gleams, still lanced through the windows, layers of brightness in the gloom, the dust motes dancing. But the shadows were deep and calming, the scents of straw and leather and horses familiar and welcoming. What a restful place it was at the end of a day.

Thea looked in on a mare and foal, who looked back at her with large unblinking eyes. A chestnut mare stretched her nose over the stall door for her visitor to scratch. And then there was The Zephyr. The mare turned her gleaming body, the faint dapples in her neck glowing in the light, and limped towards her as Thea softly called her name. And leaned against her hand, allowing Thea to scratch along the soft line of her jaw.

'Poor Zephyr! You are safe now. How frightened you must have been. I was afraid too.'

But now there appeared to be no residue of that fear. The Zephyr returned to pulling strands from a hay net, tossing her head. If she were well enough to eat, there could be little wrong. Somewhat like herself, Thea mused. She leaned her arms along the top of the door and watched, content simply to be still and quiet.

'Theodora.'

The soft voice from the open door made her fingers tighten their grip on the wooden ledge, her heart make a leap into her throat. She turned her head—and was stunned by the sight of him. And immediately wished that she had been given longer to decide what she could possibly say to him, how she could possibly respond in his presence.

Lord Nicholas stood in the shadows, just inside the door, making no movement towards her, his coat removed and slung negligently over his shoulder so that the white of his shirt glimmered. She could see neither his face, nor gauge the expression in his single word of greeting, so she made no reply. Simply waited.

'Theodora. You look better—rested. Have you eaten?' He walked towards her, his boots making little sound on the straw-strewn surface, to stop a few feet away from her. A breathing space. Now she could see him and allowed her eyes to search his face. His eyes were dark, deep blue and still as shaded pools. His mouth firm-lipped, unsmiling, as if he, too, awaited some desired outcome. She had no idea what he might be thinking. Why was the man so difficult to read? But how beautiful he was, the dark hair and well-formed features. That lithe, agile figure, which moved with such elegant assurance. Any woman would want him. She wanted him.

And when he saw her illuminated in that soft beam of dusty sunshine, all his doubts vanished, dry chaff in a breath of air. She was beautiful. She was safe and alive and free of danger. She was any man's dream of perfection. But she could be his. It was all as simple as that. He would willingly sink for ever into the depths of those magnificent dark-lashed eyes, gleaming sapphire flecked with gold. Those slender-fingered hands, so capable, which had last clung to him in an agony of fearful anguish, held his heart. The thought might terrify him. He could not wish it any other way.

'Thea—'

'I need to apologise, my lord,' she interrupted, suddenly nervous. 'I reacted without sense or courage. I have no excuses. Sir Hector and Lady Drusilla would have been ashamed of me indeed. I did not intend to embarrass you…'

Lord Nicholas waited no longer. In one stride he covered the space between them, lifting his hand to touch her lips with a brush of fingers, to stop the flow of words.

'Hush, Thea. There is no need.' He smoothed the fullness of her lower lip with the pad of his thumb, a most sensuous caress that took her breath. And his. Would she tell him the cause of her unreasonable fears? Perhaps she would eventually, but this was the time for him to take her in his arms and show her what it could be like when a man desired a woman as much as he desired her. So he silenced her and, with the supreme confidence of a man lost in love, bared his own soul to her.

'Do you still not know? Are you still so unaware? I love you. I would do anything to protect you, to stand against the world for you. I love you Thea.' He hesitated, as if he feared to reveal all, but his eyes never left hers, blinding in their honesty. 'I have known it since the moment I first saw you, first heard your voice, but refused to acknowledge it. It is not in my nature to accept a sensation so overwhelming, or so extreme. It seemed to me that you took away my choices. But there it is.' Now he lifted a hand to tease the wisps of curl on her cheek. 'I think that you are meant to be here in my arms. You are the love of my life.'

'Nicholas…'

'Does it distress you?' His laugh was low and seductive to a lady who could have dreamed of no more splendid gift than this. 'You are free to reject me, of course.'

'No. Oh, no. I am so… I cannot find the words to say it.' Thea echoed his laugh. 'The events of the day appear to have robbed me of coherent thought.'

'I wish you would say them.' His answering smile was rueful as he took possession of her wrists, to lift them and press his mouth to the soft inner skin where her pulse beat with a fever-

ish intensity that had nothing to do with her health. 'Unless it is
your intent to kill me by cruel suspense.'

'Ah, Nicholas. Don't *you* know it? I love you.' She found her
voice at last. It was easy to say the words that had been in her
mind and heart for so many weeks. 'I thought that I had destroyed
any chance of that love, and mourned it bitterly. I do not ever
want us to be apart.'

'Then there is no need. Smile at me.'

She did. Her face was radiant. When he took her hands to lift
them to his lips, she tightened her fingers around his as if she
would never let him go.

'I am not an Earl,' he murmured against her palm.

'I do not want an Earl.'

'I am not as wealthy as the Earl of Moreton.' He kissed the
soft swell of flesh at the base of her thumb.

'I am not interested in the Earl of Moreton's wealth.' Thea
held her breath.

'Theodora…' With utmost delicacy, he applied his lips to her
other palm. 'Will you marry me?'

'Yes.' There was no uncertainty here.

'I should ask Sir Hector for his permission to address you. But
I think it more important that I discover your views on the matter.' His teeth nibbled along the ends of her fingers.

'Of course.' He could hear her smile in her voice. 'As any sensible man must. Yes and yes.'

Now he looked up, released her hands. 'Then my lips will seal
the bond between us. For all time.'

'As will mine.'

And her fears? Theodora jettisoned them all. Her love for him
was too great to consider any limitations against it. She would
risk everything for the love and desire that she could read in that
moment in his face. Her fears might never happen. She would
marry her lord, her love, and consign those groundless terrors to
some deep dark spot, never to be reborn.

So when Nicholas drew her forward, close into the circle of
his arms, Thea accepted without regret. Drawing her firmly

against him, he lowered his mouth to hers. She responded with all the delight that he could have hoped for, allowing her hands to smooth over the soft, warm linen of his shirt, savouring the play of firm muscle beneath, from wrist to shoulder. Until he flinched on a gasp and pulled away.

'What is it? What did I do?' She searched his face with anxious eyes.

'A bruise. Courtesy of our lady rioters.' He shrugged against the pull of muscle and sinew where the heavy blow from a cudgel had fallen.

'Oh, Nicholas. That you should have been hurt for my sake, when I could do nothing to help myself or you…'

'It is nothing. I would do anything for you, Thea. Anything to keep you from harm or distress.'

'Then kiss me again,' she invited, 'if it will help you to forget the pain.'

So he did. The tenderness of before was now overlaid by a hint of possession. A hunger. His kiss more demanding, his arms strongly banded around her to hold her in submission against the hard strength of his chest and thighs. Until the breathing of both was heightened. And he stepped away.

'You are too desirable.'

But Thea stepped forward, surprising him, reluctant to forgo the amazing needs that flooded through her body at the evidence of Nicholas's fierce desire for her. 'And you would reject that?'

'I must.'

'You did once before, as I recall.' Thea angled her head to watch him, allowing her hands to linger on the flat planes of his chest, her eyes alight. His concern for her touched her more than she would ever tell him.

'I know.' A sudden grin lifted the tension. 'It was one of the most uncomfortable nights of my life.'

'Then why repeat it?'

She took another step until her body almost brushed his and her hands could clasp together around her neck, more than a little startled at her own forwardness.

As was Nicholas. He choked on a laugh. 'Are you *fast*, madam? What would Mistress Drew say?' His heart beat with insistent rhythm. His command of his body and his senses appeared to be slipping from his grasp, second by second.

'It seems that I am where you are concerned, my lord.' A low husky chuckle was almost his undoing. 'And Agnes would not approve.'

'Thea—' He tried for sanity, taking a light hold of her shoulders to keep her at bay. 'I would not hurt you—or give cause for condemnation in the eyes of the world, no matter the provocation.' Without thought, he turned his face against her hair. 'Do you realise how impossible it is for me to resist you? You are delicious and desirable beyond imagination.'

'Why should you resist?' In her voice the temptation of Eve, in her hands, in the softness of her skin. Her lips were so close, the warmth of her breath so sweet, 'Are you going to break your promise—of only one minute ago—to marry me? And you a man of honour, my lord!'

He was lost. Completely. Utterly. Acknowledged it with a sigh against her temple. 'No. I want you. I will not renege.'

'Then kiss me again. Unless you do not wish to, of course.' Her lips formed a delicious—and tantalising—*moue* of disappointment.

'Do you know what you ask?' He held her lightly, torn between amusement and frustration. Virgin and temptress, innocent and wanton. How could he be expected to resist her? How could any man?

He could not, of course. 'My inclination is not in question. It is my self-control that has suddenly become compromised. But you, my love, must be quite certain.'

'Oh, yes. I told my mother that if I never married I would take a lover. It seems to me that if I can do both at the same time, I would have every advantage.'

He laughed, despite himself. 'I cannot imagine such a conversation.'

'I think that Lady Drusilla did not approve.'

'But I like the sentiment. And I like you.'

'I am relieved. How humiliating it would be for me if you decided that we would not suit. After showing such lack of delicacy.' She waited, for the long beat of her heart.

His reply was quite serious, stern even. 'There will be no humiliation. It will please me to worship you with my body. There can be no shame. Nothing but the new, bright splendour of our love.' Nicholas dropped his hands to her waist and lifted her, swung her in a circle to replace her on her feet. 'What a delight you are to me.' His kiss was swift and thorough, a promise of the pleasures that he could bring to her. Then he lifted her into his arms, as if her weight was nothing, carried her to an open stall, freshly swept with a bed of sweet straw and lowered her there to her feet in the middle. Covered the straw with his ill-used coat.

'Do you realise that this is the second time today that I have begun to undress you?' he asked conversationally, even though his fingers were not quite steady at the task. 'Last time I took the coward's way and retreated in disorder.'

'Why would you do that?' There was no mistaking the firtatiousness in her voice, but she awaited his reply with some anxiety.

'It was not seemly.' He applied himself to the intricate catch of the brooch at her throat. 'Why did you have to wear something so difficult!' But the catch sprang free beneath skilful fingers. 'You were distressed—not aware of me or your surroundings. When I undress you, I want you to be aware of my every movement, every touch. Every lingering caress.' He leaned to press his mouth to the exact place where the pulse beat above the high neck of her blouse.

His reply, his action, heated her blood. 'I am aware now.'

'Also, I did not think Mistress Drew would enjoy the sight of you unclothed in my arms.' His fingers sought the buttons at her lace cuffs.

'Mistress Drew is not here now.'

'No. She is not.' A wealth of meaning spoke in this low reply, in the fierce light in his eyes as they now found and held hers. Theodora knew that she was entirely at his mercy—and rejoiced in it.

'Don't stop this time, my lord.'

'No. Not unless you would wish it.' Her cuffs were loosened, allowing him to concentrate on the row of tiny buttons from nape to waist.

'I definitely would not wish it.' Tremors of anticipation raced across her skin. But also nerves. A little fear. A heady need for the experience drove her on, but her dependence on this man was not to be taken lightly.

Reading her fears, Nicholas abandoned his task to let his hands fall by his sides. He simply wanted her. He was hard and hot and ready, driven now by his body's desire to take and own her. The blood throbbed in his loins, yet he still had a care for her inexperience. He had felt the tremors that had shivered along her spine and would not willingly push her beyond what she was prepared to give.

'I think you have no idea of your effect on me.' His voice was low to soothe, the desire for her swiftly banked. 'But it is not too late. Tell me honestly, my dear love, that this is what you want. I would not distress you. You have my love, regardless of the outcome between us this night.'

At his words of understanding, a delicate warmth touched her, dispelling her doubts as mist lifts at the rising of the sun. She raised her hand to his cheek, to brush the fine cheekbone with soft finger tips. 'How considerate you are. I am yours, Nicholas. I would like very much to be held in your arms.'

Lord Nicholas bowed. A strangely formal gesture given the circumstances and the setting. But it calmed Thea's fears. 'I will take care of you.'

Once again, with something like a hiss of frustration, he applied himself to the tiny buttons.

'I should tell you, my lord—I have no experience of this, despite my somewhat unconventional upbringing.'

'I know it.' The linen and lace blouse fell in a delicate heap to the straw.

'Lady Drusilla has been informative, but I expect she omitted some salient facts.'

'I am sure that she did.' With a grunt of acknowledgement he bent his head to the fastenings of the skirt at her slim waist.

'I have some knowledge of the marriage customs of the Bedouin.'

'Interesting. But perhaps not helpful.' The skirt sank into velvet waves around her feet to leave the lady clad in a fine linen chemise. Nicholas sighed at the fragile beauty so revealed and bent his head to press little kisses along the satin of her exposed shoulder.

'In Constantinople—'

'Thea. Be quiet!' With a smile he took her by the hand to encourage her to step from the folds, then bent to kneel before her and remove her soft boots.

'I am nervous.' Her teeth sank into her lip at the admission. 'And most woefully ignorant.'

'I, fortunately, am neither of those things. Despite my lack of knowledge of the Bedouin.' Now he stood before her again, laughter in his face, but also an exquisite tenderness. 'Is there anything other that you think I should know?'

Laughter gurgled in Thea's throat. Then stopped as she drew in her breath, for there was no mistaking the blazing passion, the rampant need in his brilliant eyes.

'I am very willing to learn,' she managed to whisper.

'Thank God!'

Nicholas pulled her down to the straw. Sat beside her to remove his boots. The sun had finally sunk below Burford Edge, allowing the deeper shadows of encroaching night to envelop them and grant them some privacy. There was no moonlight to illuminate or embarrass an inexperienced lady with intrusive shimmer.

So Lord Nicholas began his seduction of the lady who had invaded his waking and dreaming hours. Soft kisses to encourage and soothe, discovering the most delicate, most enticing curves of her face. And then her lips, softer yet, which parted beneath his urgings, inviting his tongue to take such liberties as made the lady's breath catch and quicken. His breathing deepened as he determined to slow the tender development, one caress leading to another, each touch more intoxicating than the last. His tongue traced its path down the long sweep of her throat, tasting, savouring, until he reached the feverish beat of the pulse in that most sensitive of hollows. There he paused with open-mouthed kisses, before pushing the chemise from her shoulders so that he might know the satin slide of shoulders and breast.

Theodora allowed every intimacy, astonished at the sensitivity of her skin to his caresses, even the whisper of his warm breath, as delicious shivers rippled across her skin. Daringly she pushed her hands beneath the heavy linen of his shirt to trace the play of muscle and sinew, flesh on flesh. How smooth and well defined, how fine and utterly masculine.

Thea held her breath.

'My love. My dear one.' The merest whisper against the curve. 'It is permitted for you to breathe.' He felt her laugh softly—or perhaps it was a sob—as he pressed his lips to the shallow valley where her heart beat in hectic rhythm with his own.

Gradually, imperceptibly, he sensed her softening against him as she came to know and accept his touch. Only then did he allow his hands to move where they would, to follow the path of his tongue and mouth, and then on, a gentle moulding to smooth and slide. Swell of breast, dip of waist, curve of hip and thigh.

And under that tender assault, Thea held on. Until, as her nails dug deep into his shoulders, she felt him flinch on a sharp intake of breath.

'Did I hurt you?' A soft concern.

'No. Or no more than the Maidens.' Nicholas continued to press a line of feathery kisses along one fine-boned shoulder. 'You are allowed to draw blood in such circumstances as this. But only a very little.'

'I think I am afraid.'

'The courageous Theodora admitting to fear?' He raised his head to see her watching him, eyes a little wide.

'Yes. Have mercy.'

'Perhaps. Perhaps not.' Now he drew his hand over her breast, brushing her nipple with the pad of his thumb, gently, sensuously, until it hardened and she drew in her breath on a little cry. But rather than resist she wound her arms around his neck, an invitation, which he answered by reaching to smooth one hand slowly up the glorious length from knee to thigh to waist, bringing the fullness of her chemise with it. He did not wish to remove the garment, in recognition of her inexperience, but his hands could now discover the secret delights of her. With gentle pressure he parted her thighs, stroking her with knowing fingers until she gasped. Soft, so soft. So responsive as he felt her push, a mere flex of hips, in unspoken answer against the heel of his hand. But still tense. As he captured her lips once more with his own, Nicholas knew that there was no advantage to be gained for her in prolonging the deed. It was all too new and ridden with uncertainties, no matter how skilful and patient he might be. She would suffer—but very little, if he set himself to distract, to lure her into trusting him with her well-being.

'Look at me, Thea.' He took his weight on his forearms, demanding all her attention. 'You do not need to fear.'

'But I do. You may not like me.' Admitting her most secret fear.

'I may not, of course,' he agreed, dropping the lightest of kisses on the tip of her nose.

'What will you do then?'

'If I decide that we will not suit, I will simply send you back to Cousin Jennifer.'

'Oh.' The thought made her smile. He caught the quick flash of white in the shadow. 'Do you think there is any possibility of that?'

Now he kissed her with a passion, allowing his tongue to seek the silk and heat of her mouth, retreating, then claiming her once more, delighted when her tongue touched his in ready response.

'Do you think there is such a possibility?' A little breathless now, desire riding him hard, a hunting cat with sharp claws.

'Perhaps not.'

Moving a little, he allowed his erection to press urgently against her thigh.

'Do you think I do not want you?'

'No.' He felt her arms tighten around him at this clear evidence of his need for her.

'Nor do I. I want you, Thea. Feel how much I want you.'

So he pushed against her and into her, aware of her eyes fixed on him, wide and trusting. Slowly and carefully, when all his instincts were to take and possess, until he reached a natural resistance. And held back. All her muscles were tense around him. He felt her body flinch from his at the intrusion.

'Nicholas…! I can't…'

'Hush,' he murmured. 'Think about…' What? In the circumstances he had no ideas.

Neither had Theodora. 'I cannot think about anything but you.'

'Very well. Hold on to me. Remember that I am as much in your power as you are in mine.'

For he could hold back no longer. One firm thrust and she was his. As without doubt he was hers, buried deep.

She cried out in sudden shock and would have struggled against the weight and power of his body. He felt her muscles tense around him.

'Wait. Lie still a moment.' She was immediately obedient, anxiety plain in every fine line of her body. So he kissed her. Lightly, teasingly on face and shoulders, to remind her of the more gentle pleasures of love, holding himself perfectly still. And then began to rock gently until she was accustomed to the movement. Until he felt her sigh, relax and enfold him in the softest heat.

'Better?' he murmured against her temple, still controlling every muscle in his body. Resisting the almost overwhelming urge to drive on and on.

'Oh, yes!' A sigh.

'Then, lady, let us finish it together. Move with me.' He encouraged her to arch against him, to move and slide and flex, answering every thrust of his loins until he could resist no longer. Innocent as she was, unaware of the effect she had on him, she drove him to insanity just by being here in his arms. One final thrust brought him to ultimate completion.

Afterwards they lay still until their breathing settled, Thea's arms still entwined around Nicholas's shoulders, held tight, as if in disbelief at what had just passed between them. Until

Nicholas rolled from her, but not away, so that he might look down into her expressive eyes and read the truth of what she might feel. Except that the shadows would effectively hide all trace of emotion if she chose to dissemble.

He must know! It was suddenly too important to leave unsaid between them.

'Well, my Queen of the Desert?'

'I don't know what to say.' Unusually shy, Thea hid her face against his throat. The experience had taken over all her senses, leaving her drained with a strange lassitude, yet longing to know more at the hands of this most skilful lover.

'Well—let me see. What about: I hate you? It was the worst experience of my life?'

'No!'

'I will go back to Cousin Jennifer immediately?'

'Only if you insist!'

'Perhaps then that, to your expert knowledge, the Bedouin are far more sophisticated?' She caught the gleam of a quick grin.

'No. I cannot claim that.'

Suddenly all amusement left his voice, his eyes. To be replaced by a stern intensity. 'It will be better, Thea. I promise you that it will.'

'I said that I can learn.' Was there still a hint of uncertainty there?

'You need learn nothing.' Nicholas kissed her again. 'Only how to enjoy my body as much as I enjoy yours. You are beautiful and desirable, Theodora.'

The exquisite tenderness of his mouth, his enfolding arms as he pulled her close again, brought a rose-tinted blush from the neck of her disordered chemise to the roots of her hair.

'Was it very bad?' It mattered.

'No.' Thea sighed, her breath warm against his throat. 'It was wonderful.'

'Straw does not make for the most comfortable of bedding. Next time we will do better—with a mattress and pillows.'

Nicholas helped her to her feet, helped her to dress again with careful attention, applying himself to the tiny buttons and laces, pulling on her boots, then putting his own clothing to rights. The little brooch he slid into his coat pocket for safe-keeping, then simply stood and looked at her as if she were a miracle.

'What is it?'

'I remember, when they were still living at Burford—and in London—seeing Hal look at Eleanor. As if for him there was no other woman in the world. I think I envied him such a depth of passion and commitment, but I did not understand it. Now I do. You are my world, Theodora. You are my universe.'

'As you are mine.'

'I took your innocence.'

'Do you regret it?'

'No. How could I when you are here in my arms, as beautiful as you are. But you might. Tomorrow, in the full light of day. You might regret having given yourself to me.' He feathered his fingers through her hair, removing a stray wisp of hay. 'So willingly. So generously.' In his eyes, if she could have seen them in the heavy dusk, there was a plea that she should not hold any regrets.

Nor did she. She spoke from her heart so that he might not doubt her. 'No. I am yours to take. I think that it was always so. I have been waiting for you my whole life. Now that I am yours, I feel complete.'

His heart turned over in his chest. Such a strong woman admitting to such a dependence, such a depth of emotion that would effectively place one's future happiness into the hands of another. It would take courage indeed.

'We will go in,' he said, holding out his hand. 'Tomorrow will be a new day. A new life. When I can love you in the eyes of the whole world.'

'Can I say something?' She pulled back, resisting as he took her hand to lead her from the stable. When she lifted his hand to cup her cheek, he found it wet with tears.

'Thea. What is it? Did I indeed hurt you?' He caught the tears with gentle fingers, suddenly appalled that he might have pushed her further than she wished to go. 'Is it that you can not love me so soon? Forgive me, forgive me…'

'No. It is not that.'

'Then what is it, my heart? Nothing is worth your tears. If you can not find it in your heart to love me, then you must say it.' He fought to quell the sudden rush of panic at such an eventuality.

But there was no need. 'I think you do not understand me.' He heard a hesitation of breath, but Thea's voice was clear and confident. 'This is what I wished to say. I love you, Nicholas Faringdon. I love you.'

He found that he had been holding his breath. Now he could breathe and live again. 'What more could any man wish to hear from the woman who holds his heart in her hands?'

With an arm around her waist, so that she might lean on him, her head resting on his shoulder, he led her to the house.

Chapter Nine

New York

The house still smelt of new wood and paint, but at least it was complete with walls and roof intact. Or nearly so. Eleanor could still hear sounds of hammering somewhere in the distance, but not so insistently or loudly enough to annoy. Probably the stables, she thought. The room was warm with early summer heat, despite lowered blinds and a light breeze through the opened windows. It was a boudoir, although still lacking more than basic furniture, and Eleanor was at ease. Or she would have been, she thought, if ease was possible for a lady in her condition. She shuffled on the satin day bed, trying to find a more comfortable position. She had been instructed, on pain of death, to rest her swollen ankles and, for a lady who had remained distressingly active throughout her pregnancy until the eighth month, was finding the enforced leisure difficult.

But it was merely a matter of waiting, she consoled herself. And not long now. A smile touched her lips. Pregnancy had done nothing to rob Eleanor Faringdon, once Marchioness of Burford, of her beauty. Her rich auburn hair, only loosely restrained and allowed to fall in waves onto her shoulders, shone with health, her skin glowed. And those deep amethyst eyes, eyes that had captivated Lord Henry Faringdon when she had been a young débutante making her first curtsy to polite society, shone with love and anticipation. The years between that first meeting and the present, in this new home in New York, had been long and fraught with difficulties. But now Eleanor was united with the one who held her heart and would remain so until the day of her death. If she were certain of nothing in life, it was that one incontrovertible fact.

If only she were not so hot. And so…*large*!

The dark shadows of those distant weeks in London had finally melted away. In New York, free from gossip and sly comment, critical or knowing glances, wrapped around by Henry's love and constant care, Eleanor had grown into her full maturity, content and confident in their future together. Nothing would ever separate them again. And now she awaited the birth of her second child. Henry's second child.

It was all so different, she mused, from Tom's birth, when she had been racked by guilt and anger, the child's father far distant on the other side of the world, ignorant of her situation. Now Henry was no further away than the warehouse or the stables—and refused to be lured much further until this child had arrived safely. Her thoughts naturally moved on to Thomas, her first husband, lapping her in a well of tenderness. How generous and understanding he had been, how incredibly honourable to give his name to his brother's illegitimate child. He had loved her, supported her and kept her safe through all the difficulties. Eleanor sighed a little at the sad memories, but they no longer hurt her. Her son Tom was a constant delight. And she believed that in some way Thomas knew and approved of her present happiness.

So, clad in a loose-fitting silk-and-lace robe, Eleanor sat and waited for someone to come and entertain her. Sarah had said that she would call. She would bring patterns for furnishings. And news of any local events or interesting gossip. They would pass a pleasant hour or so.

But until then—a letter lay unopened in Eleanor's lap. Her mother's astringent comments were always guaranteed to entertain. Mrs Stamford was in London for a few weeks of the Season, before going to Bath to drink the waters. She had been complaining of the rheumatics in her shoulders and hoped for a miracle at the fashionable spa. Eleanor opened the letter with pleasure at the number of closely written sheets and read for a short while.

A clatter on the stairs heralded an interruption. Eleanor smiled and folded the sheets away There would be no further quiet reading of a letter yet.

'Mama!' A sturdy child, tall for his age of almost four years, bounded into the room, with a small black dog of indeterminate origin at his heels, to slide to a halt before the day bed, the dog flopping beside him and panting loudly in the heat.

'You must come and see, Mama. We have a new horse. Papa says he is for me. That I can feed and groom him—and ride him all by myself.'

Eleanor saw the Faringdon inheritance in her son and her heart turned over in her breast. Her own eyes sparkled out of the youthful face, to be sure. But the rest was pure Faringdon. Dark hair, dense and glossy as a crow's wing. Straight nose, firm chin, the curves of babyhood beginning to disappear to reveal aristocratic cheekbones. Splendidly arched brows. And a remarkable curled lip, uncannily reminiscent of his father, at the silent reference to the despised leading rein. He was very like his father. All energy and determination, at present overflowing and uncontrolled in youth, but she had seen the adult version in her husband, combined with a certain self-assurance, arrogance even. Tom would ride the horse alone and would pester until allowed to do so. She could not help hoping that her imminent child would be a daughter with a little more of her own softer characteristics in evidence.

'I will come,' she assured her son. 'A little later in the day when it is cooler. You can show me everything then.' She stretched out her hand to touch his untidy hair, chuckling as he tossed his head with impatience. Another Faringdon trait.

'He has a black mane and tail and has no name. Papa says I can choose.'

'And so you shall. What have you been doing?' His clothes were distinctly the worse for wear and his hair had a faint sheen of dust. 'At breakfast, as I recall, you were very clean and tidy.'

'Helping Nat in the warehouse.'

Mr Bridges, she considered, deserved a gold medallion for patience. Tom was at the stage where everything must be investigated and questioned.

'You should call him Mr Bridges. Have you been a nuisance?'

'He says to call him Nat. So I do. He does not mind if I help him. He says I talk a lot for someone my size. Are you sure you'll not come now to see the new horse, Mama?' Tom hopped from one foot to the other.

Before she could reply, more footsteps approached the room. Eleanor turned her face to the door, her eyes alight with joy.

Hal. Her adored Hal.

He stepped into the room. 'I see that you are being propositioned.' And smiled. Devastatingly. Causing the colour in Eleanor's cheeks to deepen at the realisation that he was here and that he was hers.

'Yes.'

'Mama says that she will come later,' Tom explained, hoping for a change of plan now that his father, who could achieve all things, was present.

'I will bring her down to the stables when the temperature drops.'

'Promise?'

'Of course.' He grinned in understanding of the boy's enthusiasms. 'Now, why don't you go and look at the pony again—and think of a name before your mama sees him. There is a new bridle for you to use, as well.'

Tom opened his mouth as if to say more, but when Henry shook his head, his face broke into a replica grin before he clapped his hands over his mouth and giggled through his fingers.

'I didn't say, Papa. It's a secret.'

'I know. So go before you do.'

At that, boy and dog left at speed.

Which left them together.

'What was all that about?' Eleanor stretched out her hand in invitation.

'Nothing for you to worry about.' He removed his riding coat, casting it carelessly over a chairback, and covered the ground between them in easy strides.

'You can keep a secret better than your son! He'll tell me, you know.' Her eyes told him all the secrets of her heart.

'I know it. It will not matter.' Henry bent to kiss her, gently, little more than a brush of lips, but with the low heat of passion that was always there. 'Nell. You look wonderful.'

She sniffed. 'You, my love, smell of wood and…spices?'

'I have been in the warehouse. Do you object?'

'No. Better than the stables! Come and sit with me.'

He sat beside her, easing her body so that she could lay back comfortably against his shoulder and side, his arms supporting her. 'I am pleased to see that you are following orders.'

'Have I any choice?' She tilted her chin to look up at him, her lips in a little pout of mock displeasure. 'You threatened to lock me in my bedchamber and to tie my ankle to the bed if I came down to see what you and Tom were doing once more.'

He laughed. 'It will not be long.' Was there perhaps a hint of anxiety in his reassurance? Eleanor thought there was and understood.

'No. Not long.' She lifted his hand and laid it on her belly where the child kicked.

'Lively?'

'Oh, yes!' She could feel his smile against her hair.

'You are more beautiful now than the day I met you.'

'I shall be even more so when I have something resembling a waist again.'

He turned his face into her hair, kissing the elegant curve of her ear and then all the way to her temple, featherlight caresses where the curls lay damply.

'I see that you have a letter from your dear mama.' There was a dry edge to his voice. The relationship between Henry and Mrs Stamford had always had an edge. 'Now, can I guess—gossip?

Who is wearing what? Who is speaking to whom? She wishes you were not so far away—and for preference not with me?' He lifted the weight of pages. 'How can anyone write so much about so little?'

'As ever, my love—you have it in a nutshell. Although she has forgiven you, I think. She wishes that she could see the new baby, of course. It is understandable that she regrets the distance. By the by, did any news come from Nicholas in the business packet?'

'No. Why? Were we expecting some?'

'Aha! Then I have news for you, Hal. Nicholas is in London. The social thing. Probably encouraged by Beatrice.'

'Summoned more like, knowing my aunt. Very noble of him. I doubt he'll stay the pace long. Almack's was never his scene.'

'Nor yours, I remember! But he might surprise you. Mama says that he is dancing attendance on a very handsome débutante.'

Hal raised his brows. 'Well, he has done that before. He is hardly immune to the fair sex.'

'But this time he seems to be very taken. She is very handsome. With a fortune. Her father is one of our foreign ambassadors, so she is well connected. Although a trifle unconventional, according to my mama. Perhaps even a touch fast.' Eleanor's eyes twinkled at the prospect of such a lady engaging Nicholas's affections.

'That does not sound like Nicholas.'

'Mama says that she *reads*. And dances the waltz even though it is her first Season. She rides a grey Arab in the Park with considerable dash and has been seen in a high-perch phaeton—driving *alone* without a groom or maid in attendance! She is quite sophisticated—has travelled somewhere in the deserts, although exactly where Mama is unsure. I do not think that she approves.'

'Well, that is hardly surprising!' Henry considered the news. 'Apart from the grey Arab, it sounds even less like Nicholas. But perhaps he will marry at last. I wish him well if he has found a lady who can win his heart.'

'Is that all you have to say?'

'Nicholas has kissed the pretty fingers of any number of débutantes to my knowledge. Why should this one be any different?'

'Well, as long as he does not marry Amelia Hawkes!'

'Who?'

'Sir William Hawkes's daughter. Surely you recall—your neighbour's daughter at Burford Hall. Although perhaps you don't... Anyway, the poor girl has been sighing over Nicholas and his horses for as long as I can remember! And, in my opinion, without the least hope of success. I hope that I am not to be proved wrong.'

'Perhaps you had better write and tell him so! But Nicholas will do just what he likes. As always.'

'Just like you.'

'Exactly. A Faringdon failing.' He linked his fingers with hers, a symbol of unity. 'I wanted you. And look what happened. Despite all the hurdles.'

'And it took no persuasion on my part?'

'A little,' he had the grace to admit, remembering her determined occupation of his cabin on the *Sea Emerald* before he sailed back to America, her refusal to leave. Her sheer determination to ride roughshod over any principles he might have over the affair.

'And look how grateful you are.' Eleanor's fingers tightened on his.

'You do not know the half of it.' Suddenly sober, he held her and their unborn child close, unbearably moved by the memory of how close they had come to losing each other and the possibility of a future together.

Where Sarah found them some half an hour later.

Life in New York suited Mrs Sarah Russell very well. Her restrained manner, her nervous pallor, which Eleanor and Henry remembered from those anxious days in London when she had been forced by her brother to pose against her will as nursemaid to her own child, had completely vanished. She was no longer permanently ridden by guilt and shame at the despicable actions of Sir Edward Baxendale, and also of herself by his manipulation of her. The unqualified love and acceptance from the Faringdons had done much to help her heal and regain some small degree of self-respect. Now twenty-five years old, widowed and mother to an overwhelming five-year-old, she was brisk, confident and capable, enjoying an independent life, far from the powerful influence of her brother. She never mentioned him. His sins, as far as she was concerned, were too great. Likewise her sister-in-law Octavia, so weak that she would obey Edward's commands to the letter. Whatever the ease of Sarah's relationship with Henry and Eleanor Faringdon, it was not appropriate to remind anyone in this household that her own name by birth had been Baxendale.

She had left her son John with Tom and Nathaniel Bridges in the warehouse and climbed the stairs to the newly furnished boudoir, knowing that she would find Eleanor there, and set herself to entertain in these final trying days. The door on to the wide corridor was open, to catch any passing current of air, so she simply entered. She did not stand on ceremony in this house.

But the domestic scene, so relaxed and yet so intimate, made her hesitate and blush a little at her intrusion, until she saw and answered Eleanor's smile of welcome and continued into the room.

'You look comfortable.'

'It is all relative,' Eleanor muttered darkly.

'And only until she shuffles and twitches again—in about ten seconds, I should imagine, on past experience.' Henry winced a little and laughed as a sharp elbow found his ribs.

'But I am so uncomfortable—the heat and the lack of air. When I carried Tom, it was England and in winter.' Eleanor slanted a look up into Henry's face. 'I do not know why I am apologising to you, Hal! Some would say that it is all your fault!'

'Then, my love, I must accept all the blame.'

'Well, you *look* exceptionally content.' Sarah took a seat and lowered the books of furnishings and patterns to the floor to hide the sharp stab of envy. The love between them was so tangible, so all-consuming, the glance between them exclusive, effectively shutting out all others. He might well have kissed her—as he was not averse to doing in public. As a sharp stab to her heart, it made

Sarah regret her own widowed state, long for strong arms to hold her against her fears when the nights were dark, someone as intense and passionate as Henry Faringdon. She took a deep breath. Better not, she told herself quickly. Better that she should rejoice in her freedom to make her own decisions, determine her own lifestyle. She had had enough of domineering men, however attractive they might be.

'Here is someone who will appreciate Mama's news.' Eleanor shuffled into a cooler spot, a mischievous smile for Sarah.

'What's that?' Sarah untied the ribbons of her bonnet, dropped it on the floor at her side with a sigh of relief.

'Nicholas and a débutante.'

'Ah. Some London gossip.' Her eyes shone. 'Do tell. Is it serious?'

'So Mama thinks.' Eleanor searched the pages in her hand for the name. 'A Miss Wooton-Devereux, indeed,' she finally announced. 'Rich *and* beautiful. What more could he want to bring him solace as he runs the Burford acres with such fiendish efficiency?'

There was no corresponding humour in Sarah's reply. 'Oh… Oh, no.' It was certainly not the response that Eleanor had expected. 'What…what was the name again?' Sarah had become quite still. Eleanor noticed that her hands had suddenly clenched into tight fists on the skirt of her gown.

'Miss Wooton-Devereux,' she repeated, a little frown between her brows. 'Do you know of her?'

Sarah passed her tongue over dry lips, conscious that the air seemed to press down on her with a great weight so that she felt a little dizzy. 'Do you…do you know the lady's first name?'

'Mama said that it was something out of the common way. Let me see… Ah, yes—Theodora. Why…what is it, Sarah? Are you unwell?'

Suddenly finding it difficult to breathe in the hot still air, the lady pressed her hands to her face. It seemed that the past, with all its burden of guilt and intrigue, had fallen once again at her feet, to harm and destroy. 'I don't believe it,' she managed to say.

'That a malicious fate should have brought her…' Her words ended on something suspiciously like a sob.

Eleanor tried to sit up, only to be restrained by Henry, who gently extricated himself from the sofa and went to pour a glass of brandy. He returned to the stricken lady and pressed it into her unresisting hand.

'Sarah.' She looked up into his face, her own blank with shock, her mind working furiously to remember all that she had been told of this particular débutante. 'Listen to me. Drink this.' He waited until she had complied, a few sips at least. 'Now tell me. What is it? Do you know the lady? Is there a problem?' He took the glass from her and crouched at her side, holding her hands comfortingly in his.

'Yes… No… That is…I never thought to hear that name in this house—in connection with one of your family.'

'Dear Sarah. Tell us,' Eleanor encouraged. The shimmer of distress around her friend was almost visible. 'It cannot surely be as bad as all that.'

Sarah looked from one to the other. They had been so kind to her, so supportive, when she had aided and abetted her brother in bringing them such pain. And now she must tell them… Of course, she must. 'Oh, yes,' she stated, her soft voice surprisingly harsh. 'There is a problem. And it may be as bad as we could ever imagine.' She looked at Henry with frightened eyes. 'Her name by birth is not Wooton-Devereux. It is Baxendale.'

Baxendale! There was a shattering silence in the room. It seemed to echo from every corner. Even the distant hammering was silent as they absorbed that one name.

'I don't understand.' Eleanor instantly swung her feet to the floor. Sarah's remarkable statement had effectively destroyed all her contentment.

'She is Sophia Mary Baxendale and she is my sister.' Sarah announced it in firmer accents. Whatever the outcome, she must face it. Her past had just come back to haunt her and, whatever she felt about the revelation, it had stunned her audience of two.

'Your sister? I did not know you even had a sister.'

'I have not thought of her for years.' Sarah's eyes were full of sympathy as she watched the emotions flit across Eleanor's face. 'How should I? But listen. I must tell you what I know.'

Henry, reading his wife's anxiety, went to sit beside her again and took her hands, soothing the soft skin on the inside of her wrists with his thumb. And Sarah, unearthing her family secrets, gleaned from her own reluctant mother and from Edward's memories when she was a child and thus fascinated by such things, explained all. A disorganised household, increasing debts, the difficult birth. Then the arrival of Drusilla, her mother's managing sister, followed by the removal of the baby to a new home, a new family.

'So she is Sophia Mary Baxendale,' Eleanor repeated.

'Yes. But I have never met her. Only know of her from family records.'

'But the crucial question now…' Henry said slowly, considering the implications of this potentially explosive news, 'is whether there is any recent connection, any communication, between your sister and Edward.'

'I don't know.' Sarah understood the implications all too well.

'What are you thinking, Hal?' Eleanor also knew well what he was thinking, believed her thoughts ran in the same direction, but she needed him to say it aloud.

'I am thinking—what do we have here? Another Baxendale plot? An attempt to strike once more at the Faringdon family— in a desire for revenge? Presumably a revenge made even more bitter by the past failures.' There it was, laid out in stark terms as cold and flat as Henry's eyes, dark with anger.

'To lure Nicholas into marriage with a Baxendale,' Sarah whispered.

'Is the coincidence too great?' Eleanor prayed that it was so.

'Nothing is beyond Edward.' Sarah fought to hide the shame as she outlined Edward Baxendale's past sins. Something that Henry had deliberately refrained from doing, out of respect for Sarah's unenviable position. 'He was willing to use me and my child. He was willing to destroy the good name of you, Eleanor, and Thomas. He would have made your position in society untenable. What would he not be capable of? Would he not use a young sister? Even if she were innocent of his intentions, she could still be a weapon for his revenge. He cannot touch you now, however much he might wish it, but he could harm Nicholas. Simply through the humiliation of luring him into marriage with a Baxendale without his knowledge. And if my brother could get money out of it…Edward is not beyond blackmail.'

'But would the girl agree to such a deception?' Eleanor asked in disbelief. 'To deliberately set out to fix Nicholas's interest, a cruel charade for a brother she hardly knows?'

'We don't know, Nell.' Henry's fingers tightened round her wrists, forcing her to look at him and consider the weight of his words. 'We know nothing about her. But what we do know is that Edward is quite capable of playing a role—of winning the lady's compliance with a heart-rending tale of the need for justice. The evil Faringdons and the innocent Baxendales.'

'Of course he would.' Eleanor nodded her agreement. 'So what do we do? Can we do anything?'

'It could be a completely false alarm, of course.' Henry frowned down at Eleanor's hands where they still rested, enclosed in his. 'Nick's interest might have moved on to someone else, another débutante. Or your mama might have misread his gallantry. But better that he knows.'

'I agree.' Sarah sighed. 'If nothing else, Lord Nicholas needs to know that Miss Theodora Wooton-Devereux is not who she seems.'

Chapter Ten

At Aymestry Manor, Nicholas and Theodora fell headlong and effortlessly into a love affair, watched closely but with indulgence and a wry acceptance by Agnes Drew and Mrs Grant. There was no doubting the happiness that wrapped the pair around, excluding all others, so that they might as well have been living on a deserted mountain top. It did a body good, Mrs Grant informed her interested guest, to see Lord Nicholas so taken up with a young lady who clearly returned his sentiments. It was high time he had something to occupy his mind, other than the state of the summer crop or the quality of wool from his prize Ryeland sheep! And a man as handsome and desirable as he in the marriage market—he should not be burying himself in the country. It was more than time he was wed and producing an heir for Aymestry. The Manor had been empty of children for far too long.

Agnes Drew listened, but made little comment, attempting without success to ignore the concern that would not let her be. A relationship built on a lie at worst—a deliberate falsehood at best—was flawed from the very beginning. But Miss Thea was past taking advice, as held fast in love as Lord Nicholas. So she listened and watched. And hoped that fate would not manipulate events in so cruel a fashion as to bring loss and heartbreak to either of the lovers. When her conscience dictated that she should advise Thea that a return to London was both expected and eminently sensible, Agnes for once threw good sense to the winds, considered it—and kept her counsel.

They rode the estate together. Nicholas lent her one of his well-bred horses, a compact chestnut mare with a mind of her own, to replace The Zephyr, who was still recovering. Across the pasture and open meadow, so unlike the confines of Hyde Park, Thea was free to gallop. And did so. Nicholas and his lady were quick to discover their equally competitive nature and revelled in the freedom to exercise it. Who might win did not seem to matter.

He showed her Aymestry, newly aware of the pride and affection in which he held this jewel of an estate. It pleased him to see it through her eyes, the pastures and mixed woodland, the mere where the swans were still in residence with their almost-fledged young. Not a large estate, but beautiful, a gleaming emerald, in a perfect setting of green hills and sparkling streams.

Then on to Burford—the vast house with its classical architecture and extensive estate, where herds of sheep and cattle grazed the pastures.

Thea was an interested and critical observer. She heard nothing but good of Lord Nicholas. He was well received, whether on the estate or in the small town of Kingshall. After her experience of the Maidens, it would not have surprised her to sense some animosity. But here there was no threat of danger. And Nicholas's manner was easy. He stopped to speak to those he passed, he knew their names, their families and their concerns.

Her admiration grew as she saw the extent of his responsibilities. However much he might be involved in his own property of Aymestry and his dreams of breeding desirable horseflesh, the estate at Burford was never to be neglected. He told her a little about his brothers. And his nephew Tom, Marquis of Burford. If—when—Tom took over the running of the estate in his own right, he would not find it wanting.

So Nicholas was a man quick to recognise obligation and stern duty. Yet he did not crow of his achievements. And Thea had actually accused him of living on the profit and possessions of oth-

ers. How little she had known of him then! She had the grace to
feel ashamed.

When it rained and discouraged their daily rides, they gravi-
tated to the library at Burford Hall. To Thea's delight, amongst
the dusty leather volumes there were novels to be read. Scott's
Waverley and *Guy Mannering* were soon discovered. And *Ivan-
hoe*, which she declared she liked less well, the plot being more
farfetched. She devoured *Glenarvon* by Caroline Lamb, with
her sensational and outrageous dissection of members of society whom Thea was quick to recognise with wicked pleasure.
Also a remarkable choice of Gothic novels, which made her
laugh and groan at their absurdities. She gave up on Mrs Radcliffe's *Mysteries of Udolpho* and turned instead with something
like relief to Lord Byron's *Childe Harold*.

A further source of surprise was the vast number of travel
books, which it was impossible for her to ignore. Descriptions
of far-flung lands all spoke to Thea's adventurous heart. But she
had never been as happy as she was at that moment in the rural
fastness of Herefordshire. And gloried in it.

And could discover another side to the man whom she was
coming to know. For the library also contained treatises on estate improvement. She browsed through back copies of the *Farmers' Journal*, articles on making use of marls and clover and new
grasses. Reports encouraged land drainage and the use of new
implements for ploughing and threshing. Arthur Young's writ-
ings on his travels around the country were well thumbed, she
noted, as were advice on improvements to cattle and sheep breeding. And, of course, horses.

For Nicholas cared. Thea's admiration grew, as did her love.

Nicholas, for his part, was totally captivated. Theodora was
everything he could want, everything he had dreamed of. Released from the rigid convention of life in the judgmental eye of
society, she relaxed, enabling him to see her true nature: an intelligent woman, well read, well traveled, which made her a delight to converse with. Energetic, full of life, she was eager to
explore his home, to ask and discover. She was even interested

in his plans for the estate, God help him! He was lost indeed! And she laughed. Whenever he thought of her it was to see her eyes sparkling, her lips curved to show her pretty teeth, her face alight. How could he not laugh with her? What more could any man desire in a wife?

As for the physical attraction—he had never wanted a woman as he wanted Theodora. Had never been aroused so readily by a mere glance, by a simple turn of a head, by a brush of feminine fingers against his. Sometimes he did not know how he kept his hands from seizing her shoulders and dragging her into his embrace, into his bed, capturing her mouth with his. He smiled with sardonic humour. She wore his self-control to breaking point—and was well aware of it. For Miss Wooton-Devereux was, without doubt, flirtatious when the mood took her.

And, if all that were not enough, a thick luxurious layer over all was the conviction that she was meant for him. He had simply been waiting for her all his life. He woke every morning, at ease with the knowledge that he could spend the day with her. The vague dissatisfaction and unease with the future vanished as soon as Thea came to stand with him, or sit or ride. As long as she was there, life could hold nothing more.

Sometimes he saw a shadow in her eyes. It concerned him, but perhaps it was simply a lingering memory of the terror of the Maidens' attack. It had pleased him that at last she trusted him enough to tell him the truth of that disturbing episode. It had not been easy for her. They had ridden to Dinmore Hill, where they had dismounted to stroll through the woods with their new brightness of leaves and the intense hue of the bluebells.

'I should tell you, Nicholas…' She had been quiet for a little time, lost in her thoughts or in the surrounding beauty, but now she took his hand and turned to face him. She did not smile.

'Hmm?' He watched the dappled sunlight play over her hair, her fair skin. How lovely she was.

'About…about my strange behaviour.'

His brows arched in silent enquiry.

'The Maidens—when I…when I…'

'Thea—I had not thought of it again.'

'But I have. I do. It was the same when I struck out at you with my whip. I should tell you—'

'Thea.' His fingers tightened on hers. 'There is no need.'

'I think I must. There should be no shadows between us.' *Except for the one, the darkest of dark shadows, which I dare not name!*

'No. Thea—I asked Agnes. After the incident with the Maidens. When you were so distressed—I thought I needed to know.' His voice was very gentle.

'Oh. Well, then…' It took Thea by surprise. She did not know how she felt about that.

'She was very loyal, but I pressed her.'

'And she told you.'

'Yes. Enough that I might understand.' He lifted a hand to run his fingers down her cheek, a soft brush of sympathy.

'I cannot control the fear. It is the overwhelming noise—the crush of people.'

'I know. I understand, darling Thea. It is not important.'

'I feel a coward.' She turned her face to press against his fingers.

'You are no coward. You are brave and resourceful. And I love you beyond reason.'

His kiss was a confirmation of the care, the depth of compassion that she heard in his voice. Gentle, lingering, a warmth of comfort for a damaged soul until her tense muscles softened and she clung to him in relief and gratitude. Until the gentle warmth of the kiss flared into heat and need, a desire that could not be denied, when the light around them became too bright, the colours too intense. Their senses were stripped naked before the onslaught of their love, leaving Nicholas in no doubt that she was as lost as he.

But he still did not know of the reason for her strange behaviour in London, when he had been so sure that she had deliberately set herself to put distance between them. In effect, to drive him away. He dare not ask her and closed his mind against it.

Nothing must be allowed to encroach on this summer idyll.

* * *

Time came to have no meaning for Nicholas and Theodora, measured only by the days and hours and minutes—seconds, even—which they spent in each other's presence. In each other's arms. It was a compulsion, an obsession, heightened by the brush of hands, the touch of lips. Nothing outside their two selves had any meaning.

So, riding on the edge of the estate, they were unaware of the changes round them as the clear light leached from the sky. Storm clouds banked to the west with a sultry heaviness. The first presentiment that they were far from home and the weather would break was a chilling ripple of wind. The sun disappeared behind encroaching high cloud, the far hill withdrawing into an enveloping mist and the first swirl of rain. Picking up the scent of the approaching storm, the horses danced in the freshening breeze, eager for their stable.

There was, of course, the temptation of a nearby barn.

'Well, my lady? Do we take the barn?'

'Or do we get wet?' Thea's face glowed with the sheer joy of life, of being in the presence of the man she loved. Of being able to reach out and touch him whenever the thought arose.

Nicholas turned his head, picking up her mood. 'Will you then gamble. Will we run the storm?' The wildness of the approaching elements was in his blood. There was a reckless challenge in his face that she loved and it seduced her utterly. She saw the challenge and loved it, allowed the seduction.

'Yes. And yes.'

'Come, then.' He stretched out a hand in imperious demand, manoeuvred his bay close, then leaned to allow an arm to steal around her waist. A kiss. Necessarily brief, a mere meeting of mouth on mouth. But hot and hard, a thrill of passion, of burning need.

For a moment her lips parted beneath his, her heart increasing its beat, a pulse that shook her and had nothing to do with the storm, but everything to do with the fever that engulfed her at his touch, the sheer sensuality as his tongue outlined the delicate shape of her lips.

Then he released her. 'Let us do the thing.'

And they fled before the storm, the rain and wind urging them on.

A crazy ride. At full, headlong gallop, control stretched to the limit. Sleek lines and straining power, horses and riders moving as one. They leapt small obstacles, ditches and hedges. Flew as if the hounds of hell pursued them in full cry as thunder rolled over the hills of Burford Edge behind them.

And the heavens opened, a deluge that drenched them to the skin in seconds. Thea failed to suppress a shriek as cold rain fell on her heated flesh. And laughed aloud with the exhilaration of it.

Nicholas slowed the pace. 'Do we shelter?' He had to raise his voice over the lash of wind and rain.

'No. Home.'

They picked up the pace and soared over the stream that bordered the home pasture. Extending again to thwart the worst of the relentless downpour. When they clattered into the stableyard and Nicholas lifted her down, the steaming horses were turned over to waiting hands and they ran for the house. Madness was in their blood, as elemental as the lightning that flashed across the sky.

In the entrance hall they stood on the worn slates and dripped. And looked at each other.

'I am drenched.' Thea tentatively lifted the clammy skirts of her velvet riding habit.

'And I.'

'We lost the gamble.'

'Did we?'

The shock of recognition between them was beyond experience, as electric as the storm that raged without. Breathing shallow, their eyes caught and held. It was impossible to look away, one held captive in the existence of the other. Chains of pure gold bound and held them—and neither resisted the gentle but inexorable tightening of the bond.

Nicholas smiled, both tender and a demand. Held out his hand, as he had at the onset of the storm. And Thea, breath caught in her throat, was compelled to respond, palm to palm, fingers interlocked. A remarkable seduction that tempted and beckoned them on into a depth of emotion and desire which neither could have envisaged. And both fell.

'My lord.' Mrs Grant had arrived unnoticed. 'I see you were caught in the storm. And Miss Thea.' She clucked indulgently at the puddles on the floor as she approached. They looked like children daring the power of the elements, she thought. Carefree. And Nicholas—as if a boy again, shedding the responsibilities that he had so willingly shouldered. Energy and vitality burned through him, his face alight with it.

'Can I be of help?'

'No.' Her question brought them back to the present. 'Thank you, Mrs Grant. No. I will deal with it.' His smile was preoccupied.

With Thea's hand in his, they climbed the stairs together, leaving the housekeeper to watch them.

No. Lord Nicholas was no longer a boy. The expression Mrs Grant had seen in his face and eyes had nothing to do with youth and immaturity. She hoped fate would be kind to him. And stepped back into the shadows.

This vibrant, laughing girl had brought him to life again.

No further words passed between them. They were beyond speech as they came to a halt at the head of the stairs where decisions had to be made. Nicholas tightened the clasp of his hand on hers, the slightest pressure, his gaze questioning. Theodora responded by moving to his side. Answering the unspoken, he led her along the corridor to his bedchamber.

Outside the storm raged on—capricious gusts of wind swirling the rain to lash unmercifully against the windows, distant thunder rumbling ever closer over woods and hills. Thea and Nicholas stood within his room, the door barred to all, oblivious to the onslaught. Within that wood-panelled room, safe and warm and offering every comfort, the elements were set to rage no less ferociously.

'I want you. I want you every minute in the day, from the moment that I wake until the second I fall into sleep. Even my dreams are tormented by your presence. Your perfume, your voice. You are in my blood, Thea.'

'I know it. I know it because my thought mirrors yours.' How could she not know it? Love washed over her, through her, a relentless tide. She felt the power of his eyes, fierce and intense, a dark midnight blue as they held her own. In response she felt the flush of heat over her skin, a flutter of nervous anticipation in her veins. For him, her smile was answer enough.

'Shall we ride this storm too, lady?' Nicholas drew her inexorably toward him, so that he could bend his head and kiss her hands, then take her lips with his own. Impossibly gentle, a mere sensuous brush of mouth against mouth, despite the raging fire in his blood.

'We can match the glory of anything in nature's creation.' Her lips parted beneath his in confident invitation. 'Love me, Nicholas.'

'It will be my pleasure and my delight, lady.'

Now their breathing was heightened. Their movements driven by unrestrained need, as wild and urgent as the summer storm. Soaked garments, boots were quickly stripped away until nothing existed between them except the charged quality of the air. Until he lifted her high in his arms, to fall with her to the bed where they rolled, a tangle of limbs, cool damp rapidly replaced by throbbing heat as skin slid seductively against skin. The lightning that speared across the sky was no more brilliant than the passion which consumed them. Diamond bright, it wrapped them around.

Both were already aroused, he hard as stone, she hot and slick with need, desiring nothing more than to be submerged one within the other as their hands united, palm to palm, fingers meshed. Nicholas pinned Theodora to the soft mattress, hands imprisoned above her head. She needed no instruction now, but opened for him, arching her body in silent demand.

'I love you.' She gasped the words as shivers ran along her skin at his dominant power. 'I love you.'

With one powerful thrust he possessed her. And again. Deep and deeper yet. Thea took him in.

'Thea.'

His name was also on her lips. Both held suspended in that one moment of glorious joining.

'Don't close your eyes.' His voice was low and harsh. She could not look away from the fierce wanting she could see in his face as he forced himself to hold back, a brief hiatus in the turbulence that threatened to overturn all control. 'Look at me.' She could do no other. 'I want you to see me when I am inside you. As I need to see myself in your eyes.'

'Yes.'

It was all the acceptance he needed. 'Then come with me.'

The storm struck with violent intensity, overwhelming them both as they had been enveloped by the rain on the hill. As his mouth took hers, swallowing her cries, he withdrew, thrust again. And again she arched and moved beneath him, as driven and demanding as her lover. All feminine elegance, all gentle curves and sleek planes, but yet wielding total power over his senses. When her nails seared his back, he was unaware. Nothing existed but this outrageous need to own, to achieve fulfilment—and still to pleasure. For even within the rough madness of it all, this furious craving to possess, was his care for her, woven through the tapestry as bright threads of silver throughout the silken texture of it all.

'Nicholas!' Thea answered every demand with intense joy. Never had her strong mind been taken over so completely by the commands of another. Her whole world was suddenly narrowed to this one sharp focus, the man who held her captive and governed her every action with such power. When he touched her, when he looked at her, compelling her with those amazing eyes, she no longer had a will of her own—and rejoiced in the knowledge, the absolute thrill of it.

Beyond any control, Nicholas now drove on, muscles screaming, tendons stretched to snapping point. Until the tight wet heat of her body brought him to his fulfilment.

'Did we survive the storm?' Thea managed to turn her face to press a kiss against the dark hair. They lay together in the ruins of the bed.

Beyond the room the storm had moved on. In the quietness the wind had dropped and the clouds began to break, allowing the first gleam of hesitant sunshine to brighten the corner of the room. But neither lover noticed the rich glow of linenfold or the return of birdsong, both too caught up in their own world.

'I think that we might.' Still buried deep within her, his weight still holding her, his face turned into the pillow. 'When my powers of thought and movement have returned. They appear to have deserted me.'

'Your powers were amazing.' The faintest chuckle.

'I might have hoped for more finesse. You robbed me of any skill I lay claim to.'

'You were magnificent.' Thea knew he was smiling in smug satisfaction, much as she was. Her hands smoothed over sweat-slicked muscle and hard flesh. She stretched luxuriously beneath him. 'Is it always like this?'

'Hmm?'

'Overwhelming. Devastating.' She nudged him when he did not reply. 'Are you sleeping, my lord? I shall flatter you no longer if your intent is to ignore me. Now that you no longer have need of me!' She carefully placed a row of kisses along his shoulder and back again. 'But is it always like this?'

'It can be.' Nicholas lifted his head now to reply with all seriousness. Had he ever known it like this? Where control was at its thinnest, stretched beyond bearing, beyond thought, until he had no choice but to empty himself into her glorious body? No. He thought that he had never known such an unleashed hunger. 'Perhaps it is not always so…mindless,' he offered. Because he knew that the craving had driven him to be careless with her. Selfish, if he admitted the truth. She had given herself to him, but he had not brought her to her own complete enjoyment. He felt himself harden again in sharp anticipation at the prospect of doing exactly that. 'It can be better—and you deserve that it should.'

'How can it be?' A little frown touched her smooth brow. 'You have given me such pleasure. Is the fault mine?'

'How foolish you are, my dear love.' He had to kiss her into silence. 'There is no fault with you. How could there be? But I can give you more.' He withdrew from her to stretch beside her, still hard. 'Hold me.' He took her hand. Both request and demand.

With growing confidence Thea enclosed him to explore the smooth hardness, enjoying his sharp intake of breath as she stroked and touched and heat built beneath her hand. She gave a soft purr, deep in her throat, as the heavy pulse began to beat.

He caught a glint of mischief in her eyes.

'Well?'

'It seems that I am not powerless here, my lord.'

'No.' He clenched his teeth on a groan. 'And *you* once begged *me* to have mercy! I believe that you did warn me that you learnt quickly.'

'So I do. Does it please you?'

'Yes. As I can please you.' Sensing the end of control under that alluring caress, he pushed her back on to the pillows. 'Like this.' With lips and a slow drift of hands he set himself to pleasure and to soothe, to awaken every nerve ending—and then to arouse again with tongue and teeth. 'Like this.' He closed his mouth over her breast, then the other, as the bright wedge of sunshine crept round to illuminate them in a wash of gold. 'And this and this.' A ruthlessly, exquisitely gentle campaign until he had driven her to the very edge of madness. But not quite beyond. Not yet. Slowly. So slowly. A steady relentless burn rather than a fiery heat, he built it layer upon layer, flame upon flame, until she was engulfed. Refusing to release her, even when she pleaded in desperation against the intensity of the sensations, until he knew that she could stand no more. Lifting her hips, he slid within her, so easily within that silken heat, now all gilded beauty, to finally drive her over that precipitate edge. When she cried out in shocked amazement, he followed, to fall with her into oblivion. Just as mindlessly, he realised, as before.

Much later awareness returned. Thea lay against him, content to allow her thoughts to drift, her heart to settle back to its usual steady beat. But perhaps it never would. It seemed to her at that moment that life would never be the same. Her heart was no longer in her possession, yet she was quite content that it should be in the keeping of the man whose arms still held her so securely. How splendid he was, how completely magnificent. She shuddered a little at the memory of his determination to reduce her to boneless delight. His ultimate and sensational triumph.

'Nicholas?'

'My lady?' His fingers drifted lazily along her spine, setting up little shivers along its length.

'I did not believe you. That I could experience more, that there were sensations and emotions to be explored more wonderful than I had ever imagined.' Her breathing still compromised, she rested her cheek on his chest, against his thundering heart. And smiled in utter contentment. 'But it is true.'

Lord Nicholas sat at his desk in the library at Aymestry, reluctant but resigned. However delightful, however necessary for his happiness it might have become to spend time with Theodora, duty and work called loudly this morning. Some documents pertaining to the Burford Estate had arrived for his attention from Mr Hoskins, the London-based lawyer, and needed a rapid reply. Furthermore, there was an unexpected packet of correspondence from New York. The one that caught his eye was in Nell's hand, which surprised him. He picked it up, tapped it thoughtfully on the desk. Now, why should Nell write to him? And, considering the thickness of the missive, at some length.

He spread the sheets on the desk and began to read, first letting his eye travel quickly down the pages. Until picking out one name. Halted. Nicholas's fingers tightened on the paper, much as invisible hands seemed to be tightening around his chest. Returning to the beginning, he began to read more slowly, perhaps hoping that there might be some mistake that could be remedied by careful perusal of Nell's neat script. It began with personal, family affairs. Normal and comforting, reassuring that all was well. But then she reached the bitter purpose of the letter and all Nicholas's comfort fled, to leave a gaping hole of pain and disillusion.

Eventually he finished it, taking only seconds to realise its import, not the endless hours it seemed. Pushed himself to his feet to go and stand by the window, as if the light flooding into the room would offer more illumination to the content.

Surely Nell's information was wrong. Surely it was all some dreadful mistake. But Nell had written of Sarah, who would undoubtedly know the truth… His eyes focused once again on the chilling words before him.

My mama has recently written that whilst in London you have made the acquaintance of a Miss Theodora Wooton-Devereux. That you have been attracted to her. I pray that you will forgive my interference in so personal a matter, dear Nick, but Sarah and I have decided—and Henry, too—that you must be told. Or perhaps by now the lady herself has told you the truth of her birth. Lady Drusilla Wooton-Devereux is sister to Lady Mary Baxendale, the now deceased mother of Sarah and Edward. The child whom you now know as Theodora was the child of Lady Mary and her husband, but was taken by Lady Drusilla soon after her birth and brought up as her own when the Baxendale circumstances became difficult. Thus Theodora's true name is Sophia Mary Baxendale. She is sister to Sarah and Edward.

We do not know if there is any understanding between you and the lady, but we believe that you should be made aware that the lady's name is Baxendale. We fear that it is not beyond belief that she is in touch with Edward. You should have a care, dear Nick. It may be that the Baxendale desire for revenge against the Faringdon family is not dead as we had believed, and that the lady is either a willing participant or a helpless pawn in Edward's vile games. I know the anguish and despair that this can cause. I would not wish for you to be dragged into a plot, leading to heartbreak and recrimination.

Miss Wooton-Devereux, I would advise you most strongly, may not be as innocent as she might appear.

I am sorry if this will cause problems between you. Perhaps I should pray that when this letter finally reaches you, your association with the lady has come to a natural end and she is looking elsewhere for a husband.

Nicholas simply stood, staring unseeingly at the dramatic prospect of open parkland and sunlit, mature oaks before him. For some reason his mind seemed unable to function with its usual sharp perception. Could not take in the full detail of Nell's warning words. Thea was a *Baxendale*. This was the only thought that hammered in his brain, over and over again. Sister of Edward Baxendale. No—it must not be so! But if Sarah had told Eleanor that Theodora was indeed her sister, then it must be so.

What in God's name did he feel about this?

Disbelief, primarily. Then a desperately piercing anxiety that it might just be true. And beneath that emotion, a terrible burning anger and an all-consuming fear that it might indeed be all part of a further plot as Nell had hinted, concocted in Edward Baxendale's corrupt mind, to hurt the Faringdons. To hurt *him*! Was it the plan to drag him into a marriage with Thea, the lure of a lovely face and pleasing manners, and then extort money by some means into Edward's greedy pockets? Or simply humiliate him when he discovered that he, Lord Nicholas Faringdon, had taken a Baxendale bride against either his knowledge or his wishes.

But the reasons behind the charade did not matter. Theodora's possible involvement was the weapon that sliced at his heart. He loved her. He had accepted without question that she loved him. He had taken her to his bed, asked her to marry him, believing that their love was a substantial thing, of mutual satisfaction and heart-wrenching beauty. Had he been so wrong? But he must accept that he was now faced with evidence of her perfidy, that such a beautiful face could hide such deceit. But of course he knew that she had been hiding something from him, had known it since the early days in London. Was this it? Her involvement, willing or otherwise, with her brother's scheming?

All he knew was that it was imperative that he talk to Theodora. And guard his emotions when doing so. Because if she was innocent of all involvement with her brother, as he hoped and prayed, why had she not told him that by birth she was a Baxendale?

Love? Ha! He crumpled Nell's letter in a furious fist. If love did exist, and he seriously doubted it after the revelations of the past hour, it must not be allowed to blind him to realities.

As Nicholas stalked to the library door, intent on running Theodora to ground and requesting—*demanding*—an explanation, it opened. Thea stood there. Her face immediately lit with an inner glow at the sight of her lover. Stretching out her hands, she would have covered the Aubusson carpet between them with the lightest of steps to kiss him in greeting, with no intimation of the disaster which awaited her in that pleasant, book-filled room. A lethal sword of Damocles, shrouded in the form of Edward Baxendale, to destroy all her new-found love and happiness.

But she immediately sensed the tension in Nicholas's body, saw his spine held rigid, his shoulders braced, hands clenched into fists at his sides. The lines between nose and mouth were starkly engraved. And his eyes? Usually so intensely blue and smiling when they lighted on her, or burning with passion and desire—now they were the dense, flat grey of glacial ice. Thea came to a halt as if a wall had been thrown up between them.

'What is it, Nicholas?' She saw the pages scattered on the desk. 'Have you had bad news? Is it your family in New York? Eleanor…?'

'Why did you not tell me, Thea?'

His voice was soft, apparently unthreatening, but held a quality that she had never before heard. It froze the very marrow in her bones.

'What is it that I should have told you? What can have disturbed you so?' She tried to keep her tone light, but a sharp finger of warning traced its insidious path along her backbone. She could think of only one cause for this latent hostility, and did not have long to wait to learn the truth.

'That your name is Baxendale. Sophia Mary Baxendale, to be exact. And that you are sister to Sir Edward Baxendale.'

'I—' She buried her teeth in her lip, as a bottomless crevasse opened before her unwary feet. Her worst fears had just been realised, announced in one brusque statement by the man whom she loved more than life itself, in a voice that cut with rapier sharpness to her heart. What could she say? A terrible premonition enfolded her as she read the condemnation in Nicholas's face.

'I see that you do not bother to deny it.'

She found, of necessity, her voice. 'No. For it is true.'

'Why did you not tell me? What can possibly have been your motive in not telling me?'

The simmering anger in his voice, the deadly repetition of the accusation stirred her into a response. Taking a deep breath, she willed the quivering nerves in her stomach to quieten. She *would not* feel guilt or shame over a situation that was not her fault, over which she had no control. She met his cold eyes squarely.

'I thought it would cause dissension between us. And I see that I was right.'

'So you would have kept the information from me for ever?' Now the softness was layered with a thick coating of derision. 'Even if we had married? An unlikely scenario, Thea, even you must accept.'

Which Thea silently had to admit the truth of. 'Who told you? Who told you the truth of my birth?'

'Eleanor. Who had the interesting details of your little masquerade from your sister, Sarah.'

'From *Sarah*?' Thea attempted to separate the strands of knowledge that were being hurled at her by the man she loved. 'I did not know that my sister was in communication with Eleanor. Is she then in New York?'

'What is the possible relevance of that? Suffice to say that Sarah informed Eleanor of your Baxendale connection.' Nicholas waited a brief, tense moment as Theodora remained silent. 'You have remarkably little to say about it, considering the depths of your deception.'

Which spurred her into reply. 'I do not see that my connection to the Baxendale family has any bearing on what lies between us.' *But I do. I should have told you. Forgive me, Nicholas, forgive me.* She kept her lips pressed firmly together, her head high.

'No? When you must be aware to some degree at least of the damaging scandal that struck my family nearly three years ago at the hands of Edward Baxendale. And yet you thought that it had *no bearing*?' His brows rose beautifully in arrogant disbelief. 'I cannot believe that you were not aware of the gossip. Certainly I cannot believe that Judith has been silent about it.'

Thea shook her head, panic rising at the unexpected viciousness of the attack. 'Judith refused to discuss the matter, claiming that it was not her secret to tell. She was very discreet.' She tried to keep calm, to breathe deeply. How could Nicholas, her love, accuse her of such perfidy?

'Then, if that is so, it must be for the first time in her life.' Nicholas was clearly sceptical of Judith's self-control. 'Tell me, then, Theodora, are you in communication with your brother?'

'I have never met Edward Baxendale.'

'Really? I find that also difficult to believe.' His lip curled in contempt and harsh mockery.

'I do not know him.' She resisted the urge to lift her hands, to plead her innocence. 'I do not lie.'

'Your brother was a past master at the art of deception. Perhaps you, too, have the skill. You were certainly able to take me in with your winning ways and your lovely face.'

'And so you would suspect me of similar sins to those of my brother, simply because we share a blood relationship?' Thea marvelled at her ability to reply with such care when all her instincts were to succumb to the intimations of disaster, which drew the colour from her fair skin.

Nicholas shrugged. The nasty little gesture was as wounding as his words. And Thea, who had been inclined to explain her total innocence, her ignorance of any family connection until only the previous month, decided that she would not. If Nicholas was not prepared to believe her, to accept her word, what point in dragging her family complications into the open? He would take her on trust or not at all.

'I have never met Edward or Sarah Baxendale,' was all that she would say in explanation.

'But you knew of the connection.'

'Yes.'

'Yet you saw fit not to break the interesting news to me. I wish you had told me. Why did you not—if you were innocent of all involvement with your brother?'

'I feared to do so.' Theodora discovered that her control of her emotions was slipping increasingly on a knife edge. 'For so many reasons. Not least that you would reject me if you knew the truth. I tried to end the…the growing closeness between us in London, if you remember. Indeed I did, when I realised that I might be falling in love with you. I thought it best if I could create a distance between us, so that love could never bloom. So that we should never find ourselves in this impossbile situation.' She found a need to dash a stray tear from her cheek with an impatient hand. 'I think I succeeded very well. But then fate brought us together again. I knew beyond doubt that I loved you… And I feared to tell you the truth.'

Nicholas swung away, to prowl to the sideboard, as dangerous and highly tuned as a hunting cat, to pour a glass of brandy, take a long swallow, presenting his back to Thea. The silence stretched between them until she could stand it no longer.

'What did Edward do, Nicholas? Was it so bad, so unforgivable, that it will stand between us for all time?'

'Yes.'

'Why? What happened? No one who knows the true facts will tell me.'

'It is in the past and not something I care to contemplate. Certainly not something I wish to discuss with you.'

'But not sufficiently in the past that it can be forgotten.'

'No. It can never be forgotten.'

So there was the barrier between them. Solid. Bitter. Impossible, Thea realised, to breach.

'So all that we meant to each other is worth nothing in the balance with Edward's sins.'

He turned his head to look at her now. 'Tell me this, Thea. Are you part of a new Baxendale plot? You and your brother working together against us?'

'Of course not.' Seeing the abyss at her feet widen even further, Thea whispered her reply. 'But you do not trust me, do you?'

'I do not know. Perhaps I do not know you as well as I believed.' Blazing anger suddenly sprang into life between them and engulfed the cold. 'If you are an innocent party to this, you would have not left me in ignorance. Have you and Edward rejoiced together over your successes?' The thought fed the flames of his anger with dry tinder. 'Have you and Edward exchanged to your mutual delight the methods by which you might have entrapped me into marriage? What did you hope for, Thea? A financial settlement for yourself, which would benefit your brother? Or merely the pleasure of seeing me wed unknowingly to a Baxendale, perhaps with a suitable and expensive settlement to allow me to escape from such an alliance?'

Before Theodora could react, Nicholas put down the glass, closed the distance between them and pounced with lethal intent. He seized her by her shoulders, wilfully ignoring her sharp cry of surprise and protest, and dragged her into an embrace that contained all the fury and frustrated desire which had built since his reading of the letter. His mouth was hard, ruthless against her soft lips, set to take and ravage, his harsh grasp imprinting the tender skin of her arms.

Thea could do nothing but submit. Simply waited, refusing to struggle.

When he raised his head, but did not release her, there was no softening in his face.

'Is this what you wanted from me? Kisses and commitment?' His eyes burned into hers with savage fire. 'Was this all pretence? Did you feel nothing in my arms but triumph that you had fooled me into believing that you loved me? Damn you, Thea! How could you do it?' He took her lips again, a wild gesture of desperate love and despair. Then let her go, so rapidly that she almost fell, as if he could no longer bear the contact. He stalked away to pick up the brandy once more, and drank.

Then he laughed, a harsh sound in the quiet room. 'The possibilities, it seems, are endless. And none of them pleasant or flattering to either of us.' He took a breath. His voice was now cold, so cold. 'Forgive me. I suppose I should ask your pardon for handling you with such insensitivity.'

Thea listened as if from a great distance, aware only of the desperate hatred that underpinned Nicholas's rage. 'You must hate my brother very much.'

'I do. By God, I do. If indeed you do not know, I suggest that you ask him yourself.' Lord Nicholas showed his teeth in a vicious snarl. 'I am sure that he will be delighted to tell you—but do not wager that very pretty pearl drop that you are wearing around your equally pretty neck on the truth of it.'

'I think I must indeed ask him. If only to see if his version of events tallies with yours. Or perhaps it will prove that you are as vindictive and vengeful as you claim Edward to be.'

'I care not what you discover. You are hardly likely to believe my words over his, are you?'

With which words, words that would effectively destroy any hope for a reconciliation between them, Lord Nicholas Faringdon, always a model of propriety and good manners, discovered that his fury could escape his control. He lifted his arm and flung the glass and the brandy at the wall, where it smashed in a shower of crystal to the floor. The brandy ran stickily down the wood panelling to puddle below.

Thea watched the shards of crystal glitter on the carpet, shocked to the core. But not as outraged as Nicholas himself at the violent reaction that had broken free of his determination to remain cold and calm to the last.

Thea was the one to speak. Her words were very simple and from the heart. They hit home as a more emotional response might not. 'I love you, Nicholas. I cannot believe that you would put your hatred for my brother before your love for me. How shallow your love must be. Perhaps it never existed. It certainly could not stand the test of time.'

'How can you possibly decry my love for you—' he rounded on her, eyes ablaze '—when our whole relationship was based on a deceit? If you had truly loved me, you would have trusted me with your family history. You would not have kept silent on a matter that touches me so personally.'

'And you would have believed in my innocence?' Guilt brought a slight flush to her cheeks, for his words contained a grain of truth—that she had known of the dangers of silence, but had chosen not to tell him. Now she was forced to accept that such reticence was not proof of true love.

'Of course.' A flash of uncertainty might have made him hesitate, but he quickly banished it.

'I think all is plain, my lord.' Thea took the only course that she could see open to her. A step away from him, at the same time taking refuge in rigid formality, very much Sir Hector's daughter. She was now shockingly pale, her skin as colourless as the fine wax candles in their chased silver candelabra on the table beside her. She raised her chin and spoke with chilling hauteur. 'You deem me to be without either honour or veracity, my lord, capable of tricking you into a relationship purely to humiliate and wreak revenge on you. Since you would destroy my character with such unfounded accusations, there is no place for me in your life. I am clearly no longer welcome here. You offered me marriage. I refuse your offer. What a fortunate escape we have both had, to be sure! Now—if you would be so good as to provide a horse for me to ride, I can be gone from your presence and your property within the hour.'

So she would leave, with no further explanation, no need for further association with Lord Nicholas Faringdon.

Nicholas watched her, suddenly struck by the magnitude of the gulf that had widened between them in so short a time. *What am I doing? What am I saying?* She looked shattered. So pale.

So sad. Admiration, albeit reluctant, surged through him that she could stand before him with pride and composure, regardless of his deliberately cruel words and the astounding violence that had reduced him to such a lack of control. He should be whipped for this, his conscience pricked with sharp insistence. What he *should* do was take her in his arms and kiss that desolate mouth into smiling joy. How could she possibly be guilty of the sins that he had laid before her? When she had sighed in his arms, when she had shivered in newly awakened desire beneath him, when she had allowed and welcomed such intimate possession of her body—surely he must be wrong. And deserve to be cursed to the fires of everlasting hell for such insensitive handling of her. But the vicious memories returned with vivid clarity. Edward Baxendale. Smug, self-satisfied, malicious, manipulative. If he could use his wife and his sister Sarah to feed his own ambitions, so he could use Theodora. And, ultimately, Theodora had lied to him. He must not weaken, must not allow his heart to rule his head.

'No. You will not ride.' His response exactly mirrored hers. 'I will provide you with a post chaise and postilions. I do not want your safety or comfort on the journey on my conscience.'

'There is no need for your conscience to be involved.' If Nicholas could be so cold and distant, so could she. 'My welfare is no longer your concern, my lord.'

'You have no choice in the matter, Miss Wooton-Devereux. The coach will be waiting at the front steps, for your convenience within the hour.'

The sooner the better! How dare he make her so indebted to him at the last! 'Then I shall be grateful, for Agnes's sake.' There was not the slightest hint of gratitude in her face or her voice.

Of which Lord Nicholas was made painfully aware.

Theodora turned on her heel and stalked from the room before she, too, was tempted into an action of mindless, uncontrolled violence. To sweep the candles, together with their elegant silver stand, to the carpet, with the flat of her hand.

* * *

As good as his word, Nicholas arranged for a post chaise and four to be ready before the door within the hour. Always the impeccable host and gentleman, he handed the two ladies into it, ordered a fur wrap for their knees, for their comfort from the chill wind. Promised the return of The Zephyr when her sprain had healed sufficiently for her to make the journey. Added two of his own grooms to Thea's two henchmen, to ensure their safe passage. They were instructed to keep their pistols primed and eyes alert for any sign of the Maidens.

Throughout the proceedings, Lord Nicholas was as remote as the chill air quality around them, his self-control held on a tight rein. He did not allow his eyes to meet Thea's, or even to dwell on the expression on her face, afraid of what he might see there. He did not take her hand or kiss her fingers in farewell. His expression remained closed and unemotional throughout the brief leave-taking as if the whole event was a matter of little importance or interest. Thea's remained pale and set. Agnes, painfully aware of every nuance, made all the suitable farewells and necessary statements of gratitude. She did not dare ask her mistress what had occurred to cause this shattering tension between them.

Finally Lord Nicholas bowed with superb grace as the coach departed—then stalked back into the Manor without a backward glance.

The occupants travelled in taut silence for the first half-hour, both ladies pretending to admire the passing scenery. Until Agnes was aware that silent tears had begun to track down Thea's cheeks. She was crying, silently and helplessly.

Agnes sighed. 'He is hurt, Miss Thea.'

'But so am I.' Thea tried to wipe the tears away with one finger. 'Are all men so stubborn and blinkered?'

'I imagine.'

'But not as stubborn as Nicholas Faringdon!' She sniffed and turned her face away. She did not see Agnes narrow her gaze at a particularly fine sweep of woodland carpeted with bluebells.

'It's not my place to say, Miss Thea.'

'Since when did that ever stop you giving an opinion!' The bitterness in Thea's voice was overlaid by a storm of suppressed grief.

'Very well. If you want honesty from me, you should have told him.'

'I know.' An audible sob escaped. 'And now he does not trust me. With no possible evidence of my guilt. Simply because my name is Baxendale.'

Silence.

'It is not fair! And I love him so.'

'I know.' Agnes could find no words of comfort, but her heart ached for the girl whom she had known and cared for since she had come into the family as an unwanted baby, a mere four weeks old. No, it was not fair, but life was not guaranteed to hand out fairness.

'I am sorry I snapped at you, Agnes.' Thea sniffed again and used her handkerchief to great effect. 'I must not weep. It does no good.'

'No.' Agnes hid a little smile. This was more like the Thea she knew.

'I have decided one thing. I need to know the truth.' The lady tucked away the damp linen square and, once composed, turned back to her maid. 'There is only one person who might tell me.'

'So you will go to Sir Edward. Is it wise? Will you get the truth from him?'

Theodora thought for a moment, weighing the possibilities in the balance. 'Why not? I am his sister, after all. Certainly no one else is prepared to tell me what happened between Faringdons and Baxendales. I shall visit Whitchurch on our route to London.'

Thea lapsed into silence again, her thoughts taken up with that final interview between herself and Nicholas. Her emotions tore at her and gave her no rest. Guilt that she had indeed embarked on their relationship on a lie, knowing that she had not told him the truth, even when she had been aware of the dangers in remaining silent. Anger that he should believe in her culpability rather than her innocence. And frustration that he would not tell her why he was so hostile, what it was that Edward had done that was so diabolical.

But mostly it was pain that stole her breath. She loved Nicholas—yet she had lost him. And feared that nothing she could do would ever win him back. All she could see was the condemnation in his face, his eyes dark and stormy as he surveyed her with arrogant disdain, and the desolation was a band around her heart. It was a relief when they arrived in Tenbury Wells, to the surprise but casual acceptance of Cousin Jennifer, where she could retire to her bedchamber and indulge in a private deluge of tears until she could weep no more—for herself, and for Nicholas, caught up in the complicated weavings of a net from which there was no escape.

At Aymestry, denied the luxury of a confidant, Nicholas strode directly from the house to the stables, ordered the saddling of a bay gelding and informed his silent and wary staff that he would be at Burford for the rest of the day. His tone denied the need for anyone to contact him there.

'Will Miss Thea return?' Furness enquired, risking the storm clouds.

'No.'

'Do we send The Zephyr on to London when she is sound?'

'Yes.'

'Do I continue the poultices or do I turn her out into a paddock?'

'Do what ever you wish, Furness. I am sure that you know as well as I how to deal with a lame animal.'

Thus ending any conversation about horses or more personal matters. Nicholas ignored the resulting exchange of knowing glances as he rode the gelding out of the stableyard on a tight rein.

He had, he realised, no intention of going to Burford. He simply rode, hard and fast, allowing his fresh mount its head as they hit the rising ground through the park. But there was no joy in it. Anything to rid his mind of Thea's face when she had finally walked from his library, pale as the most delicate of magnolia blossoms, her expressive eyes veiled by a deliberate downsweep of thick lashes. Was it anguish from a broken heart that had brought the tension to her face, or was it shame that she had tricked him into a fraudulent relationship? How could he possibly know!

At the brow of the hill, he finally drew the gelding to a halt to look out over the acres of Aymestry to where they marched with Burford, usually a scene to soothe his heart. But today he found no satisfaction in it. He had last ridden these lanes and pastures, the shady woodland rides and the path beside the lake, with Thea. Now she had destroyed all his enjoyment in it, the pleasure in its possession and his peace of mind. And he missed her. He wanted her. His loins and his heart ached with the loss of her.

Lord Nicholas cursed fluently and long. He had known that there was some secret, some matter that had presented a barrier between them. But never this. What a stupid fool he had been, to give his heart into the keeping of a woman who, with cruel hindsight, was so clearly not what she seemed and bent on mischief. So much for love! When he married it would be for convenience, a wife to run his household, entertain his guests and carry his heirs. No emotions involved, nothing beyond a mild affection and tolerance. Henry was free to enjoy his grand passion with Eleanor. A cool calm friendship would do very well for him.

Lord Nicholas fervently hoped that he would never again have the misfortune to set eyes on Sophia Mary Baxendale.

Chapter Eleven

⟨ornament⟩

Thea was bowed into the entrance hall of the Great House in Whitchurch by an elderly servant who shuffled off to discover the whereabouts of Sir Edward Baxendale, leaving the lady to look about her. It was a lovely old house with mellow stone and graciously symmetrical lines of Jacobean origin. The main staircase and the wooden panelling was imposing enough, but gave the impression of faded grandeur. The house had seen better days. There was heavy dust on the table and settle beside her and the fireplace had not been swept of the debris of any number of fires. Curtains at the windows were worn and faded from an assault by the sun over the years. Outside the ornamental hedges were untidy and unclipped and the hinges of the wrought-iron gates were in need of repair. It spoke of a lack of servants. Thea suspected a lack of money.

But for her the most important, the most astounding, thought was that this was the house where she had been born and spent the first four weeks of her life. How strange it was to return here—and under such circumstances. How strange it would be to meet her brother for the first time in her life that she could recall. Nerves raised a shiver of disquiet along her arms. If her brother was prepared to discuss the Faringdon scandal with her, what would it reveal? And could she trust him to speak the truth?

'I remember nothing of this.'

Agnes saw the nerves and touched her young mistress's hand with light fingers. 'You would not, of course. Don't fret, Miss Thea. You must use your own judgement—whether what you will hear in this house is true or false.'

Which did nothing to ease Theodora's anxieties.

The servant returned to show her into a room that looked out over a walled garden to the rear. She sat and waited, determined to retain her composure and her impartiality. Then the door opened and a gentleman entered with quiet dignity. The first impressions for Thea were undoubtedly pleasing. Not over tall, but compact and well muscled. Fair haired with clear, friendly blue eyes, he was clad in a double-breasted coat, breeches and boots suitable for any country gentlemen, of good quality but with no extremes of fashion. His figure was good, elegant even, as was his address.

Sir Edward Baxendale. Her brother.

Yes. An attractive man, but Thea kept her council, and her expression and greeting cool. She did not know him.

Sir Edward came to a halt before her and inclined his head in gracious welcome. So this was his sister. After all these years. He had almost forgotten her very existence. Lady Drusilla had seen to that!

'Sir Edward.'

'Miss Wooton-Devereux.' With a smile as warm as the sunshine that flooded the room, he raised her hand to his lips. 'Or may I call you Theodora? If I may say—you have the look of our mother. She, too, was acknowledged to be a beauty as a young girl.'

'I did not know that.' Thea allowed a light smile in response, but remained aloof and wary. There was much that she needed to learn about Sir Edward Baxendale.

'Please sit.' He motioned to the chair from which she had just risen. 'Allow me to give you a glass of claret. I am sure that refreshment after your journey will be acceptable.'

He poured and handed her a glass, but after thanking him she placed it untouched on the table.

Edward eyed her with mild curiosity as he lowered himself to a chair beside her, close enough for easy conversation, but not so as to be an imposition. 'To what do I owe the pleasure, Theodora? I had believed that our relationship was past mending and so have done nothing to make contact with you. My mother and Lady Drusilla had nothing to say to each other. I did not even know that you were aware of the connection between us. And now here you are in Whitchurch…'

'I was ignorant of our relationship until some weeks ago. Lady Drusilla saw no necessity to tell me.'

'Ah. But she did finally.'

'Yes.'

'May I be permitted to ask why?' Sir Edward's manner betrayed nothing but a mild interest—and perhaps a sensitivity for so difficult an occasion.

'That is of no consequence.'

'Very well.' He accepted her reluctance with apparent equanimity. 'So why *are* you here today?' He watched her. Thinking rapidly, he noted the sheen of wealth, of the confidence of the rich and privileged, of high fashion. It immediately caught his interest. Here was a lady who could be of use to him. A very useful weapon, although in what manner he was not yet sure. Why had he not thought of this connection before? It would be wise to be open to any opportunity that might present itself from this unlooked-for conversation.

Equally, Theodora took a keen assessment of her brother. A gentleman, certainly. With, according to the little she had heard, a vast catalogue of unidentified sins. He looked pleasant and affable, with open features and a ready smile. Nothing sly or untrustworthy to prick her instincts. But whether he would tell her the truth, she had no idea.

'I am given to understand, Sir Edward, that I also have a sister.'

'Why, yes, indeed. Sarah.'

'Does she live near? Can I meet her?'

'Forgive me, my dear.' He rose to refill his glass, looking back at her over his shoulder. There was true regret in his voice.

'I no longer know where she resides. Sarah married a naval man against the family wishes. Not an advantageous marriage or, I believe, a happy one for my sister. Unfortunately he lacked good family and connections. Sarah, I am loathe to admit, has chosen no longer to communicate with us—despite encouragement from me. She has a child, I think. But more than that…' He shrugged as he returned to his chair and lifted his glass to his lips.

Leaving Thea with little choice but to broach the subject that had brought her to Whitchurch.

'It has come to my knowledge, sir, that there was some…unpleasantness…between the Baxendales and the Marquis of Burford. I have come here hoping to discover the truth.'

'Ah!' *The Faringdons. So that was the issue! Now, how was his sister possibly linked with the Faringdons? It would be well to have a care.* 'So that old scandal has reared its head. I had hoped for Octavia's sake that it had died a death.' A tightening of the lips was the only emotion Sir Edward allowed himself to betray.

'Octavia?'

'My dear wife. You can meet her soon. She has gone into the village on an errand of mercy.'

'I would like that.' Thea could detect nothing but concern in her brother. 'Will you tell me?'

'What is it you wish to know?'

'I would know what the issue is between you and the Faringdons.'

'Very well. We never speak of it now, as you will soon understand—but I will tell you. As a close member of family, perhaps you should know the truth.' Sir Edward leaned back, crossing one elegantly booted leg over the other. 'Tell me, are you acquainted with any members of the Faringdon family? We rarely socialize, so I am not aware…'

'Yes. A little.'

So there was something here. Perhaps something that he could use to their detriment—and his satisfaction.

'Lord Nicholas, perhaps? Or the Countess of Painscastle? If

you have moved in the first circles in London—as I am sure you have—I expect that you will have been introduced.'

'We have been introduced.' Thea watched her brother. Again, nothing in his manner to disturb her, to make her aware of the direction of her brother's calculations, the sudden explosion of insight, the chance of a sharp thrust of revenge for past injuries. And if there happened to be an understanding between Lord Nicholas and his sister...well, it would please Sir Edward greatly to destroy any chance of happiness there. As for this sister who sat so confidingly before him, he had no feelings for her, did not know her. Envied her, of course. She had enjoyed an easy, wealthy life of luxury and comfort, whilst they at Whitchurch... He owed her nothing! It would not hurt him to apply a gentle twist to a knife buried to its hilt in her hopes and dreams of love. Miss Wooton-Devereux deserved nothing from him! He smiled at Thea, all warmth and brotherly concern. He would sow a few bitter seeds, then wait and see what the harvest would bring. All carefully masked behind those smiling blue eyes, guaranteed to ease Thea's doubts. So he began his tissue of lies, as skilfully woven as cloth of the finest quality.

'It is not a comfortable tale and I beg that you will not discuss it in the hearing of Octavia. You will soon appreciate why. But these are the bones of it. Thomas, Marquis of Burford, promised Octavia marriage in the year when she was presented for a Season in London. He courted her most assiduously. She was impressionable and young, overawed by his wealth and his title— and his handsome face, of course. He seduced her and left her carrying his child.'

Edward took a sip of claret as if to removed an unpleasant taste from his mouth.

'Forgive me. It still brings me pain. The Marquis then reneged on his promise, refused to recognise the child as his own and cast her off. He married Eleanor Stamford instead.' His lips sneered.

'I see. But why?' Thea felt her heart soften towards the unknown Octavia. 'Why did he not marry Octavia?'

'Simple enough. Because although she was gently born, he

claimed that her birth was not good enough, not *appropriate* for a Marchioness of Burford. She was good enough for him to se-duce!' His bitterness on behalf of the lady won Thea's acceptance.

'So what happened to Octavia?'

'I knew Octavia—had known her from her girlhood.' His lips now curled a little in a smile at the memory. 'I married her to protect her name and give the child a home and a father. When the child was born I applied to the Marquis for financial recom-pense for Octavia's sufferings—and for the child, of course. We were refused and threatened with a court case against us if we persisted. I did persist.' Sir Edward shook his head in apparent disbelief. 'It seemed so wrong that the Faringdons should be able to reject so innocent a lady as Octavia. I took her to Burford Hall, with the child, to beg for restitution. By then the Marquis had died and matters were in the hands of his brother, Lord Henry. We were faced by the united Faringdons. Can you imagine the humiliation? Yes, they listened to what I had to say—and then promptly turned us from the door. Denied any involvement or proof of the child's paternity. Accused me of being a charlatan and Octavia—well, there is no need to explain what the impli-cations were of her. It would be too shaming to resurrect such words as we heard that day from the lips of Lord Henry Faring-don. Enough to say, they would have destroyed our credibility in society if we had pursued the matter further.'

'I did not realise…' Theodora found her thoughts almost par-alysed with shock at this appalling situation, concerning a lady who was, after all, her sister-in-law.

'It is not a flattering picture, I am afraid.' Edward's gaze was sharp and bright on his sister's face, but full of compassion.

'No, indeed. It is…it is a disaster!'

'I am sorry if it distresses you—' *now, how will she react!* '—if perhaps you had a…an understanding with Lord Nicholas?'

'No. I…'

Thea fought to bring her thoughts into some form of order. This dreadful tale of deliberate, wilful cruelty to an innocent young girl. Could Henry and Nicholas Faringdon have behaved with such callous insensitivity and selfishness? Surely she could not have been so mistaken in the man to whom she had so willingly and joyfully given her heart.

'Could I ask,' Sir Edward broke into her despair, 'what have the Faringdons said about the affair?'

She does not know the truth. She will accept anything I say!

'I could not discover the truth,' Thea confirmed to Edward's satisfaction. 'Neither Judith—nor Lord Nicholas—was willing to discuss it. I believed it was to shield the name and reputation of Eleanor, but perhaps…'

'What could they say that would not be shaming to themselves?' Edward gently increased the pain. 'They acted with complete ignominy. Octavia was better off out of their clutches.'

Thea drew in a deep breath. It all seemed so horribly possible. 'And the baby?'

'A son.' Edward acknowledged. 'Unfortunately it died. We—Octavia and I—have never had the felicity to have more children.' His lowered lashes hid any grief.

'I am very sorry, sir…'

'I, too, am sorry if it brings you pain, Theodora, but it is better that you know the truth. The Faringdons were arrogant and unfeeling, with no thought for a poor wronged girl who was preyed upon, who was robbed of her youth and innocence. I fear that Octavia has never recovered her spirit or her pure enjoyment of life. She lives in shadows, fearful and suspicious of all—other than myself.'

So there it was. Or Edward Baxendale's version of it. As Thea sat and studied her brother's face, the sorrow and concern that she could read there, it came to her that there was no reason for her not to believe the wretched tale she had just heard. But it was a terrible indictment of Nicholas and the whole Faringdon family. Anger simmered. If it were true, how humiliating it was that she had failed so completely in her judgement of human nature, had fallen in love with someone who in effect did not exist. The Nicholas she knew—caring, careful and concerned for the feelings and welfare of others—did not match this terrible portrait painted by her brother. How could she have been so wrong, have misjudged him so completely? How could she have given herself to a man who could treat a defenceless and needy woman with so little respect? *But was it all true?*

Edward watched the uncertainties flit across his sister's face and worked to preserve a bland appearance. So far, so good.

'Listen.' He stood and stretched out a hand to bring Thea to her feet. 'That will be Octavia. Now you can meet her—my very dear wife.'

So Theodora met the lady in question. A fair lady, slender almost to the point of thinness, with pale eyes that seemed reluctant to rest for long. Pretty enough, but the fine lines in the delicate skin of her face suggested a life touched with grief, perhaps nervous strain. Yet she responded to her husband with real affection and made Theodora welcome.

Thea did not stay long. She soon discovered that Octavia had little to say beyond a comment on the weather or the state of her rose arbours. Thea could well believe Octavia having been a victim. She was as insubstantial as a sunbeam on a winter's day. Yet her situation demanded sympathy. Her loss and her rejection by one whom she thought had loved her—a Faringdon—must have been hard indeed.

Thea made her farewells and felt the similarity of rejection with bitter pain.

'It would please me if you would keep in touch with us here in the country,' Sir Edward invited as Thea stood in the hall, preparing to depart. 'We do not go into society. Times are hard with us.' He hoped a slick of guilt would attack the lady's conscience. 'I congratulate you on your good fortune. Life has blessed you, with Sir Hector and Lady Drusilla.'

'It has. I must be grateful.' The comparisons between their lifestyles touched her with discomfort. As intended.

'Octavia would much enjoy your visits. To hear of events in London. We have few acquaintance who stay in town.' Sir Edward smiled again, the perfect host, the deadliest of enemies.

Thea made a non-committal reply as she curtsied her farewell. Edward kissed her hand and her cheek.

'Well?' Agnes Drew enquired as they were once more embarked on their journey and Thea showed little inclination to break the silence.

The lady sighed and turned her head. 'I do not know! I simply don't know.'

'Was it what you had hoped for?'

'No. It was worse than I could possibly have imagined.'

'Hmm. But can you trust Sir Edward? You do not know him.'

'I do not know that either.'

'And Lord Nicholas? After all, you *do* know him, Miss Thea.'

Yes. I thought I loved him. I still do. But is he a man worthy of my love? Sir Edward has cast all into doubt.

Life at Burford Hall and Aymestry Manor followed inexorably the demands of the changing seasons. Enough to occupy Nicholas, enough to fill his mind with the day-to-day affairs of running two estates and planning for the future. Enough to distract his thoughts from a blighted love affair, the final ending of which should have been a matter for rejoicing. But when he rode beneath the dripping beeches in a heavy shower, he sensed her beside him. When he rose from a troubled sleep at early light or took himself to bed—alone!—with dreams that teased and haunted him. Nicholas cursed and informed himself that Theodora WootonDevereux no longer had a niche in his life. Unfortunately he discovered, long forgotten in a coat pocket, a little diamond-and-sapphire brooch, which forced him to remember how he had removed it in the soft twilight of the stable and kissed its owner into shocked delight. For a moment he watched it catch the light with rare brilliance, then pushed it out of sight, too painful a talisman. There was no need for him to spend one second in a day in thinking of her. It would all get better with time.

It did not.

* * *

The most urgent business to confront him was the matter of the Maidens. Some days after Thea's departure, he rode into Leominster to meet with his fellow JPs at the Talbot, to discover with no surprise that the rural unrest was to be the main subject of discussion. The Maidens, with their skirts and scarves, their vociferous complaints, were extending their demands and their range of operation. Lewis Bates was still recognised as the leading voice, but the name of Samuel Dyer came often to the fore, particularly when the event involved more violence or threats of retribution than had emerged in the past. Almost every JP had some tale to tell of their activity. More old ricks had been burnt—not a great matter in itself, but a symptom of the disruption that they all understood. Two of the gentlemen making inroads into the port at the Talbot had received threatening letters, badly written but clear in their intent if the landlords did not answer their demands. Sir Thomas Clifford over towards Kingsland had suffered an actual attack on his house, forcing him to barricade his doors and windows to safeguard his wife and young family, until his neighbour could arrive and help drive the mob of drunken, swaggering labourers from their entrenched positions.

The demands were simple and clear, exacerbated by the poor harvest in the previous year and the cool spring, but there was no immediate remedy for the hunger sweeping the countryside beyond the setting up of soup kitchens, which most landlords were prepared to do. As for the desired lower rents and higher wages, it was an individual matter for each landlord. Lord Westbourne, as might have been expected, had no intention of giving in to the rabble at his doors. Nicholas winced at his lordship's forthright condemnation of his estate workers. Any attempts to ease the local suffering would receive no aid in that quarter. For himself, Nicholas arranged a meeting with his agent to see what could be done for those Faringdon tenants hardest hit. Meanwhile, the gentlemen of Herefordshire discussed the wisdom of calling out the local militia if news of further riots reached them.

For a short time, it gave considerable direction to Nicholas's thoughts.

* * *

'Well, Theodora. Sir Hector and I thought that you had abandoned us for good. I had no idea that you would find Cousin Jennifer's company so entertaining or Tenbury Wells so attractive.' Lady Drusilla regarded her daughter with close and critical attention on her eventual and belated return to Upper Brook Street.

'Cousin Jennifer liked to reminisce,' Thea informed her mother as she took a seat in that lady's boudoir and steeled herself to withstand the probing questions in the inevitable cross-examination. She had been dispatched to Herefordshire for a few days—which had mysteriously and inexplicably transformed themselves into weeks.

'She must have done. Apparently you were captivated.'

Thea ignored the dry comment, kept her lips curved into some semblance of pleasure and merely folding her hands in her lap expectantly. She must keep her wits sharp if her mother were to remain in ignorance.

'And The Zephyr. I understand that she is not with you. Why did you not bring her home?'

'A minor sprain. Some of the roads and tracks in the area of Tenbury Wells were very uneven. She will be sent on when fit again.'

'Did you enjoy the visit?'

'Yes.'

'Country life?'

'Very…ah, relaxing.'

So why do you give the impression that you are neither sleeping nor eating well? And avoiding my questions!

'And the scenery?'

'Very pretty.'

'Hmm.' Lady Drusilla clasped a chain of sapphires around her neck, watching her daughter through the mirror with narrowed eyes. 'What did you find to do in all this pretty scenery that gave you so much enjoyment?'

'What one does in the English countryside at this time of year, I expect—walk, ride, read a little on wet days, converse with Cousin Jennifer.' Thea studied her fingernails in rapt concentration.

'It sounds fascinating.'

'Yes.'

'I see.' Lady Drusilla tapped her fingers on the dressing table. Thea was as tight-lipped as an oyster, but something had occurred. Something momentous. She looked well enough, perhaps a little distracted. Tense also, by the evidence of her fingers, which she had now clenched into admirable fists as she tried to keep her mama at bay. In good health—although Thea was rarely otherwise—but with no bloom, no sparkle. And not sleeping well. The lady frowned at her daughter's image. Lady Drusilla would try again.

'Agnes had a fall, I understand.'

'Indeed. A broken bone in her wrist.' For the first time a little anxiety touched Thea's carefully bland expression. 'But it was set with great skill and now Agnes says that she suffers no pain, although it is still stiff, of course. She insisted that she was fit to travel and seems to have no lasting ill effects.'

'And the bruise to her temple? Was that acquired on the same occasion?'

'Yes.'

'So how did poor Agnes come by these unfortunate injuries?'

The reply came with the swiftness of truth—or a carefully-thought-out plan of evasion. Lady Drusilla had no doubt which of the two 'The paving stones in Cousin Jennifer's garden were uneven and slippery after a shower of rain. It was a most unexpected accident. Cousin Jennifer was quite anxious.'

I imagine! 'I see.' Lady Drusilla gave up on her daughter, but determined to have a detailed conversation with Agnes Drew.

But Agnes with an eye to her mistress's fine-drawn features, and her knowledge of the sleepless nights that caused Thea to prowl her bedchamber in the early hours, kept her own council. No point in worrying Lady Drusilla and drawing Thea into that lady's line of fire. And of course Agnes could say with all honesty that she herself had never been to Burford Hall in her life.

So Thea entered once more into the round of pleasure offered by the London Season with apparent enthusiasm and carefree enjoyment. She was soon seen riding in Hyde Park, early in the morning and also at the hour of the fashionable promenade, although not on her usual grey mare. Sometimes she could be met when tooling her mother along the open carriageways in a smart tilbury with a fine highstepping bay gelding between the shafts. The deluge of invitations for the returned débutante ensured that she graced any number of parties, soirées and drums. The Exhibition at the Royal Academy found her in attendance with Lady Beatrice Faringdon and the Countess of Painscastle, who had welcomed her back with easy affection and a deep concern. She danced until dawn and waltzed at Almack's with the Earl of Moreton, that particular gentleman both flattered and entranced by the return of the lady who had engaged his affections—Thea soon found herself the unwelcome recipient of flowers, books, a fine pair of gloves.

And could not but be overcome by a sharp guilt that she should be encouraging so honest a gentleman when her heart was in the keeping of another.

Lady Drusilla saw events moving in the exact direction that she had hoped and prayed for. Lord Nicholas Faringdon was fortunately no longer the object of Theodora's affections. He had not been seen in town for some time and there was no suggestion that he would return. Meanwhile Theodora's mama would wager any money that the Earl would declare himself within the month—in excellent time for them to arrange a most fashionable marriage before she and Sir Hector went on to St Petersburg. Thea would be well settled at last. Thus she informed Sir Hector of the delightful prospect, waving aside any objections when he expressed his undoubted satisfaction, but hoped that his wife would be kind enough to consider the state of his purse strings.

And Thea resigned herself. She liked the Earl well enough. Without doubt he would prove to be a most attractive and generous husband to satisfy the demands of all but the most exacting of young ladies. But the Earl's face was not the face that troubled her dreams and robbed her of her appetite. His voice was not the one to shiver over her skin when she remembered his words of love and desire. The sight of his distant figure in a ballroom or at a reception did not bring an instant flush of warm colour to her cheeks. And his presence was not the one to steal her breath—or reduce her to burning indignation against all self-opinionated, arrogant and impossible members of the male sex.

If the interested household at Aymestry Manor considered Lord Nicholas to be a man in torment, they would not have been in any way surprised to discover that *that* was exactly the opinion formed by the Countess of Painscastle when she met Nicholas later in the month in Grosvenor Square. Judith eyed him speculatively as he descended the steps of the Faringdon town house and approached where she stood on her own doorstep, having returned from a visit to Lady Beatrice. She sent her nursemaid on into the house with the baby and waited. Judith had not thought that Nicholas was back in town. Although no one could have faulted his bow or his general address when he halted before her, he did not look entranced by the prospect of a few days in London society—or the pleasure of her own company, for that matter. Indeed, his lips were set in an uncompromising line and his eyes did not smile. After a few weeks of Thea's brittle companionship, Judith believed that she knew the reason why.

What on earth is wrong with you two?

Since she knew that she would get a short answer if she asked the question of either of them, she decided to try a little cousinly manoeuvring.

'Nicholas. I did not know you were in town.' She gave him her kid-gloved hand to kiss and beamed at him, ignoring his lack of response. 'Does Mama know?'

'No. This is not a social visit.'

'Oh, business!' She wrinkled her nose. 'I am entertaining next week. Will you come?'

'No.'

'So what has happened to ruffle your feathers, Nick?'

'Nothing other than a trivial misunderstanding.'

'Oh.' *A trivial misunderstanding, indeed!* Judith was not getting far here. She would try another tack.

'Why are you here? What has dragged you away from Burford?' She tapped his arm before he could respond. 'Do try for more than a yes or no this time, dear Nicholas!'

At last he smiled. 'Forgive me, Judith. I am ill humoured, but you should not have to suffer the consequences. I have been to Tattersalls. Horses for sale, you understand.'

'Ah.' *Perfect!* 'Then you must come and talk to Simon. I believe he will part with his winning mare at last if the price is right.'

'I may just do that.'

'He's over at Painscastle at present'—and Nicholas was not to know that the Earl was probably sitting in the library here in Grosvenor Square with his feet comfortably propped on a footstool and a glass of burgundy in his hand—'but will be here tomorrow. Come in the afternoon. We will have tea and you can tell me what makes you such dismal company.'

Nicholas winced at the prospect. 'I believe that we can find something more entertaining to discuss. But, yes, I will be there.'

So now all Judith needed to do was to ensure that Simon be elsewhere (for there would be no opportunity for the discussion of horseflesh, if Judith had any say in the matter) and that Thea present herself for tea at exactly the same time as Nicholas arrived. Surely all the pair of them needed to do was to meet in relaxed surroundings where they could talk and sort out their differences. Two intelligent and attractive individuals who anyone could see were meant for each other. And once they had decided that the estrangement between them was not so serious as could not be remedied, then they would surely forgive her for interfering in their private affairs.

Besides, Judith decided as her worried gaze followed Nicholas to the entrance to the square, she was willing to risk all if it would wipe away the bleak unhappiness in their eyes when they thought no one was looking!

* * *

If they can only meet again.

Judith paced her withdrawing room on the afternoon of the following day, awaiting her two guests, who still lived in blissful ignorance of her devious intent.

I am certain all can be mended.

She was certain of no such thing. Theodora was undoubtedly enjoying the gratification of being one of the most sought-after débutantes of the Season. Her stamina was remarkable. But sometimes, when thinking herself unobserved, she was so sad. As if her heart was cold within her breast, untouched by the compliments and flattery, weighed down by its own secret sorrow. As for Nicholas! The expression on his face the previous day, before he noted his cousin watching him, had been both preoccupied and grave, austere even. Judith had never seen him look so *distant*.

She shook her head, refusing to accept the estrangement. All they needed was an opportunity to talk undisturbed. Which she had duly arranged. Now it was up to them. So why did she feel so uneasy? She had plotted the visit, in close discussion with her butler. Simon was instructed to be anywhere but Grosvenor Square for the duration of the afternoon. Thea was not to be announced, but instead allowed to come up alone as a close friend might, which would give Nicholas no chance to think of excuses to neither see nor speak to the lady. Unless he was prepared to forgo good manners and beat a retreat. Most unlikely!

What could possibly go wrong?

Nicholas arrived promptly as arranged. Relaxed, amiable, charming, somewhat more forthcoming than on the previous day, he put himself out to entertain and indulge Judith in her love of gossip. But the shadows were still present to add a gloss of maturity to his features. Judith found herself glancing towards the door, her fingers clasped tightly in her lap to still their fidgeting.

'Expecting someone, Ju?'

'Why, no.'

'Simon, perhaps? As that *was* the purpose of this visit, if you remember.' Nicholas smiled indulgently, having no confidence in his cousin's powers of recall.

'Simon should be here within the half-hour,' Judith assured him with a discreet lowering of lashes. 'I advised him most strictly.'

A light knock sounded. At last! Judith silently cursed the deep flush that rose to her cheeks, to contrast with her russet curls. The door opened.

'Your butler was very accommodating this afternoon, Judith. He told me to come up and announce myself. Perhaps he no longer disapproves quite so—'

Theodora came to an abrupt halt just inside the door. A delectable picture in a deep blue velvet spencer and silk bonnet trimmed with matching flowers and ribbons, her hands encased in a little sable muff against the chill breeze outside. It was nothing to the instant chill in the room. All the vivacity in her face fled, as if a bright candle had been snuffed out. The blood drained from her fair skin, leaving her pale, almost fragile.

'Why, Thea—' Judith jumped to her feet, her voice a little breathless '—is it not delightful? Look who has just come to town.'

Beside her, Nicholas, too, rose to his feet. It was impossible to read any expression there.

'My lord.' Thea inclined her head a very little. She did not smile. It was almost as if she were holding her breath.

'Miss Wooton-Devereux.' Nicholas executed a perfect bow, equally controlled. Equally severe.

And that was the end of their communication. Judith found herself standing between them, taken aback by the bleak divide.

'Thea…' Judith swallowed and launched in to her prepared speech '…Nicholas has just been telling me that he intended to call—'

'I am quite certain that Lord Nicholas told you no such thing.' Judith stammered to a halt. 'But I know that—'

'No, Judith. I know for a fact that Lord Nicholas has no intention of renewing his acquaintance with me. He has made the decision, and kindly informed me of it, that I am quite beneath his notice—my birth, my morals and my family all conspire against me. How strange that I was not previously aware of it.'

Judith looked desperately to Nicholas for help. Surely this could not be true!

'I am amazed,' Thea continued, 'that Lord Nicholas has not apprised you of my many sins. I expect that he would not consider me fit to be your friend.'

'No, Miss Wooton-Devereux, I have not in any way broached the matter to which you refer.' Now Nicholas intervened in clipped tones, to come to Judith's rescue, but not in any manner likely to reassure her of a mere trivial misunderstanding that might be healed—or to soothe the decidedly angry lady before him. 'It would be beneath my dignity to discuss with anyone such an unfortunate situation as developed between us.' He bowed again with magnificent disdain.

'*Unfortunate situation?* If that is how you wish to continue to read it…' Thea raised her brows, hostility in every line of her body.

'I have no reason to read it differently. Our differences are plain. And nothing, as far as I am aware, has occurred since we last communicated to cast a more acceptable light on them.'

Thea concentrated on breathing. Could this be the lover who had held and kissed her? Who had declared his love and desire in so splendid a fashion that she would willingly cast all caution to the winds and lay naked in his arms?

'I have not lied to you, my lord.' All she could do was to repeat her previous assertions. 'I have done nought with the intention of causing you any harm.'

'So you say.'

'I do. And I took your ill-timed advice. I have been to Whitchurch. I now have reason to see the…the *unfortunate situation* between us very differently.'

There was a little pause in the room, the tension close to snapping point with Judith still looking from one to the other in unabashed horror. Was this really happening in her withdrawing room?

'So you have been to see him! It does not surprise me.' Nicholas's smile was cold and hard and bitter.

'Yes. I told you that I would.'

'And he told you *his* version of events.'

'He told me how he interpreted the events that occurred between you, between his family and yours. Since you will not discuss it, my lord, I have to take his word on trust. I have no evidence to prove him either a liar or a charlatan. I should tell you that his description of events does not flatter the actions taken by you or by your brother.'

She ignored the gasp from Judith.

'It would not, of course.' A sneer curled Nicholas's mouth. 'And you will believe it.'

It felt to Thea that she was struggling through deep, dark water, swirling weeds grasping at her limbs to drag her down even deeper. Was there no way out of this morass of accusation and counter-accusation, when her heart cried out for one word of love from him, one softened look of sympathy and acceptance? Yet she kept her spine straight, her chin raised. She would not weaken before him.

'Whatever happened in the past, does not involve me—has never involved me. I did nothing to bring harm to you or to those you love.'

'Your family name is harm enough.' There it was again. The simple statement of indisputable fact that would separate them irrevocably, whatever arguments Thea could find to use in her own defence. It was hopeless.

So be it. She forced her cold lips to form the words.

'Since you continue to distrust me, my lord, to misrepresent my actions, to reject all that was said and promised between us, there is little point in me remaining here.'

'Thea…' He almost stretched out a hand to her. For an instant Nicholas thought, although of course he must be mistaken, that there was a sheen of tears in Thea's beautiful eyes.

'No.' She blinked the forbidden moisture away. Definitely mistaken! 'You have explained your position with perfect clarity. I understand and accept.'

'Thea, listen…' Forcing herself into action at last, Judith

would have taken hold of her hand to pull her forward into the room. 'Don't go like this—let me—' Anything to prevent her leaving in this fashion. Judith had no doubt at all of the hastily disguised sparkle of tears.

'No. Forgive me, Judith, if I do not stay.' The composure was quickly back in place, grief sternly governed. 'Mama is expecting me. And then I have an engagement to visit Kew Gardens with Lord Moreton. I am sure you will accept my apologies. And for bringing so much unpleasantness into your home.'

'If you must, of course…' Judith frowned her distress.

'My lord.' A frigid little curtsy in his direction from Miss Theodora Wooton-Devereux, all formal protocol, gained by years of experience in the Royal Courts of Europe. It was a masterpiece. 'Perhaps you will explain to your cousin the futility in setting up any future meeting between us.'

She hesitated at the door, turned back. And looked at him once more, her clear gaze holding his. Her voice was low, but she spoke without hesitation. No one could doubt her sincerity. It shook Nicholas to the core as the words struck home. 'I loved you, Nicholas. You are the only man I ever loved. It hurts me— and my pride—to discover that you are just one of those arrogant Faringdons who will ride roughshod over any who do not measure up to your superior notions or opinions of your social rank and status. It is a damnable situation.' She did not even wince at borrowing from Sir Hector's vocabulary. 'You broke my heart, Nicholas. And I did not deserve it.'

And she left the room. Her firm footsteps echoed down the polished treads of the staircase, followed by the echo of soft voices as she addressed Agnes Drew in the entrance hall.

'What?' Judith found her voice at least and wheeled to face her cousin, accusation in every gesture. 'What did she mean— about her birth—her family? Surely there is no question over her birth. She would seem entirely suitable for a Faringdon bride.' She fisted her hands on her hips, looking remarkably like Lady Beatrice. 'I understood barely half of that! What have you done to her, Nicholas? And when? Surely you have not seen her since you left town last? What can you possibly have said to her?' She lifted her hands and let them fall in frustration. 'In fact, I don't understand *any* of this!' she amended.

Nicholas flung away to the window to see Theodora walk out of the Square, Agnes in attendance, no hint of the ravaged emotions that tore at her in her graceful deportment and proud carriage of her head. He remembered the words she had used, the deliberate tense. She had *loved* him. And he had destroyed that love. Deliberately and effectively. Because she was a Baxendale. He should have felt satisfied, relieved that he had escaped the clutches of that accursed family. But in so doing he had hurt her, which rent his own heart to rags. His fingers clenched round the delicate jewelled circle still in his pocket. He should have restored it to her. What possible reason had he to keep it from her? But he could not. It was the only reminder that he loved Theodora and had once believed that she loved him. He turned his head away from the sight of her, his reactions more than a little compromised.

And he turned on Judith, the nearest target on which to vent his anger. 'Why in God's name do you instantly consider me to be at fault?'

'She was so unhappy, Nicholas.'

'And I, I suppose, am rejoicing?' All the icy control was gone. Judith watched the stormy emotions. Oh, yes, he loved her. He wore his passion for Theodora like a dark cloak, all-embracing, shrouding all other emotions.

'No. You are not,' she admitted in softer tones. 'But how could you bear to see her leave like that? Your words were so cruel. I would not have thought it of you, Nicholas.'

'It has to be. There are circumstances here of which you know nothing. Let it go, Judith. And learn from this distressing situation. It will be as well if you do not interfere—don't, for God's sake, try to bring us together again—for my sake and for Theodora's.'

'But I was so certain that you liked each other,' Judith persisted, guilt-ridden that she might have caused even more distress. 'More than liked—if you could only get over whatever separates you. Do let me talk to Thea. I thought you loved Thea, Nicholas. I still think it. I think that you have lost your heart to her completely.'

'Ha!' The laugh was harsh and brief, a mere baring of gritted teeth. 'Perhaps I have. But no—' as Judith's face lit with hope '—don't get involved. It is beyond healing. You must accept it— and allow us to have our secrets. What is there to be gained by going over the same rough ground again and again? I am tired of it all.' And indeed she saw the pale shade of exhaustion around his mouth, the disillusion and regret.

And on that bleak pronouncement, he left, for once no easy companionship between the two.

Judith was left to ponder the results of her meddling. So much hurt and anguish. And yet, when Thea had entered the room, such fire between them. It had leapt to bridge the space, burning all before it. If that were not love…! But then the flames had been extinguished, ground into ashes beneath, it would seem, Nicholas's careless and cruel heel. Judith was forced to consider that there was indeed no hope. No future. And she grieved for her cousin and her friend. Because without doubt there was a passion there that had been wilfully rejected, for what reason she did not know and could not guess.

Chapter Twelve

Some days later Judith woke to a familiar cloud of dark depression. She sat in her bed with her cup of hot chocolate, blind to the attractive picture she made against the pale green furnishings, finding no pleasure in her plans for the day ahead. The brief but explosive liaison between Nicholas and Thea was at an end. She had finally to accept it, still shocked by the anger and bitter recriminations that had assaulted her ears. Furthermore, Judith was now sworn never to interfere again. And even if she did, what possible hope was there?

She sighed at the collapse of all her planning. But Thea would become the Countess of Moreton in the fullness of time. And Nicholas would probably marry some hunting squire's daughter with no fashion sense or desire for town life.

How depressing!

As she placed her cup and saucer on her nightstand to pick up a sheaf of invitations, her depression was interrupted by her personal maid.

'My lady…'

'What is it, Martha?'

'There is a visitor, my lady. A lady…'

'At this time of day? Tell her I am not available. I am amazed that you would even consider—'

'It is a Mrs Russell,' Martha interrupted before her ladyship could get into full flow. 'She says it is of the utmost urgency that she speak with you.'

'Mrs Russell?' Judith's mind went blank. 'Do I know a Mrs Russell?'

'She is definitely a lady, madam. And most insistent.'

'Very well, I will get up. Show her into my boudoir, Martha. Ten minutes.'

Mrs Russell?

When Judith eventually emerged into her boudoir a little after half an hour, in a ruffled and lace-trimmed wrap, it was to see a fair, slight lady sitting on the edge of her day bed, certainly not at ease, and holding the hand of a robust lad of some five years who was barely containing his energies amidst such feminine surroundings.

Judith halted. Then surged forward with a little cry. 'Sarah. Oh, Sarah.'

'Judith. I know it is unforgivably early—I am so sorry…'

'No, no. I am delighted. I did not realise—I have never thought of you as Mrs Russell…' Judith flushed at the less than tactful admission. 'Oh, Sarah, I did not mean…'

'I know. The name of Baxendale has a terrible lasting quality, does it not, in the Faringdon household?'

'Nonsense! I am so pleased to see you. And John. Let me look at you! How you have grown. You were quite a baby when I saw you last.'

The two ladies embraced with a few sentimental tears. John squirmed away from the kisses. Judith laughed and told Sarah of her own entrancing infant whom she must see and admire in a little while. Another pot of hot chocolate was ordered and John was dispatched to the nursery with a willing nursemaid, who promised him a sugared biscuit if he were good.

'Now!' Judith sat herself down in a welter of ruffles beside her visitor. 'Tell me all. What on earth are you doing here? I had no idea of your return. Is Eleanor well? The baby?' Questions flooded out in typical Judith style. Knowing her hostess of old, Sarah decided to answer all the questions first.

Finally they were exhausted. 'So Why are you here? I had thought that you would remain in New York.' Judith angled her head. 'I believe you said that it is urgent—and here have I been gossiping on…'

'It might be. It seemed to me that you were the most suitable person to approach…' Sarah bit her bottom lip in a nervous little gesture which Judith remembered well. 'First I need some information. Does the…the relationship between Lord Nicholas and Theodora Wooton-Devereux still exist?'

'How did you know about that?'

'Mrs Stamford is a useful source of gossip.'

'Ah!' Judith returned Sarah's wry smile. 'But no, it does not. The attraction is at an end.'

'Thank God! If they never became deeply attracted, the damage can not be as great as I feared—'

'No…it is a tragedy!' Judith interrupted. 'You do not understand. They are made for each other. So in love—you would not believe unless you saw them together. But there has been some terrible disagreement. I cannot imagine—and Nicholas will not explain. There is no remedying it. They are both so unhappy—it is all very lowering—and Thea—she is my particular friend, you understand—is pretending that she is quite *happy*. And she is nothing of the sort! She is quite worn down by it, although she would be the last to admit it. Nicholas has taken himself back to Burford in total gloom and despondency. I despair, Sarah. It is not a relief at all!'

'So you say that Nicholas is back at Burford?'

'Yes. Or at Aymestry. He and Thea had a spectacular argument in this very house not a week ago.'

'And the lady? Is she still in London?'

'With her parents in Upper Brook Street. Allowing herself to be courted most assiduously by the Earl of Moreton.'

Sarah appeared to think rapidly over the news and with no degree of pleasure as she picked at the fingers of her kid gloves. Finally she looked up.

'Are you quite certain that they love each other?'

'Why, yes. Not a doubt in the world.'

Sarah nodded as if she had come to a decision. 'Judith. Will you help me?'

'Of course.' Judith waved aside any objections. 'Now, what is it that you wish me to do?'

'I need to meet Miss Wooton-Devereux.'

'You do?' Judith put down her cup and saucer in surprise.

'Yes. It is essential, especially if there is a serious rift. Can you arrange a meeting between us? Where I can talk to her?'

'Yes. No difficulty at all. I will invite her to come here this very afternoon.'

'It may be that I can put things right between her and Nicholas. Or at least warn her—'

'I doubt it.' Judith huffed her displeasure. 'Thea is flirting madly and Nicholas damning all women to perdition, I expect.'

'But I must try. I fear that I may have been the cause of their rift. And if Theodora is innocent… Well, Theodora needs to know.'

'Know what? What is she innocent of? I declare that you are as bad as Nicholas!' She leaned over to catch Sarah's hand in hers, concerned by the lady's distress. 'Why do you need to see her? How can you help?'

Sarah fixed Judith with her calm gaze, returning the clasp of her fingers. 'I need to see her because Theodora Wooton-Devereux is my sister.'

'What?' It was almost a squeak.

'Her name is Sophia Mary Baxendale. She is my sister.'

'Well!' Judith sat back, lips parted. 'I did not know you had a sister!'

'Nevertheless…'

'And so she is also sister to Edward. Well, now! So that explains…' Judith had picked up on the nuances of the relationship with remarkable speed.

'Yes, it does. Because if Theodora's relationship with Edward would not cause a rift between her and Nicholas, I do not know what would. And I, wrongly as it may be, informed Nicholas of the connection through Eleanor's letter to him. I need to discover from her…' Her words dried, her eyes dropped before Judith's inquisitive glance.

'What?'

'It shames me to admit it—but I need to discover if my brother has had any hand in these events, using Theodora as he once used me. Or if she is an innocent, caught up in a cruel twist of fate. Whatever I discover, my sister needs to know the truth about our brother. It is not beyond belief, is it?'

'No.' Judith rose to her feet to stride to the window and back with a stirring of ruffles, in some agitation. 'We know of what Edward is capable. But I would never suspect Thea of being involved in anything unseemly.'

'Unseemly? Edward's actions were far more than unseemly, if you recall. And very manipulative.'

'True.'

'And also, as you most assuredly recall, I too became involved! I became as guilty as Edward in that disgraceful deception. There is no guarantee that Theodora is blameless, that she has not been drawn into my brother's web of deceit.'

'Oh, Sarah.' Judith sank down beside Sarah again, hugged her in remorse at the unhappiness that had begun to resurface. 'You were never as guilty as Edward. How could you be? Oh, dear! How tangled it all is.'

'Yes. And I must do all I can to stop Thea falling into any mischief, now or in the future, dreamed up by my brother.'

'I think it may be too late.' Judith admitted with a rueful look. 'Thea said—now, what was it?—she said, "I have been to see him." I did not understand at the time. But it made Nicholas angrier than ever.'

'Oh. I imagine it would.' Sarah nodded. 'It is even more imperative that I speak with her.'

'Well! It is easy enough to arrange.' Judith rose again to pick up pen and paper. 'But how is it that she is your sister? Perhaps you would like to tell me a little more of these amazing events

while we have something stronger to drink than this chocolate.
Perhaps a little ratafia…'

Judith's depression had instantly lifted.

Later that morning Theodora received a little gilt-edged invitation, delivered by hand by a maid who, she informed the lady in breathless haste, had been instructed by her mistress to await a reply. Thea opened it.

The Countess of Painscastle requests the pleasure of Miss Theodora Wooton-Devereux's company this afternoon for tea at 3 o'clock.

Thea tapped the card thoughtfully against her hand. Sat at her little escritoire in the morning room and dashed off a reply before she could change her mind.

Thank you, Judith. But I will not come if Nicholas is to be there. I am certain that it will be better if we do not meet again. Your dear friend, Thea.

She despatched it, only to receive another missive by the same maid some little time later. The handwriting was hasty and informal with one careless blot.

Thea—do not be difficult. Nicholas is back in the country. Imperative that you come at 3 o'clock. Do not disappoint. Judith.

So it was settled.

When Thea walked into Judith's withdrawing room, promptly at three, it was to see her ladyship in deep conversation with another visitor unknown to Thea. They rose to their feet as Thea entered. The lady was older than Thea, in her mid-twenties. Slightly built, fair haired, but not as burnished as Thea's, blue eyes, but not as deep a hue. An attractive woman, quietly dressed, with a calm composure and confidence. She smiled at Thea as if she might know her.

'Thea.' Judith spoke. 'At last. Here is a lady come to see you. From New York. Mrs Russell.'

'I don't…' Thea glanced questioningly at her hostess, but the unknown lady kept her attention.

'I am Sarah,' the lady explained gently. 'Sarah Baxendale. Your sister. And you are Theodora. I am sorry that we have not met until now.'

'Sarah!' Astonishment flooded her cheeks with colour.

'I decided that I needed to come to see you,' Sarah continued, giving Thea time to gather her wits. 'To ensure that you learnt the truth about our family and our past involvement with the Faringdons, not some terrible mischievous version from Edward. And I think it may be that I need to ask your forgiveness.'

'Well!' Thea selected her most immediate thought. 'I asked Edward about you. He said that he did not know where you were.'

Sarah nodded complacently. 'Much as I would expect. Edward lied. He knew that I had gone to New York. We have much to talk about, Thea.'

'I think so.'

Judith went to the door with a quick smile and an encouraging pat on Thea's arm as she passed. 'I will leave you two ladies as I am not needed here. I will be in the nursery.'

'How tactful she is being.' Thea smiled, perhaps a little nervously.

'Yes. Judith has been a good friend to me.' Sarah now took the time to survey her new sister. Her lips curved into a genuine smile of pleasure at what she saw. 'How smart you are. And how beautiful. I think that you are very like our mother.'

'Ah…' Thea laughed lightly, shaking her head at her inability to take in what was happening. 'How difficult this is.'

'It is. And we have no shared memories to help us through it.' Sarah's composed maturity was soothing in itself. 'Come and sit and I will try to explain why I needed to come.'

Thea obeyed, but with a sudden frown between her brows as

her present predicament swept back into her mind. 'You warned Nicholas about me, didn't you?'

'I did. Eleanor wrote the letter.'

'You cannot imagine the extent of the damage it caused.' There was a chill in Thea's voice. Here it seemed, sitting in Judith's withdrawing room, was the source of all her ills.

'Perhaps I was wrong.' Sarah showed little remorse. 'But there were reasons. Good reasons. I was afraid.'

'Then tell me. Tell me about my family's connection with the Faringdons. Because it has broken my heart.' It was spoken quite matter of factly, but it could not hide the sadness in those glorious eyes or the brief flash of blame.

'Of course.' Sarah felt the urge to take Thea's hand as she sat beside her, but resisted. There was a need to build trust between them before this splendid sister would accept any intimacies from her. 'First tell me this—you have seen Edward?'

'Yes.'

'What did he say to you? I presume that you asked him the same question as you now ask me.'

Thea took a breath, bringing all the words to mind. And repeated them to her sister in all their bitter detail. Only coming to a halt, to run her tongue along dry lips, as she recalled the damning final condemnation of the man she loved. 'He said that Lord Henry and Lord Nicholas were content to consign Octavia and her young son to the gutter to safeguard the reputation of the Faringdon name.'

'Thea... What can I say?' Sarah's eyes had widened in distress. 'Is it true?'

'It is all lies. Every word of it.'

'But how can I know that?' It was Thea who stretched out a hand to Sarah for honesty and comfort. 'Judith and Lord Nicholas will not talk of it. And even if they did, their version would perhaps be quite as selective as Edward's. How am I to know what is truth and what is falsehood?'

'I will tell you the truth.' Now Sarah linked her fingers firmly with Thea's, as if the unity between them, of blood and the flesh, would prove her veracity.

'How do I know it? I have only known you for fifteen minutes!'

'You must be the judge, little sister. But what I have to tell you is painful and does not cast me in a good light. It shames me to tell you. But you need to know how Edward is skilled at subterfuge and manipulation. He must not be allowed to use you against the Faringdons. For that is what I feared most in New York, when it was impossible to know what had transpired.'

'That is certainly what Nicholas believes.' Thea huffed a little breath. 'But Edward has no part in this,' she assured. 'I have only met him the once. I did not even know of his—or your—existence until some few months ago when my mother—Lady Drusilla, that is—told me. My meeting Nicholas—that was a matter of pure chance. Or mayhap fate.'

And Sarah believed her as Theodora sat before her, her heart in her eyes. Without doubt, she loved Nicholas Faringdon. 'That is good.'

'But Nicholas would not believe me.'

'No. He was wrong, I know.'

'He would not listen. He was so intransigent. Nothing like the sensitive, compassionate man I thought I had come to know…'

'There are reasons, Theodora.'

So Sarah filled in the missing facts for Theodora. The truth that Edward had so skilfully manipulated. How Edward introduced Octavia as his sister, legally married to Thomas, with a child, at least a year before Thomas's fraudulent marriage to Eleanor. Thus Octavia should be presented to society as the Marchioness of Burford. Edward claimed the whole estate and title on her behalf and that of her son. Which would have disinherited Eleanor and her child, with all the attendant gossip and social ostracism when the *on dit* became public knowledge. Eleanor would be cast adrift with no appropriate settlement for her as party to a false marriage. Far from driving them from the door, Henry and Nicholas had agreed that Edward and Octavia take up residence in Faringdon House here in Grosvenor Square.

'Did Edward have proof of his accusation?' Thea had listened in silent astonishment at this version of events. How outrageous the plot had been!

'Oh, yes. He had all the necessary legal documents. They certainly fooled Mr Hoskins, the Faringdon lawyer. Octavia's brother, a clergyman of dubious habits, was easily bribed into producing the appropriate papers for the marriage and the birth.'

'I see. Octavia's baby—it died, did it not?' Thea still felt a sharp tug of sympathy for the frail figure in the garden at Whitchurch. She held on to it amongst all the turmoil in her brain as her preconceived ideas were destroyed one by one.

'No. It did not.' Sarah's voice had acquired an edge that made Thea note the faint lines of tension around her mouth. 'Octavia never had a child.'

'Then how? How did she claim to be the mother of Thomas's child?' Now she saw a stricken look on Sarah's face.

'Edward used me. And my son. He presented John—my little boy—as Octavia's son. And I…I played the role of nursemaid. As you see, I am not innocent in all this.'

'Oh, Sarah.'

Tears gathered in Sarah's eyes, to roll helplessly down her cheeks. 'I have no excuses. My husband had recently died… I was widowed and without resources. Edward offered me money and a home for my compliance. And, God forgive me, in a moment of despair and weakness, I agreed to go along with his nefarious plan.'

'And Edward could do that?'

'Oh, yes. He had the perfect scheme to feather his own nest from the Faringdon coffers. It was a very clever scheme. It almost succeeded.'

'So how was it foiled?' Thea found herself caught up in the incredible drama.

'Hal and Nick discovered the truth of Octavia's brother. And I…I turned evidence. I spoke out against Edward and told the truth. My conscience would not allow me to do other.'

'And you went to New York.'

'Yes.'

'With Henry and Eleanor.' There was the faintest question in Thea's voice that Sarah could not ignore. A smile lit her countenance as she replied.

'They understood and forgave me, you see. And gave me a home. Hal and Nell gave me a life and hope, with no recriminations or blame for the damage that I helped to bring them.' She held Thea's gaze with her own. 'I love them both. So I must repay them. I must not allow you to be used by Edward to hurt Nicholas.'

'No, Edward did nothing to hurt Nicholas.' Thea sighed. 'I think I have done that on my own without any assistance! I have done a dreadful thing, Sarah—because I did not fully understand. I accused Nicholas of overbearing arrogance and cruelty. Of putting too little value on our love. Of destroying it for a hatred that I could not accept. Now I understand why he detested Edward— the very name of Baxendale. And so he should.'

'Perhaps. But don't exonerate Nicholas too lightly. He should not have been so quick to judge—he should have listened to you.'

'I know. But *I* should have been honest with *him*. I did not tell him that I knew of my birth, so, when Eleanor's letter arrived…my denials did not carry much weight. Sarah—how I wish that we had met before.'

'And I. Do you believe me, Thea?'

'Yes. I do.' Thea realised that she had not one doubt that Sarah's heart-wrenching tale of ruthless and vindictive plotting by their brother was the truth, because, in so doing, she had heaped blame on her own head. On impulse she put her arms around Sarah's slight shoulders and hugged her. 'It must have brought you great pain to relive it all again.'

'I hoped never to have to refer to it again. But sins have a habit of returning to haunt. Now we must try to heal the wounds.'

'Dear Sarah. I think there is nothing to be done and your journey has been in vain. Nicholas will not talk to me—or I with him, I have to confess. Our lives will take different paths. We had our chance at love—and it was not to be. I fear that any hope of love between us is at an end. Can love survive such anguish? I do not know.' Her fingers curled into claws. 'Is it right to hate one's brother? I certainly hate Edward for all the lives he has touched.'

'You are not alone.'

'What will you do, Sarah?'

'Speak honestly to me. Do you love Nicholas still, after everything that has been between you?'

'Yes. For we were both at fault. He fills my sleeping and all my waking moments. Yes, I love him.'

'Then this is what I shall do. I shall go to Aymestry. Tell Nicholas what I know—of your innocence and of Edward's continuing lies.'

'Will he listen?' She looked doubtful.

'I think so. I think I have one argument that he would find impossible to refute. There is one thing I would ask.'

'Of course.'

'Will you come with me? To Aymestry.'

'Yes.' With typical courage Thea thrust aside all her doubts and grasped the one positive opportunity to salve her own conscience and perhaps bring some peace to Nicholas's troubled mind. Her love for him insisted on it. 'I will come with you. I think I must. Whether Nicholas wishes to see me or not, I have my own apologies to make, for I think I cannot live with myself or my lineage until I do. I will not allow Edward to continue to influence my life in any manner. I will come with you to Aymestry. I will ask Nicholas's forgiveness—and if it is his will that we part, then so be it.'

Thea walked slowly back to Upper Brook Street from Grosvenor Square, preparing to inform Lady Drusilla and Sir Hector that she had spent the past two hours in the company of her sister, learning unbelievable horrors about Edward, things no sister should ever have to learn about her brother. Sarah, with her years of knowledge, had recounted the events with calm acceptance of his culpability. For Thea it was all too shockingly new and painful.

Now she knew. All the secrets and tensions that had worked so effectively to destroy her relationship with Nicholas. The perfidy of her brother. The Faringdon pride in their family name and the protective instinct of Nicholas towards Eleanor and her child, the security of the estate in the absence of the Marquis. After a mere two hours in Sarah's company, all was clear.

Thea entertained no doubts concerning Sarah's revelations. On her return from the nursery with Sarah's little boy in tow, Judith had confirmed every word when she knew that Sarah had told Thea everything that was to be told. The Faringdon scandal was thus in Thea's domain. And with it came recognition, explaining Nicholas's intransigence and suspicion. Thea, her Baxendale birth disguised, was most probably implicated, a matter of terrible and inescapable logic. And because she had deliberately hidden the truth of her birth from him, it had provided the final bitter conviction for him.

Oh, Nicholas!

And now Thea found herself committed to going to Aymestry Manor with Sarah. What on earth would that achieve between her and Nicholas? Forgiveness, perhaps. Understanding, of course. Some sense of closure for the whole affair. But love? For a fleeting moment Thea wished that she had not made the impulsive promise to Sarah. Almost retraced her footsteps to tell her sister that she could not go. Really, she could not.

Did love not need deep and fertile soil in which to grow and flourish? All that lay between her and Nicholas was surely hard and stony ground. No sooner had they discovered each other, acknowledged the bright passion that stirred their blood and demanded that they be together, than they had been torn apart by the legacy of Edward's stirring of a deep, dangerous pot of envy and greed, indiscriminately selecting the Faringdons as his quarry. Would this provide sufficient soil for even the most robust shoot to survive?

No. Thea did not relish the prospect of this visit. But as she had told Sarah, she needed to make her peace with Nicholas. Only then could she look forward. And perhaps there could be a contented future for her with the Earl of Moreton—if she were able to banish Nicholas from her mind and her heart.

She really must not dwell on that.

Miss Wooton-Devereux arrived back in Upper Brook Street with no recollection of her journey, thoroughly damp from a persistent drizzle that had begun as she left Grosvenor Square. She winced in discomfort, realising that her little satin slippers were definitely the worse for wear, and untied the ribbons of her bonnet with clammy fingers. A vivid memory caused her to halt on the first step of the staircase, of that previous glorious occasion when she and Nicholas had been caught in the storm. Soaked to the skin, it had not seemed a matter for depression at all. She flushed a little at the intimate pictures in her mind. But now? Why, even the clouds wept in unity with her, she decided, as she surveyed the limp ostrich plumes of her bonnet with dismay.

Chapter Thirteen

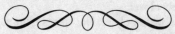

Four days later Sarah and Theodora and also Agnes Drew, whom Lady Drusilla had insisted accompany them to stand guard against all unforeseen dangers on the journey, stood in the familiar entrance hall at Aymestry Manor before a surprised Mrs Grant. The housekeeper's face broke into an instant smile.

'Miss Thea. And Mistress Drew. What a pleasure.' She peered closely at the third lady. 'It's Mrs Russell, isn't it? Well, now. We were not expecting you. But come in, come in. How is your little boy, madam?' She remembered Sarah from her living at Burford Hall with Henry and Eleanor, when she had on occasion visited Aymestry Manor.

'John is well and growing. I have left him with the Countess of Painscastle in London since I anticipate this visit being very brief. He still talks of you, Mrs Grant.'

'Does he enjoy gingerbread pigs as he used to?'

'He does.' Sarah laughed. 'I will tell him that you remembered him.'

'Of course. Now, was it Lord Nicholas you wished to see?'

'Yes.'

Mrs Grant shook her head. 'His lordship must not have known. He's over at Burford. Been there all week. But come into the parlour where there is a fire and I will bring tea.'

They did, grateful for the warmth and comfort. It had been a relatively easy journey made in style, thanks to Sir Hector's post chaise, but for Thea fraught with anxieties. She had worked hard to keep her spirits and her confidence high. Soon all would be put to rights, with Sarah standing as her friend. And then… Well, she would wait and see. Her heart beat rapidly at the prospect of seeing Nicholas again, but her palms were damp with nerves. She pressed them surreptitiously against her muslin skirts, ashamed of her lack of composure as the end of the road—and Nicholas's presence—grew closer.

And now he was not here. Her spirits plummeted to the level of her little kid boots.

'Do you expect his lordship to return?' Sarah asked Mrs Grant when the housekeeper returned to usher in a maid carrying a large tray.

'Why, no, madam.' She busied herself with the china and tea caddy, selecting a key from the chain around her waist. 'Probably not until next week. There are horse sales in Hereford, I believe. And the assizes in Leominster in two days.'

The tea was made and the ladies left to drink it, Mrs Grant assuring them that his lordship would wish them to remain at Aymestry for as long as they desired.

'What do we do now?' Thea turned to her sister. She felt very much an interloper in this house where she had not been invited, where it was very possible that she would not be made welcome. Sarah had no such qualms about their taking up occupation.

'We follow Nicholas to Burford, of course.' Sarah's decisiveness sometimes sat at odds with her apparent but deceptive fragility. 'We cannot sit here and wait.'

'No.' In a moment of chicken-hearted weakness, as Thea castigated herself, the lady thought that she would rather do just that. And found herself forced to admit it with a deep sigh. 'Sarah—I fear the outcome. I have ridden across the deserts of Syria and explored the ruins of more ancient cities than you could imagine—but I fear a meeting with Nicholas. How can that be?' Her eyes flashed with something like annoyance or even anger at her shameful weakness. 'It is so frustrating and not a little humiliating. That one man should reduce me to such cowardice. I would rather face a whole band of desert robbers. Or even the Maidens—and they were frightening enough. As if the blame is all mine—which it certainly is not! Nicholas was overbearing and insensitive—and I have no idea why I should care what he thinks or says! Or even if he wishes to see me. Indeed, I think I should go home now!'

'I think it has something to do with the nature of love!' Sarah smiled, acknowledging her sister's dilemma with deep compassion. 'So here is my plan. Stay here with Agnes. I will take the coach, go on to Burford and attempt to talk some sense into his lordship! Tell him that you are waiting here with the best of intentions. How he could believe that you could be in league with Edward I will never understand! Then, when he is in possession of all the true facts, it will be up to him to make the grand gesture. You have come all the way from London to acknowledge your guilt, as you see it, although I cannot agree with you. The least he can do is travel the few miles from Burford to Aymestry. But do not yield too quickly, Theodora. In my opinion, it is good for a man who is used to wielding authority with ease and a high degree of success to be put under some pressure and be unsure of the outcome. And Nicholas is certainly more authoritarian than many!'

'How devious you are, dear Sarah.' Theodora chuckled, her perspective somewhat restored by her astute sister. 'I think you understand Nicholas very well.'

'Not devious. Determined.' Sarah raised her fair brows. The family resemblance was suddenly clear. 'And don't forget that I lived in the same house as Nicholas for a little time. He was younger then, but he has always had what might be described as a strong character and a flair for getting his own way. As do all the Faringdon men. But I have a strong affection for him. He was very kind to me when life was difficult and my self-esteem was at its lowest ebb, and he never once blamed me for—' She caught herself up on the unhappy thoughts. 'But that is long ago now. I want the best for both of you. I am of the opinion that it would be better if I see Nicholas when you are not present. Then I need not mince my words.' She took Thea's hand in both of hers and pressed it warmly. 'Don't worry so. Mrs Grant will look after you very well. I think you will not have long to wait.'

'Well!' As Sarah left the room to continue her journey, Agnes rose to her feet to enquire about a room for her mistress, a thoughtful expression on her face. 'A forceful lady—crafty, even—in spite of appearances to the contrary. I can well believe that she is your sister, miss!' She turned her head as she reached the door, a little smile deepening the lines on her face. 'I don't give much hope for Lord Nicholas if that one has her way. With both of you hunting him down, the man does not stand a chance.'

'Indeed, dear Agnes, I hope not.'

'I think there is no need for you to lose any more sleep over it, Miss Thea. It would not be good for it to affect you looks, now would it? I think we should expect Lord Nicholas before the night is much advanced. And then perhaps at last we can all get back to a more placid lifestyle!'

Ignoring the dark mutterings, but none the less accepting the sense of them, Theodora followed Agnes from the room, praying for the success of her sister in persuading Nicholas to see the light.

'I have come here, Nicholas, to illuminate a few basic misconceptions concerning my sister Theodora.' No sooner had she alighted from the coach than Sarah had stalked into the library at Burford Hall, not even waiting to remove her bonnet and gloves. She now stood defiantly in the centre of the room, the light of battle in her eye. The clear gaze that she fixed on Nicholas held a severity, a conviction, of which he had no recollection. New York, it seemed, had allowed the somewhat reticent and self-conscious Mrs Sarah Russell to blossom into a lady with a core of steel. He admired it.

Yet, on this matter he was not to be intimidated.

'Then I am afraid that you are doomed to be disappointed and your journey a wasted one. Sister or no, she is the last person of whom I wish to speak.'

'Nevertheless, I have travelled from New York for this sole purpose. Because I felt that I owed a debt to your family and to my sister. And unless you forbid me the house, I shall say what I feel I must.'

Nicholas discovered with not a little surprise that he had taken a stance behind his desk, as if to put the expanse of polished wood between himself and the lady who had arrived a mere few minutes ago, her impressive post chaise and escort pulling up on the gravel sweep with considerable dash. The last person he had expected to see was Sarah Russell, believing her to be comfortably established on the far side of the Atlantic, probably in domestic harmony with some worthy American gentleman. Yet here she was breathing fire, and, it appeared, hell-bent on taking him to task.

As he watched her with a degree of caution, his thoughts fell into the painful and familiar pattern that he had signally failed to banish. He did not want this…this *interview*. He had persuaded himself that the death of his liaison with Theodora with all its attendant suspicions was a matter for rejoicing. *Almost persuaded!* He felt his jaw clench. It continued to amaze and infuriate him, as every day passed, that his existence without Thea's warm smile and infectious laughter, the slide of her silken skin beneath his fingers, was disagreeable in the extreme. He could not stop thinking about her. Could not stop wanting her. A disease that had got a hold and would not let go! Would it be a lifelong ailment?

Oh, God!

And here was Sarah Russell to stir and reignite the banked sensations even further. From the beginning he set his mind and his will against her.

'Very well. Say what you must—and that can be the end of it. It is of little consequence.' He picked up a sealed document from the desk, one which he had been working on when Sarah arrived, as if this conversation was a mere interruption to his daily routine.

And it would not be an easy conversation, Sarah realised, as she took in the discouraging set of his jaw and his shuttered expression. She assessed him with some interest. Here was a power. Not dormant as in his youth, but tightly leashed. Here in the high-bridged nose, the elegantly carved cheekbones, the decided chin, was not the careless, smiling boy whom she remembered. Nor in the cold hauteur as he regarded her across the desk, brows raised, disapproval in every inch of him. Thea was right. Matters had become dangerously difficult between the two of them.

'I have left Thea at Aymestry, Nicholas,' she informed him before he could change his mind and be tempted to show her the door. And that nugget of information, she was delighted to note, forced him to focus on her and to concentrate on her words. The expression of supercilious boredom had vanished entirely. She took immediate advantage, embroidering the truth a little. 'The poor girl is waiting there, quaking in her kid slippers.'

At Aymestry. Theodora was at Aymestry. His pulse took a fast leap in response. She was at Aymestry, his own home. So close that he could be with her within the hour, could hold her in his arms and claim those smiling lips with his own. His heart would urge him to take a horse and ride through the growing dusk, to throw himself at her feet and ask forgiveness for any false accusation. He took a deep breath against that impulse. For there would lie disaster. His mind, proud and hurt, questioned why she had come, refused any spirit of compromise and so forbade it. But his willpower was severely tested. Nicholas turned his mind back to Sarah, who patiently awaited his response, no sympathy at all in her expression.

'Theodora is not a poor girl. Neither does she quake.' His words were brusque, voice cynical, eyes cold. 'She is the most headstrong female I have ever had the misfortune to meet. There is nothing between us.'

'Nevertheless, she is afraid. Of you primarily, although she would find it difficult to admit to such a weakness. Your possible reactions to her if she had accompanied me here to Burford. Of the depth of emotion that has taken over her life and will give her no peace. But she forced herself to come here because she believes that she wronged you. I cannot think why.' Sarah frowned at Lord Nicholas. 'It seems to me that *you* were far more to blame in all this.'

The document crumpled as his hand clenched. 'Your confidence in me and my judgement of a situation where you were not yourself present is most flattering. Thank you, Sarah!'

She ignored the bitter irony and pushed on, aware only of the controlled emotion in his face and the bleak grey of his eyes, a symptom of unhappiness if she knew anything about it. 'You should have believed her, Nicholas. Her integrity is beyond question. I have known her less than a week, but that is clear to me. She is no more Edward's tool against you than...than...' Suddenly Sarah could not find the words as the horror of the past and her own part in it rolled back to swamp her with regret and shame.

Nicholas sighed, the taut muscles in his face relaxing. 'Than you are now, dear Sarah.' He replaced the manuscript back on the desk, carefully, smoothing it with his hand. The softening of his expression and the deliberate kindness in his words were almost her undoing.

'Yes. That is what I would say.' She took a breath to steady herself again. 'Theodora is innocent, Nicholas. There was no plot between her and Edward. No deceit. The rift in the family a mere month after her birth was final, all connections between the Wooton-Devereux and the Baxendales cut. Even I had almost forgotten my sister's existence until Mrs Stamford wrote to Eleanor about your interest in the lady.'

'Eleanor's mama! I should have guessed.' Nicholas snorted in grim amusement at Mrs Stamford's involvement.

Sarah clenched her still-gloved hands before her, willing Nicholas to listen and believe. 'Thea did not know of her birth until after you had met in London. She was not aware until Lady Drusilla told her of it. Lady Drusilla did not know much of the old scandal, but warned Thea that nothing good would ever come of a relationship between Baxendale and Faringdon—and suggested that it would be best if it were ended before it could become a matter for pain and heartache between you.'

'Ah. Now I understand.' A faint line touched his brow. 'So that is why she tried to end it.'

'I know nothing of that—but it certainly explains why Thea decided no good would come of telling you that Edward Baxendale was her brother. Her mother—Lady Drusilla—had warned her well. You should have talked to her, Nicholas. Indeed you should.'

As Sarah's impassioned words bit, forcing his mind to reconsider, Nicholas prowled to the fireplace. Kicked a smouldering log into life. Returned again to face her, running fingers through his hair, an impatient gesture that almost made her smile. How often had she seen Henry do exactly that when assailed by frustrations and doubts.

'I know,' Nicholas admitted at last. 'I know it. I wish that she had told me. It made me think that…that she had a motive for her lack of openness. Then afterwards, when I had accused her of baiting a trap to lure me into marriage—then it was too late for explanations, for either of us.'

'So I understand.' At last. A hint of regret. Sarah felt for the first time a relaxing of the tense muscles in her shoulders, but still she did not cease her attack. 'You did not explain to her why you should hold the name of Baxendale in such hatred, which left her thinking you to be capricious and unreasonable.'

'No.' He raised his eyes to Sarah's. 'Neither of us was very wise, I think.' His lips curved in a bitter parody of a smile. 'The past casts a long shadow, Sarah, whether we wish it or not?'

'Yes. I too remember the torment Eleanor had to live through.' Sarah at last dropped her eyes from his fierce gaze.

'Forgive me, Sarah. I would not have resurrected all this for the world. I can see that it brings you pain.'

'Yes, it does. I hate the need to remember. I still feel the shame. But the legacy is here before us and we must deal with it.' She could no longer prevent a tear escaping to track down her cheek.

At which Nicholas abandoned his entrenched and distant position to stride round the desk, and took her in his arms as any brother might and kissed her damp cheeks. 'Don't think of it, Sarah. There is no blame attached to you. You have proved your loyalty to this family time and again. You know that you are loved and respected here.'

'Yes.'

He led her to a chair and sat beside her. Leaned forward to rest his forearms on his thighs, hands clasped loosely before him, and set himself to bare his soul.

'What should I say to you? I think—if I am honest—that the portrait you have painted of Thea's innocence is no stranger to me.' For a long moment he dropped his head into his hands. Tempting Sarah to reach out to touch his dark hair in compassion. But now was not the time to weaken. She must push the message home. As if picking up her thought pattern, he raised his head to look at Sarah. The longing in his eyes struck at her heart, even before he spoke. 'I have made such a mess of things, Sarah. You would not believe... When I received Eleanor's letter—it brought it all back. And then everything went wrong, layer upon agonising layer. We said things that would deliberately hurt and tear. Neither of us would step back and reconsider.'

'Headstrong! I knew it!' But there was a smile now in Sarah's voice and a sigh of relief. 'You are both the same.'

'Yes. I fear so. And pride. And the legacy of Baxendale is still too close to ignore. The name is still an anathema,' he admitted, 'however much I might wish to bury it.'

Sarah remained silent for a long moment. She knew exactly how to destroy these chains that still bound Nicholas to the past. And set herself to do it.

'Nicholas—do you love Theodora?'

'Yes. I cannot get her out of my mind. But is it now too late? I fear that I have killed her love for me.'

'Of course you have! That is why, foolish girl that she is, she was prepared to travel all the way across the country, simply to make her peace with you! Have a little sense!' She curbed her impatience at the blindness of men, and hid a triumphant little smile. 'She has so much courage Nicholas. It astounds me.'

'I know. I see the same courage in you.'

'Never! But Theodora… What are you going to do about her?'

'I think it is all beyond remedy.'

'You say the name stands between you. Think about this. Do you have any friendship for me?'

'Of course.' He looked puzzled. 'Do you need to ask?'

'No. Do you trust me?'

'Of course.'

'Then what is the problem?'

'I fear that you have left me wallowing in unrequited love!' At last she saw a glint of appreciation. 'You will have to explain.'

'It is very simple, Nicholas. How you have failed to work it out for yourself is beyond belief. You rejected Theodora, the love of your life by all accounts, because her name was Baxendale.'

'I…' A hint of colour flared along his cheek bones at the re-alisation of how empty and futile and ridiculous it sounded in Sarah's words.

'Of course you did. But I, too, am a Baxendale—or have you forgotten?' She slanted a surprisingly mischievous glance at him. 'If you can trust me and care for me a little, why is loving Thea any different? And you adore her! Her name should not stand be-tween you. It cannot. As a man of logic, you must realise it.'

Nicholas searched Sarah's face as he absorbed her undoubted logic. Then he laughed, as if a weight had been lifted from his heart. 'Sarah… What have I been doing all these weeks? Perhaps I needed you to put it so simply that even a child would see it.'

'Or beat you over the head with it! I wager no one has had the temerity to do so, unless it be Lady Beatrice.' She watched him shrewdly, rewarded by Nicholas wincing in reluctant agree-ment. 'It *is* simple. You love her and she, for some reason which I cannot fathom, loves you. Her name is irrelevant. Besides, she is my sister and I love her and want her happiness. She has de-cided that she can find it only with you. Now if *I* were in need of a husband—' there was a distinct twinkle in her eye '—I would have given the Earl of Moreton more of a chance. He is so much easier to deal with. The Faringdons are never easy!'

She was relieved to see humour creeping back into the stern lines of Nicholas's face to dispel the bleak misery. 'You are a managing female, Sarah. I did not realise it. Moreton does not know of his lucky escape. So I must go to Aymestry, it seems.' He rubbed his hands over his face as if he had just awoken from a dire nightmare.

'Of course you must. What is taking you so long? You should have saddled a horse at least half an hour ago.'

'Will you come?'

'No. I have travelled enough in recent days. And I should most decidedly be in the way.'

'Perhaps.' He kissed Sarah's fingers, then her cheek. 'My thanks are beyond expression. It may be that you have just given me back my life.'

As she accompanied him to the door, Sarah gave him some parting advice. 'If you love her, Nick, don't lose this chance.' She touched his arm lightly, amazed at the courage she had shown this night in speaking so candidly to this most complex of Faringdon men. 'You know how it is between Henry and Nell. You have seen it for yourself. It is beyond magnificent. The affection and the caring—and the blazing passion that only grows with time. If you and Theodora achieve only half of the love that they have, it would be enough for a lifetime. Don't throw it away, Nicholas. You would regret it for the rest of your life.'

Nicholas bent his head, kissed her cheek again in heartfelt gratitude.

As he strode from the house toward the stables, Sarah's words echoed in his mind, clear and strong. So much advice, confirming what he had known all along and been too blind and proud, too bent on revenge, to accept. It was time that he faced the truth and old hatreds were buried. His future happiness depended on it.

At Aymestry Manor, whilst Sarah was taking Nicholas to task at Burford Hall and advising him, much as Lady Beatrice might, on the only course of action open to a man of common sense, Theodora brooded and awaited the outcome. The day gradually drew on into late afternoon as she watched the road with anxious eyes. She could not possibly expect him before dusk. Nevertheless she watched and waited impatiently. Clouds heralding oncoming rain began to gather on the horizon to the west. Time hung heavily. Thea's patience became thinly stretched.

She visited the stables where she became reacquainted with The Zephyr. The beautiful mare bloomed with health, her coat gleaming in the late sun, and seemed perfectly sound as she trotted across the paddock at Thea's voice. Furness was encouraging, already lamenting the loss of the little mare when she returned to Thea's possession. Thea admired the new foals. Played with an enthusiastic litter of spaniel puppies who at least made her laugh and forget her woes.

Still he did not come.

She strolled in the gardens with Agnes, mentally stocking them with her favourite flowers. Aquilegia and hearts' ease, honeysuckle and… and… But what was the purpose in such wishful thinking? She would like to grow herbs and…. No. She must not think of it. It would never come to that if Nicholas decided that her Baxendale connection created too great an obstacle.

And still no sound of hooves on the road or on the track that dropped down through the woods.

Of course he might reject everything that Sarah could lay before him in her sister's defence. Theodora cursed the name of Edward Baxendale in language that would have drawn her mama's deep disapproval.

She took herself to the kitchens out of interest to see Mrs Grant's kingdom. And spoke with the lady, who readily conversed about the running of such a household and the particular likes and dislikes of his lordship, whom she had known since a young boy. So Lord Nicholas disliked sweetbreads, did he? Well, so did she! Thea would have enjoyed the experience if nerves had not begun to flutter with persistent wings in her stomach.

Dusk shrouded the house and candles were lit. Still no Nicholas.

Thea and Agnes shared a meal, neither having much appetite. Then Agnes was sent off to her bed, leaving Thea to pace the library, without even a pretence at finding solace in one of the many volumes that hemmed her in. He would not come. Not now.

Then, at last, noises outside. Muted but just discernible. Hooves and voices. Thea stopped her pacing, gripped the back of a chair with her hands and watched the door.

But no Nicholas. On a hiss of frustration at what could possibly be detaining the man—probably a mare in foal!—she went to the window to peer out. It was dark with the now-heavy cloud covering the moon so she could see nothing. But that was not right! There were figures, black on black, on the carriage drive to the left. And there! A flash of light—and another from torches. And in the light from those torches, Thea was able to see the truth. Figures clad in skirts and shawls. The Maidens. Torches. Now they moved quietly as one led away a horse. Voices deliberately kept low, but there was no doubt in Thea's mind that their presence was a threat and their intent evil. As they disappeared from view towards the stables, Thea fled. First to the kitchens, where by chance Furness was lifting a jug of ale and enjoying a pipe as he exchanged opinions with Mrs Grant.

'Miss Thea?' Mrs Grant immediately rose to her feet. 'Is there a problem…?'

'Master Furness…'

He put down his ale in concern at the lady's wide eyes and breathless state.

'The Maidens are paying us a visit,' Thea gasped. 'I have seen them. Heading to the stables, I would say…with torches—' Before she had finished, Furness was on his feet with the agility of youth and out of the room at a run.

Without thought, Thea followed.

Nick rode to Aymestry, his mind full of Sarah's forthright words. And hope surged through his veins with every mile as he took the track through the woods, despite the falling light. Every instinct persuaded him to reach his manor with all speed. He knew Sarah well enough, had enough experience of the innate honesty that had troubled her conscience and driven her to expose the deceit of her brother. And so he had believed her every word. Thea would be waiting for him. She was entirely innocent, as he must assuredly have known. The shame of his lack of trust crawled beneath his skin, yet the prospect of his loved one quaking made him smile again. What a delight it would be to hold her and kiss her and calm any fears she might have. But he would have to ask forgiveness first, for indeed it was his fault that he had judged her without cause. Surely she would not reject him. If she had come all this way she could not be cold to his advances. He winced under Sarah's biting criticisms. But he could put it right.

Joy leapt in his blood as he rode out of the trees where the track began its descent to the manor. It was late, but not too late. She would be awake, watching for him. A light rain began to spatter on his shoulders, but he would soon be home. He kicked his horse into a controlled canter, making use of his intimate knowledge of the track. But then with an oath reined in, staring forward to where the house nestled in the shallow depression.

Lights. Too many lights. Indeed, they were flickering torches. And shouts. Some crisis had occurred. The possibilities jostled in his mind as the unease grew. And then the truth was clear, for the first tongues of fire climbed into the sky from the corner of the stables, the wing where the mares and foals were kept for their safety at night. The unease blossomed into desperate and fully-fledged panic.

Fire!

The stallions and mares would die if the alarm was not raised. And if the flames got a hold on the stables, they would spread to the house with its plaster and dry beams before anything could be done to save it. His home, where Theodora awaited him.

Nicholas applied his heels to his horse and galloped heedlessly towards the looming disaster.

The scene in the stableyard rushed towards her, swamping Thea with terror, every sensation in her body under instant attack, every instinct to freeze in abject fear or to run for her safety. It was a scene straight from the torments of hell. Flames were already licking along one side of the three wings of wood-timbered buildings, stonework already blackened. Within the enclosed space, illuminated by torches and fire, chaos reigned. Figures loomed and dispersed through the billowing smoke. Shouts and cries of anger and encouragement filled the air. There appeared to be few skirted figures—certainly not as many as when Thea had met them on the road—but in their midst, urging them on with wild, triumphant gestures, was Samuel Dyer.

Violence had broken out between the stablelads and the intruders. Blows falling, from fists and wooden staves and pitchforks, wielded on both sides with bloody intent. A firearm was discharged to her left with a flash of fire and a loud retort, causing her to retreat a step. By the stable door lay the deep and ominous shadow of a body on the floor, friend or foe impossible to tell. And over all, the shrill, heartrending cries of horses in a state of ultimate fear and panic as smoke and flames invaded the stalls.

Furness had already taken command, to set a line of men to bring buckets of water from the stream that tumbled down the slope from the distant woods, and struggle with a cumbersome water-pump. But it was so little and so ineffective compared with the blazing wood and plaster! Thea found herself watching in despair the meagre efforts to quench the flames, thwarted at every step by the Maidens.

Now Furness had turned his attention to the horses. It was imperative to get into the stables, to overcome their terror and liberate them into the paddocks where they would come to no harm.

'Open the doors!' His voice cracked as acrid smoke engulfed him.

The bolts were drawn, the huge doors dragged back.

'Get the mares out—the foals will follow! Turn the stallions loose.'

He and others plunged into the hell of noise and flame within, with little thought for their own safety. Smoke thickened as the dry timbers caught. Sparks flared and blew in the light wind, threatening the house itself. If the house took, there would be nothing they could do.

Thea stood on the edge. Familiar cold settled on her senses. Noise. Violence. Danger. A constant swirl of movement that seemed to draw her in and enclose her into its deadly centre. She knew it all, had experienced it all, and knew her probable reaction to it. It was as if she stood at a distance, outside herself, and watched as the rigid panic assailed her limbs, gripping her chest with iron-tipped claws. She struggled to breathe. She could not move.

Even when a terrified mare was led out, only yards from her, her offspring following, wide-eyed and distressed.

From that safe distance, trapped within her mind, Thea focused on the scene, forcing her conscious thoughts to stay in contact with the horrors she was witnessing. She could not let the horses die in such agony. Or Nicholas's men. Not when she had the power to move her limbs and help. She could not stand by in a fit of useless and selfish panic and let others take the risks.

A stallion was sent out with a hard slap to its neck and rump, with tossing head and rolling eyes, and turned loose to canter off into the darkness.

The Zephyr is in there. Do something! Don't think—just do something!

A group of bodies pushed and swayed between her and the stable, arms swinging. She could hear the grunts quite clearly as the blows made contact. They would not stop her. They must not stop her. She took a breath. Too much at stake. And pushed between, looking neither left nor right, dodging the blows, ignoring a pistol fired close by. She followed Furness into the stable.

'Get out, Miss Thea.' The head groom cast one horrified glance in her direction. 'Too dangerous. No place for you. What his lordship would say if you was harmed…' He coughed in the smoke, wiping a filthy hand over red-rimmed eyes. 'Get out and up to the house.' But he was too occupied to force her to obey.

'No. You need all the help you can get.' She seized a blanket, submerging it in a water trough. 'Wrap yourself in this.' She did likewise. And joined the men struggling to release the horses. Aware only of wildly lashing feet, wicked teeth. It was hot dangerous work. She did not once stop to think what she was doing.

Outside shouts went up from a dozen voices. Matters appeared to be coming to a head, which prompted Thea to make a detour to collect one of the coachman's pistols from the room that stored harness and saddles. She had no idea whether it was loaded or not and did not stop to look. It might serve its purpose and there was no time to do more, certainly not to prime a pistol in the dark. Back outside, the first sight that met her horrified gaze was Sam Dyer with a flaming torch, stooping to apply it to the inner wing.

'Stop.'

By some miracle her voice carried in a slight lull in the general pandemonium. Dyer looked up, torch held high, across the space that separated them.

'Do that and I fire.' The blanket falling from her shoulders to the floor, she held the pistol in both hands and aimed it at his chest.

Dyer halted. Looked at her in amazement. And laughed in terrible mockery—but he lowered the torch.

'A real woman, lads.' He waved to draw the attention of his associates. 'No false skirts here. Get her. Or she blows my head off!' Before Thea could respond or even be aware of those around her in the shifting shadows, the pistol was knocked from her hand to the ground and she was seized from both sides in a rough grasp.

The panic rose within her chest. She could hear her own heartbeat thundering in her ears. Her breathing became tight and difficult.

But surrender she would not.

She struggled furiously, resisted every effort to restrain her. Surprised her captors into letting her go free, with jeers and amused comment, now that they had possession of the pistol. A mere woman who could do no harm. Instantly she dashed across the courtyard toward Dyer, who still held the torch in close proximity to the walls and a pile of straw that would provide superior tinder. What she would do she had no idea. But she could not stand by and watch him burn down Nicholas's home. Dyer caught her by the arm.

'Oh, no, you don't.'

'Take your hands off me!'

'So his lordship is using women to defend his rights now, is he? And a pretty one too.' The grin was sly in the flickering light. 'How does he pay you? In kisses?' He ran his hand down her arm in a terrible intimacy and leered. 'Perhaps you would be willing to kiss me, my lady. If you want me to set you free.'

'Let go! You cannot stop me. I will not let those animals burn to death.' She fought furiously, digging her nails into his hands. 'You disgust me—you have no quarrel with the Faringdon estate. To stop me you will have to either kill me or tie me up!' She brought the edge of her heel down heavily on to his instep, so that he grunted with pain. And looked at her with reluctant admiration. The gilded hair impossibly ruffled. The stylish gown soiled and singed beyond recognition as a creation of Bond Street. Her face smeared with soot, but determination writ clearly on every feature.

'Well, now. A firebrand. Which shall it be then, my lady, a bullet or a rope? It matters little to me.'

'Neither.' The cool voice cut through the heat of the situation. 'I suggest that you take your filthy hands from the lady.'

There in the courtyard stood Lord Nicholas Faringdon, pistol raised and aimed, with far more precision than Thea's earlier attempt, most dangerously at Dyer's head.

'Well, my lord. We did not expect to see you here this night. Come to watch your pretty house burn?' Dyer grinned, gestured at the dire results of his work, full of confident bluster. 'We will be glad to accommodate you.' But he gripped the torch firmly as he kept a wary eye on the icy rage that emanated from the motionless figure before him. Lord Nicholas was never to be underestimated.

'Let her go!' Lord Nicholas snarled. Ignored the blatant threat to his property. 'Or, by God, you may be sure that I shall not miss if you give me cause to fire.'

Thea found herself instantly released. Without a glance at the two men she set about her self-imposed task, running back towards the stable door where a foal was engaged in a full panic, refusing to follow its mother. Grabbing its mane, she pulled and cajoled until it consented to escape into the safety of the darkness after the mare.

The two men faced each other. 'If you shoot me, my lord, it will not save your precious buildings. They'll still go up in flames. As all landlords should, damn their black souls to hell!'

'But you will be in hell first.'

'Would you shoot an unarmed man?' Dyer challenged. 'A man who is fighting for a wage to put bread into the mouths of his family?'

'Perhaps not.' Lord Faringdon seemed to give the matter some consideration. 'But you will pay for this night's work.'

A split-second decision, Nicholas leapt the distance between them, fast and sure, a short left jab to Dyer's ribs, followed by a powerful straight right to his jaw. The man fell to the floor, dropping the torch, as if struck by a blow from a heavy club. When he struggled to regain his feet, his lordship hauled him to his feet and hit him again.

This time he lay still. Until Nicholas, not wasting any further words, dragged him to his feet and summoned two of his lads to take him up to the house, with instructions to lock him in the cellar. Then he was free to turn back to the disaster unfolding before him. To assess the damage and the possibility that the manor house in its entirety would be nothing but a blackened shell by the morning.

The flames still leapt with crackling intensity. Horses were still being brought out. Nicholas strode forward to relieve one of the smaller lads of a recalcitrant stallion. Although the rest of the Maidens had suddenly melted away with the obvious defeat of their leader, their work had been done with terrible efficiency. The walls well lit, flames encroaching onto the roof. Water was still being ferried in a chain, but it was a desperate race against time. Surely the house would catch.

Then the rain began. The threat that had been evident throughout the evening came to their rescue when they least expected it, drenching everyone and everything. Damping down the flames. Nature achieving what they could never have done alone. They stood and watched, in mingled horror and relief, the results of the night's attack.

'Master Furness.' Nicholas turned to his head groom who emerged from the smoke-blackened inferno to stand beside him. 'Be so kind as to get those burning walls pulled down to stop the spread of the flames. Keep damping down those not yet burning. And pray that the rain continues.'

'Thea. Look at you. You should not have risked yourself.' Nicholas pulled her from the soaking mire of the stableyard into the shadows of the dovecote. The doves whirled in silent panic in the dark above their head. 'Are you hurt in any way? You should not—' He bit down on the terror and fury that had gripped him since he saw her in Samuel Dyer's ungentle grip, and drew an unsteady hand over her wet hair in a rough caress.

'We saved them.' Thea found herself holding on to the sleeve of his coat as if her life depended on it. 'The horses—they are all alive, I think. And The Zephyr. I don't know about your people.' Her eyes were wide, her breathing disordered, her clothing beyond repair. But there was no hint of panic about her. Only a wild sense of achievement that they had thwarted the Maidens.

'Thea…' The wet and soot and grime did not matter. His eyes sought her features as if he could not quite believe that she stood safe and unharmed before him. The dangers had been so great. Ignoring her squeak of surprise, he dragged her into his arms and captured her mouth with his in a kiss as hot and fierce as the flames themselves, marvelling at the strength and courage that she had shown. It was an insistent demand, pressing her close from breast to thigh, a unity against those who would threaten and destroy. Thea responded with equal fervour. Faced with possible death and certain destruction, with weakness and surrender, she had stood firm. Here in his arms was life and power—and, she was certain, forgiveness.

Nicholas could not get enough of her. He held on, oblivious to wet and discomfort.

Then sense reasserted itself, the demands and problems of the moment taking precedence, to release her from his close embrace, yet sliding his hands to encompass her wrists, unable to let her go.

'Thank God you are alive.' He touched his lips to her forehead, a tender blessing.

'And you.' Thea spread her hands, fingers wide, against his chest, needing the muscular solidity of him, the firm beat of his heart against her palms.

'The danger was yours. I saw you.'

'And you saved me.'

Their eyes held in the dark, their fingers linked at last.

'I did not panic.' As Thea realised her achievement, her breath caught on a sob. But there was no place for tears. 'I wanted to. I wanted to flee. But I did not.'

'I know. You have all my admiration. I cannot say it.' What a marvellous woman she was. How he loved her.

'I think the rain has saved us.' A soft laugh shook her when Thea became aware of the heavy drops pattering on her head and running down her smoke-smeared face.

'Yes. But now you must go.'

'No.' Her fingers tightened, preventing any separation. 'I will stay with you.'

Nicholas shook his head, gentle but firm. 'Go to Burford, Thea. There is little you can do here now and I have to know that you are safe. I will send someone with you. Take my horse.' When she would still have resisted, he made a plea from the heart. 'Go to Burford for my sake, if not for your own. I could not bear it if you were hurt now.'

'I don't—'

'Don't argue. It will be easier for me if you are not here in all this debris. You have done enough this day.'

'Very well.' She accepted the force of it. She would achieve nothing through dissension.

For a brief moment Nicholas held her close, to imprint her on his mind and body—then led her to his horse, suddenly aware of the shivers that began to attack her in her thin gown now that the dangers which had driven her were finally past. Taking off his own coat, he pushed her arms into the sleeves even as she objected. 'You are cold. You will need this on the journey.' The warmth from his body enveloped her, to soothe and comfort as if his arms were still around her. He helped her to mount before summoning two of the stable lads. His instructions were brief and plain.

'Take Miss Thea to Burford Hall, Sim. Take care of her. Do you understand? Any danger, anything at all that gives you cause for unease, don't fear to use the pistols. And shoot to kill.'

'Yes, my lord.' Sim was already mounted, the pistols stowed away. 'The lady will come to no harm.'

Nicholas watched her go. Watched her turn to look back once, her face a pale blur, before swallowed up in the rain-sodden darkness. So much to say. So little chance to say it. But tomorrow he would.

For now, he walked back into the stableyard to see how much of his property had survived the vicious attack of the Maidens.

Later, much later, once he was certain that all at Aymestry was secure, Nicholas arrived back at Burford Hall. Waiting for him in the entrance hall, in a borrowed lace bedrobe, was Theodora.

'You should have gone to bed.' He spoke softly, the great house silent around them.

'I could not—not until I knew that you were safe.'

He shrugged out of his coat, grimacing at the discomfort, to stand before her, grimy, smoke blackened, wet to the skin from the rain that was still falling. His clothes were in ruin, his hands and face hopelessly smeared. 'I am not fit, Thea—' He halted, as if words failed him.

'Is the house safe? And your people?'

'Yes. The rain was a blessing. Some cuts and bruises. A sore head or two. Singed hair and eyebrows, I expect. But no lives were lost.'

'And the horses?'

'Yes.'

Exhaustion was imprinted on every engraved line on his face.

'What of the Maidens?'

'Dispersed for the moment. Samuel Dyer is spending tonight locked in one of the store rooms off the stables here, with a guard!' The muscles along his jaw clenched. 'I will deal with him tomorrow.'

'And you, my lord?' Despite all that had passed between them, Thea found it impossible to reach out to touch him. Even though she needed to convince herself that he was here and he was safe.

He managed a smile. 'I took no harm.'

The gulf between them appeared to Thea to be as wide as ever. It was not the time to say the words in her mind, but she could wait no longer.

'I am so sorry. I did not mean to lie, but I did not tell you the truth. I never meant to hurt you. I had to come here to tell you that.'

'I know. You have an excellent champion in Sarah.' A weary smile touched his mouth. 'She argued your case most persuasively. And left me in no doubt of her opinion of me!'

'I do not know Edward Baxendale. But I now know the depths of which he is capable. I understand the pain and the hurt he brought to you.'

'Thea…' Nicholas ran his hands through his dishevelled hair with a sigh. 'I have my own apologies to make.'

'You are exhausted.' At last she touched his arm lightly.

'Yes. But I should thank you. You saved my home and the bloodstock from certain destruction. I cannot find the words to express my gratitude—or not tonight, in any event.'

'I could do no other.'

'I saw you face Sam Dyer. I shall not forget it.'

She shook her head. 'You need rest. Go to bed, my lord.'

'I will take your advice.' Yet he could still find the grace to take possession of her hand and raise it to his lips. Then walked slowly to the stairs.

'Good night, Thea. Tomorrow we will talk.'

Which left Thea curiously dissatisfied. But she held to that moment in the stableyard when he had snatched her away from the noise and the chaos for one long moment. Had held her and kissed her as if he would never let her go.

Chapter Fourteen

On the following morning Sarah sat at a leisurely breakfast in
one of the parlours, allowing her mind to drift with possibilities
for the future. Nicholas would claim the bride he so clearly
needed. Soon—she rubbed the crumbs from her fingers with an
inner delight—she could return to London and her darling John.
A little frown settled to mar her brow. For then a decision would
have to be made over what she should do next. Stay in London
or return to New York. Sarah did not know. If she stayed, there
would be the problem of where she would live and how she
would find financial security for herself and her son… But she
would not think of that yet.

Her thoughts were interrupted by Nicholas, who entered the
room to take a seat at the opposite side of the table with a groan
in acknowledgement of his aching muscles.

'I feel as if I have not slept this sennight.'

Sarah studied the faint prints of exhaustion beneath his eyes,
the lines bracketing his mouth, but also saw the absence of tension in his arms and shoulders. Cleansed of all the soot and
grime from the previous night, he looked remarkably at ease despite some evidence of singed hair at one temple. Sarah smiled
across at him, her own anxieties dispersed, then rose to pour coffee when he sank into a chair, placing the cup before him, fight-

ing a need to take him in her arms and offer comfort as she would her son. Instead she seated herself again, elbows on the table, chin propped on her hands to hear the news. 'I heard a brief account of the events, when Thea returned. Is the damage very great?'

'No.' Nicholas stretched and yawned. 'It could have been worse. Far worse, if Dyer had had his way. He has no personal quarrel with me, but in his eyes all landlords are tarred with the same brush.' A shrug, a tightening of the lips, the only comment he would make on the man who had threatened his livelihood. And, far greater in consequence, the life of the woman who was everything to him. At the thought, without his knowledge, Nicholas's fingers clenched around the cup to the imminent danger of the fragile porcelain. 'The house is intact apart from one corner of the roof on the south side, which caught before we could get the flames under control. Thank God for the rain. Without it the whole house would have been a charred ruin by this morning.' He rubbed his hands over his face as if to erase the memory of the hopeless battle against the fire. 'The stables have gone, of course.'

'But Thea said that the horses are safe.'

'Yes.' He shook his head to dislodge the tragic images of what might have happened. 'Thank God also for sympathetic neighbours. William Hawkes has agreed to take the mares and foals for as long as need be—we'll keep the stallions here. And Tom Clifford has offered to collect Dyer and take him off to Hereford Goal before the day is out.' He pushed himself a little wearily to his feet, restless still. 'At present he is locked in one of the storerooms with a guard watching his every move. I shall be relieved to have him away from here in case one of my people is tempted to take a bloody revenge. It was nasty work last night. Lives could have been lost.'

'I hear he already has a black eye and a bloody nose.' Sarah's raised brows begged for enlightenment.

'I know nothing of it.' But Nicholas rubbed the skinned knuckles of his right hand absently.

'No, of course not. I merely wondered if you were as talented with your right arm as your brother.'

'He taught me well.' The soft laugh acknowledged the accuracy of the prompting. 'And Thea. I owe her so much.' Now he looked back from where he stood by the window, face suddenly alight. 'You should have seen her, Sarah. There she stood in a gown as rich as amber, firelight in her hair, her eyes ablaze…' He stopped to savour the memory, his lips drawn back in a snarl as he recalled the pleasure of his personal dealing with Dyer. 'You have a remarkable sister, Sarah.'

Sarah smiled at the dynamic picture. 'Theodora benefited from an adventurous upbringing by Sir Hector and Lady Drusilla. Not by our mother, who could not bring herself to venture into the kitchen if the cook was so much as wringing the neck of a chicken. Lady Drusilla is made of much sterner stuff.'

'I know.' He came to sit again. 'I was so wrong. Last night proved it beyond all argument, beyond all doubts. What it must have cost her to stand within the noise and chaos around her, the men and the horses jostling in fear and panic… She did not flinch. Had no thought for her own safety. She has all my admiration.'

'And you are going to put it right with her, dear Nicholas.' Although she did not understand his reference, Sarah rose to walk round the table and lay a hand on his shoulder.

'Assuredly.'

She watched him with silent sympathy as he came to terms with his own doubts and faults and the enormity of what might have happened, emotions chasing each other across his face before he spoke again.

'I have hated Edward Baxendale with every fibre of my body. I think it is within me to have killed him without compunction for his sins. I would have challenged him to a duel if Hal had not prevented it. He has been the enemy for nearly three years or more, but the passage of time has not lessened that hatred. I despise him today as much as I ever did.'

'I know.'

'And Thea?' Nicholas continued, looking up into Sarah's understanding face. 'Well, she too is a Baxendale. What hope would such a fragile emotion as love seem to have against such destructive power? Against such hatred and bad blood?'

Standing outside the door, Thea listened with mounting horror to the words of condemnation in Nicholas's bleak confession to Sarah. She repeated them in her mind, again, and then again, as if she could not believe that she had heard them. But she had and must accept. Of course nothing had changed. His kiss, his embrace, his heated words of the previous night—she had completely misread them. They had only been in response to the immediacy of fear and shock of fire and violence. And gratitude for her role in the rescue of his precious horses! She was still Edward's sister. That could never be altered. Any warmer feelings, any lessening of the disgust that Nicholas felt towards her, that was simply the result of the desperate circumstances.

It was not love that had coloured his words and actions. Gratitude, perhaps. Obligation. But not love. How could she have allowed herself to so foolishly be mislead? How could *he* have so carelessly, thoughtlessly, allowed her to believe that there was any deeper emotion on his side other than obligation!

Fury surged through Thea, heat replacing the winter cold in her veins. How could he! Before she could change her mind, she pushed open the parlour door, to step over the threshold, to face him.

'Theodora…' Nicholas would have risen to his feet with a smile of welcome and outstretched hand, but was instantly aware that the lady was in no mood for pleasantries or platitudes. Waves of temper shimmered round her. Ice over fire.

'How could you have misled me? How could you have held me in your arms and kissed me? I thought you loved me, Nicholas. And that all could be right between us.' Her voice was low, controlled even, but could barely disguise the flood of anger and despair.

'Thea… No…' Sarah's attempted intervention merely stoked the flames. The flash of Thea's eyes silenced her.

'And now I hear from your own lips that nothing has changed.'

Thea continued to face the man who had captured her heart, toyed with it, and then shattered it. 'Nothing! How could you be so callous—so cruel! You despise me as much as ever—'

'It is not so, Theodora—'

'Do you dare deny it? I heard you tell Sarah… What was it— the fragility of love against—?'

'No… Enough, Thea!' The firm note of authority now crackled in his voice, bringing Thea to a breathless halt. Lord Nicholas compressed his lips, brows drawn into a straight and forbidding line. He stalked to the door and opened it. 'Sarah. I need a conversation with your sister. An urgent, private conversation.' He stifled a sigh at the prospect of explaining to a lady who gave every appearance of being beyond reason. 'If you would be so kind…'

Sarah diplomatically made her exit. This was no place for her. Nicholas closed the door behind her, leaned against it to watch the love of his life clench her hands into admirable fists.

'Say what you have to say, my lord.' She deliberately turned her back against him, to focus on the pink showers of roses that bloomed around the terrace windows. And to hide the tumbling emotions that she feared might slip from her control. She could sense his presence behind her. And she trembled. Why was love so very painful?

Nicholas said nothing, but let his gaze travel over her, her straight shoulders and upright spine. So, she would resist his explanation. He would allow her that self-indulgence for a little time. But not for long, by God! Moving past her to the sideboard, without bothering to ask her preference, he poured two glasses of claret, then walked to her side to hand her one of them. Without a word, she took it with fingers that clenched around the fragile stem. He watched her with, for Nicholas, infinite patience. Her face was stormy. Beautiful. Magnificent in its determination to freeze him to the marrow. Or to fry him in the fires of hell.

Not in a million years!

But he also, to his surprise, saw fear. She was afraid of what he would say, of what she had overheard and what might be settled for ever here in this quiet room. So that made two of them!

His mouth was suddenly dry, as dry as the cinder and ash in the remnants of his stableyard, at the realisation that the outcome here meant as much to her as it did to him.

He glanced at the glass still clasped so forcefully. 'You may throw it at the wall if you wish.'

Thea glared at him before quickly looking away, then putting the glass down out of temptation, because she was sorely tempted. She raised her chin a little. 'I am not so far beyond control and good manners, my lord.' There was no thaw in her expression. Thea was far too busy concentrating on the erratic behaviour of her heart, which thudded hard against her ribs.

Lord Nicholas, with applaudable cunning, tried for a minor distraction. 'I have some property of yours, Thea.'

Theodora raised one brow in polite and glacial enquiry.

Lord Nicholas removed from his coat pocket a small object, which he had carried like a talisman. It lay on the palm of his hand, glittering ice-white and fiery blue in the strong light.

Thea made no move. 'And will you return it?'

Nicholas thought of pinning the little brooch to the bodice of her gown where lace met ivory flesh... No. That was not his plan.

'Not yet.' He placed it on the table amidst the breakfast cups where it continued to sparkle.

Then simply stepped to stand before her. It was time to settle matters between them, with no opportunity for misunderstanding. When she would have automatically taken a pace back, he reached out to frame her face, with his hands so that she could not retreat. Lowered his head and kissed her. Brief and hard, allowing her no escape. Looking down into her face he noted with satisfaction the shocked surprise in the deepening wash of rose, in her widening eyes and parted lips. So he kissed her again, a forceful demand with lips that allowed for no compromise. And again until he felt her mouth quiver, her lips part against his.

Only than did he slide his hands slowly, gently, very much at odds with the masterful demands of his mouth, along the slim column of her throat to rest on her shoulders, thus to hold her still. Only then, when he was certain that he had her attention, did he say what he had to say—needed to say.

'Listen to me, Theodora. You misheard. If you had waited… This is what I need to lay before you—and you need to know. I was wrong—desperately wrong—when I accused you of deliberate deceit. I did not know the true facts—did not even stop to think about the distress that I would cause. And now, because of Sarah, I do know the truth. I should have trusted you, but I let the past with all its bitterness colour my judgement. My treatment of you was beneath contempt, utterly unworthy of a man of honour and integrity. I have no excuses. The blame is all mine. I need to ask your forgiveness. If you cannot give me that, then I must accept that there is nothing between us.'

'Oh.' She blinked. As before with Nicholas, Theodora found herself in unknown territory, lost for words. She had never expected this. That he should take the burden of guilt fully on to his shoulders, when she had accused him of wilful and vindictive hatred without cause, sufficient to destroy their love without evidence of her involvement in any deception. After all, her accusation had been equally as ill-founded as his.

'Consider well, Thea. I don't deserve your forgiveness, but I will get to my knees if it will help.' His fingers tightened against the fragile bones of her shoulders as he waited to hear her verdict. A decision that could shatter his future. Without this lady, this glorious woman, he had discovered his life to be an empty existence, bringing nothing but loneliness and dissatisfaction. His hands clenched further, only loosening when he felt Thea wince under his fingers.

Thea watched him, searching the now familiar lines of his features, saw the lingering pain and uncertainty there. He had hurt her. But so too had she hurt him.

'I could forgive you,' she announced carefully, keeping her voice light.

Nicholas took a breath. And another against the hope that slammed into his belly.

'Then there is more. You are wrong, Thea. I know what you overheard between myself and Sarah, but you are wrong.' He still held her, but more gently, despite the frustrations burning in every tense line of corded flesh and muscle. 'If you had waited longer, you would have heard me tell Sarah what I truly feel. That love is not a fragile emotion. It is stronger than forged metal, certainly stronger than past hatreds and enmities. I love you. I care not whether your name is Wooton-Devereux or Baxendale. I love you. I find that I cannot live without you. I do not *want* to live without you. I can never envisage living without you.'

'Oh.' *Could she find nothing other to say?*

'I once asked you to marry me and you accepted. Later you rescinded your agreement. I will not allow that. I intend to keep you to that promise. You will marry me—I shall speak to Sir Hector as soon as I can. Do you understand me?'

'Yes.' *Of course she did.*

'Since you have already lain in my arms, shared my bed, you are in no position to be maidenly.'

'No.' She blushed a little, for it was the truth.

'You belong to me, Theodora. You are mine. Do you hear me?'

'Yes.' *Was he always so masterful?*

'You will not marry the Earl of Moreton.'

'No.' *So uncompromising?*

A little shake punctuated every point.

'There—I have said it all. Now, what do you have to say?'

What could she say? He had offered her the sun and moon and all the planets to hold in her hands, as rare and costly as a jewelled necklace.

'Do I have any choice in the matter?'

He laughed softly at the unexpected reply. 'No. None at all.'

Suddenly Theodora's face was bright and shining, her eyes aglow as if from an inner flame. She could not hide it. Her lips curved in a smile of utter delight. Nicholas saw it and knew that the battle was won. The relief of it swept through him as a wind through summer trees. So knowing finally that she was his, he retreated a little, allowing her at least a little space.

'You only have a choice, my dearest love, if you do not love me and cannot bear the thought of living at Aymestry as my wife.'

Again she studied him, head tilted, savouring the warmth that touched her skin and tinted her face with delicate colour. She supposed that she would have to put him out of his misery—although the smoothing of the lines of strain around his mouth suggested that he knew the victory was his. But it was *their* victory, as she well knew. Stepping forward, standing on her toes, she pressed her lips to his in the most tender of kisses.

'Very well. I will marry you.'

'Is that all?' One brow rose a fraction of an inch in astonishment.

'Is that not enough, dear Nicholas?'

'It is.' A soft sigh. 'So much more than enough. You can never know.'

He touched her cheek, a light brush of his fingers against the satin curve, as if he could not quite believe her reply. Or when she turned her face into his caress.

'I thought that I would have to persuade you, you know.'

'And how would you have done so, my lord?'

He smiled against her palm, where he had pressed his lips, at her deliberately predictable response. 'Like this, of course.'

Releasing her, he slid his hands up, and up, until he could draw her close, imprisoning her against his chest within his embrace. His mouth was warm and most persuasive, brushing softly at first, encouraging her to accept the delicious caress of his tongue as her lips opened willingly in acceptance of so intimate an invasion. Her skin was soft, so very soft and seductive. Whereas he… He held her body firmly against his, so that she might know her power over him, for the desire made him hard as stone. But who seduced whom? With a little cry Thea stretched her arms to slide around his neck and angled her head to allow his mouth to take even further liberties. So much heat, so many impossible sensations that raced through her body, leaving her totally at his mercy. It stunned her that he could take her over, demanding and receiving every shivered response to his touch. It stunned them both, a mutual joy and possession that stole their breath and raced through their limbs, a promise of even deeper passion. Control was destroyed, replaced by a simple desire to love and be loved, to pleasure and be pleasured. When his kiss became hot, now a demand rather than a request, it demolished her defences against him utterly, as his, too, were destroyed.

Nicholas lifted his head, as sense prevailed to restore some element of self-control in the breakfast parlour in the full light of day, but not before kissing her closed eyelids in gracious acknowledgement of her power over him.

'Would I have persuaded you, do you think?'

'I think you might.' Thea turned her face into the curve of his throat, a little shy of the depth of emotion that had wrapped around, enclosed them like a velvet cloak.

'I thought I had lost you,' he murmured. She felt his lips against her hair. 'The flames still haunt my dreams. It brought me to my senses as nothing else could. I need you in my life, Theodora.'

'Nicholas—are you sure?'

'Of what?'

'That you love me. I think…I think I might be difficult to live with. I like my own way.' Now she looked up into his face as she confessed. 'You may have noticed.'

'I would never have guessed it! But I think I am no easier.'

'But when we argue—will you not call me a *scheming Baxendale*?'

'Never!'

'Good. I would not like it.' The sparkle in her eyes was a delight to him.

'As long a you do not insist on referring to me as one of those *damned arrogant Faringdons*.'

Laughter sprang between them at the lessening of tension, to cauterise the wounds of the past, even though both realised and accepted that they would undoubtedly find space for disagreement. Both were too strong willed to make for a placid relationship. Somehow, it no longer mattered as long as they were together.

'Besides,' Nicholas reassured his love, 'you will no longer be a Baxendale. You will be a Faringdon. Will that be acceptable to you, my lady?'

'Most acceptable, my lord. I think that I have loved you for ever—since the day I struck at you with my riding whip.' Confession came easily, she decided, as she touched his hand where the old scar had long since faded into less than a shadow.

'The scar has gone from my hand, but if you had refused me, my heart would have been scarred for ever.' Meshing his fingers with hers, Nicholas brought their joined hands together against his chest.

'I thought I had ruined everything… And Edward told me such lies. So that when we met at Judith's…' Thea shook her head. That image still had the power to wound her. 'Can you truly love me in spite of all the hurt and malice of the past?'

'Let me show you how much I can love you. Come, my affianced wife.' Only then did Nicholas allow distance between them, but he kept her hand firmly in his as he led her to the door. 'Let me show you the depths of my love.'

The splendour of Nicholas's sumptuous room at Burford Hall became witness to this most private of moments. They stood in the centre, making no overt move, a little shy of each other. The tension in the air sparkled as if an entity in itself, much like the brooch, which now lay forgotten in the breakfast parlour. The rift between them had been so wide and vicious, words spoken so accusing and bitter. But now it was in their power to set all aside and become free of the past. Nicholas took his love's hands in his, the first step to renewing his knowledge of her, to renewing his promises and avowals of love, which had been so cruelly broken.

Her eyes were captured and held in his, in the dark fire. She knew him now. She understood him so much better now, what had driven him to judge and condemn. And she had forgiven. She would trust this man with her life. He had saved her from harm, had given her comfort. He had rescued her from possible death. He loved her. She closed her hands tightly around his wrists, bonds of love and trust. Now she must convince him that the past was indeed dead and would cast no long shadows unless they allowed it.

As he must convince her.

Nicholas wanted nothing more then to take her, to love her. The bed was there, beckoning with its cool sheets and soft pillows. Such a little distance. There was nothing now to separate them, nothing to prevent them reaffirming the love that had been strong enough to withstand impossible strains. But Lord Nicholas Faringdon, for once, was uncertain, his confidence undermined. He knew that he must have a care of her after the pain and hurt of the past weeks. Guilt and self-disgust slicked his skin. The beautiful woman who stood before him, encircling his wrists with silken chains, willing to giver her heart into his keeping, had every reason to turn her back and marry her Earl with her parent's blessing. But she would not. She would not leave him and wed another. She had said that she loved him. She would trust him. And Theodora was not a woman to break her word—or give it lightly. It was more than he could have hoped for. Now he acknowledged in his heart and soul a need to heal the hurt he had caused and to rebuild the trust before they could look to a future together.

So he set himself to woo her again, without words, but with every muscle and sinew of his body, as if he had no knowledge of her nor she of him and it was all new discovery. As indeed it was. As if she were an untried virgin again, who needed—and deserved—the most exquisite care and cherishing at his hands. Which was not so. But Thea, aware of her lover's torment, allowed him with joy the luxury of the tender seduction.

Gilded by evening sun, stroked by its warmth, he set his mind to control the urgings of his body. Dedicated every skilful touch of mouth and hands to create a delight and a pleasure for her. Lovingly. Tenderly. Yet claiming her as his own. For she must be left in no doubt of the strength of his need for her. His unshakable faith in her. His love for her.

Thea stretched and arched languorously beneath this relentless assault, absorbing the weight and fluent power of her lover. Admiring the controlled restraint even as she fought against it. Clever hands and skilful mouth, rediscovering the secrets and textures, the satin sweep of breast and waist and thigh. The perfumed invitation of softest skin. All thoughts were obliterated in that delicate, sensual onslaught.

For Nicholas it was in the way of a promise that nothing should stand between them. Never again. He had allowed fear and suspicion, arrogance and hatred to separate and wound. He shuddered at the memory of it as he traced the line of her ribs with heated kisses, smoothed the warm skin with a slow trail of fingers. Lingering as she gasped on an intake of breath. And poured all the love of which he was capable into that magnificent courtship as he covered her body with his own.

Thea had read her lord well. The depth of hurt and regret. The need to make restitution. So she allowed him the dominance and the freedom to make amends in his own way, seeing his need to do so, as she took on her own delicious role to soothe and reassure. Following the paths he took, the slow, thorough awakening of every nerve, of every desire, she responded to every demand. The choices were his. Yet it was no hardship for her to follow. Or to use her own experience with him to tease and arouse with a delicious sense of power. Passion was built on passion, layer on enticing layer, until Thea's heart raced and her breath sobbed, the heat built her body crying out with desire for fulfilment. She placed a palm against Nickolas's chest, fingers spread where his heart was as tumultuous as hers. Tears sparkled on her lashes.

'Don't cry, Thea. It breaks my heart.'

'They are tears of joy. I do not regret them.'

He dried them with gentle lips, cradling her against his heart.

'I will not break, Nicholas.'

'No. You will not.'

Silent, they smiled, lost in each other in that instant of perfect stillness, the air around them heavy with emotion, knowing at last that the future was theirs to make of it what they would. And then, only then did Nicholas allow the pace to explode into brilliant heat. Patience was abandoned. He claimed the authority for himself, giving Theodora no choice but to allow herself to be swept along on the storm waves of impossible longings. His mouth took and took. She gave all.

With her name on his lips, did he allow his mind to be flooded, erasing all thought but of her, to thrust deep, sheathing himself within her and claiming her for ever, taking her with him as he drove them both to shuddering delight and ultimate release.

Epilogue

New York

In the intervening weeks since she had received her mother's letter, Eleanor's boudoir and bedchamber had lost the intense smell of newly sawn wood, the spicy tang of resin, and gained a certain sophistication, particularly in the way of new furnishings. The lengthy discussions between Eleanor and Sarah, the apparently endless choosing and discarding of fabrics and patterns, had resulted in tasteful curtains at the windows with matching hangings for the bed. It was now a haven of tranquillity in shades of blue and cream, always Eleanor's preferred hues. The deeply cushioned chairs and window seats invited and encouraged one to sit at ease.

But now the bedchamber held an even more recent item of furniture.

'D'you like it, Mama?' Tom traced the intricate carving along the foot with a grubby finger.

'Of course I do.' Eleanor, newly returned to her previously slim figure and her easy tolerance of the heat, smiled at her elder son. Perhaps she looked a little tired, her fine skin pale against the lace of her wrapper as she rested back against the banked pillows, but her eyes glowed with amethyst fire, heralding both pride and achievement. And a fierce love. 'It is quite beautiful.

You are such a clever boy, Tom. How could you guess what I would exactly like?' She leaned to smooth the palm of her hand over the rounded edges of the cradle. Its occupant, astonishingly new to the world, slept on, unimpressed with the surroundings, the admiration or the company.

'We guessed.' Tom shrugged his nonchalance, a miniature copy of a gesture that Eleanor had seen so often in Henry and now made her laugh softly. 'Papa said you like plants…and things.' Tom followed the outline of what might have been a daisy. 'Like this.' The cradle was made from cedar and polished to enhance the grain, the decoration at head and foot a riot of deeply incised leaves and flowers, more to do with enthusiasm than elegant taste, but still a work of love and therefore of delight. 'I chose the flowers,' Tom confided, shuffling impatient feet in pleasure at the success of the gift.

'And you made it? All by yourself?'

'Well…' Honesty got the better of him. 'Papa helped. A bit. D'you think the baby likes it?'

'I am certain.' Eleanor kept her solemnity in place as she pushed the black hair from Tom's forehead. The honesty had cost him! 'Look how well he sleeps. It must be so comfortable for him. I think he looks very pleased to be here.'

'I suppose.' Tom peered in with a frown. One baby, after all, looked much like another.

But not to Eleanor. She was aware only of the dark hair, the straight nose. And she knew that this time their child's eyes were blue, dark as the columns of delphinium that graced the flower borders at Burford Hall. Another Faringdon. Another son.

'I have to go.' Tom abandoned his brother without shame. 'I haven't seen my pony today. He'll be missing me.' He came to a sudden halt at the doorway and turned back. 'The baby won't be able to ride yet, will he?' The anxiety of personal ownership was written across his face, a burning concern. He looked to Henry, a silent and amused observer of the previous interchange, who saw and understood.

'No,' he answered his son's unspoken concern plainly enough.

'He is far too small. The pony is yours, Tom. When the little one is older, we shall buy another for him.'

'Yes. That's what I thought.' Life was as simple as that. Tom took himself down the stairs with a rush and slide of feet on the polished treads. Eleanor did not bother to tell him not to run.

'I fear a pony holds more attraction for our son than a baby.' Henry pushed himself upright from where he had been half-sitting against the open window frame, arms folded, to stride across the room with his habitual long-limbed grace. Moved to sit on the edge of the bed, where he took Eleanor's hands in his, raising first one and then the other to his lips. 'He is very fine, Nell. Was Tom like this when he was born?'

'Oh, yes.' Eleanor tightened her clasp in instant sympathy and a sharp twist of grief to put an edge on her happiness, surprised by a sudden desire to weep. Of course. Hal had missed all the early promise and progress of his firstborn son, but could now relive it through the first weeks and months of the life of this new child.

The baby snuffled in his sleep and yawned, but did not wake.

Henry grinned at the innocent gesture as he bent his head and kissed the palm of Eleanor's hand. 'Richard, then. Are we agreed?' And, when she nodded her compliance, 'We are indeed blessed,' on a little sigh now that the pain and his fears for her safety through the dangers of childbirth were past.

'I would wish the same for Nicholas. And perhaps even the unknown Miss Wooton-Devereux—if he truly loves her.' Eleanor fretted a little at their enforced ignorance. 'We know so little of what is between them now. Do you suppose that she was indeed in league with Edward Baxendale? I hope that she hasn't quite broken Nicholas's heart.'

'I don't know.' Henry continued to hold his wife's hands enclosed in his, as if he feared that she might still be snatched away from him. 'But Sarah will write when she can. All you need is patience, my wife. And confidence in Nick's good sense!'

'Where a lovely woman is concerned?' Eleanor's tone spoke her scepticism of all men in such circumstances.

Henry lifted his hand, palm up in the formal gesture of a swordsman, in acknowledgement of the accurate hit.

'*Touché*. I have never had any sense where you are concerned! But Nicholas has a strong will and a liking for going his own way. He always had. Perhaps he was a little overshadowed as a boy because he was the quietest of the three of us, but his calm acceptance of life disguised a determination to achieve his goals in the way that best suited him.' Henry's mouth curved, his eyes softened at the memories of a happy boyhood at Burford. 'Before you knew what he was about, he had done it—whether it was to persuade our far-from-indulgent father that he could not survive without a new horse, or to charm the affections of one of the maids at the inn in Burford. Whatever the future, Nick will work out his own salvation, with or without the débutante.'

'Well, I am sure that you read your brother correctly. I just hope that the lady is innocent of all subterfuge and that Nick loses his heart to her and has to kneel at her feet. I think it will do him good not to get his own way quite so much!' And then, 'I miss Sarah.'

'I know. But she has her own life to live, and that of John to consider, and it was her decision to make. I do not think that she made it lightly.'

'No.' Eleanor remembered the final leave-taking when Sarah had wept. 'But still she believed that to return to England was necessary to meet with her sister.' Whether Sarah would remain in London—or return again to New York—only time would tell. Eleanor set her teeth. Again a matter for patience! Her somewhat melancholy mood was interrupted by a shout of laughter from below the window as Tom indulged in some childhood pastime. Then the sound of running feet, followed by a distant shriek of joy.

Her face lit, the sadness swept away. 'Tom never told me, you know.' Eleanor smiled into Henry's eyes. 'Your *secret*. Sometimes I thought he would burst with the overpowering desire to do so.' As a smug smile was all the answer she received from her lord, her expression became suspicious and not a little stern. 'How did you do it?'

'I think it would not be honourable for me to divulge my methods to my wife,' Henry replied in all seriousness. 'Not in so vital a matter between a man and his son.'

'So it involved money!'

'You have no confidence in my powers of persuasion, Nell!'

'Oh, Hal. Bribery!'

Henry laughed at her affronted, yet still amused expression. 'What else? It was in an excellent cause.'

'And it is a splendid cradle.'

'As is the child. Both of them.' The pride in Hal's face made her catch her breath. 'Thank you, Nell. Dear Nell. I shall be always in your debt.' He slid his arm around her shoulders to pull her close as he leaned to touch the infant's clenched fingers which flexed in response—tiny fists and perfect nails. 'What a clever girl you are, my love.'

'Shall I tell you a secret?' For a moment she turned her face against his shoulder.

'Is it very terrible?'

'No. Just that I wanted a daughter.' She felt him smile against her hair. 'But I have decided that Richard is quite perfect and I find that it no longer matters.' She lifted her face. 'And he is so like you, Hal.'

'Perhaps next time.' Henry folded his arms around her, touched his lips to hers in the tenderest of caresses. 'We will make a good life here, Nell. Whatever the future holds for us.'

'I have no doubt of it.' Eleanor leaned her head against him and smiled her perfect contentment.

Some months later, far from New York in Herefordshire, Nicholas was indeed working out his own salvation in his own way. Now Nicholas took the steps at a run and strode into the entrance hall at Aymestry Manor, a man at ease in his surroundings and with the life that he had chosen for himself. It was clear that his involvement in that life was complete. His hair was ruffled from physical exertion, his shirt sleeves rolled up, cravat loosened, boots and breeches covered with straw.

'Thea?' No reply. No sound. She could be anywhere at this time in the morning. 'Thea!' His voice echoed. He would have shouted again but then heard her feet, in riding boots, hurrying along the oak boards of the corridor to the head of the staircase. He would recognise the sound of her quick, light footsteps anywhere now. He stood hands on hips, head thrown back, until she came to look down over the balustraded landing above him. As full of vibrant life and as beautiful as the first day that she had struck him with her riding whip and in so doing had turned his life upside down.

'What is it?' she asked. 'Are you hurt?—no of course you are not! You look far too healthy.' Smiling down at him, she was aware of the tingle in every nerve ending as his smile banished the austere lines from his face, the warmth in her blood when his eyes swept over her, even after six months of marriage. He still had the power to make her want him, to need him. To feel herself at one with him, body and soul. And, it appeared—she flushed with delight at the realisation of the miracle—he needed and wanted her just as much.

'Come down!'

She did.

'You are very dirty, my lord.'

'And you are very smart, my lady. I like the riding rig.'

'I like the boots and breeches better.' Her smile was openly teasing. 'But this is more appropriate! I am going to see Mrs Calke at Burford and I must not shock the tenants!' The velvet of the long skirt and closely fitted jacket was in her favourite deep blue. Her eyes reflected its depth of colour and her hair, worn a little longer these days, was a rich gold. Nicholas could not resist sliding his arms round her slim waist, pulling her close, regardless of the dusty state of his clothes. And since she did not object over much—indeed, she wound her arms around his neck and tilted up her face in blatant invitation—he kissed her, hard and fierce.

'I will accompany you.' Nicholas still had moments of sheer horror when he recalled in vivid detail the dangers that she had faced, moments when his blood froze at the certain knowledge that she might have met her death here in his own home. He knew that those fears would never leave him, but chose to say nothing, carrying the weight of care close within him. It must not be a burden on her. His lady must be free to fly if that was her wish. Yet he often found excuses to be with his wife, to accompany her when she rode off estate land.

As if she did not know! Thea hid her smile because she understood and valued his care. Knowing his fears, she would never refuse his subtle planning.

'But before we go—I have something to show you, my lady. Close your eyes.' He pulled her arm securely through his to aid her steps. 'No looking, now!'

The stables! She surmised from their direction when they left the house. Newly constructed, Nicholas's prized horseflesh were once more in residence. They had been brought over from Burford only the previous week and appeared to be well settled into their fine accommodation. Her smile bloomed. 'Can I guess?'

'Of course not! No guessing. No peeping.' He tightened his hold on her arms. 'Take care here—the pavings are still somewhat uneven.'

But she knew why he had come to find her. What he had brought her to see. Her feet clattered on the cobbles of the courtyard. Then soft darkness, intermittent rays of sunshine, with the sweet scents of hay and horses closed around her—but she remained obedient with her eyes closed. Nicholas led her forward.

'Now look.'

Of course. The Zephyr stood in the centre of the large stall. At her feet, a foal, newborn, its coat still damp, but determined to manage its long legs and gain its feet. By their side stood Furness with handfuls of straw with which he had been wiping down the little grey's hot sides. He looked up at Thea with pride and the suspicion of a grin on his lined face.

'Oh Nick.' Thea leaned against the half-door to see the new arrival. It was a roan, the dark bay taken from its sire, Nicholas's recently acquired stallion, but with the arched neck and small head of the Arab mare. Liquid eyes with absurdly long lashes blinked at them as sunshine came through the high windows.

'A colt, my lady,' Furness explained. 'Give him two or three years on his back—he'll be an asset to our breeding programme here at Aymestry. What do we call him, my lord?'

'I think Faringdon Pride. He will be the bedrock of our future.' Nicholas looked at Thea. 'Do you agree, Thea? You have part-ownership, after all.'

'Yes. I approve.'

Thea stroked The Zephyr. Admired her baby. Then Lord Nicholas and his wife walked back into the sunlight to sit on the stone balustrade that delineated the formal garden and look out over the home pastures.

'I feel so happy.' Thea laughed aloud, eyes sparkling.

'Even after all of six months?' Nicholas knew what she meant. Their love was still as new and bright for him too. He stripped a late rose bud from the bush beside them, handing it to her with solemn formality. 'Even though I only married you to stop your taking The Zephyr away from me?'

Thea raised the unfurling flower to her lips as she slanted an arch glance at her companion. 'There now! And I thought it was for my own sake.' Then on a thought, 'Will they ever return, Henry and Eleanor?' Thea asked as she leaned back within the shelter of her lord's arm.

'No. This was never the life that Hal wanted. And although the title is rightfully his, he would never claim it. It would ruin Eleanor's reputation, you see. It is better that the world here continue to see Tom as Thomas's child, rather than Hal's, born without the sanction of marriage.'

'The strait-laced Faringdons!' Her smile was a little sad for all the anguish and scandal of the past.

'True. But Tom might return. One day. When he is grown and can decide for himself. Burford is his, after all.' He glanced down at her. 'Are you content, Thea? Managing acres that are not ours? Perhaps it is no more secure for you than residing in a foreign embassy. You once told me that you had no settled home, had never had one—and that is what you wished for above all else.'

How delightful that he should remember. And was concerned that she should not be dissatisfied with any one part of their life here together. Nicholas's sensitivity to her emotions was something which still took her by surprise. Thea shook her head, eyes clear, meeting his without shadow.

'Aymestry is your own. I am here because it is yours, and thus it is mine too. I feel that it has been waiting for me all my life, and I have come home at last. Just as I felt that you and your love had been waiting for me to discover the glory of it. Fate has determined that we be together.'

He could not look away from the love that shone from her face. 'You can still travel, you know, if you become restless. It was never my intention to chain you to life in rural seclusion. We are not buried here.'

'I know.' And was grateful for his promise, although she no longer needed it. 'But we have a beautiful home here. I predict that Faringdon horses will be famous.'

Lord Nicholas would have risen to his feet, pulling her with him. But Thea detained him with a hand on his arm and a thoughtful expression.

'What is it, my heart?'

Her fingers tightened on his, to the detriment of the neglected rose bud. 'It is just that I have been thinking… Perhaps we should consider securing our own inheritance for the future—for Aymestry Manor.'

'I think it an excellent idea,' he replied promptly, as solemn as she.

'Ha! Why do I think that you always manage to get your own way?'

'How can you say that? Certainly, in my younger days I usually managed to do so.' His fleeting grin, devastating as ever, melted her bones. 'Until, that is, I met a certain wayward débutante who challenged all my preconceptions.'

'I cannot imagine what you might mean, my lord!' Thea could

not repress an answering smile as she tucked her hand cosily into her husband's arm with satisfaction at her achievement. 'So we have decided that we need an heir for Aymestry.'

'I believe, my dear love, that we have.'

Which was exactly what Lord Nicholas Faringdon wanted after all.

* * * * *

Don't miss the third instalment of

THE FARINGDON SCANDALS,

The Enigmatic Rake
coming in January 2010

A Damnable Rogue

by

Anne Herries

Anne Herries lives in Cambridgeshire, where she is fond of watching wildlife and spoils the birds and squirrels that are frequent visitors to her garden. Anne loves to write about the beauty of nature and sometimes puts a little into her books, although they are mostly about love and romance. She writes for her own enjoyment and to give pleasure to her readers. She is a winner of the Romantic Novelists' Association Romance Prize.

The sparkling final instalment of Anne Herries's Regency trilogy, A SEASON IN TOWN, is available next month from Mills & Boon® Historical romance. Don't miss *The Mistress of Hanover Square.* Coming in January 2010

Chapter One

'I cannot tell you how sorry I was…' Sir William Heathstone looked at the young woman standing so silently before him. In truth she was not so very young, being less than two months from her twenty-seventh birthday and therefore unlikely to marry. In the light of events this past year, she had a bleak future before her. 'As you know, Emma, your father was my lifelong friend…'

His tone and sympathetic expression made Emma's eyes smart with tears. The shocking manner of her father's tragic death had stunned her, and her mother's near collapse on hearing the dreadful news had given her no chance to grieve. For the past eleven months she had devoted herself to the care of her mother and the estate, which left little time for thinking about her own life.

Nor was there time for tears now. The future must be decided before Sir William and Lady Heathstone left for their long winter holiday in the warmer climes of Italy.

'It is because of that friendship and your kindness that I have dared to ask so much,' Emma Sommerton replied with quiet dignity. 'If Mama is forced to spend the winter alone at the house I think she may sink into a decline and die.' Her clear eyes were deeply expressive, carrying as they did a look of appeal, which touched the older man's heart.

'If it had not been for that damnable rogue!' he exclaimed with a flash of temper. 'He led Sir Thomas into a trap, my dear… taunted him the way he does all his victims, from what I've been told.'

'I have heard that the Marquis of Lytham is scrupulous in matters of play,' Emma said, managing to control the rage she felt inside against the man who had ruined all their lives. 'Papa's lawyers assure me that he was warned not to put up his whole estate to the marquis that night, but ignored all advice. And the marquis has been considerate in the matter of claiming his rights, you know. His lawyers assured us that we must continue here as if nothing had happened and that he would not trouble us until our year of mourning had passed. He has been as good as his word, for we have heard nothing from him. We were told we might apply to the lawyers if we needed anything, but of course we have not. Mama has her own small income and we have managed on that.'

'Oh, I am not saying there was any question of anything underhand,' Sir William said frowning. 'Just that Lytham managed to get underneath your father's skin, driving him to do something that I am convinced he would not otherwise—'

'Please, sir,' Emma said, blinking hard against the sting of tears. 'It does no good to speak of these things. Papa was foolish to gamble, but he chose to do so that night with...' she choked back a sob '...disastrous consequences.'

'I never realised Thomas was so desperate,' Sir William said, looking distressed. 'He must have known I would have helped him.'

'I dare say he was too proud to ask,' Emma replied. 'Besides, it seems there was nothing of any consequence left.' She lifted her head proudly. She was not pretty by the standards of the day, her thick hair dark brown and drawn back in a sleek style that made her look older than her years, but her eyes were extremely fine, a wide clear grey, and her mouth was attractive, especially when she smiled. 'Which brings me to my request. Will Lady Heathstone take Mama with her to Italy? I know it is a great deal to ask...'

'Stuff and nonsense!' Sir William said stoutly. 'It was our intention to ask you both to come and live with us when Lytham takes over the estate. Your mama and Lady Heathstone have always dealt well together, and we shall all put our heads together in the matter of your future, my dear.'

'I thank you for your kindness,' Emma said and smiled. It was a smile of rare sweetness and made Sir William catch his breath for a moment. Had his own sons not already been married he would have welcomed Emma as a daughter-in-law, for she would surely make some worthy gentleman a good wife. He knew of one or two widowers who were comfortable enough with regards to money, and he might see what could be done to help the gel towards a suitable match. 'But all I ask is that Mama shall be taken out of herself this winter. As for myself…' She drew a deep breath. 'I have found myself a position as a companion.'

'A companion? No!' Sir William was outraged. 'You a companion—that is impossible, my dear. Most unsuitable, Emma. I am sure your mama would never allow it.'

'I am afraid poor Mama has no choice but to allow it,' Emma replied. 'As you know, Papa quarrelled with his family some years ago, and Mama has none living. There is no one to whom we could apply for help other than you, Sir William—and although I am grateful for your offer of a home, I believe it would not be right. I am young and perfectly capable of earning my living, and as long as I know that Mama is well…'

'I must beg you to reconsider.'

Emma shook her head as she saw the anxious look he gave her. 'I assure you I shall be quite content, sir—which I should not be if I were a burden on you and dear Lady Heathstone. Not that you would consider me such, I know that, but—'

'It would not sit comfortably with your pride?' Sir William was thoughtful. Emma Sommerton was a woman of independent spirit, and perhaps it was as well for her to be allowed a little freedom for once in her life. She had not taken in her season for some reason, and after that her mother's delicate health had kept Emma tied to her apron strings. Perhaps it would be a good thing for Lady Sommerton to learn to do without her daughter, and it might give Emma a chance to live her own life. Who knew what might happen then? Emma was not pretty, but there was something attractive about her. It might be that she would catch the attention of some worthy gentleman, a man in his later years perhaps who would appreciate her qualities. 'Then I shall not interfere with your plans, my dear—but you will give me your promise that, if you are ever in need of help, you will come to me?'

'Who else would I turn to?' Emma said and took the hand he offered her. 'You have always been as a kind uncle to me, sir— and Lady Heathstone is a good friend to Mama. I shall be able to leave her with a quiet mind now.'

'Then you must do as you wish, Emma. When do you take up your position?'

'At the beginning of next month,' Emma replied. 'I shall then be almost at the end of my mourning and can go into company without fear of giving offence. The position is with a lady who has recently come from Ireland. Her name is Mrs Bridget Flynn and she is a widow.'

When Emma had spoken of becoming a companion, Sir William had imagined it would be to a lady of quality, and to discover that she was planning to work for an Irish woman of no particular family shocked him.

'But you cannot!' he exclaimed. 'She sounds...common.'

'I know her to be extremely wealthy,' Emma said, a little amused by his expression. 'Her husband was a distant cousin of the Earl of Lindisfarne, and a favourite with the earl apparently. She herself comes from a good family, though gentry, not aristocracy, and the earl is sponsoring her in society.'

'Lindisfarne? I have heard the name, though I know nothing of the man. This all sounds a little dubious.' Sir William was still doubtful, his heavy brows lowered as he looked at her for some minutes. He was a worthy man of broad stature, and kind, though perhaps not the most imaginative of fellows. 'Are you perfectly sure this is what you want to do, Emma?'

'Yes, perfectly,' Emma replied, crossing her fingers behind her back. She had not told her generous friend the whole story and hoped he would not learn of the true nature of Mrs Flynn's relationship with the earl. 'I—I knew Bridget a little when I was younger. We attended Mrs Ratcliffe's school together. Bridget's parents were in India, her father was a colonel in the British army, and she was left at the school for a year before she went out to join them. I think that was where she met her husband, who was a major before he was killed.'

'And she returned to Ireland after her husband was killed.' Sir William nodded. One of his own sons had served with Wellesley in India some years previously, and a widow of a British major naturally assumed more respectability in his eyes. 'She is to spend some time in London? And she will be sponsored by Lindisfarne?'

'Yes.' Emma crossed her fingers once more. 'Bridget is a year younger than I am, sir. I believe the earl hopes that she will find happiness again.'

'Yes, she is young to be a widow,' Sir William agreed. He was not sure why he felt that Emma was not telling him the whole truth, for he could not see why she should lie to him. However, at the age of six and twenty she was at liberty to do whatsoever she pleased with her own life, and, since he was not her legal guardian, he could not gainsay her. 'Then I shall not question you further, for you have made up your mind on this. Yet I ask you to remember your promise to come to me if you are ever in trouble.'

'You have been kindness itself, sir.'

'Then I shall take my leave of you,' he replied and held out his hand. She gave him hers and he pressed it warmly. 'We shall call for your mother on Monday next—and you leave a few days later for London. Will you be comfortable here alone for that time, Emma?'

'I shall not be alone,' Emma replied. 'I have received instructions from the marquis's lawyers that all the servants are to be retained, and that I am to await his coming at the beginning of next month.' A flash of temper showed in her eyes. 'When he will presumably wish to be shown whatever treasures the house contains. I am afraid he will be sadly disappointed. Papa had sold off most of the silver and pictures before he threw away the estate.'

'So you will have Mrs Monty with you—that will be a comfort to you, Emma.'

'And Nanny—at least until I leave here,' Emma said. 'Poor Nanny has talked of retiring to live with her brother for years, and at long last she may do so. I shall be sad to see her leave, but pleased that she will not have the trouble of looking after us in future.'

Sir William thought privately that in recent years it was Emma who had cared devotedly for Nanny as well as her mother, rather than the other way around.

'Well, I must wish you happiness, my dear. And now I must go.'

Emma went to the door with him, pausing as he climbed into his carriage and was driven away, then sighed as she turned back to the house. That was her first hurdle over, now for Mama…

Her expression was determined as she went upstairs to her mother's boudoir, for she knew that Lady Sommerton would resist being sent off to Italy with her kind friends. She had been insisting on staying to meet the marquis, and was prepared to throw herself on his mercy in the hope of retaining her own home. Emma, however, was not. Nor was she willing to allow her mama to debase herself to that…that monster!

What had Sir William called him? Ah, yes—a damnable rogue! Indeed, he must have been a rogue to provoke Sir Thomas to gamble away his entire estate. Not that there had been so very much to gamble, Emma admitted privately, for she better than most knew that her dearest papa had been worried to death about various debts. He had, she knew, been contemplating the sale of yet another stretch of land by the river, and it would have gone on that way until they had nothing left.

Why must men throw their fortunes away at the gaming tables? It was a mystery to Emma, and although she did not entirely blame her father's gambling for their troubles—there had also been unwise investments—she believed it was a curse.

She put her distressing thoughts away, smiling as she went into her mother's room to find her lying on a daybed, a kerchief soaked in lavender pressed to her forehead.

'Are you feeling any better, dearest?'

'A little.' Lady Sommerton raised her head. 'I am sorry to be such a trouble to you.'

'You could never be that, Mama,' Emma said and meant it sincerely. Her decision to give up all thought of marriage to look after her mother had not been entirely the fault of a disappointment in love. She had been happy at home with her parents, despite their faults, of which she was perfectly aware, and she had long ago made up her mind that she would never make a marriage of convenience. 'I have some wonderful news for you, dearest. Sir William was just here. He and Lady Heathstone have begged for the favour of your company on their travels this year.'

'No…no, I could not possibly leave,' Lady Sommerton replied. 'I must be here to greet the Marquis of Lytham when he arrives. Besides, there is Tom. Supposing he should come home?'

'That is unlikely, Mama,' Emma said. 'If Tom had wanted to come home he might have done so at any time these past months. He must surely have heard of Papa's accident.'

'My poor boy is dead,' Lady Sommerton declared dramatically, pressing a hand to her breast. 'I know that he would have come to me if he could.'

Emma wondered if that might be the case. Her brother had disappeared three years earlier after a terrible row with his father and they had not heard from him since. Like his father before him, he had a temper when roused. It was quite possible that he had done something foolish, which had resulted in his death.

'I am sure that is not the case,' she told her mother, despite her own fears. 'Please do not distress yourself, dearest. It may be that Tom has gone abroad to take service in the army. You know he always wanted to be an officer.'

'If his father had only bought him his commission,' Lady Sommerton said with a sigh as a tear rolled down one cheek. 'But he would not and now I have neither son nor husband—and that wretched man will take my home away from me unless I am here to throw myself on his mercy. He will want to see everything. I must be here to greet him, Emma.'

'Not at all, Mama,' Emma replied serenely. 'I shall do all that is necessary myself.'

'That would not be proper, Emma.'

'I shall keep Mrs Monty with me,' Emma said. 'And I also have dear Nanny. It will be perfectly proper. Besides, I am hardly a green girl in the first flush of youth, am I?'

Lady Sommerton looked at her doubtfully. 'No, and of course I have perfect trust in your good sense, Emma…but I still think I should be here with you. We must take the greatest care not to alienate him, my dear. He might decide to let us stay here if I ask him.'

'Supposing he refuses your request, Mama—would you not find that embarrassing? Besides, there is the rest of the winter to consider. You know that I am pledged to Mrs Flynn and you will be here alone.'

'But I cannot live with Sir William and Lady Heathstone for the rest of my life…' Lady Sommerton choked back a sob. 'If only your papa had not quarrelled with Tom.'

'There is nothing Tom could have done to prevent this,' Emma said. She too had often wished that Sir Thomas had not disowned his only son after their violent quarrel, for it was only after their breach that his gambling had become much worse. 'It is useless to upset yourself, Mama.'

'But why has Tom not been in touch with us if he is alive?'

'I do not know, but he must have his reasons,' Emma said as she had a thousand times before. 'Do not fret so, dearest.'

'I do not know what is to become of us when Lytham turns us out,' Lady Sommerton said and dabbed at her eyes.

'Sir William and Lady Heathstone have offered you a home for as long as you need it, Mama,' Emma said, trying not to see the tears in her mother's eyes. 'It really is the best thing for you. Even if Lytham were to allow you to stay here, you could not manage on your income. This house is far too expensive to run. But if you accept Sir William's offer, you can afford to buy your own clothes and make your hosts the occasional little gift. Otherwise, you will have to manage with what I can give you, which will be very little.'

'Oh, no, I do not wish to be a burden to you,' Lady Sommerton said instantly. 'You have already given up too much for my sake.'

'I have given up nothing, Mama,' Emma said and smiled oddly. 'You know very well that I did not take in the drawing rooms of London.'

'I have never understood that,' Lady Sommerton said. 'I remember thinking that one or two of your suitors would definitely come up to scratch.'

Emma reflected that they might well have done so given the slightest encouragement but, in the throes of first love for a man who was not the man she'd imagined him, she had positively discouraged the more worthy gentlemen who might have offered for her. Her father had suffered some reverses at the card table that season, which had meant that she had never again had a chance of another season, something she did not particularly repine.

'Are you sure this is what you want?' Lady Sommerton looked at her daughter. 'I am aware that Mrs Flynn was a friend when you were at school, but what will she be like as an employer? Have you thought of that, Emma? People often change when they go up in the world, and if she is to be sponsored by her husband's relative…'

'Oh, I think I shall be quite happy with Mrs Flynn,' Emma replied. 'She is very eager for me to go to her, and though she means to pay me a wage, she says I am to think of myself as her guest.'

'Then I suppose I must let you go to her.' Lady Sommerton pressed her lavender-scented kerchief to her head. 'There is nothing else for it, Emma.'

'No, Mama.'

Had things been different, Tom might have managed to save something from the ruin of their estate, but as it was there was no hope—either of saving the estate or of his returning.

There was nothing else for either of them to do. Sir Thomas's folly, followed by his tragic death, had left them little choice but to accept the generosity of their friends.

'I don't see why you have to go down there yourself.' Tobias Edgerton looked at Lytham with a lift of his brows as they sat in the marquis's library sharing a bottle of exceedingly fine claret. 'Why don't you send Stephen Antrium to look it over for you? He is a good fellow and does well by your own place. The Sommerton estate is bound to be in a ramshackle way, stands to reason… Sir Thomas wouldn't have been so desperate otherwise.'

'I fully expect to find it will be more of a burden than a pleasure,' Alexander Lynston, Marquis of Lytham, said to his friend. 'But what else can I do? The son is missing and we must presume him dead, for otherwise he would surely have come forward this past year. I know there was some scandal concerning him, but nothing was ever proved and I fully expected him to demand his rights of me, which is one reason I have waited so long before doing anything. There *is* a widow and a daughter—of the spinster type, I am told. They have been left destitute and their minds must be set at rest. My lawyers told them to apply for funds if they were in need, but they have not done so and I cannot think how they have managed all this time. It was not my intention to leave them in poverty.'

'Damn it all, Alex, you weren't to blame for what happened to Sommerton. Why should you take on the responsibility of two women who are not related to you? You told the fool to call it a night—'

'In such a way that he practically threw his estate on to the table,' Lytham replied. His handsome face belied the nature of the man, which could at times be Machiavellian, his eyes just now as black as the midnight sky and just as mysterious. He smiled at the younger man, of whom he was fond in his own careless manner. 'The devil was in me that night, Toby. Sommerton was a fool, but I did not imagine he would deliberately walk in front of a speeding carriage and horses the next day. The only mercy was that he died instantly and did not linger—but it was so unnecessary! Had he kept his appointment with my man of business as I requested, all would have been well.'

'You could not have known he was that desperate,' Toby said. 'Besides, you won fair and square—pay and be paid, that's my motto. His estate was forfeit. A man should not gamble if he cannot afford to pay.'

Lytham smiled inwardly. It was easy for the young man to speak of such things; the only son of a wealthy father, he had never known what it was to want. Toby's fair good looks and blue eyes won him friends easily, and he had never experienced the loneliness that can haunt a man possessed by fear.

Lytham had understood the look in Sir Thomas's eyes that night, and knew that a part of his recklessness had come from his desire to punish, to seek revenge. It was because of Lytham's brother that he had cast his son out, and the suffering was there in his eyes. It must have cost him much pain, though he had held it within, where it had festered and clung like a limpet, bursting out of him in uncontrollable hatred the night he found himself so deeply in debt to Lytham that he could never pay him. He had wanted to best Lytham at any cost, and in pitting his wits against him had lost everything.

'I do not want his damned estate,' Lytham replied on a note of irritation. 'Nor do I want the trouble of running down to some village in the back of beyond.'

'Steady on, old chap, come from Cambridgeshire myself. Ain't that bad…some pretty villages, and the city has some damned fine buildings.'

'Cambridge is well enough, but this wretched estate is off the beaten track—out near somewhere called Ely, I understand.'

'Been there once,' Toby supplied helpfully. 'Got a cathedral—built in Ethelreda's time.'

'Good grief! Are you turning into a bluestocking?'

Toby blanched at the suggestion. 'Not me, Alex—please! Just a bit of information I picked up along the way.'

'Well, spare me your lectures,' Lytham replied, his amazingly dark eyes bright with mischief. He flicked back a lock of almost black hair that was too long for fashion, and might have given him the look of a poet had his features not been too strong, too masculine. He looked, rather, what indeed he was, the last surviving scion of a noble family who had descended into debauchery and decay, squandering much of their fortune on their merry way to hell. 'You disappoint me, Toby. I quite thought you had nothing in your head but horses and clothes.'

The Honourable Tobias Edgerton was known for his elegance, which far outshone that of his careless friend. Somehow, however, it was always the marquis who commanded attention whenever they were together.

'Bamming me,' Toby said mournfully. 'Might have known—thought you meant it for a moment. Suppose you know all about the place anyway. Ain't much you don't know, Lytham.'

He looked ruefully at his friend. Lytham could be a devil when he had the bit between his teeth, but he was also the best of men when you really knew him. His rather satanic good looks were universally admired, and he was spoiled by adoring mamas and their hopeful daughters alike; his ready wit and undeniable charm won him many friends in high places. The Regent always made a beeline for Lytham whenever they met in company, although the marquis was not one of his intimate cronies—through choice.

'Trouble is you ain't one to let on what you're thinking.'

Toby studied his friend thoughtfully. Bit of a dark horse, Lytham! He was in his mid thirties, having escaped the matrimonial market when younger by virtue of having been forced to supplement his living in the army.

'It comes of necessity,' Lytham said, a reflective expression in his eyes. 'I never expected to inherit the title—wouldn't have if Father had had his way.' He frowned as he thought of the circumstances that had brought him into line. His two elder brothers had died, Henry from a putrid infection of the lungs and John Lynston from a fall from his horse. John was said to have been drunk at the time, a normal state of affairs, and riding recklessly. His sudden death had precipitated Alexander's hasty return from the army for the tenth marquis had not long survived the demise of his favourite son.

'Father and my brothers had done their best to ruin the family estate, as you know. Needed my wits about me to manage when Father cut me off and I learned to keep my own counsel.'

'Well, you've turned the estate round these past three years. My father says you've one of the best heads for managing your affairs that he's come across, but he thinks you're a mystery—can't see why myself.'

'You put up with my moods, Toby,' Lytham said. 'Not everyone is blessed with your good nature.'

A wry smile touched his mouth as he reflected on his life. He supposed others must find him an uneasy companion at times, for he was prone to moods. He thought of them as his devils; they rode on his shoulder, prompting him to do or say things he often wished unsaid.

'My father, for one, thought I was a rogue and a wastrel. Our quarrel was never resolved.' There was a slightly bitter taste in his mouth as he remembered his father's words as he cast him off.

'My hope is that I shall never see you alive again. You are no son of mine!'

Alex had always been aware of his father's dislike, even as a child. He supposed he ought to find an ironic pleasure that it was he who had eventually inherited the estate and rescued it from ruin, but that would have been a meaningless triumph. His life was empty in many ways, his heart untouched by love. He had had his share of mistresses over the years, young and beautiful women who had offered their favours, but none of them had ever meant more than a fleeting pleasure to him.

'Lady Rotherham and her daughters seem to find you fascinating,' Toby teased recklessly. 'And I can think of a few more who wouldn't say no to becoming the new Lady Lytham!' Toby knew that, since Lytham's return from the army, both aspiring mamas and women of another kind had relentlessly pursued him.

'Or to my reputed fortune,' Lytham replied, an odd expression in his eyes. 'You know, of course, that Rotherham is facing ruin if he can't marry those girls off to a fortune?'

'Well, I'd heard a tale,' Toby said. 'But you always seem to get to the bottom of these things, Alex. I'm damned if I know how you do it.'

'Your faith in my powers of omnipotence is flattering, Toby—but I fear you are sadly wrong. Had I, for instance, been privy to that fool Sommerton's state of mind, I might have prevented a tragedy.'

'Well, that's different, desperate men do desperate things,' Toby said. 'What are your intentions? Planning to let the girl and widow stay on?'

'As my dependants?' Lytham gave him a withering smile. 'Now what gave you such a foolish idea? I shall naturally turn them out into the snow.'

'Ain't snowing,' Toby observed, knowing that his friend hated to be thought generous. 'Ain't likely to for months.'

'In that case I shall have to wait for my wicked pleasures—or I might pack them off to keep Aunt Agatha company. She is always complaining that Lytham Hall is like an empty barn. A widow and a spinster daughter should be just the thing to keep her busy.'

'Get her out of your hair for a while?' Toby grinned. Lady Agatha was the best of her family and the only one who had ever had a kind word for Alexander, which was perhaps why he cared for her opinion. A redoubtable lady of seventy years with hair as red as a hot poker—and only a fool would suggest it was a wig in her hearing!—she had a sharp sense of humour and an even sharper tongue. 'I pity the poor widow.'

'Then you waste your pity,' Lytham remarked, carelessly flicking at a speck of dust on the sleeve of his immaculate blue cloth coat. He was dressed in casual fashion in riding breeches and a simple white shirt and neckcloth, but his boots were of the finest leather and polished until they reflected his valet's face; he had a natural air of style and authority that made him the envy of lesser dandies. 'Agatha will mother them both. It is the best solution to the problem. I have been considering whether or not to keep the estate, but I think a quick sale—and a trust fund for mother and daughter…' A look of relief came to the midnight eyes as he made his decision. 'Yes, that should be sufficient.'

'Your lawyers could arrange that,' Toby suggested. 'Save you the bother of a troublesome journey.'

'I think it would be best coming from me.' Lytham finished his wine. 'I had intended to wait until the end of the week, but I think I'll go down tomorrow. Get the business settled before I visit my aunt.'

'Come with you if you like,' Toby offered nobly.

'My gratitude for your friendship is always boundless,' Lytham drawled, his mouth lifting in what others would see as a sneer but was actually self-mockery. 'But I fear your absence at this time might hinder your attempts to secure the beautiful Miss Dawlish. No, Toby. Stay and win yourself an heiress if you can.'

'Don't care for her fortune,' Toby said. 'Inherit one myself one day. Trouble is, not sure Lucy really cares for me—enough to marry me, anyway.'

'My advice is to be persistent.' Lytham smiled oddly. 'The heiress has a bevy of suitors, but half of them are interested only in her fortune. If she is as wise as she is beautiful, I believe Lucy Dawlish will soon begin to sift the dross from the gold.'

'Can't call Devenish dross,' Toby said gloomily. 'Still, she might notice me eventually, I suppose.'

Being an exceptionally observant man, Lytham believed the elusive heiress had already noticed his friend. Although not in line for an earldom as were some of Miss Dawlish's suitors, he was undeniably a very eligible *parti,* besides being good humoured and easy going. Lytham thought the heiress would have to be stupid to take Devenish instead of Toby. However, he was not in the habit of paying his friend compliments and kept his thoughts to himself.

At any other time he would have been glad of Toby's company on what was certain to be a tedious errand, but it might prove embarrassing if he was as unwelcome a guest to the Sommerton family as he fully expected.

'Don't forget to take your shawl, Emma,' Nanny said as her former charge, now become friend and comforter, prepared to leave the house. 'It is nearly October and the weather can turn nasty of a sudden.'

At that moment they were enjoying what was often termed an 'Indian' summer and the afternoon was both warm and sunny. However, Emma draped the shawl over her arm to oblige Nanny before she went out.

It was two days since Lady Sommerton had departed for the Hall with four large trunks full of her personal possessions, one or two of which might reasonably have been called part of the estate. Since no one had bothered to take an inventory in the months since Sir Thomas's death, there was no need to worry that Lady Sommerton might be accused of theft. However, Emma had been scrupulous in packing her own trunks. She would in any case be unable to take as much as her mama, and had decided to dispose of some of her unwanted clothes.

She imagined that the Reverend Thorn's wife, Mary, might know of a few deserving cases in the village and surrounding cottages, and it was to discuss the matter and take leave of her friend that she had ventured out this afternoon.

The walk to the Vicarage was pleasant on a warm, dry afternoon and Emma took the shortcut, avoiding the village by going across the fields. For once she had not bothered to put up her heavy dark hair into the usual coronet of plaits, and it hung loosely on her shoulders. She felt a release of the tension that had hung over her these past weeks and even sang a few bars of a popular melody as she walked.

Mary Thorn was as delighted to see her as Emma had known she would be. She was taken into a pretty parlour, given tea and cakes and thanked for the offer of the clothes.

'You know we can always find a use for them, Emma—but are you sure you won't need them?'

'Mrs Flynn has told me not to bring too much as she intends to buy clothes for herself and me,' Emma said. 'Besides, I had three new gowns last year and they are quite adequate. If my evening dress is too shabby, Mrs Flynn will no doubt provide something.'

'Your future employer sounds very generous.' Mary Thorn looked at her curiously. 'How did she know you were in need of a position?'

'She heard that Papa had died,' Emma replied, a break in her voice. 'And since she needed a respectable woman to keep her company, she wrote to ask if I would go to her.'

In fact, Bridget Flynn had written a long and revealing letter, begging Emma to stay with her. She had a most urgent need of female companionship, and had perhaps confided more than was wise in the letter to her old schoolfriend.

The earl has agreed to sponsor me in society, Emma, Bridget had written. *But he vows he loves me and I believe he is determined to make me his mistress. I find him fascinating for my part, but I am determined not to succumb. It is marriage or nothing…except that he makes me feel so very delicious…*

'Was that not the most fortunate thing!' Mary Thorn was thrilled by Emma's good luck. 'I hope you will enjoy yourself, dearest Emma—but should you have reason to leave Mrs Flynn, you know you may always come here for a visit. The vicar would be happy to see you.'

Emma thanked her. She felt that her true fortune lay in having friends like Sir William and Mary Thorn, and she felt a little guilty at deceiving them. They would both have been utterly shocked had they guessed that her future employer had confessed to being on the verge of becoming the Earl of Lindisfarne's mistress.

Emma was not sure what would happen if Bridget did give way to the earl's persuasion. He was obviously a great temptation to her, but since the earl was unmarried there was no real reason why he could not offer her marriage. However, Emma had heard a whisper that he was a notorious rake, who had had a string of mistresses.

She was thoughtful as she began her walk home. The sky had clouded over and she realised that Nanny's advice had been sound as she hugged her shawl about her. She would undoubtedly have been wiser to look elsewhere for employment, since she could not afford the loss of reputation that she might suffer if there were to be a scandal. Yet her life had been so quiet of late and she felt that this might be her last chance of having a little fun…a little excitement.

As she entered the house, Emma noticed the hat and fashionable travelling cape in the hall. She was surprised as most of her father's friends had already called to pay their respects to her mother and she was not expecting company.

Indeed, the house was looking sadly neglected, for many of the little items that had made it a home had gone with Lady Sommerton, and the whole impression was rather more shabby than usual. Emma had fetched a few bits and pieces from the attic to fill up the empty spaces, and the Chinese vase in the corner with an arrangement of dried flowers did not look too bad if you did not look at the crack, which she had turned into the wall. Not that it mattered, for nothing could disguise the fact that the house had not been refurbished in an age.

About to enter the small back parlour, which was the room she and her mother had most used these past weeks, she heard Nanny laugh.

'You are the veriest rogue, sir! None of your flummery, now... Ah, here's Miss Emma back from her visit.' Nanny greeted her with a smile of welcome. 'Now here's a surprise, my love. The Marquis of Lytham come to see us a few days early...'

Emma had been studying the rather large gentleman who was standing before the fireplace, wineglass in hand, apparently completely at home in the parlour he seemed to make smaller by his very presence. Her first thought had been that he was remarkably good looking, but as his dark, challenging eyes turned to survey her she felt a surge of anger. How dare he look at her in that way? She was aware that her hair was windblown and her cheeks pink from the cold, and wished that she had gone upstairs to tidy herself before meeting her guest.

'My lord,' she said, head up, eyes flashing with unconscious pride, 'we had not anticipated your coming until the weekend...' When she had confidently expected to be on her way to London and beyond his reach.

'I believed too long had passed with no word from me,' Lytham replied, hard gaze narrowing as he read her hostility. 'I am sorry to have missed Lady Sommerton, and glad that I have managed to catch you before you left for London.'

'Indeed?' Emma's tone was cool, her manner dismissive. 'I cannot imagine why, sir. Your lawyers have made all clear. I fear the estate may not be what you hope.'

'Since I hope for nothing, that matters little,' he replied, as cool as she now. 'However, I dare say something may be salvaged.'

'Nanny—would you arrange some tea, please?'

Emma waited until her nurse had left the room before rounding on him. 'You may do as you please with your own property, my lord. I shall make arrangements to leave first thing in the morning.'

'You will do no such thing,' Lytham said in a tone that brooked no denial. 'If it offends you to have me beneath your roof, I can stay at the inn.'

'You will find that uncomfortable.' She was angry and her words were perhaps too harsh, too hasty. 'Why was it necessary to come earlier than planned? We might have avoided any unpleasantness.'

'I made it clear that you and Lady Sommerton were to remain here as my guests. I ought perhaps to have come sooner, but I did not wish to intrude on your grief—and was uncertain what to do for the best.'

'There was no need for you to concern yourself. We have made our own arrangements.'

'Your mother's visit to Italy with friends is perfectly acceptable,' Lytham said. 'But I cannot allow you to continue with this foolish idea of becoming a companion to a woman whose situation in life is below your own.'

'*You* cannot allow…' Emma was indignant. 'I beg your pardon, my lord. I was not aware that you had become my guardian. I am almost seven and twenty, and even Papa would not have spoken to me in these terms.'

Damn it, but there was fire in those eyes! Lytham was surprised and amused to discover that he had been so misled as to the nature of Sommerton's daughter. He had been told she was a confirmed spinster and well past her last prayers, but that was clearly not the case. She was not pretty like the enchanting Lucy Dawlish, but she was certainly a woman of spirit.

'I spoke as a gentleman, as a man of honour…' He saw the disbelief in her face and smiled inwardly. The little firebrand was not above showing her contempt. 'Believe me, Miss Sommerton, I had no desire to win your father's estate in that card game. I suspect it will be more trouble to dispose of than it is worth…' In saying that he was not speaking only of financial matters, but Emma was not to know that she herself was destined to be the cause of more bother than her father's debts.

'You intend to sell, then?'

'I do not imagine you could afford to continue living here if I offered you the opportunity? And, since there has been no word from your brother, I think I have little choice.'

Emma looked into his eyes and then away as her heart caught, stopping for a moment and then pounding wildly for some unaccountable reason.

'I imagine you know our circumstances as well as we do, sir.'

'Yes. I have been into your father's affairs thoroughly, Miss Sommerton, and I believe what he did was a desperate act. Had he held the winning hand, he might have been able to stave off ruin for a time—for there was a considerable amount on the table that night.'

Emma's face was pale as she stood before him, hands clasped in front, to stop them trembling. 'I am aware of Papa's debts. Will the sale of the estate cover them?'

'I believe with some small attention to detail it may do a little more—there may be a small sum…' For some reason Lytham was reluctant to inform her of his intentions to invest that money on her and her mother's behalf.

'Not equal to what my father would have won, though?'

'No, not that much.' Not by a half or a quarter, but he would never tell her that.

'Then he cheated you…'

'Sir Thomas was desperate. A desperate man may do many things.'

He had not denied it! Emma was silent. She was mortified and thought guiltily of the small treasures her mother had taken with her; nothing had been of great value, but still…she ought not to have removed things like the enamel and ormolu gilt clock from the drawing room or the best silver tea service.

'I am sorry my father deceived you.'

'You have no need to be. I accepted the bet, knowing the estate could be worth little. I should have refused to do so, of course. Perhaps then—'

'He would still be alive?' She read the answer in his eyes. 'Yet he would have continued until there was nothing left. After the quarrel with Tom, it seemed that nothing else would content him but to gamble it all away.'

'I am afraid it is often the way with unlucky gamblers. Please accept my condolences for your loss, Miss Sommerton,' he said, his eyes dwelling intently on her face as he watched her struggle for control. He saw anger, grief and despair register and then fade into resignation. 'I feel in part responsible for what happened— and it is therefore my intention to offer you…' He paused uncertainly. He had meant to offer a home, but she was too proud to accept charity from him. 'The post of companion to my aunt. She is a wonderful old lady, but needs young company about her. Aunt Agatha would like you, Miss Sommerton—and I believe that you might like her.'

Emma was surprised. She had the oddest notion that he had intended to say something entirely different.

'That is considerate of you, my lord—but unnecessary, as you must already have realised. I have a very comfortable position to go to. Mrs Flynn is an old friend, and I have promised to join her at the house she has taken in London.'

'An odd time to visit London,' he said. 'The season is over. You will find there is very little going on at the moment.'

'I believe Mrs Flynn has her own reasons for visiting at this time. Besides, I think she means to retire to the country after a while—or perhaps to Bath. Her plans are not quite formed yet.'

'I see…' Lytham gave her an enigmatic look. 'Will you not change your mind? I believe my Aunt Agatha would be a more suitable person for you to know than this Mrs Flynn would be.'

'How can you say that since you know nothing of Mrs Flynn?' Emma's hostility towards him had waned, but now it came flooding back. How dare he presume to dictate to her? 'I thank you for your consideration, my lord—but I can manage for myself.'

'Can you?' He seemed doubtful. 'I take leave to wonder.'

'What does that mean, sir?'

'For goodness sake, call me Lytham,' he burst out. 'I have not come here as your enemy, Miss Sommerton.'

Emma's answer to that was forestalled by Nanny's arrival with a maid bearing a tea tray. She beamed at them innocently, clearly having taken to the marquis at first sight.

'Here we are, then,' she said. 'Isn't this nice, Emma dear? It's always pleasant to have a gentleman in the house. Shall you pour?'

'Please excuse me,' Lytham said. 'I must forgo your kind offer to stay the night, Miss Sommerton. I have pressing business elsewhere.'

Emma caught the mocking tone of his voice, but he had her at a disadvantage. She knew that she had been less than polite, especially if he had come all this way to offer her and her mother help.

'Oh, must you go?' Nanny said in the slight pause that followed. 'Surely you will stay one night, sir? He would be very welcome, would he not, Emma?'

'Yes, of course,' she said stiffly. 'It is too far to return to town this evening, my lord—and the inns are not always reliable.'

She saw a gleam in his eyes and knew she had fallen into his trap, but what choice had he given her? He had been sure Nanny would react exactly as she had.

'Then of course I shall stay. I am delighted to accept your hospitality, Miss Sommerton.'

'My lord…' She raised her head, receiving a little shock as she looked into those devastating eyes and saw the imp of mischief that resided there. 'I shall leave you to your tea while I speak to Cook about dinner.'

'Oh, there is not the least need,' Nanny said innocently. 'Cook has been planning dinner ever since his lordship arrived. That is why you must not even consider leaving, sir. She would be most upset.'

'We cannot have Cook upset,' Lytham said, somehow managing to look almost as innocent as his new-found admirer. 'Especially if she is a good cook!'

Emma saw that he was laughing inside. She raised her head, giving him a reproving glare. Did he imagine she was to be won over so easily…even though it had been seldom that she had discovered a similar sense of humour to her own in a man?

Sir William was right about the Marquis of Lytham after all. He was a damnable rogue!

Chapter Two

There was to be no escape for Emma until much later that evening, apart from the half an hour it took her to change for dinner. After tea, the marquis had asked to be shown the house, which Emma had felt obliged to do herself. He had made encouraging noises about it being an attractive property, and possibly more valuable than he'd thought, and had spoken of staying until the end of the week so that he could ride over the estate with Sir Thomas's bailiff.

'I am inclined to think that something may yet be accomplished here, Miss Sommerton. It would be a pity to dispose of a substantial property too hastily. I shall have to think seriously before I decide. Had your mama still been here, I might have suggested you both remain in residence, for a while at least.'

'Mama needs company and the sunshine of Italy will be good for her,' Emma replied. She had decided to retreat behind a mask of cool dignity. His arrival earlier had taken her by surprise and she had been betrayed into a shocking display of temper, but now she was in control. Her hair was wound into its usual coronet of plaits and it was a different Miss Sommerton who dined with the marquis that evening.

Lytham was intrigued by the change, both in her appearance and her manner. Who did she imagine she was fooling by this calm, spinsterish behaviour? He might have been deceived for a while had he not seen the real Emma, but it was too late for pretence. Intrigued and amused, he discovered that what he had thought would be an awkward visit was actually proving enjoyable. He had been growing bored of late in town, and this was just what he had needed to divert him.

'You must, of course, do just as you please,' Emma told him when he announced his intention of staying on. 'But Nanny is due to leave the day after tomorrow and I shall bring my own journey forward by one day. It would not be proper for me to be alone with you in this house, my lord.'

'No, I dare say it would not,' he agreed, the light of mischief lurking in his eyes had she dared to look. She was a challenging minx, and worthy of the contest. He was going to enjoy this tussle of wills. 'But I believe Nanny might delay her journey by one day if I asked her—and then, you know, we might travel together. I am sure you would find my carriage comfortable, Miss Sommerton.' He smiled across the table at Nanny, who was dining with them at Emma's insistence, and she immediately agreed that it would be no trouble at all to delay her journey.

'For you know Sir William has put his gig at my disposal, Emma—and you were to have travelled on the Mail coach because you feared it would be too expensive to travel by post chaise, dearest. Think how much more comfortable it will be to travel in his lordship's carriage. It is excessively good of you, sir, and I am sure Emma is most grateful.'

Inside, Emma was fuming, but she could only accept her defeat and agree that it would be more comfortable to travel in the marquis's carriage than by public coach. She had felt it necessary to save what little money she had, and had not been looking forward to the journey. However, she was not pleased by the way she had been persuaded to agree, but her attention was diverted by the marquis's next words.

'You shall not go anywhere in a gig, Nanny,' Lytham said and earned Emma's instant approval. 'I am sure you would find it more comfortable to travel by chaise—and you will allow me the privilege of paying your expenses.'

'But it is merely a distance of ten miles, sir.'

'Which you may as well travel in comfort. Indeed, I insist and shall be hurt if you refuse me,' Lytham said and was rewarded by a beaming look from his elderly devotee.

There was no doubt that the marquis could be a charmer when he chose, thought Emma. However, she had no fault to find with this latest evidence of his generosity. The expense was nothing to a man of his fortune, of course, but it was nevertheless a kind thought.

Without her realising it, Emma's manner towards the marquis had thawed slightly, and before she knew what was happening he had refused a solitary glass of port in favour of taking tea with her and Nanny in the parlour. His manner was exactly what it ought to be, gentlemanly and courteous, and his stories of what was happening in town were vastly entertaining. It was only when the longcase clock in hall struck ten that she was aware of time passing.

'I must bid you goodnight, sir,' she said as the clock finished striking. She stood up, signalling her intention to retire. 'We have kept poor Nanny from her bed long enough. I fear we have not been used to late hours here.'

'Forgive me…' Lytham sprang to his feet. 'Goodnight, Miss Sommerton…Nanny…'

'You must stay and take a glass of brandy,' Emma said. 'I believe you may find my father's cellar tolerable—what is left of it.'

He inclined his head, a flicker of amusement back in his eyes. Miss Sommerton was most definitely a challenge, and of all things Alexander Lytham enjoyed pitting his wits against a worthy opponent.

She was determined on taking up this post as a companion, and it seemed nothing would change her mind. There was really no reason why she should not do as she had planned, but he would use every effort to deter her. He had no charge to level at this Mrs Flynn, and yet his instincts told him something was not quite as it should be.

Miss Sommerton had looked a little odd once or twice when she mentioned her future employer. Now why should that be? Lytham could not decide, but that inner sense that had always directed him was seldom far out. It was telling him now that he would regret it if he simply abandoned Emma Sommerton to her fate.

Alone in her room a little later, Emma took the unusual step of locking the door both to her dressing room and her bedchamber. She did not imagine that the marquis would wander in his sleep, but it was best to be careful.

She suspected that he was a man used to having his own way. However, he was undoubtedly a gentleman and she was not really afraid that he would seek to abuse her hospitality. No, she was just being prudent.

She undressed, donning a plain white, much-washed nightgown and her shabby old dressing robe. Then, having brushed her hair until it shone and fell in gentle waves to her shoulders, she went to stand at the window and look down at the garden. The moon had shed its soft light across a swathe of lawn, shrubs and trees, turning them to a curious silver. She felt a pang of regret as she remembered that she would soon be leaving it for good. Yet there was no point in repining and she was looking forward to a change in the slow pace of her life.

What was that? She stiffened as she saw something moving…a man's shadow in the shrubbery? Had the marquis gone out for a walk in the gardens? It seemed the most logical explanation, and yet the shadowy figure had seemed too slight for the man she had dined with earlier, and its movements had appeared slightly furtive.

For a moment Emma was tempted to go in search of the elusive figure, but then she remembered that she was scarcely dressed for such an excursion. Besides, she could not be sure that she really had seen something out there. It might have been a trick of the light—a cloud falling across the moon, perhaps?

Going over to her bed, Emma slipped between cool sheets. It felt strange to think that she was sharing her home with a man she had only met that afternoon—a man she ought to hate and despise.

She had believed that she hated him for what he had done, but during the evening she had discovered that she could not do so.

She hated and despised what he stood for—this careless society that allowed the ruin of a man's life, and his family, on the turn of a card. Gambling was surely an abominable practice and ought to be banned. And yet…perhaps it was only her father's own weak character that was at fault?

Emma decided that she did not entirely dislike the marquis, but she certainly did not trust him. No, indeed she did not! There was something hidden…something that went much deeper than the charming manner he had shown them over dinner. Yes… something hidden. She felt that he was a man of secrets, a man with a past.

It could not matter to her what kind of a man he was! She was forced to accept his company for the next few days, but once they reached London they would each go their own way. She would never need to see him again unless she wished.

Feeling vaguely restless, Emma reached over to blow out her candle. It had been a long day and she was feeling tired.

'Goodbye, Nanny. You must write to me once you are settled.'

Emma felt the sting of tears as she kissed her nurse's soft cheek. She had been prepared for this parting, but it was still difficult now that it had come. She was, after all, being torn from all that she held dear—home, friends, and family. Nanny had been almost a second mother to her and she knew that she would miss her sorely.

After Nanny had been seen safely on her way, it was time for Emma to take her seat in the marquis's comfortable carriage. It looked new and she thought the springing would be better than on her father's old coach, which had been most uncomfortable. Despite its smart appearance and the obvious quality of his horses, she noticed that it did not carry his coat of arms on the side panels. Most men of his importance would have had their family crest emblazoned on the sides, but Lytham had chosen not to. She wondered why, then forgot it as she saw that inside it was every bit as comfortable as she had expected, with cushions and a travelling rug to keep her warm.

Lytham was travelling with her and had insisted that one of the more responsible maids should accompany them for the sake of propriety.

'It would be too exhausting for you to travel the whole distance in one day,' he had insisted. 'We shall stay overnight at a good posting inn, and you will need the assistance of a maid.'

Emma had tried to protest that such consideration was not necessary. Indeed, she would have preferred to complete her journey in the shortest possible time, but she was given no say in the matter.

'There is still time for you to change your mind,' Lytham said, pausing with his foot on the step. 'Give the word and I shall take you to my aunt instead.'

'I believe I have made my wishes clear, sir,' Emma said, her eyes sparking at him. 'Indeed, I think I have done so several times these past two days.'

'Then I shall ask no more,' Lytham promised and gave the order to move off as he climbed into the carriage.

'Thank you.'

Lily, the young maid travelling with them, was overawed by the marquis's presence, and had scarcely uttered a word since accompanying Emma from the house. She looked frightened to death at the thought of leaving familiar surroundings, and even a reassuring smile from her mistress did not take the anxious look from her eyes.

Emma leaned back against the squabs. It was an exceedingly comfortable conveyance, much better than Sir Thomas's antiquated travelling carriage. She closed her eyes with a little sigh, hoping that the marquis would take that as a sign that she did not wish for conversation. He immediately followed suit, crossing his long legs and, when Emma dared to peep, gave every appearance of intending to sleep throughout the whole journey. This had the desired effect of making Emma open her own eyes and begin to look about her at the countryside through which they passed.

Sitting with her back to the horses, Lily had shrunk back into her corner and was looking fixedly out of the window.

From the tension in her manner, she was apparently expecting disaster to strike them at any moment.

'And so…' Lytham said when they had been travelling in silence for some half an hour or more. 'Does Mrs Flynn hope to entertain much? As I believe I have told you before, I think you will find London thin of company just now.'

His sudden question startled Emma, for she had been dreaming, but she recovered quickly, meeting his eyes, only to look away again almost at once.

'I believe Mrs Flynn seeks to purchase a new wardrobe,' Emma replied. 'And then we may go elsewhere for the winter months. It has not yet been decided.'

Lytham nodded, his eyes narrowing intently. She appeared so cool and calm, completely in control of her emotions, but he suspected it was a pose and that the real Emma was lurking behind the façade she showed to the world. He would swear there was something Miss Sommerton was hiding, but it was clear that she would not be drawn.

'You will keep me in touch with your movements, Miss Sommerton?'

'Oh—why?' Emma arched her brows. 'I really see no reason—'

Whatever she had meant to say was brought to an abrupt ending because the carriage came to a sudden halt and she was thrown across the space between them into the marquis's arms. She gave a startled cry, looking up into his eyes in alarm, but he merely smiled reassuringly, his strong grip saving her from falling to the floor. Lily screamed once, but hung on to the tassel hanging from the corner of the carriage and retained her seat.

'Are you all right, miss?' she asked after a moment, looking shaken and nervous.

'Yes, thank you,' Emma replied and straightened her bonnet. 'Are you?'

'Yes, miss…I think so…'

From outside Emma could hear shouting and some curses from the coachman and groom, and then, as the marquis gently righted

her on the seat opposite him, an anxious face appeared at the
window.

'Beggin' your pardon, my lord. I hope neither you nor the
young ladies were harmed?'

'I think not,' replied Lytham with a sharp look at Emma, who
nodded to indicate that she was merely shocked. 'But it was most
unfortunate—what caused the incident?'

'There is a fallen tree across the road, my lord. I think we can
clear it, but it will take time.'

Lytham's groom opened the door for him and he got out to
view the situation himself. It was actually only a large branch,
but it had blocked the narrow road, which wound between dense
woods on either side, and had given his driver no choice but to
pull the horses to an abrupt halt.

'I think the three of us should be able to clear this,' Lytham
said, and took off his coat, tossing it inside the carriage, where it
lay on the floor until Lily retrieved it, folding it neatly on the seat
beside her.

Emma glanced out of the window and saw that the three men
were tugging the heavy branch, which looked like the whole top
part of a large elm, to the side of the road. One of the horses was
moving restively, and Emma thought it wise to get down in case
the nervous animal, which had already been unsettled by the sudden halt, should make a sudden lunge.

'I think I shall get down,' she said to Lily. 'You stay here for
the moment.'

'Yes, miss—but be careful…' Lily hesitated as if wishing to
say more, but held her tongue.

'Yes, of course.'

Emma descended from the carriage and went to stand at the
horse's head, reaching up to pat it reassuringly. She actually had
her hands on the harness when the shot rang out, and she felt the
immediate pull of the frightened horse. Instinctively, she braced
herself for the jerk she knew would come as the horse tried to
bolt, and felt herself almost lifted off her feet by its wild plunge.

'Whoa there, old fellow,' she said in a voice of command.
'Steady…steady, boy…'

Her calm voice and the fact that she was already at the horse's head when it was frightened probably saved it plunging blindly into the men ahead and dragging the carriage and other horses with it. The men had stopped pulling at the fallen branch and were staring down at someone lying on the ground. For some minutes, Emma was too busy calming the horses to see what had happened, but then, as the groom came hurrying to take over from her, she gave a cry of distress as she saw for herself what had happened.

The marquis had been shot! He was back on his feet as she began to run towards him, but he was clasping his shoulder and she could see the crimson staining his shirt.

'Oh, my lord,' Emma cried in distress. 'Are you badly hurt? What happened—did you see who shot at you?'

Lytham grimaced and took his hand away from his shoulder for a moment to look at the powder-burned hole in his shirt.

'I think it is a flesh wound only,' he said. 'I saw nothing for my attention was all on our task, but whoever it was must have taken a pot-shot from somewhere in the trees.'

'The shot came from behind us,' the driver said. 'I felt the wind as it whistled past me, my lord. Whoever did it must have been hidden in those trees as you said, sir.'

'He must have been waiting there...'

Emma had taken a small penknife from her reticule and approached him purposefully. 'May I slit your shirt and look at the wound, sir?' she asked. 'I think some attempt should be made to staunch the blood for it will be a while before we can reach a doctor.'

'You should return to the carriage,' Lytham said. 'That rogue may still be lurking in the woods.'

'I shall be pleased to do so if you come with me,' Emma said. 'Your men can finish clearing the road. Besides, I doubt a poacher would remain long once he had so misfired as to hit you.'

'A poacher?' Lytham frowned, then nodded. 'Yes, perhaps it might have been. I dare say there are small deer in these woods, and certainly a few rabbits.' A smile flickered in his eyes as he looked at her. 'You are remarkably calm, Miss Sommerton. Most young ladies of my acquaintance would be screaming or lying prostrate on the ground from a faint.'

'It was not I who was shot at,' she replied, her lips curving in response to his expression. 'And I do not think you need another incident of that nature. Please come inside the carriage, sir, and let me see what I can do to stop that bleeding.'

'I am in your hands, Miss Sommerton.'

Emma allowed the groom to hand her into the carriage, and then watched as Lytham followed. Her heart was thumping madly and she was not in the least calm, but she had no intention of letting him guess it. He was also putting on a mask, for she suspected that he was in some pain, but was refusing to let it show.

Once he was seated, she knelt on the seat at his side and slit the shirt, taking the large kerchief he offered her to gently wipe away the blood oozing from the wound. Since she could see only a shallow gash across the skin and there did not seem to be a hole in his shoulder, where the ball might have entered, she decided that it was as he had said, merely a flesh wound. He had been fortunate, it seemed, which relieved her mind.

Lily watched with huge rounded eyes, clearly too upset by what had occurred to offer assistance to her mistress. Naturally a timid girl, she sniffed into her kerchief a couple of times, as if overcome by the terrible things that had happened.

'I think we might use your neckcloth to bind the wound,' Emma said. 'If you would permit me?'

'Please feel free to do whatever you wish with me,' Lytham said mockingly. 'I am entirely at your mercy, Miss Sommerton.'

'I shall be as gentle with you as I can,' she promised and began to deftly unravel the folds of his white cravat, which she then used to pad and bind his arm, fastening the tatters of his shirt around his shoulder with a pin when she had finished. 'There…that should hold until we reach an inn,' she told him with satisfaction. 'I fear I have nothing to give you for the pain…unless you happen to have some brandy amongst your luggage?'

'You are an amazing woman,' Lytham said. 'Do you always carry emergency supplies with you?'

Emma smiled and shook her head at his mockery. 'I have often found a penknife useful, my lord—and what respectable woman would go anywhere without a few pins or a needle and thread?'

'No, indeed,' he replied. 'That would be shockingly bad form, would it not?'

'Shockingly,' Emma agreed, a smile quivering at the edges of her mouth. 'I suggest that if you have no brandy amongst your things, you should close your eyes for a moment.' She glanced out of the window as she heard the groom shout something. 'I believe we are almost ready to move off. I shall tell the driver to take us to the nearest inn.' She leaned out of the door and beckoned to the man, giving him the required direction, then sat back. The marquis had taken her advice and was leaning his head back against the squabs, his eyes closed. 'There, now, we shall soon find somewhere comfortable where you may rest for a while.'

Lytham opened his eyes and looked at her. 'My intention in escorting you was to take care of you, Miss Sommerton. It appears the roles have been reversed.'

'It was nothing,' she assured him. 'Yours is not the first wound I have bound, my lord.'

'Indeed? You interest me, tell me more.'

'You have not forgotten that I have a younger brother?' She could tell from his expression that he was interested in learning more. 'As a child Tom was always in trouble. Once he stuck a pitchfork through his leg and it was I who stanched the bleeding and bound the wound.'

'And where is your brother now, Miss Sommerton?' Lytham asked with a slight frown. 'I had hoped that we might hear from him before this. He is, after all, the heir to your father's estate.'

'I wish I might tell you,' Emma replied. 'As for being the heir…Papa cut him off without a penny years ago. My brother was always in trouble, but he did something unforgivable, and Papa would not have his name spoken in his presence. Mama was broken-hearted, but even she agreed that Tom had gone too far.'

Lytham tensed, waiting for her to go on, but she did not. He was well aware of the reasons for Tom Sommerton's quarrel with his father, but he was not sure how much she knew of it.

'May I ask what this terrible sin was?'

Emma bit her lip. 'I am not perfectly sure, for I was never allowed to hear the whole story—but as I understand it, my brother was accused of cheating at the card table.'

So she did not know it all; well, he would not be the one to tell her, though he knew she might learn of it from others. Her brother had been suspected of causing the accident that had killed Lord John Lynston, Lytham's own brother. He was said to have been having an affair with John's wife, something that was suspected but not known generally, though Aunt Agatha had told him it was true.

'That is a serious crime,' Lytham agreed. 'But I would not have thought it enough for a father to disown his son.' He probed gently, for it was important to know just how much she either knew or suspected. She must blame him for her father's untimely death, but did she also lay her brother's disgrace at his family's door?

'I believe there was more,' Emma said with a frown. 'Mama whispered to me that a friend of the man who accused Tom of cheating said that Tom had insulted his wife, and I believe he took a horse whip to him. A few days after that the man who whipped him was thrown from his horse and died of his injuries…and Papa…' Emma faltered. 'Papa believed that Tom might have been involved in the accident, but I am sure that, whatever else Tom might have done, he would not have caused another man's death.'

Lytham frowned as she stopped speaking.

'Do you know the name of this gentleman?'

'No, my lord. I only know that Mama became ill after my father and brother quarrelled, and my brother stormed from the house, vowing never to return.'

'I see. And you have not heard from him to this day?' Lytham's gaze narrowed. It seemed that she was in ignorance of the facts, which he had not known himself until this past year when he had asked his lawyers to investigate the estate. It was his agent, Stephen Antrium, who had told him the full facts of the case.

'We have heard nothing in almost three years,' Emma said. 'My brother is three years my junior, my lord, and I have missed him for we were very close as children.'

'It was unfortunate for the family,' Lytham said. 'Tell me, would you accept your brother if he tried to contact you?'

'Yes, of course,' she replied, head lifting proudly. 'I do not for one moment believe that Tom had anything to do with the death of that man. He may have flirted with a married woman—my brother was a flirt by all accounts—and he may possibly have cheated at cards, though I cannot think it, but he would never murder anyone.'

'You seem very confident that he would not have stooped to murder?'

'I do not believe my brother is capable of such infamy, sir.'

'Would you be happy for me to make certain inquiries concerning his whereabouts? I have not done so thus far, for I imagined he might come to me.' He had expected Tom Sommerton to demand his rights of him, but it had not happened. Why? Was he afraid that Lytham might press charges against him? Or was there another more sinister reason for his silence?

'But why should you want to help Tom?' She blushed as she looked at him, finding his intent gaze unsettling. 'Surely my family has caused you enough trouble, sir?'

'At the moment my most pressing problem is to get you to use my name,' he said, lips quirking. 'Would you prefer to call me Alex as my friends do?'

'Certainly not,' Emma said at once. 'I should not dream of being so presumptuous, Lord Lytham.'

'Lytham…' he murmured and grimaced as he felt the pain in his shoulder. 'You know, I think I shall take your advice and try to rest for a few moments.'

'Of course. I shall be as quiet as a mouse.'

He smiled as if he doubted it, but she was as good as her word. He put his head back and closed his eyes, but sleep did not come for his mind was far too busy.

He had been told that his elder brother John had been involved in an unpleasant scandal shortly before the accident that had killed him—something involving a young man he insisted had insulted his wife. There had been an ugly brawl, and John had had to be restrained, pulled off the man before he beat him to death. Yet until the fateful night when Sir Thomas Sommerton had gambled away his estate, he had not bothered to go into details.

John had been a brute and a selfish hedonist; it was little wonder that his wife had sought comfort elsewhere. Yet Lytham could well believe that his brother might have been jealous of his beautiful wife, and would have done whatever he thought necessary to rid himself of a rival. It might prove fruitful if he were to seek an interview with Maria, though he was not sure that his brother's wife would confide in him. Why should she? Nearly three years had passed since her husband died, and no doubt she wanted only to forget all the distress it had caused her.

Stephen Antrium had said that there was no doubt the accident was purely that, the result of John's recklessness, but supposing there had been more? Supposing the rumours had been true and Tom Sommerton had been in some way responsible?

Lytham did not believe the pot-shot taken at him from the trees had been a poacher misfiring, but as far as he knew he had no particular enemies. Unless… A young man disowned by his father, perhaps because of an injustice, and now his inheritance stolen from him at the gambling tables by the brother of the man who had ruined him—sufficient cause for an attempt at murder? He wondered. It might be if Tom Sommerton was desperate enough—and yet Lytham was not convinced.

Who else would like to see him dead? Lytham reviewed the possible candidates in his mind… Who had he upset recently? He was often lucky at the card table, but few men were so foolish as to throw their estates into the pot, and most could afford to lose what he won from them. He had stolen the occasional mistress from beneath the nose of a rival, but such things were usually taken in good part.

Who would benefit from his death? There were some distant cousins in the north, but he had never met them to his knowledge and could not think that they would go to such lengths to inherit his estate. Especially as he believed they were quite wealthy themselves.

It seemed, then, that Tom Sommerton had the most reason to wish for his death.

Emma was relieved when they reached the inn after some twenty or so minutes more on the road. Although the marquis was able to descend from the carriage without assistance, she had observed that he looked pale and she knew that the wound had opened again when he moved, for there was a fresh bloodstain on his shirt.

The innkeeper was quick to bustle round and organise rooms for them both, and a doctor was immediately sent for. Emma was left sitting alone in the parlour, Lily having gone off with their hostess on some errand of her own, when the doctor came in to tell her that he had finished attending the marquis.

'His lordship asked me to tell you that he would be remaining in his room for a few hours,' he said. 'I have repaired the damage, Miss Sommerton, and given him something to ease the pain. Providing that he does not take a fever, he should be well enough to continue his journey tomorrow.'

'Thank you,' Emma said feeling relieved. 'Shall you be calling again, sir?'

'Not unless you send for me, Miss Sommerton—which you may do if you have cause for concern.'

'We shall see how we go on,' she replied and thanked him once more.

Emma felt at a loss after he had gone. It was far too early for her to think of nuncheon, for she had eaten only an hour or so before they set out on their journey, and she was restless. Since she could hardly go up to visit the marquis in his bedchamber, she decided to go out for a walk.

'You should take care, miss,' the innkeeper advised as he saw her about to leave his house. 'There are some bad people about these days—and you don't want to get yourself shot like his lordship.'

Emma thanked him for his advice, and said that she did not intend to stray too far from the inn, but she had not taken more than a few steps before Lily came flying after her.

'Oh, miss,' she said breathlessly. 'I saw you from the upstairs landing and came to warn you.'

'To warn me of what?' Emma said, a little amused by Lily's expression. 'I shall not wander as far as the woods. I am not so foolish after what happened to the marquis.'

'I didn't like to say, miss...not with the marquis there...'

'To say what?'

'I saw someone following the carriage, miss...almost from the time we left home.'

'You saw someone following?' An icy prickle ran down Emma's spine as she stared at the girl. 'Do you mean a man on horseback?'

Lily nodded, her cheeks pink. 'He kept some distance behind as if he didn't want to be noticed, and then he disappeared into the trees when we got to the woods.'

'You mean he could have ridden ahead and...' Emma was shocked. 'But that would be a deliberate act, Lily...almost planned.'

'Yes, miss.' She bit her lip. 'I was too upset to think proper at the time. I should have mentioned it, shouldn't I?'

'Don't worry,' Emma said as she saw the girl's awkward look. 'I shall tell the marquis later—and it wasn't your fault. No one could have dreamed something like that would happen. Besides, it may have been an accident.'

'Yes, miss.' Lily hesitated. 'It's just that there have been tales of a highwayman...a local man...'

'That is the first I've heard of it,' Emma said and frowned as she saw that Lily was looking hard at the ground. 'What do you mean—a local man?'

'I'm sure I don't know, miss.'

'Yes, you do.' Emma took hold of her arm. 'What have you heard in the servants' hall, Lily? What is it you don't want to tell me?'

'There have been half a dozen robberies on the London road,' Lily said. 'They say he knows the area too well to get caught, although there have been attempts to trap him.'

'And what else do they say?'

Lily's cheeks were bright red as her mistress gave her an impatient little shake. 'Cook said it was all nonsense, but others said as it was Master Tom.'

'Are you saying that my brother has become a highwayman?'

Lily hung her head. It was obvious from her manner that she had heard the tale, and that she believed it.

'And you think it may have been him following us?' Emma saw the truth in the other girl's eyes. 'But why would Tom shoot at the marquis?'

Lily was silent and Emma frowned. Surely it was nonsense? Why would her brother try to kill the Marquis of Lytham?

Oh, no! Surely he could not be out for revenge for what had happened to their father? The thought was so shocking that Emma felt sick. Tom would never deliberately try to murder someone— would he?

She remembered the quarrel between her father and brother. She had heard them shouting at each other in the library. Tom had bitterly denied his involvement in the crimes his father had accused him of and then he had stormed from the house. At the time she had not attempted to stop him, for she had imagined he would return when tempers had cooled, but he had not. She and her mother had deeply regretted the breach, and Emma suspected that her father had also come to wish he had not banished his only son, that he had brooded over it and his unhappiness had led to the increasing recklessness in his gambling.

She had thought Tom might come home after her father's death, had half-expected to see him at the funeral, but there had been no sign of him, and she had given up hope as the weeks and then months passed.

A memory stirred in the back of her mind. She had seen someone in the gardens outside her bedchamber on the night that the marquis had first come to the house.

Had that been Tom? Had he been watching the house, waiting for his opportunity?

Such an idea was very distressing to Emma, and she dismissed the thought almost immediately. Why should Tom have skulked in the bushes like that when he might have come into the house? Had he had something to say to Lytham, surely he could have said it face to face? The brother she remembered would certainly have done so—but had he changed? Had she ever really known him?

'You are to say nothing of this to the marquis,' she told Lily. 'I shall tell him you think someone may have been following us— but I want none of this foolishness over highwaymen, or that there is a tale about my brother. It is all gossip and I will not have it— do you understand me?'

'Yes, miss,' Lily said. 'I am sorry if I've made you angry, miss.'

'No, I am not angry,' Emma said. 'But this is a foolish tale, Lily, and I want you to forget it. If there is a highwayman haunting the road between Cambridgeshire and London, it is not my brother.'

'No, miss…if you say so.'

'I do say so,' Emma said. 'Now, go back to the inn and see if you can make yourself useful to his lordship. Knock at his door and ask if he wants anything, and then go to my room and wait for me.'

'Yes, miss.'

Lily hung her head as she retraced her head to the inn. It was clear that she felt her mistress had been sharp with her, which was a pity and not what Emma had intended—but she could not allow such tales to reach Lytham's ears.

She decided that she would take up his offer to try to trace Tom. She had already been toying with the idea of employing an agent to try to find her brother, and now she realised that it might be more important than she had previously thought.

She wandered as far down the road as she dared, finding a wooden seat that overlooked a pretty view of the river, and sat down to ponder her situation. Could Tom have taken that shot at

Lytham? Were the rumours of his having arranged an accident to bring about a man's death by some remote chance true? No, she could not believe it and yet…

Emma sat there for some moments, staring at the brown water as it weaved its way sluggishly through reed beds and lapped against willow-fronded banks. She had wondered how Tom was managing to live, cut off from home and family. She had thought he might have joined the army, for he had spoken of wishing he might when they were children—but to become a highwayman!

That was indeed a desperate act, and one that made Emma feel shivers down her spine. It was a hanging matter if he was caught…but…no, she would not believe it. The servants had got hold of some foolish tale and made it more than it was…

'Emma? It is you, isn't it?'

Emma jumped as she heard the voice, spinning round to stare in bewilderment at the man who had spoken so tentatively. She rose to her feet, feeling as if she were in a nightmare. Tom here? Then it must have been him Lily had seen following them.

'Tom…is that you?' Her face was as white as a sheet, her heart beating wildly. 'Oh, Tom! I was just thinking about you.'

'Lily spotted me, didn't she?' Tom came towards her a little awkwardly. 'I saw her looking out of the window and thought she might have seen me—that's why I dodged off into the woods.'

'Oh, Tom!' Emma went to greet him, her hands outstretched. 'Why didn't you come home for the funeral? Why didn't you come to see Mama and I after Father died?'

'I wasn't sure I would be welcome,' Tom said. 'Besides, I've only just recovered from…a nasty chill.'

Emma was sure he had been going to say something else.

'Tom…' It was a terrible thing to ask, but she had to be sure. 'You didn't take a shot at someone earlier today, did you?'

His eyes lost their look of uncertainty, becoming angry. 'If that's what you think of me, I may as well go now.'

'No!' She took a step towards him, catching at his arm. 'I didn't think it was you, but Lily told me…'

Tom pulled a wry face. 'I can imagine what she said.' He paused and then squared his shoulders. 'It's true, Emma. I did take to the road for a while. I was desperate and I fell in with someone…a bad lot.'

'Oh, Tom…' Her heart caught and she looked round as if fearing someone might hear his confession. 'That is so dangerous.'

'I know.' He looked rueful. 'Someone took a pot-shot at us some months ago, and I was wounded. I've been ill of a fever, and then I went into hiding because I was told they were looking for us. That's why I couldn't come home for the funeral—because I might have been arrested.'

'Are you in danger of being arrested now?'

'I've given up the life,' Tom said. 'I doubt if anyone has proof that I was involved in any of the crimes we committed. But the man I was with is threatening to murder me if I don't help him with something he has in mind.'

'What is that?' Emma sensed that he was nervous. 'You might as well tell me, Tom.'

'I think he took that shot at Lytham,' Tom said after a moment's hesitation. 'He had me watching the house for Lytham's arrival but…when I guessed what he intended, I refused to help him with the rest of it. But I saw someone skulking in the woods just after the shot, and I think it may have been him.'

'The rest of it?' Emma felt the chill run down her spine. 'What are you talking about, Tom?'

'I shouldn't have told you so much.' Her brother glanced over his shoulder. 'He would kill me if he knew—but I wanted to warn Lytham to be on his guard. If *his* attempt to murder the marquis has failed this time, he will try again. He hates him and has vowed to see him dead.'

'Who is this man?' Emma hung on to his arm as he tried to turn away. 'You have to tell me, Tom.'

'I don't know his name, not his real name—and that's the truth,' Tom said. 'All I know is that he hates Lytham. He swears he has a score to settle…and that was said when he was drunk one night. Usually he is tight lipped and keeps his plans to himself.'

'You are afraid of him, aren't you?'

Tom nodded but said nothing.

'Why did you get involved with him?'

'I was drunk and near to desperate,' Tom said. 'It seemed I had nothing left to hope for…I thought I might as well be hung as a thief since everyone already thought the worst of me.'

'Oh, my dearest brother…' Emma saw the hurt in his face and her throat tightened with emotion. 'What can I say?'

'Only that you believe me,' Tom said. 'Believe me, Emma, however desperate I might be, I would not kill, except in self-defence. I am not a murderer, and I did not arrange the death of Alexander Lytham's brother.'

She stared at him in horror. 'It was Lytham's brother—the man with whose wife you were supposed to have had an affair? It was Lord Lynston who fell from his horse and was killed?'

'Yes. I thought you must know.'

'I had no idea. Mother told me a part of it, but Father never mentioned the man's name. I don't think she knew that.'

'There was something between Maria and I,' Tom admitted, his cheeks pink. 'You are not to tell anyone else that, Emma. Give me your word!'

'Yes, of course.'

'I did not do anything that might have caused him to fall that afternoon. I give you my word.'

'Of course you didn't! I never believed it,' Emma cried.

'Thank you.' She was rewarded by a slight smile from Tom. 'But you thought I might have taken a pot-shot at Lytham today—why?'

'Because of what happened to Father and the estate.'

'He is welcome to the estate,' Tom said, a note of bitterness in his voice. 'Had I inherited there would have been nothing left. What I hoped for—what I wanted—was a career in the army, but Father would not fork out for a commission for me. He insisted I must look after the estate, but he had ruined us before I had the chance to try.'

'I am so sorry, Tom.'

He shook his head. 'It was not your fault—or Mama's. I have thought of you both often, but I believed it better not to involve you in more trouble. I'm going to find honest work if I can and then I'll do something to help you and Mama.'

'How can I reach you?' Emma asked as he began to move away from her again. 'Tom…don't go just like that, please?'

'It is better you do not try to contact me,' he said. 'If I need you, I'll be in touch.'

Emma stared after him as he ran towards the woods, where she thought he must have tethered his horse.

What was she going to do now?

Chapter Three

Emma had the rest of the day to consider her options, for the marquis did not appear before seven that evening when he came downstairs to join her in the private parlour for dinner. She saw that he had somehow managed to dress himself, struggling into his coat, which was foolish and unnecessary since they were to dine privately. He looked tired and pale, but seemed otherwise no worse for his injury, and denied feeling any great pain when she inquired.

'Thank you, but apart from a little soreness I believe I have taken no ill, Miss Sommerton.'

'Should you not have supped on a little broth in your room?' Emma asked. 'I am certain the innkeeper's wife would have been happy to have brought up a tray.'

'And that would have left you to fend for yourself,' Lytham said. 'I have already caused too much distress, and I can only apologise for it, Miss Sommerton. I thank you for remaining here and not finding yourself an alternative way to finish your journey.'

'I should not dream of abandoning you while you are unwell,' Emma said. 'And I could quite easily have had my dinner upstairs—could do so now, if you would prefer to return to your bed.'

'This is not the first time I have been wounded,' Lytham said. 'I had the privilege of serving under Wellington, and received a slight injury in the Spanish campaign. I was with him in France, too, and left him only after Boney had been beaten.'

'You were a soldier…' Emma nodded as if that confirmed something in her own mind. 'That was what my brother wanted above all things—a commission in the army.'

'It would probably have saved much unpleasantness had your father allowed him to have his way.' Lytham's gaze narrowed as he saw her blush. 'Have you considered that your brother may have joined the army already?'

'I…I am not sure that he would have joined the ranks, and anything else would have been out of the question.'

'Because he did not have the money?'

'That, and the shadow hanging over him.'

'Ah, yes, that accusation of cheating.'

Lytham's gaze narrowed as she avoided looking at him. Now what was she hiding? She had told him she knew nothing of her brother's whereabouts, but it seemed she had not told him the entire truth. He was certain she did know something, but his questions had to wait because the innkeeper's wife was bringing in their supper. She had prepared vegetable soup, which smelled delicious, and informed them that stuffed pike and a tender roast duckling would follow it.

'For I didn't want to cook anything too heavy for his lordship, miss,' she explained. 'Not but what there ain't a nice bit of roast beef if he should fancy it.'

'You are too good, madam,' Lytham said. 'We shall see how we go on, thank you.'

'So, what is it you don't want to tell me?' he asked once the woman had retired after serving the soup. 'It would be best if you deal honestly with me, Miss Sommerton. Be sure that I shall know if you lie—and I do not care for liars.'

'Lily saw someone following the carriage from the moment we left Sommerton House.'

'But she did not see fit to tell us?' He arched his brows. 'Why was that, I wonder?'

'I dare say she was frightened of you,' Emma replied. She glanced down at her dish, toying with her spoon. 'Besides, it does not follow that the man who was riding behind us took that shot at you.'

'It is not necessarily the case,' he agreed, but his eyes were hard and suspicious. 'Who was following us—your brother?'

Emma's gaze flew to his face in surprise. 'What makes you say that?'

'Although some may make the mistake of thinking it, I am not a fool, Miss Sommerton. When did you know your brother had been following us?'

'Not until after—' She bit her lip. 'Tom said it was not he who shot you and I believe him.'

'Indeed? Should I believe you? I wonder?'

'I am not in the habit of lying.'

'I do believe that,' he said. 'You should never play cards, Miss Sommerton. You have the most expressive face and it gives you away every time.' He studied her as she choked over a spoonful of soup. He had hardly touched his own, she noticed. 'Come, now, it cannot be that bad.'

'You are pleased to mock me, sir!'

'Yes, it does please me,' he admitted. 'But tell me—what has your brother been getting up to now?'

'Nothing…why should he?'

'You told me he had not been home since his father's death. There must be some reason for that, would you not agree? I would have thought it was an excellent opportunity for him to visit his mother and sister. And yet he approaches you now.'

'He has been ill…'

'Ah, so he has been ill. I wonder what kind of illness?'

'A fever, I believe.' Wild horses would not have dragged the truth from her!

'Yes, but what had he been doing before he became ill?' Lytham mused. 'Clearly you do not mean to tell me, Miss Sommerton. Has your brother given you an address where we may contact him?'

'No. He…he said he would come to me if he needed me.'

Lytham nodded. 'Then, whether you know it or not, he is involved in something.' He saw that she was staring at the table again. 'You may tell me the truth, you know. I have no intention of bringing more harm to your family—any member of your family.'

Emma glanced up, meeting his eyes. 'My brother is in some kind of trouble,' she admitted. 'I cannot tell you what exactly for I do not know—but he said that I was to warn you of danger to yourself.'

'It is a little late for that, do you not think?'

'He did not know you would be shot at,' Emma said, though she could not be sure that Tom hadn't had some idea of it. Why else would he have been following them? 'He says that some-one... A man he knows has a score to settle, but he does not know the man's name, only that he is a bad lot. I believe this man may have been committing acts of highway robbery these past few weeks.'

'Ah, now we are getting to it,' Lytham said, nodding his head. 'Your brother has been involved, but draws the line at murder—is that it? No, you do not need to answer, for it would incriminate both you and your brother.'

'Tom is not a murderer. He told me that he did not arrange your brother's death.'

'I am sure that John's death was the result of his own reck-lessness,' Lytham said. 'Your father should have known better than to believe such rumours. There were bound to be some after what happened—but I shall make inquiries and do my best to clear your brother's name...of this at least.'

'I do not believe he cheated at cards either,' Emma said, hold-ing her head proudly. 'He always maintained his innocence, but he was not believed.'

'It is a difficult thing to disprove,' Lytham said. 'But this also I shall look into—there, does that make you more inclined to trust me?'

'I have had no reason to distrust you, sir.'

'And yet you continue to hold me at arm's length.'

'How else should I behave, sir? We are destined to part in another day or so.'

'Perhaps.' His mouth curved in a mocking smile. 'Why is it that I do not believe that, Miss Sommerton?'

Her heart raced wildly as she saw the laughter in his eyes. He was a very provoking man and she had a good mind to tell him so, but she did not quite dare.

'Perhaps because you do not wish to believe it, sir.'

'That may be true. I have always taken my responsibilities towards others seriously. Until I believe you safely settled, I could not simply abandon you.'

'Even if I prefer to be abandoned?'

'Even so.' He inclined his head. She thought he looked a little uncomfortable, but he was intent on questioning her and she did not ask if he was too warm, though his face was flushed. 'Did your brother give you a name or any other clue to this rogue's identity?'

'None, sir. He said merely that you should be on your guard. I do know that Tom is afraid of him, whoever he is. Apparently, he has threatened to kill him if he does not help him do whatever it is he intends to do.'

'Murder me, do you think?' Lytham's brows rose. 'And yet will there ever be a more perfect opportunity than this morning in the woods? I feel that the shot that winged me was a warning in itself.'

'But why?' Emma frowned as she posed the question. 'Have you an enemy, sir? Someone who would like to make you suffer…someone for whom a quick death would not be enough?'

'That seems a likely explanation, does it not?' His brow furrowed. 'I have not been able to think of anyone I have offended to that degree, except your brother. I believe he may feel he has cause to wish for my death. There is the matter of the quarrel with his father, which led to his being disowned, and, if that were not enough, I am responsible for your father's death. Please believe me when I tell you I wish I could have prevented that, but it happened and there is no denying it. Your brother has more than one grievance that might make him wish to kill me.'

'It was not Tom who shot you!'

Lytham looked at her gravely, then nodded. 'You know, I am inclined to think you may be right. Your brother is clearly a hot head, Miss Sommerton—and whoever planned this has taken his time.'

'Who would benefit from your death, sir?' Emma asked. 'Have you no brothers or cousins?'

'I have distant cousins in the north,' he admitted. 'But I do not know them. I cannot think they covet my fortune to such a degree—and I am the last of my immediate family.'

'Then you must have an enemy—someone who hates you,' Emma said. 'Are you sure you cannot think of anyone? Perhaps someone with a grudge against your family, if not you personally?'

'I believe my father and John may have made enemies,' Lytham said, looking thoughtful. 'Your brother was not the only one to have been ruined by them.'

'Then that is perhaps where you should look.'

He shook his head and she noticed again that he looked flushed. He was sweating now. Was he ill and too stubborn to admit it?

'But they are dead,' he said as if to convince himself. 'Would such hatred continue beyond the grave?'

'It seems unlikely, sir—but unless it was merely a poacher…' She left the sentence unfinished, hesitating for a moment, then, 'No, Tom risked much to warn me. You do have an enemy, sir. You must look deeply into your past and think of someone you have injured.'

Lytham frowned. 'There was once a man who might have hated me, but he is dead. I heard that he had been killed in a bar in Spain after he was court-martialled.'

Emma saw that he was thoughtful. 'You have remembered someone who might have cause to hate you enough to kill you?'

He drew a deep sigh and did not answer at once. She could swear that he was feverish and his eyes had an odd brightness about them. She believed that it was taking a supreme effort of will to sit there talking to her as if nothing was wrong.

'He was reported killed,' Lytham said. 'But if he lived…yes, Pennington might hate me sufficiently to make me suffer before he killed.'

'What did you do to him?'

His face was hard as he returned her accusing look. 'What makes you imagine that I did anything?'

'Forgive me, but you did say he might have cause.'

'I was unwittingly the cause of his downfall,' Lytham said. 'He committed the unforgivable sin of raping another officer's wife while under the influence of drink, and I was the first on the scene afterwards. I did what I could to help her, and then went to her husband. He challenged Pennington to a duel, and for that he received a severe reprimand—but Pennington was court-martialled and dismissed from the service in disgrace.'

'And so I should think!' Emma cried. 'In my opinion, he deserved more than that.'

'He received more,' Lytham said and something flickered in his eyes. 'Some of the other officers got together after he was dismissed. They whipped him and spat at him, humiliated him in all manner of unspeakable ways, and finally drove him out without a decent rag to his back.' He saw that she had turned pale. 'Forgive me, that was not a tale to repeat to a lady.'

'It was no more than he deserved,' Emma said, recovering from the shock. She rather liked it in him that he had told her the whole tale. Most gentlemen would think it too terrible for her to hear. 'But why should that make him hate you? Unless you were one of those officers?'

'No. I was aware of their plans, but I did nothing. I have often thought that I ought to have reported them, but I was disgusted at what he had done, and although I did not join them, I condoned what they did. That was wrong and has been a shame to me ever since, Miss Sommerton. I have told no other.'

'Then I am honoured by your confidence, sir. You may rest assured that it will go no further.' She looked at him uncertainly, taking note of the beads of sweat on his brow. The stubborn man was obviously ill, but refusing to admit it. What ought she to do?

'Thank you. You are a remarkable woman, Emma Sommerton.'

'You are certain this man was killed in a brawl?'

'I was told it was certain, but I had no evidence. I wished to put the whole incident from my mind.'

'Yes, I can understand how you felt,' she agreed. 'But I think you should try to make further inquiries—don't you?'

'Yes, perhaps.' He laid down his spoon. 'This is excellent fare, but I do not feel I can eat much more. Will you excuse me if…?' He rose to his feet, gave a sigh and then staggered, crashing into the table.

Some instinct had Emma on her feet in time to prevent him falling. He leaned on her heavily, muttering an apology as she assisted him to a wooden bench.

'You are ill, my lord. You should have stayed in your room.'

'Forgive me,' he said and gave her the sweetest smile. 'I was feeling perfectly well when I came down.'

Emma placed her hand against his brow. 'I think you have a slight fever, sir. Will you allow me to help you upstairs?'

'Call the landlord,' he said thickly. 'It is not fitting for you to help me to bed.'

'I dare say he is busy just for the moment,' Emma said. 'If you can lean on me I believe we might make it up the stairs…if we go slowly.'

'Yes, I think I could manage if you help me. I am so sorry.'

'Hush, you foolish man,' Emma replied. 'Put your arm about my waist and we shall do the best we can.'

He obeyed her, clearly feeling much worse than he would allow. Emma marvelled that he had managed to hold a sensible conversation with her for so long. He was obviously suffering both a great deal of pain, and judging by the heat coming from his body was also in fever.

She drew him from the parlour into the hall, just as a party of rather rowdy gentlemen was being ushered into the larger parlour next door. One of them laughed and nudged his friend, who leered at Emma suggestively. They seemed to imagine she was assisting a drunken man, and probably thought the worst.

Emma ignored them, concentrating on getting him up the stairs. She had managed to get halfway when one of the maids came hurrying to help them.

'Is the gentleman ill again, miss?' she asked. 'He was very hot earlier and I offered to fetch the doctor, but he wouldn't hear of it.'

'I think we must send for the physician as soon as he is in bed,' Emma said, ignoring the muffled protests of the man she was half-carrying by now.

It was difficult to get him to his room, but once they had him on the bed the maid hurried away to fetch the stable lad, who would ride at once for the doctor. Emma left the marquis for a moment as she went down the hall to her own room and summoned Lily.

'The marquis is ill,' she said. 'We must get him into bed and sponge him down to cool some of the heat before the doctor gets here.'

'You can't do that, miss,' Lily said, looking horrified. 'You can't go into a gentleman's bedchamber—not a lady like you.'

'I have already been into his bedchamber,' Emma said, ever practical. 'Besides, no one need know if we do not tell them. It will be our secret, Lily.'

'Why don't you let me look after him, miss?'

It was exactly what she ought to do, of course—but Emma could not simply abandon the marquis to his fate.

'We shall do it together,' she said. 'No one can say it was improper if you were there, can they?'

Lily opened her mouth and then shut it again. She had not forgotten that her mistress had been sharp with her earlier, and she did not want to upset Miss Sommerton again.

'No one need know, miss…if that's what you want?'

'It is what I want,' Emma said and smiled at her. 'Thank you, Lily—and I'm sorry if I was sharp with you earlier.'

'Oh, that's all forgot now, miss.'

'Follow me, then.' Emma led the way back down the hall to the marquis's bedchamber. He was lying where she had left him, but as she entered he moved restlessly and called out a name. Emma could not make out whom he was calling to, but she imagined it was a woman—perhaps the woman he loved, she thought.

She laid a hand on his brow, frowning as she felt the heat. 'It is all right, my lord, the doctor will come soon.'

He muttered something she could not hear again, and Emma turned as Lily brought a bowl of cold water to the bed.

'Had we better undress him, miss?'

'Yes, I think we ought,' Emma said. 'You start with his boots and I'll bathe his face, and then we'll take off the rest of his things.'

'You'd better turn your back when we get to his breeches,' Lily said. 'I've seen a naked man before when I nursed my father, but I dare say you haven't, miss.'

'No…' Emma swallowed hard. 'Yes, perhaps that would be best, Lily. I'll help with the rest and leave that to you.'

She bathed his face, and then began to take off his neckcloth and then his coat, waistcoat and shirt. He winced as she tugged at his coat, and she wondered at the strength of mind that had got him into it with his wounded arm in the first place. He was clearly a stubborn man, but now he was suffering for his reckless behaviour.

Lily had discarded his boots, and she began to pull down his skintight breeches, warning Emma when it was time to turn her back.

'It's all right, miss. I've covered him with a sheet. He's decent now. You can turn round again.'

Emma turned back to the bed. She saw that the top half of his body was still uncovered, which was enough to make her stomach clench with the oddest sensation. She had never realised that a man's naked body could look so beautiful, and half-regretted that she had dutifully turned her back as Lily finished undressing him.

Lily had begun to sponge his shoulders and arms while Emma looked on. He muttered in his fever a few times, but she thought that he was not really aware of what was happening.

'He's proper poorly,' Lily said. 'It's a terrible shame, miss— and him such a fine figure of a man, too.'

'Yes, he is, isn't he?' Emma said, her voice sounding husky. 'I should imagine he is quite strong.'

'Oh, yes, miss—but it's often the strongest what the fever takes.'

Emma wished that her maid would be a little more cheerful, but she held her tongue. Lily might be needed in the next few days and she did not want to upset her again.

'I think you should go back to your own room now, miss,' Lily said. 'It would be better if there was just me here when the doctor comes—don't you think?'

'Yes, I suppose so. But you must tell me what he says as soon as he has gone.'

Emma was reluctant to leave, but it would not do her reputation any good if she remained, and so she went out into the hall and started to make her way towards her own room.

'Ain't he no good to you this evening, lovely lady?' a voice asked, and Emma looked into the flushed face of one of the men she had seen downstairs a few minutes earlier. 'I could show you how a proper man behaves with his woman.'

'Please allow me to pass,' Emma said haughtily, disliking the suggestive leer on his face. 'Stand aside, sir—or I shall call for the landlord.'

'No call to take offence,' the man replied, swaying slightly on his feet. 'Just being friendly—doxy!' His taunt was clearly meant to wound because she had refused him, but Emma did not care to answer, merely going into her own room and locking the door.

It would stay locked until Lily came!

Several hours passed before Lily came at last to tell her that the doctor had been.

'Doctor Fettle gave the gentleman something to ease him, miss. He says someone needs to sit with his lordship all night—and the innkeeper's wife is there now. She told me to get some rest. You should too, miss. You haven't slept at all, have you?'

'I couldn't rest until you came,' Emma said. 'But I shall try to do so now.'

It was in any case difficult to sleep since Emma was unused to sharing a bed. She dozed for a while, but when Lily began to snore got up, dressed, and went down the hall to the marquis's room.

The innkeeper's wife put a finger to her lips as Emma entered.

'You shouldn't have come, miss. It isn't fitting for a young lady.'

'I had to know how he was faring.'

'A little better, I think. Go back to bed, miss. I can manage here.'

'I would rather just sit here quietly for a while. You have been sitting with him for hours now. Why don't you go and get some sleep? I am sure you have much to do in the morning.'

The woman looked at her uncertainly. 'That's true enough…if you're sure, miss?'

'Perfectly sure,' Emma said and took her place by the bed. 'Thank you for being so kind to us.'

'It was no more than anyone would do. Such wickedness to shoot down a fine man like that. 'Tis a wicked shame that such a thing should happen, that a man cannot be safe anywhere these days. I hope they catch whoever did it and hang him!'

Emma nodded, but did not speak again. She was watching the marquis as he slept, and got up to place her hand on his brow as the other woman went out. Was it her imagination—or did he seem a little cooler than he had earlier in the evening?

She wrung out a cloth in cool water and bathed his face and neck, smoothing the cool linen over his shoulders, then sat down by the fire again. The logs were still smouldering, though no longer giving out much heat and she shivered as the chill went over her. Had Tom been telling the truth when he said he had not shot Lytham? She did hope so for she did not think she could forgive him if he had…especially if the marquis should die. But he would not die! He was strong and despite what Lily had said earlier, she believed that he would beat this fever.

'Please, God, let him live,' Emma prayed aloud. 'Do not let him die. But he will not die! He is much too strong to let something like this defeat him.'

'Water…' She heard the harsh whisper and went to him, seeing that his eyes were open. 'Please…water…'

There was a jug of water beside the bed. She poured a little into a cup, and then saw that she would have to help him to drink.

'Help me…'

'Yes, of course,' she said and put her arm about his shoulders, lifting him so that he could sip from the cup she held to his lips. 'Just a little at a time, not too much at once.'

'You are a good nurse,' he muttered and she realised that the fever had broken. His eyes were open and looking straight at her. 'But you ought not to be here.'

'Others have been sitting with you,' she said. 'Lily and the innkeeper's wife. I have merely come to give them a rest.'

He sighed as she laid him back against the pillows. 'Damned fool…all right now. Go to bed, Emma.'

'In a little while,' she agreed. 'When I see you are settled.'

'Sleep now,' he said and his eyes closed.

Emma sat with him for another hour or so, but he seemed to be peaceful and she believed the fever had gone. It was as she had thought; he was strong and had been able to fight the sickness off more easily than some others might, and she thanked God for it.

Lily came just as dawn was breaking.

'You should get some rest, miss,' she said. 'I'll sit with him now—unless you need me?'

'No, you stay here,' Emma said. 'But I think you will find he is much better. I dare say he will wake and call for his breakfast soon.'

'He's sure to be weak for a few days,' Lily said in a voice of doom. 'And just because he's settled it doesn't mean the fever's gone. It can come back worse, so they say—the fever does for many a man what seems strong as a horse.'

'Thank you, Lily,' Emma said and smiled inwardly. Did Lily enjoy being the forecaster of ill fortune?

She was fairly sure in her own mind that the danger time had passed and was able to rest on her bed for a few hours before she rose and went down the hall once more to look in on the marquis.

As she had suspected, he was propped up against his pillows and eating what looked like a milky porridge. He set the bowl aside as she went in and gave her a disapproving look.

'I believe I told you last night—you ought not to be here, Miss Sommerton.'

'In fact, you called me Emma last night,' she said and smiled at him. 'I see that you are feeling more yourself, my lord. I shall not stay to disturb your sensibilities, but go down at once and break my fast.'

'I shall come down later.'

'You would be foolish to try. Why do you not stay in bed for today? You should rest for the morning, at least.'

'But you will wish to continue your journey. Mrs Flynn will be expecting you.'

'She will not worry too soon. Travelling is always uncertain, and she will merely think there has been some delay.'

He looked amused. 'Are you always so calm?'

Emma smiled, but would not be drawn. She had felt less than calm on several occasions recently, and most of them were due to this man.

'You know that is not so, my lord. I believe I treated you to a most unseemly display of temper the first day you arrived at Sommerton.'

'Ah, yes, but I took you by surprise, didn't I, Emma? It was Emma I met that afternoon, and it was Emma who gave me water last night—but you are Miss Sommerton now.'

'Surely Emma and Miss Sommerton are one and the same?'

'Oh, no,' he said and his eyes gleamed with humour. 'I can assure you that they are two very different people.'

'I shall not question your judgement,' Emma replied. 'One should always humour an invalid, especially when fever is present.'

With that she went out, a little smile on her lips as she heard his laughter. How was it that he had penetrated her secret self in a way that no one else outside her family had for years? She was not sure that even her beloved mother truly knew the real Emma. She had subdued her passionate nature long ago, knowing that a life of duty caring for her mother quietly at home was likely to be her lot, but just now and then she had allowed herself to dream.

She shook her head, dismissing the foolish dreams that had started to come into her mind since…since never mind! She would not be wise to let Emma loose, and would do better to keep up the pretence of being the calm, serene Miss Sommerton who was always ready in an emergency.

Fortunately, the emergency seemed to be over. Lytham took her advice and stayed in his room until late that afternoon, coming down in time to order dinner for them both in the private parlour.

'Are you feeling better, my lord?' Emma asked, noticing that he had sensibly not tried to force himself into his elegant coat this time, but allowed it to rest over his injured arm. 'You certainly look less flushed than you did yesterday evening.'

'My wound is still a little sore and my shoulder feels stiff, but I believe I am on the mend now. I must apologise for causing you so much trouble last night, Miss Sommerton.'

'I really had very little trouble from you,' Emma assured him. 'You should thank Lily and Mrs Bennett—she is the innkeeper's wife, you know. It is Mrs Bennett who has been put to some trouble, for we are occupying rooms that were promised to someone else.'

'Yes, I dare say,' Lytham said. 'I shall have to give her a handsome present to make up for it—and Lily, too.'

'Shall you feel able to continue your journey tomorrow, my lord?'

'Yes, certainly. I am sorry to have delayed you, Miss Sommerton.'

'As I believe I told you, it is no matter.'

Lytham inclined his head, but made no further apology. He sat with her in the parlour and they discussed various books they had read, discoursing on the merits of Byron, Shelley and the quieter, whimsical work of Charles Lamb, exactly as they might have had they been in any London drawing room.

Dinner was served at six o'clock, which was early by town standards but quite late for country hours. Mrs Bennett had done them proud with soup followed by roast pork, a baked ham, trout and a side dish of baked potatoes and parsnips.

Emma was pleased to see that the marquis did this excellent fare justice, and she herself indulged in two of the custard tarts provided as a sweet course. Afterwards, they took their mulled wine to sit by the fire, the evening having turned quite chilly.

Their conversation had graduated to music and politics, and they had a lively debate on the merits or otherwise of the Corn Laws. The law had been passed that March to forbid the importation of foreign corn until the price was sufficiently high to enable the farmers to make a decent profit, but had unfortunately led to a four-pound loaf rising to the astronomical price of one shilling and tuppence.

'Well, I dare say we shall never see eye to eye on such matters,' Emma said with a smile after they had argued the subject long and hard. 'For I think of the poor villager in his cottage, and you think like a wealthy landowner.'

'Commerce must have its way,' Lytham said, amused that she had forgotten to be Miss Sommerton during her impassioned defence of the rights of the common man. 'But if the villager in his cottage were paid a fair wage might he not make his own choice about whether or not he wished to buy a loaf or bake his own?'

'Now that is another debate altogether,' Emma said and was startled by the striking of the clock in the hall. 'Do you know it is ten o'clock, sir? We have sat here all evening talking, and it is time you were in bed if you are to be fit to travel on the morrow.'

'And you must be tired since I kept you from your bed last night.'

Lytham rose with her, catching her hand, as she would have turned away. She gazed back at him, and something in her face got through to him. Before he realised what he was doing, he had drawn her close to him and, as she made no attempt to pull away but looked up at him fearlessly, her eyes dark with emotion, he bent his head to kiss her lips. His kiss was soft at first, but deepened, becoming fiercer and more passionate than he had intended.

The effect was startling for them both. Emma felt a sensation such as she had never experienced before; it seemed to burn its way through her body like slow fire, making her melt into his embrace helplessly, all resistance gone. Dimly at the back of her mind she knew that she ought not to allow this, but the over-whelming pleasure she felt prevented her from breaking away. She had never dreamed that a kiss could be so sweet! For his part, Lytham was aware of a fierce desire to scoop this woman up in his arms and carry her off to his bedchamber.

The madness lasted no more than seconds, for both remembered where and who they were and broke away almost simultaneously.

'Forgive me,' Lytham muttered, fighting the urgent need she had aroused in him. 'That was unforgivable in the circumstances.'

'It was foolish,' Emma replied. 'But understandable, my lord.'

'How so?' His brows arched. How would she seek to make such a kiss commonplace?

'You have had a brush with death…men must be forgiven much in such a case, so I have heard.'

He gave a crack of laughter. 'No! That is doing it too brown, Miss Sommerton. I am not in the grip of a fever now, I promise you—at least, not a fever induced by that slight wound to my shoulder.'

'Not so slight, my lord. You were quite ill last night. Lily was very fearful that you would succumb to your hurts.'

'Then Lily is a foolish girl,' Lytham said and frowned. 'There was never any danger of my dying from such a paltry injury. Goodnight, Miss Sommerton. I would debate this matter further with you—but the hour is late and I have taken too much advantage of your good nature already.'

'Goodnight, my lord. I wish you pleasant dreams,' Miss Sommerton said, but Emma's heart was saying something very different.

She went from the parlour hurriedly, knowing that once again she had betrayed herself into unseemly behaviour. It was fortunate that the marquis was a gentleman, for otherwise she might have been in some trouble.

Hurrying up to her room, Emma found that Lily had turned down the bed and passed a warming pan between the sheets. She assisted Emma into her nightgown, and then retired to the truckle bed that Mrs Bennett had set up.

'I thought it best, miss,' Lily said. 'You did not sleep well last night, and my snoring will not disturb you so much if I am not beside you.'

Emma thanked the girl for her thoughtfulness, but she was so tired that she did not think anything would keep her awake, even the memory of that kiss.

She closed her eyes and soon drifted into a pleasant dream...of kisses that never ended and a man who spoke of love.

It was a fine dry morning, and Emma woke early to discover that Lily had brought a breakfast tray to her room.

'The marquis requested that you breakfast early, miss,' she explained. 'He has been out already, making sure that everything is ready—and one of the grooms from the inn is to ride with us so that his lordship's own groom may keep a sharp eye out for anyone who might follow us.'

'Has Lord Lytham asked you anything about the horseman who followed us the other day?'

'He did ask me when I first saw the man, miss,' Lily said and blushed. 'And he asked me to tell him if I noticed anything in future. I said I would, miss—was that all right?'

'Yes, of course.'

Emma discovered that the marquis was wearing his coat in the normal fashion, and from his manner when she went down seemed perfectly recovered. Indeed, had she not seen him in the fever, she would not have thought that he had had a moment's illness in his life.

'I am sorry to appear impatient, Miss Sommerton,' he said. 'But I thought we should continue with all speed. Mrs Flynn will begin to worry if you do not soon keep your appointment with her.'

Since he seemed impatient to deliver her to her employer, Emma could only think that he had regretted his impulse of the evening before. It was as she had suspected, a moment's madness on his part. She imagined that he kept a mistress, and that he was used to dealing with experienced women. He had had no intention of encouraging any pretensions in her, and she was sure that she would not have been his choice had he been considering marriage. So it was just as well that she was a sensible woman who could put an unimportant incident from her mind and behave as if nothing had happened.

'I am certain you also have business, sir,' she replied briskly. 'The sooner we arrive in town and you can deliver me to Mrs Flynn's door, the better.'

Lytham nodded, but made no further comment. When he had helped first her and then Lily into his carriage, he climbed in himself, settling down with his long legs stretched out before him and his eyes closed.

Emma waited for him to begin a conversation as he had on the first day, but as the miles passed and he did not speak, she realised that he had withdrawn into himself.

Clearly he did not wish to become further involved with a woman whose family had caused him nothing but trouble, and she could not find it in her heart to blame him. She could wish that he had allowed her to go her own way from the start, but there was no sense in repining over what could not be altered.

She had suffered reverses before and coped...but something told her that it would be many nights before she ceased to dream of that kiss.

Chapter Four

Lytham roused himself from his reverie to make casual conversation for the final hour or so of their journey. He was, he told Emma, planning to go out of town for a few weeks.

'I have some business to complete, but after that I may be gone for nearly a month.'

'You are to visit your estates perhaps, sir?'

'I must visit my aunt,' he said. 'She has complained that I never do so, although I spent a month at my estate earlier in the year.'

'I dare say she is lonely. Perhaps you should bring her back to town with you?'

'I have suggested such a visit, but she has always declined,' Lytham said. 'However, the idea of a companion was a good one. I must see what can be done.' His gaze was thoughtful as it rested on Emma. 'I shall not forget your affairs whilst I am away. You may expect a visit from me on my return to town.'

'As I believe I told you, I am not certain where we shall be.'

'A letter to my London address will keep me informed.'

The tone of his voice made it a command rather than a request, and Emma gave him a speaking look. However, it was reasonable to suppose that he might have some business to discuss with her, and she nodded once to show that she acquiesced.

'Good.' He gave her a look of approval. 'We made an unfortunate beginning, Miss Sommerton, but there is no reason why we should not progress.'

Emma was not certain what he meant by this, but she made no demur. Indeed, she was pleased rather than dismayed at the idea of seeing him again.

'There is, of course, no need for us to meet in the future as other than friends,' she agreed. 'Should I be able to assist you in the matter of disposing of my father's estate, I shall be happy to do so.'

'As to that…' Lytham paused. 'Well, we shall see. I have not made up my mind yet.' He glanced out of the window as their carriage slowed to a decorous halt. 'It seems we have arrived.'

Lytham jumped down as soon as they had stopped outside the tall but narrow house in an elegant square, handing both Emma and Lily from the carriage. The front door opened instantly at his knock, and a very pretty young woman dressed in an elegant lilac dress came flying past the rather staid-looking servant who had answered it. Her pale spun-gold hair was caught up in ringlets that bobbed about her face and were tied with satin ribbons.

'Emma!' cried Bridget Flynn. 'I have been worried to death thinking that some accident had befallen you. But you are here now and all in one piece so everything is all right.'

Emma saw the expression on Lytham's face and smiled inwardly. She was not sure what he had expected, but the very fashionable young woman who spoke without the trace of an Irish accent was evidently a surprise to him.

'Bridget…or perhaps I should say Mrs Flynn.' Emma accepted her friend's impulsive hug and laughed. 'May I introduce you to the Marquis of Lytham, who very kindly brought me to London in his own carriage.'

'But isn't he the one—?' Bridget bit back the embarrassing words and offered her hand to him in a friendly manner that robbed the situation of any awkwardness. 'It is a pleasure to meet you, sir. Especially if you have been kind to my dearest Emma.'

'Thank you, ma'am.' Lytham's mouth twitched slightly. This dazzling creature was far from the wretched widow he had been imagining as Emma's future employer. 'No doubt you are eager to be alone with Miss Sommerton, so I shall not trespass on your hospitality.' His eyes challenged Emma. So this was the reason for that odd, secretive look in her eyes! 'I had not perfectly understood your situation. Please excuse me, I have other business.'

'Pray do call on us another day,' Bridget invited with an appealing innocence that he did not believe for one moment. She was a minx and those flashing eyes would be the downfall of many a man, especially now that she was a wealthy widow. 'As yet we have few engagements, though I hope for more once it is known we are in town.'

'This is not the best time of year for social occasions in town,' Lytham said. 'My advice would be to visit Bath for a few months and come back in the spring, ma'am. I believe you might find that quite diverting.'

'Yes, perhaps we may once I have something decent to wear. I have only recently come out of blacks for my dearest Bertie, you know, and I am eager to buy a new wardrobe—in fact, we shall both buy new clothes. I must tell you, sir, Emma was my dearest friend at school, and I am determined to make up to her for the unhappy time she has had of late.'

'I wish you both good fortune.' Lytham bowed to her, gave Emma a very odd look and took his leave without more to-do.

'Well…' Bridget said, glancing naughtily at Emma as she drew her into the house. 'That was a shock. I had no idea that the dastardly marquis was so attractive. No wonder your journey took so much longer than it ought.'

'Pray do not imagine anything until I tell you the whole story,' Emma said, but her heart lifted as she looked at her friend. It was such a long time since they had been together at school, and although they had always exchanged letters, she had almost forgotten how much fun it was to be with Bridget. 'Let me start from the beginning. We have had such a time of it!'

Her story unfolded, leaving nothing she considered of importance out, apart from that kiss…which had been a mere moment of madness and consequently not worth repeating.

'So you did not tell him about us,' Bridget said. 'That must account for his look when he first saw me. Do you suppose he thought I was a woman of the lower orders?'

'He may very well have done so,' Emma said and gave a little giggle. 'Perhaps it was wrong of me to deceive him, Bridget— but he was so autocratic at first. He had come to make us his dependants and it quite took the wind out of his sails when he discovered that Mama had escaped to Italy with friends, and that I was determined to become a companion.'

'Oh, pooh to that!' Bridget cried. 'It sounds very well—and we must appear to be completely respectable, Emma dearest—but you know that I invited you here to be my friend.' She pulled a naughty face. 'I shall need you to protect me once Lindisfarne arrives. He is determined to seduce me, and I am determined that he shall not.'

'Oh, Bridget,' Emma said. 'If only I could believe you.'

Her friend gave a little giggle of sheer pleasure. 'You cannot imagine how good it feels to be pursued again, Emma. I was married for nine months to my dear Bertie and I have been a widow for more than a year. Does that sound fair to you?'

'Not at all,' Emma replied. 'I told you in my letter how sorry I was for your loss.'

'I wept forever when he was killed.' Bridget pulled a face, her eyes shadowed by sadness. 'It was just like him to race his horse like that…in such a mad fashion. Bertie was such a dashing man, Emma. I wish you could have met him.'

'So do I…' She looked at Bridget and saw the haunted expression in her eyes. 'But I am sure he loved you and would not want you to grieve forever.'

'Oh, no, he absolutely forbade it,' Bridget replied. 'When we were courting he told me he'd had a premonition that he would not live long, and he made me promise that if I were to become a widow soon after we were married I would return to England and set the town on fire with his money.'

'Did he really say that?' Emma felt a little shiver down her spine. 'What a very exceptional man he must have been.'

'Oh, he was, the best,' Bridget said. 'He had nothing when we first met, you know, but then his uncle died and left him lots of lovely money—and Bertie was going to buy himself out of the army. We had planned to come back to London and set up house here.'

'And so you decided to come alone. I think that is very brave of you.'

'It is a promise, you see,' Bridget said. 'Only I didn't expect to like Lindisfarne as much as I do.'

'Ah, I see…'

'I went to call on him because Bertie talked about him so often. Lindisfarne is the black sheep of the family, Emma. The wicked earl—a terrible rake, gambler and altogether not the kind of man a young woman should know. She especially shouldn't fall in love with him.'

'Except that you have?'

'I think I may have,' Bridget admitted. 'I did not believe that I would ever love anyone again, but this is different. Bertie was like a part of me. We were so close that we might have been twins. Lindisfarne is different. He excites me and yet he terrifies me.'

'Yes…' Emma nodded her understanding. 'It is strange that you should say that, but there is a difference.'

'That is how you feel about the marquis, of course.' Bridget laughed and clapped her hands. 'Oh, do not bother to deny it, Emma—I saw it in your face. You never were very good at hiding your thoughts.'

'So I have been told. I hope that Lytham could not read me as easily as you could.'

'Oh, I doubt it,' Bridget replied blithely. 'Men are not as perceptive as we are…as the general rule. But were you in love the other way once?'

'It was during my first season,' Emma said. 'He was a very shy young man and we met only a few times. He picked up a glove for me once, and smiled at me. He sometimes sought me out at gatherings. I thought he liked me because he read poetry to me and told me I was different to the other young women he had met…but then he discovered Papa's estate was heavily encumbered and married an heiress.'

'Oh, poor Emma,' Bridget said. 'At least I did not have my
heart broken in that way. I may have lost Bertie, but I know what
it is like to be truly loved, and to be happy.'

'Yes, you were lucky and you must never forget that,' Emma
said. 'I cannot truly say my heart was broken, though my confidence received a severe setback. I did not take well in my first
season, you know, and I was never given another chance.'

'You were a late developer,' Bridget said, looking at her con-
sideringly. 'I think you could be startling in the right clothes.'

'That sounds ominous,' Emma said. 'I am not sure that I wish
to be startling.'

'You know what I mean,' Bridget said. 'You have that remote,
proud look, rather like a princess or a queen. I think you could
be a heartbreaker, and I shall take great pleasure in dressing you
as befits royalty.'

'A few clothes I can accept, but there is no need to go over-
board, Bridget.'

'Oh, pooh to that,' Bridget replied. 'I have far too much money
to spend it all on me, Emma, and I am determined on this. I want
us both to take the town by storm. Would you not like to be all
the rage…just for once in your life?'

'Well, I suppose…' Emma was tempted and the mischief in her
friend's eyes made her laugh. 'Just what are you planning?'

'Oh, nothing very much,' Bridget said. 'But I shall be very
interested to see what the Marquis of Lytham makes of you when
he sees you next time.'

Lytham frowned as he flicked through the pile of letters awaiting him at his London house. Even after a few days there was
always some pressing matter of business that must be attended—
and for once in his life he was not in the mood for making more
money.

He tossed the notes aside as he went over to the sideboard and
poured himself a brandy—far superior to any that he had tasted
in the past week. He sipped it reflectively as he went to stand by
the fireplace, one immaculate boot resting on the fender.

His valet had near fainted at the sight of the Hessians he had worn into the country, but these were superbly polished and he was once again dressed in the elegant but understated dress he adopted for town.

It seemed that Toby had made some headway with his heiress, and he was invited to an intimate gathering of friends, which might possibly turn out to be an engagement party. It was in two days' time, and would mean that he would need to stay in town a day later than he had planned.

He could make his excuses, of course. Or he could request an invitation for two friends.

A smile tugged at the corners of Lytham's mouth as he recalled the wistful note in Mrs Flynn's voice. An endorsement from him would mean that she was launched into society, here or in Bath…and that might be amusing.

He had seen something in the widow's eyes that touched a chord in his own heart, and he believed she meant to cut a dash in town. She had an unusual style, and he imagined that, once started on her way, she would cause quite a sensation.

And if the widow were invited everywhere…that would necessitate her companion accompanying her and their paths were bound to cross—especially if Lytham dropped a few hints.

'Now what are you up to?' he asked himself softly, lifting a glass to his own reflection in the mirror.

He had been unable to separate Emma from Miss Sommerton, but perhaps Mrs Flynn might succeed where he had failed. And whereas he had felt only a passing interest in the fate of the calm, reserved Miss Sommerton, he was very much more concerned with Emma. For it was Emma who had given him water when he woke from his fever, and Emma who had returned his kiss in a way that had made him want her with an urgency he had not felt in an age.

As for his ultimate intentions? That was something that even he did not know as yet. He had not thought that he cared to marry, his only experience of family life having been far from happy.

His parents had neither loved nor liked each other, both taking lovers whenever the fancy suited them, and his elder brother had picked a cold beauty as his wife, which was perhaps the reason that they had had no children.

Did he want children? Lytham stared broodingly into the fireplace. He certainly would not want to subject any child to the kind of childhood he and his brothers had been given, left to the care of servants who might sometimes be kind and at others take a cruel delight in punishing the offspring of their employers. Perhaps that was why his brothers had grown up the way they did, taking their pleasures with no thought of others, hurting any who offered them love. Was he not the same in his way? For he had never allowed himself to love and there was an emptiness within him that he had never found a means of banishing as yet.

Were all families the same? His brow wrinkled as he considered. Emma had suffered at the hands of a careless father, though she had not complained of him, had seemed to care for all her family…even the troublesome brother.

Lytham frowned as he finished his brandy. Emma was a challenge, and might prove amusing to watch over—but what was he to do about the brother?

Tom had been involved in crimes that would lead to a hanging if he were caught. And that would be disastrous for them all. Before Lytham could even consider his own affairs, he must rescue Emma's brother from his folly and set him straight—if that was possible.

The first step was probably to clear Tom Sommerton's name of any lingering scandal, and that might in part be achieved by a visit to his own home in the north-east of England. He had not bothered himself with John's personal papers, but he knew that his wife Maria still lived in the Dower House. He had seen her a couple of times briefly, to ask if she needed anything, but he usually left the day-to-day running of the estate to Stephen Antrium. Maria was his responsibility now that he was the head of the family and he had told Stephen to make any repairs to the Dower House she requested. She had retired there after she was widowed, refusing to think of coming out of her mourning, but as far as he knew she had made no demands of the estate.

He could call to see her on the pretence of business and then ask casually what she knew of the affair. She might be prepared to tell him the truth of that quarrel between Tom Sommerton and his brother, which could set the rumours of murder straight—but the charge of cheating at the card table was another matter.

It needed to be investigated further, and for that he must talk to a few of his late brother's friends. They would remember the tale and if there was any truth in it.

There was much to be done, he thought. In the meantime, Toby would oblige him with that invitation.

'Oh, look,' Bridget cried as she opened the exciting envelope the following afternoon after they had returned from a rewarding visit to her dressmaker. 'We are invited to a small evening party tomorrow.'

'Mrs and Mrs Dawlish invite you to dinner and a musical entertainment,' Emma read as Bridget handed her the card. 'That is curious. I would have expected to be invited to something more formal for a start. Do you know these people, Bridget?'

'No…' Bridget had seen something scrawled on the back and leaned over to read it. 'Ah, that explains it. Turn the card over, Emma.'

Emma did so and read aloud, 'I understand you are friends of the Marquis of Lytham, and he has personally requested that you be included, and it is therefore my pleasure to request your presence at what is to be an intimate gathering.'

'Wasn't that sweet of the marquis?' Bridget said. 'I shall wear my blue silk—and you must wear the green gown we bought today. It was fortunate that Madame Fontaine had something to fit you, Emma. It needs to be taken in a fraction at the waist, but it will be ready for tomorrow.'

'Do you mean to accept?' Emma stared at the scrawled message a little doubtfully.

'Oh, certainly,' Bridget said. 'This is just what I hoped for. Lindisfarne will take us up once he arrives, but he seems to have been delayed for some reason. Besides, it will be very much more comfortable to know some people before we go down to Bath.'

'You have made up your mind to take Lytham's advice, then?'

'Oh, yes—and if Lindisfarne is not here by the time we leave so much better,' Bridget said with a naughty look. 'It will show him that I am not to be taken for granted.'

Emma nodded, but her mind was wandering. Why had Lytham gone to the trouble of securing an invitation for them? Something warned her that he would be present at the gathering, even though he had expected to be leaving town almost at once.

'You look wonderful in that gown,' Bridget said the next afternoon as Emma twirled in front of the long mirror for her. 'Now, let me see—what shall we do with your hair?'

'What is wrong with my hair?' Emma glanced at her reflection. 'I think the style very suitable for a companion.'

'Perhaps—but not for my best friend,' Bridget said and began to unwind the plaits. 'It suits you back off your face, but I think we could make it a little fuller at the sides, and then catch it back in a big swirl like so...' She glanced at Emma's reflection in the mirror. 'Yes, that is much better. I shall instruct my maid to teach Lily how to achieve this style, and I shall lend you some of my pins to make it look special for the evening.'

It was impossible not to catch Bridget's enthusiasm, and Emma was suddenly looking forward to the prospect of their first evening engagement since she had come to town. She was vain enough to know that she would be looking very much more stylish than she had for years, and to wonder what Lytham might think of the change in her.

'You're a deep one,' Toby said, giving the marquis an old-fashioned look. 'I thought you meant to banish the old-maid daughter off to deepest Yorkshire?'

'It seems she had other plans,' Lytham replied coolly. 'And since neither she nor Mrs Flynn has any acquaintance in town, I thought it behoved me to give them a helping hand.'

'You're up to something,' Toby said. 'I know you too well, Alex, and I ain't a slowtop. No cause to imagine you can pull the wool over my eyes. Besides, Mama has seen Miss Sommerton, and she says she is rather—' He had been going to say attractive, but happened to be staring across the room as two young women entered the salon. 'Good grief! Are they the widow and the companion you asked Lucy's mother to invite? Pray tell me at once, which is the widow and which the companion?'

'The dark one is Miss Emma Sommerton,' Lytham replied with a lift of his brows. 'The blonde beauty is Mrs Bridget Flynn— why do you ask?'

'Because they are both beautiful, but *she* is stunning.'

'Mrs Flynn?' Lytham gave him a quizzing look. 'I thought your interest was fixed with Miss Dawlish?'

'Yes, of course it is. You know I am devoted to Lucy,' Toby said, a faint colour in his cheeks. 'Matter of fact, there may be something announced this evening…but that doesn't stop me appreciating beauty and *she* is rather special.'

'I admire a woman with style,' Lytham said, deliberately obtuse. 'And I grant you that Mrs Flynn has a certain dash about her.'

'You know very well I meant Miss Sommerton.' Toby gave him an indignant stare. 'Mrs Flynn is lovely, but her companion—' He broke off, lost for adequate words.

'Puts her in the shade? I dare say most women would find it difficult to compete with Emma.' He had spoken the name without thinking and cursed himself as he saw Toby's gaze sharpen with curiosity. 'I meant Miss Sommerton, of course.'

'So that's the way of it,' Toby said and grinned, delighted at having caught his friend out, which was exceedingly rare. 'Mama was sure of it. She said she had never known you to take the slightest interest in a decent young lady before and that there had to be a reason for your doing so now.'

'Your mama always was inclined to let her tongue run away with her,' Lytham said, brows lifting. 'It would be most unfortunate for Miss Sommerton's chances if such an unfounded rumour were to take hold, Toby. I have no thought of making her or any other lady an offer of marriage.'

'Can't be thinking of making an offer of *carte blanche*,' Toby said. 'Not to Miss Sommerton, anyway—the widow is another thing, of course.' Lytham fixed him with a stare that made him subside into silence. 'Sorry, mind my own business.'

'May I offer you congratulations on your own engagement?' Lytham said. 'I shall have to find a pretty gift for Lucy before I leave town.'

'Oh, are you going to Yorkshire?'

'Tomorrow—and now you must excuse me. I ought to greet Mrs Flynn and Miss Sommerton.'

He nodded, feeling slightly off balance as he walked leisurely across the room in the direction of the newcomers. He had known Emma would dress well, but that gown brought out reddish highlights in her hair. Or perhaps it was the new style that did that. She had looked beautiful when he first saw her, hair windswept and a fresh colour in her cheeks, but this evening she had been transformed into another person. There was a brilliance about her, a vitality that shone from her lovely eyes, and he felt that he was witnessing the awakening of a woman who had lain dormant for too long.

Toby had been right, she was stunning. She had poise, style… and watching her smile at her hostess, charm. With the right backing she could be the toast of the town. He was sorry that he would not be here to oversee her success, but he believed that she would need little help from him.

It was a pity she had no fortune, of course, but that need deter only the fortune hunters. A man of sense would admire her for all the qualities she possessed. She turned to him as he approached, a slightly guarded look in her eyes.

'Miss Sommerton,' he said. 'How delightful to see you here this evening—and Mrs Flynn. I had hoped we might meet again before I left town. I have something I wished to tell you. It could have been put into a letter, of course, but I always prefer to communicate in person where possible.'

He offered her his arm and they walked through the first reception room into the next, which was less crowded. Lytham steered her towards a small sofa set near the long French windows.

'Will you not be seated for a moment, Miss Sommerton?'

'Thank you, my lord.' Emma glanced at him as he sat beside her. She was not sure what she had expected, but his serious manner had set off flutters in her stomach, and she was a little disappointed that he had not mentioned her appearance. 'Something has happened? I do hope you have suffered no more attempts on your life?'

'You may rest easy on that,' Lytham assured her. 'I dare say you were right in the first place and that it was merely a poacher misfiring.'

'Oh, but...' She was quelled by his look.

'The matter concerns your brother. I was able to make certain inquiries last night, and I discovered that the accusation of cheating came from a close friend of my own brother...' His gaze was intent on her face. 'You do realise what this may mean?'

Emma was silent for a moment, then, 'You think your brother may have put his friend up to it—because he wanted to ruin Tom?'

'I think it possible,' Lytham said. 'My brother—indeed, both my brothers and my father were capable of such behaviour. There is or was bad blood in my family, Miss Sommerton. My father and his heir did their best to ruin us, and my second brother was little better. Had he inherited instead of me...' He shrugged his broad shoulders. 'I doubt there would have been an estate by now. My mother's loose behaviour in her youth may only be excused by virtue of her having been badly treated by her husband.'

Emma was a little shocked by this revelation, which she absorbed in silence and without comment. 'But what would your brother have gained by such vindictive behaviour, my lord?'

'For all his faults, I believe John was in love with his wife. That does not mean he treated her well or that he gave up his pleasures for her sake...any of his pleasures. You understand me?' Emma nodded. She understood perfectly, for, if her mama were to be believed, even her papa had taken a mistress when he was young. 'If Maria decided to console herself in the arms of a young and handsome man, I think John might have done almost anything in his rage.'

Emma's face had turned pale. 'Then the whipping…it was all part of the same plan to destroy Tom because he had dared to flirt with your brother's wife.'

'That part of it is mere speculation as yet,' Lytham said. 'I tell you only what I think possible. If Maria is willing to tell me her story, I may soon have more to report.'

Emma nodded, her eyes dark with emotion as she gazed up into his face. 'It would clear Tom's name of cheating, but would it not make it all the more likely that—?' She halted and could not go on.

'You think that anger might have driven Tom to take his revenge?' Lytham read the answer in her expressive eyes. 'But did he not swear that he was innocent of all the crimes of which he stood accused?'

'Yes, but…'

'Have faith, Emma,' Lytham said. 'Believe that I shall do nothing that would harm either you or your family more than they have already been harmed.'

'You are generous, sir. I do not know how to thank you.'

'You will thank me by enjoying your life, Emma. You now have an opportunity that has, I believe, been denied to you for a long time. You should take what is offered with both hands.'

She blushed as she realised he had now twice called her by her name, and his mouth twitched at the corners as he saw the look of accusation in her eyes.

'You *are* Emma tonight, you know—and it suits you very well.'

So he had noticed the change! She chided herself for having expected a more effusive compliment. Bridget had called her stunningly beautiful, but of course she was not really.

'It is an elegant gown,' she said. 'I dare say that makes the difference.'

'Ah, but the woman maketh the gown,' Lytham said and she could see the mischief in his eyes. 'I believe you will receive more exquisite compliments before too long has passed, Emma—but I am not in the habit of flattery.'

'I do not require flattery, sir!'

'Oh, Miss Sommerton!' His tone and look mocked her. 'I have never yet met a woman who did not enjoy being complimented—if she spoke truly.'

'You, sir, are a rogue!'

'Yes, I believe you are right,' Lytham agreed, a smile on his lips. 'I have been called worse by some, I dare say. But it does not hurt me so I do not regard it—though I should not like to think I had offended you. Are you cross with me, Emma?'

'Will you not be serious, sir?' Emma fixed him with a straight look. 'You are leaving town soon, I think. Please take care—and do nothing that might endanger your own safety for my sake. Or, I may add, that of my brother.'

'Why, Emma, I believe you are concerned for me,' he teased and laughed softly as he saw her blush. 'No, no, I am the veriest rogue to tease you so. I promise I shall not be caught by surprise again as I was in the woods. I shall be very careful, I promise you—there, will that content you?'

She shook her head at him, but her hostess was bringing a young man and a young lady towards them, and she was obliged to give her attention to the introductions.

'Miss Sommerton—may I make you known to Mr Tobias Edgerton and my daughter, Miss Lucy Dawlish.'

Lytham got to his feet. He bowed to the younger lady, and congratulated her on what he said he expected to be a happy night for her, threw an outrageous wink at Mr Edgerton, stayed only a moment to wish them both happiness and then turned to Emma.

'For I must be early to bed if I am to rise early.' He bowed to Emma. 'It has been a pleasure to spend a few moments in your company, Miss Sommerton. I shall hope to see you on my return—if not here, then I shall most certainly see you in Bath.'

With that he walked away, leaving her to stare after him while everyone else in the room nodded to one another and considered that his most particular behaviour had confirmed what they all suspected.

The Marquis of Lytham was obviously very interested in Miss Sommerton and that could surely mean only one thing! Since she appeared to be a respectable young woman, he must be thinking of taking a bride.

Emma, of course, had no such thought in her head. His revelations had given her much to think about, and her rather absent-minded manner that evening did nothing to dispel the rumour that had firmly taken root.

It was obvious that Miss Sommerton was interested in the marquis, and he had made his intentions perfectly clear.

Emma had no idea that Lytham's interest in her was the reason that several invitations—to dinner, card parties and even a small dance—began to arrive the next day. There were nowhere near as many as there might have been had it been during the season, of course, but there were still a number of hostesses in town who had for various reasons not yet retired either to their country houses or Bath for the winter. Sufficient anyway for both Emma and Mrs Flynn to discover that they had not one free evening for the whole of the two weeks they planned to spend in town.

'This is such fun,' Bridget said to Emma as they discussed what they would wear to the dance, which was being given to celebrate Miss Dawlish and Mr Edgerton's engagement. 'I think I shall wear the crimson silk—and you must wear that blue gown we bought from Madame Veronique. It suits you very well, Emma.'

'You should not have bought it,' Emma replied. 'It is beautiful, Bridget, but it was so very expensive.'

'And worth every penny,' Bridget replied. 'If you had not come to me, Emma, I should have had to employ some crabby old matron to lend me consequence, and I dare say we should not have been invited to a half of the houses we have been these past few days.'

If Bridget had some idea of why they were being so well received by the cream of society, she did not enlighten her friend. Although the daughter of gentry, Bridget knew that her marriage had done nothing to give her the entrée into London drawing rooms, and had Bertie brought her to London himself as they had planned, it would have taken much longer for them to be accepted.

* * *

It was a stroke of good fortune to be introduced by someone like the Marquis of Lytham, and Bridget was determined to make the most of her chances. She had let it be seen that she was not averse to dancing now that she was out of her period of mourning, and her fortune saw to it that she was never short of partners at Lucy Dawlish's dance.

She was asked to dance by several men she shrewdly assessed as being fortune hunters, but there were others who could not be said to have come from the same melting pot. She was enjoying herself very much, and if the truth be known had hardly given Lindisfarne a second thought until he walked in towards the end of that evening.

He came towards her as her partner returned her to Emma's side at the end of that particular dance, and her heart missed a beat as she saw the look in his eyes. It was the look of a predator hunting its prey!

'He is here!' She touched Emma's arm, her pulses racing. 'He has come at last.'

'Lindisfarne?' Emma turned to look at the man approaching them, and she felt an icy trickle down her spine. There was something about the earl that she instinctively distrusted. 'Oh, Bridget…'

Bridget was gazing at him in much the way a rabbit might gaze at a stoat. The earl was undoubtedly one of the most handsome men Emma had ever seen, in a dark, almost saturnine way, his eyes piercingly blue, his hair as black as jet, thick and wavy, but cropped short to his head. He had full, sensuous lips that seemed to Emma to curl back in a sneer, and he had an air of menace about him that she found slightly threatening.

Why did Bridget find him so fascinating? Emma could not understand it. There were several gentlemen here this evening that had as much and more to recommend them, and to her dismay Emma found herself immediately disliking him.

'My dear Mrs Flynn,' Lindisfarne said, his voice softly purring as he bowed over Bridget's hand. He reminded Emma of a great cat prowling around a helpless mouse, waiting its time to pounce. 'Have I come too late to secure a dance with you?'

'I fear my card is full,' Bridget said in a slightly breathy voice. 'I did not expect you. Had you sent me word, I might have saved one for you.'

'Business delayed me,' he said. 'But I am here now, and I shall claim my rights in future, believe me.'

The look he gave Bridget was so blatantly sensual that Emma gasped. What did he mean by behaving in such an intimate manner in company? Had he no thought for Bridget's reputation? And *she* seemed to have lost all her natural common sense as she stared adoringly up at him.

'Mrs Flynn, I believe this is our dance?'

'Oh…yes, of course.' Bridget gave her hand to the young man who had come to claim her. 'Excuse me, Lindisfarne. Please— you must stay and keep Miss Sommerton company.'

Emma frowned as her friend was whisked away to the dance floor. She herself had no partner for this particular dance, and she wished that she had not been left to make conversation with a man she instinctively felt was dangerous for her friend, and perhaps for both their reputations.

'Miss Emma Sommerton…' Lindisfarne's eyes turned on her, narrowing with sudden interest. He had ignored her in his assault on Bridget's senses, but now he was aware of her. Emma squirmed inwardly as she felt his gaze intensify. 'Ah, yes, Mrs Flynn's companion. I believe she did mention having invited you to bear her company for a while.'

'Yes, my lord,' Emma replied coolly. She could have wished that she was not wearing the blue gown that became her so well or that she had dressed her hair in the prim style of old. She did not like the way he looked at her! 'We have been friends for a long time. I am very fond of Bridget.'

She was not sure why she had stressed that to him, unless it was to make it clear that she knew his intentions and had decided to do all she could to thwart them. For she felt that Bridget would be making a terrible mistake if she consented to be this man's mistress—or, indeed, his wife. He was not a nice man, Emma felt it deep down inside her, and was sure that he would cause Bridget only unhappiness if she allowed him his way.

The earl's eyes narrowed, and she knew that he had sensed her hostility. 'I am sure Mrs Flynn's generosity must make her generally liked, Miss Sommerton.'

Emma blushed. Was that a hint that he knew Bridget had paid for the gown she was wearing?

'Bridget is a good friend.'

'Mrs Flynn has no notion of how to take care of her fortune,' the earl said. 'That is why she came to me—and I intend to take care of her, to make sure that she does not fall foul of hangers-on and fortune hunters.'

Was that a warning? Emma knew that this man would make a bad enemy. She believed that her expressive eyes had betrayed her. He had seen that she neither liked nor trusted him, and was on his guard now—and he would do all he could to lessen Emma's influence on Bridget.

Bridget would do as she pleased in the end, of course. Emma had no right to influence her one way or the other, unless she asked for advice. Should she do so, Emma would advise severing any connection at once. This man was a ravenous wolf and he would gobble up her poor friend and her fortune in an instant.

Bridget would be a fool to trust either her person or her fortune to his care, but she had fallen under his spell. Emma was not sure that it was not already too late to save her from him.

Emma knew she would have to take the greatest care or she too might find herself being devoured by this man.

Chapter Five

'Should you care for a visit to Bath, Aunt?' Lytham asked as he handed Lady Agatha Lynston a glass of her favourite port. 'You could take the waters for your health and gossip with old friends.'

'Most of 'em are dead,' his great-aunt snorted with something between triumph and disgust. Her face was deeply ingrained with the lines of old age, but her eyes were as intelligent and bright as those of a much younger woman. 'Gave up that lark when I realised they were dropping about me like flies. Might be contagious.'

'Not you, Agatha. You'll live to be a hundred, I dare say.'

'Buttering me up, Lytham?' The sharp, knowing eyes swept over him. He was the best of his family, most of whom had been bad to the core. Of course, if Lady Agatha's suspicions were correct, he wasn't the old marquis's son. And a good thing, too! Not that one word of the forgotten scandal would ever pass her lips. There were cousins ready to pounce on the estate he had restored and extended. He deserved his good fortune, and her suspicions would die with her. 'What are you up to?'

'I was thinking of visiting Bath myself.'

'Who is she?' Lady Agatha demanded instantly. She was like a little terrier after a rabbit as she sensed a secret. 'Or ain't she decent?'

'Miss Sommerton is a very respectable young lady.'

'Good thing, too! We don't want more bad blood in the family. We've had enough of that.'

'I couldn't agree with you more, Aunt.' He smiled at her fondly. She was the only person who had ever offered him affection and he always enjoyed his visits with her.

'Thinking of getting hitched at last, eh?' She looked at him with satisfaction. 'I never expected to see the day, thought your parents had given you a distaste for it.'

'It wasn't that so much,' he told her. 'I saw no reason to marry.'

'And now you do? She must be an exceptional gel.'

'Yes, she is.' Lytham smiled as his memory jumped back in time to the moment Emma had brandished her knife at him in the woods, ready to bind up his wounds. 'I believe you will like her.'

'Want me to look her over for you?'

'Good lord, no!' He laughed. 'I merely want you to meet her— without appearing too particular.'

'Not still shilly-shallying? Pull yourself together and take the plunge, Lytham. You're not getting any younger.'

'I am not quite in my dotage yet.'

'Want a son, don't you? Better get on with it before it's too late. You'll be past your prime soon and we don't want a knock-kneed runt as the heir, do we? Old men's children are always sickly creatures.'

Lytham choked on his port. He had been used to thinking himself at the height of his sexual powers, and to be told that he would soon be past his prime in such a forthright manner was something of a shock.

The gleam of mischief in the elderly lady's eyes amused him. Agatha Lynston had been born in a more bawdy age and had never hesitated to call a spade a spade. Or anything else by its right name, come to that. Emma was not quite as forthright, but she too had the courage of her convictions, which might be why he admired her.

'I don't know where you got your spirit, Agatha Lynston, but they should bottle it and feed it to the army.'

She cackled with laughter, her skinny, age-spotted hands clapping in appreciation of his reaction to her provocation.

'Say one thing for you, Lytham. You ain't high in the instep like your father. For all his selfish, bad ways, he was a damned snob. You must be a throwback to your great-grandfather. He was a fine man, but his son married into bad blood.'

'Perhaps…or perhaps Mama went astray,' Lytham replied with a lift of his brows. He had never been able to dismiss his father's last words to him, spoken in anger, but unforgettable.

'You are no son of mine!'

'Stuff and nonsense!' Agatha lied stoutly, though she knew it was very likely the truth. 'Your father would have disowned you from birth if he'd thought that.'

'Perhaps he couldn't be bothered. He had two elder sons, after all. He could not have expected that I would inherit the title.'

'Only Lady Helena could have told you the truth of it,' Agatha said. 'And she can't because the old devil finally broke her heart.' She snorted as she saw Lytham's sceptical look. 'You may be a rogue, Lytham, but you are unquestionably a gentleman. It's time the family became respectable again.'

Lytham looked at her affectionately. 'It always has been, Aunt—and always will be while you live.'

'I ain't going to live forever—so oblige me by producing an heir, Lytham. And now I think about it, a trip to Bath might be just the thing to set me up for the winter.'

The chaise carrying them towards Bath was both fast and comfortable. Emma could only be grateful that Lindisfarne had chosen to travel on horseback. It was bad enough that he had insisted on escorting them, and she did not think she could have put up with his company the whole way, for her dislike of him had grown each time they met.

The earl's arrival in town had meant that Bridget had delayed their journey a week to fit in with his plans. She seemed to be completely under his dominion, willing to do anything he asked—other than become his mistress.

'I am certain he loves me,' she told Emma on her return from being driven to the park the afternoon following Lucy Dawlish's dance. 'But he insists that we have no need to marry.'

'You should continue to hold out for marriage,' Emma told her, hoping that she would come to her senses in the end and see him for what he was. 'It is all very well for him to say there is no need for you to marry, but if you wish to continue to visit the best houses you must protect your good name. An affair could only tarnish it.

'I know that Maria Fitzherbert was received everywhere when she was the Prince of Wales's mistress, but that was a different case. Many believe he went through a form of marriage with her, that she is in fact his true wife, but even had that not been so they would have accepted her. And other women do carry on affairs without censure, but they usually have some consequence or the protection of an influential man. Remember what happened to Lady Caroline Lamb. She made a scandal with Lord Byron and that led to disastrous consequences for her and the family. It would be even worse for you. I dare say some hostesses would receive you, but have you considered what might happen if you should part from Lindisfarne?'

'I know you are right,' Bridget said. 'But sometimes when he kisses me I feel... Oh, you cannot imagine how it feels to be kissed like that!'

Emma could imagine it very well. She had not forgotten the kiss Lytham had given her that night at the inn, and the temptation she had felt in his arms. In that heady moment she might have counted the world well lost for love, but she had no fortune and no prospects. Bridget was a wealthy widow with every chance of remarrying if she did not throw it all away for the sake of a man who would only ruin her.

Emma was becoming increasingly wary of the earl. She had not been invited to drive out to the park with them on three separate occasions during the week they remained in London. She was aware that the earl had every intention of excluding her whenever possible. However, he had reckoned without Bridget's genuine affection for Emma and she refused to attend parties without her. She also retained enough sense not to be alone with him in the parlour. A drive in an open carriage was another matter, of course, and even Emma could not find reasons why she might not go with him.

Emma reflected that she was fortunate not to have been consigned to the baggage coach with their maids. Lindisfarne had made it clear that he thought her presence unnecessary and she knew from little things that Bridget had let slip that he was actively discouraging her from giving Emma presents.

Since Emma had herself tried without success to curb Bridget's excessive spending she did not object to this, though she did wonder why the earl seemed to take such an interest in her friend's fortune.

She knew that it would be impossible to warn Bridget against trusting him. Even a hint of censure was enough to bring a frown to her friend's brow. Emma was wise enough to realise that she must only offer advice when it was asked for; to press her opinions when they were unwelcome could only destroy their friendship.

In her heart, Emma knew that Bridget was already too deeply involved with Lindisfarne to draw back. It was, she believed, merely a matter of time before she became either his wife or his mistress.

In either case it would mean an end to their arrangement. Emma knew that the earl would never allow her to remain in his home if he decided to marry Bridget—and if she became his mistress it would not be possible for Emma to stay with her.

Besides, he would probably carry her off to his castle in Ireland, and Emma had no intention of ever living under the same roof as the Earl of Lindisfarne!

Glancing out of the window, Emma saw that they had drawn up outside an inn. It was almost evening, and they would be staying here overnight.

Lindisfarne came to assist Bridget from the carriage and escort her inside. He did not offer assistance to Emma, and she was left to jump down herself. She followed the others into the inn, feeling rather like a gatecrasher at a private party as she watched them laughing and putting their heads together.

Lindisfarne glanced back at her once, and the cold expression in his eyes sent a shiver through her. She knew that he was her enemy, and she wondered how long it would be before he tried to dislodge her from her position as Bridget's companion.

It was clear to Emma that she must start to make plans for that eventuality. She would have to make discreet inquiries while they were in Bath, and in the meantime she must be careful.

Lindisfarne was ruthless, she felt it instinctively, and he would not hesitate to use any means at his disposal of making it impossible for her to stay in Bridget's employ.

Emma pondered that word employer... For her first few weeks with Bridget there had been no reason for her to feel other than a valued friend, but she had noticed a slight difference recently. Had Bridget withdrawn from her slightly?

'Oh, do come on, Emma,' Bridget called looking back at her. 'It is chilly out here. Let us go into the parlour and get warm while Lindisfarne sees to the matter of our rooms.'

Bridget's smile allayed Emma's fears for the moment. Lindisfarne was doing his best to dominate her friend, but he had not quite succeeded yet.

Emma stood watching from the side of the bath as Bridget moved about in the warm waters of the spa. She was not the only woman to indulge, for there were several dowagers taking advantage of its medicinal benefits. However, she was the youngest and most beautiful, and it was she who was attracting the attention of the gentlemen who had come more for the sights than the waters, for her bathing gown clung most revealingly to her figure.

On this their second visit to the baths, Emma had taken a few sips of the drinking water in the pump room, finding it unpleasant to the taste, and the idea of stepping into the bath with only the flimsiest of garments to cover her naked body was something she had steadfastly refused.

'Why do you not follow Mrs Flynn's example?'

Emma had been allowing her attention to wander, and the earl's soft voice startled her. She turned to look at him, seeing the menace in those cat-like eyes as they watched her.

'Mrs Flynn is much braver about these things than I, sir.'

'I suppose you think it beneath you?'

'Indeed, I think no such thing, sir. It must be perfectly proper if Lady Thrapston feels it respectable to indulge. It was she who recommended it to Bridget.'

The earl's full lips curled back in a sneer. 'But you know differently, do you not? You despise those who are prepared to show off their charms in such a vulgar way, is that not so?'

'Please do not put words into my mouth, sir. I have no opinion one way or the other. I dare say it is a very pleasant experience, but I do not care to try it.'

'You are a little prude, Miss Sommerton,' the earl said, his eyes sweeping over her. Emma had taken to styling her hair into the staid coronet of plaits about her head rather than the softer style Bridget favoured. 'I doubt a man has ever laid a finger on you.'

'That, sir, is my business and not for discussion.'

The earl's hand snaked out, catching her wrist. She could feel the burn of his fingers bruising her flesh, but resisted the temptation to snatch her arm away.

'I've a mind to see if I can get beneath that prim mask you wear. I would swear there is a whore wriggling beneath that delicate skin of yours.'

'Take your hand from my arm, sir. Or you will force me to make a scene. I think that would be most embarrassing for us both, and Bridget would not care for it.'

Lindisfarne's eyes narrowed with anger. 'There are other places and other times,' he hissed. 'Do anything to turn Bridget against me and you will wish you had never been born.'

Emma turned as he released her, walking from the bathing chamber into an adjoining room and then into the pump room. She was outwardly calm, but seething inside. It was the first time the earl had put his hostility into words, and she had a feeling that she had not handled it as well as she might. She must try harder to keep her distance from him, but she would not allow his spite to overset her.

'This is foul stuff, Lytham. Give me a glass of good Madeira any day.' The words accompanied by a cackle of laughter drew Emma's eyes across the room to a rather odd-looking lady. She was clearly of advanced years, but her hair, which she wore in a mass of curls beneath a rakish hat more suited to a woman half her age, was bright red. 'Pah—that stuff will kill anyone fool enough to take it regularly, and as for the baths…'

Emma's gaze travelled on to the gentleman standing beside her. He was tall, broad of shoulder and well dressed, though in a more casual style than many of the gentlemen present, and the sight of him made her heart turn over.

She saw that he had noticed her, and he smiled as he touched the arm of his companion, nodding in Emma's direction. The elderly lady looked towards Emma, then raised her hand and beckoned imperiously. Emma had been wondering whether she ought to approach them or not, but now felt able to do so without fear of intrusion.

She realised that she was being intently scrutinised by the lady, who had very bright, inquisitive eyes, and felt her cheeks getting a little warm as she instinctively made a slight curtsey.

'Well met, Miss Sommerton,' Lytham said a faint smile on his lips. 'I had hoped we might see you somewhere. Please tell Mrs Flynn that it is my intention to call soon.'

'Good morning, my lord.' She smiled at his companion. 'Did you wish to speak with me, ma'am?'

'Know my nephew here, don't you? He tells me your name is Miss Emma Sommerton, and that you are a respectable young woman—is that right, miss?'

Emma was a little startled to be addressed in such a forthright way, but found it amusing. 'Yes, ma'am, I believe I am. I try to behave properly whenever I can.'

'Not too mealy-mouthed, I hope? Can't stand all these modern young woman who are too frightened to say boo to a goose. We were not like that in my day, miss.'

'No, indeed, ma'am, I can see that you were not.'

Lady Agatha Lynston stared at her for a moment, and then gave a shout of laughter, which caused a few heads to turn in their direction.

'I like the gel, Lytham. She has spirit…yes, I think we shall deal well together.' She turned her eagle eyes on Emma. 'Give me your arm, gel. Walk me about a bit. I've a mind to see what they are getting up to in the baths. Now that ain't decent, though I indulged when I was younger—when I had a figure to show off. You don't care for it, miss?'

'No, though my employer Mrs Flynn is bathing at the moment. I came to bear her company.'

'Got bored, did you? Thought you would see what the gentlemen looked like in the pump room. Young woman like you, bound to be thinking of marrying. Take my advice, gel—get yourself a good man with a sense of humour and plenty of money. I never married. I had the money through my grandfather and didn't see why I should be at some man's beck and call all my life. Besides, the right one never asked me.'

'I do not imagine I shall marry,' Emma replied. 'I am not in the happy position of having my own fortune, ma'am, and I dare say I shall need to work for most of my life.'

'Oh, I dare say you may marry,' Lady Agatha said, giving her a knowing look. 'Men ain't all fools, m'dear, and some of 'em ain't even bothered by the lack of a fortune. Mind you, there ain't many I could recommend to you as a husband, but if you're sensible you may do well enough.'

'Perhaps,' Emma said, not wishing to argue. Lady Agatha's hand was gripping her arm tightly as if afraid she might make a bolt for it.

'That fellow over there—the one staring at us in that peculiar manner.' Emma looked and saw that she meant the Earl of Lindisfarne. 'Now I wouldn't recommend you to take someone like that. He's a scoundrel by all accounts. I knew his father. Bad blood there.' She glanced at Emma. 'Why is he staring at you?'

'He is a friend of Mrs Flynn's,' Emma replied. 'He is staring at me because he does not like me…and I do not like him.'

'Be careful of him, Miss Sommerton,' the old lady said. 'Lytham is a rogue, but he is also a gentleman—that one is not.'

'I shall be careful,' Emma told her. 'But I thank you for your warning, ma'am.'

'You are a sensible gel,' Lady Agatha said, her eyes sweeping over the ladies and gentlemen in the water. 'Look at those old fools! What do they think they look like? Only one of them shows to advantage, and that's the blonde beauty. I'll bet she's no better than she should be.' She felt Emma stiffen and glanced at her. 'Your employer, is she? Well, my advice to you would be to find a new position. You may take me back to my nephew now. All this splashing about in water has given me an appetite. Lytham shall take me somewhere for something decent to drink and a slice of cake.'

Emma made no reply as she escorted Lady Agatha back to the pump room, where she discovered that Lytham was deep in conversation with another man. He glanced in her direction, smiled, but made no attempt to delay her as she turned away.

Emma was slightly disappointed that he had been content to let his elderly aunt monopolise her, for she would have liked some conversation with him. However, it was not for her to push herself, and he would no doubt seek her out when and if he had news for her.

When she returned to the baths it was to discover that Bridget had left the water, and she hurried to the dressing rooms, arriving only just in time to help Bridget gather her things.

'Where have you been?' she asked in what was an unusually irritable tone for her. 'I thought I should have to leave without you. Lindisfarne wants me to drive out with him to a beauty spot this afternoon, and I must go home and change.'

'I happened to see the Marquis of Lytham and made the acquaintance of his great-aunt, Lady Agatha Lynston,' Emma said. 'She is a remarkable lady, but she kept me talking and I was perhaps longer than I ought to have been. I am sorry if I kept you waiting.'

'So the marquis has come to Bath, has he?' Bridget's mood of irritation seemed to slip away. 'I wonder why?'

'To accompany his aunt, I imagine.'

'Oh, surely he would not come just for that—would he?' Bridget wrinkled her forehead. 'Well, it does not matter. We must hurry. I do not want to keep Lindisfarne waiting.'

Bridget shivered as they went out into the keen air of a dull winter day, and Emma looked at her in concern.

'Do you think it wise to drive out in an open carriage this afternoon, Bridget?'

'Why ever not?' Bridget said with a slight frown. 'It is just chilly after the heat of the baths. You did not bathe, so you cannot realise what it feels like to come straight out into the cold air.'

'Did you enjoy bathing, Bridget?'

'It was well enough as an experience,' Bridget replied with a shrug of her shoulders. 'I only did it because Lindisfarne thought I should—and Lady Thrapston recommended it.'

'Was it Lindisfarne's idea?'

'Yes. Why do you ask?' Bridget looked at her oddly, but Emma merely shook her head. 'Oh, don't look like that! I know you didn't approve. He told me that you thought I was making a show of myself, that it was indecent.'

'No! That is not true, Bridget. I said nothing of the sort. It is perfectly respectable, but I do not care for the idea for myself, that is all.'

Bridget was silent for a moment as they walked along the street together, clutching their scarves and shawls about them. The wind was much cooler and Emma saw her friend shiver several times.

'You dislike him very much, don't you?'

'Who?' Emma glanced at her, seeing the stubborn set of her mouth. 'I am not perfectly sure what you mean, Bridget.'

'Lindisfarne. You disapprove of him, and he feels it dreadfully. He is afraid that you will turn me against him.' Bridget looked at her accusingly. 'Is that what you want to do, Emma?'

'I would not dream of turning your mind against anyone,' Emma replied carefully. 'I do not particularly like the earl, but it is not my place to influence you in such a matter.'

'He said that you despise him!'

'Surely it is not what I feel that matters?' Emma said. 'I am here only as your companion, Bridget—because you asked me to come and help you resist the temptation he offered. If you wish to dispense with my services, you must say so. I do not wish to interfere with your pleasures.'

They had reached the house Bridget had rented, and she swept in ahead of Emma, two spots of bright colour in her cheeks. It was obvious that she was angry, but undecided what to do. Emma waited as Bridget unburdened herself of her scarves and shawls, then ran upstairs. She followed more slowly, knocking at the door of Bridget's room.

'Oh, come in,' Bridget answered impatiently. She was at the wardrobe, pulling at some of her gowns. 'What shall I wear? The white muslin or the yellow silk?'

'The silk would be a little warmer,' Emma said. 'Would you like me to leave, Bridget?'

Bridget whirled on her. 'For goodness' sake, don't look at me in that prim and proper way. I did not think you had changed so much from the girl I used to know.'

'I am sorry if I have changed.' Emma thought it was Bridget who had changed under the influence of Lindisfarne. 'I have tried not to be critical, even though I cannot like him, Bridget. I cannot think you would be happy as his wife.'

Bridget looked at her haughtily. 'I did not ask for your opinion, Emma. Please go away now. I need to send for my maid. I haven't time to argue with you. We shall talk about this another time… when I have made up my mind.'

Emma felt herself dismissed, exactly as if she were a paid companion, which of course she was. It would not have hurt so much if Bridget had not insisted at the start that they were friends and Emma was to think of herself as guest in her house.

She turned away and went into her own room, sitting on the edge of the bed and staring at her pale reflection in the dressing mirror. The rebellious spirit inside her wanted to start packing immediately, to leave before the situation deteriorated too far, destroying happy memories. But she knew she could not afford to be so impetuous. Bridget had showered her with costly gifts, but she had not actually given her money. Emma had only a few shillings in her purse, which would not even pay her fare home.

Besides, she was going to have to learn to accept this sort of behaviour. Employers were often fickle and could be pleasant one moment, and demanding or irritable the next. She had been led to expect something different from Bridget, but it seemed that their old relationship was over.

* * *

It was at about four that afternoon when the maid came to call Emma and tell her that they had a visitor.

'The gentleman asked for Mrs Flynn, but when I told him she was out, he said he would talk to you, Miss Sommerton.'

'What name did he give, Maisie?'

'The Marquis of Lytham, miss.'

Emma's heart skipped a beat, her mood lifting a little. 'Very well, I shall come down at once.'

She glanced hastily in the mirror, smoothing her gown and her hair, which were both immaculate. Her complexion was a little pale, but that could not be helped and she refrained from pinching her cheeks to make them pinker.

'Ah, Miss Sommerton,' Lytham said as she walked into the small parlour. 'Forgive me. I thought Mrs Flynn might have been at home, but I came to deliver an invitation from my aunt and could not leave without delivering it.'

'That was kind, sir,' Emma replied. 'I am sorry Mrs Flynn was not at home. She will be sorry to have missed you, I am sure— but she went out driving this afternoon.'

'Not in an open carriage, I hope?' Lytham glanced at the window. 'It has been raining this past hour or more.'

'Has it?' Emma had been engaged in reading a book to take her mind off her problems, and had not noticed. She crossed to the window to look out. The rain was heavy, slating down on the pavements, and it looked as if had been raining for some time. 'Oh, it is a heavy downpour. Bridget will be soaked to the skin if she is caught in this.'

'We must hope that her friends have had the sense to take shelter somewhere.'

'Yes, we must certainly hope that is the case.' Emma did not tell him that Bridget had gone with only the earl, for she sensed that he would not have approved, and his next words confirmed it.

'My great-aunt tells me that Mrs Flynn has formed a friendship with Lindisfarne, Miss Sommerton.'

'Yes. I think they met in Ireland when she went to him for advice after her husband died. I understand he is a distant relative of the late Captain Bertram Flynn.'

'It is none of my business, of course—but I think you should warn your friend that Lindisfarne is not the kind of man she wants to know. He is dangerous and bad…I mean really bad, Miss Sommerton. I am not talking of a charming rogue who gambles and drinks a little.'

'What do you mean?' Emma felt a little shiver run down her spine.

'There are unsavoury rumours connected with Lindisfarne's name,' he replied frowning. 'Rumours of women treated in an unfortunate way and other things that I would not care to repeat to a lady, even one as broad-minded as yourself.'

'I fear that it is useless to speak to Bridget,' Emma said and looked anxious. 'I believe that she is besotted with him and will listen to no criticism of him at all.'

'Indeed, then, that is a pity for he may ruin her—financially as well as her reputation.'

'She will not listen to me. I have no influence with her in this matter or perhaps in any other.' She was still smarting from Bridget's behaviour towards her earlier and something showed in her manner.

'Emma! You must listen,' Lytham said suddenly urgent. 'My aunt is not the only one who disapproves of Lindisfarne. I have been here but one day and already I have heard whispers. If Mrs Flynn continues to be seen everywhere with him, she will soon begin to be thought of as fast—and if you stay with her some of that may rub off on you.'

'I am aware that she must not be seen to be alone with him.'

'That is not enough,' Lytham said. 'Surely you must realise that people love to gossip? His pursuit of her is so blatant, and some think that she may already have succumbed, that she may be his mistress.'

'No, that is not true. I know it to be a lie.'

'I did not say that it was true, only that people may begin to believe it, and then you know it would not be long before some ladies refused to meet her at social gatherings. They would cut her if she attended the assembly, and she would not be invited to the best houses. What is permissible in a lady of high rank is not tolerated in someone of Mrs Flynn's position. Unfair, I grant you, but unfortunately the case.'

'I am sure she knows that…' Emma raised her head a little. Why must he lecture her when she had already warned Bridget of the pitfalls associated with the relationship? 'But I do not believe that will change her if she has made up her mind to have him.'

'She would not think of marrying him?' Lytham was shocked.

'It is all she dreams of—and who am I to lecture her?'

'You must warn her against such an idea,' Lytham said. 'For her own sake, Emma. He would run through her fortune in no time, and then he would mistreat her. He has been married once before, you know.'

'Married? I had no idea. I do not think Bridget is aware of that—indeed, I am sure she is not. What happened to his wife?'

'She died a few months after their wedding…' Lytham frowned. 'He was much younger then, of course. She was an heiress, a sweet child by all accounts, though I cannot claim to have known her. I have heard stories, however, and they are not pleasant.'

'How did she die?'

'In an accident, I am told. She fell down the stairs and broke her neck, apparently when she was feeling unwell. There was some talk of her having been mentally disturbed, but the rumours were hushed up and have been forgotten by all but a few.'

'Your aunt remembered it?' Emma nodded as he was silent. 'Yes, she told me to be careful of him because he was a bad man. Was the earl thought to have been involved in his wife's death?'

'Nothing could be proved, but it was rumoured at the time, I believe.'

'This is terrible. Bridget may be in some danger.'

'You should warn her, Emma.'

'I do not think she will listen. She is already angry because I have shown my dislike of him.'

'Then you will think about leaving Mrs Flynn's employ?'

For some reason Emma could not give him the answer he sought. She had already given the matter some thought, but she knew he meant to offer her help and her pride would not let her accept.

'I shall think about it,' she agreed. 'But I cannot simply walk out on Bridget just like that. If tongues have already started to wag, think how much worse it would be for her if I were to leave too suddenly. Besides, if Lindisfarne is so dangerous…' Emma shivered as she thought of her friend at the mercy of such a man.

'If she insists in her foolish behaviour it is no more than she deserves.'

'But I cannot—shall not do it,' Emma said. 'I shall talk to Bridget when she returns, but if she decides that she can dispense with my services I shall stay with her until she can replace me.'

'Do not be a fool, Emma!'

'I cannot desert her,' Emma said. 'She has been generous towards me, and though I do not approve of her behaviour I cannot desert her.'

'You refuse to listen—because the advice comes from me, I suppose?' Lytham glared at her. 'You can be too stubborn for your own good, Emma.'

'That is a ridiculous statement!'

'Ridiculous, is it?' His brow furrowed. 'Or have I mistaken your intentions? Can it be that you approve of Mrs Flynn's behaviour, that you see nothing wrong in her becoming that man's mistress? Perhaps you hope that one of his dubious friends will show an interest in you?'

'How dare you?' Emma lost her temper. 'I believe you have said enough, sir. Will you please leave now?'

'Is that it?' Lytham advanced on her, a glitter in his eyes. 'Did you come to her knowing her intention from the start?' He saw something in her eyes and thought he understood. 'That's it, isn't it? You always knew that it might happen.'

'Please leave,' Emma said. 'I do not think we have anything further to say to one another.'

'Do you not?' Lytham towered above her, anger sparking out of him, driven beyond reason by her apparent calm. 'Then let me tell you this, Emma—I have much to say on the matter. Should you decide to sell your favours to the highest bidder, think of me. I am perfectly willing to offer you *carte blanche,* and I am far richer than Lindisfarne or any of his cronies—but I never take another man's leavings. Think carefully before you make your choice.'

Emma's hand shot out, catching him a glancing blow across the cheek. He grabbed her wrist, pulling her in hard against him so that she could feel the heat of his breath on her face, and the anger pulsing through him.

'Let me go!' she demanded. 'Let me go this instant, sir.'

But he would not let her go. He held her fast, imprisoned against him so that she could feel the throbbing of his manhood, feel the heat of him as his mouth took possession of hers, her lips parting to the insistent probing of his tongue. Emma struggled, angry at this abuse of her feelings, but her body would not deny him much as she wished it; she felt herself melting into him, her mouth responding to the delicate touch of his tongue.

She tangled her fingers in his hair, unable to resist as his kiss explored and thrilled her, his leg curved around her so that she was pressed into him, moulded to him like a second skin. She felt that she would faint from the sheer pleasure of being in his arms like this and almost stumbled as he abruptly let her go.

He was breathing hard, a strange look in his eyes as he stared at her. She felt that he was angry and yet triumphant, as if he did not understand his own feelings.

'Do not look at me that way,' she said, a hot flush creeping up into her cheeks. 'You took advantage. I—I forgot myself. I did not mean to allow you to do that again.'

'You lie, Emma—you lie with every breath you take.' He grabbed hold of her arm and thrust her in front of the mirror. 'Look at yourself in that mirror! Where is the woman I saw that first afternoon—where the elegant creature I met at Lucy Dawlish's house? You hide her but she is there. Beneath that prim exterior is a passionate woman. Why do you hide her, Emma? Or is it that you only wish to hide her from me?'

She turned away from the mirror. Did he not understand that she was trying to protect herself from Lindisfarne and others like him? He had lectured her and now he accused her of doing the very thing he had been advising! He was an impossible man, and she did not understand him.

'Please go away, my lord,' she said in a choking voice. 'We have nothing more to say for the moment.'

'I am going, Emma, for I must. If I stayed, I could not trust myself to behave as I ought. Remember what I have told you.'

Emma did not turn to look at him. She was ashamed that she had once again betrayed her feelings for him. If he misunderstood them, then so much the worse.

'I have no wish to be your mistress, sir.'

'Oh, Emma—you know I did not mean to insult you.'

'Please go away!'

'Emma…' He hesitated but she shrugged away when he laid a hand on her shoulder. 'Well, I suppose you are angry with me, and perhaps I deserve it. I shall leave you to think about things, and we shall speak again another day. You know that I would help you if you needed my help. If you are in any trouble, you must come to me. Promise me you will!' His eyes bored into her, making her tremble inwardly but she turned her face aside, refusing to be won by his passionate appeal.

She would not answer him, and at the last he turned and went out without speaking again. Emma waited until she heard the front door slam and then she ran upstairs to her own room, locking the door behind her.

Chapter Six

Bridget did not return to the house until quite late in the evening. Emma had sat for hours alone in the parlour, having taken a light supper on a tray when it became apparent that Bridget would not return in time.

'I believe Mrs Flynn must have decided to dine with friends,' she told the servants when they asked her what they should do. 'But you must be prepared to provide a cold supper should she require it when she returns.'

By half past nine Emma was beginning to think that there must have been an accident and was wondering whether she ought to raise the alarm. However, just as she was thinking of setting a search in motion, Bridget came in, looking slightly flushed and guilty.

'Forgive me,' she said, glancing awkwardly at Emma. 'We were caught in a terrible storm and had no alternative but to take shelter at an inn. Lindisfarne bespoke dinner and there was no way I could let you know what had happened.'

'I was beginning to be a little anxious,' Emma replied in a dignified manner. She had no wish to quarrel with Bridget over this unfortunate business. 'But I thought perhaps you might have met friends and gone on to dine with them?'

'Oh, yes, that was the way of it,' Bridget said airily. 'It was all quite respectable and we were not alone.'

Emma saw the flush in her cheeks and sensed that she was lying. Bridget could not meet her eyes and there was something different about her this evening. She looked excited and yet ner-

108

vous. Surely she had not done anything foolish? Emma's heart sank. She was truly fond of Bridget and felt real concern for her.

'Lytham called this afternoon with an invitation to dinner for tomorrow evening. I was not sure of your engagements, but he said a reply in the morning would do well enough.'

'Oh…yes,' Bridget said carelessly. 'We may as well go. I have nothing else planned. Lindisfarne has to go up to town for a day or so.'

'Then perhaps you will send a note in the morning.'

'Yes, of course.' Bridget looked at her awkwardly. 'Are you still cross with me, Emma? I did not mean to quarrel with you this morning, and of course I do not wish you to leave.'

Emma hesitated. For her own sake she ought to look elsewhere for employment, for Lindisfarne's reputation could only do her own harm, but Bridget was giving her a tentative smile by way of an apology and she did not want to leave her in the lurch.

'I shall stay for the moment if you want me to,' Emma said. 'But I must tell you that people have begun to talk—about you and Lindisfarne. It is not serious as yet, but I think you should be careful.'

'Lindisfarne says the same,' Bridget replied, surprising her. 'We shall be more discreet when he returns. I may decide to take a house in the country for a few months.'

Emma felt a sense of foreboding. What had happened that afternoon to bring about this change in Bridget? Had she given into the earl's persuasion to be his mistress? Had she allowed him to make love to her? Just where had they spent the evening?

It was Emma's sincere hope that she had not been foolish. She would not have censured her friend had Lindisfarne been other than he was. There were discreet affairs going on around them all the time, but Bridget had been careless and Lindisfarne blatant in his pursuit. Society would forgive the rich and titled much, but Bridget was in no position to flout the rules so openly. Even Caroline Lamb had been censured for her behaviour with Lord Byron, and Mrs Flynn was a mere nobody in comparison. If she went too far she would be cut in the street, and then her hopes of cutting a dash would be at an end.

* * *

Emma worried about her friend as she undressed that night. It was not that she did not understand Bridget's feelings. She did— oh, she did! But it was so dangerous. Bridget might lose her heart, reputation and her fortune. Even her life…

The thought came unbidden and was terrifying. No, surely there was no danger of that! Lindisfarne was not so evil—was he?

She was letting her imagination run away with her! There could be no benefit in Bridget's death for Lindisfarne. Or could there? He was a distant relative of Bridget's husband and the money had been inherited from another cousin. Wills were sometimes strange. Might it be that Lindisfarne would inherit if Bridget died?

Emma struggled to put her fears from her mind. She was being ridiculous. Lytham's tale of the earl's tragic first wife had filled her mind with foolishness.

'Lytham…' Emma had tried not to think of that last stormy interview. All evening she had struggled to put him out of her mind but now it came back to her. How could he offer her *carte blanche?* It was cruel and insulting, and it made her want to weep.

His kindness to her, his apparent concern for her brother, and his teasing had given her cause to hope for something more. She had been foolish to do so, of course, but his manner had misled her. He did find her attractive, that had been evident from his physical arousal that afternoon—but he thought of her as someone he would appreciate as his mistress.

She knew that many young women in her situation, with no prospects of improvement, would have accepted such an offer, had it been made in a different way. Lytham had flung it at her in a temper, making her feel it was an insult, but of course it was not.

Lytham was a generous man. A woman in Emma's position need not fear that she would be cast off without a penny at the end of their affair. He would no doubt settle enough on her to enable her to live quietly somewhere. It might be preferable to a life at the beck and call of a selfish employer.

What was she thinking? Such an arrangement was an outrageous suggestion! She was the respectable daughter of a gentleman. She would never consider becoming any man's mistress for a moment. When she thought about it, she decided that Lytham had probably only said it to punish her for her stubbornness in refusing to leave Bridget's employ.

Yes, that must be it. She would allow herself to believe in the excuse that she had invented for him, otherwise she might find it difficult to meet him in company. And she must do so. She could not ignore the man who had introduced her to society in the first place.

Emma and Bridget spent the next day visiting the shops and the lending library. They met several ladies they knew and were greeted politely, though Emma thought with less warmth than on previous occasions. But perhaps that was merely her imagination?

Whenever she was given the chance she made a point of telling their acquaintance that they were dining with Lady Agatha Lynston and the marquis that evening. She was asked straight out by one lady where Lindisfarne was, and replied that she believed he might have gone out of town, hoping that her tone implied that she neither knew nor cared—which was the truth.

Bridget looked at her sulkily when they returned to the house to discover that only two visiting cards had been left that morning, when they had been used to receiving a dozen or more—and both belonged to gentlemen whose own reputations were dubious.

'I suppose the old tabbies have me down as a hussy?' she said to Emma with a scowl.

'I think there has been some gossip, but if you are careful in future perhaps no real harm has been done.'

'Oh, I do not care for them,' Bridget said and shrugged carelessly. 'Besides, when I marry Lindisfarne they will have to acknowledge me.'

'Are you going to marry him?' Emma asked. 'Has he proposed to you?'

'No—but he will. He will…' There was a note of near desperation in her voice. 'He must!'

Emma did not press her further. She sensed that Bridget was unhappy, but was reluctant to risk another quarrel. At this moment they were relieved of Lindisfarne's presence and for Emma that represented a breathing space—time for her to decide what she ought to do.

The evening went off better than she had imagined. Lytham was a perfect host, taking care of his aunt's guests and behaving in exactly the same way with the elderly ladies who were old friends of his aunt's as he did with Emma and Bridget. There was no hint of censure in either his manner or his speech, and she could almost have believed that their quarrel had never happened had it not been for the look in his eyes.

However, it was for her one of the most pleasant evenings they had spent since coming to Bath and Emma was feeling more relaxed as they prepared to take their leave.

'I hope we shall see you at the Assembly next week, ladies,' Lytham said as he kissed their hands before they departed. If he held Emma's for a fraction too long she tried to ignore it, and the beating of her heart. 'I shall expect two dances from each of you.'

'I am sure we shall be pleased to save them for you—shan't we, Emma?' Bridget fluttered her eyelashes at him flirtatiously.

'Yes, of course,' Emma replied, but did not look at Lytham.

She was very conscious of his attentions as he escorted them to their carriage, handing them in and remaining on the path to watch as they were driven away.

'Well,' Bridget said when they were finally alone. 'It is obvious that Lytham is interested in you. If you were to give him the least encouragement, he might marry you.'

'I am very sure he would not,' Emma replied. 'I am seven and twenty and I have no fortune. If Lytham were looking for a bride it would be to a young woman of some consequence.'

'Then why do his eyes seem to devour you wherever you go?'

'If Lytham were to make me an offer, it would not be of marriage.'

'Oh…' Bridget sighed. 'And of course you would refuse any other. Men are beasts sometimes, aren't they? I wonder why we love them?'

'I suppose it is a woman's nature to love,' Emma said thoughtfully. 'Mama still cared for Papa despite his gambling.'

Perhaps that was why she had this persistent ache in her heart, Emma thought. Of course she didn't love Lytham! Oh, why was she lying to herself? She had loved him almost from the beginning.

Perhaps not immediately; she had been prepared to hate him for what he had done to her family, but somehow she had not been able to sustain that first anger he had aroused. When had she begun to love him? Certainly she had known from the moment he had become ill. She had realised then that she could not bear it if he should die, and yet she had subdued her feelings, hiding them as she had so often in the past.

Lytham had once accused her of being two people, and perhaps she had been, but it was becoming harder and harder to subdue the Emma who wanted to live and love.

Two gentlemen called to take tea the next afternoon, and Mr Howard brought his sister Jane, who was a lively intelligent girl. Emma liked her and gathered from hints Jane let fall that Edward Howard was more than a little interested in Bridget.

Since he was a personable young man of moderate but adequate fortune, Emma thought how wonderful it would be if her friend were to marry him or someone like him. She mentioned the idea to Bridget as they went up to change for the evening.

'Oh, Edward is very pleasant,' Bridget said with a little pout. 'But not exciting. He does not make my heart race the way…someone else does. Edward might be a good husband, but do you not think he is a little dull?'

Emma made no reply. If Bridget enjoyed playing with fire there was nothing she could do to stop her, and perhaps she ought not to try.

Bridget seemed a little pensive when they left for the theatre that evening, but she remarked on Emma's appearance.

'That blue dress always looks lovely, and I'm glad you've done your hair in the softer style. It makes you look altogether different, Emma.'

A faint blush stained Emma's cheeks. She felt a little self-conscious, as though there was something wrong in having tried to make the best of herself for once. Of course there wasn't! Why shouldn't she look attractive? It didn't mean that she was setting her cap at Lytham.

Yet in her heart Emma knew that she did want him to think her attractive. She wanted him to smile at her, and she did not wish to quarrel with him.

She looked for him at the theatre that evening, wondering if he might be there with his aunt, but he was not and she was conscious of a sharp disappointment. Nor did she see him about the town on several occasions that she visited the library or the shops in the next day or so.

Could he be avoiding her? She tried to tell herself that she was imagining things, but her hopes of seeing him by chance before the Assembly were dashed.

For the next few days they lived an unexceptional life, walking in the town, driving out with the Howards to a beauty spot, and dining al fresco on a clear bright day that seemed to deny the season.

But the evening of the Assembly arrived at last, and Emma wore her blue gown once more. It was by far the most elegant of the gowns she owned, and made her feel special. She dressed her hair in the softer style, which she was adopting most of the time now and was moderately pleased with her appearance.

Her heart was fluttering as they set out, which was nothing to do with the fact that Lytham had said he and his aunt would be attending, of course.

Their arrival at the Assembly that evening seemed to cause a little stir. At first Emma was not particularly aware of anything amiss. They were greeted by several gentlemen, who took spaces on their dance cards as usual, and one or two of the younger ladies smiled and nodded in passing. It was only after some twenty minutes or so that Emma realised that the stricter ladies, who were the important hostesses, had not appeared to notice them. It was not that they were being deliberately ostracised—not yet—but some of the ladies had clearly decided they would not go out of their way to be friendly.

However, Bridget seemed quite content in the company of several young women, who were actually thought to be a little fast, and she was certainly not short of dance partners. Her laughter rang out often, and Emma wondered if she had noticed the difference and was putting on a show of bravado or whether she really wasn't aware of the slight coolness towards them that evening.

It was not until they had been at the Assembly for an hour that Lytham and his aunt arrived. They did not immediately come to greet Emma, for they were made much of by several dowagers who had not seen Lady Agatha at such a gathering for an age. However, after perhaps fifteen minutes, Lytham approached Emma. His eyes seemed to go over her and approve of what he saw.

'You look well this evening, Miss Sommerton,' he said. 'May I ask if by some chance there is a dance left for me?'

'You instructed me to save two for you,' Emma said, a flicker of amusement in her eyes. 'I believe there are actually four spaces remaining, so you may choose what you will.'

Lytham took the card she offered and scribbled his name in three places, including the supper dance. Emma made no comment, although to dance with him three times might cause some comment.

'Thank you, my lord,' she murmured as he returned the card to her. Since he had left the immediate dance free a partner did not claim her, and they had time to stand and talk to one another for a while.

'Lady Agatha looks as if she is enjoying herself,' Emma remarked. 'I believe you told me once that she did not go out much in company these days?'

'Foolishly, she had allowed herself to become almost a recluse,' he said with an affectionate glance towards his aunt. 'I believe I have convinced her that she ought to take a companion and make her home in Bath for a few months of the year.'

'I am sure it would be more congenial for her than being alone in the country.'

'I spend most of my time in London, which Agatha finds too rackety these days,' Lytham said. 'But I may perhaps be spending a little more time in the country in future.'

'Oh…' He did not elaborate and Emma was not inclined to ask for more than he wished to tell her. 'I am sure that will please your aunt.'

'Should my plans proceed as I hope, my aunt will soon have little cause for complaint.'

The enigmatic look that accompanied these words caused Emma's heart to miss a beat. Just what was he saying? She could not guess for his expression gave nothing away.

At the start of the next dance a young and rather shy young man claimed Emma. He was not a good dancer, and several times almost stepped on her toes, but she smiled at him encouragingly, not wanting to make him feel embarrassed.

'Thank you so much, Miss Sommerton,' he stammered awkwardly as their dance ended. 'I am afraid I am very clumsy.'

'Not at all, Mr Exening,' she replied. 'It was very pleasant. I enjoyed myself.'

'You are so kind,' he said and blushed a fiery red. 'And so pretty. I do not care what Mama says, I hope we shall be friends, Miss Sommerton.'

'I hope so, too, sir,' Emma replied and wondered what his mama had said to cause him to look so embarrassed. However, she did not ask and in another few moments she was claimed for the next dance by a man who held her a little too tightly and gave her what she could only construe as suggestive leers.

Emma survived the dance and thanked him politely, reminding herself to do her best to avoid that particular gentlemen in future until her card was safely filled. His hot hands had made her feel rather too warm and she made her way to the ladies' cloakroom to splash her face with cool water.

It was as she was refreshing herself behind one of the screens provided that she heard two ladies enter and begin at once to talk in rather loud, excitable voices.

'I tell you she is Lindisfarne's mistress,' one of them said. 'They were seen, my dear—coming from the direction of the bedrooms at that inn. Jonathan said it was quite obvious what they had been doing…'

'What a fool she is,' the second woman replied. 'Has she no idea of his reputation…or of what this will do to her own?'

'She is obviously beyond caring. Men of that ilk cause women to lose their heads, Ellen. It is so foolish of her. They say she has a considerable fortune and could do much better for herself.'

'It is the companion I feel sorry for. She cannot know what is going on, surely?'

'Well, as to that—how can one be sure?'

Emma did not wait to hear her own character torn to shreds. She emerged from behind the screen and was given the satisfaction of seeing the ladies turn bright scarlet. She nodded to them but did not smile, leaving the cloakroom with her head held high.

Inside she was churning with fury. Of course she had known that people were talking, but surely Bridget had not been so foolish as to share a bedroom with Lindisfarne at an inn? She must have known that there was a chance she would be seen!

Returning to the ballroom, Emma looked for her friend and saw that she was dancing. She seemed to be perfectly happy, though whether that was a front to cover her embarrassment Emma could not tell. She herself was smarting with humiliation and wished that she had not happened to overhear the women gossiping.

She recovered her composure in time for her first dance with Lytham, though she immediately noticed something a little different in his manner.

'We must talk privately,' he said to her when the music ended. 'Not this evening—tomorrow. Please be at home tomorrow at noon, Emma.'

Her heart jerked uncomfortably. 'Does it concern something you have heard this evening, my lord?'

'Yes…' He gave her a sharp look. 'Have you heard it, too?' He raised his brows as she nodded. 'For the first time?'

'Yes,' she whispered her cheeks warm. 'I had wondered, but I was not perfectly sure of the facts. And I did not wish to think it might be so.'

'I imagine it to be widely believed,' Lytham replied. 'Remember, I shall call tomorrow—and now you must forgive me. I must cancel my other dances with you, I am afraid. My aunt wishes to be taken home. I think she is feeling a little fatigued.'

'Yes, of course. I do hope it is nothing serious?'

'I am sure it is just over-excitement,' he said. 'Forgive me.'

Emma nodded, but could not smile. Her eyes were stinging with the tears she must not shed. Clearly, he had decided that he did not wish to be seen dancing with her too often after hearing what was being said about Bridget.

She watched him leaving with Lady Agatha, who did look a little tired, but she was convinced that it was merely an excuse on Lytham's part. His leaving meant she had no partner for the supper dance, and therefore no one to take her in. She was about to go in alone, when she heard a voice behind her.

'Well, if it ain't the doxy from the inn…'

Emma shivered as something stirred in her memory, and she turned to see the young man who had accosted her the night she was leaving Lytham's bedroom. He looked surprised as he saw her, and for a moment she thought that he was confused by the change in her appearance. He had believed that he had recognised her, but now he was not quite certain.

Emma looked through him, turning away to make her solitary walk into the supper room. She was aware that the young man had followed her and was still staring at her intently. She refused to look at him or give any sign that she had recognised him, and after a few minutes he walked away to greet some friends.

Emma's heart was racing. How unfortunate that he should be in Bath—and that he should remember her! If he were sure of his facts he might talk, and with all the scandal Bridget had caused,

Emma would be ruined. She knew that some of the ladies were already inclined to tar her with the same brush as Bridget simply because she was her companion—but if there were to be gossip about her having been in a man's room at an inn her reputation would be finished. She would never be able to show her face in society again and any hope of securing a post with a respectable lady would be at an end.

'Why the long face?' Bridget came up to her, accompanied by two gentlemen and Miss Jane Howard. 'Why are you all alone, Emma? I thought you were having supper with Lytham?'

'He had to take his aunt home because she was unwell,' Emma replied and forced herself to smile. 'I am quite content to have had one dance with him. Are you enjoying yourself this evening, Bridget?'

'Oh, yes, of course,' Bridget replied. 'As much as I can when…'

She left the sentence unfinished, but Emma understood. She meant as much as she could without the presence of the man she loved. Despite wishing that Bridget had not been so foolish as to give her heart to Lindisfarne, Emma could feel sympathy for her. She knew only too well what it felt like to love unwisely.

The rest of the evening passed without incident and it was not until they were being driven home that Bridget let slip her true feelings about the evening.

'If it were not for Jane Howard I think I should leave Bath at once,' she confided to Emma. 'Jane says that the old tabbies have set their faces against me, but she does not believe a word of the scandal and has assured me that she and her brother will remain my friends no matter what happens.'

'Oh, Bridget,' Emma said. 'I am sorry if you were made to feel uncomfortable this evening. I know some of the ladies were talking. It appears that you were seen at the inn with Lindisfarne.'

'I do not care what they may say.'

'But you will if you are ostracised,' Emma said. 'It did not happen completely this evening, but if the Howards were to turn against you…'

'Why should they?' Bridget hunched her shoulder. 'It is only until Lindisfarne returns anyway, which he may do by tomorrow evening.'

'What will you do then?'

'I shall go with him if he asks me,' Bridget said. She pulled a face as Emma looked at her unhappily. 'You do not understand how it feels to love as I do.'

'I understand more than you imagine,' Emma said. 'But I ask you to think carefully before you decide, Bridget. If you become his mistress openly you can never go back. I know that there will be some houses that are open to you as his mistress—but what if…?' she faltered uncertainly.

'You mean when he is finished with me, I suppose?' Bridget stared ahead of her in the darkness of the carriage. 'My life will mean nothing to me then, so what does it matter?'

Emma was silent. Bridget had clearly decided that she could bear anything but to be parted from Lindisfarne—which was possibly why he had taken this trip to London, to teach her a lesson and bring her to heel.

They finished the short journey in silence, parting at the top of the stairs with no more than a subdued farewell. Emma was thoughtful as she undressed. Why had Lytham made such a point of wanting to see her privately? Was it to lecture her once more? Or was it perhaps to renew his offer of *carte blanche?*

It was obvious that she could not expect an offer of marriage now. Her reputation had already become tarnished by the scandal concerning Bridget, and might suffer more if that young buck from the inn spoke of his belief that she had been a man's doxy. It did not matter that Lytham would know the truth, the damage would already have been done.

Emma went to bed with her mind in turmoil. Lytham had not requested her to be at home, he had ordered it—and she did not feel inclined to obey. Indeed, she would make sure that she was not at home when he called.

Bridget awoke with renewed energy and declared that she was going shopping. She said that she felt like spending money, and was determined to spend some of it on Emma.

'I must pay you some wages, too,' she said, looking thoughtful. 'I promised I would and I haven't.'

'You've given me lots of presents already.'

'That was my choice,' Bridget said and went over to the little writing desk with its secret drawers. She took six gold sovereigns from it and gave them to Emma. 'I do not have much spare money on me at the moment. I can pay for anything I need by a draft on my bank—but I want you to have this.'

'I shall not refuse, because I may need it,' Emma said and looked at her sadly. 'You know that I shall have to leave you when Lindisfarne returns, don't you?'

'Yes...' Bridget sighed. 'You do not like him and he does not like you. It is impossible for me to have you both.'

'And you choose him.'

'I have no choice,' Bridget replied. 'He makes me come alive, Emma. Without him I might as well be dead—as I was inside after I lost my dear Bertie.'

'Would Bertie have wanted you to do this, Bridget?'

'Oh, don't ask me that, Emma! It isn't fair.'

'I think it entirely fair,' Emma replied. 'I know you will be angry—but Lindisfarne is not a good man. He will make you unhappy.'

'I am miserable without him,' Bridget replied. 'If I can have a few months of happiness with him, it is all I want. After that...' She shrugged her shoulders.

Emma decided to say no more. There was nothing she could say that would change Bridget's mind. She realised that all she could do was to enjoy this last morning of shopping with Bridget; if Lindisfarne were expected to return at any time, she would have to leave as soon as he did.

They spent the morning shopping and managed to enjoy themselves despite being cut in the street by a woman who had once been delighted to welcome them both to her home. Bridget stuck her head in the air, determined not to mind, but Emma felt it keenly both for herself and her friend.

She tried not to think of what her life would be like when she left Bridget. It would be almost impossible to find work as a companion to a lady of quality, for any prospective employer would turn her away if there was the merest hint of scandal attached to her name.

It might be that she would have to return to the country and throw herself on Mary Thorn's mercy. She could perhaps stay there for a few weeks until she made inquiries about finding a position.

Perhaps she ought to change her name? She could use her mother's maiden name. It was a risky thing to do, for should she be unmasked she would immediately be asked to leave. However, she could choose her new employer carefully and if it were an elderly lady who seldom left her country home she might possibly get away with it for a time.

Emma's thoughts on that subject were not the happiest, but she managed to conceal them from Bridget, pretending to enjoy their outing—and she tried not to think about how angry Lytham would be when he discovered that she had disobeyed him.

However, on their return to the house, Emma discovered a note waiting for her. It was from Lytham and begged her to forgive him for not keeping his appointment with her. He was pleased to tell her that his aunt was much recovered and hoped that Emma would visit her soon. He himself had been called away on business and would return within a few days, when he would call without fail.

Emma folded the letter away. She felt that it was merely an excuse, and believed that Lytham had decided against continuing their friendship.

He had warned her what would happen if she stayed with Bridget, and now he was ready to wash his hands of her. Well, she had only herself to blame. Had she listened to him in the first place, she might have been his aunt's companion and settled comfortably in the country—something that was now out of the question.

Emma found no comfort in her own thoughts, or in the cry of surprise and delight that came from Bridget as she opened her own letter.

'Lindisfarne is back!' she cried. 'He says that he will call and take me to the theatre this evening.'

'I am pleased for you,' Emma said. 'If it is what you truly want?'

'Yes…yes, it is.'

'Then all I can say is be happy.' Emma went to kiss her cheek and then walked upstairs.

She sat on the edge of her bed and looked about her. It was too late to make any arrangements for travelling today, but she would certainly start her packing first thing in the morning.

She was not sure what the future held, but she would go home and seek the advice of friends before she decided.

Lytham cursed the ill fortune that had caused him to leave Bath just at this time. He was aware that several rumours were being circulated about Mrs Flynn, and he did not like them—for Emma's sake.

Had his business not been so urgent he would have kept his appointment with her and tried to persuade her to leave her friend before it was too late. However, one of his agents had important news for him, and he knew that it was something that could not be ignored.

It seemed that the man who had accused Tom of cheating might be in some kind of trouble with his creditors, and that it was not the first time he had come close to finding himself in a debtor's prison. At that time he had somehow managed to find the funds needed to clear his debts—the very time when he had caused Tom Sommerton's name to be blackened.

His investigations so far into the scandal of Tom Sommerton being accused of cheating and then thrashed had convinced Lytham that his brother's wife had indeed taken a young lover, and that that lover was Tom. The theory followed then that John had not only arranged for his rival to be accused of cheating, but also that he had probably hoped that the young man would die of the beating he had given him.

This being the case, it could lead to the finger of accusation being pointed at Tom Sommerton over Alexander's elder brother's death. It would do Emma's brother no good to clear him of cheating and then have him arrested for murder, and so he had set agents to search for evidence that Tom could not possibly have been involved in what he was still convinced had been an accident.

There was also the matter of his enemy. Had Tom Sommerton taken that pot-shot at him in the woods—or had that been the work of a man he had believed long dead? He must set further investigations in hand if he was to get to the bottom of this mystery.

But it seemed at last that he was about to get some answers. Only then would he be able to tell Emma of what was in his mind and heart.

Chapter Seven

Bridget begged Emma not to leave until her own arrangements were fixed, and she could do no less than agree. On the morning after Bridget's trip to the theatre with Lindisfarne, Emma asked if she would mind if she went to visit Lady Agatha.

'Providing you do not wish me to come with you, I do not mind what you do,' Bridget said and sighed. 'I have such a terrible headache. I think I shall stay in my room and rest all day.'

Emma sympathised. Bridget did look unwell, her face pale and shadows under her eyes as if she had not slept all night. She promised to have a soothing tisane sent up to her, and then collected some books she wished to return to the lending library and set out.

Her trip to the library was uneventful for it was early and she saw no one she knew either in the street or while she was choosing some new books for Bridget, but on the return journey she met two ladies with whom she was slightly acquainted and was surprised when they crossed the road rather than acknowledge her.

Emma had not expected to meet with such rudeness so soon, and felt distressed. She hesitated outside the little tea-room where she had sometimes stopped for tea and cakes, and then turned away, feeling that it might be too embarrassing if she were to be snubbed again.

'Emma—do wait!'

She glanced round and then halted as Jane Howard came hurrying up to her. Jane was looking extremely stylish in a gown of green-striped sarcenet and a heavy wool pelisse to keep off the chill air. Her bonnet was dark green velvet and trimmed with curling black feathers.

'I am so glad I caught you,' Jane said. 'Were you thinking of taking tea? I should be glad of the chance to speak with you.'

'I am on my way to visit someone,' Emma replied, 'but I should be glad of your company if you would consent to walk with me.'

'Willingly…' Jane gave her an uncertain smile. 'This is a little awkward, Emma. I am not perfectly sure where to start.'

'You may have heard certain rumours, perhaps?' Emma said, deciding to help her out. 'Please do not be afraid to speak of them, Jane.'

'Yes, yes, I have. I must tell you that they made me extremely angry and I do not believe them for a moment. And nor does my brother.'

'I think Mr Howard would believe nothing ill of Mrs Flynn,' Emma said with a smile. 'And I am very glad, for she may need friends in the future.'

'My brother refuses to listen to gossip about Mrs Flynn, and he will always continue her friend—but this concerns you, Emma.'

'Me…' Emma stared at her, a cold chill creeping over her. 'You have heard gossip concerning me?'

'Yes, and most unpleasant it was, too,' Jane said, her cheeks warm. 'You were supposed to have been seen supporting a drunken man up to the bedchambers of an inn.'

'Ah, yes,' Emma said fighting for calm. She curled her fingers into her palms and took a deep breath. 'I thought that young man had recognised me. However, he was the one who was drunk at the time, and the man I was helping upstairs was ill. He had a fever and had almost fainted. I know that the situation appears to have been compromising, but there was really nothing improper about it.'

'I knew there could not be,' Jane said and looked relieved. 'Was the gentleman a friend or a stranger you had helped out of kindness?'

'His identity and the circumstances must remain confidential,' Emma replied. 'For your own information, I will say that the gentleman was Lytham and his illness was the result of an injury. But I do beg you not to reveal that to anyone. I have confided in you alone because of your staunch friendship towards Bridget and myself.'

'Then I shall not repeat what you have told me to anyone,' Jane said. 'Shall we see you at the Assembly this week?'

'I believe not.' Emma hesitated. 'I am thinking of going home for a short visit. Mrs Flynn may also be leaving Bath soon, but I am not yet certain of her intentions.'

'My brother will be sorry to hear that.' Jane frowned as though the news that Bridget might be leaving Bath had upset her. 'I think I must part from you now. I am sure we shall meet again soon.'

Emma nodded, but had nothing further to say. She was grateful that Jane had gone out of her way to tell her about the latest gossip, but she knew that not many ladies would be so easily convinced of her innocence. Gossip, once it began, was difficult to stop. Coming on top of the gossip concerning Bridget, it made Emma's position even more difficult, and she realised that her departure from Bath could not long be delayed.

Arriving at the house where Lady Agatha was staying, she hesitated and then decided she would continue with her visit. Lytham's great-aunt would surely allow her to give her side of things. She could always confirm it with Lytham herself. Besides, Emma felt it would be impolite of her to leave Bath without saying goodbye to a lady who had treated her kindly.

A stern-face butler admitted her to the house and asked her to wait in the small parlour while he went to inquire if his mistress was in. Emma stood looking out of the window that fronted on to the street, noticing that it had just begun to drizzle with rain. She turned expectantly as the butler returned.

'Lady Agatha begs you to forgive her, Miss Sommerton, but she is not receiving visitors this morning.'

'Oh…' Emma's cheeks burned. 'I hope she is not ill?'

'As to that, I really couldn't say, miss. I was just told that she was not at home this morning.'

'I—I see,' Emma said, her cheeks flaming. She was so embarrassed! The message could not have been clearer. Lady Agatha was not at home to her. 'Forgive me for troubling you.'

'I am sorry your journey was wasted, miss.'

Emma avoided looking at him as she allowed him to show her to the door. Oh, this was so terrible! She had not minded being cut earlier by two ladies she only knew slightly, but to be refused by a lady she liked and admired hurt more than she cared to admit.

Emma's insides were churning as she walked briskly back to Bridget's house. She had called with the best of intentions and now felt humiliated. It was all so unfair. She had suffered a loss of reputation when she had really done nothing wrong.

Inside the house, she took off her bonnet and pelisse and went into the parlour to deposit the little parcel of books she had brought for Bridget. She was startled to see a gentleman standing by the window and was about to make a hasty retreat when he turned and looked at her, his cold eyes sending a chill down her spine.

'I suppose I have you to thank for this?' The tone of Lindisfarne's voice left her in no doubt that he was furious and blaming her for whatever was causing his anger.

Emma was startled by the accusation. 'I fear I do not understand you, sir.'

'Bridget has refused to see me…' His gaze narrowed in dislike. 'Do you tell me this is none of your doing?'

'I believe she has the headache.'

'A convenient excuse, no doubt.' He moved towards her, his expression so menacing that Emma's pulses jumped in fright. 'I'll swear you put her up to it. No doubt you have lectured her about the perils associated with a rogue like me?'

Emma's head went up. She had had enough for one morning, and she was not going to put up with this!

'I have told her from the beginning that I think her unwise to continue her friendship with you, sir. It can do her reputation only harm, but—'

'Damn you!' His lips had gone white with temper. '*You* to speak of reputation—when it is all over town that you are little better than a whore yourself.'

'That is a vicious lie!'

'You pretend to be such a meek little thing,' he muttered, beyond listening to her so caught up was he in his own fury. 'But I have suspected there was fire beneath the ice. Very well, since I am to be denied Mrs Flynn I'll have you!'

Emma gasped as she read his meaning and turned to flee from the room, but he came after her, catching her arm in a viselike grip and swinging her round against him. She gave a little scream and kicked out at him, but he twisted her arm behind her back, making her cry out in pain, and then, imprisoning her with his other arm, he lowered his head to kiss her.

His kiss was horrible, meant to punish and humiliate as his teeth ground against hers and he hurt her. She tasted blood in her mouth and struggled, turning her head aside and gagging for air. He took a handful of her hair and pulled her head back, tugging it at it so that tears came to Emma's eyes. Holding her with his leg curled about her and one hand, he pulled at the neckline of her gown, and it tore in his hand as she jerked wildly, spurred on to a desperate effort as she guessed what he meant to do.

'Let me go, you beast,' she cried but he jerked on her arm and made her scream out. 'Let me go! I want nothing to do with you.'

'I am going to teach you a lesson, whore!' Lindisfarne hissed. 'You shall learn what it means to defy me. I had *her* eating out of the palm of my hand. She was ready to do anything I asked and now…'

'You want her fortune more than you want her! You are a wicked evil man and I—'

He struck Emma across the face, making her head jerk back. 'Be quiet, jade. The money is necessary, but I want Bridget—she's mad for me and I intend to have both her fortune and her.'

He grabbed Emma tighter and began to force her backwards towards the sofa, and she gasped as she realised what he had meant by teaching her a lesson. He was going to violate her!

'What is going on here?'

Bridget's voice startled them both. Lindisfarne let Emma go immediately, his face stamped with surprise and guilt. He had been sure that Bridget was safely in her room and would not venture down, but here she was wearing a loose wrapping gown and looking pale as if she really were suffering a headache.

'Bridget dearest…your companion pretended to faint,' he said and then with more confidence, 'She then flung her arms about me and made a scene because I would not embrace her. She is jealous of you, because she knows she is unlikely to stir any man to passion.'

'Liar!' Emma said. She had retreated to stand as near to the door as she could, prepared for flight. 'Don't listen to him, Bridget. You know he is lying. You know I dislike him and that I would never throw myself at him or any man.'

Bridget pressed a hand to her head. She was suffering dreadful pain and she stared from one to the other of them in indecision.

'Oh, I do not know who to believe,' she said and tears of self-pity sprang to her eyes. 'I wouldn't have believed you capable of this, Emma—and yet why should Lindisfarne want you when—' She broke off on a sob.

'She accused me of wanting only your fortune,' Lindisfarne said, pressing home what he sensed was his advantage. 'I was about to tell her that I adore you when you came in.'

'Bridget…' Emma appealed to her but saw that she was wavering, obviously wanting to believe her lover. 'Very well, if that is what you wish to believe, please excuse me.'

She walked from the room with her head lifted high, holding on to her torn bodice and the shreds of her dignity. Bridget must know in her heart that she would never throw herself at Lindisfarne in the way he had described, but she was prepared to believe him because she could not bring herself to accept the alternative.

It was time she was leaving. Emma went up to her room and took off her torn gown, throwing it on the floor of her bedchamber in disgust. Even if it had not been ruined she could never have brought herself to wear it again. The memory of Lindisfarne's hateful lips on hers made her shudder. She scrubbed the back of her hand across her mouth and then went over to the washstand

and poured cold water from the jug into an earthenware basin. She was not sure that she would ever feel clean again, but she was going to try and scrub the taste of him from her mouth.

And then she was going to leave this house.

'It is unfortunate that Mrs Flynn should take up with such a man,' Mary Thorn said as Emma unfolded her tale some hours after her arrival at the vicarage. It had taken two days on the Mail coach, but she could not afford the luxury of travelling by post chaise and had been worn out by the time she had finally walked the last few miles to her friend's home. Most of her luggage had been left behind at the depot, and she had had to arrange for it to be sent on by carrier. Mary had taken her in instantly, insisting that explanations could wait, and now it was after supper and they were comfortably settled in Mary's small but pretty parlour in front of a warming fire. 'If I may say so, I think you have been treated shamefully, Emma dearest. And I am very glad you came to us.'

'It is only for a short while,' Emma assured her. 'I shall write to various agencies and see if they can advise me of any vacancies for a lady's companion, and I shall read the advertisements. I dare say it will not take too long to find something.'

Emma sounded more confident than she felt, for she knew that many prospective employers would expect a reference from her last employer and she was not sure that Bridget would give her one should she apply to her.

Emma had not spoken to her former friend after that unpleasant scene in the parlour, feeling that she did not wish to be accused of throwing herself at a man she had always disliked. If Bridget could think that of her then their friendship was clearly at an end, and the only sensible thing left for Emma was to put the whole sorry episode from her mind.

She had left a note for Bridget before she left, telling her the truth of what had happened, and assuring her that she wished her only happiness in the future, and then she had sent for the porter to fetch her trunk to the coach station. She had taken only one or two of the gowns Bridget had bought for her, leaving the most expensive behind. She would, after all, have no use for elegant ballgowns in future, and Bridget might be able to have them altered for herself—or more likely give them to one of the maids as a gift. Emma had no wish to keep them after the way her former friend had behaved. She was not bitter, but she knew that if they were ever to meet in the future, she would not be able to feel towards Bridget exactly as she had previously. Bridget ought to have taken her word, the fact that she had not had been both hurtful and humiliating.

During the uncomfortable journey on the Mail coach, which had involved a stay overnight at an inn and contrasted vividly with the one in Lytham's carriage a few weeks earlier, Emma had had a great deal of time to think. She made up her mind that the only way to deal with all that had happened to her was to bury it deep in her subconscious.

Emma had managed to subdue her feelings many times before when it was necessary, but she had already begun to discover that it was not going to be so easy this time. Lytham would not be banished from her thoughts no matter how she tried, and the memory of those kisses he had given her had disturbed her sleep too often already.

However, she had accepted that she could expect nothing more exciting of life in future than a position as companion to an elderly lady, and knew she must expend all her energies on seeking that post. Mary Thorn had welcomed her warmly, but she could not stay with her kind friends for more than a few weeks.

Emma had wished several times since her departure from Bath that she had taken Lytham's offer to become a companion to Lady Agatha, and yet perhaps that would not have served. For her foolish heart would still have misbehaved, and she knew that if he were to be wounded again she would not hesitate to do exactly as she had the first time.

Emma reflected that it was a sad thing to be a woman and at the mercy of spiteful tongues. Had she been a man and noticed on the stairs of an inn with a whore, she would have been thought a bit of a devil and no one would have censured her. It was unfair that she should have suffered a loss of reputation through a kind act, but it would just have to be forgotten along with all the rest.

Emma tried not to think of what might become of her if she could not find the kind of situation she was looking for—but she would not allow herself to have such thoughts. It was surely only a matter of time before the right opportunity presented itself, and in the meantime she would keep busy helping Mary with all her parish work.

'I believe it may be my fault that she left Bath so abruptly,' Lady Agatha said to Lytham as he towered over her that morning some six days after Emma's departure. 'Please do sit down, Lytham. This is a small parlour and you make it seem smaller when you stand there so aggressively. I did not mean to offend her, of course. I had not heard those unkind rumours then, and I was feeling unwell the morning she called. I told my maid to give Miss Sommerton the message herself, but she delegated it to Smithers and goodness knows what he said. He must have upset her for she went off that same day.'

'If she had heard the rumour herself, she may have thought that you did not wish to receive her,' Lytham said and frowned. 'It is my fault. I should have kept my appointment with her that morning before I left for town and made all clear.'

'Do sit down, Lytham, and stop pacing like a caged animal,' his aunt said a trifle impatiently. 'Your restlessness is disturbing.'

'Forgive me.' Lytham sat in the large wing chair opposite her but still looked as if he were a coiled wire spring ready to snap.

Lady Agatha smiled inwardly, wickedly deciding to tease him a little more. 'This story going around—you think there is no truth in it?'

'My dear aunt,' he replied between his teeth, 'I can only imagine that the young fool spreading this gossip is referring to the night I was taken ill of a fever on our journey to town. Since I was the gentleman in question, I can assure you that I was in no case to ravish her that particular evening.'

'I trust you would not have done so had you been perfectly well,' his aunt reproved him with a frown. 'Emma Sommerton is a lady—and although you are a rogue, Lytham, I believe you to be a gentleman. Gentlemen do not take advantage of innocent young ladies, however much they might wish to sometimes.'

Lytham's mouth twisted in a wry smile. 'You are telling me that I am to blame for Emma's predicament, I think.'

'Well, if it was you she was helping upstairs, you are certainly the indirect cause of her loss of reputation, and I think you must instantly repair it.'

'You are very right, Aunt,' Lytham agreed. 'I shall see the young idiot in question—Rotherham's boy, I believe? By the time I've finished with him he will be ready to grovel to Emma on his knees.'

'All that is necessary is that a correct version of the story be circulated,' his aunt reproved. 'It would be best to make a jest of the tale if you can find the way to do it. People will always wonder a little—no smoke without fire, as the saying goes—but if you handle this properly no permanent damage may result.'

'You know my intentions, Aunt.'

'Yes, but Emma may feel differently,' Agatha said. 'You must do what you can to re-establish her reputation before you press your own desires on her, Lytham.'

'You mean she might feel that she is being forced to accept me because she has no other choice?'

'Yes, that is exactly what I mean,' Agatha said. 'Your first duty is to put the story straight here in Bath, and you must also call on Mrs Flynn and ask her if she knows why Emma left so suddenly—and where she went.'

'Yes, I believe you are right,' he replied thoughtfully. 'I think I shall have a few words with Jane Howard. She and Emma had been quite friendly I think, and she may be able to shed some light on Emma's decision to leave.'

Lytham was thoughtful as he set out for the Howards' lodgings, and was fortunate enough to meet with Jane, as she was about to set out on a visit to the pump room.

'I was hoping we might have a word, Miss Howard?'

'Why, certainly, my lord,' she replied and smiled at him. 'If you mean to ask me about these ridiculous rumours circulating about Miss Sommerton, I can tell you my mind is quite at rest over them. Emma told me in confidence that you were unwell that evening, and that she merely assisted you up the stairs. I have told anyone who will listen that that is the case, though I did not use your name as Emma particularly requested I should not.'

'Did Miss Sommerton seem upset to you when she spoke of the affair?'

'No, indeed, she was remarkably calm,' Jane Howard replied. 'I should have been most distressed had she been upset as it was I who told her about the stupid tale going around. I believe she was on her way to visit someone.'

'Yes, my aunt,' Lytham said, 'who was unfortunately not well enough to receive her.'

Jane looked at him thoughtfully. 'I had wondered why she left Bath that day, for she had mentioned a visit to her home but she had not said it was imminent. When I spoke to Mrs Flynn concerning Emma, she seemed a little odd. It was in my mind that they might have quarrelled, but I cannot be sure of that.'

'Thank you for your confidence,' Lytham said and smiled at her. 'I think I must call on Mrs Flynn immediately.'

'You will not find her at home,' Jane told him and smiled a little oddly. 'My brother has taken her driving this afternoon, but I believe she means to visit the Assembly this evening.'

'Then I shall see her there and make an appointment to call—' Lytham's gaze narrowed as he caught something in Jane's look. 'Forgive me if I presume too much—but am I right in thinking your brother and Mrs Flynn have an understanding? When I left Bath I thought someone else was her constant companion?'

'That is all changed now, I am happy to say. There is nothing official as yet,' Jane assured him with a little blush. 'But now that Mrs Flynn has ended her friendship with Lindisfarne, I expect to hear happier news of her very soon.'

'That nonsense is definitely ended then?' His brows rose.

'Oh, yes, my brother says it is quite over. She had found *him* out, you see, and turned to Edward for advice in the matter of some investments a certain person had been trying to force her into—and of course he told her that they would be a mistake. He assured her that she would be much better not to break the trust her husband's lawyers had set up for her, which was what any honourable person would do, of course. It is rumoured that the very next day Lindisfarne left Bath in a terrible rage. I believe there was also a personal reason for the split, but whatever the cause…' she gave a little satisfied nod '…I am perfectly certain that it is over.'

'All Mrs Flynn's friends must be glad of it, I am sure.'

'Oh, yes,' Jane said and gave a little shudder. 'One should not speak ill of another if one can help it, but that man is despicable!' She made an expressive face of disgust.

'Exactly,' Lytham said. 'You are a sensible young woman, Miss Howard, and I am glad I came to you first.'

'I do hope you will go after Emma,' Jane said. 'Her friends will always support her, for none of us could believe that kind of Banbury tale.'

'I am sure she will be glad to hear that, and as I hope she will either return to Bath or spend some time in London next spring, I hope you will call on her.'

'You may depend that I shall.'

They took their leave of one another in perfect harmony, Jane convinced that her suspicions about a certain gentleman's intentions towards her friend had been correct all along, and Lytham to make his rounds of the fashionable meeting places in order to begin the reparation of Emma's reputation.

'Oh…' Bridget gave Lytham a guilty glance as he came up to her at the Assembly that evening. 'If you are looking for Emma…'

'I believe I am seeking an explanation,' he said before she could continue. 'Did you perchance quarrel with Emma, Mrs Flynn?'

'Yes, and it was most unfair of me,' Bridget replied with a shamefaced look. 'She had warned me that Lindisfarne would ruin me and indeed he would have had…he not made that mistake. I heard some of their quarrel, you see.' Her voice tailed away to a whisper.

'I imagine your tale would be better told in private,' Lytham said as he saw her embarrassment. 'May I call on you in the morning—say at eleven-thirty?'

'Oh, yes, I am sure that is best,' Bridget said and turned as Edward Howard came up to her. 'Pray excuse me, sir. I have promised this dance to Mr Howard.'

And most of the others on her card from what he had been able to observe, Lytham thought. Clearly Mrs Flynn had recovered from her passion for Lindisfarne much more quickly than would have seemed possible, and was probably seeking a safer attachment for the future.

He wondered what Lindisfarne had done to cause her to come to her senses so suddenly, and wondered if it concerned Emma. If that swine had harmed her…! But he must wait for the morning in patience. It would not do to march Mrs Flynn from the ballroom and force her to repeat what was sure to be a harrowing tale.

It was in any case too late to set out for the country that evening, and Emma was probably quite happy staying with her friends for the moment.

He stayed only to dance once with Jane Howard, and then took his leave. As soon as he learned the truth of Emma's hasty departure, he would set out to find her.

It was only when he arrived back at Lady Agatha's lodgings that he realised his journey would have to be delayed for a few days.

Almost two weeks had passed since Emma left Bath, and her hopes that Lytham might follow her had faded. It had been foolish of her to allow herself to hope even for a moment, but she could not control her heart. Despite everything, it continued to race wildly at the mention of his name—something she tried hard to hide from Mary.

'Why do you not apply to the marquis for help?' Mary asked when her first two inquiries for the post of companion ended in disappointment. Both positions had been advertised in a local paper and she had thought it might be easier to get work locally, where she might be known as Sir Thomas's daughter. Indeed, she had received a very kind letter from one lady who said that she knew Emma's mother and would have gladly given her the position had it not already been filled. 'I am sure he would recommend you to someone he knows.'

'Oh…I prefer not to ask for favours if I can avoid it,' Emma replied. She had been encouraged by the kind letter and was only waiting for the next edition of the paper to see if any more likely situations were offered within its pages. 'I believe I shall—' She had been about to say that she was thinking of placing an advertisement herself when Mary's little maid came in with a silver salver. 'Is that for me, Annie? Thank you.'

She slit the letter open with a pearl-handled knife, and saw that it was from one of the agencies she had approached soon after her father's death. She had written to them again to ask if they knew of anything, and it seemed there was a suitable position with an elderly lady living in Northumberland.

'This sounds as if it may suit me,' Emma said, holding it out to Mary when she had finished reading it. 'What do you think?'

Mary read the letter and frowned. 'It says that their client is a difficult lady and that her recent companion left suddenly. I think she may be the sort of person who makes life uncomfortable for her employees, Emma.'

'Yes, I dare say,' Emma replied, for she had guessed something of the sort herself. 'But I do not have a great deal of choice, Mary. I must find a position soon.'

'You know we are delighted to have you here.'

'You have been very kind,' Emma said. 'But I must not stay too long, Mary dearest. If I do not wear out my welcome, then I may come back to you whenever I am in need of a temporary home.'

Mary made no further protest. She would have liked to offer Emma a permanent home, but she knew that would not be comfortable for any of them. At the moment her two sons were sharing a room, but when Mary's daughter was old enough to leave the nursery she would need a room of her own. For a week or two at a time they could manage, but the Vicarage was not large enough to accommodate them all indefinitely.

'I thought I would take a walk up to the house this afternoon,' Emma said. 'Lily told me that they go on as usual and I wanted to see how everyone is. Lytham will surely not let things continue as they are forever, and when I return next time there may be new people living there.'

'Well, it is cold, but I do not think it will snow,' Mary said, glancing out of the window. 'A little walk may do you good, Emma. You may use the time to think about this position you have been offered and decide what you wish to do for the best.'

'Yes, that is what I thought,' Emma agreed. 'I shall write this evening and let them know one way or the other.'

It was easy to speak of making a decision, Emma thought as she began the walk to what had once been her father's estate. She had chosen to take the longer route through the village for the fields were muddy and, though it was cold, she did not think it cold enough to freeze. Better to take the road and avoid getting stuck in the mud. The trees were beginning to lose their leaves and it would not be long before winter set in. The prospect of spending the coming months at a place she did not know with an employer of uncertain temper was not a happy one but, try as she might, Emma could find no alternative.

Everyone was delighted to see her up at the house. It was clear that Lily had told her fellow servants that they had left Bath hurriedly after a quarrel with Emma's employer, though she had been unable to give them more details since Emma had not communicated them to her.

Lily was back to her old work as a parlour maid, apparently quite content to be home from her travels. She welcomed Emma to the servants' hall, but did not stay to listen because she was summoned by the ringing of the doorbell.

'Well, miss, you're looking very healthy,' Cook told her as she sat down at the table with them as she had often done in the past. 'You could have knocked me down with a feather when Lily said you was back so soon. Shall you be staying long, miss?'

'Only for a few weeks,' Emma replied. 'I am looking for—' She turned as Lily came back in, looking pink-cheeked and flustered. 'Did you want me, Lily?'

'It's his lordship, miss…the marquis himself,' Lily said in a voice breathy with excitement. 'He recognised me and asked me how I was.'

'I hope you didn't tell him I was here?' Emma's heart sank as she saw the look on Lily's face. 'You did and he asked to see me, of course?'

'Yes, miss. He said he would take it as a favour if you would consent to take tea with him in the parlour.'

Emma cursed the ill fortune that had caused Lytham to arrive on the very afternoon that she had chosen to visit her old servants at the house. He would think she was taking liberties, but there was no help for it. She could do no other than comply with his request.

'I shall go up at once,' she said. 'Please wait a few minutes before you bring the tea, Lily.'

'Yes, miss—his lordship said twenty minutes and no sooner.'

Clearly Lytham was in charge here, but she must expect that. The estate belonged to him now, and she was merely a guest under his roof—an uninvited one at that. She put her hands to her cheeks in an effort to cool them, taking a moment to recover her composure before knocking at the parlour door.

'Come!' Lytham barked, then glared at her as she entered. 'I imagined it was Lily. Why did you knock? This is your home, you may enter without seeking my permission.'

'It was once my home,' Emma corrected with dignity. 'I must ask you to forgive me for this presumptuous visit. I came only to see old friends before—'

'Running away again, Emma?' His brows arched. 'You have less courage than I believed. I did not think you so easily cowed.'

'Forgive me. I do not think I understand you.'

'Why did you run away from Bath—was it because of that stupid tale making the rounds? Or because you quarrelled with Mrs Flynn?'

Emma clasped her hands in front of her, trying for calm. He had obviously been listening to the gossip, and though he knew the truth of the scurrilous tale put about by one young gentleman, he must think ill of her or he would not be giving her such looks!

'If you know that I quarrelled with Bridget, you must know why I left,' she said, refusing to be drawn.

'I know that that rogue Lindisfarne told Mrs Flynn you had thrown yourself at him, and that for a few moments she chose to believe him.' He glared at Emma. 'But that was no reason for you to run away. You might have known that she would realise the truth of the matter when she'd had time to reflect.'

'I knew no such thing,' Emma retorted. 'Bridget was in love with him, and I believed she had chosen to believe him over me. I did not care to be disbelieved in that manner. Besides, there were other reasons for me to leave.'

'Such as that stupid tale circulating?' His brows rose. 'I have put that to flight, Emma, and I think you will hear no more of it—and my aunt was unwell that morning. You were supposed to have received that message, but perhaps it was not put to you in quite those terms?'

'No, it was not,' Emma replied, a flush in her cheeks. 'I believed Lady Agatha had heard the gossip and did not want to receive me.'

'She was afraid that was what had happened,' Lytham said, 'and she asked me to beg your forgiveness if indeed you were made to feel unwelcome in her house.'

'It was not exactly that,' Emma said, not meeting his eyes. 'Jane Howard had told me about the gossip, and I fear I may have jumped to a hasty conclusion. When Lindisfarne also accused me of being a whore—'

'Damn him! The man deserves to be horsewhipped for the way he behaved towards you—and Mrs Flynn. Had he not taken himself off to Ireland I might have been tempted to teach him a lesson myself.'

'Has he indeed gone?' Emma was relieved as he inclined his head. 'Poor Bridget must be desperately unhappy.'

'That was not the case when I last saw her,' Lytham said. 'She seems to be making a remarkable recovery under the tender care of Mr Howard and his sister.'

'Oh, I know they will take care of her, but Bridget was desperate. I cannot believe her nature to be so shallow that she is not hurting inside.'

'Then it is your own nature you follow, not hers,' Lytham replied with a frown. 'I have found most women to be inconstant, and to find comfort very quickly in another lover.'

'That is unfair of you, sir!' Emma's eyes flashed fire at him. 'I do not know what you may have experienced in the past, but not all of us are so easily content to pass from one man to another. Some of us having once given their heart may never give it to another if disappointed.'

'Is that what happened to you, Emma? Is that why you have hidden your feelings for years?'

'I do not know what you mean.' Emma turned away from him and went to stand by the window, looking out at the park. Her pulses were racing and she did not trust herself to speak for the moment. She must do and say nothing that gave her feelings away, though her heart raced wildly when he looked at her.

'So—what are your immediate plans?' Lytham asked, his change of subject surprising her.

'I have been seeking for work as a companion,' Emma replied, without looking at him. 'There is a post that I might consider with an elderly lady.'

'Is that really what you want?'

'I may have no choice. Once there has been talk there are always some who will believe it, and I may not be able to find more congenial employment.'

He was silent for a moment, then, 'There is always my offer...'

Emma's heart stood still. She felt a tingling sensation sweep over her. He was asking her to be his mistress! For a moment she was angry that he could press his scandalous offer at a time when she was so very low. Yet in an instant the anger was gone as she realised how wonderful it would be to be held intimately in his arms...to sleep in his bed after having experienced his loving.

Her cheeks were burning as she felt the confusion and shame mingle in her mind, and knew that she was sorely tempted to accept his offer. She ought to refuse it, of course. She ought to storm from the room and never speak to him again …but it was her last chance of ever knowing the happiness of a man's love. Even if that love were a transitory thing that would burn itself out.

She couldn't do such a wicked thing! She would be throwing everything away, her reputation, the respect of her friends, all hope of a return to society. But as she gripped her hands together tightly, she knew that she was going to be reckless for perhaps the only time in her life.

'You are asking me to be your mistress,' she said, still not looking at him. 'I refused you the first time, but have given your offer much consideration since we parted, sir, and—and I have decided to accept.'

Lytham was stunned. Surely she could not mean it? He was not sure what devil had prompted him to remind her. In Bath, he had thrown the offer that she might care to be his mistress at her in a moment of temper and never for a second had he believed she would accept—nor had he truly wished for it. Even now, he had expected her to fly at him in a rage, and then of course he would have taken her in his arms and told her that she was quite wrong. He had always had something quite different in mind for Emma, but now that little devil was on his shoulder, tempting him to see how far she would really go. Supposing he let her believe that he truly wanted her as his mistress?

'If you mean that, Emma, I should be both honoured and delighted with the arrangement. I assure you that you will be well taken care of financially.'

'Oh, I know that, my lord.' Emma turned to face him. She was in command of herself now, though her heart was pumping madly and she thought her cheeks might still betray her inner agitation for they felt heated. 'I have realised for some time that you were both generous and fair. I am therefore quite prepared to be your mistress for—for as long as you are satisfied with the arrangement—and to retire to a discreet distance when you are…tired of the situation.'

'That may be a very long time, Emma,' Lytham replied. If she was struggling for composure, then he—the rogue!—was struggling to stop himself laughing out loud. 'You are a lovely woman, and I admire beauty for its own sake, but I think you also know that I enjoy your company, and that I have certain feelings for you.'

'Yes…' Emma's cheeks were definitely burning now and she could not have met his eyes to save her life. 'I was aware of that when…when you kissed me, my lord. I—I found it a pleasant experience. Had I not, nothing would have induced me to accept your offer, but I think we may deal well together and—' She found it too difficult to continue.

Lytham decided to rescue her. He moved swiftly towards her, taking her into his arms and pulling her close to him so that she felt the heat of him. As he pressed his mouth to hers in a kiss of possession that left her close to swooning, Emma felt an overwhelming surge of relief and happiness.

It did not matter that this would not last, that one day she would taste bitterness and despair when he no longer wanted her—for now, she was happier than she had ever been in her life.

'Does that answer your question, Emma?' He gazed down at her, a look of devilish amusement in his eyes. 'If you were in any doubt about my feelings for you, that must surely tell you that I want you very badly.'

'Yes, my lord,' Emma said, a smile tugging at her mouth. 'Had this been a conventional arrangement, I should have had to pretend that I was ignorant of your meaning or that I was too shy to respond—but I believe you would have known that to be a falsehood?'

Lytham chuckled, realising that she was an even more remarkable woman than he had believed, and that he was extremely fortunate that he had found her.

He ought, of course, to tell her at once of his true intentions towards her, but the pleasure to be got from teasing her a little longer was irresistible.

'Your response was very satisfactory for a beginner, Emma,' he replied. 'But I shall teach you the way a passionate woman behaves with her lover—there are many things for you to learn, my darling. Shall you be willing to learn them, Emma?'

'I think you will find me an apt pupil,' she replied. It was so good of him to make a jest of this, she felt, easing her through what might otherwise have been an awkward situation. She was well aware that her behaviour was shocking in the extreme, but just for the moment she did not care.

'Oh, I am convinced of it,' Lytham said, eyes alight with mischief. 'But I think we shall not begin your lessons just yet, Emma. I do not want to shock your friends and household. No, I shall take you somewhere that we may be private…a little love-nest that will enable you to become the woman I know you can be.'

'You are always so thoughtful, my lord.'

'I really must insist that you call me Lytham, Emma.'

'Yes, certainly, Lytham,' she replied and her lovely eyes were brilliant with the love she had no idea that she was betraying. 'You see, I shall be very good from now on.'

'Oh, yes, I see it,' he replied and smiled inwardly. It was a good beginning, but he could not wait for her to wake up and realise just what she had agreed to.

Chapter Eight

Lytham insisted on accompanying Emma back to the Vicarage, declaring that he would have the carriage brought round since dark clouds had blown up and there was a likelihood of rain. She could not but be grateful; it did indeed begin to bucket down long before she could have walked to the Thorns' house.

'There you are, my love,' Mary said welcoming them into her parlour where a fire was merrily burning. 'I was beginning to think you would get a terrible soaking, but his lordship has seen you safely home as I might have expected he would.' She smiled at the marquis, clearly approving of him. 'My husband had heard you were come, sir. It is nice to see you back again.'

'Thank you, Mrs Thorn,' he responded warmly to her welcome. 'Emma could have remained at Sommerton for as long as she wished, of course. However, she wanted to return here until we leave tomorrow. I am taking her to my family estate, ma'am, where she will be quite safe.'

'There—did I not say his lordship would make all right if you applied to him, Emma?' She beamed at him. 'My mind is completely at rest now, sir. I know *you* will take care of her.'

'Thank you, Mrs Thorn. You may indeed rely on me to do just that.'

Emma wondered how he could respond so easily. For herself she was determined to say as little as possible about her intentions for the future. If Mary knew the true situation she would be terribly shocked. Emma hoped that she would never need to tell her.

146

* * *

Her courage ebbed during the night when she lay for some hours, staring into the darkness and trying not to think about what she had done. By agreeing to become Lytham's mistress, she had effectively cut herself off from her family and friends, none of whom would approve of what she was doing. She knew that she was being reckless, but the alternative was so bleak…and she did love him. It would be heaven to be with him, to be loved by him, even if for only a short time.

No, she did not regret her decision, not for a moment! She would think only of the time to be spent with him, the man she loved, and forget that a lonely future might await her one day.

Emma slept at last, dreaming sweetly of a cottage with roses growing up the walls and a man who looked remarkably like Lytham carrying a young lad on his shoulders, who she instinctively knew was their son. All quite ridiculous, of course, she reflected on waking. Lytham lived in a large house and their relationship was hardly likely to last long enough for her ever to see him playing with children of their union.

She had slept longer than she intended and there was a last-minute rush to be ready for the carriage, with Emma searching for trinkets she had somehow mislaid, and Mary trying to organise the final packing of her bags. The last hour went so swiftly that she did not have time to be nervous, and the carriage was at the door before she realised it.

'You must write to me when you have the leisure,' Mary Thorn said as she kissed Emma goodbye. 'But I know you will do well now, dearest Emma. The marquis is a fine man and he will take care of you.'

Emma blushed then as she wondered for a moment if Mary had guessed the truth. She seemed to be suggesting a relationship of an intimate kind between Emma and Lytham, but of course she could not know anything. She probably imagined that Emma was to live with Lytham's aunt as a kind of unpaid companion, Lytham's dependent. Of course that must be it.

Kissing Mary goodbye, Emma smiled at Lytham as he came to hand her into the carriage. He nodded but said nothing, though his eyes seemed to study her face thoughtfully before he went to take his leave of Mary Thorn.

'I wish to thank you for taking care of Emma for me, ma'am.'

'It was nothing, sir. The Vicar and I are both fond of her.'

'But I am grateful none the less. Should your husband ever wish for preferment to another living you will apply to me, ma'am. I shall be happy to promote your family's interests now and in the future.'

'Oh, sir,' Mary said, overcome. 'I am sure I don't know what to say.'

'You need say nothing, ma'am. Simply pass on my message to the Reverend Thorn and he will know what to do.' He took the hand she offered, saluting it with a chaste kiss before leaving her to climb into the carriage with Emma.

'What have you been saying to Mary?' she asked, having witnessed their leave-taking but not overheard the conversation between them.

'Merely politeness,' Lytham replied with a careless shrug of his broad shoulders immaculately clothed in a coat of blue superfine. She could not help noticing how very good looking he was and experiencing a little shiver of anticipation. 'I am glad to see you looking so well, Emma. I trust you slept well?'

'Tolerably well,' she replied, eyes downcast, lashes long and dark against her cheeks. 'There are always slight anxieties when one embarks on a new venture, but I am content now. I know that you are experienced in these matters and I need only follow your lead.'

Lytham's mouth twitched at the corners, but he managed to hide his amusement. Did she imagine that it was his habit to carry off innocent maidens and make love to them? What a delicious idiot she was! This was proving even more enchanting than he had thought. He was a wicked rogue to carry on this deception, but he had not been so diverted in an age. She would make an entrancing mistress!

He gave her no answer, stretching out his long legs as he leaned his head back against the squabs, and admiring her lovely face and apparent composure from beneath lowered lids. She was a picture of serenity. She could not possibly be that calm inside—

could she? A young woman of good family about to become an outcast from society by becoming his mistress—what must be going through her mind? Had she thought ahead, to a time when he might no longer want her? No, he was sure she had not. She was behaving recklessly in a way that was foreign to her nature and soon now she would wake up and realise that she could not go through with this masquerade—and then he would tell her that he had something else in mind for her.

He reviewed in his mind the women who had been his mistresses in the past. Not one of them could hold a candle to Emma for poise or looks, although all of them had been exceptional in some way. Some had been young and beautiful, others had possessed different qualities, but none had been everything that he could desire in one woman.

The first woman he had ever made love to had been a lady some twenty years his senior. He had been fifteen and she had been married, a friend of his mother's. Lady Lytham had died a few days previously and Alexander had been feeling bewildered by his grief; although his mother had never shown her love for him, he had cared for her.

Anne Hemsby was a gentle, pretty woman who had initiated him into the pleasures of the bedroom, teaching him how to please her as well as himself. He had always been grateful to Mistress Hemsby for her patience and forbearance with a clumsy youth, and they were still good friends.

He was on good terms with most of his former lovers, though there was the notable exception of the fiery opera dancer who had driven him from her dressing room with a vase directed at his head at the stormy end of their relationship.

'Why are you smiling like that?' Emma asked, bringing him out of his reverie. 'You have a positively wicked expression on your face, Lytham. Tell me what you are thinking?'

'I was contemplating all the pleasures in store for us, my darling,' he replied in a tone that caressed her, sending a flush of heat through her body and making her tinglingly aware of him. 'I think we should have a period of retreat so that we may get to know one another well—and then perhaps a trip to Paris to buy a wardrobe fit for—my love.'

Her cheeks were on fire now, her heart racing wildly. He had deliberately avoided using the word *mistress* so as not to embarrass her. His consideration for her feelings was remarkable.

'I should enjoy that very much,' she said once she could trust herself to speak. 'I—I am not perfectly sure what you expect of me, Lytham. Oh, I know that there are…certain duties…but do you intend me to live in a separate establishment and…' Her voice tailed off in confusion as she saw the expression in his eyes. 'No, do not laugh at me, Lytham. I really do not know how these things are conducted.'

'Be assured that I know exactly what I require of you,' he said. 'You need only give yourself up to the pleasures in store for you, my love. You should, however, be aware that my passion for you is no slight thing. I intend to spoil and indulge you, Emma. You need not worry about anything.'

'Then I shall not,' she replied. 'I shall rely on you entirely to show me what is expected of your…' Once again she hesitated and he came to her rescue gallantly.

'My lover,' Lytham supplied and knew himself a wicked rogue. A gentleman would do the decent thing and set her mind at rest, but the rogue in him was enjoying this far too much!

Emma was not sure what she had expected once they left the Thorns' house, but Lytham's behaviour was exactly what it had always been—polite, courteous, and casual. Oh, there were those burning looks, of course, and the occasional touch of his hand, which turned her insides to liquid fire, but he had made no attempt to make love to her during the three days of their journey.

She had been treated in every respect as a lady, sleeping alone in her own room after dining with Lytham in the parlour at the inn in which they stayed overnight. She had wondered on that first night whether he might wish to begin their relationship, but her look of inquiry had met with an enigmatic smile.

'We have plenty of time, Emma.'

'Yes, of course,' she had replied, her heart racing.

And now they were approaching the house Lytham had described as a perfect retreat. She was a little surprised to hear the cry of seagulls and to smell the salty tang of sea air, and then their carriage rounded a long, gentle curve in the road and she saw the sea glistening in the distance.

'Oh—are we to stay near the sea?' she cried, looking at him in delight. 'I have only been to the sea once, Lytham. Papa took us to Newquay for a few days when I was a small child.'

'I trust you do not have a dislike of sea air? Our north-east coast can be a little bracing, but there are some excellent walks and on a mild day it can be beautiful.'

'Certainly not,' she replied, eyes sparkling. 'I loved my visit and wished we might have stayed there forever. I believe I cried when it was time to go home.'

Lytham looked amused. 'This is not a developed resort, Emma, merely a small, rather private cove. My mother was advised she needed some sea air for her health's sake soon after I was born and she bought a house here with a legacy from her aunt. She came alone often, but a few times I was allowed to accompany her and I have retained some good memories of the place. The house was left to me when she died and I have maintained it in good order. I visit from time to time.'

'I am glad you brought me to your mother's house,' Emma said, craning her head to look from the carriage window. She gave a gasp of pleasure as the house came into view. It was set in a bend in the road, sheltered by the hill from the full blast of the sea wind and from public gaze as it faced the sea. The walls were painted white and looked dazzling even in the weak wintry sunshine, the long sash windows at the back were sparkling as they caught the rays. 'It looks beautiful.'

It had no front garden as such, just a sweep of grass that gradually sloped to the cliff edge. Two of the windows at the front were bowed and dressed with lace curtains, but the main entrance was at the side and approached by a gravel drive flanked by evergreen bushes of some kind. The black painted door stood between two pillars of white stone, and opened at their approach.

A woman who was clearly the housekeeper came out to greet them as they got down from the carriage. Tall, thin, dressed in a suitable grey gown with a white lace collar and a bunch of keys worn on a chain at her waist, she had obviously been expecting them and bobbed a respectful curtsey.

'Your lordship...Miss Sommerton. I am Mrs Warren. Everything is ready for you, sir.'

'Thank you, Mrs Warren. If you would be so good as to take my ward to her apartments. We have been travelling for some hours and I know Emma would like to rest before we dine.'

Emma's cheeks felt warm. He had spoken of her as his ward to the housekeeper to save her blushes presumably, but their true relationship would become apparent once...they were sleeping together. There, she had faced it in her own mind. She had become accustomed to the idea now. At first she had been shocked at her own brazen behaviour, but Lytham's casual manner had robbed the situation of any embarrassment. Indeed, his behaviour had been so circumspect during their journey that she might well have been his ward.

'Would you come this way, miss?'

Emma followed the housekeeper through a small entrance hall to a reception room set out with various chairs and sofas into a larger hall with an open and rather impressive staircase, which gave the house a light airy feel. She looked up to the floor above, thinking that it had an Italian feel about it—or as she had imagined an Italian villa might look from pictures she had seen. The marble statues of naked boys added to the feeling that the person who had furnished this house had liked the Italian style.

'It is a long time since his lordship visited,' Mrs Warren informed Emma as she led the way upstairs. She stopped in front of a pair of double doors at the end of the upper hall and opened them with a flourish. 'These rooms were always used exclusively by Lady Lytham herself. I hope you will be comfortable here, miss.'

'Oh, how very pretty!' Emma exclaimed as she stepped inside the first room.

She had never seen such elegant furnishings. The colours were gentle shades of pink and cream with the occasional touch of deep crimson, as though it had been flung there to startle the senses, the furniture of some pale wood with panels of intricate inlay. There were display cabinets containing delicate porcelain cups and tiny teapots, and some exquisite figurines that looked as if they came from the Derby factory, also a lady's desk with a leather top and a gilt rail above the little drawers. Sofas, gilt-framed chairs and an embroidery frame all combined to make it the most charming room Emma had ever been in.

Further exploration showed her an equally charming bedroom, beyond which was a dressing room and a door leading where— into another bedroom, perhaps? Emma tried the door and found it locked. She turned to see Mrs Warren looking at her.

'His lordship will be occupying the next suite, miss. He has the key, of course, but you have a key to the dressing room.'

'Oh…thank you. I suppose these are meant for the master and mistress?'

'Yes, miss.' The housekeeper was clearly thoughtful. 'Was there anything more?'

'No, thank you. I shall come down in half an hour or so… Perhaps some tea in the parlour?'

'Yes, miss. Her ladyship always used the back parlour in the winter, miss. She said it was warmer.'

'Then I expect we shall do the same,' Emma said and turned away to look about her once more. The housekeeper's gaze had made her feel slightly uncomfortable, but she was determined not to be affected by any other consideration other than her own feelings. It did not matter what Lytham's servants thought of her. She would not allow such considerations to weigh with her.

After the housekeeper had gone she took off her heavy travelling cape and went to investigate the contents of two large armoires in the dressing room. Her trunks had been sent on ahead in the baggage coach, but although her own gowns were hanging there she saw that the clothes she had left behind in Bath had also been placed in the armoire. Had Lytham been so sure of her then?

Dismissing the unworthy thought, Emma was about to select one of the gowns when a knock at the door made her turn. A young maid was standing there, holding an elegant silk gown that Emma had never seen before.

'I'm Betsy, Miss Sommerton. I've been pressing some of the new gowns his lordship had sent from town. I brought this one back—and Mrs Warren said to ask if you needed any help, miss?'

'I was about to change into this green afternoon dress,' Emma said. 'But the one you have pressed looks rather nice. Perhaps I shall wear that instead.' Betsy held up a bronze silk gown that was more stylish than anything else Emma possessed and had clearly been chosen by someone with an eye for colour. 'Yes, I shall wear that one, please.'

Lytham must have been planning this for some time, Emma thought as she allowed Betsy to help her to change into the beautiful dress. He could not have known she would be forced to leave Bath so suddenly—and yet perhaps he had been expecting it. He had warned her of the consequences if she continued as Bridget's employee, though he could not have known what Lindisfarne would do.

Emma had found it difficult to accept Bridget's apparent change of heart. How could she be desperately in love with one man, and only a few days later be seemingly content to be courted by another?

She was glad that Bridget had come to see how unworthy Lindisfarne was, but still hurt that she could carelessly cast off her friend for a man she was now prepared to forget. Lytham had told her that Bridget was very apologetic for the way she had behaved and hoped that they might be friends in the future, but Emma did not think it would ever be quite the same between them.

If their circumstances had been reversed Emma would never have been so careless of another's feelings, especially someone who was in an awkward position, but then, she would not have become so involved with a man like Lindisfarne in the first place.

She had in her own way been as reckless as Bridget, though. The only difference was that Lytham was being discreet. They were unlikely to meet anyone who knew them here, which meant that their affair could be kept secret. At least until they went to Paris.

Surely she would not need so many new clothes? Lytham had chosen several gowns for her himself, and she had those Bridget had given her. The trip to Paris was not necessary. Unless Lytham wished for it, of course.

He would not choose to stay here for long. Emma realised that he must mean this to be a temporary situation…just until she had got used to being his mistress. And she meant to show him that she was perfectly capable of carrying the role he had given her, which was why she had chosen to wear the bronze gown.

She was not some green girl to shy at the first hurdle. Lytham had offered his protection and she had accepted, that meant she must expect to have gowns bought for her and presented as a *fait accompli*. A wife would be given an allowance and expected to choose her own things, a mistress must accept what she was given. And, judging by this dress, Lytham had given her beautiful things.

By wearing this gown she was showing him that she was perfectly happy to accept his terms.

Lytham looked out at the pretty back garden, which was protected from the full blast of the sea air by the house itself. There were rose walks, herbaceous borders and the summerhouse at the end of the long walk. It was all rather bare at the moment, the only things blossoming a few winter heathers and shrubs. He had remembered it as a garden full of roses, but he had never visited in winter before. Perhaps he should have gone straight to Lytham Hall—and yet that perverse devil inside him wanted to see just how far Emma would push this masquerade of hers.

She would surely not go through with it to the end? She would realise what she was doing, beg his pardon for having misled him and ask to be allowed to leave—and then he would tell her of his true intentions.

He wondered what she would make of the gowns he had ordered for her from town. They had been intended for her use at Lytham, just a temporary measure until he could arrange for her to join him in London in the spring, when she would be able to buy whatever she desired. She was certain to be outraged when they were presented for her use with no explanation. She would never wear them...at least until he told her the truth, which was that she would need some warmer clothes because the winters in these northern climes could be very cold.

'I hope I have not kept you waiting too long?'

He turned to look at her, experiencing a shock as he saw her standing there in the bronze silk. He had always known that the gown would suit her. It brought out the richness of her hair and gave her skin warmth—but he had not expected to find her quite so beautiful. Nor had he imagined she would choose to wear one of the gowns he had bought for her. He was uncertain for the first time since he had begun this charade.

'You look…beautiful, Emma,' he breathed, feeling a sharp, urgent desire to make love to her now, this moment.

'It is the gown,' she said and laughed softly. She looked so confident standing there, almost a different person. Was it the gown—or had something else happened to her? He could not decide, but there was one thing certain in his mind. She was no longer the prim Miss Sommerton she had pretended to be, but a lovely desirable woman. 'Whoever chose this had good taste.'

'I chose it for you from a range shown to me by a French seamstress. When I mentioned your name she said that you had visited her showrooms and she had your measurements, though you had not bought anything from her.'

'Madame Alicia,' Emma said. 'I recognised her style. She did indeed measure me for a gown, but I decided she was too expensive for my gowns, though Bridget bought from her.'

'She may be expensive, but I think the cost worthwhile.'

'I am glad you approve,' Emma said. She thought he was about to say something more when a knock at the door heralded the arrival of the tea tray. It was a few minutes before they settled again, and by then the moment had passed.

'You were looking at the garden when I came in,' Emma said as she poured tea the way she knew he liked it, with just a spot of cream and no sugar. 'I imagine it is very pretty in the spring and summer. Did I see roses climbing up the wall just beneath my window?'

'Yes, I believe so,' Lytham replied. 'I had not realised it would look so bare at this time of year.'

'I should imagine the views from the edge of the cliff are quite spectacular. Perhaps after tea we could take a walk there? Is there an easy route down to the cove—or must one go all the way back along the road that brought us here?'

'There is a path,' Lytham said. 'But the incline is quite steep and I believe there has been a rock fall quite recently. If you use the path you must take the greatest care, Emma. I should not want you to slip and hurt yourself. A tumble could only result in serious injury.'

'I promise to be careful.' She sipped her tea, then picked up the silver pot. 'May I refill your cup, Lytham?'

'Thank you, no.'

His eyes watched her thoughtfully as she refilled her own cup, adding one lump of sugar with the silver tongs. She was perfectly at ease, her manner that of a lady at home in such a drawing room, which of course she was. Except that he had thought she would be nervous of being alone with him. He had anticipated the moment when she would throw herself on his mercy and then he would laugh, take her in his arms and tell her the truth.

But this woman was too assured, too confident to act in the way he had imagined. By heaven, she was not going to shy off! She was actually going to go through with it. Why? She was not that desperate—not as desperate as she had been when she left Bath, for he had told her that the rumour was scotched and she must know that many doors would be open to her if she were to return to society.

As she turned her lovely head and looked at him he saw the expectancy in her eyes…the hint of excitement. He had seen that look in other women's eyes, across a crowded room, at the theatre, and he knew what it meant.

She wasn't afraid of becoming his mistress. Indeed, she was ready for him to make love to her now if he chose. That thought made his blood race and he felt himself hardening as his desire for her burned ever brighter. It was women such as this who had turned the course of history! Cleopatra might have come to Caesar in just this way, he thought and smiled as he realised where his thoughts were leading him.

He had underestimated her courage and her determination. He had been misled because she had run away from the scandal in Bath, but now he began to see that she was much stronger than he had imagined. It was obviously time for his confession. He could not allow the masquerade to continue.

He rose to his feet and took a few steps towards her, stopping just short of the sofa she had chosen to sit on. She glanced up at him inquiringly and he held out his hand to her.

'Come here, Emma.'

She rose gracefully and came obediently, but there was nothing subdued or submissive in her manner. Her head was up, her clear eyes meeting his fearlessly. She stood without moving as he reached for her, then her lips parted invitingly as he drew her against him. As their lips met in a hungry, yearning kiss, she melted into his body, and he could feel the completeness of her surrender. Her mouth told him that her hunger was as great as his own, and he felt the throbbing need in his loins.

'I want you, Emma,' he said hoarsely. 'Oh, God, I want to make love to you so much.'

'Yes,' she said, gazing up at him. 'I think it is time.'

'Go up to your room and wait for me.'

She smiled and for just one second there was uncertainty in her eyes, but then it had gone.

'I shall lock the sitting-room door to the hall. You will come through the dressing room?'

'Yes…'

He watched as she left the parlour, his hungry eyes devouring her. This was not at all what he had planned! It was wrong, a mistake. He could not destroy her innocence this way even though she was brave enough to give herself to him, and yet he sensed that it was what she was waiting for, wanted.

Lytham paced the room like an angry beast. Why had he not spoken out? What had he done? This foolish masquerade had been carried too far. It had amused him to tease her, but to use her so basely would be a betrayal of all he felt for Emma.

He would go up and tell her that he had never intended her to be his mistress. She was the woman he loved…the only woman he had ever loved like this. He wanted her as his wife!

Yet she was waiting for him, expecting him to make love to her. His mind saw her as she would look with her hair loose on her shoulders, clad only in a flimsy nightgown and he knew that if he once touched her he would be lost. If she offered herself to him as she had a moment ago, he would not be able to control himself. No, he could not, would not use her so scurvily!

Cursing himself for creating a situation that need never have arisen, he went to the door and walked out into the hall. Instead of following Emma up the stairs, he let himself out of the main door and began to walk across the sweep of grass to the edge of the cliffs.

He needed to cool his fever before he spoke to Emma again, to control the raging desire that had sprung up inside him at the sight of her in that bronze gown. Until that moment he had not really understood the depth of his own feelings for her, and though he had known that he intended to ask her to be his wife he had not realised just how much he wanted and loved her.

It was the fault of his damnable humour, that quirk in his nature that drove him always to test others, and more often than not to find them sadly wanting. This time it had rebounded on him, for Emma was so much more than he had ever guessed, so much more than he deserved. Her reserved manner had hid so much that was valuable and fine in her, and only now did he know her for the woman she was—the woman she could become given her rightful place in society.

He was not sure that she would appreciate the jest he had played on her. Indeed, he thought she might be very angry, and rightly so. He had been a very knave to play such a trick upon her.

She might think that he had deliberately tried to humiliate her and that he had belittled the sacrifice she had been prepared to make for his sake. He knew that she was capable of anger and he feared that she might believe herself insulted.

It was that imp of mischief inside him, the perverse devil that drove him close to the edge only too often. Had it not been for that stubborn streak in his nature this situation would never have come about. Emma's father might still be living, she still residing quietly in her own home—and yet that would have been such a waste. She would have faded into a lonely spinsterhood, and the world would have been so much the poorer. With his help she could shine in the drawing rooms of society as she had always been meant to do. He comforted himself with the thought that he had at least done this for her.

In another moment he felt a surge of disgust with himself for trying to excuse the inexcusable. Emma had been forced to go against all she had been taught. What had seemed amusing to him must have been torment for her, but she had been brave enough to go through with it.

Why? Why had she been willing to go so far? He knew her too well to think it was for what she might gain financially. The only explanation that came to mind was that she cared for him sufficiently to consider her world well lost for love.

Lytham had never been offered that kind of love, had not imagined it truly existed beyond the covers of a book. Indeed, he could not believe himself worthy of it.

Most women he had known took as much and more than they gave—and yet he *had* seen love in Emma's eyes, he had known that she cared for him. He *had* known in his heart that she had not accepted his careless offer—an offer he had never truly intended to make—for the sake of his wealth.

Fool! Damned fool! He was a damnable rogue as his father had once called him during one of their frequent quarrels. He was going to hurt Emma when he told her that he had been deliberately leading her on just for his own selfish amusement. She might turn from him in disgust, refusing to believe that he truly loved her— and who could blame her? Who could blame her!

He had planned mischief and he was the one caught in his own toils. Staring down at the angry sea, as it boiled and thrashed around the jutting rocks below, driven by a bitter wind from the north, he knew a moment of utter despair. He had discovered something wonderful and there was a good chance that he was going to lose it almost immediately through his own carelessness. What a stupid fool he had been!

'Lytham!'

He turned at the sound of a man's voice and faced his enemy— a man he had believed gone to his grave in a foreign land until recently, when his investigations had warned him that Luther Pennington might still be alive and returned to England.

'They told me you were dead in a brawl…'

'I ought to have died,' Pennington replied, a bitter tone in his voice. His face was aged beyond his years, his long unkempt hair streaked with grey. He had the look of a man who had suffered abuse both at the hands of others and by his own hand through wild living, a man desperation had brought to his lowest ebb. 'You and your friends did your best to destroy me.'

'I took no part in that,' Lytham said, staring into his hate-filled eyes. 'Your court-martial—yes, that I admit. You deserved that, Pennington, for what you did to another man's wife.'

'It was a moment of foolishness under the influence of too much wine. She had been leading me on for weeks.'

'Yet that did not give you the right to act as you did. You raped a woman, a lady of gentle birth. Even a whore deserves better than that.'

'Are you so pure that you can afford to sneer at me?' Pennington snarled, his mouth curled back in a sneer of contempt. 'Why did you bring Sommerton's daughter here unless it was to make her your mistress?'

'Damn you!' Lytham said furiously, his anger directed as much at himself as the other, for he had laid her open to such rumours by his careless behaviour. 'I will not have you abuse her name. Miss Sommerton is none of your business—and for your information I intend to marry her.'

'A pity you did not marry her sooner. She might have been a rich widow,' Pennington muttered. 'I've been following you for weeks, waiting for the right moment. I don't want to make another mistake…'

Lytham saw that he was holding a pistol. Pennington's intention was clear. He had planned his revenge for a long time, feeding on his hatred for what had been done to him and his opportunity could not have been more inviting. Lytham was alone and unarmed, the last thing on his mind that afternoon the possibility that an unknown enemy might take the chance to kill him.

'You won't get away with this…'

His only chance was to keep Pennington talking. Lytham took a few steps towards him, hoping for a chance to wrestle with him, but the pistol was cocked and ready.

'Don't be a fool, man. We can talk about this…'

'You ruined my life,' Pennington said. 'Money won't buy yours.'

He raised his arm to fire, but even as his finger pressed down on the trigger another shot rang out from some distance behind him. Lytham heard the first shot seconds before the force of Pennington's ball struck him in the shoulder and sent him staggering back, teetering for a moment on the edge of the cliff. And then, losing his balance and falling over, he went slipping and sliding down the face of the craggy cliff where the rock had fallen in recent storms. He clawed at the loose boulders desperately, until his head knocked against one larger than the rest, robbing him of all conscious thought.

He did not see the man who had fired the first shot come racing across the lawn, stop to glance briefly at the man he had killed, and then look over the edge of the cliff. Nor did he see the moment of indecision before Tom Sommerton began to make his way down the treacherous path.

Emma was wearing only a thin night chemise when she heard the frantic knocking at her door. She hesitated, but Mrs Warren was calling to her urgently and Lytham would surely not come now. She had waited nearly an hour. Something must have happened to delay him. Reaching for her wrap, she pulled it on and went to unlock the door.

'Yes, Mrs Warren? I was just having a little rest.'

'You must come at once, miss. There's been a terrible tragedy. His lordship…' The housekeeper choked on a sob of near hysteria. 'Benson says he heard two shots out the front a while ago. He went out to investigate and—'

'Has the marquis been shot?' Emma asked, her heart catching with fright. 'Someone attempted to kill him a few weeks ago—has he been badly hurt?'

'We—we don't know yet, miss. Benson found a dead man near the top of the cliffs, but there's no sign of his lordship. We think he may have gone over the edge, though whether he fell or was pushed—'

'But how could he fall?' Emma felt sick with anxiety. This was like a nightmare. How could such a thing have happened? 'What are you doing to find him?'

'Benson has everyone out searching, miss. There's only me left here to tell you what happened.'

'I shall dress and come down,' Emma said. 'Give me a few minutes, Mrs Warren. We must get more help. Is there a village near by? Yes, I recall that we passed it. We must send there.'

'I believe Benson has already sent one of the grooms, miss.'

'Then we must pray that Lord Lytham is soon found.'

Emma's eyes were smarting with tears as she returned to the bedroom and pulled on one of her older gowns. She would join the search herself. They must find Lytham. They must!

She felt as if her heart were breaking. How could she bear it if he were lost to her now?

It was growing dark by the time the villagers began to search the beach with their dogs and lanterns. Standing at the top of the cliff, her cloak caught by the fierce wind that had blown up, Emma stared down at the angry sea and felt the despair wash over her. It was somewhere here that they thought Lytham must have fallen, for there were signs of loose rock having been disturbed. Just below her she could see what seemed to be a shelf of rock, which had been caused by the erosion of this part of the cliffs. Below that was a sheer drop to the jagged rocks that protruded from the sea like dragons' teeth.

How could he survive such a fall—how could anyone? He would either be dashed to pieces on the cliff itself or drowned in the swirling current about those spurs of jutting rocks. No one could have lived through that—and he might also have been wounded before he fell. She felt such a surge of despair that she swayed towards the edge as though she would cast herself down to join him in his watery grave.

'Come back to the house now, miss.'

Emma felt someone tugging at her arm. She shrugged away from the housekeeper's grasp.

'He must be there somewhere. They have to find him—they have to!'

'They will find him if they can,' Mrs Warren said. 'But these tides can sweep a man away. The sea does not always give up its dead.'

'He isn't dead...he can't be dead...' Emma's words were torn away by the wind and lost. 'I love him so...I love him so...'

'Yes, miss. He was a good man. He will be sorely missed.'

Her words were so final, so dismissive of any chance that they might find Lytham alive that Emma felt the rebellion surge within her. She would not give him up so easily!

'He must not be dead!'

'No, miss. Perhaps he isn't. Come away back to the house now. You can't do any good here tonight. The men will keep searching. The locals know this cove better than anyone else could. If he's there, they will find him.'

Emma wanted to defy her. She wanted to keep a vigil here at the top of the cliff until he was brought in, but she could barely see anything now other than the lights of the lanterns on the beach. Nothing could be gained from staying here and she would be needed in the sickroom when they eventually brought him home. Because they would in the end. They must! Otherwise she might as well die with him.

She took a step towards the edge, then something inside her made her draw back. No, she was not such a weak fool. She would not give him up for dead, though others might.

Chapter Nine

The wind was bitterly cold, whipping about her fiercely as she walked along the beach, constantly searching. Her eyes moved over the face of the cliff, looking for a crack or crevice where Lytham might have crawled to hide after his fall, but there were none that she could see. She turned towards the sea itself, straining as if she would penetrate its stormy waters and find him.

How could he simply have disappeared? It was more than a week now since that terrible night, a week of such anguish that Emma did not know how she had lived through it. She had hardly slept in all that time, spending every daylight hour out searching for him, and every dark hour was torment because she was forced to remain within the house.

People had been to the house, people from the village. The Vicar had tried to tell her that God had a purpose for all he did; neighbours came wishing to offer advice or condolence. Emma had turned her face to the wall, closing her ears to the Vicar's advice to pray.

Did he think that she had not already prayed a hundred times, her prayers sometimes an entreaty, at others a curse that this could happen? Why had Lytham been taken from her? Was it because of the sin they planned? No, no, she would not believe that. Love such as she felt for him could never be a sin. She knew that her life would be empty from now on for she would never love another man.

As yet, Emma could not even think about the future or what might become of her now that Lytham was dead. She did not want to think of a world that did not include him, her mind able to cope only with an hour at a time, counting them one by one as the darkness lifted and she could once again go out to begin her lonely vigil.

The villagers had given up the search after the second day. Everyone had told her that all hope was gone: Lytham was dead. He must have fallen unconscious into the sea and been swept under by the current. It was not possible that he had survived in such weather.

Emma refused to give up. She could not believe that it was hopeless. If they had brought her a body she might have accepted it, but without proof her stubborn nature would not give in.

He had to be alive because if he was dead then she wanted to die, too. He must be alive. He must!

'Oh, my darling,' her heart cried out to him. 'I love you. Come back to me. Please come back to me, for I shall die if you do not!'

There was only pain in the world, nothing but pain. Around him was merely darkness, no light or heat or warmth…no love or…what was it he was trying to reach? He did not know what he called for in the rare moments when he was aware of someone roughly tending him, but he knew that there was an even greater pain inside him than that in his head and shoulder.

Day was night and night was day, nothing was as it should be in this place of terrible pain. He was lost, wandering in an ocean of misery, needing something that was lost to him…lost to him forever.

'Forgive me…' he whispered as just for a moment the darkness lightened and he sensed someone bending over him. 'I did not mean to hurt you…forgive me.'

'Poor devil,' a soft, female voice said close to his ear. He felt a hand stroking his forehead. 'I doubt he can last much longer like this. It would probably have been better if you'd let him go into the sea.'

'I couldn't just let him drown. I have to keep him alive somehow.'

'I heard tell they were searching for him. Why don't you tell them where he is—fetch a doctor to him?'

'Because they will hang me,' the second voice said. 'I killed a man, Belle, and unless he vouches for me I'll be taken as Pennington's accomplice and hanged. They'll say it was thieves falling out.'

'You killed to save an innocent man's life.'

'I was seconds too late to stop that devil firing,' Tom Sommerton said ruefully as he looked at the pretty young woman bathing Lytham's forehead. 'You've got to help me, Belle. I can't watch him the whole time, and I need to collect wood for the fire. He ought to be given something…gruel or…' He shook his head despairingly. 'Damn it! I don't know. What do they give people who are this sick?'

'That wound in his shoulder looks nasty,' Belle said. 'I'll fetch Granny Robins to him, she'll know what to do.'

He grabbed her arm as she turned away. 'Can she be trusted? She won't go blabbing?'

'You don't know her,' Belle said. 'She ain't like the rest of us. Some say as she's a mite touched in the head—she sees things we don't—but she knows a bit about healing. If the wound needs the hot iron she'll do it, and she'll give him something to ease the pain.'

'Fetch her, then—but remember, if anyone follows you here I'm done for. Unless he can prove that I saved his life I'm for the drop.'

'And wouldn't that be a pity, handsome lad like you!' Belle laughed at the man she hardly knew but had taken to her bed and her heart within minutes of seeing him hunched up in the corner of the inn parlour, looking like he had all the worries of the world on his shoulder. She had wondered where he went to when he left her father's inn, but it had taken her a week to discover his secret, and it was a fearful one. Belle knew that she could earn a fine reward for information leading to the injured man, but she wasn't going to turn her young lover in for a few pieces of silver. Besides, if his lordship recovered because of her and Granny Robins he would likely give her more. 'Don't you worry, my luvver.

I'll be back and there won't be no hangman running behind nei-ther.'

Tom watched as the saucy barmaid ran off, then went over to look at Lytham once more. He ran his fingers through his hair, wondering why he was risking his neck by staying here. If he had any sense he would cut and run, and let Belle turn the marquis in if she chose.

'Oh, Lady Agatha,' cried Mrs Warren. 'I was never so glad to see anyone in my life. I've been at my wit's end to know what to do with the poor lass. She won't eat a thing I give her—she hardly touches a cup of tea and I'm sure she never sleeps. She was a pretty girl when she came here, but she's hardly more than skin and bone now.'

'Why on earth did you not send for me sooner?' Agatha Lyn-ston demanded. 'All I knew was that Lytham was missing, and I saw no reason to come charging up here when he might very well turn up in Bath at any moment.'

'We didn't want to worry you, ma'am. Besides, no one ex-pected the poor girl to take on like this. I think it must have turned her mind. She seemed bright enough when she came.' She bit her lip and looked rather awkward. 'I wasn't sure you knew about her, ma'am. I thought she might be—'

'Well, spit it out, woman!' Lady Agatha said crossly. 'What bee have you in your bonnet? I am beginning to think that it is you who have lost your wits!'

'Begging your pardon, ma'am, but it did cross my mind that she might be his lordship's lady love.'

'Stuff and nonsense! Where on earth did you get that idea? Miss Sommerton is a respectable young woman. Lytham was in-tending to marry her, but he wanted to get to know her a little better first. I had hoped for an announcement at any time.'

'His lordship's fiancée...' Mrs Warren looked shocked. 'Oh, forgive my foolishness, Lady Agatha. His lordship said she was his ward, but he asked for her to have the suite next to... Well, that's none of my business.'

'It most certainly is not,' said Lady Agatha sharply. 'Well, I must be thankful that you decided to make me aware of the situation—what is it, three weeks after it happened?'

'We did tell you his lordship was missing, ma'am.'

'But you did not make the situation clear. Had you done so, I should have been here long before this. Now don't look so indignant, woman. I am not entirely blaming you. There are others who might have informed me. And I am here now, so we shall say no more about it. Where is Miss Sommerton now?'

'She is walking on the beach, ma'am. She begins at first light and does not return until the evening is drawing in.'

'Walking on the beach in this weather? Good grief! It's a wonder she doesn't take her death of cold. Send someone to fetch her this instant!'

'Yes, ma'am—but I doubt if she will come. She just stares through anyone who tells her to come home. I told you, I think she has lost her mind.'

'She will come if she is told that I am here and want to see her about something most urgent.'

'She will think there is news of his lordship...'

'Exactly. If that doesn't fetch her, then I shall begin to believe that you are right and she has lost her wits.'

Mrs Warren went away to detail the errand to one of the maids, a girl who had sometimes managed to get through to Miss Sommerton. It seemed a bit cruel to raise unfounded hopes, but perhaps it was the only way to shock her out of the apathy she had fallen into since that terrible night...

Emma heard the voice calling to her as she continued her walk along the beach, but she did not choose to turn round. There was only one person she wanted to see and she could not find him. She had searched and searched until her mind was so weary that she no longer really knew what she was doing, but there was no sign of him, no clue as to what had happened to him.

She was like someone sleepwalking, repeating a pattern for its own sake without knowing why. She was so tired...so terribly tired...but she had to keep on searching or she would die.

'Miss Sommerton!' Betsy caught at her arm, forcing her to turn and look at her. 'There's someone up at the house to see you. Lady Agatha Lynston has something urgent to tell you.'

'Lytham's aunt?' Emma's head went up, a glimmer of hope in her red-rimmed eyes. There could surely only be one reason for Lady Agatha to make the long journey here! She must have news of Lytham. Gathering up her skirt in one hand, Emma began to run along the beach towards the steep path that led up to the greensward. She had climbed it many times now and it held no fears for her. Besides, it was the quickest way. And if Lytham had been found she must hurry. Pray God he was still alive! But she would not think beyond the fact that there was news at last.

Betsy had not followed her, preferring the longer, safer route to the top, but Emma did not look back. She was running as hard as she could, her chest tight with pain as she fled across the grass towards the house and burst in.

Seeing Mrs Warren in the hall, she clutched wildly at her arm, her breathing so ragged that she was gasping as she asked, 'Where is she—what news?'

'Mercy on me!' Mrs Warren cried as she saw her wild look. 'Whatever shall we do with you? She's in the parlour, miss…'

She shook her head as Emma went flying through the hall. The poor girl was out of her mind, and the disappointment of discovering that there was no news was likely to send her right over the edge. In the end they might have to lock her away for her own safety. Well, well, she had warned against it, but Lady Agatha had always gone her own way. She frowned and muttered to herself as she went back to the kitchen. Would this tragedy never be done?

'Lady Agatha!' Emma cried as she rushed into the parlour. 'Has he been found? Is he alive? Oh, please let him be alive!'

Agatha stared at her in horror. She had thought Mrs Warren must have been exaggerating until she saw Emma for herself. Her face was drawn; there were dark shadows beneath her eyes and her cheeks were hollowed. She did indeed look as if her grief might have deranged her mind.

'Come to the fire and get warm, my dear,' Agatha said, her pity aroused. 'I had no idea you were suffering all this time. That foolish woman, to leave me in ignorance.'

'Lytham,' Emma gasped. Her chest was heaving as she tried to recover her breath, but for some reason she could not. She felt pain in her chest and her head, and her vision was blurring. 'Please, tell me…'

'There is no news,' Agatha said and then wished she had not as Emma gave a scream of despair and then collapsed into a heap at her feet. 'Oh, you poor foolish child. What has that rogue done to you? Let him only come back and he shall have a piece of my mind! What can he be thinking of to upset you like this?'

She tugged at the bell rope impatiently. It was quite clear that Emma had exhausted her strength. A doctor must be summoned at once, and Emma would need constant nursing if they were not to lose her, too.

Lytham was aware that the pain had lessened since the strange old creature had begun to nurse him. She was so ugly, and so bent up that she looked like one of the witches from *Macbeth!* At first he had thought her something he had dragged up from hell— the hell of his nightmares—but now he knew that the girl had brought her here.

He tried to remember the girl, but he was certain that he had never met her in his life—but how could he be certain when he did not even know his own name?

There was a man here too sometimes. He kept in the shadows as if he were frightened of being recognised, and yet something about him seemed familiar. Why could he not remember this man—and, even more importantly, who he was?

The girl had told him that he had had a terrible accident. He had fallen from some cliffs and it was only the bravery of the man in the shadows that had saved his life.

'If Tom hadn't gone down the cliff after you, you would have fallen into the sea, been dragged under by the current and drowned. You owe your life to Tom, sir, and that's the truth of it.'

'Thank Tom for saving my life,' he muttered weakly. 'Can I have some more water?'

'Remember, just sips,' the old woman hissed at her from her chair by the fire. 'And don't be bothering him with your talk, Belle. I don't want all my good work wasted on account of your tongue.'

Belle turned away to fetch the cup, holding it while he swallowed a few sips. He grasped her wrist, as she would have moved away.

'Who am I?' he asked hoarsely. 'Tell me if you know, girl. Who am I and why am I here? Have I no home to go to?'

Since the darkness had receded a little, driven out by the light of the fire and the lanterns, he had realised that he was in some kind of a hut. It looked a bit like those used by woodcutters on the estate... What estate? Did he have an estate and, if so, why wasn't he there?

Why did he remember that there was a play about witches called *Macbeth* and yet he couldn't recall his name? There were all kinds of things jumbled up in his brain, fragments that seemed to lie just behind a curtain of mist in his mind. He thought it must be his whole life, but until he could somehow reach out and tear down that curtain he could not reclaim it.

'Ask Tom if he knows who I am,' he whispered. 'Please, I must know.'

Tom came forward out of the shadows and stood looking at him from the end of his bed, which was little more than a pile of straw covered by sacking.

'Can you not remember anything?' Tom asked. 'Do you not remember what happened just before you were shot?'

'I was shot?' Yes, he could feel the soreness in his shoulder and he seemed to remember the old woman applying the hot iron. The pain had been so unbearable that he had fainted, returning to that place of darkness from where it was such a struggle to return. He might never have returned if he had not seemed to hear a voice calling to him, begging him to come back. Yet he did not know who called to him in his dreams. 'Who shot me—was it you? Were we fighting a duel?'

'Someone tried to murder you,' Belle said before Tom could answer. 'Tom shot him and saved your life when you fell over the cliff. If he hadn't come after you you would have tumbled into the sea and drowned for sure. And now he's in trouble with the law.'

'Belle!' Tom warned. 'Lytham doesn't want to hear this, at least not yet.'

'Is my name Lytham?'

'Yes. You are Alexander Lynston, Marquis of Lytham,' Tom replied, 'and I'm Emma's brother, Tom Sommerton.'

'Emma?' Something seemed to stir in his mind and Lytham was aware of pain, pain from within rather than physical, though he did not know what had caused it. 'Is Emma my wife?'

'I don't know what she is to you,' Tom said and glared at him. 'The last thing I knew, she was companion to Bridget Flynn, then I spotted you leaving Father's estate with her and followed you. And it's a damned good thing I did. I was coming to the house to have things out with you when I saw that devil shoot you.'

'Who shot me?'

'Pennington…' Tom frowned. 'I didn't know his name at first, but he got drunk one night and confessed the whole sorry story. He blames you for his court-martial, because you reported that he had raped a fellow officer's wife. He had been waiting his chance to kill you for ages.'

'Away with you!' Granny Robins muttered, elbowing Tom to one side. 'Enough talking for now or you will kill the poor man. Now then, sir, drink some of this good broth and rest. Time enough to talk later when you're feeling more yourself.'

'Yes, I must rest,' Lytham said and fell back against the pillows, his head spinning from weakness. 'You won't go, Tom? I need you. Help me and I'll help you, whatever you've done. Please don't leave me here alone. I need your help to find myself.'

'I wasn't going anywhere,' Tom said, but Lytham's eyes had closed.

'You've worn him out with your chatter,' the old woman scolded. 'Let him rest now. He'll be stronger next time he wakes.'

'So, you are feeling a little better,' Lady Agatha said as she visited Emma that morning, two days after her arrival. 'You foolish chit! You had me quite worried about you for a while, but Mrs Warren said you took a little chicken soup this morning.'

'Indeed, I am sorry to have caused you so much bother,' Emma said, her cheeks pink. She was feeling rested because the medicine the doctor had given her had made her sleep peacefully for the first time in an age. 'You should not have come all this way for my sake.'

'Should I neglect the lady my foolish nephew had decided to marry?' Agatha Lynston fixed her with a stern gaze. 'He would not thank me when he returns to find you wasted away to a shadow of your former self.'

Emma clutched at the straw of hope her words conveyed, ignoring the misconception of an engagement between her and Lytham for the moment.

'Do you believe he will return?'

'Lytham is not so easily disposed of,' Agatha said. 'I doubt not that there has been some mischief here. The authorities have at least established the identity of the dead man—a disgraced officer who apparently once served with Lytham. My nephew played some part in his court-martial and it was believed Pennington had died abroad. It seems Lytham had been making inquiries about the fellow recently and that he may have cause to think that Pennington was intending to murder him.'

'Murder…' Emma shuddered as another shooting incident crossed her mind. 'Oh, no! He should have been on his guard. It happened once before—the shot that scraped his arm in the woods! It occurred when he was escorting me to London. I begged him to take care.'

'That was when he was taken ill of a fever and you helped him up the stairs of an inn to his room, I presume?'

'He—he told you of that?' Emma's cheeks were heated as she met the knowing gaze of the elderly lady standing at the foot of the bed.

'Certainly. I must apologise for any distress caused you on the day you called on me in Bath, Emma. I do hope I may call you that, my dear?' She smiled as the girl nodded. 'I was unwell and I had not heard that scurrilous rumour making the rounds in Bath. I hope Lytham told you that he had scotched it?'

'Yes. He did say something about it.' Emma felt terrible. Lady Agatha was being so kind to her. What would she say if she knew the true situation?

'Well, Emma, what are we to do?' Agatha looked thoughtful as the girl was silent. 'This is a pretty coil, is it not? Lytham disappeared and you here alone, at the verge of collapse when I arrived. It won't do. It won't do at all.'

'I could not leave here while there was hope.'

'This house has never suited me, being so close to the sea, especially in winter. Those winds do my bones no good at all. I think I shall take you home with me, my dear. Lytham made Lynston Cottage over to me as a present soon after his father died. It is smaller and more comfortable than that rackety mansion of his. Yes, we shall go home and wait for him to contact us.'

'But supposing...' Emma's protest died on her lips. She had no right to remain in this house indefinitely. If Lytham was lost— her mind could not accept the word dead—she had no place here. She would have to leave eventually and she did not know where to go, for she could not impose on Mary Thorn again so soon. 'You are very kind, ma'am. I will come if I shall not be a trouble to you.'

'Stuff and nonsense!' Agatha said. 'I am not an easy person to live with, Emma, but I dare say you could fare worse. And I am all Lytham has apart from some distant cousins. We shall support each other through this trying time.'

Emma might have continued her protest, but she caught a glimpse of the vulnerability beneath Lady Agatha's show of strength. She must be more than seventy years of age and, though of stout heart and constitution, would find the loss of her only close relative hard to bear.

'I should like to stay with you for a while, ma'am.'

'If Lytham had not wasted so much time you might have been his wife.' Agatha's hand trembled, but she clutched the bed rail to steady herself. 'I dare say the wretch is caught in some card game and will return when he thinks fit.'

Emma did not reply. She could not believe any such thing, though she did wonder why Lytham had gone out when he had told her to wait for him in her room. Why had he changed his mind? Why had he gone out instead of coming to her? It was so puzzling.

In her first wild grief she had not taken the time to wonder why he had not come to her, but now the question was beginning to nag at her. Had she done something to displease him—been too eager for his kisses? Or had something lured him out to those windswept cliffs where he might have met his death? *Oh, please let him not be dead!*

Perhaps her unrestrained passion had been too revealing? Perhaps he had not wanted her to fall in love with him, fearing that she might cling, become an unwanted burden. Yet his passionate words had seemed to indicate something very different.

Why had he gone for that fatal walk on the cliffs? And why did Lady Agatha imagine that he had intended to take Emma as his wife?

It was a mystery and one that she had no way of solving. She was aware that her first tearing grief had settled to a dull ache in her breast. It would come back to haunt her sometimes, bringing tears and a return of the unbearable pain his loss had woken in her, but she was feeling calmer, more able to cope with life than she had been before Lady Agatha's arrival. And perhaps there was still a flicker of hope.

'Tell me again, Tom,' Lynston asked as he leaned heavily on the younger man's arm. They had come out for some fresh air because he was in need of it, though not yet strong enough to walk out alone. 'I have grasped who and what I am, and a few pictures have begun to remind me in flashes of my past—but though you have told me so much, I am not yet clear about your own involvement. There was some scandal linking us through my brother, you say?'

'I swear I had nothing to do with your brother's death,' Tom said. 'At least, not directly. I was with his wife that day. Maria and I had spent the afternoon together at the Dower House. It was always her favourite place, for she did not like the Hall. She lives there now, of course. She said her husband would not come to the Dower House and we met there often—but I think he may have discovered that we went there.'

'Why do you say that?'

'Because…' Tom looked awkward. 'That afternoon I saw him. I had gone to the bedroom window to look out and I saw him staring up at the house. Until that moment I had not thought he cared what Maria did. He was a careless husband, neglecting her and going his own way, but he seemed distressed, staring up at the house more in grief than anger. He may even have seen me.'

'So he rode off in some kind of a mood and was thrown from his horse.' Lytham nodded. He could not remember his brother, but something told him that he had felt no love or friendship towards the man he could not picture. Besides, he had come to trust Tom in the past few days and believed his story. 'It fits in with what you have told me. But you were accused of murder— and your father threw you out.'

'Because I told him the truth. He was in such a rage. He said that I was guilty of murder even if I had not planned it. My behaviour had driven Maria's husband mad with jealousy and so he rode carelessly—and perhaps Father was right. I had not thought John Lynston a loving husband, but perhaps I wronged him.'

'My brother was always a careless brute with horses! It is not surprising that he was thrown, nor the first time, I dare say.'

Tom stared at him. 'Have you recovered your memory, then?'

'No. I have no idea where that came from,' Lytham admitted. 'It was instinctive. But I believe it to be true. It seems that fragments come back to me when I least expect it.'

'Perhaps everything will return in time.'

'I must hope so.' Lytham frowned. 'Now, tell me if you will, what was my relationship with Emma?'

Once again he felt that peculiar little pain about his heart. Why should he feel that way when he spoke her name, as if something very precious was lost? He tried to pull aside the curtain and remember what he knew instinctively was very important, but could not.

'I do not know,' Tom admitted. 'I had wondered that myself.

You may have felt yourself in place of a guardian towards her. I know there were rumours…'

'What kind of rumours? And who told you of them?'

'Maria.' Tom went slightly pink. 'I visited her a few weeks ago and she told me you had been to see her. You asked her questions concerning her husband's death, but she had told you nothing of the afternoon we spent together.'

'Yet she might have saved you from disgrace.'

'And brought ruin on herself. I forbade her ever to speak of it.'

'That was noble if a trifle foolish, my friend.'

'Would you have done otherwise to save a lady you cared for from scandal and disgrace?'

Lytham hesitated and then smiled wryly. 'Would I? That is the question and an important one, I think. Unfortunately, I cannot answer it for the moment. I fear that I may have done many things that might not bear the light of day.'

'I have heard you spoken of as a damnable rogue, but I do not think it, my lord.'

'Do you not?' Lytham murmured, smiling oddly. 'We must see what can be done to restore your fortunes, Tom. What is the wish closest to your heart?'

'I once wanted to be an officer in the army, but my father would not hear of it. He demanded that I do my duty by the family, but he had already ruined us. When you won the estate from my father he was deeply in debt and had sold too much land. It was not worth what you had hazarded against it.'

'Do you believe you could restore the estate—given a free hand and the necessary funds?'

'Be your agent?' Tom thought for a moment and then nodded. 'Yes, I think I should enjoy that—but are you sure you trust me? As I have told you before, you won it fairly.'

'I cannot think that I meant to take your father's estate even though he had foolishly thrown it away at the tables, though I have no memory of that night. Yet I believe I would find such business distasteful. The estate is yours by right. Show me that you can manage it properly and I shall restore it to you. As for the matter of your good name—I shall see what can be done once

I have recovered my health and know a little more about my own fortunes.'

'Granny Robins has healed you,' Tom said, feeling rather emotional and wishing not to show it. 'But it is surely time you sought a softer bed to sleep in, my lord? You own a house close by and it is a matter of a short journey only.'

'Yes, you are right, Tom. I shall do so, in another day or so. At the moment I am as weak as a kitten. The day after tomorrow you will oblige me by taking me to my house for, unless you show me, I have no idea of where I live.'

'Of course,' Tom said and grinned at him. 'And I must make Belle a handsome present before we leave for she helped me care for you when you were in a fever.'

'I shall make both her and Granny handsome presents when I am in funds again,' Lytham said with a wry smile. 'I believe you did tell me that I am a wealthy man?'

'I am given to understand that is the case, my lord. There was a reward for information as to your whereabouts of five hundred guineas,' Tom told him. 'Belle could have taken it, but she did not out of loyalty to me.'

'You are fortunate in your friends, Tom.'

'Belle is an honest woman, and she has been a good friend to me in this business. It was I who begged her to keep silent.'

'You were afraid of being accused of involvement in the attempt to murder me,' Lytham said. 'We must make up some tale to cover your neglect, Tom.' He smiled a little mockingly. 'I think that will not be beyond the resources of our imaginations, my friend. Fear not, you shall not end at the hangman's noose on my account.'

Chapter Ten

'What a pretty house,' Emma exclaimed as the carriage pulled up outside the thatched cottage. The walls were of faded rose brick, the windows of grey glass and thick, but hung with pretty lace curtains. 'I have seldom seen anything I like more.'

'I am glad you approve of my home,' Lady Agatha said. 'I am very fond of it. My father restored it for the estate manager some years ago, but Lytham provided his manager with a more modern establishment. This was built in Queen Anne's time, but it has been recently refurbished to my taste and I am content here.'

'It must certainly be easier to manage than the Hall,' Emma replied with a smile. They had passed an impressive Elizabethan house on their way through the park. 'That needs a large family to fill it, I think.'

'Exactly what I've been telling Lytham since he came home from the army,' Agatha Lynston said with a harsh cackle. 'And why he spends most of his time in town, I dare say. Especially in the winter.'

'Yes. I imagine it must be very cold at this time of year.'

Emma had learned to control her feelings these past few days. Her tears were shed in private now, during the restless nights when her thoughts returned again and again to those last moments when Lytham held her in his arms and she had counted the world well lost for love.

'If my nephew had any sense he would pull most of it down and build a modern house in its place,' the elderly lady said as her groom came to assist her from the carriage. 'Thank you, Bennett. It is far too cold to stand out here talking, Emma. Come inside, my dear. I am in sore need of refreshment.'

A smiling, buxom housekeeper welcomed them into the hall, assuring Lady Agatha that tea would be served in the parlour as soon as she was ready.

'There's a good fire ready for you, my lady, for I knew you would be cold when you arrived. 'Tis a raw, bitter day so it is.'

Emma admired the warm and comfortable room to which her hostess led her. It was furnished in restful tones of blue, grey and a delicate pink, with deep cushioned couches and dainty little tables and cabinets, very much a lady's room full of knick-knacks and personal items. A sewing box stood opened on a stool by the fire, books lay everywhere as if they were always at hand when their owner needed them, and a writing box stood on the desk under the window, its lid up as though it was often used.

'Such a clutter,' Lady Agatha clucked as she watched Emma's eyes wandering about the room with interest. 'But it is comfortable so and I am a creature of habit, as you will soon discover.'

'I think it delightful,' Emma replied with a smile. 'Very like my own dear mama's parlour at home before she went to Italy with our friends.'

'Have you heard from your mother, my dear?'

'There was one letter waiting for me at home when I returned from Bath,' Emma said. 'Mama and her friends had hardly reached their destination when it was sent. I have heard nothing since, but letters are often delayed coming from abroad and I have been moving around myself a great deal.'

Lady Agatha nodded, holding her hands to the fire to warm them. 'There, that is much better. I declare I shall not stir again until the spring. Indeed, why should there be the least need? Now that I have you, my dear Emma, I shall not be in the least lonely.'

'You are very kind to say so, ma'am.'

'Not at all,' she replied. 'I have been thinking, Emma. Should Lytham not return, I should like you to make your home with me. Not as a paid companion, you understand, but as my friend. I should settle an allowance on you so that you need not be beholden to me for your personal expenses, of course. It is less than would have been yours had Lytham lived, but may recompense a little for your loss—financially. I know that nothing can repair your true loss, my dear.'

Emma dropped her head, her cheeks flaming. Now was the time to make the situation plain to Lady Agatha, but she could not find the words to tell her that Lytham had asked her to be his mistress and not his wife.

'I do not say that he will not return, for I believe he will,' Lady Agatha said firmly, though there was a slight tremor in her voice. 'But if the worst should happen, I would like you to make your home with me.'

'Thank you, ma'am. I should be happy to do so.'

Emma had not the heart to refuse for she had grown fond of Lady Agatha. As for the deception…well, perhaps it did not matter. No one but she and Lytham knew what had been said between them, and nothing had actually happened. Indeed, he had called her his ward when introducing her to Mrs Warren, and as far as Society was concerned there was no need for anyone to know the truth.

Perhaps it was wrong of her to deceive her kind hostess, but Lytham had offered her the post of companion to his aunt at the beginning and that is what she would be in all but name from now on.

And what if he returned? Emma had not solved the mystery of his apparent change of heart. Until he came to unmask her, it was surely a harmless masquerade?

'My lord!' Mrs Warren turned pale as she saw him walk into the house. 'God be praised! We thought you dead this last month.'

'I have been ill,' Lytham replied with a slight smile. 'And I must ask you for your patience, ma'am. My memory was affected by my illness and unfortunately has gaps in it. Your name seems to escape me for the moment.'

'Mrs Warren, sir. Warren and me have kept house here for the past thirty years or more, since when your mother was alive and first bought the house, God bless her soul.'

'Ah, yes, Mrs Warren.' He nodded and turned to his companion. 'This is Mr Tom Sommerton. He is my guest. It was Mr Sommerton who saved my life when I was shot and stumbled over the edge of the cliff. He found me on a rocky ledge and carried me to safety or I might have fallen unconscious into the sea.'

'Miss Emma's brother? Yes, I can see the likeness, sir. Well, fancy that. I suppose you was on your way here to see her.' Mrs Warren frowned. 'The poor lady near died of grief when we thought you lost, sir. Begging your pardon—but it seems strange your lordship did not let us know you were safe.'

'I had lost my memory and Mr Sommerton thought there might be other rogues waiting their chance to attack me. He considered it best to tell no one of my whereabouts and kept me hidden until I was better.' His face had gone white from the effort of talking to her. 'The parlour, Mrs Warren—may I ask you to direct me?'

'Of course, my lord. You're still not well and here I am keeping you gossiping in the hall!'

She hurried before him, throwing open the door.

'Some brandy for his lordship,' Tom said. 'I think he is faint.'

'Yes, sir. At once.'

She hastened away, troubled and confused by the change in her master. He was thin and looked as if he ought to be in bed. And what she was to make out of his loss of memory she did not know.

'You are sure he is not an impostor?' her husband asked her when she related her tale in the kitchen. Cook and the kitchen wench stared at her in amazement, for everyone had believed the marquis must be dead.

'Take the brandy in yourself. I would swear it was him, but much changed.'

'And no wonder if he has been ill all this time!' Cook said and crossed herself. 'It is quite shocking…shocking!'

'I shall decide this matter for myself.'

Warren picked up the tray and went out, leaving the women to exclaim and shake their heads over it again. He was shocked when he saw the change for himself, but he did not doubt his master's identity. He served the brandy to both gentlemen.

'Is there anything else, my lord? Would you like to retire? I will have a warming pan heated and passed between the sheets immediately.'

'Thank you, Warren, but I shall not retire just yet. I would like you to ask Miss Sommerton if she will join us please.'

'Miss Sommerton is not here.'

'Not here? I thought Mrs Warren spoke of her distress over my disappearance?'

'She was here until a few days ago, my lord. Lady Agatha took her back to Lytham Hall with her. Miss Sommerton was beside herself with grief. Mrs Warren thought she had lost her mind. We sent for your aunt and she took your young lady away.'

'My young lady?'

'Your fiancée, my lord. Lady Agatha told us you were to be married. And indeed, Miss Sommerton broke her heart over your disappearance. Like someone possessed she was. Walking along the beach at all hours and in the worst of weather, looking for you, refusing to give up when everyone else thought you lost. In the end she was ill herself, but she is better now.'

Lytham felt the pain smite him in his breast. Emma had become ill because she was so distressed over his disappearance. She must love him—but did he love her? He wished that he could remember.

'I see. Thank you, Warren. We shall dine at six. Please tell Mrs Warren that I shall want something light, but Mr Sommerton will expect a decent dinner.'

'Do not trouble overmuch for me. A baked ham and a capon or some such thing will do well enough if you have it.' Tom looked at the marquis as the door closed behind the butler. 'So you were engaged to Emma. Had I known, I would have risked being accused of complicity to save her pain. I had no idea she was in love with you. I had thought it might have been something else and this relieves my mind in that respect, though I feel terrible for letting her suffer as she did.'

Lytham's brows rose. 'Did you imagine I might make her my mistress? Alas, I have no memory of how things stand between us, but I could not have offered less than marriage to a young woman of good family.'

'There was some scandal, as I told you.'

'You did not tell me the whole. Perhaps you should.'

'Emma was seen helping you upstairs at an inn. The tale was that you were drunk and she by inference a whore—but it was the night that Pennington shot you the first time.'

'Yes, that would make sense of the rumour.'

Lytham was thoughtful as he sipped his brandy. This damnable loss of memory! It would seem likely that he had asked Miss Sommerton to marry him out of a desire to restore her reputation. It would be the action of a gentleman and he hoped he was that— but if that were so, why would Emma almost die of her grief?

And why did he feel this overwhelming sadness each time her name came into his mind? What had he done to her?

He was too weary to set out in search of her today. He would rest here for a day or so and then continue his journey.

'Do you think we should send word to Emma and Lady Agatha?' Tom asked, breaking into his thoughts. 'They must have been wretched over this business. I had not realised Emma would be so distressed or...' He looked contrite and anxious as he paused.

'You would have reported my whereabouts?' Lytham smiled. 'It was a terrifying risk, Tom, for had I not accepted your word you might have been hung as an accomplice. I can guess what your sister might feel about that!'

For a moment the curtain in his mind seemed to shift. He saw the picture of a woman's anxious face looking at him; they were in a wood and she had something in her hand.

'Emma is very beautiful.'

'Yes. I always thought she could be if she had the right clothes,' Tom remarked. 'Have you remembered her?'

'I saw a woman in my mind, a lovely woman. Is Emma dark-haired with wide clear eyes and a soft, generous mouth?'

'Yes, but don't be fooled by that calm manner of hers. She has a temper when roused,' Tom replied with a grin. 'You will remember that fast enough when you see her.'

'One must hope so,' Lytham said.

He finished his brandy. It had restored him a little, but he found it frustrating not to be able to remember. He should be able to recall the woman he was going to marry!

'No, we shall not send word,' he said at last. 'I understand that my estate is not far from here. We shall be there almost as soon as a letter. I would rather tell my aunt and Emma our story in person, Tom.'

He did not know why he was reluctant to let his family know of his survival. There was something regarding Emma lurking at the back of his mind, but he could not pull that curtain aside for long enough to discover it.

Emma had decided that she needed some air. Lady Agatha's cottage was very warm and she had been used to walking often at her own home. Besides, she was curious about the Hall. They had sent word up to the big house and Lytham's agent had called to discuss the situation.

'There are distant cousins,' Stephen Antrium told Emma. 'But I do not feel duty bound to inform them of the matter as yet. I shall wait for a few months and then discuss the way forward with his lordship's lawyers.'

'Lytham will be back long before it comes to that,' Lady Agatha said. 'You mark my words, Mr Antrium. I feel it in my bones.'

'I pray you are right, ma'am. His lordship has done wonders with this estate and I should not care to see it go to rack and ruin once more. He is an excellent landlord, far better than his father and brothers were, and there are other good deeds of his that he would not allow me to speak of, but there, I must say no more.' He smiled at Emma in a friendly manner. 'Should you wish to be shown over the estate, Miss Sommerton, you have only to send for me.'

'You are very good, sir,' Emma said, feeling like a fraud. 'It might be interesting to look over the house one day.'

'Mrs Williams will be delighted to show you. I shall tell her to be ready for a visit from you.'

'Thank you, but it will be an informal visit. She must not go to any trouble on my behalf.'

Emma had not intended to visit the Hall that morning, merely to walk in the extensive gardens and look at the house from outside. However, as she approached through the rose garden, where the earth had been raked winter clean and the bushes cut back to the stems to preserve them through the worst of the weather, Mr Antrium came out of the house to meet her.

'I chanced to see you walking this way from the window of my office,' he said giving her a welcoming smile. 'Will you come in and take some refreshment, Miss Sommerton?'

'Thank you. I am afraid I am taking you away from your business. I meant only to walk and observe, not to intrude. I hope I am not disturbing you, sir?'

'No, indeed, you are not hindering me,' he said. 'Mrs Williams is excited at the prospect of your visit. If things had been as they ought... You must know that we are all devastated by his lordship's disappearance, as you must be, Miss Sommerton.'

'Yes, I am,' Emma admitted truthfully. 'I loved him very much.'

'Of course. We have heard how ill you were and that is why we all wish to make you welcome here, to make up as best we can for the terrible time you have suffered.'

Emma felt herself blush. How kind these people were and how guilty she felt for allowing the misconception to continue. Yet it had begun innocently enough and now she could do nothing. To confess the true situation would be too shaming.

She walked into the house with the young man at her side. He was not a handsome man, being snub-nosed, with sandy hair and pale eyes, but he was, she sensed, sincere and honest. She liked him and felt herself responding as he began to show her some of the main reception rooms.

It was a very fine house, though old; some repair and refurbishment had been done to the main wing in the last century, though it was in need of much more. The furniture consisted mainly of heavy oaken pieces, heavily carved and bought at the time the house was built, the silky surface of each piece polished to a brilliant shine over the years. The stone walls had at some time been panelled in oak, and that too had mellowed to a soft golden sheen, and there were huge paintings in many of the rooms of rather dour-looking men and women in period costume. Clearly Lytham's ancestors, Emma thought.

She looked for some resemblance to the present marquis and found none. One room, though, had been decorated in soft shades of green and the furniture here was of a more recent period, fashioned of mahogany and extremely elegant, though not new. There were pad-footed tables, comfortable wing chairs by the fireplace, a magnificent cabinet with a towering swan-necked pediment and a large writing bureau with its own elbow chair. On the far end wall as you entered, a portrait of a pretty woman dominated the room. Gazing up at it, Emma found what she had searched for elsewhere in vain and knew without being told that this was Lytham's mother.

'This is a lovely room,' she remarked. 'So different from the rest of the house.'

'It belonged to his lordship's mother. He has kept it exactly as it was, though I believe he seldom comes here. He prefers the library. My office is close by, which makes it convenient for business. His lordship does not care to stay in the country overlong.'

'Yes, Lady Agatha told me he prefers to stay in town.'

'His house there is beautiful,' Mr Antrium said. 'He had it done over recently and his lordship's taste is excellent—but you will perhaps have seen it for yourself?'

'No. I was staying in Bath before—' She broke off, unable to continue for the tightness at the back of her throat. 'I did not have the opportunity to visit.'

How terrible it was to keep up this deception. She felt as if she were committing a crime, but managed to regain her composure as the housekeeper came to greet her.

'Will you stay for nuncheon, Miss Sommerton? Then I could take you on a tour of the rest of the house this afternoon. You might like to see the bedrooms?'

Emma hesitated and was lost. She ought to refuse, of course, but this might be her only opportunity. 'Would it be a trouble to you? Could a message be sent to Lady Agatha so that she does not worry?'

'It would be a pleasure,' Mrs Williams assured her, beaming. 'I know we all want to tell you how happy we were to hear the news of your engagement.'

'Well, I am not sure that…'

'Oh, we know it hasn't been officially announced, miss,' Mrs Williams said. 'I suppose you were waiting to tell your mother as is right and proper, but Lady Agatha let the cat out of the bag, as it were. To tell the truth, it's what we've all been waiting for since his lordship came home from the wars. It's more than a body can do to keep such a thing secret. You wouldn't expect it, miss?'

'No, I suppose not.' Emma blushed. 'Thank you for being so kind.'

She allowed herself to be shown into a small parlour, where two places had been laid for nuncheon. Mr Antrium held out the chair at the head of the oval gate-legged table, and then took his place beside her. He engaged her in friendly conversation as the meal was served on delicate porcelain in a pretty turquoise blue pattern. It consisted of several courses, beginning with a delicious vegetable soup served with freshly baked bread, followed by cold capon, a pie of eels, which Mr Antrium clearly relished, a warm pork pie and side dishes of creamed potatoes, buttered parsnips and a quince tart.

'Goodness, does Mrs Williams always serve such a variety at midday?' Emma asked, feeling spoiled by the excellence of the meal and used to something lighter. 'Or was this in my honour?'

'I do believe she might have been planning to impress you,' Mr Antrium said with a smile. 'I have been eating rather more lavishly than I am used to of late.'

Emma smiled and nodded, making a special point of remarking on the quality of the fare served to them when Mrs Williams returned to show her over the house after their meal.

'Shall we begin with the main wing, Miss Sommerton?' Mrs Williams asked. 'The other wings are not much used and the furniture is kept under covers unless his lordship is in residence, though we have been used to keeping this part of the house in readiness. He sometimes pops in on us of a sudden. You never quite know with his lordship.'

'I see…' The housekeeper seemed to think like Lady Agatha that the marquis would turn up in his own good time. Pray God that he did! She thought that she could bear anything if she could only see him again.

It took some time to tour the bedrooms on the first floor, for they were in better case than many of the reception rooms, because the marquis wanted his guests to be comfortable in their beds, according to the housekeeper.

'This is the master suite,' Mrs Williams said, stopping at the far end of the hall. 'Part of it is actually in the old wing, though it has been done up, as you might imagine. There are five rooms in all, Miss Sommerton. Perhaps you would like to explore on your own for a while? If you need help, please ring and I shall come at once.'

'Oh, I think I can find my way back,' Emma assured her. 'I have kept you too long from your duties already. I must thank you for your kindness and I shall not trouble you before I leave.'

'It was no trouble, miss. I hope we shall see you here as mistress very soon.'

Emma smiled, but made no answer. Her hand trembled as she opened the door and went into the first room, which was a pretty parlour, clearly a lady's room and decorated in shades of yellow, gold and cream. It led into a bedroom, also a lady's room, furnished in the style of perhaps twenty years earlier with pieces that must have come straight from Mr Chippendale's workshops.

Here there was little sign of the oak that filled most of the rest of the house; it had been replaced by smooth shining mahogany, wrought into tasteful designs: elegant elbow chairs, a pretty desk under the window, a cabinet with figurines set out on the shelves, little chests at the side of the bed, and a five-drawer chest at one end. On the dressing table there was a pretty mirror set on a stand and all manner of expensive trifles, including blue scent bottles with silver gilt clasps, silver boxes, silver buttonhooks, combs and brushes and an enamelled patch box.

Passing through the dressing room, Emma entered what was clearly the master bedroom, her heart catching as she caught the scent of cedar-wood. This was Lytham's own room! It was a scent she had noticed on his clothes on a couple of occasions.

The room was furnished in what was usually described as the Empire style, with imposing pieces of furniture that had obviously been commissioned to match. Everything was made of some dark wood that she did not immediately recognise and had stringing of a paler wood with some gilding and the Lytham coat of arms cut into the bed-head.

There was a dressing robe lying on a chair next to the bed. It was dark blue striped with a dusky gold. She approached it slowly, her heart racing as her hand moved towards it, then drew back. She had no right to touch his things, and yet the aching need to be near him was in her, making her eyes smart with the tears she had believed long cried out of her. How could she face the future without him?

'Oh, Lytham,' she whispered, allowing herself to touch the soft fabric at last. Her chest was tight as she fought the longing to pick up his robe and hold it to her face, to breathe in the remembered scent of him. 'Where are you, my love? Please come back to me. I need you so.'

So overcome by her emotions was she that she did not notice the door open behind her, and it was only when she heard a slight noise that she turned, expecting to see Mrs Williams. Her heart caught as she saw him standing there watching her, an odd expression on his face; for a moment she thought that she might faint. Had she conjured him up out of her need and longing? Was he flesh and blood or merely a figment of her fevered imagination?

'Lytham…' she whispered hoarsely, her throat so tight that she could scarcely speak. 'Is it truly you?'

'Emma?' he seemed to question, frowning as he hesitated. 'You really are beautiful. I had hardly believed my visions, but now I see you for myself.'

'My lord?' She was puzzled both by his words and his manner. He seemed unlike himself. And, indeed, there were marked changes in his appearance. 'Please, tell me I am not dreaming! I fear I must sit down or I may fall down.' She sat heavily on the edge of the bed as her legs almost gave way beneath her. 'Do you not know me? What is the matter? Are you truly alive and well?'

'Perhaps not truly well,' he answered, seeming to wake as from a trance. 'Forgive me if I frightened you. Williams told me these were my rooms and I had hoped that seeing them might bring back my memory, but it does not seem to have worked thus far.'

'You have been ill?' Emma caught at the only part of his speech that made sense to her. She gazed at his face, seeing the new-wrought lines of strain that illness had brought. 'Yes, I see a change in you. What happened, my lord? You must know that everyone has been very worried about you. We feared you might be dead.'

'Yes, I believe that was generally thought,' Lytham said. 'And I must apologise for it, Emma—but Tom thought it best until I was recovered lest another attempt was made on my life.'

'Another attempt—but surely Pennington was killed?' Her gaze narrowed as she looked at him. 'Are you speaking of my brother, sir? Was Tom involved in this?'

'He saved my life. Apparently I stumbled over the cliff when I was shot and though I fell on to a ledge, I might have died there if Tom had not carried me away and nursed me back to health.'

'How did Tom come to be there?' Emma demanded, feeling angry. If Tom had known…all this time! Surely he could have let her know?

'He had followed us from your home,' Lytham said, his eyes narrowing as he sensed her anger. 'He was not aware that my disappearance might cause you pain and distress, Emma. Tom had no knowledge of our engagement until we reached my house.'

'Our engagement...' Emma stared at him, her cheeks suddenly hot as she realised what he was saying. 'My lord, I should tell you at once—'

'No, please do not be angry with your brother,' he said with a smile of such sweetness it took her breath away, leaving her unable to continue. 'You must know that Tom had his reasons. He told you that he was afraid a man he had been riding with might try to murder me, I believe?' She nodded, unable to go on, though she knew she must speak out. 'And I believe you know the nature of their business? Had he been suspected of complicity in the attempt on my life, he might have been hung.' Emma nodded again, her heart pounding. 'Tom is finished with the life as you know, but it was fortunate that he decided to follow us that day or I might not be standing here today.'

'My lord.' Emma looked at him oddly. 'You mentioned a loss of memory just now—how complete is that?'

'I fear I can remember nothing before waking to find an old hag caring for me in some deserted shack. If it had not been for Tom, I might never have known who I was. I owe him so much, Emma, and I have decided that he shall manage the estate that was your father's for a year. I shall give him money to help him get it back into good heart and if he is successful, which I am certain he will be—it will be his own, as it ought always to have been.'

'Do you know how it came into your possession?'

'Tom told me everything. He was very honest. I like your brother, Emma. I should have liked him if we had met in other circumstances, but as it is I think he has become like a brother to me—which he will be soon enough in truth.'

'You mean our marriage?' She could not look at him for fear of betraying herself.

'Yes, of course. I do not know what we had spoken of in the matter of setting a date, but I think we must postpone it until the spring—if you do not object too much? By then I shall hope to recover all the parts of my life that are still eluding me.'

'Do you think that will happen, my lord?'

'Lytham. You should properly call me by my name, Emma.' His dark eyes dwelt on her thoughtfully. 'I am not perfectly sure of the depth of my feelings for you at this moment, though I believe I must have loved you very much. It must be best for our hopes of happiness if we spend some time together, getting to know one another.'

'Perhaps…' She could not go on for her heart was full.

'You are hurt by my speaking so plainly?' he asked. 'I thought it was best since there is no hiding the truth. To have pretended things were otherwise might have caused more hurt.'

'Yes, that is perfectly true.' Emma's heart was racing as she looked at him. She must speak out now, she must in all honesty! And yet she could not bring herself to say the words that would make him turn from her in disgust. She had allowed Lady Agatha to bring her here under false pretences and gained the friendship of his servants. He would be angry if he discovered her masquerade, accuse her of trying to force his hand, of duping him into something he had never intended. Yet it was too difficult to speak, to watch the smiles of those people she had come to like turn to icy coldness, as they must. In time he would remember and then she would leave, but for a little longer she would linger and bask in the delight of a future that could never be hers. 'Yes, of course. I would say only this to you, Lytham. Should you discover that there has been a change in your feelings, for any reason, I release you from any promises you may have made me. If that happens, I shall go away and you may forget me.'

'Forget you, Emma?' He moved towards her, feeling an urgent need to take her in his arms and taste those lips. Her face had haunted his dreams since that first time of remembering and he wanted to make sure she was real, not just a figment of his imagination. She did not move away as he reached out for her, allowing him to draw her close, to kiss her softly on the lips. A great surge of desire flowed through him as he felt her instant response and he knew that he had done this before—that he had wanted her desperately once before—but something had stood in the way. He released her and drew back, seeing the way her mouth had softened with desire, her eyes smoky and languorous as though she too had wanted their lovemaking to continue. 'I do not think that once a man had held you, kissed you, he would ever willingly forget you, Emma.'

'I think we must see how you feel once you have come to know me,' Emma replied, finding it difficult to breathe. When he looked at her like that she felt close to swooning! She loved him so and to leave him would break her heart, though she must do it in the end. But he would regain his memory and then he would tell her to leave, his anger driving a wedge between them.

'I do not believe that I shall change my mind,' he said and for a moment he looked as he had before his illness had wrought a change in him, the old mocking expression there in his eyes once more. 'But perhaps we should go down. Mrs Williams will think I have seduced you if we stay here alone much longer. Besides, I know that Tom is anxious to make his peace with you.'

'I shall have some things to say to my brother,' Emma said, a gleam in her eye. 'I forgive you for not letting me know you were alive, Lytham—but Tom could have come to me. He must have known I would not betray him.'

'Apparently he was not sure that you truly believed it was not he who shot me the first time, Emma.'

She made no answer. The shock had made her forget everything but her pleasure in seeing him alive once more, but now she was remembering…the agony of believing him dead had almost killed her.

'Your aunt has been most distressed, Lytham. I think you must allow me to tell her that you are here—but she will want to see you at once, I know.'

'Then perhaps you will both dine with me this evening?' His smile set her heart racing again and she longed to be in his arms once more, to be truly his as she would have been if he had come to her that afternoon. 'And I shall have my carriage take you home.'

'It is not necessary, my lord,' she replied. 'I believe I shall walk. It is not far and I would have time to be alone with my thoughts for a while.'

'Of course. This has been a shock. I should not have come upon you unannounced, but I had not realised you were here.'

'I never intended...' Emma blushed. 'I was walking and Mr Antrium insisted I take some refreshment. That became lunch and a tour of the house. Mrs Williams left me here to explore these rooms alone.'

'I trust that you liked what you saw? Though truth to tell, I think there must be some changes made here. I had no idea it was such a mausoleum.'

'You have forgotten,' Emma said with a smile. 'Perhaps you always meant to change things but were too busy.'

'My man of business tells me that there is much to be done after my absence,' Lytham said and frowned. 'But this house must be a priority for I could not expect my wife to put up with it as it stands. You must advise me, Emma, tell me what you like and what you don't.'

'Yes, of course,' she said, though she could not meet his eyes. Oh, dear, this was becoming worse and worse. She had no right to oversee the refurbishing of a house in which she would never live. 'But now I must go or indeed Mrs Williams will think me lost to all propriety.'

'I shall see you this evening?' He caught her hand as she would have passed him, pressing it to his lips, his eyes meeting hers. 'You will not disappear into the mist like the myth I thought you must be when I first dreamed of you in my fever?'

'If I go, you will know why,' Emma said. 'I promise I shall not run off without your leave to go.'

'Then you will never leave me,' he said and smiled at her. 'At least only for a short time. As soon as we are truly comfortable with one another again I shall arrange the wedding.'

Chapter Eleven

'**D**id I not tell you it would be so?' Agatha Lynston gave a harsh cackle of laughter. Instead of being overset by the news, as Emma had feared, she was triumphant. 'I knew that scoundrel Pennington was no match for my nephew!'

'I can still scarcely believe it,' Emma confessed. The long walk home had helped her come to terms with Lytham's sudden arrival, the wind blowing some colour into her cheeks. Her eyes held a sparkle that had been missing of late. 'When I saw him first I thought I had imagined it, that he was but a dream.'

'A substantial ghost, Lytham.'

'He is much thinner than he was and he looks drawn. I think he is not truly recovered yet.'

'He is *alive,* gel. Give him time and he'll be back to his old ways, I dare say.' Lady Agatha frowned. 'You say he has lost his memory?'

'That was part of the reason Tom did not inform us of his whereabouts.' Emma hesitated and then decided to tell Lady Agatha the whole story.

'Damned young fool!' the old lady snorted. 'What would he have done if Lytham had died, as he might? He would have been a fugitive all his life. He might at least have told you the truth.'

'I scolded him roundly for it,' Emma replied. 'But, indeed, he was already contrite. He did not know how much it would mean to me to know that Lytham was safe.'

'Well, he has not heard the last of it for I mean to have my say!' Lady Agatha pulled the bell-rope and ordered tea from the maid who answered. 'So we are to dine with Lytham this evening. I hope he means to send his carriage. My servants are getting too old for jaunting here and there at night.'

Her grumbling disguised the relief she felt at knowing that Lytham was home. She had never let Emma guess how deep her doubts were, but she had been afraid that she might not see her great-nephew again. As her eyes swept over the younger woman she wondered what was troubling her. Emma was obviously happy that Lytham was alive, but something was on her mind.

'What is wrong, my dear?' she asked. 'He ain't called the wedding off, has he?'

'No.' Emma blushed as Lady Agatha's keen gaze dwelled on her face. 'It is merely delayed until the spring—so that we may get to know one another.'

'Are you afraid he won't feel the same as he did before his illness?'

'I suppose that is possible.'

'Rubbish! He cannot fail to love you, as I do myself. And so I shall tell him if he tries to cry off.'

'You must not,' Emma pleaded. 'I do not know what his feelings are. He could not remember me, other than as the woman to whom he had been told he was pledged in marriage.'

'Hadn't got round to giving you a ring, had he?' Lady Agatha's gaze narrowed and she looked thoughtful. 'Always was slow to make up his mind. Not that there was ever any doubt in my mind. He could not have done less after that damned young fool besmirched your name.'

Emma's heart lurched. Was that why Lady Agatha had believed that they were to marry? Of course it must be. She had told him it was his duty, but he had decided otherwise. If she had refused his offer of *carte blanche* perhaps...but she had not. She had been already so desperately in love with him that she was ready to cast aside everything for his sake. Therefore she was not entitled to wonder if he might have been thinking of asking her to marry him.

'Damn my idle tongue!' Lady Agatha said as she saw the doubts in Emma's eyes. 'I've made you think that was his reason for offering you his name, and of course it was never that. I knew as soon as he asked me to visit Bath that he was in love with you.'

If only she could believe it! Emma wished with all her heart that it were so. Yet would he have asked her to be his mistress if he truly loved her? Emma could not think it.

'Even if he loved me then, he may not do so now,' she replied. 'Who knows how his illness may have changed him? If I thought he had changed his mind, I should, of course release him.'

'Stuff and nonsense,' Lady Agatha said briskly. 'Go upstairs and rest before you change for the evening, Emma, as I intend to do. I hope Lytham has not forgotten that I keep early hours. My digestion will not stand town hours these days.'

'If he has forgotten, Mrs Williams will not,' Emma reassured her with a smile. It would be a wrench to part with her friend when the time came for her to leave, but at least Lady Agatha would not be alone. She would have the marquis to care for her and one day he would take a wife.

Lytham had spent almost an hour acquainting himself with the personal items in his room. He picked up combs and brushes, sniffed at pomade for grooming his hair and found it smelled pleasant, though he was not sure that he would use such a thing. Opening the huge armoire in the corner of the dressing room, he discovered that it was full of clothes, most of them comfortable plain garments for riding and country living, but there were also some fashionable coats that must have come from the best tailors. In fact, everything he discovered was of the finest quality, which seemed to indicate that he had fastidious taste.

He had hoped that something in the room might trigger his elusive memory, but even an exquisite miniature, which stated on the reverse that it was of the tenth marchioness and therefore his mother, brought no flicker of recognition. Damn it! He ought to remember his own mother. She was beautiful, but he thought she looked a little haughty, even cold—and he smiled as he considered the lady who would be his wife. Emma was flesh and blood, as warm as she was lovely.

Yet there was something that troubled him about her. It was a damned nuisance that he had no memory of his relationship with Emma! Especially as he suspected that she was hiding something from him.

There had been no doubt about her shock at seeing him alive, or the pleasure that had swept over her as she realised that he was actually there in the room with her. Nor could he doubt her response to that kiss. He had not meant to do that so soon, but the need to hold her had been so strong that he had not been able to resist.

The scent of her had lingered long after she had gone, arousing and frustrating him. He had wanted her so badly! Yet he could not remember anything that had passed between them.

From all he had been told and heard, and from the warmth of her lips beneath his, he believed that she cared for him, as he believed he had cared for her. No, surely she was in love with him? He had known other willing women, but none had been like her—how could he know that? He had no memory of those other women, but he knew that they had meant nothing to him.

Emma's face and name had been haunting him ever since Tom had spoken of her. Why? Why did he feel that he had done something to hurt her? She had not reproached him or given any indication that he had displeased her...but there was some reserve in her. Was it because he had changed physically or because he had requested that they wait until the spring to marry?

Yet how could he marry her until they had had time to know one another? She had not lost her memory, of course, but he was at a disadvantage. He did not know what would please her—and he wanted to please her. He knew that he had hurt her. She had not complained of the anguish she must have felt while he was missing—but he knew how she had suffered, for Mrs Warren had been forthright about it. He had been affected powerfully by the knowledge of Emma's grief, and it had made him even more determined never to hurt her again.

It would take a little time to break down this barrier between them, he thought, but he must not rush her. It was important for the future that they should be comfortable together. Yet when he recalled the urgent throbbing in his loins as he held her, he wondered how long he could wait to claim her as his own.

'So you've come back to us,' Agatha Lynston said, her questing eyes going over him. 'You look terrible, Lytham. No wonder Emma thought she had seen a ghost.'

Lytham laughed and kissed her cheek. 'Someone warned me that your tongue was sharp, Aunt.'

'It used to amuse you. You were always the only one of my relatives I cared for. Your father and brothers were bad, Lytham—bad blood. They did their best to ruin the family. It's as well they're gone, but I should be obliged if you would get yourself an heir before you disappear again.'

Her gruff tone held concern for him. He sensed it instinctively. He could not remember her, but knew that their relationship had been special.

'You must forgive her, Emma,' he said in a teasing tone. 'My aunt has always been one to call a spade a spade, I believe.'

'I ain't mealy-mouthed, never have been,' Lady Agatha said. 'Emma doesn't mind me. She knows what I mean.'

'I am sure Lady Agatha has your best interests at heart, my lord.'

'Lytham,' he said. 'Will you never learn to say it, Emma? Or is it only that I have displeased you again?'

His eyes widened as he spoke, for the words had come into his mind unbidden, and he had the strangest feeling that it was not the first time he had said something similar to her.

'You have not displeased me,' she said but her eyes would not meet his questing gaze. 'Forgive me, Lytham. I sometimes forget that we are engaged.'

He glanced at her hand. 'It seems I have been neglectful in buying you a ring. Perhaps I meant to have it made. No matter. Give me your hand if you will, Emma. This will suffice until I go up to town.'

Emma offered her left hand reluctantly. The ring he slid on to her finger was a small cluster of fine diamonds in the shape of a daisy and fitted well.

'Stephen reminded me that it was in the office strongbox,' he said with a little frown. 'It belonged to my mother. I understand it was her father's gift to her when she was wed. I am sure she would want you to have it.'

'It is beautiful, my...Lytham.'

'A trinket until something more suitable is arranged.'

'Thank you.' Emma's guilt rose up to haunt her. This was terrible! Why had she not spoken out long ago?

It was not easy to recover from the embarrassment of accepting a ring to which she had no right, but as they progressed into the dining room she felt the awkwardness alleviate. Lady Agatha was eager to hear everything Emma had told her from Lytham's own lips, and Mr Antrium put himself out to entertain his employer's fiancée, Tom joining in the conversation from time to time, but looking thoughtful.

'I am so relieved that I did nothing precipitate in the matter of his lordship's cousins,' Mr Antrium confessed. 'And I am sincerely happy to have him back home.'

'You will be invaluable to him in the coming weeks,' she said. 'It must be so awkward, so uncomfortable, to remember nothing of your past life. He will need good friends to help him.'

'I have heard of such cases,' the young man said with a serious expression. 'Sometimes the memory returns of a sudden, though there is apparently no certainty of it.'

'Then Lytham must learn his life all over again.'

'His lordship is a very intelligent man. I do not doubt that he will cope with a situation that others might find intolerable.'

It was clear to Emma that Mr Antrium was both fond of and an admirer of his employer. From the respect in the manner of his agent, and the happy smiles on the faces of his servants, Emma realised that all his people held him in affection.

Later, when it was time to leave, Mrs Williams brought Emma's cloak for her, fussing over her as she placed the soft velvet garment about her shoulders.

'Is it not the most wonderful news, Miss Sommerton?'

'Yes, wonderful,' Emma agreed. 'I think his lordship has had a marvellous escape.'

'And due to Mr Sommerton,' the housekeeper said with an approving beam at Tom as he came to take his farewell of his sister.

'I shall call to see you in the morning,' Tom said as he kissed Emma's cheek. 'I must hope that you will one day forgive me for keeping you in ignorance of the situation concerning Lytham?'

'Of course,' she said and smiled up at him. 'I was shocked when Lytham told me the story and cross with you, Tom, but I understand your dilemma. It was an awkward situation. Yet you ought to have known that I would support you.'

'I did not realise that Lytham meant so much to you. Had I done so, I would have taken the risk of coming to you.'

Emma blushed and shook her head. 'I was naturally distressed. Anyone would be.'

She felt that someone was staring at her, and looking up, met Lytham's dark gaze. His eyes seemed to express doubts and regret, but he smiled as he came to say goodnight and to escort them to the carriage, assisting first Lady Agatha and then Emma.

'I have things to discuss with Stephen, which I imagine must keep me busy for the morning, but perhaps we could ride together in the afternoon. Do you ride? Forgive me. I am not sure.'

'How could you be? I did not ride in London or Bath, though I enjoyed the pastime at home when it was possible. Father had reduced the stables before he died and did not possess a horse suitable for my use, though Sir William allowed me to use something from his stables sometimes.'

'Stephen tells me I have one or two horses that might suit you, Emma. I beg you will use them whenever you wish.'

'Thank you. I shall ride with you tomorrow. At what time shall you be ready?'

'Why do you not come for nuncheon? I should have finished my business by then and shall be free to spend some time with you.'

'Thank you. I may walk back with Tom after his visit to me.'

Lytham kissed her hand, his thoughtful eyes dwelling on her face. Something was definitely troubling her, though she was trying to hide it.

'Goodnight, Emma. I shall look forward to our ride.'

'Goodnight, my lord.'

She turned away as he gave the order for the carriage to move off.

Emma was thoughtful as she undressed that night. What did she truly know of Lord Lynston? She had met him only a few times, but her defences had crumbled before the force of their mutual passion. In truth, she had learned more of his true nature from his servants than she had known of him previously.

It seemed that he was a better man than she might have expected from what was whispered about him, for he was certainly not the damnable rogue her friend Sir William Heathstone had believed him. Why then had he asked her to be his mistress? Thinking it through, she realised that it was not the behaviour of a gentleman. Although her name had been linked to scandal because of Bridget's indiscretion, and that night when he had been taken ill, she was respectable and of good family. He should properly have offered her marriage.

And she ought to have refused the offer he *had* made her!

Emma's cheeks were hot with shame as she recalled her own behaviour that afternoon. She had melted into his arms, offering herself and her love to him without reserve, like any wanton from the streets. What had she been thinking of?

It would shame her if Lytham recalled her unbridled passion and his own distaste for it. She had come to the conclusion that it must have been something in her that had sent him out to walk on the cliffs. What other reason could there be?

She ought to leave here as soon as possible, before she was exposed. Something in Lytham's gaze that evening had warned her that he had some doubts. She would not be able to bear it if his manner should become cold and distant, which it must if her deception were discovered.

Yet it was difficult to leave. For one thing she had very little money. She could ask Tom to lend her some but he would want to know why she needed it, and what could she tell him? He had the prospect of a secure future at the moment; if she told him the truth he might call Lytham out. And then there was the matter of her own future. If she was to leave she would have to find work somehow. There was no way out of this web into which she had walked of her own volition. For the moment she must go on as she was, and if Lytham should remember—then his natural disgust would make it easier to leave him.

Lytham paced the floor of his bedchamber, feeling much like a caged beast. Why would his wretched memory not return? He knew that something important was lurking behind that misty curtain in his mind, mocking him.

Several times that evening Emma had deliberately refused to meet his eyes. What in heaven's name had he done to her?

He must have done something to hurt her! Her eyes seemed almost to accuse him and she was holding back from him. He had had the leisure to observe her as she spoke to others and saw none of the reserve that she held towards him. Had he not been told of her desperation after his disappearance, he would have assumed that their engagement was merely a matter of convenience on both sides. For him it would be the obligation of providing an heir and for her…security?

He must have felt himself responsible for her welfare after her father's untimely death. Having talked at length with Tom and Stephen, he now understood the matter much better. Apparently, he had challenged Emma's father at the card table, goading him into gambling away his estate. He had no idea why he should have done so, but it seemed clear that he had, an unfortunate circumstance that had led to Sommerton's death. It would seem clear that he had an obligation to the family, made even more acute by the scandal caused by his illness at that inn.

Yet if that were all, why did his senses become inflamed at the mere mention of her name? That kiss had brought him almost to the point of no return, making him throb and burn for her, and only his fear of frightening her had made him draw back. Was it possible that they had been lovers? Would he have anticipated their wedding night?

It was not the behaviour of a gentleman, but was he a gentleman in the true sense of the word? Even Lady Agatha had admitted that there was bad blood in the family.

He could not know the truth and was frustrated again, cursing as he resumed his pacing.

What kind of a man was he?

'I meant to come earlier,' Tom said as they began their walk to the Hall that morning. 'But Lytham suggested I might like to talk to Stephen Antrium about Father's estate and I clean forgot the time.'

'It does not matter,' Emma assured him with a smile. 'I am glad to see you taking so much interest in the estate, Tom.'

'I want to make a success of it, prove that I'm not quite the fool Father thought me.'

She caught the note of defence in his voice, understanding how much the quarrel with their father had hurt him, and reached out to press his arm. 'I have never thought you a fool, Tom, just a little hot-tempered, as Father was himself.'

By this time they had reached the Hall and were welcomed by the housekeeper. She provided a warm drink to drive away the chill of their walk, and within ten minutes Lytham and his agent joined them. The two men were in close conversation when they arrived, but business was forgotten as they all went into nuncheon.

Once again several courses were served, though Emma refused to take more than cold meat and some bread and butter.

'You eat very little,' Lytham remarked, regarding her thoughtfully. 'You must order the menus as you wish them, Emma. Mrs Williams has consulted me, but I was not sure of what you would like.'

'I need only something simple in the middle of the day,' she told him. 'But you and Mr Antrium must not be deprived on my account. It is not for me to make changes to your arrangements.'

'I was thinking it might be easier if you and my aunt were to stay here at the hall—'

'Oh, no,' Emma said hastily and blushed as he raised his brows. 'Lady Agatha loves her home and we are quite comfortable there.'

'As you wish.' He frowned as if her refusal had displeased him, but said no more on the subject.

The meal was at an end. Tom and Mr Antrium took their leave and Emma was invited into the parlour next door to drink a dish of tea.

'I have asked for the horses in half an hour,' Lytham told her. 'I thought we might enjoy the opportunity to talk alone for a while.'

'Yes, of course,' Emma said. 'How are you feeling now? I believe you look a little better. Did you sleep well?'

'Tolerably well,' he agreed, though it had been hours before he had finally fallen asleep. 'Do you like to dance, Emma?'

She was surprised by the sudden change of topic and replied without thinking, 'Very much. Why do you ask?'

'I thought we might hold a small dance here to announce our engagement. Stephen is arranging for an advertisement in *The Times,* but I would like to give a dance to celebrate—and it would be a good way for me to get to know my neighbours again.'

'Yes, I am sure that it would.' Emma was hesitant. The trap seemed to be closing ever tighter. How could she let him tell everyone that they were to be married and then withdraw? If he announced it to the world, she would not be able to draw back then without causing a terrible scandal. She got to her feet and walked across to the window to look out at the park. 'I agree that you would find such an occasion a convenient way to rediscover friends—but are you sure you wish to announce our engagement just yet?'

'You are thinking that you may wish to withdraw if my memory does not return?'

'No, of course not...' She faltered and then turned to face him, her shoulders squaring as she decided that she must at least tell him a part of the truth. 'It is a little awkward, but there is something you should know.'

Lytham rose and came to stand before her, his eyes intent on her face, studying her, reading her discomfort. 'Have I upset you in some way, Emma? I really was ill for some time, you know. Once Tom told me who I was I could have sent word, but I was lost…alone in a world that made no sense. I did not know you were waiting for me or if anyone cared whether I lived. You cannot imagine how frustrating it is to have no knowledge of yourself other than what you have been told.'

'I do understand that this must be terrible for you,' Emma said, sensing his frustration and hurt. 'I am not angry with you, nor do I blame you for what happened.'

'Then what is bothering you? Please tell me, for I know something is—I can feel a reserve in you towards me and I think I have done something to harm you.'

'Oh, no, it is only that…you had not asked me to marry you,' Emma said, her cheeks pink. 'When Lady Agatha arrived at your mother's house she told everyone that I was your fiancée and insisted that I come here with her. I did not know what to do. I had been unwell and she was so kind—but then everyone believed we were engaged and I did not know how to tell them it was not so.'

Lytham smiled and experienced a sense of relief. 'You feel as if you are guilty of deceiving everyone, including me—is that it, Emma?'

'Yes.' She dropped her gaze as she felt his eyes intent upon her. 'It was very wrong of me. I should, of course, have made it clear at once that you had not spoken…but somehow I did not and then it was too difficult.'

'Emma, Emma,' Lytham chided and the look in his eyes caused her heart to miss a beat. 'Is that your terrible secret? Clearly I was at fault for being tardy. As I understand the situation, I must have confided my intention to my aunt. Indeed, I imagine that it was a matter of honour. After your reputation suffered because of my carelessness there was no other option open to me as a gentleman. Besides, I already feel deeply attracted to you and I believe you care something for me?'

She could not deny it when he looked at her that way, and it was now even more impossible to confess the shameful truth.

'Yet I think we should wait before we announce our intentions,' she said quietly. 'If by the spring you are sure of your feelings…'

'I shall not change my mind,' he said before she could finish. 'We shall marry next March and announce our engagement at Christmas. The dance may wait until then. Will that content you, Emma?'

It wanted no more than three weeks to Christmas, but she could not refuse. 'If you are of the same mind I—I am content.'

'It occurs to me that my proposal leaves something to be desired, Emma,' Lytham said and laughed. 'However, let us make it clear so that there may be no more doubts between us—I do most sincerely want and desire you as my wife, Miss Sommerton. Will you do me the honour of accepting my offer?'

Emma's heart caught, for the way he looked at her seemed to show sincerity and a depth of feeling on his part that was all she could ask of the man she would marry.

'I am honoured by your proposal, my lord, and if you still wish it in the spring I shall marry you.'

'Then we are agreed,' he said and reached out to touch her cheek with his fingertips. 'Do not look so anxious, my love. I dare say my memory will return long before then.'

'Yes, we must hope so.'

He glanced at his pocket watch. 'I believe the stables are expecting us—shall we go? I thought you would like to choose your mount yourself since it is your first time.'

He held his hand out to her and she took it, her heart fluttering wildly. She had told him as much of the truth as she dare and he had dismissed her fears with laughter. He wanted to marry her, had asked her to be his wife, and God forgive her for the deception, but she wanted to marry him.

Alone in her room later that evening, Emma looked at herself in the mirror. Was what she was doing so very wrong? Lytham seemed to know what he wanted, and he *had* asked her to marry him—but would he have done so if he had remembered that afternoon when she had so very nearly become his mistress?

He had told her after their ride together that he was planning to take a short trip to town to visit his lawyers, and to consult a doctor that Stephen had told him about, to discover what the chances were of him ever remembering his past.

'You will not mind staying here with my aunt?' he asked, gazing down into her face, his dark eyes seeming as if they would pierce her very soul. 'I believe she is not always as well as she pretends and I must make some arrangement for her to have a companion. Otherwise it will be a wrench for her when we are in town or on some jaunt of our own.'

'Yes, I think it would be good for her to have a companion,' Emma agreed. 'Though she will have company when we are in residence at the Hall.'

'Do you enjoy living in the country, Emma?'

'I have been used to it,' she said with a smile. 'We lived very quietly at home, Mother and I, you know.'

'Where is your mother? May I fetch her to you? You will want her to be at the wedding?' He frowned. 'Forgive me. I had not realised until this moment that you had a parent living. No one had thought to tell me of Lady Sommerton's existence. Where is she and how is she managing to live?'

He looked upset at this lack, and she felt her heart go out to him. How terrible it must be not to be able to remember anything about yourself or the people you see every day.

'You did not know, how could you? And that is my fault for neglecting to tell you,' she said softly. 'My mother is in Italy for the winter with good friends. She will return in the spring.'

'Ah, then I must see if any letters have come for you. I dare say she will write care of the estate.'

'Tom will send them on,' she said. 'But letters take a long time to come from that distance and I dare say Mama will not write often. Indeed, I hope she is enjoying herself too much to think of it.'

'I shall be gone no more than a few days,' he said, his serious gaze dwelling thoughtfully on her face. 'But there are matters I must attend to, Emma. In the meantime, I ask you to make free of my home. Use it as you will—and perhaps you might make a friend of Maria.'

'Your late brother's wife?' Emma frowned. 'Lady Agatha sent a note when we first came here, asking her to dine with us, but she declined. Do you think that I should call on her?'

'It may be that she is embarrassed to meet you, because of her involvement with Tom. I have not called to see her thus far, but I shall certainly do so when I return from town.'

'Then I shall call on her in the meantime,' Emma said. 'For we are bound to meet from time to time and I would have no awkwardness between us.'

'Nor should there be any,' Lytham said. 'It is not for me to say, Emma—but I believe that in another year or so Tom may think of marrying and it is possible that he will ask Maria to be his wife. I know that he intended to pay her a visit before he left Lytham this afternoon.'

'You think that he cares for her?'

'Maria could have cleared him of all suspicion of my brother's murder, but he would not let her speak,' Lytham said. 'He was more concerned for her reputation than his own, and that I think shows a certain feeling between them. I shall do my best to re-establish Tom's reputation, for he undoubtedly saved my life, and I owe him more than I can ever repay.'

'Then I shall definitely call on Maria,' Emma said. 'I must make a friend of her for my brother's sake.'

She would do so in the morning, she decided as she finished dressing for dinner, glancing at her reflection in the mirror. She was wearing one of the gowns Lytham had had made for her and sent to the house by the sea, for the maids had packed them with her own and she had not realised until they were at Lynston Cottage. The gown was fashioned of heavy silk in a dark amber shade, very similar to the one she had worn the afternoon that Lytham went missing.

He was dining with them at the cottage that evening, and she wondered if the gown she was wearing might help to trigger something in his memory. She could not wish him never to remember, though she knew that when he did he might turn from her in disgust. However, she had decided that she must risk that happening. To run away now would be cowardly. Besides, she loved him and it might be that he would never remember that he had meant her to be his mistress and not his wife.

Chapter Twelve

Emma saw a rather lovely woman picking yellow chrysanthemums in the garden of the Dower House as she approached the next morning. The weather was fine though chilly, and she was wearing a thick cloak over her gown, the hood pulled up over her head, but the woman picking flowers was wearing only a shawl as she placed them in her basket. She glanced up as Emma's shoes made a scrunching sound on the gravel, seeming startled at first and then resigned.

'Good morning, Miss Sommerton,' she said. 'I have been expecting you to call, though I was not sure you would want to meet me socially.'

'You are Lady Lynston?' Emma asked and received a nod in return. She knew instantly why her brother had fallen in love with this young woman, for she had large, soulful eyes that seemed to speak of an inner sadness, reminding Emma of a puppy Tom had once rescued from drowning and brought home. 'I am very pleased to meet you. Why should I not be?'

'You must know that I was the cause of your brother's disgrace?'

'I do not think that is quite the case,' Emma replied gently. 'My brother is a man of some four and twenty years, and well able to choose for himself. Besides, it was someone else who accused him of being a cheat—and as for the suspicion of murder, that never came to anything. My father was furious, of course, and it caused the split between them, but if had not been that it would have been something else. They were always out of sorts

213

with one another, perhaps because they both have a temper when roused.'

Maria's dark brown eyes rested on Emma's face for a moment longer and then she smiled. 'Tom assured me I would like you,' she said. 'I should have come to see you before this, but I was afraid that you would be angry with me.'

Emma judged her to be two or three years older than Tom, perhaps a little more, but she had the kind of face that would be beautiful until the day she died, with high cheekbones and slanting eyes, the lashes long and silky against the cream and rose of her skin. Her hair was a reddish brown and pulled flat on the top of her head, curled into a large knot at the nape of her neck, as though she tried to hide her beauty by every means she could.

'I believe Tom cares for you,' Emma said. 'Therefore I could not be angry with you, Maria. I came to visit you in the hope that we shall be friends.'

'Yes, I think we may,' Maria said. 'I must admit I have been lonely here for the last year or two, though Lady Agatha invites me to dine from time to time, but it will be pleasant to have the company of a young woman.'

'Lytham is to give a dance to celebrate our engagement,' Emma said. 'I hope that you will come, Maria?'

'I have not been into company since…the accident,' she said and looked uncertain. 'Do you think I ought? I mean…there was a great deal of scandal after my husband was thrown from his horse.'

'I am certain you should,' Emma assured her. 'It would be a shame if you were to live in seclusion for the rest of your life. Indeed, I shall not allow it. If we are to be friends, I must insist that you come to my dance.'

Maria laughed softly. 'How refreshingly positive you are,' she said. 'I am not surprised Lytham is in love with you. I thought he would never marry. I am so glad that he has found you, Emma, and I shall be very happy to come to your dance. Now, will you come in and share a dish of tea with me?'

The morning spent with his lawyers had proved more than useful, Lytham thought as he walked down Bond Street towards the jewellers that he had been told he usually patronised. He was in a better position to understand his own affairs than he had been, and could now direct his attention towards the matter of a ring and a gift for Emma.

'You might have let me know you were alive!' An indignant voice accosted him, the gentleman's hand clasping his shoulder from behind. 'Damn it, Alex! I knew you were missing, but until I went to White's last night I had not heard that you had been found. Now I see you as large as life and still no word from you.'

Lytham turned, looking at the young man who was grinning at him, his words more accusing than his expression. He was blond, blue-eyed and extremely handsome and Lytham felt instinctively that he was fond of this man, who was perhaps five years his junior.

'Forgive me,' he said. 'I would have if...'

'If you had thought about it, I suppose,' Toby Edgerton said. 'It's as well that the wedding invitations have not gone out. I've a good mind not to send you one for your neglect.'

'I hope you won't cast me off. I am in need of friends,' Lytham said a trifle ruefully. 'Since you are about to be married and an expert on such things, tell me what I ought to buy as an engagement gift.'

'So you're going to marry the beauty,' Toby said his grin widening. 'I knew it when you asked me to invite her and the Merry Widow to my engagement dance. Mrs Flynn has married Howard, so I hear. They have taken the sister and gone off abroad for a while, but I dare say Miss Sommerton has already told you that?'

'I do not think Emma has had a letter from Mrs Flynn, though it may be waiting for her. I must hope that Tom will send her letters on when he reaches his estate.'

'Tom Sommerton? Given it back to him, have you? Of course I knew you would—you never wanted the damned thing in the first place. If Sommerton hadn't behaved so badly that evening you would never have allowed him to wager it, but we all knew he could never cover a half of what he had wagered. Anyone else would have had him thrown out of the club as a cheat. Still, all's well that ends well, what?'

'Yes, certainly,' Lytham said. 'I was thinking of visiting a jeweller's this morning, but that will keep—shall we go to the club together?'

'On my way there,' Toby agreed easily. 'I thought I might have a little work out later.' He gave Lytham a playful punch in the arm. 'You look as if it would do you no harm to go a few rounds in the ring.'

'Why not?' Lytham replied and smiled lazily.

'Morning, Lytham. Good to see you in town. Toby—I hope to see you and the lovely Miss Dawlish at my house next week.'

'Of course, Hattersly. Lucy is looking forward to it. In the country at the moment with her Mama but she'll be back next week.'

'I trust you are well, Hattersly,' Lytham said, thinking that this chance meeting with Toby was a piece of good fortune. The young man must be Tobias Edgerton, for he had looked through his engagement book at his town house and recalled the name, also that Toby was engaged to a Miss Lucy Dawlish. He was learning much that he needed to know—and without telling his friend that he had lost his memory, something he was reluctant to do unless he was forced.

'You were remarkably polite to Hattersly,' Toby remarked as they moved on. 'First time I've known you to do more than nod to him in passing.'

'I must be mellowing,' Lytham said and raised his brows, his mouth curving in a mocking smile. 'I dare say it is because I almost died.'

'There was some talk of a shooting,' Toby said. 'Sounded rather suspicious to me—something about a court-martial while you were serving abroad?'

'We all thought Pennington had died in a bar brawl in Spain,' Lytham replied. 'The man carried a grudge against me—if it hadn't been for Tom Sommerton I might have been dead, if not of my wounds then of drowning.'

'Good grief,' Toby said looking amazed. 'That's a turn up—after the scandal with your brother.'

'Tom Sommerton was quite blameless in that,' Lytham replied.

'He has a cast-iron alibi for the afternoon John was thrown, and I do not for a moment believe he ever cheated at the card table. That tale was my brother's doing—and I dare say you may guess the reason behind it, though I am not at liberty to say.'

'Well, it just goes to show...' Toby said. 'We all thought Sommerton had gone for good after his father threw him out. What had he been doing?'

'I believe he went abroad,' Lytham replied vaguely. 'Now tell me—when is the wedding to be?'

Toby began to describe all the arrangements for his wedding in great detail as they walked. He was hailed by several gentlemen, and answered all of them by their names. As most of them also addressed Lytham he was able to add their faces to the growing list of his acquaintances. A very little persuasion brought more personal details from his companion, which helped him to form a picture of these men and the way they fitted into his former life.

It seemed that he was rather particular and had few close friendships. Most were no more than acquaintances, and he was able to merely nod in passing when addressed by strangers without causing undue offence.

At White's, where it seemed he was a member, and welcomed by the staff, who said they were glad to see him back, he was able to pick up the names of the gentlemen they met from the general conversation going on about him. He and Toby bespoke a light nuncheon, and then refused the offer of a game of cards, taking themselves off to the club run by a former professional pugilist. Here again, Lytham discovered that he was known and welcomed by the owner, who offered to spar with him for a few rounds.

'You look as if you need the exercise, my lord. You've lost some muscle and need to build your strength up again.'

'He would do better to spar with me, George,' Toby said. 'You'll be too much for him. He's been ill, you know.'

'You would hardly be a match for Lytham,' a voice drawled behind them. 'From what I've heard you are something of a pugilist, Lytham. I should be pleased to go a few rounds with you—

if you want some real sport.'

'Good grief, Lindisfarne,' Toby said and looked sick. 'Don't take his challenge, Lytham. You're not up to his weight at the moment, he'll slaughter you.'

'Indeed?' Lytham was not sure why that name had put his hackles up, but he knew instinctively that he did not like or trust this man, and also that he would never dream of refusing a challenge from him. 'I think Toby is right and I am a little out of form, sir—but if you care to indulge me I shall accept your challenge.'

'Mistake…' Toby hissed. 'Man hates you.'

'Then I shall be on my guard,' Lytham replied in a similar whisper.

Stripped to the waist and eyeing his opponent minutes later in the ring, Lytham knew immediately that this was not to be a friendly bout. Lindisfarne was out for blood, and he sensed that there was some quarrel between them, though of course he did not remember it.

They began to spar equally enough, each man landing a hit about the other's body to the encouraging praise of Gentleman George as the prize-fighter was generally known. He had been a much-admired champion in his day and, like others who had excelled in the sport, now earned his living teaching gentlemen to fight.

'A little sharper, Lytham,' he commanded. 'You are giving your opponent too much time and space to come at you. Lord Lindisfarne—you are aiming too low. Above the belt, please, gentlemen.'

'Watch him, Alex,' warned Toby as Lindisfarne suddenly came at him with a flurry of blows. 'He's a sly hitter. He'll catch you if you don't watch…' He groaned as the blows found their mark, sending Lytham stumbling back so that he lost his balance and fell on his back, his head hitting the floor with a resounding crack that appeared to knock him out. 'I warned you!'

Climbing into the ring as Gentleman George held Lindisfarne at bay, Toby bent over his friend anxiously, patting his face and crying his name. Lytham's eyes flickered and then opened. He grinned and put a hand to his cheek.

'That was a cracking facer,' he said. 'Not from you, Toby? The last time I fought you—you couldn't swat a fly.'

'If you're going to insult me, I shan't warn you in future,' Toby said, greatly relieved by his friend's mockery. 'I told you—you aren't up to Lindisfarne's weight yet. You've lost a couple of stone by the looks of you while you were ill.'

'Lindisfarne...' Lytham looked beyond him to where Gentleman George was handing his opponent a towel to dry himself. 'Did he knock me down? I must have been in a daze, can't seem to remember.'

'I warned you not to fight him.' Toby gave him a mournful look. 'But naturally you wouldn't listen, but that's no more than usual, of course.'

'Naturally,' Lytham said and smiled. 'Give me a hand up, Toby. I must congratulate Lindisfarne on his win.'

He was feeling a little odd as he got to his feet, his memory seeming to have strange gaps in it. What on earth was he doing here—and why had he agreed to go a few rounds with Lindisfarne? The man was a disgrace and after his behaviour towards Mrs Flynn and Emma...

Emma! Good lord! What must she be thinking?

Lytham went through the motions of shaking hands with his opponent, his mind working frantically as he tried to make sense of his thoughts. Why was he here? Surely he had been with Emma at his mother's house...and then he was shot! He remembered turning as Pennington spoke and the gun had gone off almost immediately, giving him no chance to avoid the ball. The force of it in his shoulder had sent him staggering towards the edge of the cliffs and then he had known no more until he woke to find himself being tended by an old woman. He recalled his thoughts to the present with some difficulty.

'Splendid hit, Lindisfarne,' he said, his expression giving nothing away. 'Perhaps you will allow me my chance of revenge another time?'

'Any time you like,' Lindisfarne sneered and went off towards the dressing rooms.

'You are out of condition, my lord,' Gentleman George said, giving Lytham a severe look. 'I believe you have been ill, my lord. You must begin a regimen to recover your muscle strength, and refrain from boxing over your weight until you are completely well again.'

'Thank you, George. I shall be pleased to follow the routine you set me when I first came to you—though I am planning on returning to the country soon.'

'Come to me when you can, my lord. If you were in peak condition, you would not have been such an easy target for the earl.'

'No…' Lytham moved his jaw gingerly. 'Yet I think I have learned something from him.'

He had left Emma to walk alone—why? Good grief! Now he remembered it all. What must she think of his behaviour? He shook his head as if to clear it, but the memory of those last moments remained to haunt him, not a hallucination then, but a product of his damnable humour!

'You can't be serious about going another round with Lindisfarne?' Toby asked after Lytham had taken a shower beneath the pump. 'I thought you despised the man?'

'Yes, I do, don't I?' Lytham said and grinned at him. The cold water had done its work, helping to refresh his mind and clear the last remnants of confusion. 'All the more reason to teach him a lesson, don't you think, my friend?'

He was feeling wonderful as the last gaps began to fill up in his memory, because now he could remember the man he had been before his illness and everything that had happened since.

He recalled Emma's embarrassed confession that he had not asked her to be his wife. What an intolerable position he had left her in! She must have been in torment since his disappearance. It was little wonder that she had been at her wit's end! Or that she had accepted his aunt's invitation to stay with her.

Because of his damnable behaviour she had been left without a home, and if the truth were known concerning her situation, a loss of reputation from which she could not hope to recover. She could not possibly have told his aunt what she believed to be her true situation, and must have suffered terribly at being forced to live what she thought was a lie. And it was his fault!

How alone and desperate she must have felt before his aunt took her home with her, and bless Agatha for acting so sensibly. He shuddered to think what might have happened to Emma had his great-aunt not taken her under her wing. And all because he had been enjoying a jest, amusing himself at Emma's expense! It would serve him right if she turned from him with the disgust she was entitled to feel.

Yet she had agreed to marry him. Was it because she loved him? Surely she must to have agreed to his outrageous offer in the first place?

What had possessed him to make it? If he had thought it a jest, it was in very poor taste. No, he seemed to recall that he had been testing her, to discover whether or not she truly cared for him. He might have married a score of respectable young ladies, some of them rather beautiful, but none of them had touched his heart, nor had they loved him. His position in Society and his fortune had made him a good catch—and Emma's manner had often been reserved towards him. The plain truth was that he had not been sure of her feelings towards him…until that afternoon.

He remembered kissing her, the way she had melted into his embrace, giving herself up to him with such honesty and such loving trust that he had been horrified at what he had done. His passion had been such that he dare not confess his true intentions to her for fear that he would not be able to control his longing to make love to her. He had gone out to take the air and gain control of his feelings…and disappeared! Emma must have been distraught.

He ought to tell her at once that he had regained his memory, to explain and apologise, but if he did that she would be embarrassed—and he feared that her reaction would be to run away from him. He knew that he could not bear to lose her now, and must marry her even if she despised him for the wicked devil he was— had been. The prospect of life without her was intolerable, for he could never return to the aimless life he had known before meeting her. Something had changed in him, though he did not know whether it was his illness or the love he felt for Emma that had brought about this change.

He had never loved anyone as he did Emma. He had loved his mother as a child, but she had been a cold, reserved woman and he had soon learned not to run to her with a cut knee. His father's hatred had taught him never to expect a kind word, and his experience with the women he made his mistresses had been that he must pay for favours.

Emma had given so much of herself with little reason to trust him, and he could not risk losing her. Perhaps it would be better to keep the return of his memory a secret until after they were married.

'You look lovely, Emma,' said Lady Agatha, complimenting her on the new gown she was to wear that evening. Lytham had ordered it for her in town from a dressmaker she had used in the past and it fitted her perfectly. 'That colour becomes you, my dear. I like that shade of midnight blue on you, and the style is a little out of the ordinary.'

Emma smiled and thanked her. They were staying at the Hall for Christmas to make entertaining their guests more convenient. Lady Agatha had told her it was Lytham's habit to invite her for a few days at that time of year, and indeed Emma had not wanted to decline. She had found nothing but pleasure in her developing relationship with Lytham these past weeks, and had almost managed to quell any doubts. He was unfailingly courteous, always considerate, and she had already known that he could be a charming companion.

They had discovered many pastimes in which they shared a common interest, including poetry and literature, attending the theatre and listening to good music. They rode nearly every day when the weather permitted and dined together at least three times a week, either at Lady Agatha's home or the Hall.

Emma had been persuaded to make a list of all the changes she considered necessary to the main reception rooms and had found it a task she thoroughly enjoyed. There was much to do to make it a comfortable family home, and she looked forward to continuing her work over the coming months and years. Already new curtains ordered from an exclusive establishment in town had arrived for the drawing room and the rich shade of crimson, banded with gold braid, had given the huge chamber more warmth and colour.

Lytham had ordered a suite of furniture in the style of Mr Chippendale to replace the worn sofas that had begun to look sadly weary. Yet in many of the rooms Emma had decided that rearranging the existing pieces, but adding to them small comforts such as cushions and flowers, had made all the change necessary.

'Yes, I like this shade of blue,' Emma said in reply to Lady Agatha's earlier remark. 'I had something similar made when I was in town—but this certainly has more style. I dare say it was expensive.'

'What does that matter? You deserve a little spoiling, my dear.' Lady Agatha smiled at her benevolently. 'You must wear the pearls Lytham sent you, Emma. They are a family heirloom and given to brides on the day of their engagement. My nephew consulted me on what he ought to send for from the bank and I thought of the pearls—though I believe he intends to make a personal gift of some kind.'

'Oh, no,' Emma disclaimed. 'I have already been spoiled shamefully.'

'And why not?' Agatha Lynston demanded, her eyes bright and decidedly wicked. 'Lytham has far more than is strictly necessary. It will do him good to spend some of it on you.'

Emma laughed. 'Why are you so good to me, ma'am? I am sure I do not deserve it.'

'I never did hear such nonsense,' Lady Agatha replied. 'You are both lovely and good-natured, and my nephew is very fortunate to have secured you as his bride. Well, I shall go down now and leave you to finish your toilette—do not be long, my dear.'

Emma smiled, but said no more. She had almost stilled her doubts concerning her relationship with Lytham, or at least banished them to a far corner of her mind. Surely his manner towards her showed a deep tenderness? And, if he loved her, would it not simply spoil things if she told him the truth now? Her conscience pricked her from time to time, but she had decided it was something she must live with for the present.

She fastened the shorter length of pearls about her throat, choosing between the three strings of large, lustrous beads. Each one had a diamond clasp, and all three could be linked together if so desired by a diamond pendent. However, she preferred the simple choker, which sat neatly at the base of her throat. She was just preparing to leave the room when Lytham knocked at the door and asked if he might be admitted. His eyes went over her appreciatively as she opened to him, resting on her face for a moment.

'You look beautiful,' he said. 'The Lytham pearls look well on you, Emma. They were Aunt Agatha's suggestion, but I thought this might improve upon tradition.'

He handed her a small box with an oval-humped lid, which she opened to discover a bangle of pearls and diamonds.

'Oh, that is lovely,' Emma said, slipping it over her hand so that it hung loosely on her wrist and holding it up for him to admire. 'Thank you. It is a wonderful surprise and goes well with the necklace.'

'And it is your own, never worn by any other Lytham bride,' he said. 'Now your hand please, my love.'

She offered him her hand and he removed the diamond cluster from her finger, replacing it with a large clear sapphire surrounded by fine diamonds.

'There, that is much better.'

The small diamond cluster lay abandoned on the dressing table, but Emma slipped it on to her right hand. 'Your ring is beautiful, Lytham, but I think this has become like a part of me. I shall continue to wear it, if you do not mind?'

'You may do as you wish, Emma.' He reached out to touch her cheek, moving a wisp of hair that curled in a tiny ringlet at her ear. 'You must know that I want only to make you happy?'

'Thank you.' She blushed at the tenderness in his eyes. 'I am very happy.' Her eyes gazed up at him, searching for any sign that he might have changed his mind and finding none. 'If you are still content?'

'How could I be otherwise, Emma? You are the woman I have waited for my whole life.'

Emma's hand trembled slightly as his strong fingers closed about it. She smiled and allowed him to lead her from the room.

'Tom brought me a letter from my mother when he came this morning,' she said. 'She is well and enjoying herself. She says that the Heathstones have invited her to make her home with them, but she may wish to go home when she knows that Tom is living there. I shall write at once and tell her.'

'And your own news, I trust? She may wish to return for the wedding. You know that your mother will always be welcome to stay with us for as long as she wishes?'

'You are very good.'

'Not at all. I think myself fortunate to have found you, Emma, and your family's happiness is my pleasure, not a duty.'

Her heart was full and she would have said more, but they had reached the drawing room where Tom, Lady Agatha and Maria were waiting for them. Tom was standing next to Maria and from his deferential manner as he listened to something she was saying, Emma thought it likely that Lytham was right concerning his intentions towards her. If Maria were his choice, she would not object, for she wanted him to be happy.

'Oh, you do look lovely,' Maria said as Emma went up to her and kissed her cheek.

'I'm so glad you came,' Emma said. 'Your dress is most attractive, Maria. Is it new?'

'No. I had it made some time ago, but I have not had the occasion to wear it.'

'Well, I think that shade of green is very much your colour.'

'Thank you. I like what you've done with the house. I was never allowed to make changes.' For a moment Maria's eyes were shadowed by unhappy memories. 'But I am delighted to see the changes you have made, Emma.'

'Lytham says I have not done half enough,' she replied and threw a laughing glance at him. 'But I have hardly started yet.'

Their guests had begun to arrive. Some were staying in the house and had waited to come down until their hosts were ready to receive them, some were at the houses of neighbours or other houses on the estate. One of the first to arrive was Toby Edgerton, his fiancée and her mother.

Watching Lytham's easy manner with his friend, Emma realised that he was very much more at ease than he had been in the first few days after his reappearance, but that was only natural. He was looking much better now, more like he had been before the illness that had almost ended his life.

She had noticed a slight difference in his manner when he returned from his visit to London, but had assumed that he was beginning to feel more at home with himself. He had told her that he had met several old friends in London, but she noticed that there was no awkwardness in his greeting to any of the guests. He was behaving exactly as if he had known them all his life.

He had known many of these people for a long time, of course, but he seemed so easy in his manner with them that Emma was slightly puzzled. She still found it difficult to recall everyone she had met since coming to Lytham Hall, and some of the guests were completely unknown to her. Yet Lytham seemed to have no difficulty in identifying them, or in finding some mutual topic of conversation.

'You look anxious, Miss Sommerton,' Stephen Antrium said to her and she turned to look at him. 'Is something bothering you?'

'Oh, it is nothing,' she said and smiled at him. 'I was merely wondering how Lytham is managing to remember everyone.'

'I believe he has spent many hours memorising names and facts,' Stephen replied. 'And he has visited every house in the district where we are on terms with the owners since his return.'

'Oh, I see,' Emma said and turned away as Toby Edgerton and Lucy Dawlish came up to her. 'Thank you, Stephen.'

'You look beautiful,' Toby said and he kissed Emma's cheek. 'You and Lucy will have much in common—our wedding next month, you know. I hope you and Lytham mean to come to it?'

'You must know that we could not possibly miss it,' Emma said and kissed Lucy on the cheek. 'That is a pretty dress, Lucy. You must tell me the name of your dressmaker.'

'Yes, of course,' Lucy replied and dimpled. 'That is if I can recall it—I have bought so many new dresses that I cannot remember exactly where every one came from.'

'Her papa swears she will ruin him,' Toby said. 'But I don't care if she spends a fortune on pretty things—she is worth every penny.'

'I am glad to hear it,' Emma said and laughed as they passed on and more guests came to greet her.

It was some time before she was released from greeting newcomers to mingle with the guests, who were drinking champagne and waiting for the dancing to begin. Card tables had been set up in another room, but most of the younger men had already been selecting their partners for the various dances.

Emma was to open the dancing with Lytham, of course, and they had selected a waltz as the first of the evening. Emma smiled as he bowed and asked her formally for the pleasure of taking her on the floor, enjoying the sensation of being held close to his heart as he gracefully whirled her about the room.

'We danced like this once before,' she told him. 'In Bath, I believe?'

'In my dreams I have held you in my arms many times, Emma.'

'Or was it in London—at Toby's engagement ball? I cannot perfectly remember.'

'Perhaps we danced then and in Bath,' Lytham said, gazing down at her face. 'What are you thinking, Emma?'

'Just that I like dancing with you,' she said and smiled up at him. It was foolish of her to test him like this. If he had recovered his memory, he would surely have told her. Why should he not?

'Then I shall dance with you all night and no one else.'

'You cannot do that,' she replied and shook her head at him. 'You have guests and you must ask the young ladies to dance, and Maria. Yes, you *must* dance with her, Lytham.'

'I shall certainly dance with Maria,' he said. 'It would not do to ignore her or to seem to slight her. I noticed that one or two ladies were a little distant with her when they arrived. I would not have her ostracised so I must do my utmost to show that I approve of her—and your brother, Emma. I have set certain rumours in circulation in London, and I hope to repair much of the damage to Tom's reputation very shortly.'

'That woman in the crimson gown,' Emma said. 'Lady Leamington, I think…I noticed that she was very frosty towards Maria.'

'Lady Leamington is an old tabby,' Lytham replied. 'I understand she actually cut you in Bath, Emma, but I believe she had changed her tune this evening.'

'She was quite friendly,' Emma said. 'Yes, I remember now—she did cut me the evening that you took Lady Agatha home early.'

'My aunt reminded me of it,' he said. 'We were bound to invite her, because she is a distant cousin of sorts—but you need have little to do with her except at such affairs as these, Emma. She will not expect to be invited to weekends. We have never been on those terms.'

'I am glad to hear it. I cannot say I like her.' She supposed he could have learned these things from his aunt, but it gave her pause to wonder. Just how much of Lytham's memory had returned to him?

They completed the rest of their dance in silence, and then Emma was claimed by a succession of gentlemen who wished to dance with her. She danced with Lytham again just before supper and he took her into supper afterwards, where they were joined by Toby Edgerton, Lucy and several more of the younger guests.

Emma was talking to Lucy about her extensive shopping trips, some of which had been in Paris, and she was not immediately aware of the conversation between some of the gentlemen, until a burst of laughter caught her attention.

'Lytham was out of condition, of course, or Lindisfarne could never have landed him a facer,' Toby was saying. 'I look forward to the return bout. If I'm any judge, Lytham will teach him a lesson once he is fully fit again.'

'I believe I am almost that now,' Lytham replied. 'I shall not go out of my way to challenge Lindisfarne, but I must admit I do not much care for him.'

'You told me once you thought he was a blustering bully and a blaggard,' Toby said. 'It would do him good to be on the wrong side of a thrashing.'

'Personally, I would like to take a horsewhip to the man,' a gentleman who had his back towards Emma said harshly. 'I never could stand the fellow. I remember the time you went ten rounds with that black, Lytham. No one would take a bet on you—they all thought he must win because he was a professional—but you knocked him down in the end. How did you manage it? He was bigger and heavier than you.'

'It's all a matter of science,' Lytham replied and laughed. 'You have to watch your opponent, learn where his weakness is while keeping on your toes and out of reach—then when you are sure of him, you go in for the kill. The black was heavy and a bruising fighter but he had one fault. He had a habit of dropping his guard every so often. I waited and then I went straight in and it took only the one punch to lay him out.'

The colour drained from Emma's cheeks as she heard the general laughter. It was an amusing story, more suited to a gentleman's club perhaps, but she did not object to a little sporting talk—but how could Lytham have remembered in such detail?

And why had he not told her about the sparring bout he had taken part in with Lindisfarne? Was it over her? Had Lindisfarne insulted her?

'Is something the matter?' Lucy Dawlish inquired. 'You look quite pale, Emma.'

'I believe I am a little warm,' Emma replied, turning hot now as a tide of embarrassment washed over her. If Lytham had regained his memory, he must remember that afternoon at his mother's house! 'Would you excuse me, Lucy? I think I shall go upstairs and tidy myself.'

'Yes, it is warm at these affairs, isn't it?' Lucy said. 'I think I shall follow your example, Emma. My cheeks feel quite pink.'

Emma was forced to accompany Lucy upstairs, but at the top they parted and Emma hurried to her own bedchamber, where she splashed water on her heated cheeks and looked at herself in the mirror. Was it true—had Lytham's memory finally returned? And when had it happened? He had said nothing to her...made no mention of that afternoon.

When she thought about it, she had noticed an increase of confidence on his return from London, yet she had not really taken so much notice until this evening. It was his manner towards Toby that had alerted her. She had always known that they were very good friends and the warmth between them was apparent. Could their relationship have reached such ease if Lytham was not able to remember him?

Somehow she did not think that was possible. So that meant he remembered Toby well enough to feel at ease with him. She knew that some things had come back to him from time to time— but to remember so much of a boxing match? No, she did not think that held true. Did that mean that Lytham had remembered all his past life? If that was indeed the case, why had he not spoken to her of the afternoon when she had so nearly become his mistress? Was he waiting for her to confess it to him?

She pressed her hands against her cheeks, feeling the shame wash over her. What must he be thinking of her? Her first wild thought was to flee from the house so that she need not face him, but then in an instant she knew it was impossible. She could not make the situation worse by causing a dreadful scandal on the evening of their engagement. She must wait a little longer and then...she did not know what the outcome must be, but she must obviously ask him for the truth and be prepared for his scorn when he told her that he knew her terrible secret.

She finished tidying herself and left her bedchamber, going back down to the ballroom, where everyone was assembling for the dancing again. She was engaged for the next several dances and it was not until the guests were beginning to take their leave that Lytham came to her.

'I believe everyone enjoyed themselves,' he said, looking down at her. 'I hope you found the evening pleasant, Emma? It is good to have friends to visit sometimes, is it not?'

'Yes, of course, my lord. Lucy and Toby seem very happy. She is excited about the wedding, of course.'

'Yes.' He frowned as he caught the note of reserve in her voice. 'Is something wrong, my love?'

'No, of course not. Why should something be wrong? The evening went extremely well.'

'I meant with you—you seem not quite as happy as you were. Has something upset you?'

It was her chance to have it out with him, but now was not the time. 'You are quite wrong, Lytham,' she said. 'It is merely that I am a little tired and shall be glad to seek my bed.'

'I see.' He took her hand and kissed it. 'Then I wish you good-night, Emma, and may your dreams be sweet.'

'Thank you—and yours also,' she said, but as she walked away from him she knew that her dreams would be anything but sweet. It would be a wonder if she could sleep at all!

Chapter Thirteen

After some considerable persuasion Maria had agreed to go with Emma to London for the wedding of Toby Edgerton and Lucy Dawlish. She had been reluctant at first, but when Emma explained that Lady Agatha had cried off she had agreed.

'Then I cannot refuse you,' she said and laughed. 'How can I? For otherwise you would have no chaperon, Emma. How shocking that would be. And my consequence can do so much for you.'

She was teasing, of course, and they laughed together. For Maria suspected that Emma's pleading was as much for her sake as her own. She and Lytham had clearly hit upon the plan of reintroducing her into the broader society of London and she could not deny their kindness: especially if she did not wish to spend the rest of her life in seclusion at Lytham.

Emma laughed at her friend's teasing, but was reminded of what had gone before and a faint blush came to her cheeks. Maria would not think it so very funny if she knew the truth!

As yet Emma had had no opportunity of speaking to Lytham about the recovery of his memory. Some of their guests had stayed on over Christmas, and afterwards Lytham had had business that had taken him elsewhere for some days, making it impossible for her to see him alone. Now they were here in London to attend the wedding of his particular friend and it was certain that Emma could not make a fuss until that was over and they returned to the country. She was not sure what she ought to do then—unless she confessed her shame to Lytham and took the consequences.

She had almost settled it in her mind that she would do so at the first opportunity and because of that she had withdrawn from him slightly. It would not do to show her feelings too plainly, for there might be painful decisions to be made in the near future.

She was dressing for a ball given by friends of Lord and Lady Dawlish two nights before the wedding when Lytham sent up a note to tell her that he would not be able to escort her and Maria.

Forgive me, but something has come to my attention, he had written. *I shall hope to join you later in the evening. I am sorry to inconvenience you, but there is no reason why you and Maria should not attend alone.*

'How provoking,' Maria said when Emma told her. 'It is always so much more comfortable to have a gentleman with one, is it not?'

'Yes—but Bridget and I went to parties without an escort, Maria. It is perfectly proper for you to do so and I am scarcely a green girl. I was Bridget Flynn's companion.'

'Yes, I know.' Maria refrained from saying more, but Emma understood how she felt.

'I believe it must have been important or Lytham would not have cried off at the last moment,' Emma said. 'Shall we stay home?'

Maria hesitated, then lifted her head, a martial light in her eyes.

'No, we shall not,' she said. 'We have neither of us done anything wrong and I do not see why we should cower at home and hide our heads just because Lytham is not there to lend us his consequence.'

'Bravo,' Emma said and smiled. 'That is exactly my own feeling, but I would not have forced it on you.'

'I must make an effort,' Maria said, her eyes dark with remembered sadness. 'There was so much scandal after John died and I felt responsible—but I refuse to hide away for the rest of my life. We shall go and be damned to the gossips!'

The ballroom was hot and crowded. Emma had been aware of some curious stares from certain of the dowagers as she and Maria entered alone, but although one or two had given them rather frosty looks, most people had been friendly.

Toby had named his friend a very scoundrel for not having sent him word. 'For I could easily have called for you. Lucy would not have minded coming with her mama,' he said. 'But now that you are here you will naturally join our party.'

His care of them had made it very much easier for he had danced with them both, and other gentlemen had not been long in seeking to add their names to both cards, once it was seen that Maria was willing to dance.

Emma had been dancing for most of the evening, but she had kept the supper dance free on purpose in case Lytham arrived. However, he had not done so by the time the music struck up and she decided that she would go out on to the balcony for a few minutes to cool herself before supper.

It was provoking of Lytham to stay away so long, almost the whole evening was over and she missed him. She realised that if she were forced to leave him eventually it would break her heart.

The balcony overlooked a very pretty garden with some exciting statuary and what would be magnificent rose beds in the summer. One thing she had not yet started to improve at Lytham was the garden, but she would begin that in the spring...if she was still there.

'So you are alone,' a voice said behind her, startling her. She spun round to find herself staring at a man she had hoped never to see again. 'Has he deserted you for his mistress already? Or is a whisper I heard the truth—that you were his mistress?'

Emma's face drained of colour as she looked at Lindisfarne. 'You have no right to speak to me like this,' she said and tried to go past him and back into the ballroom. He moved to prevent her, a sneer on his lips. 'Please allow me to pass, sir.'

'When I am ready,' he said and the menace in his voice sent a shiver through her. 'You were always a proud bitch, Emma Sommerton, but undoubtedly a beauty. If you had had Bridget's money, I might have married you.'

'I do not wish to listen to this,' Emma said. 'I prefer to have nothing to do with you. Now allow me to pass. I refuse to listen to any more of—'

'You will do as you're told, damn you,' he hissed, his hand snaking out to grasp her wrist in a viselike grip. 'We have some unfinished business, you and I, Emma Sommerton.' He was pushing her backwards, away from the light to a dark corner of the balcony. She struggled, but his hold on her was too strong and she felt herself knocked against the wall, a cry of protest breaking from her as his mouth came down on hers.

Emma gagged in disgust as he tried to invade her mouth with his tongue, pushing at him and struggling for all she was worth as his hands clawed at the neck of her gown.

'Scream if you want to,' he suggested. 'It will make a fine scandal—especially when I tell everyone that you were my mistress before you became Lytham's.'

'That is a lie!' Emma cried and clawed at his face. He pulled back from her, putting a hand to the wound and looking at the blood on his fingers in disbelief. 'No one would believe you.'

'I'll make you pay for that...'

Lindisfarne raised his fist to strike her, but even as he did so Emma heard a growling noise and then someone grabbed Lindisfarne's arm and spun him round. In the next instant that same person threw a punch that floored the earl, splitting his lip.

'Damn you, Lytham,' he muttered as he lay sprawled at Emma's feet. 'You will meet me for this!'

'Willingly,' Lytham replied, eyes glittering in the light of the moon which had that moment sailed out from behind the clouds, giving a ghostly yellow backdrop to the scene Emma found so terrifying. 'In the ring, with swords or pistols, at your convenience.'

'No...' Emma cried, covering her face with her hands. 'You must not fight over me.' But she was not truly aware of what they were saying, feeling too embarrassed and ashamed to listen to what passed between them.

'This swine deserves to be taught a lesson he will not forget,' Lytham said, his face white with anger. Emma had never seen him look like this and she trembled. 'Well, Lindisfarne—name your pleasure.'

The earl had struggled to his feet, though it was clear he was still suffering from the effects of the blow that had made his lip bleed profusely.

'They tell me you are a better shot than a swordsman—so I'll take the swords,' he sneered. 'That was a lucky blow, Lytham, I was not expecting it. But a thrashing in the ring is not satisfactory. Because of you and your whore, I lost the chance of a fortune.'

'You will do me the honour of asking your seconds to call upon me,' Lytham said in a voice that would have cut glass. 'Let me assure you that it will give me great pleasure to instruct you in the art of swordplay, Lindisfarne. Someone ought to have taught you to mind your manners years ago.' He gripped Emma's arm, propelling her towards the door that led back inside. 'I think we should leave. The stench out here is appalling.'

Emma allowed him to take her back inside. She was feeling bemused and confused over what had gone on out there—all that talk of a thrashing in the ring and fencing lessons. She had been so shocked that she was not really sure what the two men had said to one another. All she could think about was the tear at the neck of her gown and was praying that it would not be noticed. She held her fan in front of her in an effort to hide it.

'What on earth possessed you to go out there with him?' Lytham growled next to her ear.

'Nothing would have persuaded me to do so,' Emma replied in a shocked whisper. 'How can you think it? I went out for some air and he must have followed me. Until he accosted me I did not even know he was here this evening.'

Lytham said no more, but a nerve was working in his throat as he led her through the ballroom to a small chamber near by that was for the moment deserted.

'Did he hurt you?' he asked in a softer tone.

'No, not very much. My gown is a little torn, but I have a pin in my reticule.'

'I shall send for your cloak. If Maria is not ready to leave, I dare say Toby will escort her home.'

'I am sure she will be ready.' Emma was upset and beginning to be angry now. 'She was not sure whether we ought to come alone, and now I think she was right. I am sure Lindisfarne would not have dared to act so badly if you had escorted us.'

'Perhaps not.' He saw the proud tilt of her head and understood her feelings. 'You are angry with me, Emma. Forgive me. My business was important or I would not have cried off.'

'It is not that alone.' She felt close to tears, but would not let him see it. 'How could you accuse me of having gone to the balcony with that man? After the way he behaved in Bath I would not have spoken to him unless forced. Indeed, I dislike him intensely.'

'I was angry. I spoke without thinking. Forgive me.'

She turned her face aside, feeling the sting of humiliation. How could he have thought such a thing? Yet she had agreed to be his mistress and a moral woman would have refused. Clearly she had forfeited all right to his respect. She felt the sting of humiliation and could not bear to look at him.

'I should like to leave now please. My head has begun to ache.'

'Yes, of course.' He looked at her anxiously, but she kept her face averted, not wishing him to see her distress. 'I shall send for your cloak and ask Maria to join us here.'

Emma gave him no answer. She was unbearably hurt. If Lytham thought so little of her he could not love her. She had agreed to become his mistress because she loved him, but his behaviour had shown her that he had no respect for her.

Maria joined her a few moments later. Emma had used the opportunity to put a pin in her gown and she was able to greet the other woman naturally.

'Is something wrong, Emma?'

'I have a little headache, nothing more,' Emma replied. 'I am sorry to spoil your evening, Maria.'

'There is nothing to spoil,' Maria assured her. 'It has been pleasant enough, but I am ready to leave. I am sorry you are unwell, Emma. You look rather pale.'

'I shall be better soon.'

They were prevented from saying more by the arrival of servants with their cloaks, closely followed by Lytham. Emma accepted his help, but she did not smile at him as he placed it about her shoulders or when he handed her into the carriage.

The journey to his house in Hanover Square was accomplished in near silence. Maria refrained from chattering because she believed Emma unwell. Emma and Lytham both had their own reasons for remaining silent.

'Emma,' Lytham said as they went into the spacious front hall. It was furnished in the style of Adam; its floor tiled with Italian marble and serviced by a magnificent curving staircase of gilded wood and ironwork. 'May I speak with you for a few moments in private, please?'

'May it wait until the morning?' she asked. 'My head is aching quite badly.'

'Yes, of course, if you wish.' He took her hand and kissed it. 'Please believe me when I say I never wished to cause you pain— not ever. I have always loved you, Emma.'

Emma's heart caught. For a moment she wished that she had agreed to speak with him. Why was he looking at her so oddly?

'We shall talk tomorrow,' she said. 'Goodnight, Lytham.'

'Goodnight, my love.'

Emma ran on up the stairs. Tears were burning behind her eyelids and it was not until she had undressed and sent her maid away that she was able to think properly and to remember. There had been some mention of a fist fight and fencing lessons—but she had been too overcome with shame at Lindisfarne's attack on her to take much notice. What exactly had Lytham said? She had been trying not to listen, but now it was suddenly important that she remember. Lindisfarne had mentioned pistols...Lytham was surely not going to fight a duel?

No, it was impossible! Duels were frowned upon these days. She had heard that the Regent had forbidden them. It would merely be a sporting contest, much like the one that had taken place in the boxing ring. Yet there had been an odd look in his eyes when he bade her goodnight…the way he had told her that he had always loved her… He was going to fight a duel!

Why had she not realised it immediately? But she had been in such distress. She had been so shamed by his apparent lack of respect for her, but that was no longer important. He was going to fight a duel over her. It must not happen. It was so foolish. He had arrived in time to stop the earl really harming her.

She must speak to him at once! She must make him see that this duel was too dangerous. He might be injured. He could die of his wounds. Emma could not bear to contemplate such an eventuality.

She pulled a heavy silk dressing robe over her nightgown and went out into the hall. Candelabra were still burning as her bare feet pattered softly over the thick carpet. She hurried to the room she knew was Lytham's. The door opened almost instantly to her knock and she saw that he had removed his coat, but was still wearing his breeches and shirt, though it was opened down the front as if he had been about to remove it.

'Emma—why have you come?'

'I did not realise,' she said. 'Tell me the truth, Lytham. Are you going to fight a duel with Lindisfarne?'

'Of course. You did not think I would refuse his challenge?'

'I was confused, distressed, and I did not hear perfectly. I thought it was merely a contest—like the sparring match you spoke of at our engagement dance.'

'You heard me speak of that?' he asked and frowned. 'You should not be here dressed like that, Emma. Someone may see you.'

'Do you think I care for that when you may be badly wounded or killed? I have not forgotten that I was to have been your mistress, if you have—' She broke off as he grabbed her arm, pulling her inside and locking the door.

'No, Emma, I am not about to ravish you, though dressed like that you tempt me sorely. I am making sure that no one walks in on us. Servants like nothing better than to gossip. I would not have them hear or see anything they ought not.'

'You do not deny that what I said was true?'

'Only in that it does not go far enough.' His expression was grave. 'I must beg your pardon for my despicable behaviour, Emma. I always meant you to be my wife, of course. It was a jest—no, not even that. I was not sure how you felt until that afternoon. I suppose I doubted that you could love me, as I loved you. I wanted to see how far you would go before you drew back.'

'You had given me no sign that I meant any more to you than any other woman you had taken as your mistress,' she replied indignantly.

'Did I not? I must have missed my vocation in life. I should clearly have been an actor.'

'Lytham! You mock me.'

'Only myself, dearest Emma.' He reached out to touch her cheek. 'You must know I love you?'

'Why did you not tell me you had recovered your memory?'

'Because...for the same reason as you did not tell me what a rogue I was. When I realised that you would not withdraw, that you really meant to be my mistress, I was overcome with shame. I am a very rogue for putting you through such torment, Emma. If I had come to you then, I could not have held my self-control. I wanted you so badly that I was afraid of losing my control.'

'I thought I had disgusted you by responding too freely.'

'Oh, my sweet, foolish Emma.'

Lytham reached out and drew her into his arms, kissing her tenderly but with such hunger that she trembled and clung to him, feeling as if she would melt for sheer pleasure.

'How you must have felt when I vanished! You had no home, no money to speak of—and I had put you in an impossible position, which must have led to a loss of respectability if it had been known. It is a wonder that you did not hate me for it.'

'I searched for you every day for as long as there was light,' she said, reaching up to touch his beloved face. 'My life meant nothing to me without you. If your aunt had not come, I think I should have died.'

'And then I would not have wanted to live.'

'You must not fight Lindisfarne! If you should be hurt or killed, I could not bear it.'

'I am reputed to be one of the best swordsmen in London, Emma. I shall not be killed, I promise. Besides, I cannot draw back. It is a matter of honour.'

'Honour be damned,' Emma cried and he laughed huskily, drawing her close to him once more so that she could feel the throbbing heat of his arousal and sensed his need. 'I care nothing for honour, Lytham, and everything for you. That is why I would have been your mistress and counted the world well lost for a little time of love.'

'My sweet, darling Emma,' he murmured, caressing the side of her face with his hand. 'Go to your bed and sleep peacefully, my dear one. The duel cannot take place until after Toby's wedding. I assure you that it will be no more than a fencing lesson to me. I shall bring Lindisfarne to his knees and make him write an abject apology to you.'

'You are so sure?' She gazed into his eyes.

'Return to your bed before I take you to mine, Emma.' He smiled and let her go. 'I think we must bring the day of our wedding forward or I shall go entirely mad.'

Emma laughed. Perhaps she was making too much of it. She had been right the first time—it was merely a contest of skill and honour, which would be satisfied at the first blood.

'You promise me that nothing terrible is going to happen if I leave you?'

'You may sleep and dream of our wedding night,' he said. 'Go now, my love—or I shall not be able to keep from making love to you. And I am determined you shall be my wife before that, Emma.'

She left him then, feeling reassured. Whether she would have slept so peacefully if she had known that Lytham's friends were to wait on him at six the next morning was another matter.

Emma did not wake until the maid brought in her breakfast tray the next morning. She yawned and smiled at the girl, feeling surprised that she had rested so well. Then she realised that things had been settled between her and Lytham and she had no more need to wonder how she would leave him. She would never leave him!

'Thank you, Betsy. You are spoiling me. I had intended to get up and come down for breakfast.'

'It was his lordship's orders, miss. He said you were to be allowed to sleep in—and that I should bring breakfast to you this morning.'

'Well, it is pleasant to be spoiled sometimes. Is Lady Lynston awake yet?'

'Yes, miss. She had her breakfast an hour ago. I think she is writing some letters in the small parlour.'

'Thank you. Please tell her that I shall be down shortly.'

Emma nibbled a sweet roll, glanced through a small pile of notes that had been sent to her, drank her chocolate and then rang for her maid to help her dress. She chose a walking gown of dark green velvet and a hat with a jaunty feather.

'Have you seen his lordship, Betsy? Do you know if he is down yet?'

'I'm not sure, miss. I could ask his man, if you like?'

'No, do not disturb Brunnings. It does not matter,' Emma replied. 'I had promised to go shopping with Lady Lynston. I shall write a note for Lytham and you can give it to Brunnings to deliver.'

'Yes, miss.'

Emma did not notice the look of relief in the girl's eyes. She was feeling much too happy to notice a slight hesitancy in Betsy's manner that morning. At last she had discussed *that* afternoon with Lytham and *he* had apologised. After all her soul searching and fear that he might despise her, it was a relief to know that he had been ashamed of his own behaviour and did not despise her for hers.

She would take him to task for it once all this other silly business was over. How could he have played such a trick on her? Yet she admitted to herself that she had not given him much idea of her true feelings for him until that afternoon. Aspiring mothers and their daughters must have relentlessly pursued him since he had inherited the title and it was little wonder he had doubted her love. Her reckless behaviour that afternoon must have convinced him that it was he she wanted, rather than his fortune.

Her mouth curved in a little smile as she recalled the way he had kissed her the previous night. He was wicked to have kept his recovered memory a secret from her and yet she understood his reasons for they were much the same as her own.

She was still smiling as she went downstairs to join Maria in the parlour. She was staring out of the window and seemed startled as Emma asked if she was ready to go shopping.

'You still mean to go?' she asked.

'Why not?' Emma's blood ran cold as she saw her friend's expression. Had Lytham lied to her about the duel? Her hand crept to her breast as if to still her racing heart. 'He told me the duel would not take place until after Toby's wedding—'

'Of course he did,' Maria said. 'He was afraid of your tears, Emma. It took place at eight this morning. I could not sleep and came down to fetch a book. I heard them talking in the library before they left. Toby was with him and Mr Charlton.'

'But it is already past ten!' Emma cried, her eyes flying to the pretty gilt mantle clock. 'Surely they should be back before now?'

'Yes, I would have expected to hear something by now. Unless...' Maria stopped speaking as she saw Emma's distress. 'But we would have heard if—'

'What is that?' Emma's head went up as she heard voices in the hall. 'Someone has come!' She ran to the door, her heart stopping as she saw Toby and another gentleman supporting Lytham. 'He has been wounded!'

'It is a flesh wound,' Lytham said and straightened up. 'I have lost a little blood, but I shall be better in a day or so.'

She moved towards him, feeling as if she were back in the nightmare of his disappearance. She could not bear this! It was too much. His right arm was in a sling, his shirtsleeve shredded where the blade had torn through it. His coat had been placed over his shoulders to protect him from the cold, but he could not have worn it because his arm was padded and bound with thick bandages.

'You promised me it would not happen,' she said in a voice thick with emotion. 'You said the duel was not until after Toby's wedding.'

'Forgive me, Emma. I did not want you to be awake all night worrying.'

'He needs to rest,' Toby said in an apologetic tone. 'We must get him to his bed.'

'Yes, of course. All this can wait.'

Several servants had come to assist their master and Emma went back into the parlour to join Maria.

'He has been wounded—' she said and broke off on a sob.

'I feared as much, but at least they have brought him home. You need not wonder if he is alive or dead.'

'He looks so pale,' Emma said and Maria came to put an arm about her, holding her until the brief storm of tears was over.

'Lytham has suffered worse and survived,' Toby said, coming into the room as she was drying her tears on Maria's kerchief. 'He served with Wellington, you know. I just wanted to tell you not to worry. I must leave you now. Much to do, you know— wedding tomorrow.'

'Yes, of course. I must thank you for taking care of him.'

'Doctor patched him up. He ain't too bad. Lindisfarne is in a worse case. Touch and go whether he survives, I dare say—not but that he didn't deserve it. Lytham would have retired after pricking him the first time, but he pressed the fight.'

'We must pray that he does survive,' Maria said. 'Lytham might otherwise be in some trouble.'

'We kept it all right and tight, plenty of witnesses to prove that Lindisfarne was at fault. It ain't as easy as it used to be, but Lytham's a favourite with the Regent. Brush through it, I dare say.'

'Providing they both recover,' Emma said with feeling.

'Just so,' Toby agreed and took himself off before she could add to this. 'Hope to see you both tomorrow.'

'Men!' Maria exclaimed as he went out. 'Why must they do these foolish things?'

'Lytham said it was a matter of honour.' Emma's voice broke on a sob. 'I do not know what I shall do if—'

'Begging your pardon, miss,' Betsy said as she came into the parlour at that moment. 'His lordship has asked if you would be so kind as to go up to him.'

'Yes, of course. I shall come at once.'

Emma almost ran from the room, her heart pounding. Had he taken a turn for the worse? She was out of breath when she arrived to discover that he was lying on top of the bed, propped up against a pile of pillows.

'Are you feeling worse?'

'Stop looking so terrified,' he said and smiled at her. 'I am a little drunk, Emma. They gave me brandy to kill the pain while the surgeon patched me up. I was unable to walk by myself, but once I have had time to rest and drunk some strong coffee, which Brunnings is fetching for me now, I shall be fine. Believe me, Emma, it is no more than a scratch.'

'You wretch!' Emma cried as the relief swept over her. 'I thought you were dying.'

'I know.' The amusement danced in his eyes. 'That's why I asked for you to come as soon as I was settled. I might not be able to stand straight, my love—but I am not so far gone that I did not realise how upset you were.'

'Once we are married I shall not let you out of my sight. You cannot be trusted not to get into trouble!'

'I hope that nothing like this will happen again. I assure you that I do not make a habit of duelling. If Lindisfarne recovers, which I pray he may, I do not think he will be a danger to anyone again.'

'Oh, Lytham,' Emma said, tears trickling down her cheeks. 'Why do I love you so much?'

'Perhaps because you cannot help yourself,' he said softly. 'It is very much the same for me. I think I fell in love with you the day you came home with your hair windblown about your face and looked as if you wanted to throw me out of your house. If it was not then, it must have been when you took out that knife and prepared to patch me up after I was shot in the woods. My only regret is that I did not ask you to marry me then and there.'

'I should probably have refused,' Emma said with a rueful laugh. 'I was fighting my feelings for you then, and it was not until some time later that I knew I loved you.'

'You were adept at hiding your feelings and caused me much heartache, Emma Sommerton.'

'I am sure I have never caused you the least trouble,' she replied.

'That, my love,' he murmured as he held out his hand to her, 'is palpably not the case...'

Chapter Fourteen

'You are surely not intending to accompany us?' Emma asked as she saw Lytham come down the stairs the next morning. 'I am sure Toby would understand your reasons for not attending his wedding.'

'I dare say he might,' Lytham replied. 'But I have no intention of missing it. This coat is not the one I had intended to wear, but it will suffice. At least I was able to get it on, which did not please Brunnings for he has always disliked it. It has no style, you see.'

'You look well enough,' Emma said, her eyes moving over him with love as she recognised that mocking smile in his eyes. He was certainly himself again! 'But I think you foolish when you might be resting.'

'I believe you had a letter from Italy today, my love,' he said, changing the subject. 'Tom told me had sent it on to you—from your mother, one would suppose.'

'Provoking creature!' Emma cried, her eyes flashing at him. 'But, yes, the letter was from my mother—she writes to tell me she thinks she will stay in Italy for a year or two. She has made some friends there—the Count Grattini and his sister Maria. I believe there is a possibility that she may marry again.'

'Then she will not return for our wedding,' Lytham said, looking thoughtful. 'We must write and let her know when it is, of course, but perhaps we might take a trip to Italy ourselves—if you would like that?'

'Could we really?' Emma said, looking at him excitely. 'I think I should like that very much.'

'It could be a part of our honeymoon trip,' he said. 'And it may be a good idea if we were to marry as soon as possible, quietly, and then leave the country for some months.'

Emma looked at him anxiously. 'What have you heard? Has Lindisfarne…?'

'I do not think so. However, I have been advised by a letter, which comes from the Regent's secretary, that it might be better if I were to remove myself from town for a few months. I do not think that I shall be charged with any offence, but to save making more scandal it might be better to comply with Prinny's request. He has made quite a thing of stamping out the practice of duelling and he cannot be seen to take sides in this. The newspapers delight in scurrilous attacks on him, without my making things worse. In a few months we may return and it will all be forgotten. Especially if Lindisfarne recovers, which I trust he will.'

'Yes, I see.' Emma gazed up at him. 'You know that I am ready to marry you whenever you wish, my love—and I would prefer a small private ceremony in any event.'

'Then we shall arrange it for next week by special licence at Lytham,' he said. 'A few of our closest friends may care to come; as for the others, we shall not mind if they prefer not to know us for the moment.'

'That is just what I want,' Emma said. 'I shall enjoy being a guest at Toby's and Lucy's wedding, but I would not want to have such an affair for myself.'

'Then if we are agreed I think we should leave before Maria grows tired of waiting for us.' Lytham said and offered her his good arm.

'You look wonderful,' Lady Agatha said, her eyes misty as she saw Emma dressed in her wedding gown. 'That pearly grey looks so well on you, my dear, and just a touch of midnight blue on the bonnet—charming.'

'Lytham saw this bonnet in town and bought it for me,' Emma said. 'I thought it would look well with the dress. He is forever buying me things.'

'It is very dashing,' Maria said and came to kiss her. 'And just right for a quiet country wedding.'

'Thank you,' Emma replied and smiled. Maria had promised to keep a friendly but unobtrusive eye on Lady Agatha while they were away, and a new companion had been hired who was to travel to Lytham after the wedding to take up her post. 'I think we should go down now, don't you? I do not wish to keep Lytham waiting.'

'Pooh!' Agatha Lynston said. 'It will not do him the slightest harm to wait a few minutes for his bride. He has kept me waiting for this day far too long.' She smiled and patted Emma's cheek with her gloved hand. 'But I have no fault to find with his chosen bride.'

Emma gave her a quick hug, which made her maid exclaim and fuss round her, repairing the damage to her toilette. Then they all trooped downstairs to where the carriages were waiting.

Lytham Church was small, hardly big enough to hold the sixty guests that had been invited—none had refused—and a crowd of well-wishers from the estate had gathered outside to cheer the bride as she arrived.

Tom was with her and he smiled cheerily at her. His future brother-in-law, who had managed to secure a confession from the man who had once accused him of cheating, had solved his most pressing problem.

'That is where I went the night I cried off taking you to the dance,' Lytham had confided to her when they returned from attending Toby and Lucy's wedding. 'I was asked to meet someone, who I may say was in hiding from his creditors. Apparently, it was not the first time he had been in Queer Street and he told me that my brother John had paid him to accuse Tom of cheating.'

'I suppose you paid him to sign his confession?' Emma asked, but received only an enigmatic smile.

'Provoking creature!' Emma cried, but she had not been cross with him. How could she when he had managed to secure the proof of Tom's innocence?

It was all she needed to complete her happiness and she suspected that it might not be too long before there was another wedding in the family.

Entering the church on her brother's arm, Emma saw Lytham waiting for her with Stephen Antrium at his side. It was another proof of his loyalty, she thought, for there must have been a dozen gentlemen he could have asked to stand up with him, but since he could not have Toby (who was, of course, on his honeymoon) as his best man, he had chosen his agent. Something that she knew had pleased Stephen Antrium very much indeed.

As she began to walk down the aisle towards him, Lytham turned his head to watch for her and the look of love he gave her made Emma's heart beat wildly. She had never believed that she could ever be so happy or that she would be loved this much.

Even the sun managed to break through the clouds, penetrating the gloom of the old church and sending showers of colour from the stained-glass windows onto the flagstones.

And then the bells were ringing out joyfully as she walked out of the church on her husband's arms, to be met by a shower of dried rose petals. A little girl came forward shyly to present her with a token tied up with blue ribbons, and several had posies of winter flowers.

Emma's own flowers had been grown at Lytham and were Christmas roses and some fragile fern from the hothouses, tied up with trailing lace. When all the villagers had paid their tributes, Lytham handed Emma into the carriage and scattered coins for the children. Emma waved as the horses moved off, and then turned to her husband with a smile.

'Well, my love,' he said and reached across to touch her cheek. 'Are you happy?'

'You know that I am,' she replied. 'This is the happiest day of my life.'

'There will be others equally as happy,' he promised and laughed ruefully. 'If I kissed you as I would like, I should ruin your gown. So I shall wait until we are alone.' He took her hand, turning it up to drop a kiss within the palm. 'Hold that until later.'

'I shall give it back to you,' Emma promised. 'You ask if I am happy—what of you, my husband? Are you content with your bride?'

'Do you need to ask?' he murmured huskily. 'Look at me like that, Emma, and you will not see much of your guests.'

'Behave yourself,' she warned, tapping his knee in mock reprimand. 'We have the rest of our lives to indulge ourselves, Lytham. We must not disappoint our friends, for some of them have travelled a considerable distance to be with us.'

'Indeed, you do right to chide me,' he said, a wicked glint in his eyes. 'For I am sorely tempted, my lady.'

Emma shook her head at him, but her heart was racing. If truth were told, she could hardly wait to be alone with him.

'At last,' Lytham said as the carriage taking them to the house where they were to stay for a few days before beginning their journey to Italy. 'I quite thought we should never be able to escape!'

'My impatient love,' Emma said and leaned over to brush her lips against his. He seized her, pressing her close and kissing her hungrily. 'But I must admit that I almost lost my patience with Aunt Agatha at the end. She kept remembering things she thought I ought to know about you, Lytham.'

'I hope she did not tell you what a terrible rogue I was?'

'Oh, yes,' Emma assured him naughtily. 'She has told me that many times, but I am well aware of your faults, my lord.'

He put a finger to her lips. 'Lytham,' he commanded. 'Or Alex if you wish. Anything but "my lord"!'

'I shall know exactly how to punish you if you displease me,' Emma teased and reached up to stroke his cheek.

'I hope that I shall never displease you,' Lytham said. 'I trust that you do not mind returning to my mother's house for our wedding night? It is but a short journey and I did not want to share you with others.'

'I think I shall like the house, if only we can exorcise the dreadful memories of that time,' Emma said. 'Besides, it is convenient for our ship and, as long as you do not decide to go walking alone, I shall be content.'

'If you think that anything will keep me from your bed this time,' Lytham said, 'you are sadly mistaken, madam.'

And nothing did keep him. He came to her with love in his eyes, pulling her hard against him to kiss her tenderly, his hands caressing the nape of her neck, then travelling down, pressing her against him. The passion flamed between them and Lytham swept her up in his arms, carrying her to the bed. The ghosts of the past were exorcised as he made love to her, tenderly at first but then with a hunger that consumed them both, carrying them to a far shore.

Afterwards, they lay in each other's arms, touching and kissing, whispering their secrets until the desire flamed once more.

'You are so beautiful,' he whispered as he bent his head, his tongue flicking at the rosy peaks of her breasts, sending thrills of pleasure through her entire body. She arched sensuously, feeling the burn of his arousal against her thigh, knowing that he wanted her again, and that she wanted him as urgently. Her hands moved down the firm contours of his back, tracing the scars that bore witness to earlier injuries that she had never guessed were there, her lips pressing against his shoulder as her breath came faster. 'I never lived until I met you, Emma. You are the mistress of my heart, my world, and my heaven.'

'You are everything to me,' she said. 'I had no hope of finding happiness until you began to take an interest in me. When you asked me to be your mistress I knew that even a few weeks or months of being with you meant more than a lifetime without you. To be your wife is more happiness than I could ever imagine.'

He pulled her against him, his hands moving down the silken arch of her back, cupping her buttocks so that she was conscious of his throbbing arousal, hot and hard as she curled into his body. There was no need for words, because the tenderness and love between them was saying all that they would ever want to hear.

Giving herself up to his loving, Emma smiled in the darkness. She wanted nothing more than this man, to be with him like this, to be his wife and, if God blessed them, to bear his children.

* * * * *

Regency

HIGH-SOCIETY AFFAIRS

Rakes and rogues in the ballrooms — and the bedrooms — of Regency England!

Volume 1 – 6th March 2009
A Hasty Betrothal by Dorothy Elbury
A Scandalous Marriage by Mary Brendan

Volume 2 – 3rd April 2009
The Count's Charade by Elizabeth Bailey
The Rake and the Rebel by Mary Brendan

Volume 3 – 1st May 2009
Sparhawk's Lady by Miranda Jarrett
The Earl's Intended Wife by Louise Allen

Volume 4 – 5th June 2009
Lord Calthorpe's Promise by Sylvia Andrew
The Society Catch by Louise Allen

Volume 5 – 3rd July 2009
Beloved Virago by Anne Ashley
Lord Trenchard's Choice by Sylvia Andrew

Volume 6 – 7th August 2009
The Unruly Chaperon by Elizabeth Rolls
Colonel Ancroft's Love by Sylvia Andrew

Volume 7 – 4th September 2009
The Sparhawk Bride by Miranda Jarrett
The Rogue's Seduction by Georgina Devon

NOW 14 VOLUMES IN ALL TO COLLECT!

M&B

Regency

High-Society Affairs

*Rakes and rogues in the ballrooms – and the
bedrooms – of Regency England!*

Volume 8 – 2nd October 2009
Sparhawk's Angel by Miranda Jarrett
The Proper Wife by Julia Justiss

Volume 9 – 6th November 2009
The Disgraced Marchioness by Anne O'Brien
The Reluctant Escort by Mary Nichols

Volume 10 – 4th December 2009
The Outrageous Débutante by Anne O'Brien
A Damnable Rogue by Anne Herries

Volume 11 – 1st January 2010
The Enigmatic Rake by Anne O'Brien
The Lord and the Mystery Lady by Georgina Devon

Volume 12 – 5th February 2010
The Wagering Widow by Diane Gaston
An Unconventional Widow by Georgina Devon

Volume 13 – 5th March 2010
A Reputable Rake by Diane Gaston
The Heart's Wager by Gayle Wilson

Volume 14 – 2nd April 2010
The Venetian's Mistress by Ann Elizabeth Cree
The Gambler's Heart by Gayle Wilson

NOW 14 VOLUMES IN ALL TO COLLECT!

A wanton widow

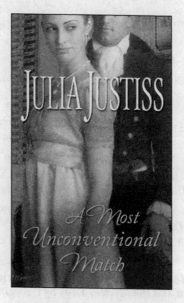

JULIA JUSTISS

A Most Unconventional Match

Hal Waterman has secretly adored newly widowed Elizabeth Lowery for years. When he calls upon Elizabeth to offer his help, his silent, protective presence awakens feelings in her that she does not understand.

Elizabeth knows that society would condemn her, but Hal's attractions may well prove too much to resist!

Available 18th December 2009

Sparkling ballrooms and wealthy glamour in Regency London

Immerse yourself in the glitter of
Regency times and follow the lives
and romantic escapades of
Stephanie Laurens' Lester family

He could marry her — or ruin her!

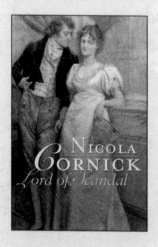

London, 1814

Scandalous and seductive, Hawksmoor is a
notorious fortune hunter. Now he has tasted the
woman of his dreams, Catherine Fenton, and
he will do anything to make her his.

Though heiress to a fortune, Catherine is trapped
in a gilded cage and bound to a man she detests.
She senses there is more to Ben, Lord Hawksmoor,
behind the glittering façade. She believes he can
rescue her — but has she found herself a hero, or
made a pact with the devil himself?

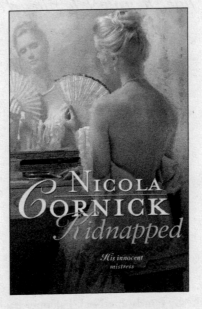

Orphaned and vulnerable, Catriona is doing her best to resist the skilful seduction of the scandalous heir to the Earl of Strathconan. Then her newly discovered inheritance places them both in terrible danger.

First kidnapped, then shipwrecked with only this fascinating rake as company, her adventure has just begun...

*To unmask her secrets, he will
have to unlock her heart!*

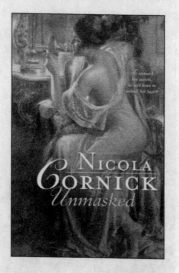

Wickedly handsome Nick Falconer has been
sent to stop a gang of highwaywomen.
But the woman he suspects of leading them
is intoxicatingly beautiful and Nick sets
out to seduce her.

Mari Osbourne's secrets are deeper and
darker than Nick could ever imagine.
Will trusting the one man she wants lead
Mari to the hangman's noose?

Wanted: Wife

**Must be of good family, attractive
but not too beautiful, but calm,
reasonable and mature...
for marriage of convenience**

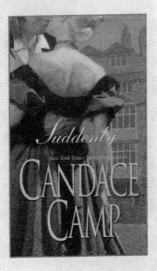

Spirited Charity Emerson is certain she can meet
Simon "Devil" Dure's wifely expectations. With
her crazy schemes, warm laughter and loving heart,
Charity tempts Simon. However, the treacherous trap
that lies ahead, and the vicious act of murder, will put
their courage – and their love – to the ultimate test.

GENERIC_04

millsandboon.co.uk Community

Join Us!

The Community is the perfect place to meet and chat to kindred spirits who love books and reading as much as you do, but it's also the place to:

- Get the inside scoop from authors about their latest books
- Learn how to write a romance book with advice from our editors
- Help us to continue publishing the best in women's fiction
- Share your thoughts on the books we publish
- Befriend other users

Forums: Interact with each other as well as authors, editors and a whole host of other users worldwide.

Blogs: Every registered community member has their own blog to tell the world what they're up to and what's on their mind.

Book Challenge: We're aiming to read 5,000 books and have joined forces with The Reading Agency in our inaugural Book Challenge.

Profile Page: Showcase yourself and keep a record of your recent community activity.

Social Networking: We've added buttons at the end of every post to share via digg, Facebook, Google, Yahoo, technorati and de.licio.us.

www.millsandboon.co.uk